THE PARADINE CASE

ROBERT HICHENS

THE PARADINE CASE

A NOVEL

DOUBLEDAY, DORAN & COMPANY, INC.

Garden City   *New York*

1934

PRINTED AT THE *Country Life Press*, GARDEN CITY, N. Y., U. S. A.

TO MY FRIEND
MAUD VALERIE WHITE

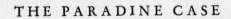

THE PARADINE CASE

THE PARADISE LOST

I

SIR MALCOLM KEANE, K. C., put on his fur-lined coat in the cloak-room of the Cleveland Club at the corner of Pall Mall, picked up his soft black hat, doeskin gloves and closely furled umbrella, and came out into the big square hall where a huge fire was burning on the wide hearth. A group of men stood before it smoking and laughing. Among them, rather to his surprise, he saw Lord Hor-field, the Judge, with whom he had just been spending half an hour in the smoke-room upstairs. So Horfield had followed him down, after picking up an evening paper and apparently settling himself in a big leather chair to read the last of the news.

Silver-voiced Horfield with the witty, unscrupulous tongue, the unravelling brain and the surely pitiless heart! Keane admired his brilliant capacities, his determined will and acute intellect, but there was something fundamental—at any rate he believed it to be fundamental—in Horfield's nature which obscurely quarrelled with something surely fundamental in his own. Perhaps it was cold quarrelling with heat, or the cruelly intellectual quarrelling with the fiercely emotional, ice and fire at odds one with the other. There was certainly some separating quality which Keane was usually conscious of when he was in company with the Judge. On the plane of humour, however, they got on very well and they always found many subjects of conversation. Horfield was excel-lent company when he chose. A pity you couldn't really respect him. Somehow—and this was perhaps a proof of the naïveté that had not even now been expelled from Malcolm Keane's fiery temperament—the brilliant advocate had a secret desire to respect the Judge before whom he was forced to plead. The Bench, you know! But there were reasons that made it hard going when a man wanted to set Horfield on high. As a Judge he was eminent; as a man he was sometimes startling. But he probably didn't care much what any individual thought of him. Keane believed him to be a profound cynic.

"Going home to your wife, Keane?" said the Judge, turning a little from the men by the fire and stretching his thin lips in a faint smile.

"Yes. I'm taking her to the Haymarket Theatre this evening, and then more work."

"Give her my compliments. She knows I'm her victim."

"I wonder if she does."

"All women know which men are under their spell and which are not."

"Gay is delightfully unconscious. That's part of her charm, I think."

"She doesn't like me. But tell her I'm still at her feet."

"I will, but she may not believe it."

"That's not essential."

He turned again to the fire. The flames from the logs flickered over his meagre figure—he was excessively thin—his pale, pointed features and long, narrow, yet strongly intellectual head. A large man with a face that always looked as if he had not fully recovered from an attack of the mumps spoke to him. As he moved away Keane heard the silvery sound of the Judge's voice in reply, then a burst of laughter. Something amusing, no doubt. It must be rather wonderful to be naturally witty and totally untroubled by any deep emotions. Physically, of course, Horfield was of the Satyr breed. So at least it was more than whispered. But now he was a Judge perhaps he controlled himself for the sake of his calling, or at the least was circumspect in his public behaviour, although remarkably untrammelled in his speech. But he was in the depths unemotional. Keane was certain of that. And Keane himself was by nature almost fiercely emotional. That was partly why he had attained to such success as an advocate.

Out in the misty cold of a November evening, Keane set off on foot up the Haymarket. He was a fresh air man, tall, strong, athletic, and perpetually conscious of the urgent necessity of keeping himself in the pink of condition. A tremendous worker, he never neglected his body, for he was proud of it, had been proud of it ever since he had been an exceptionally handsome and finely made boy, good at all games, a runner, hurdler, football player and horseman. It was natural to him to be fond of physical exercise and sport. But he had another reason than that for the attention he gave to his body; he was sharply conscious of the importance of health, complete health, sound and vigorous, to his brain. Talent combined with ambition had brought him to where he was. Now he had got to stay there or go higher. He mustn't neglect any weapon in the fight to keep at the top. And strong health was perhaps the most important weapon in the whole armoury. Look how Ravenstone had dropped out because of his drinking propensities. Gresham, too, had become almost negligible because he had overworked, overtired his brain. That mania of lawyers for getting into Parliament had been the ruin of him. He, Keane, had been asked to stand several times but had always refused. The Law should be his sole Mistress. Thank God he wasn't driven by an ambitious wife at home, crazy to shine in Society. Gay didn't wish him to be in Parliament. If she had believed that he really cared to be there, wasn't happy away from Westminster, she wouldn't have stood in his way. She was unselfish, and cared for him so much that she couldn't be happy seeing him discontented. But luckily in this, as in so many other matters, they thought alike. So Politics could go hang for him, and he could give his whole mind to the Law, and have enough time left over to keep himself splendidly fit.

The Keanes lived now in Portland Place. Formerly they had lived in Westminster, in a quite small house in Cowley Street, Westminster, but as Keane's success grew and money poured in, they had enlarged their borders. Keane, in his leisure moments, liked picking up pictures, china, good pieces of furniture. He was a big man, too, standing over six feet, and had a passion for space. His frame was big and his gestures were big, and he liked a big house and a big life. The niggling, as he called it, was abhorrent to him. True, their house in the country, not far from Tilford Common, was small, but there was one enormous room in it, and the size of that room gave the impression, and to Keane the feeling, that the house itself was of ample size. When he thought of it he always thought of that room. And now, in London, there was the Portland Place house big enough for a large family.

But Gay and he had no children.

He did not greatly regret this, though sometimes he had wished to have a son. But he and Gay had always got on so well in their married life, and were such good comrades as well as lovers, that they needed, he thought, nothing to link them more closely to-gether. After ten years of marriage, he was still under her charm. And the coming of children might, perhaps, have diminished that. For her charm was compounded of physical and mental attributes, and children, even delightful children, sometimes rob their mother of graces. It is not always so, but often it is so.

Gay was thirty but remained very young, girlish almost, in her great naturalness and pleasure in life. She seemed always expectant of good things, and so, perhaps, attracted them to her. Many called her "a lucky woman," and she thought herself lucky. Believing in her luck, or her happy destiny, she was morally fearless, not afraid of the arrows of fortune.

Keane crossed the Circus into Regent Street with a pleasant feeling of anticipation. He was not far from home now. A boy came up to him shouting something and carrying newspapers. Keane bought one. At the Club he had talked to the Judge and hadn't had time to look at the news. Gay didn't care for news-papers. She was in some ways a curious being, holding herself, but without self-consciousness, apart from the rough-and-tumble of life. She seldom denounced the ugliness of life, but seemed in-stinctively aware of it and disinclined to have anything to do with it. Partly for that reason, perhaps, she had never been into a Court of Justice to hear her husband plead a case. He seldom talked over his cases with her, though he had been in many *causes célèbres* since their marriage. But now and then he had asked for her opinion, when he had had the defence of a woman accused of some crime in his hands. And he had found her clear-headed and remarkably instinctive about human nature, not cruel, but penetrating in her judgments of character and motive. She was not great in reasoning, but seemed able to arrive at the truth by a species of instinct that to him bordered on the mysterious. So now and then, in a difficulty, he came to her. Generally, however, he preferred to keep her out of his legal life as much as possible, and she never seemed to wish to be in it. He was unlike many men in that he did not require en-couragement in his profession. He was full of self-confidence. That indeed was one of his great assets, and had always helped him to happiness. He believed in himself, and had confidence in his ability to influence others. But he had a fiery temper and sometimes lost control of it. There were Judges who did not like him. Sometimes he wondered whether Horfield was one of them. Difficult to know! For Horfield, with his silver tongue, was not easy to read, in spite of the bitterness he often mingled with his honey. He could be very agreeable. He had been so in the smoke-room of the Cleveland that afternoon. But one didn't know—with Horfield.

Gay wasn't fond of him.

"I'm sure there's a lot of vinegar in Lord Horfield's blood," she had once said of him. "And I don't like vinegar."

When he had passed the Church close to Queen's Hall, Keane began to walk faster. The air was brutally cold, seemed to grow colder in the wide thoroughfare of Portland Place, as if Regent's Park sent a blast from its winter to meet him. But he wasn't afraid of it. His 'make-up,' physical and mental, was hardy and English in spite of his emotional temperament. He loved his country and was not afraid of its climate. Although in his early youth he had studied abroad, both in Germany and in Paris, and was a good linguist, he always felt most at home in England. But there are many more emotional Englishmen than people are willing to admit, and Keane was one of them and not ashamed of it. He had won too many cases by emotional outbursts in Court not to know the value of strong feeling. He had often carried away a Jury by being carried away himself. For his emotions were not forced, but natural. Nevertheless, Horfield had said of him:

"An excellent actor was lost to the English stage when Keane went to the Bar."

When someone had repeated this remark to Keane, he had said:

"As to that, I often feel I could have done pretty well on the stage."

And he was a great favourite with stage people. He liked them, felt at home with them, knew many of them well. Both Gay and he were often seen at 'first nights.' They were due at one that night, and Keane was already looking forward to it.

Number fifty-three! He stood before the tall green door and put his key into it. He was awfully fond of his big house, and proud of it, too. Its spacious beauty was a witness to his success. He had earned it by his own talent and assiduity. For he was a great worker.

In the hall he left his outdoor things, went into an inner hall and opened a door on the left of it. Gay would surely be there in her favourite sitting-room, curled up on the big sofa by the log fire with a book. She nearly always managed an hour's reading before she dressed for dinner. Afternoon parties of any kind were not in her 'line.' But she was oddly indifferent to society, though they knew many people.

Gay was there as he had anticipated. She turned her brown head as he came in, and a smile curved her pale lips. But she didn't say anything. She was often silent when another woman would certainly have spoken, and her ease in her silences delighted Keane. It was so unusual and so characteristic of her.

"What are you reading?" he said, going to the sofa and touching her hair.

She held up her book.

"Nietzsche!"

He looked at the page.

" 'The night song of Zarathustra!' "

He stood for a moment with the book in his hand. When he gave it back to her there was moisture in his eyes.

"Gorgeous!" he said. "But it pains."

He looked down at her and a penetrating expression came into his large dark eyes.

"Where do you live, Gay, when you're alone?" he asked.

"All over the place. Now here, now there! This evening"—she stretched out a narrow hand to the book—"in that blinding light. To-morrow I may be in the darkness of Gorki. I'm going to read his *Asile de Nuit*. Yesterday it was *Hannele*."

"You're like a bird flying from branch to branch."

"That's my way."

"And how much of it all remains with you?"

"I never bother about that. What I really like sticks."

Keane dropped down into an armchair and stretched out his long limbs. He laid the evening paper down on an arm of the chair without glancing at it. He was busy with Gay.

"Someone at the Club has sent you a message by me," he said.

"Yes?"

She didn't look interested but rather aloof.

"Would you like to guess who it was?"

"No; I hate guessing. It's a waste of time. Tell me."

"It was Horfield."

"Lord Horfield? You've been with him?"

"Yes, for about half an hour. When I was leaving he said: 'Give your wife my compliments. She knows I'm her victim.' And he added a minute later: 'She doesn't like me. But tell her I'm still at her feet.' By the way—why don't you like Horfield—if you really and truly don't?"

Gay looked at him for a moment steadily under her level brows. She seemed to be considering something. At last she said:

"Why should I like Lord Horfield? Because he's a Judge?"

Keane smiled.

"That would hardly be a reason. But he's always very pleasant to us."

"I don't think he cares much for you."

Keane felt slightly startled by this unexpected remark and immediately a hostile look changed his mobile face.

"What makes you suppose that?"

"Nothing particular. I just seem to feel it. He's a cold nature, you see."

"And what am I?"

"Too volcanic."

Keane looked thoroughly disconcerted.

"Why that 'too'?" he said. "I daresay I am rather volcanic, but I think that has often helped me with Juries."

"But we weren't talking about Juries!"

"No. But I believe a good deal of my success comes from the fact that I feel my cases intensely."

"Well, I hope you'll never have a big case before Lord Horfield."

"Gay! What do you mean? I have been before him. You know that."

"Of course. But I mean in a crucial case. I think he would enjoy taking the wind out of your billowing sails. And your sails do billow, you know."

"I believe you're a sarcastic wretch."

"I don't think I am sarcastic. But Lord Horfield is. And I think he's rather a nasty old man, too. So let us forget him. Oh, by the way, Malcolm, Sir Simon telephoned this evening, from Flaquer and Flaquer. He thought you might possibly be in. He wants particularly to see you to-morrow—any time that suits you."

"Got a case for me, I suppose."

"I don't know."

"I shouldn't wonder if we meet him and Lady Si to-night at the Haymarket. What are you going to wear?"

"Something *I* like, but perhaps nobody else will. That reminds me. I ought to dress."

She gave him a butterfly kiss on his broad, powerful forehead, from which the dark hair grew back, smooth and thick, and went out of the room. At the door she looked back at him for a moment intensely, slightly screwing up her yellow-brown eyes. She was a little short-sighted and it gave her sometimes a peering look which fascinated him still, after ten years. It was wonderful to be married to a woman who could fascinate you—after ten years.

When the door was shut behind her, Keane sat still for a moment looking at it, and his face was very soft in expression, tender even. There was something in Gay that called forth at times all the tenderness that was in him. "And what a strange emotion deep tenderness is," he thought, sitting there by the log fire. "It seems to come from such a depth. It seems to mean so very much, something beyond all we know, all we can experience here. It's surely the feeling that was born in the far-away land and brings us the mystic message from there. It teaches the man who has it— me in this case—that besides what he knows here there is something that he *must* know hereafter."

Gay! Till now in his life—and he was close on fifty—she alone had given him a glimpse into his further destiny.

After sitting quite still for two or three minutes, Keane put a hand down on the arm of his chair. It came on the evening paper which he had forgotten. The paper rustled faintly. The touch, the answering tiny sound, recalled him.

"By Jove, I must have a look at the paper."

He picked it up. Across the top of the first page in leaded type he saw these words:

"Warrant issued for the arrest of Mrs. Paradine."

He bent over the paper with an expression of intense concentration.

II

"Palest lemon colour—isn't it, Gay?"

"Yes."

"Well, *I* like it. And that's the main thing, I suppose. Isn't it?"

"After being married for ten years, in these days! You really think that possible?"

"For us all things are possible."

"But that would include bad things."

"There are destinies, I think, for God's creatures. Always when I look at you I see a shining destiny like a halo round your life. You are a precious thing and you will be protected."

Gay's smile at him seemed to say:

"I have that feeling, too."

"The car is here, my lady," said the butler, opening the door.

"We shall be just in time," said Keane.

Gay's maid came with a white cloak. They went out to the motor.

They reached the Haymarket Theatre five minutes before the curtain went up, and made their way to the stalls, which were already nearly full. All the usual 'first night' faces, critical and important, were to be seen.

"The Jury are ready to try the case," said Keane, nodding here and there to people he knew.

"How the poor souls behind the scenes must hate us on first nights," said Gay. "But I can say this for myself: I always long for the play to be a success."

"Ah, but you are rare. You never wish ill to anyone. I don't see the Flaquers. I hope they are coming. I might have a word with him between the acts. Hulloh, there's Horfield in the stage box!"

"I believe the only first nights he ever comes to are at the Haymarket. Is Lady Horfield there? It's too far for me to see."

"She's very much there! What *can* have induced him to marry her?"

"I think she loves him very much. Perhaps it was that."

"Isn't it abominable that even love can seem only grotesque in certain people?"

"Not—only!" said Gay. "It always contains a redeeming principle."

"Oh, there are the Flaquers! That's good."

He sat down just as the lights were dimmed.

When the first act was over he said to his wife:

"D'you mind if I leave you for a few minutes, darling? I see Sir Simon is going out, and I want to catch him and find out why he wants to see me to-morrow."

"Of course go. I'm perfectly happy."

She said the words lightly, trivially even, as women say such words in such moments of pleasure. And he heard them as if lightly, trivially too. But afterwards he remembered them in a different spirit and thought of them with a tragic intensity.

As he went out many people looked at his towering figure and handsome, expressive head, and some of the men envied him his success and his not unpleasant self-assurance, and some of the women envied Gay for having such a husband.

"She's kept him all these years, and she's safer than ever with each year that goes by."

Not every woman lies on roses without any thorns, like Gay Keane. It made some women bitter to think of it. And yet women liked her, for there were in Gay no undercurrents of 'cattiness.'

Lord Horfield, standing up in the stage box beside the seated figure of his prodigiously fat and distressed looking wife, put up a small pair of opera glasses and glanced along the stalls. Presently the glasses showed him the tall, slight figure of Gay in a pale lemon-coloured dress, an empty seat beside her. He put down the glasses, said something to his wife, who replied with a movement of her large head and an awkward gesture, and went out of the box.

Meanwhile, Keane, outside in the foyer, was looking for Sir Simon and being spoken to by many of the men who had passed out of the stalls to have a cigarette. It seemed that almost everyone knew him and that most of his acquaintances wanted to have a word or two with him. Evidently he was a popular man.

"One moment, Balgate!" he said in a moment, to a large, rosy young man, who had been extravagant enough to light an enormous cigar, though the interval was announced as one of ten minutes only. "Forgive me! But I see Flaquer over there and I've got to speak to him."

"Another big case, is it?" said the large young man, who was a popular journalist, looking suddenly keen.

"I've no idea. I'm your man for golf next Sunday if the weather's possible. Yes, Woodcote Park."

He moved away towards a small, very smart, even dapper elderly man who was standing perhaps fifty yards off looking keenly about him through double eyeglasses from which hung a black ribbon. This was Sir Simon Flaquer, the cleverest and most celebrated solicitor in England, a devout son of Israel, and the repository of the deadly secrets of practically the whole of London Society.

"Oh, there you are, Keane! I was looking for you. Someone told me you were here and your wife, too. How is she?"

"Very well. But she's never ill, thank God. Her ethereal appearance is deceptive."

"And enticing. I hope she never loses it. Poor Lady Horfield! And—poor Horfield!"

"Oh, I don't pity him. I'm sure he knows where to go for consolation."

"D'you think so?"

It was characteristic of Sir Simon that he often put a question in the place of an indiscretion. "So am I!" seldom came on his lips.

"But just come into this corner for a minute. There isn't much time and I've got something to say to you."

Walking lightly in his marvellously polished evening shoes, Sir Simon led the way to a seat in a comparatively quiet part of the foyer, sat down and crossed his thin legs letting, at the same time, his eyeglasses go to the length of their ribbon. Keane sat down beside him.

"What is it, Sir Simon?"

"Have you seen the evening paper?"

"Yes."

"Mrs. Paradine's been arrested. Inevitable, of course. I'm acting for her."

"I thought you probably were, though there was no mention of the fact in my paper."

"Well, Keane, I shall want you with me. This is going to be a big case. We shall have all our work cut out, and I'd rather brief you for the defence than any man in England."

A bell sounded.

"Curtain going up already!" said Sir Simon, getting quickly to his feet. "We must have a conference. If possible, not later than to-morrow. Are you free to see me any time?"

"Only the luncheon hour, I'm afraid."

"That'll do. Come to lunch with me in Bewly Place. Can you be there by one?"

"I think so, or five minutes after."

"That'll do."

They were now close to the entrance to the stalls. Keane felt a gentle pressure on his left elbow.

"Do you know Mrs. Paradine?" came Sir Simon's voice in his ear.

"No."

"Ever seen her?"

"Never."

"A most fascinating woman, a beauty from the North. But difficult to read, *very* difficult."

And then they parted.

When Keane dropped into the stall beside his wife, he whispered to her:

"You haven't been bored all alone, dear, I hope?"

"But I wasn't alone. Lord Horfield kept me company. He's just left me. He was most agreeable and said several funny things."

"Then you take back what you said to me about him this evening?"

"Not a word of it. Did you find Sir Simon?"

"Yes. He wants me for a big case."

And then the curtain went up on the second act.

Keane didn't see Sir Simon again that evening, but as he and Gay were leaving the theatre they met Lord and Lady Horfield on their way to the portico and stopped to speak to them.

Lady Horfield was older than her husband and showed it. There was something portentous about her appearance. She towered and was alarmingly stout, yet had thin arms and small flapping hands that seemed to belong to another type of woman and to have nothing to do with her. Her face was very red and always looked congested; a distressed expression was stamped on it. A dark and very wiggy wig crowned her person. From beneath its fuss of curls peeped a pair of agitated, but obviously well meaning, small dark eyes. Gay could never see her without feeling sorry for her. Nobody seemed to know, or probably ever would know why Lord Horfield had married her. She looked as if she might once have tried to preside over a boarding house. That night she was dressed in plum colour.

They spoke of the play.

"My wife liked it," said the Judge, raising his tufted eyebrows, below which twinkled a pair of intensely sharp, steel-grey eyes.

"Oh, I don't know!" said Lady Horfield, with a sort of alarmed haste. "But I thought there were some—a few—pleasant moments. Still I hardly think perhaps I *really* cared for it. It's so difficult when you've only seen a play *once* to—to———"

She glanced, as if for help, to her husband.

"Pity the poor critics who have to make up their minds after only one performance!" said Horfield. "Their mental rapidity is a lesson to us all."

"But they are *paid* for it, Horfield!" said his wife, as if that explained the phenomenon.

"To be sure! That accounts for it. Money makes the mind go. What was your view of the piece, Lady Keane?"

"I thought it clever but not very true."

"And I'm sure you prefer truth to cleverness."

"Perhaps because I understand it more easily," said Gay.

"Does she?" said the Judge, turning to Keane with an expression of whimsical inquiry on his pointed face.

"I believe so," said Keane. "Anyhow I know she has an art of getting at the truth of both events and people."

"Then she would be very dangerous in cross examination," said Horfield. "Ah, there's our car! Good-bye, Lady Keane. I wish I had that art of yours. It would be very valuable to a Judge. Goodbye, Keane. Come, Sophy!"

Lady Horfield's terribly high shoulders moved on through the crowd.

"The tower of Pisa *en route!*" murmured Keane.

When he and his wife were on their way home he said: "The Horfield marriage is to me the most inexplicable marriage in London. What can have brought it about? She didn't have money, I'm told."

"I think it was the persistence of terrified devotion that did it," said Gay from her corner.

Keane took her hand.

"Would that weigh so much with a fellow like Horfield?"

"Perhaps when he was young and uneasy."

"Uneasy?"

"About himself and his powers. She may have been the first to reassure him."

"How?"

"By her terror and worship of him. I think that must have been it."

"And now?"

"Oh, they're an old story now!"

"Aren't old stories sometimes the best? What about ours?"

"Malcolm dear, you're said to be a brilliantly clever man."

"And do you deny it?"

"No. But as it is so haven't you discovered something about us?"

"What?"

"That we are exceptional people. Others grow out of things but we grow into things. That's why our old story is so different from the sad fading old stories that surround us in London."

"Evidently we aren't modern."

"Nor old fashioned either. We are just two exceptional people."

"Stickers, eh? Two strongly adhesive beings!"

"Don't talk of us as if we were stamps!"

The car drew up before the big green door.

And then, very soon, Keane got down to work. He often worked till far into the night getting up briefs.

He had a case in the Courts the next day but got away in good time to keep his luncheon appointment with Sir Simon Flaquer in Bewly Place. Sir Simon was the soul of punctuality and method in business hours. Out of them he allowed himself occasionally a little Bohemian carelessness, and now and then a button flew, as it were, off his mind with a pop letting through a glimpse of his underlinen. He enjoyed all the good things of life, was a frequent and generous host, revelled in good conversation, was, like so many Jews, an ardent lover and supporter of music and the theatre, and was also a devoted family man. He had a young son in his business, and two daughters at home, one, Amy, whimsical and secretly full of sentiment, the other, Judith, twinkling with humour and almost as acute as her father. (What a solicitor she would have made!) His wife, a beautiful Venetian Jewess, was tremendously intelligent and also tremendously kind. This family had an unique position in London. Although of course they knew all the important Jews, and one met many Jews at their house in Hyde Park Gardens, they had acquaintances innumerable among many who seldom went into Jewish Society. Sir Simon was valued for his extraordinary astuteness and discretion by many members of the English aristocracy, who made friends with him and his wife and daughters; the artists who flock to London from all over the world, when they were of real value—not otherwise—were warmly welcomed in Hyde Park Gardens, were often given the best legal advice gratis and were strongly backed up in their efforts to gain public favour; and many 'floating foreigners,' as Judith Flaquer called them, who were 'all right' as well as cultivated, gay and agreeable, found their way at one time or another to the 'Palace in the Park,' Society's name for the Flaquers' big London home. The Flaquers, in fact, were in touch with nearly all worlds, and the only wonder was that they found time to do all that they did without ever getting exhausted. But they were all of them dowered with zest, that best gift of the gods to the children of this world. Never did their eyes look dull; never were their unforced energies abated.

Mrs. Van Rennap, the American novelist and traveller, had named them 'the quicksilver family,' and they lived joyously up to the name.

The church clocks of London had just struck one when Keane's motor car turned into Bewly Place, a quiet *cul de sac* not far from Bond Street, at the end of which stood the large elderly house belonging to Flaquer and Flaquer. Keane was welcomed respectfully by a rosy old hall porter who, backed up by his beehive chair, had received in his time some of the greatest people in Europe, from Royalty downwards through the governing classes and the rich middle classes, to cocottes and blackmailers. Terrified women had tipped him with trembling hands as they begged him to get them a moment with the great Sir Simon; pale, stricken men, sometimes with great names, had besought him to carry their messages in spite of his quiet assertion that Sir Simon had given strict orders that he was not to be disturbed for the next hour. He was not merely a hall porter, he was a trusted janitor, known in legal circles as 'the terror that walketh in daylight,' but he looked like a chubby old coachman and his blue eyes, even when they gazed upon a blackmailer, were full of respectful courtesy.

"Good morning, Sir Malcolm. Sir Simon is just ready for you, Sir," said 'the terror' to Keane. "I'll ring for the lift."

And he moved across the square hall, followed by Keane.

"How's the bronchitis, Warwick?"

"Not started yet, Sir, I'm glad to say. But I've been to Sir Simon's own doctor and he has promised to keep it at bay, Sir."

"At bay? That's good."

"Yes, Sir."

And then Keane went up in the lift to the second floor above the main offices and was shown by a manservant into a lofty, but not large, dining-room where Sir Simon was already waiting for him, by a round table spread for lunch, with a large gardenia in the buttonhole of his double-breasted and braided black jacket, below which appeared a pair of perfectly creased grey trousers, drooping over white spats and shining black shoes.

On a Chippendale sideboard were some silver dishes keeping hot over spirit lamps. Having shown Keane in, the manservant immediately went out of the room softly shutting the door behind him.

Sir Simon held out a welcoming hand.

"You're to the minute, Keane. We shall have plenty of time. Now what will you have?"

He walked lightly across the red and blue Afghan carpet and lifted the silver covers, showing what was beneath them.

"Roast mutton for me and potatoes in their jackets."

"And I shall have curry. What will you drink?"

"Only water."

"Not barley water? You know my recipe for it?"

"To be sure. Then barley water."

"And I'll keep you company. My luncheon asceticism increases my joy in good wine at dinner."

"Yes. But I have to be careful even at dinner. Briefs! And now you've another for me?"

"Yes. Have some red currant jelly, and I'll have chutney. Yes, I've got a devil of a brief for you this time."

He ate for a moment, took a sip of barley water and then said:
"She asked for you."

"Mrs. Paradine?"

"Yes, Mrs. Paradine. 'If it comes to the worst,' she said—(and of course she knew it must some time ago)—'get Sir Malcolm Keane to defend me.' It seems she's followed the big cases in the papers with a great deal of interest for some time. I wonder—" he laid down his knife and fork for a moment, and his eyes rested on Keane with a meditative and yet piercing look—"I wonder whether she ever had a premonition that she would be in one herself some day, whether the shadow of coming events was on her when she followed those cases."

"That's possible, I suppose."

Keane seemed to hesitate for a moment, then to make up his mind to something.

"Have you formed any opinion as to her guilt or innocence?" he said. "That premonition you just mentioned as a possibility rather suggested to me a—what shall I say?—an instinctive preparation for an act that might have consequences."

"Well, I'll confess that I'm always inclined to be rather suspicious of people who, not being of the *métier*—as you and I are—pore over criminal trials. It suggests to me a bias towards crime. On the other hand, as we all know, crime is a subject that has a natural interest for the greater part of humanity."

"As sex has."

"Precisely. So one mustn't deduce too much from the fact of an amateur showing a rather acute interest in reports of exciting trials. Otherwise one might begin to suspect that every amateur criminologist was a potential criminal. And that wouldn't do. Have a little more mutton?"

"I will, thank you. It's delicious. Nothing like perfectly cooked Welsh mutton."

"And I prefer curry. The oriental touch, perhaps."

Standing at the sideboard Sir Simon carefully carved another slice from the small haunch on the silver dish. As he carried the plate back to Keane he said:

"In some fairly remote past an ancestor of mine trekked here from India."

He sat down again.

"To return to Mrs. Paradine. We shall of course have to struggle
against great prejudice on the part of the public, which will
include the Jury—I except the Judge; as a rule the judges are splendidly impartial—on account of the husband being a V.C."

"And blind!" added Keane.

"Exactly! And blind! The combination is really a terrible one
for the defence. We shall have our work cut out for us. The
national feeling for those who made great sacrifices in the war will
certainly tell against us. Of course she realises that fully. But she
seems to realise everything. She has a very clear brain."

He frowned. His forehead showed suddenly a mass of wrinkles
below his thick, undulating grey hair.

"You'll find that!" he added, glancing at Keane and immediately
looking down.

"All the better. I hate a muddle-headed client. There's nothing
like confusion in another for confusing you."

He smiled and added:

"But I'm talking to a man who could never be confused."

Sir Simon accepted the compliment with a faint smile.

"Mental confusion isn't, I hope, my leading characteristic," he
agreed. "But there are times when I am greatly in doubt."

"What about?"

"Human nature. This Mrs. Paradine, for instance."

"She's Scandinavian, isn't she?"

"Yes, she's a Dane."

"No other blood?"

"Her mother was Swedish. She's extraordinarily good-looking
in a blonde Northern way. In fact, such looks as hers might get a
woman almost anywhere. And yet she married a blind man."

"But was he blind when he first knew her?"

"Yes, he never set eyes upon her. They only met long after he
lost his sight. In addition to the handicap we've already touched
upon, there's another—the origin of this lady."

The last word he spoke with a slightly ironical accent, or so
Keane thought.

"It seems she was originally a maid servant, when she was very
young."

"How old is she now?"

"Thirty-four, she says. She doesn't look more. In fact, I

shouldn't have given her more than twenty-eight at the most. But she's very fair indeed, and these fair women often look younger than their years. And then her manner—I think that's rather young in some subtle sort of way, though she doesn't give any idea of innocence—specially—or of ignorance. She's a very remarkable person. If you met her without knowing who she was it would, I'm sure, never occur to you that she could have been a servant. But she wasn't one for very long. And she was evidently treated in a rather special way while she was in service."

"How was that?"

"Well, she was taken as a servant by a philanthropist."

"Danish?"

"No. He was an American diplomat accredited to Denmark and living, of course, at Copenhagen. First Secretary at the time. Evidently he was a born altruist doing good by stealth. It seems that Mrs. Paradine's parents—or at any rate the father, I'm not so sure about the mother—were a poor lot. She must have been a lovely girl. When she was very young, barely sixteen, they got her into a barber's shop in Copenhagen. While there, she made the acquaintance of a young devil who was connected with a gang of criminals, thieves. He evidently thought she might be very useful to his gang as a decoy, and made love to her. Pretending that he could get her work in a film studio, he persuaded her to leave the barber's, and took her to live with an elderly woman who was a pal of his and, of course, one of the worst. God knows what would have been her fate if it hadn't been for a stroke of what I suppose we might agree to call luck. Before she had been in the house more than three or four days it was raided by the police. The matter got into the papers and our American Secretary, who was often on the job helping the fallen, came forward and took the girl, against whom nothing could be alleged, into his service as a maid."

"Was he married?"

"Yes."

"His wife didn't object to his special brand of philanthropy?"

"One doesn't know for certain. Anyhow, Mrs. Paradine stayed in the service of these Americans for a time in Copenhagen and eventually went to America with them."

"Scandinavia Americanised! By the way, one point occurs to me."

"Put it."

"You said the young devil who wanted to use Mrs. Paradine as a decoy made love to her. How far did it go?"

"She says not the whole length."

"Do you believe her?"

Sir Simon got up to change the plates. As he did so he said: "With women in such matters it's very difficult to know what to believe and what to disbelieve. There's no evidence, as far as I know, either way."

He touched a bell. The manservant came in almost immediately with *Crêpes Suzette*, *Macedoine de fruits*, and cream cheese. When he had served them, Sir Simon said to him:

"Coffee in ten minutes, Blake."

"Yes, Sir Simon."

"She was a very short time in his hands. It may have been all right for her. And she says that it was."

"I can't make out exactly what is your attitude to this unfortunate lady," said Keane.

"Well now, that shows your perspicacity. For, upon my soul, I don't quite know what my attitude is."

"Do you believe her guilty of the murder of her husband?"

"Keane—I don't know what I believe about her. She is an enigma to me. But, mind you, I like her."

Keane looked rather surprised, and pursed his very expressive lips, keeping his splendid dark eyes, which had impressed so many journeymen, fixed on Sir Simon for a moment. The word 'like' had rather taken him aback. He hadn't expected it. If Sir Simon had said: "But, mind you, she fascinates me," he wouldn't have been surprised. But about the word 'like' there was a homely intimacy which was unexpected.

"Then she's evidently not a vamp," he said.

"Good gracious! Do you think any woman can vamp me?" said Sir Simon, with quite a broad, and not at all subtle, smile.

"It didn't seem likely. But is any one of us absolutely immune?"

"I'm nearing sixty. I must leave that sort of thing to you."

"I have—Gay," said Keane, very simply.

"A lovely protection from vamps of all breeds!" said Sir Simon, and apparently quite without sarcasm.

III

It was half-past two when Keane left Bewly Place, after a long and earnest colloquy with Sir Simon which had greatly increased his interest in this new case. He realised that it was likely to be one of the most sensational which had ever come his way. There were elements in it which were quite certain to fix the attention of the world upon it, and upon all those prominently connected with it. He was a strongly ambitious man, more ambitious than was suspected by his closest friends and most admiring colleagues. For he was very human and this quite natural humanity of his hid the extreme force of his ambition from those about him. Even Gay had never fully realised the extent and persistence of it. Everyone, Gay among them, knew of course that Keane exerted himself to the fullest on behalf of his clients, never spared himself in a case, but his strongly emotional identification of himself with those he was working for diverted attention from the latent egoism which goes hand in hand with ambition. A man who evidently felt so much for others would surely not be so keenly preoccupied about himself as the greatly ambitious man must necessarily be. It had become almost a joke at the Bar that Keane had only to undertake the defence of a man or a woman automatically to believe in his client's innocence.

This, however, was not the case. Keane had occasionally secured acquittals of people whose innocence he had not believed in. But while he had been pleading for them his strongly developed sense of the dramatic and his driving ambition, which made success in all he undertook almost as necessary to his soul as the air he breathed was to his body, had caused him to simulate belief so intensely that for the moment he had been able to trick his own brain. It had only been afterwards that his brain had again taken command and he had realised, or suspected, the guilt of the client he had 'got off.'

Yet he never thought of himself as a trickster, and in the ordinary affairs of life, and in his relations with others, he was known as a most sincere man.

As a great surgeon is delighted to have the chance of proving his skill in an exceptionally complicated surgical case, so a great advocate is delighted when a *cause célèbre* comes his way. When Keane left Bewly Place that day he felt like a man who has just taken a powerful tonic, and was already beginning to feel its action upon him. His brain had fastened on this Mrs. Paradine, her life and her desperate situation, had fastened on her and them like a steel trap on the wild creature caught in it. A new interest, which was to increase with the passing days, had suddenly come into his life. He walked to the Law Courts turning over all that Sir Simon had told him at lunch and after; he left the Law Courts in the late afternoon thinking about Mrs. Paradine, this evidently unusual woman whom he had never seen, but whose fate, perhaps, was being given over into his hands.

What a responsibility! His handsome face grew stern as he thought of it.

And the man had been blind! His mind kept dwelling on that, the blindness of the man whose death was to be investigated by the Law, blindness brought about by his sacrifice of self to Country. For Colonel Paradine had rejoined his Guards regiment directly the war had broken out, though there had been no obligation on his part to do so, having regard to his age—he was close on fifty, and had been out of the army for years—and had known, of course, that he would be sent to the front. But he had been one of those men who had been determined to get to the front as quickly as possible.

The sort of man the whole of England admired.

A V.C., too!

It was going to be, as Sir Simon had implied, a devil of a case. But that made it all the more enthralling. And the ambition in Keane seemed to move in him as a wave moves, rising with foam on its crest.

He walked to Pall Mall and turned in at the Cleveland Club. Although he was so devoted to Gay, he didn't as a rule hurry straight home to her. He knew it was necessary that he should frequent the society of clever men in order not to get rusty, and as he usually gave his evenings to Gay and their domestic happiness, he dedicated this hour to male intercourse. At the Cleveland he met men who, in his view, were worth meeting.

It happened that in the vast hall of the Club that day, before the fire, three men were gathered smoking and talking, two of whom were well known to Keane. Of these two one, Martin Latrobe, who was Assistant Editor of one of the big London papers, was an ardent amateur criminologist and had written two clever books about crime; the other, Vernon Cartwright, was in 'big business,' and entertained largely, at his house in London and his country place near Windsor. The third man, whom Keane did not know, was a Bishop.

As Keane, after leaving his outdoor things in the cloak-room, came up to the fire, he heard Latrobe say:

"She's probably condemned already in the eyes of the public whether she's guilty or not guilty. I pity the Defence. Hulloh, here's Keane! Perhaps he can tell us something about it."

Keane greeted his two friends, and was introduced by Latrobe to the Bishop, a small, energetic-looking man who travelled Europe in the service of the Anglican Church, and then said, in perhaps a rather stiff tone:

"Who is the unfortunate female who is probably condemned already in the eyes of the public?"

"Colonel Paradine's widow, Mrs. Paradine, to be sure," said Cartwright, a man with an amazingly broad face, the most notable feature of which was an enormous mouth with thin lips.

" 'Judge not that ye be not judged!' " said the Bishop, but not at all seriously, rather with a slightly ironical intonation, as if he were probably thinking of humanity's incessant disregard of that injunction.

"Oh, that's all very well, Bishop," said Latrobe, in his sharp, clear and authoritative voice, "but humanity without an opinion would be as flaccid as a fish without bones. And our opinion is practically our judgment. Now, as to this Mrs. Paradine! There are several things that are terribly against her. In the first place the murdered man, if he was murdered, was blind; in the second place, he was—going away already, Keane?"

"I'm sorry, but I have to write a letter," said Keane. "I'll see you later, perhaps."

And he walked towards the lift, disappeared into it and went up.

There was a moment of silence among the three men by the fire.

Then Cartwright said:

"What's the matter with Keane?"

"Your friend didn't seem to be in a very happy mood," said the Bishop.

Latrobe sat in silence for a moment. Then he jerked up his head. "I have it! I have it!" he said. "I'll bet you anything you like he's going to be in the case and doesn't want to talk about it. It must be that. In a case like this the defence would be sure to brief Keane. Wonder why I didn't think of it before."

Meanwhile, Keane was out of luck. He had made his way to the upstairs smoke-room, where he had intended to have a quiet tea and think over his colloquy of that day with Sir Simon Flaquer. But directly he entered the room he came on Lord Horfield, who was standing alone close to the door in the act of lighting a cigarette.

"Good day, Keane. Come and have tea with me. I'll treat you for once."

Keane was forced to acquiescence. He accepted with secret reluctance, remembering Gay's remarks about the Judge on the previous evening. But how could he refuse? It would be unreasonable on his part to be unpleasant to the Judge, and he had no valid excuse ready. Horfield's *bonhomie* did not give him much pleasure, for now he was thoroughly convinced that Horfield really disliked him. Gay's instinct about people he knew by experience was nearly always correct. And Horfield's evident attraction to Gay repelled him. He wasn't jealous. That was impossible, knowing and trusting Gay as he did. No; but he disliked what he suspected to be the Judge's outlook on women. There was, he was sure, no chivalry in it and a great deal of ugly lust; and Horfield's almost blatant display of his admiration for Gay did not trick Keane, though he believed it was meant to.

Over tea the Judge first talked in his airy and often satirical manner of topics of the day. He was something of a gossip, and enjoyed exercising his smiling malice at the expense of his fellow-creatures. His silvery voice contrasted with his sharp-edged mind and, in the contrast, made a piquant combination. He seemed full of contradictions, yet they were underlaid by a strong sense of logic; it was, to Keane, impossible to conceive that he had ever felt, or could ever feel, deep emotion. He had a darting mind and undoubtedly revelled in humour. His favourite modern author was George Bernard Shaw. Among the dead he delighted in Sterne, upon whom indeed he had written a monograph. Deeply serious people he saw—he himself confessed it—in caricature.

"Their minds are all chin," he said of them. "Their conversations remind me of sackcloth and ashes. Their souls are set upon Judgment Day and I don't believe in it, being a Judge."

When tea was over, however, and they had lit cigars, Horfield dropped his characteristic airy manner. Something had been said casually by Keane about the career of a man they both knew, and Horfield said:

"He has never had a career in the true sense of the word. It has been all ups and downs."

"But can't a career have ups and downs?"

"Not as his has had. Ups and downs there may be, but beneath them all there must be something inexorable, a moving onward. Without the inexorable something in him, a man is incapable of having a career."

As he said the last words, he looked at Keane with considering eyes.

"Without it," he then added, "there will come a moment when a man will betray himself. The greatest enemy to a career is emotion, unless it is held in stern control."

Keane felt sure this was meant for him. He was touched on the raw and showed it.

"I don't agree with you," he said, rather warmly. "I believe that emotion is a great driving force and that without it a man can do nothing worth doing."

"I said—unless it is held in stern control," observed Horfield, in his most mellifluous tone.

"I get a little tired of our English mania of self-control. I think it tends to keep our feelings in ice until they rather resemble the frozen meat that comes to us from the Antipodes. I prefer the homebred article with some of the fresh blood still in it."

"Le bœuf saignant! Yes, I think you do."

Again Keane felt irritated.

"The word legal is often used as if it were synonymous with dry," he said. "Anyhow, I don't intend to be turned into dust by my profession. After all, we deal in humanity."

"Usually of a somewhat inferior class," observed Horfield. "But I must say for you, Keane, that you have managed to preserve a singular freshness, almost an impulsive boyishness, if you'll forgive me for saying so, which is remarkable among counsel."

"If I do it seems to have answered," Keane couldn't help saying.

"So far!" dropped out Horfield. "Have you anything big on just now?"

His intention entirely to change the mode of their conversation was obvious. Keane felt as if he had been dismissed.

"I saw Flaquer to-day," he said, trying not to sound sulky in his effort to conceal intense irritation. "He wants me for the Paradine case."

"Ah!"

Horfield looked down at his thin knees for a moment. He was a very slight man, almost elegantly slight. His figure and carriage went well with his voice and the usual tone of his mind. Then he looked up and said:

"She is a very interesting-looking creature."

"You know her then?"

"Not at all. I have never seen her. Have you?"

"Never. But then how——"

"I saw a photograph—I should think an extremely good one—in a shop window in Regent Street to-day as I was walking to the Courts."

"What is she like?"

"Do you read Strindberg?"

"I'm afraid not. Gay does, I believe. She seems to read everything."

"Mrs. Paradine looks to me like a Strindberg woman. When you go home ask your wife what is meant by that."

"Oh, I seldom talk about my cases to Gay," Keane said. "I prefer to keep her out of them."

"Then you are not one of the many men who go to their wives for their opinion and rely on their wives' judgment rather than on their own?"

"I am not!" said Keane decisively.

"These cigars are excellent, don't you think?" said the Judge.

"They are indeed. Where do you get them?"

"Masinger's in Jermyn Street."

"Your judgment on *cigars* would never be upset on appeal," said Keane imprudently.

(In a recent important case Horfield's judgment had been upset.)

Horfield smiled.

"I'm glad your opinion marches with mine," he said. "If you'll allow me I shall send you a box—at Christmas."

"Oh really, Judge, you're too good!" said Keane, feeling as if the Good Samaritan's oil were running all over him.

"Christmas being the season of attention to the physical man. Even good Christians, it seems, have a material side which they consider it suitable to gratify on Founder's Day."

Keane knocked the ash off the end of his cigar, which really was exceptional. He wanted to get back to Mrs. Paradine's photograph, and had already realised that his temper had carried him into folly. That left-hand reference to Horfield's upset judgment had been most incautious on his part. He knew Horfield well enough to be certain that it would not be forgotten.

"That photograph you saw to-day——" he said.

"Yes?"

"What was the type? I'm naturally interested to know, as Mrs. Paradine is to be my client. What *is* the Strindberg type, as you called it?"

"Well, I don't know whether Lady Keane would confirm my impression of the Strindberg characteristic woman. Perhaps not. I conceive of her as exquisitely pale, with large, pale, very pale eyes, and that wonderful hair of the North almost flaxen but with golden lights in it. Hair, by the way, can tell you a lot about a woman. (Perhaps that's why so many women dye their hair. For fear of its giving them away!) Features? Well, with that pallor, those eyes, and that hair, it's marvellous how little a man worries about the features. Mrs. Paradine's however, in the photograph I saw, are perhaps a little bit, only a little bit, on the rough side. They are not what we call neat features. The nose seems blunt, the chin is round and decisive, the mouth isn't small. But I thought it a most lovely mouth, mutinous, perhaps, the lips meeting but not tightly pressed together. The teeth were not shown, but I have no doubts about them. Perfect teeth must certainly be behind those lovely expressive lips. And to think that the blind husband never saw them! I would rather be deaf than blind, though deaf people seem always more troubled by their affliction than the blind. The lady was casually dressed."

"Casually?"

"Yes. None of your ropes of pearls, and long dangling ear-rings, and Chanel's latest creation put on to be photographed in. Sports clothes and a sort of beret, which showed the hair of course. It would have been a crime worse than murder to have hidden it. And now for the Strindberg touch!"

He shot a side glance at Keane full of twinkling malice.

"It was a beautiful, one might almost say a mystically calm, and a self-possessed face, but one felt that it was the face of a woman in whom there might be latent hysteria. Does that recall any recollections of Strindberg to your mind?"

"But I'm sorry to say I've never read him."

"Mention it to Lady Keane. She'll know what I mean. Strindberg, you know, had madness in him, and, in my opinion, he put madness into several of his creations. Hysteria isn't actual madness. But it creeps, so I feel, along the borderland without going over. Madness can be a nuisance, and generally is, I expect. But in hysteria—let's still call it latent hysteria—there may be an element that is deeply interesting and even extraordinarily fascinating. It seems to add to rather than take away from in some cases. It comes like a breath from an unknown land. It whispers of the unexpected, of the incalculable, of the uncontrollable."

"In fact of the emotional on which just now you were down."

"Ah, but in a woman!" said Horfield. "We are talking of women now, not of K.C.s—with all respect to our admirable profession."

"I don't think I feel particularly drawn towards hysterical women," said Keane with a touch of contempt, and thinking of Gay.

"But towards the incalculable?"

"Nor towards that either,"—again thinking of Gay.

"Now, d'you know, I think you are doing an injustice to your emotional side. But perhaps you have never met the Strindberg woman."

"Probably not."

"And now," said Horfield musingly, "you are going to meet her —in the cell of a prison."

IV

KEANE passed rapidly through the hall of the Club and purposely avoided looking towards the fireplace as he traversed it. The three men were still by the fire, and Latrobe observed to the Bishop:

"He's determined to have nothing to do with us."

"Perhaps he has a hatred for aprons," said the Bishop. "I always think that ecclesiastical custom is rather hard on the Church. I shall never forget my feeling as a small boy when I first saw a clergyman wearing a shovel hat. I ran to my nurse crying. It seems to me, as I look back, that I thought the wearer was the Devil."

"I bet you we shall see in the papers to-morrow that Keane's been asked to defend Mrs. Paradine. And he's already deep in her case."

"Well, he'll have his work cut out for him," said Cartwright. "Would you wager on the verdict?"

"Things have not gone far enough yet for anything of that kind."

"But——"

Once more they fell into conversation about the Paradine case.

Keane walked home by Regent Street. He looked very carefully at the window of a certain shop, but he didn't find the photograph he was searching for. That night he said nothing to Gay about his conversation with Horfield, but he mentioned to her that he was going to lead for the defence in a case that was certainly going to be a *cause célèbre*. Gay asked him what case it was and he told her he was going to defend a Mrs. Paradine who had been arrested on a charge of having murdered her husband, a Colonel Paradine in the Guards.

"Poor woman!" said Gay, in her curiously casual and yet sympathetic manner.

Evidently she had not seen anything about the case in the papers though there had been a great deal about it in the last days.

"You say 'poor woman,' Gay. But what if she's guilty?"

"Then ten times more poor woman for having been able to do such a frightful thing. But don't you believe her to be innocent as you are going to defend her?"

"I've never seen her. It's impossible for me to form a definite opinion yet as to her guilt or innocence."

"But suppose you form the opinion that she is guilty?"

"I shall still do my very best for her. That's my duty."

Gay was silent. By her silence Keane knew that her heart didn't assent to his last remark.

"That's our British conception of the best way, indeed the only way, to get at the truth of a matter, and so to reach what we're aiming at—Justice," he said, in his most persuasive manner. "Each side puts as forcibly as possible all the evidence there seems to be for and against. When that has been done and the Judge sums up the Jury decides. Can we do better than that? Would you have no defence put up even for one who may be a criminal?"

"I don't say that. But I could never plead with any conviction for anyone who I was certain was guilty. Have you often done it?"

She fixed her eyes, her shortsighted but beautiful eyes, on him earnestly as she spoke.

"I haven't asked you before," she added. "Perhaps I oughtn't to ask you now. I know you're not fond of talking to me about your cases."

"No. I prefer to keep you out of that side of my life. There are so many ugly things in life that I have to come into contact with, but that you needn't be mixed up in."

"And—my question?" she said.

"Occasionally I have. Not very often."

"I'm sure if I were in a Court of Justice and you were pleading for someone you were sure was guilty, however wonderful you were, however eloquent, I should know that you didn't believe what you were saying."

"I'm not so sure of that, Gay."

But she said quietly:

"Yes, Malcolm, I should *know*."

"Well, you've never heard me in Court yet, and probably you never will."

"Why don't you wish me to?"

"I believe I should be awfully nervous if you were there. And somehow I've always had an odd instinct to keep you out of it all. I scarcely could tell you why. But you don't seem to belong to that side of life."

He paused, then said, prompted, perhaps, though he wasn't aware of it.

"What have you been reading to-day? *Asile de Nuit?*"

"No, Strindberg."

Keane was startled, thoroughly startled. And yet afterwards he asked himself whether he hadn't put the question because the unknown fact had pushed him to it.

"Strindberg!" he said. "And what was it?"

"A play called 'The Father.' About an appalling woman. But oh! she had brains! The play is just crammed with brains. But a terrible woman! A real dyed-in-the-wool Strindberg woman."

"Ah!"

He waited, then, as she said nothing more, he asked:

"And what's a real dyed-in-the-wool Strindberg woman? As you know I haven't time to read very much, except in the vacation."

"Well," said Gay, as if musing seriously, "it isn't easy to describe. Strindberg's women are so extraordinary. There's something merciless in them, terribly merciless. And they're brainy with a horrible sort of perching braininess. And they keep at it—yes, they keep at it."

"What d'you mean exactly by that?"

"I hardly know how to explain. You know what nagging is?"

"Yes, of course, though not from you."

"Their keeping on is worse by far than nagging. It's goading, driving. You know the awful habit donkey boys in the East used to have of making their donkeys run by pushing a goad into an open wound—well, it's like that. I could imagine a Strindberg woman persisting until murder might happen."

"On the man's part?"

"Yes, of course."

The question seemed to strike on her mind.

"Why are you asking me this—about Strindberg's women?" she said. "You have a reason, haven't you?"

"Yes. But I don't want to tell it to you now."

"Then, of course, don't. I am not really curious. And besides I trust your reluctance."

"I never knew any woman so full of trust as you are, Gay."

"With you, not with everyone. You have taught me to trust."

"If so I've only fostered what was already there."

"When you married me the world hadn't taught me yet not to trust," she said, simply.

"And now?"

"Well, one has to be careful, even against one's will," Gay said, with a little sigh. "There are a good many people here in London whom I'm afraid I could never trust."

"Even so I can't see you ever degenerating into a cynic."

"I hope not. Do you think you will ever tell me why you asked about Strindberg's women?"

"Then you are a little curious?"

"I suppose I must be."

"Probably I shall. But I don't want to now."

And why was that? Was it because Keane was for the defence and was therefore already instinctively defending Mrs. Paradine by not handing on, even to Gay, Lord Horfield's comment on her photograph, which might create prejudice against her?

He asked himself the question and didn't then supply the answer.

That night—they dined out with some friends in Leamore Place —as usual he sat down to do some work when they came home. But he found it difficult to concentrate. His mind was already full of this Mrs. Paradine.

"Horfield's put me up to it," he thought. "And Sir Simon's put me up to it, too. The woman's evidently made a very strong impression on Sir Simon. And even her photograph took a pretty tight hold on Horfield. I was a fool with Horfield to-day."

And then resolutely he bent over his brief.

On his way to the Courts on the following morning he visited a photographer's shop in Regent Street.

"Do you happen to have a photograph of Mrs. Paradine, who has just been arrested, for sale?" he asked.

"Yes, Sir Malcolm," said the young man to whom he had put the question, smartly, gazing at him with obviously eager interest. "I'll get it for you."

He hastened away and came back with a cabinet photograph.

"There she is, Sir Malcolm! A beautiful woman, Sir!"

"Will you kindly put it in an envelope for me?" said Keane rather curtly, and without looking at the photograph.

The young man seemed rather dashed but he only said:

"Certainly, Sir Malcolm, with pleasure," and went to get an envelope.

"Some of the wind gone out of his billowing sails!" thought Keane, remembering, half humorously, half wrily, Gay's remark to him.

He left the shop with the photograph in the breast pocket of his coat. Later that day, in his home, he studied it intensely.

"My client!" he muttered, bending over it.

While he was looking at it he heard a step and knew it for Gay's. Immediately he hid the photograph.

V

THERE was no novelty for Keane either in a prison or in a prison cell, but when he drove up to Holloway with Sir Simon Flaquer for his first interview with Mrs. Paradine, he was surprised to find that he had something of the feeling of a man paying a first visit to a place of gloom about which lingered harsh memories of crime and despair. And he realised immediately, with acuteness, what a beautiful woman must feel when being driven there under arrest, freedom gone, possibly for ever.

"It's extraordinary how calm they often seem!" he said to Sir Simon, in whose car he was driving.

"Who? Persons just taken into custody?"

"Yes."

"It is. I've often thought so. But the shock of arrest is usually tremendous. I'm sure of that. The hand of the Law laid upon you must feel like the weight of a world. Suddenly no more your own master—as if one ever was, by the way! That's the terrific moment, the unforgettable moment. The bones like wax in most cases, I fancy. And yet there will always be crime in plenty, always be the strange people who are ready to take the great risk. Gambling on the chances! Extraordinarily interesting problems they offer us. I wouldn't exchange my profession for any other. Sometimes I look round London and I say to myself: 'Simon Flaquer, there's nobody who has such an interesting life as you have.' And I thank Jehovah."

"Is your life more interesting than mine, do you think?"

"I do. You see, I have so many cases that never come into Court. Half my time is spent in keeping cases out of Court. And such cases!"

"What reminiscences you could write!"

"And never shall write a line of them. Here we are!"

The car drew up before the prison.

At the door of the room where they were going to see Mrs. Paradine, Sir Simon said softly, in his slightly guttural voice:

"I shall be interested later on to hear what your impression of the lady is, and whether it accords with mine."

"Is yours quite definite?"

"I wouldn't say that. Still, of course one has an impression."

And then they went in.

The room, which contained a table and three chairs, had an out-side wall of glass, and was rather like the office of a large commercial warehouse. Sir Simon and Keane waited there for a moment, and then the prisoner came in escorted by a wardress, who at once withdrew, but remained in the corridor, out of hearing but able to see all that passed between the prisoner and those who were visiting her.

"Well, Mrs. Paradine," said Sir Simon, with a sort of brisk cheeriness, taking a long white hand in his, "I've got the great man for you and here he is. Sir Malcolm Keane—Mrs. Paradine."

And Keane shook hands with her, and found her hand cool and dry and steady in his.

"I am very glad you will act for me, Sir Malcolm," she said. "I wanted you from the first. I told Sir Simon so, and asked him to get you if possible. I shall need all the help I can have. I know that—yes."

The voice was not a light voice, and there was a veiled, slightly husky sound in it which was individual and pleased Keane, he scarcely knew why. He noted a soupçon of American accent and there was a trailing accentuation of certain words such as he had noticed in Swedes talking English. Everything about her, he thought, suggested the North and the strangeness and fascination of the North. She was as different from a Latin almost as a grey sky above snow is different from a blue sky above palm trees. Her manner was quiet and composed, and suggested to him, her situation and the moment being taken into account, an amazing steadiness of nerves, even a complete lack of what is generally called nervousness. She was not dressed in black. (Absurdly enough, considering his experience, he had expected that she would be.) She wore a grey dress, very simple with the simplicity that comes from the best Paris houses. It took his mind to the country. He scarcely knew why, for it wasn't a sports costume. But there was nothing of town about it. And in it, though so very well dressed, she looked somehow like a woman who very seldom went to parties, and who probably didn't care for them much when she did. Something remote and casual about her. The material of the dress had a roughish look, but just the right kind of roughness. She of course didn't wear a hat and Keane fixed his eyes on her hair. It was certainly marvellous hair, pale, very pale, yellow with gold lights in it here and there. There were ripples in it, not the corrugated ripples of the permanent wave, which were abhorrent to Keane, but soft, lazy-looking ripples almost suggesting disorder, as if she didn't care how she looked but just happened to look wonderful.

The hair was exceedingly thick, and long at the back, and curling outwards in some mysterious way all round the back of her milk-white neck, which wasn't thin though it was long. Her head had a look almost of roughness as the material of her dress had. But it was a roughness that was splendid and enticed far more than a perfectly and obviously neat head ever could. This was a woman who certainly could never look as if she came out of a bandbox. She didn't seem to be at all made up. There was no colour in her face, just a wonderfully smooth fair whiteness. Her eyes were enormous and exceedingly pale, Keane thought the palest pair of eyes he had ever seen in a woman's head. He supposed they were silver grey. Afterwards, when he looked at them, he often thought they were very pale blue. The young-moon shaped eyebrows above them were not yellow but, he thought, mouse-coloured. (Perhaps a woman would have named their colour differently.) She was tall for a woman, probably at least five foot ten in height, and naturally slim, very slim indeed, as a greyhound is whom one cannot imagine ever being anything else. Her white hands were long and very narrow, with long narrow fingers and narrow thumbs. Everything of her was in harmony. And she had a curious distinguished look which made it very difficult to believe that she had ever been a servant. And yet she had. Keane had Sir Simon's word for that. In that very first moment of seeing her, Keane was specially struck by two things. One was that this woman's face could certainly look blank and yet be very beautiful in blankness; the other—and this startled him—was that in her somewhere, and he couldn't say where, there lurked some faint, surreptitious resemblance to Gay.

As she sat down, he thought he had never seen a more natural, less self-conscious movement. It was even careless in its slouching grace. But when she stood she was straight as a wand.

"Good Heavens, what a woman!" Keane said to himself. "And won't she help—with a Jury!"

Already he was thinking about a Jury in connection with Mrs. Paradine. And that was horrible. Why wasn't this woman free, like other beautiful women?

There was about her something brooding. And yet she continued to remind him mysteriously of Gay. Why was that? How could it be? Two women so different the one from the other! And this mysterious resemblance, which he couldn't define, couldn't pin down to any characteristic of appearance or manner, which seemed evasive as will o' the wisp, puzzled and obscurely distressed him.

He said something polite in his charming and cordial way in reply to her little speech. Sir Simon had brought with him a leather portfolio and he laid it down, and they drew up chairs, and immediately there was something of business in the atmosphere. No time to waste in desultory conversation. They must get to work.

"And now," said Sir Simon, "we must go into things."

And then at once Keane remembered that he was counsel for the defence of this woman, stood perhaps between her and the hangman. He cast a glance at her beautiful long throat that wasn't thin.

"What a responsibility! What a responsibility!" he said to himself. "But I'm going to bring it off. Nothing shall stop me. Nothing shall prevent me. I'm here for that. My gifts were given to me for that. And she asked for me. She felt I was the man and I'll prove to her that she was right."

But what was hidden in her?

He leaned his arms on the table. Although he wasn't conscious of it, he was devouring her with his eyes.

In the discussion that followed—it might almost have been a board meeting at moments—Keane found out, he believed, a good deal about this woman whom he was going to defend. He found out that she had a clear intellect with a quick grasp of important points. That was one thing. He found out that she had moral courage, a possession that is rare enough though such an immense number of people, men and women, have physical courage. She was evidently ready to face all the danger that was likely to befall her, didn't want or intend to shrink away from anything. She proved this by pointing out calmly things that would tell against her in the examination that was close upon her.

"My past is against me," she said quietly, in the rather husky and not light voice. "I was once a servant."

"Any harm in that?" interjected Keane, in his impulsive and fiery way.

"Do the English like a woman to rise from being a maid-servant to being a rich woman who has lived in luxury and could live in luxury still if she were acquitted?" asked Mrs. Paradine.

"They'd be damned snobs if they didn't!" said Keane, with contempt.

"But perhaps—are they *not,* some of them?"

"Of course they are," said Sir Simon, in his swift common-sense way. "She's right," he added to Keane. "They'll think: 'How did she force herself out of domestic service? Must be something wrong there!' That's what they'll think."

"And then my beginnings!" said Mrs. Paradine, always in the same slightly hoarse voice with the trailing accentuations. "It was not my fault. But they were very bad. They will say to themselves: 'She came from the mud—surely she must be muddy.' "

"Undoubtedly we shall have to contend against the bourgeois prejudices of a British Jury!" said Sir Simon.

"You can trust me to get over those," said Keane, confidently. As he spoke instinctively he drew himself up and opened out his broad, but not clumsy, chest. He had a splendid figure and knew that in his profession it was an asset.

"Then my husband was such a remarkable man, such a very fine man. One of the rare men! And his sacrifice was so great, and all for his country. They will think beforehand: 'If this woman did what she is accused of doing she is not an ordinary murderess, she is a fiend.' To crush a worm is not so very much. But to crush a glowworm, something that is giving light—that is not the same thing. And he glowed and gave light."

Evidently the mention of light reminded her of the saddest circumstance connected with the dead man, for, after an instant of silence, she added:

"And then his blindness! One of the bravest of the brave and yet to be helpless! The one that could strike at a helpless man who was splendidly brave—what must she be? His blindness was against him in the last years of his life. But now it is against me. It is *my* enemy."

"Of course, I realised that at once," said Keane. "And yet there's the other side of that blindness question which, properly handled as I shall handle it, will tell immensely in your favour."

"Yes?" she said, quietly, without any excitement.

"Weren't you his eyes?" said Keane, leaning forward and looking at her with a piercing intensity which he wasn't aware of.

"I was, of course. I had to be."

Sir Simon gave vent to a slight dry cough, which somehow seemed rather a deliberate comment than an unwanted affliction. Keane turned slightly and looked sharply in his direction.

"We won't get it like that in Court," he said.

It wasn't absolutely obvious to which of the two he was speaking. Sir Simon coughed again and then said:

"No; not quite like that."

"Why not?" said Mrs. Paradine, apparently in the dark. "He was blind. I was his wife. Hadn't I to be his eyes?"

"It was natural you should be. But don't you see our point?" said Sir Simon. "The word 'had' rather suggests compulsion. There must be no suggestion of compulsion. Were you not gladly, eagerly, eyes for this unfortunate—hero?"

He said the final word with a faintly ironic intonation, as if anxious to save himself from being melodramatic.

"He *was* a hero!" she said, and there was a sudden sulky sound in her voice.

"Indeed he was!" said Sir Simon, with a very brief glance at Keane. "The whole world knows it. The Victoria Cross attests it. And so you were proud and glad to be his eyes. That is the point."

"Oh, I see now," she said.

"When giving your evidence, you must be very careful not to put things in an ugly way," said Sir Simon, with a definiteness not far from severity. "By that, I mean in a way that would tell against yourself with the average man or woman. No doubt there will be some women in the Jury."

"I will try, of course," she said, with a touch of impatience.

("This woman seems very sincere!" Keane thought.)

"No heroics either," continued Sir Simon. "British people always distrust heroics."

"Not quite always!" commented Keane, dryly.

Sir Simon smiled.

"They mustn't come from her," he said. "In a great speech for the defence, perhaps, but certainly not from a witness."

"I'm with you," said Keane.

"Can't I just be as I am?" asked Mrs. Paradine.

And her broad white forehead showed a slight contraction.

"If I try to act a part I shall make many slips. I know that. I want to be natural."

"I'm not sure you could be anything else," said Keane, looking for a moment half-amused. "All we want, Sir Simon and I, is to be sure you don't do yourself any harm by your naturalness. In a trial it is possible to be too natural."

"Is it?" said Mrs. Paradine.

And just at that moment Keane had the feeling that she was one of the most extraordinary women he had ever encountered. She seemed so strangely unaware of herself, in that general unawareness being included unconsciousness of the effect she was making on those she was with.

"Is she even thinking about us?" he asked himself.

And yet she didn't seem to be thinking about herself, except when Sir Simon and he obliged her to. And then she seemed to do it with an almost stubborn reluctance. Could she be mulish? Certainly, she didn't, so far, seem to be malleable. It was possible, he began to think, that they might have trouble with her. But she was full of a curious, mutinous fascination.

"We don't want you to act a part," said Sir Simon. "Certainly not. You would be found out."

"Oh!" said Mrs. Paradine.

"English Judges are not easily deceived and they have to direct the Jury. If it was the Jury without the Judge! Ah then!"

He lifted his rather oriental-looking hands in a very un-English gesture.

"But the Judge tells the Jury—even more than the average outsider thinks."

"Nevertheless, Judges can be influenced, even conquered," said Keane, squaring his shoulders.

"Not all Judges. What about Horfield, for instance?"

"Oh—Horfield!" Keane exclaimed. "We shan't have him in this case, I hope."

"It's quite possible that we shall. He's one of our best criminal Judges."

Keane pressed his lips together, frowned and, for an instant, looked heavy, almost old. His eyes met the pale eyes of Mrs. Paradine.

"But are not all English Judges *just* men?" she asked.

"Judges, like all other men, are subject to likes and dislikes," said Keane. "And Lord Horfield——"

A warning look from the bright eyes of Sir Simon stopped him. He had been on the edge of saying a very imprudent thing.

"——is a rather difficult Judge to plead before," he said slowly. "There's something frosty about him that—that dries people up. But—well—that's beside the point."

And then they got down to the evidence.

When the interview was over and Keane was saying good-bye to Mrs. Paradine, he asked:

"How do you pass your time? Have you anything to read?"

"Oh, yes," she said, in the trailing voice. "I am reading a book called *Les Grands Initiés*. It is interesting. It has a motto, too."

"What's that?" said Keane.

" 'L'Ame est la clef de l'univers.' "

"I don't know it," Keane said, after a pause.

As he said that he wondered whether Gay knew it. Probably she did.

And then they said good-bye to Mrs. Paradine and she went away with the wardress.

VI

WHEN Sir Simon and Keane left the prison that day they drove to Bewly Place for further discussion. At first they were silent in the motor car. Keane seemed plunged deep in thought. Sir Simon, wrapped up in a fur-lined coat with a sable collar, looked out of the window on his side into the murky gloom. As usual he had an air of being brilliantly alive. By the side of Keane his slim smallness and numerous hints of the East were emphasised. And his nearness to Keane emphasised the latter's bigness, which wasn't bulkiness.

Presently Sir Simon turned from the window. Perhaps he was tired of looking out at the gloom of London.

"Thinking over the difficulties of this case?" he asked, in his thin carrying voice.

Keane lifted his head.

"I was—naturally."

"Specially troubled about any one of them?"

"Yes, I am."

"Perhaps I could tell you which it is."

"Do, do!" said Keane.

"This damnable contrast between the magnificent public character of the dead man, dashing bravery, self-sacrifice, patriotism carried to dizzy heights above zero and his private character."

"Yes, that was what I was brooding over."

"She is bitterly aware of the danger that lies for her there, isn't she—eh?"

"Did she show it?" said Keane, and there was a touch of defiance in his voice.

"Her intellect—a very good one, by the way—accepted it as a fact. That woman faces facts."

"Yes. She's no coward."

"If she'd committed a crime one might predict that she'd have the courage of it."

"And if she hadn't she'd have all the fighting courage of innocence."

"Certainly! Certainly!"

Sir Simon said nothing more for a moment. During that moment, being amazingly quick in receiving impressions, he was acutely aware that Keane was not feeling quite so friendly to him as he usually did.

"It's unfortunate," he said, at length, as Keane kept silence, "that there will probably be a number of witnesses to the ugly side of Colonel Paradine's character."

"The evidence of servants isn't difficult to discredit as a rule," said Keane, with some contempt in his voice.

"Still even servants can be dangerous in certain cases. And then there are others. The Paradines lived in the country, and the country is more of a glass house than the town."

"But they were all very proud of him, and naturally so," said Keane. "A V.C. sheds glory on his neighbourhood."

"Of course! But still many of the neighbours were fully aware of the discrepancies between Colonel Paradine's record as a soldier and his record as a private gentleman. She is chivalrous about him, of course."

"Very much so."

"The question is—why? Is she chivalrous because she senses the danger to her if Colonel Paradine's objectionable characteristics are fully exposed, or is she chivalrous because she loved and admired him in spite of them, and so wishes no speck of black to rest on his shining memory?"

"Your answer to that question, I should say, must depend on the conception you have formed of the lady's character."

Again Sir Simon was sharply aware of a creeping unfriendliness in Keane.

"Do you think Mrs. Paradine is an easy woman to read?" he said.

"No, I shouldn't care to say that."

"Nor should I. Ah, here we are! Come up and we'll go into it all more thoroughly."

It was two hours later when Keane came away from Bewly Place, and during the whole of the time he had been shut up alone with Sir Simon a certain question had never been broached between them: the question of Mrs. Paradine's innocence or guilt. They had skirted round it, of course; they had even debated what were likely to be the views of others in regard to it; what they had not done was to speak personally with frankness about it. Sir Simon had not said to Keane: "What's your impression? Is this woman guilty or not guilty?" And Keane had not said to Sir Simon: "Tell me frankly what you believe about her now. Is she a murderess or not?"

They had avoided that surely obvious question. And why? Sir Simon knew why. He was not quite certain whether Keane knew or not. Their intellects were not akin really though both were remarkable. Sir Simon was essentially and at all times a realist. He had warm feelings—his wife and family knew that—but he assembled facts, and saw them just as they were. He made no mistake about them. Keane, however, had a strongly romantic tendency and this often coloured his view of things. Golden clouds of glory or black clouds from the Brocken swept through his mind. Had his intellect marched closely with Sir Simon's the fundamental question of their respective views of Mrs. Paradine would surely have been settled. It wasn't that day. And when Sir Simon was left alone in his room in Bewly Place he muttered, as he touched the electric bell to summon his junior partner, Harold Wigston, a valuable fellow whom he had made valuable:

"The boy in him! The boy in him! Now a Jew, even if he were really a boy, couldn't have taken it quite like that. But he'll plead for her magnificently—because——"

And then the bell was answered and he turned his mind to other things.

That day Keane didn't look in as usual at the Cleveland. He was in no mood for casual conversation even with clever men. Moreover he didn't want to meet Horfield. But he did very much want to meet Gay as quickly as possible, for he wished to trace and identify that strange resemblance which he had noticed in Holloway Prison between her and Mrs. Paradine.

On his way home he called at a well known French library near Charing Cross.

When he and Gay met, just before dinner—for Gay was out when he reached Portland Place—Keane put a question to her.

"Do you know a saying—'L'Ame est la clef de l'univers'?"

"Why, Malcolm," she said, evidently surprised. "Have you been reading *Les Grands Initiés?*"

"No. I haven't much time for that sort of reading unfortunately. I suppose I'm too successful. Success brings such a lot of toil with it."

"Then where did you see that saying?"

"On the cover of Schuré's book. I saw it lying—somewhere—recently, and was struck by that saying. It goes very deep."

"Yes, terribly deep."

"Why do you say *terribly,* darling?"

"Because I think the soul is so, *so* difficult to get to, the naked soul. It hides, and it knows *how* to hide."

Keane took her by the shoulders and gazed into her face.

"Why?" she asked.

But he didn't tell her why. He didn't want to speak to her about Mrs. Paradine just then.

They dined at home that night, and no one was with them. Although, knowing many people and being fond of first nights, the opera and concerts, they went out a great deal at night, both of them loved a quiet evening when, after an excellent little dinner, they sat by the log fire in the big sitting-room downstairs which adjoined the spacious dining-room, and talked, while Keane smoked a cigar, or each read a book. This room was at the back of the house and was very quiet though in it they were sometimes aware of faint sounds from the great City. In these peaceful evenings Keane savoured his domestic happiness and his worldly prosperity and knew himself for a fortunate man. He had succeeded in love and he had succeeded in law. And he was still in the prime of life and had excellent health. Often, looking across at Gay's slim figure, her lovely body which seemed at home everywhere, and in every posture, her long neck and delicious head with its shining brown hair and yellow-brown eyes full of confidence and serenity, he thought: 'And I have found the one woman and she is for me,' and felt the peculiar peace which comes only to those whose feet are set on rock that shifts not beneath them. And then the curious contrast between his professional life and his private life gave him cause for, usually fleeting, reflection. So often his work lay among criminals, so often he had to probe into and try to untangle the meshes of sin, so often his money was made from the horrors of life. That very night, when Gay had gone up to her bedroom, he would sit down to study the intricacies of the case in which that woman from the North was involved. And that woman would be sleeping, or lying awake, that night in Holloway Gaol and wondering whether freedom was beyond her possession for ever.

And she was somehow like Gay.

Gay was deep in a book on the other side of the fire, her little dog, Sausage, a thoroughbred Dachshund with yellow eyes, lying close to her, resting his chin on her left foot and looking like a tiny toy elephant. Keane put down his book, *Histoire de l'Art Moderne* by Elie Faure, leaned back in his deep armchair, cigar in hand, and looked at her, seeking where a resemblance lay.

Gay, though the whole effect of her was an effect of almost luminous fairness and fluid grace and airiness, was darker than the woman from Scandinavia. Her hair was brown and her eyes yellow-brown, and her eyebrows were narrow and long, not curved in the sickle-moon shape shown above the pale eyes Keane had seen that day in the prison. Her face was small and oval, and her skin was very white and had a transparent look. She was surely a nymph strayed into modern London. Her features were more delicate, more ethereal than Mrs. Paradine's. Her profile, with the slightly tip-tilted nose and extraordinarily sensitive nostrils, always made Keane think of Echo, lover of Narcissus, Echo when she was no longer a chatterbox but had been punished by Hera. But this Echo loved him and had no thought of Narcissus, and only his arms might hold her. Mrs. Paradine, Keane now realised, had a marked definiteness in her appearance which was not characteristic of Gay. And now that he was with Gay he was aware that in Mrs. Paradine there remained something, very subtle, however, which at moments might suggest to an acute observer that she was not the thorough-bred that Gay obviously was. Both she and Gay were tall, very slim, very natural in their movements and had long narrow hands.

But even now he had not detected where exactly the resemblance of the one to the other lay, though he knew he had not been wrong. There was a resemblance between them. There was even, he believed, a charm that was common to both though perhaps not in the same degree.

A sudden feeling of dislike shot through him, dislike of this subtle resemblance. It seemed to him that he wanted to, but could not, deny it.

Gay put down her book and sighed, and the sigh was echoed by Sausage.

"What's the matter, Malcolm dear?" she asked.

"The matter!" he said, startled.

"Yes. You are not quite happy this evening."

"I believed I was."

"Till I spoke. But now you know you are not."

After a moment of hesitation, Keane said:

"I have a big case on my mind. That's it. I've been to Holloway Prison this afternoon to learn more about it. To-morrow I shall have to study it."

"Is it that case of Mrs. Paradine?"

"Yes."

"Poor woman! What is she like?"

"I think she's a little like you."

He hadn't wished to say it, but he had said it.

"Really!" Gay said.

And Keane noticed that there was a sound of reluctance in her voice as if her mind wanted to push away from it his statement as untrue.

"Perhaps it's my—— I may be wrong. You are such different types."

"Are we?"

And then the conversation dropped. Sausage turned over on his back and lifted his four paws towards the ceiling at the same time yawning. This meant that he was ready to go out.

"I'll give Sausage his run," said Keane.

"Yes, do. I'll be here when you come back."

"Come, Sausage!"

Sausage turned rapidly over and got to his feet, uttering his usual short muffled bark which meant: "I am ready."

He followed his master out of the room, his wagging tail pointing cheerily upwards.

It was a foggy and humid night typical of November in London. While Sausage was busy investigating several area railings and selected segments of the street Keane walked a little way in the direction of Regent's Park. He was conscious of a slight depression of spirits and regretted having spoken of the Paradine case to Gay just now. His instinct to keep her always out of his cases had been a right instinct. Professionally he was remarkably self-sufficient and always had been. Much as he loved Gay he did not need help from her in his profession. He was not one of those husbands who are to be heard saying proudly: "Without my wife I should never have got to where I am." If he had never seen Gay he would still have been Malcolm Keane, famous as an advocate, impetuous, passionate in his work and successful in it. And he had been less thoughtful than usual when he had blurted out that remark about Gay's likeness to Mrs. Paradine. Gay hadn't liked it. Perhaps she had felt that it seemed to connect her with a sensational life, a life she had nothing to do with. Or—anyhow she hadn't liked it, and it had created a momentary coldness between them. Just a tiny passing coldness that meant really nothing. But still——

He heard a patter behind him. Sausage was at his heels quite ready now for his basket. Keane returned to the house. He went rather eagerly to the sitting-room where he had left Gay by the fire. But it was empty.

So she had changed her mind and had gone up to bed.

And he had to study the Paradine case. He felt a sudden reluctance to do that, a sickness of work. But it must be done. But couldn't work get in the way of something that was greater than work? Couldn't it be, or become, a separating quantity, a barrier rising up between a man and something that was dearer to him than any ambition?

He had never thought of his work in this way before, literally never in all his years. Hitherto he had always gloried in his work. What was the matter with him to-night?

Sausage ran merrily out of the room. He had gone upstairs to his basket on the first landing. Keane rang the bell for the butler to turn out the lights and lock up and followed the rocking patter of Sausage.

He found the little fellow already ensconced in his basket, a yellow eye showing in sign of good night. He bent to touch the brown head, then turned into his dressing-room.

"Gay!" he called.

"Yes?" came her voice from the adjoining bedroom.

"So you didn't wait?"

"No. I think I'm tired to-night."

He went to the door between the two rooms. He still felt a thin barrier between them.

Gay was in a white silk wrapper in a large armchair near a bright little fire before which lay a beautiful Persian rug. He thought of the other in Holloway and felt almost ashamed of their luxury.

"And I was thinking that I didn't want to do any more work to-night."

"Must you?"

For an instant he was ready to give it up, not to go to the library that was on the same floor near their bedrooms, to stay with his wife and forget the Paradine case.

"Well——" he said.

He hesitated.

"I ought to," he added.

Gay said nothing.

"You see I've got such a lot on hand."

"Yes?"

"And this is such an important case, terribly important—for my career."

He had been going to say something different, and substituted the last three words hurriedly, as a man might who felt he was on the verge of making a slip.

"But your career is made, isn't it?" she said.

"Made? Success is always in danger. One has to work to keep at the top. It's a strain, Gay."

At that moment he was longing for the sympathy she was usually so ready, so eager to give.

"It must be. Don't overdo it, Malcolm. Why take so many cases? It isn't as if we were poor. And if there wasn't so much money coming in we could easily live more economically."

"Oh, I couldn't drop out!" he exclaimed.

The mere thought of such a thing startled him, struck a blow against his ambition.

"Besides—I don't want to seem conceited, but there are certain coups which I feel could perhaps only be brought off by me. I think I have been given capacities, powers which no other English counsel has in quite the same degree. Oughtn't I to use them, isn't it my bounden duty to use them, when I have the chance, when the fate of a human being depends upon whether I do or not? Gay, there's an enormous responsibility in being leading counsel for the defence in a great trial. I mustn't be weak. I mustn't give in. I must do my very best. I mustn't leave anything to chance. If I did I should be horribly unworthy, and if—if things went wrong because of any dereliction of mine, I should never forgive myself."

While he was speaking his reluctance to work that night left him, was replaced by an almost hot eagerness to get down to it.

"You understand that, don't you, darling?" he added, suddenly struck by her complete immobility in the chair and her lowered eyelids.

"I wonder if I do—quite!" she said.

"Surely——"

"There are so many threads in the web of any one of us. It's difficult to unravel them. But one goes on trying. Don't be too late to-night."

"I won't. I promise you."

But it was after two o'clock when he went to bed. And Gay seemed to be sleeping.

VII

COLONEL PARADINE! What manner of man had he really been, in the depths of him? That was what Keane had been trying to come at that night between leaving his wife and returning to her, after completely forgetting her. (For when he concentrated on a case he forgot everything else.)

Colonel Paradine had been a *beau sabreur* of our modern days certainly; a magnificent Guardsman, a man's man, a heroic figure bound to win the admiration of every woman with a heart for the great adventure, of every man who thrilled to the trumpet call of courage. He had been a patriot *pur sang*. But he had quite evidently been much else.

The woman now accused of his murder had been his second

wife. His first wife had had a bad time with him. Women, it seemed, had always pursued Colonel Paradine from his earliest youth. They had tried to spoil him. And evidently they had succeeded in their pertinacious attempt. Under the apparent modesty about his own efforts which the Englishman of a certain class considers obligatory Colonel Paradine had probably concealed, or partially concealed, an inordinate vanity. A splendid soldier, he had perhaps not been vain about that; but he had been vain about his successes with women. The soldier side of him had been first-rate. Not a doubt could exist about that fact. But apart from the soldier, with his bravura, his fearlessness, his thoughtless readiness for self-sacrifice, Colonel Paradine had surely been far less than admirable. Kind to his men, careful always for them, he had been cruel with women and brutally thoughtless about and indifferent to their happiness and peace. There was abundant evidence of it.

Unfortunately!

Unfortunately for the defence!

And already Keane was, in brain and soul, passionately on the defensive.

Murder without a motive; such a charge may not be difficult to repel. But when there is a very strong motive for murder the defence is often hard put to it. As he studied his brief Keane wished fiercely that Colonel Paradine had been a man of a different type. What woman would be likely to murder a blind hero who had been splendid in battle but also splendid to her? Unless of course she had a lover and was being kept from him by the presence of her husband.

And hitherto Keane had not found any evidence that Mrs. Paradine had had a lover while she had been married to Colonel Paradine. If she had had one his traces were lost. It was possible of course that there had been a secret marvellously kept. Keane's experience of women in big cases had taught him that when a woman wishes to keep a secret she is, as a rule, a greater adept in deception than a man. So that possibility could not be ruled out in this Paradine case. But as Sir Simon had said to him: "Look as one may one doesn't come on a lover."

That was well for the defence, a strong point in favour of Mrs. Paradine.

But, against it, there was Colonel Paradine's treatment of her.

During the interview at Holloway Prison she had not said a word against him. Her 'line' evidently was to defend his memory if it was attacked. And of course it would be attacked. Now there might be one of two reasons for her defence of her husband's memory. She might have loved him very deeply and, as a loving woman will, instinctively now tried to act as a shield against his attackers. Or she might have realised how important it was for her to minimise those faults in his nature which might furnish a possible motive for hatred of him on her part.

Keane weighed up these alternatives in the knowledge that he now had of Mrs. Paradine. But Sir Simon, a penetratingly sharp man with an unrivalled experience of women in contact with the Law, had said that she was very difficult to read, and Keane found himself, in his solitude, mutely assenting to the assertion. Had she loved her husband or not? Which was in the ascendant in her, heart or brain?

She had made upon Keane the impression of a woman with an excellent brain. Yet there had been suggestions of a curious naïveté in her. Keane had not forgotten her apparent misunder-standing about the reason of his and Sir Simon's objection to that phrase of hers 'I had to be,' —meaning 'I was obliged to be his eyes.' Her eventual 'Oh, I see now' after Sir Simon's explanation, had been spoken with such simplicity that it was almost impossible not to accept it at its face value. But of course it might possibly have been a blind.

Keane, however, was inclined to think not. But then that told—didn't it?—against the excellence of Mrs. Paradine's brain. For surely a quick-witted woman would have grasped instantane-ously their reason for objecting to the phrase 'I *had* to be.'

Could a 'Strindberg woman' have missed the point there?

And then Keane's thoughts went for a moment to Horfield. He didn't want Horfield to judge the case of Mrs. Paradine. He would prefer that any Judge rather than Horfield should sit on the bench at the Old Bailey when the case came up for trial. And yet, as Sir Simon had remarked, Horfield was one of the best criminal Judges England possessed, if not the best.

But he was unsympathetic. Rather a feeble reason, perhaps, for Keane's objection to him as Judge in a case in which he, Keane, would be concerned. Keane's legal brethren would laugh at such a reason if they knew of it. But beneath Keane's striking presence, towering stature and self-assured demeanour was a great deal of sensitiveness. And what Gay had said about Horfield's dislike of him had not been forgotten by him. She was right. If Horfield, publicly, could take the wind out of the billowing sails of Keane K.C., he would surely do it, and enjoy the doing of it. There was a lively malice in him.

"And she might possibly suffer then on my account!" he said to himself, his mind again reverting to Mrs. Paradine. "That mustn't be."

And at that moment he came to a strong resolve. If by any evil chance it should fall to Lord Horfield to judge Mrs. Paradine— for the case would certainly go to trial after the hearing before the Police Magistrate—Keane would do his utmost to get on good terms with Horfield before the hearing at the Old Bailey. He often met Horfield in private, at the Cleveland and in Society; he would use his opportunities. He knew that he was perhaps rather too apt to show others what he felt towards them. Certainly he had made one or two slips with Horfield. That stupid allusion to a case upset on appeal had been one of the worst. Well, he'd be more careful in the future. He'd walk warily. He knew the natural heat of his temper. He'd look to that. A great mistake to be too impulsive; a cardinal mistake to be impulsive at the wrong time! There were moments, great moments, when he was bound to let himself loose. Such moments would come, must come, when Mrs. Paradine was put on her trial. But till then—care, control, the keen intellect rather than the play of the hot impulses!

And Horfield must be cultivated, on the chance of his being Judge of the case, which God forbid!

"Let's get up a little dinner for the Horfields, shall we, Gay?" Keane said to his wife. "It's ages since they've set foot here. Don't we owe them a dinner?"

"No. But if we are going to ask them I'd rather do it without owing them anything."

"I never knew a woman less given to arrière-pensées than you, Gay," said Keane, feeling slightly ashamed of himself.

For he was sure that she had at once detected that he had a reason quite other than hospitality for suggesting this dinner.

"The fact is," he added, perhaps realising that as she was not subject to even the most delicate deception it would be wise to be frank, "I want to be on good terms with Horfield, really good terms, not apparently good ones. He's a first rate Judge and not a bad fellow, and I'm a first rate K.C.—aren't I?—and not a bad fellow either. So why should there be any difficulty between us? Can you see a reason?"

"If there is a reason I wonder if a dinner will get rid of it," said Gay. "But we might try. Whom shall I ask if the Horfields accept?"

"Let's find out first if they'll come."

A day was fixed upon and an invitation sent and the Horfields did accept. Keane thought he was glad. They decided to invite the Flaquers—Papa and Mamma and the lively and acute Judith Flaquer, who was always good company—and three others, not legal, to make up a dinner of ten. They invited Martin Latrobe. Then, as the dinner was fixed for a Sunday night, they asked Mrs. George Blason, the famous actress, and Arthur Lieberstein equally famous as a pianist. Both these well-known artists were great successes in Society, and noted as talkers as well as for their remarkable gifts.

"No need to be a dumb fool because one has a talent which one has taken out of its napkin!" as Mrs. Blason said.

Some of her sayings were devastating but she had never been known to be dull. She was also extremely good looking in a thoroughly un-English way, and often expressed the opinion that she must have been found in the bulrushes instead of, as her middle-class parents affirmed, having been born in Putney Vale on a Bank Holiday.

Lord Horfield admired her and was also amused by her.

The problem of this dinner, as of every dinner the Horfields attended, was how to bring Lady Horfield through it without falling on disaster.

Lady Horfield's intellect was difficult to deal with because it nearly always seemed to be in a state of confusion. She made statements as a rule only to withdraw them—evidently in fear that they might otherwise be combated or perhaps even refuted. She was sure of nothing; Mrs. Blason said not even of her own existence. She was probably very shy but at times felt it incumbent upon her to assume an anxiously haughty demeanour. It couldn't be said with truth that she had no conversation. On the contrary when nervous—and she was always nervous when her husband was present—she talked a great deal, running on vaguely about nothing particular, perhaps in the hope of presently striking an epigram. And she had an unfortunate faculty of spreading uneasiness round about her like an atmosphere.

"I think I can keep her quiet," Keane said to Gay, just before their guests arrived. "Latrobe will be on her other side. We can manage her between us unless Horfield is in his impish mood, or Mrs. Blason happens to be possessed by the Devil."

"I wonder sometimes what Lord Horfield really feels about her," said Gay, in her delicately meditative way.

"He seems to rejoice in her absurdity."

"That may be a mask. I think it is."

"You don't think he is fond of her surely?"

"I don't know. But I believe she could be—" Gay paused and seemed to think unselfconsciously—"tremendous in a tremendous moment."

"Tremendous—Lady Horfield?"

"Yes. And I think he knows it. Perhaps she has shown it to him during their married life. Lady Horfield may be preposterous but I think there's something in her that is wonderful. She is one of the few people in London I should like to know much better than I do."

"In a minute you'll make me find her interesting."

"Believe me, Malcolm, she is—but not in her words. They are like a dust in the air. But there's fire underneath. I'm sure of that."

"Sir Simon and Lady Flaquer, Miss Flaquer . . . Lord and Lady Horfield."

Lady Horfield was in bright red that evening. She had no taste, but wore clothes that showed an almost frightening definiteness of view about her array. Whatever she wore suggested that she had been to a good dressmaker whom she had overpowered in battle and left practically for dead upon the stricken field.

The dinner went off quite well. Gay was between Lord Horfield and Sir Simon. Mrs. George Blason sat next to Sir Simon and had Latrobe on her other side. Judith Flaquer was between Lord Horfield and Lieberstein.

Horfield greatly appreciated Miss Flaquer but not as he appreciated Gay. Gay appeared to him as a delicious ethereal woman who attracted him by her exquisite femininity. In Miss Flaquer—he called her 'Judy'—he found well-springs of humour which were rare in an English girl.

"But she isn't English," he said of her. "She's a radiant cosmopolitan who would be at home anywhere except perhaps in the Ghetto. Israel has made her what she is yet she secretly laughs at Israel. As a solicitor she'd have been an outstanding success. Even her own Father wouldn't have got the better of her. She's a bird of Paradise who's managed to make friends with the London sparrows."

Sexually she meant nothing to him. For there was nothing yielding in 'Judy.' But she could be kind, very kind. She was much beloved by artists of outstanding talent. Second rate artists were rightly afraid of her. She pierced their pretensions as a needle pierces a blister. She had no pity for assumption unless it was backed up by genius. Then it might be as arrogant as it pleased.

"No need for the Gods to eat humble pie!" she said. "They are quite right to demand big goblets of nectar."

Mrs. George Blason gave beautiful performances on the stage, full of truth, observation, and the charm that has its roots deep in humanity. Off the stage she was usually a clever buffoon. Her sense of the ridiculous was so great that apparently she could not control it. Someone had accused her once, at rehearsal, of being inhabited by seven devils.

"You're one out!" she said. "There are eight of them."

When a party was small Keane was fond of general conversation. But that was to be avoided when Lady Horfield was present, for her natural nervousness and consequent ineptitude were greatly increased by a multiplication of hearers, and if she knew that several persons were listening to her, among them being her husband, she confounded herself in astonishing statements followed by immediate and piteous withdrawals. The only chance with her was to keep her if possible engaged in strictly private talk. And this Keane set himself to do, rather neglecting Lady Flaquer, who, however, understood perfectly the why of his behaviour, having often entertained the Horfields in Hyde Park Gardens, and knowing the necessity for clever management where the poor lady was concerned. Thus it was that Keane and Lady Horfield passed a great part of dinner in a sort of uneasy dual isolation, about which surged the general conversation of the rest of the party. Lady Horfield, though confused, had a strong sense of her social obliga-tions, and she set herself with a will to the task of holding her host's attention. Though Keane had no idea of it she secretly admired him very much and thought him a great lawyer, and because of that she wished to impress him. Keane, for his part, had Gay's startling statement about Lady Horfield still in his mind.

Lady Horfield—tremendous! Was that possible, in Gay's sense of that word? Tremendous she was, of course, in the physical sense. She towered and was red. Her high shoulders heaved themselves above the shoulders of other women. But was there not something piteously small and plaintive in the inner woman who lurked in hiding behind the important physical envelope? And yet Gay was generally right in her instincts about people. And this woman had long ago been married to Horfield.

There must be something.

He tried to find it, but in vain. Lady Horfield's uneasiness and confusion of mind baffled him, yet obscurely he felt that she was not unsympathetic. She gave him the impression of something struggling in a net the meshes of which were unbreakable. She wanted surely to be free. But from what? He couldn't tell. From time to time her small dark eyes, surrounded by red pouches of skin, roved anxiously to the opposite side of the table where her slim husband was sitting in gay conversation. His silvery voice came to them detached by its peculiar timbre from other voices that were eagerly talking. As the dinner progressed, although she drank no wine, her face, beneath the dark wig, showed increasing signs of congestion, and an expression of nervous excitement pushed its way, so Keane felt, through her features and remained stamped on their redness.

She was surely conscious of the effort Keane was making to keep her talk to himself, or to keep his talk all for her. Perhaps even she discerned his unflattering reason. But she made no attempt to break away. On the contrary she seconded him, leaning side-ways towards him and uttering her contradictory remarks in a low and almost confidential voice, as if she and he were discussing some subject which they must keep to themselves.

"Horfield has a great opinion of you, Sir Malcolm. At least —well, I believe so, though indeed it's difficult to be sure with Horfield. Isn't it? He is so full of whims. Not that—I don't mean that he is whimsical. I shouldn't like to say that. But he—he plays with ideas, don't you know, and one can scarcely tell sometimes—and yet no one can be more clear and definite than he. The most decisive Judge now on the bench, they call him. But I mean in ordinary life it amuses him to see how people take things. You mustn't think I mean he is sly. I shouldn't like you to think that. For he really has a hatred of—but he loves to play his fish—not with you, of course. He would never dream—he has such an opinion of you. And you like him—don't you?"

"There are few men I enjoy a serious talk with more than with your husband."

"Ah, yes, he *can* be serious! But——"

At this moment a peal of laughter greeted some remark of Mrs. Blason's, which was added to, perhaps amplified, by the Judge. Lady Horfield's small folded-in mouth tried to unloose itself in a smile, though she had not heard what was said.

"He thinks it a duty to be lively when dining out. 'We don't meet together to be tragic, Sophy,' he has said to me often. At least, I'm not sure he used the word tragic. It may have been—but I know what he meant. One must try to keep up other people's spirits. There's so much that's—at least, we can't go through life without—a Judge knows that better than anyone, and of course——"

Suddenly she fixed him with a pair of eyes that looked almost fiercely intent.

"Could you be a Judge? Could you pronounce sentence?"

"Of penal servitude?" he asked.

"Of death?" she almost whispered.

"I would rather defend than judge," Keane said. "But both defence and judgment are necessary parts of the machinery of the Law."

"When Horfield has to put on the black cap, I'm frightened. At night when he comes home and I know he has done it——"

Another peal of laughter broke in upon this extraordinary conversation. Lady Horfield looked distractedly at the other guests. But she was not to be diverted from the matter in hand. Evidently she was a woman of some obstinacy when she was roused. She leaned a little nearer to Keane.

"When he comes—after *that*," she said, in the low, almost whispering voice, "I don't know how to be with him. It isn't his fault. I know that. But still——"

Her little flapping hands tapped the table nervously. Suddenly Keane felt deeply interested.

"I understand your feeling fully," he said. "And respect you for it."

"Do you? Really?"

"But isn't he more upset than you are? I have often thought of that."

"Of what?"

"Of the evening, the night passed by a Judge in his own home after he has sentenced a man or woman to be hanged. Can he sleep? Don't you find him altered when he comes home on those awful days?"

"No; just the same—apparently."

"Ah?"

"But he acts to me. He won't let me see that he's upset. He acts—wonderfully. If it wasn't that I know—but I do know. There's pity in his heart but——" her voice, in spite of its whispering quality, became portentous—"he would rather die than show it. People misunderstand him because he's so witty and amusing. But *I* know what he is."

The fierce intensity had not left her small excited eyes, which seemed demanding assent from Keane to all that she had been saying. Her idol was placed on its pedestal; was there not to be even one worshipper besides herself?

"He likes you. He appreciates you," she murmured. "At least, I——" Her voice subsided.

"I'm glad," Keane forced himself to say.

And then he felt the need of disentangling himself from this amazingly unexpected intimacy, and he drew Latrobe into the conversation. Looking down the table he saw Gay's imaginative eyes fixed upon him, and there was a curious scrutiny in them. No doubt she was remembering their conversation before dinner. He heard Mrs. Blason saying:

"You are wrong, Lord Horfield. Only women know how to

worship without experiencing degradation. There's nothing selfless in a real man. The unselfish man is always half feminine and so something of a monster. Women know that and invariably give him a bad time. To see a beetle is to wish to put a foot on it. The unselfish man is the human beetle. We women have the instinct to crush him."

"Ah, you are the cruel sex when all's said and done!" said the Judge. "Do you know that since women have been allowed to serve on Juries, I have had two cases before me in which the Jury couldn't agree. And in each case the disagreement was caused by women holding out for a condemnation when the men were for an acquittal."

"And on which side was the sense of strict justice most developed?" asked Judith Flaquer. "That's the point. You, as a Judge, ought to know."

"She ought to have been a solicitor, Flaquer," said Lord Horfield. "She'd have cut you out completely."

"You're evading my question, Judge," said Miss Judith. "I shan't let you ride off on the horse Adulation."

"As both cases must be re-tried, I mustn't express an opinion."

"When they are re-tried, perhaps the women will be vindicated," said Mrs. Blason. "I should like to sit on a Jury. I wouldn't let the men browbeat me."

"And I'm sure you would cheek the Judge," said Lord Horfield. "You have no sense of reverence."

"Why reverence a wig?"

"I don't ask you to do that. I ask you to reverence the brain that has won its way to the wig."

"Imagine winning one's way to a wig!" said Mrs. Blason. " 'Fo. Heaven's sake don't get in my light! I'm *en route* to the toupet!' What a goal! To see far off on the road of life—a wig! Beckoning one ever onward!"

"Can a man live without symbols?"

"Woman can because she is the great realist. She alone sees a Judge as he really is. Don't you agree with me, Lady Horfield?"

And Mrs. Blason turned her white face, her large, laughing and impudent eyes towards the red monument on the right hand of Keane.

"I don't know. I'm not sure. Of course, if a Judge is a married

man, his wife—— And yet, even a wife can make mistakes——"
She looked appealingly at her husband.

"Surely not, my dear!" he corrected her gently. "Surely the
making of mistakes is the prerogative of the unfortunate spinsters."

"Oh, I suppose it is. And yet, of course—but unmarried women
do certainly sometimes——" (She caught Judith Flaquer's humorous gaze.)—"but there are others who—I'm pretty sure that *some*
girls see nearly as far as we married women."

"If they do, will they ever marry?" asked Mrs. Blason, earnestly.

"Oh—but think of the position, Mrs. Blason!"

"And then the population!" said Mrs. Blason. "That has to be
considered, too. And the alimony."

"The alimony?" said Lady Horfield, evidently in great confusion
of mind.

"Yes, the alimony when the happy woman has as last been
lucky enough to wheedle a divorce out of a soft-hearted Judge,
quite different from your husband!"

"I confess," said Judy Flaquer meditatively, "that I'm sometimes
tempted to take the great plunge by the thought of the alimony
at the end of the matrimonial journey. Alimony! It's a heartening
word in a woman's ears!"

She made her pronounced features look dreamy.

"Mind *you* go full out for it, Lady Horfield, when *your* case
comes before the Court," said Mrs. Blason. "All we women shall
be with you heart and soul. We know what you've suffered."

"Oh, but really, I should never—there's no question of Horfield
and I—I know it's rather different on the stage, of course, with all
those temptations—but——"

And then Gay managed to catch Lady Horfield's distressed eye
and got up with unusual definiteness.

When the women had gone to the drawing-room on the first
floor of the big house, Keane got up and moved to the other side
of the table.

"What are you drinking, Judge?" he said, pulling up a chair
between Horfield and Sir Simon, while Latrobe and Arthur Lieberstein got into conversation.

"Some of this remarkable port. Thanks to my daily ride in the
Park, I'm still able to drink port. I haven't seen you out these
last few days."

"No. The fact is, I've been sitting up so late at night—your fault, Sir Simon—that I've been forced to sleep late on these winter mornings."

"Shall I withdraw a brief or two from you?" said Sir Simon. "What do you say? I might begin with the brief for Mrs. Paradine."

"Any brief rather than that!" said Keane, with an attempt at humorous lightness.

"You are deeply interested in that case, no doubt?" said Lord Horfield, lifting his glass to his thin lips.

"Oh, I see a great chance there!"

"Ah! Well, of course, the case is going to be talked about a lot. In fact, everyone in London seems to be discussing it already."

Latrobe and Arthur Lieberstein had stopped talking and turned towards the three older men.

"When does it come up before the Magistrate?" asked Latrobe.

"Immediately," said Sir Simon, rather curtly.

As a rule, he greatly disliked discussing legal matters in which he was concerned in Society, especially when journalists were present. He had made a slip in mentioning Mrs. Paradine, and now realised it.

"I knew Colonel Paradine, poor fellow," said Lieberstein, speaking with a strong foreign accent.

"Did you?" said Keane, evidently surprised.

Sir Simon fixed his keen eyes on the pianist, who was a thick-set man of not more than thirty-two or so, with the usual pianist's mane of hair and Slavonic features.

"Yes. I met him in Spain when I was very young and he was military attaché in Madrid. At that time he was a magnificent man, adored by the women. And Spanish women, you know, are not reticent in showing their feelings."

"Unlike our dear English patterns who, however, can be very effective in action," murmured Horfield.

Keane pursed his lips together. At that moment he was thinking of Gay.

Lieberstein looked at the Judge and smiled. Sir Simon accepted a little more wine. Latrobe, who was not drinking, lighted a cigarette.

"Poor Paradine! He devastated Madrid at that time!" said Lieberstein. "It was tragic to see him after the war, decorated and deprived of practically everything that made life worth living for a man such as he was. He loved music, and when I was over here I used sometimes to go and play to him. It upset me—it upset me. Music, like perfumes, has a special power of recalling the past. And sometimes, when I was playing, I felt that I was making Paradine suffer till he could scarcely bear it. He was not a musician, but simply loved music, and, like many military men, was specially fond of music I should call sentimental. For instance, he always made me play to him Liszt's 'Liebestraum.' That gives you his measure."

Sir Simon nodded.

"But good—in its way," he said.

"Oh, yes. Genuine stuff of the sentimental kind."

"I hate it," said Latrobe.

"Now we have *his* musical measure!" said Horfield. "These little things are very revealing."

"I usually ended my programme for Paradine with 'Liebestraum,'" said the pianist. "But one twilight—it was in this month, I remember—I was tempted—by the Devil, I'm nearly sure—to add another piece, though I had the definite sensation that poor Paradine was near the breaking point. And I played a transcription of my own of Strauss's 'Blue Danube.'"

"I've heard you play it," said Sir Simon. " 'Youth in Vienna.' Terribly upsetting!"

"Miss Judith likes it."

"Loves it. So do I."

"His second wife, this famous Mrs. Paradine, was there on that occasion. It was the only time I met her. He always wished to be alone when I played. I think because he was so moved by music and didn't wish to show it. A soldier, you know. But that night she was there."

He stopped and seemed to consider something, throwing his powerful head back.

"Perhaps that was why I played my 'Blue Danube' transcription," he said. "It never occurred to me before. She was beautiful in a Northern way."

Lord Horfield smiled and his pale tongue showed for a moment feeling its way round his lower teeth.

"A strange face but beautiful somehow. There was a painful scene when I had played the last bar. Paradine got up from his chair and began to make his way towards the door. His face—it was quite awful. No one should have seen it. No one should ever see a man's face when—there are things that should be hidden from everyone. He stumbled against an armchair. Then she went to him, to help him away. When she touched him—he broke up altogether. The knowledge that a woman was seeing him in that state seemed to drive him mad. He said something to her that I shan't forget. He thrust her away and managed somehow to find the door for himself and get out. We were left together. And then I must say she was marvellous. She began to discuss—of all composers, Mozart! No word of allusion to what had happened, but —just Mozart! A most extraordinary woman!"

"Any more wine, Lord Horfield?"

"No, thank you, Keane. I've had my allowance."

"And won't any of you——? Then shall we go upstairs?"

As they got up Lord Horfield said to Keane:

"Just Mozart—eh?"

In the drawing-room Arthur Lieberstein presently sat down at the Steinway piano and played his transcription of 'The Blue Danube.' While he was enchanting them all, Lord Horfield, over a faint smile, watched Keane, who sat with his long legs crossed, looking down.

As Sir Simon was leaving later on with his wife and daughter, he whispered in Keane's ear:

"We shan't want Lieberstein as a witness, shall we?"

VIII

WHEN their guests had gone Keane, who was looking preoccupied, said to Gay:

"Nearly midnight! They stayed late so I hope they enjoyed it."

"We didn't go in to dinner till twenty minutes to nine. And then Arthur Lieberstein's playing!"

"Marvellous, wasn't it? But I quite understand that——"

He stopped short.

"Yes—what?" said Gay.

"There's something tormenting in that music, and in the way he plays it. It might easily cause a terrible ache for *tempi passati* in a sensitive—that is in anyone who's been happy, a great success, perhaps, and then fallen upon tragedy."

Against his intention there was something so significant in his voice that Gay wondered. She of course understood the drift of his remark, for she was acutely musical, more musical than he was, but she felt that it had been prompted by something which she couldn't divine, something that had not been within him but had reached him from outside.

"Yes," she said.

She waited, and then added:

"What made you say that, think of it?"

He looked at her and she saw refusal in his eyes.

"Oh, it just struck me when Lieberstein was playing. I thought, 'Thank God, I'm happy. Otherwise I simply couldn't stand such music!' "

"That was it!" said Gay. "Well—bedtime. Must you work to-night, Malcolm?"

"I'm afraid I must, dear. But I'll try to make it short."

As she was going out of the room Gay said over her shoulder:

"I don't know how you manage to get back to your working brain at midnight after hearing music like Arthur Lieberstein's. I couldn't."

"I have to," said Keane. "It's my life job."

And he felt, for the first time, that she was resenting his work. For a moment he thought of giving it up and staying with her. But what Lieberstein had told him that night about Colonel Paradine had acted as a spur to his working brain. He longed to be shut up alone in his library.

When he was there he opened the long drawer in his writing table and took out the photograph he had bought in Regent Street. It had lain there face downwards. He had long ago taken it out of its envelope. He sat down, placed it in front of him on the table and studied it for a long time.

Although he had, with the passion that was natural to him, and sprang partly from his driving ambition and partly from his abounding humanity which was tinged with romance, determined to save the woman in the photograph from the hangman, he had not been able to make up his mind about her. He believed, was not absolutely sure but believed, that Sir Simon thought she was probably guilty of the murder of her husband. Already he resented this belief in Sir Simon. Without intending to he had even once or twice shown this secret resentment. It was that which had prevented him from frankly discussing the question of Mrs. Paradine's innocence or guilt after the visit to Holloway Prison. He had instinctively wished to avoid any declaration on the part of Sir Simon. It would have hurt, even angered, something in him if Sir Simon had definitely stated that he believed his client to be guilty of the crime of which she was accused. Keane didn't want to hear that. He was now even determined not to hear it, never to hear it, if avoidance was possible. To hear it might weaken him, for, like most men in the Law, he had reason to know that Sir Simon's mind was penetratingly clear and that his judgment of a human being with whom he came into any close relation was seldom at fault. If Keane had made up his own mind about Mrs. Paradine, possibly he would have felt differently about this question of Sir Simon, but he knew that he was still undecided. Or at any rate he told himself that he was still undecided and was determined to believe that.

"Mind you, I like her."

Sir Simon's odd remark about Mrs. Paradine had stuck in Keane's memory. He remembered it now as he gazed at the photograph. So, apart from fascination, a condition in which sex plays its part, there was a something in this woman which drew liking from that keen solicitor and man of the world, who, perhaps, was sceptical of the virtue of her.

"Why does Flaquer like her?" Keane said to himself.

And then, without answering that, he added to himself:

"And why do I like her, too?"

Like was a homely word, but this woman surely was not homely. She was strange, enigmatic, perhaps, full of a very peculiar and individual beauty that must appeal strongly to certain people but that might not attract everyone; but she was not homely. There was something remote in her appearance. And then that very curious blank look which had puzzled him once or twice when he had been with her! Nothing homely about that! Was it a natural look that came without her knowing that it came? Or was it an expression deliberately assumed by her? Or was it merely a sort of trick, a mannerism? He could not be sure about that. Anyhow, when it came, it rendered her quite unreadable. One looked and saw the shutters up. And one was completely baffled. A white blankness with great pale eyes under hair that was palest yellow. Were there, perhaps, many secrets behind it?

Suddenly Keane found himself wondering what Gay would think of this woman?

Gay, he knew, entirely lacked the curious and immediate instinctive hostility which so many women feel and show to a man who speaks of another woman with any interest, any hint of admiration. He had never detected in her any petty jealousies. She had a warm liking for several women and was even capable of admiring the appearance of a woman better looking than herself. A rare creature! What would she think? What would be her impression?

He had a great wish to carry the photograph to their bedroom, show it to her and say:

"What sort of woman is that? Tell me frankly what you think about her."

He had a great wish; he had also a great reluctance. And he took up the photograph, dropped it into the drawer and shut the drawer on it.

He wasn't going to do that, wasn't going to show the photograph to Gay. Gay had nothing to do with his cases, and this was a case.

And now to study it once more.

IX

THE magistrate before whom Mrs. Paradine's case came up at Bow Street was Sir Charles Draker, the premier magistrate of London, a man whom Keane knew well and greatly respected. The proceedings ended, as Keane and Sir Simon had foreseen, in the committal of Mrs. Paradine for trial at the Old Bailey, bail being refused. During the hearings before the Magistrate the public were, according to the usual practice, not admitted, but the press were, and long accounts of the proceedings appeared in the principal papers. In consequence all the world began to talk about the case and Mrs. Paradine's name was in every mouth. Her character was debated, her antecedents were discussed, her probable fate was canvassed, and her photographs were sold by the thousand.

Mrs. Paradine was admirable throughout this prelude to the great ordeal of her trial. She pleaded of course not guilty, and by the advice of her solicitor reserved her defence till the trial. Her demeanour in the police court was perfect. She was simple, composed, unemotional, yet gave no impression of hardness. She had no tricks, no feminine wiles intended to create an effect upon the Court, did not seem either cast down and fearful, or brazenly confident. Nor did she strike the pathetic note. Yet in what might perhaps be thought her detachment there was nothing inhuman. She was not a woman deliberately presenting herself as an enigma. She seemed an unusual woman not trying to be unusual but being simply herself. Sir Simon believed that the impression she made upon the Court was excellent.

"When she has to go into the box at the Old Bailey I believe she'll make a wonderful witness," he said to Keane. "She's certainly not a bundle of nerves like so many women."

"Let's hope she'll do herself justice," Keane said.

There were moments when he felt at a disadvantage with Mrs. Paradine on account of her simple self-possession, and almost uncanny lack of self-consciousness, moments when he felt a sort of guilt dawn in him because he was looking at her with the question in his eyes: 'Are you guilty or not guilty?'

As a practised lawyer he realised that the evidence against her was strong.

There was unfortunately no doubt that Colonel Paradine's death was not a natural one. He had been done to death, either by himself or by someone else. If he had not been blind it might, perhaps, have been possible to convince a Jury that he had committed suicide, but a blind man could not have managed deliberately to poison himself, as Colonel Paradine had been poisoned, without assistance. And if his wife had helped him to death, even at his own request—and this she absolutely denied—it would be practically impossible to make a Jury believe that she had not been an intentional murderess, acting from self-interest and not under the influence of the dead man. A Jury might easily be induced to think that such a man as Colonel Paradine was known to have been had found life in blindness sufficiently intolerable to wish to be out of it. Keane could imagine himself with exquisite subtlety leading them step by step to such a conviction. But though they might even sympathise with a desire for, and an intention to commit, suicide in such circumstances, that would not save Mrs. Paradine if they suspected her of being an accessory.

When brooding over the case Keane's mind incessantly returned to one figure in it who was going at the trial to be called as a witness by the Crown, Paradine's valet, William Marsh.

This man, who had been a private in Colonel Paradine's regiment and had at one time been his batman, had not held the position of an ordinary valet in the Paradine household. Owing to his master's affliction of blindness he had been more in his intimacy than a valet generally is with the one whom he serves. He had often taken the Colonel out, gone with him for walks, kept him company when he would otherwise have been alone. They had been more together than master and servant are as a rule. The Colonel depended on William Marsh and there seemed little doubt that Marsh had a fanatical admiration for, and devotion to, the Colonel.

Fanatical! That was the point, that was the danger point in connection with William Marsh, and Keane always had it in his mind when he was brooding over the Paradine case. A fanatic, yet full of the major virtues, faithful, courageous, warm-hearted, implacably honest. Decorated, too, like his master though not with the Victoria Cross. The sort of man the British public responds to with all the heat of its boiling sentimentality, the sort of man to carry immense weight with a British Jury.

And this man was hostile to Mrs. Paradine; this man apparently believed that she had murdered the blind man.

Apparently!

When Malcolm Keane sat up at night in his library on the same floor as the room in which Gay was sleeping, or perhaps lying awake, it happened that those two words, 'fanatical' and 'apparently,' continually recurred to his mind, and often they came together, as if there was a link between them.

The man of the world, if he is at all acute, is soon trained by life to be doubtful of appearances. As he goes on in life he is apt to distrust these until, with time, he becomes a hard-boiled cynic. Often he distrusts them too much. The man of the world, who also happens to be a lawyer—the Malcolm Keane in fact—has an additional reason for becoming distrustful and a cynic; he is continually up against men and women who are trying to get the better of the Law by dust throwing, acting, and lies. The clever lawyer should be, and usually is, the last man to accept things at their face value.

When Keane's sympathies were strongly engaged Keane was capable of casting all distrustfulness to the winds and becoming an even fervent believer—for the time at any rate—in human righteousness; but when his sympathies were not engaged, when for instance he had to deal with one whom he looked on as the enemy of a cause to which he was devoting all his powers, he realised acutely human depravity. No man was more suspicious of an enemy than Keane was. And because he was for the defence in the Paradine case William Marsh, a hostile witness, was his enemy.

Suppose that William Marsh, in spite of all the virtues attributed to him, some of which he certainly possessed—he had been a courageous soldier, an extraordinarily capable servant, a strictly honest man in money transactions—suppose he was one of the cunning breed of men who do so much harm in the world? A cunning man can have virtues, a cunning man can show affection, even devotion, a cunning man can be strictly honest when honesty is prompted in him by devotion or is considered by him as the most useful policy he can pursue. But a cunning man at certain crucial moments in his life is bound to play the devil and be exceedingly dangerous.

The question Keane asked himself again and again was whether such a crucial moment had come in the life of William Marsh.

As he had a photograph of Mrs. Paradine which lay always in the long drawer of his writing-table, a drawer which he kept unlocked, so he had a photograph of William Marsh. He had been at a good deal of trouble to procure it. Often, in the night, he had it before him on his table. Sometimes it lay side by side with the photograph of Mrs. Paradine, and, bending over the photographs, he studied them both.

Marsh's photograph showed him half-length, and without a cap, in his Guards' uniform, a man of about thirty-five with square shoulders. His hair was very dark and his eyes were bright blue. The bony structure of his face was prominent and noticeable. The cheekbones stood out. The mouth was firm with large lips. The chin was bold and had a cleft in it. The temples were marked—something cruel about them, Keane thought. It was an amazingly handsome face, seizingly handsome and unusual, and very animal. There was a very strong resemblance to a panther in it. And yet in the eyes, tremendously steady eyes, there was, mingled with the curiously animal remoteness—eyes watching distances not nearnesses—something surely of the Knight-errant look.

On the left breast three medals were shown: the D.C.M., the M.M. and the Mons Star.

Keane had seen and heard William Marsh at the Bow Street police court, as he had seen and heard Mrs. Paradine in Holloway Prison. Nevertheless he bent over his writing-table in the night and pored over these two reproductions of them—for he had a theory that sometimes a photograph will tell a keen observer something that's hidden by the living man or woman under a play of feature that may be designed to deceive, that may be deliberate trickery. The thing at the back often gets to work in the living creature, throws an honest expression into the eyes, curves the lips in a good-natured smile, sets a wave of apparent kindness rippling over the face—for a purpose. In the stillness of a photograph there is sometimes revelation. So Keane sometimes studied photographs of which he had seen the originals.

He had studied Marsh in the Magistrate's court, and had been struck at once by his remarkable, and unusual, good looks, and by the animalism of his appearance mingled with something else and quite other than animalism. His manner and bearing had been rather typical than exceptional. In the witness box he had at first given Keane the impression of an upright 'soldierly' man, definite, fearless, honest, English to the bone, typical in fact of the best kind of Englishman of the lower middle class, the sort of man likely to be thoroughly appreciated by his countrymen. He had been a good witness, and at first, in spite of his decidedly unusual and remarkable appearance, Keane had thought of him rather as a type than as a very definite individual, not to be confounded with any other individual or mass of individuals. But by degrees that impression had worn rather thin, and Keane had begun to realise that there was something quite unusual in this man's character which perhaps matched his appearance, and to seek about for what exactly it was. And presently he had found, or believed that he had found, an emotional fanaticism working in this man Marsh. Marsh was surely, underneath his keen, soldierly and typical demeanour, a man of fierce and perhaps complicated feeling, and consequently capable of many things which the ordinary man is incapable of. He had a sort of rough art of concealing this fact —Keane believed it to be a fact—which probably would deceive most people, but Keane eventually felt 'in his bones' that Marsh was fierce, complicated, strongly emotional, and he believed that he felt it so intimately because of his own emotional quality, his own secret fierceness of which he was well aware. There was something in Marsh that was akin to something in himself, and like recognises like.

That Marsh apparently did not wish this fact of his nature to be perceived by others might be due to one of two things: to his inherent Englishness or to cunning. Was he a cunning man?

One night, as Keane in his study leaned over Marsh's photograph, a startling idea took shape in his mind. It was this: "Am I looking at the murderer of Colonel Paradine?"

So far as Keane knew, it had never occurred to anyone as probable that Marsh had murdered his master. Even Sir Simon had never suggested it as a probability, although of course it was obvious that, owing to Marsh's position in the Paradine household, it was, must be, a possibility. Marsh could have committed the crime because he was about Colonel Paradine in intimacy, had access to him perpetually in private. But there was no conviction in 'could.' Marsh had been ruled out of suspicion because his devotion to his master was so well established, so proved, so thoroughly accepted by everyone who knew him and what his relation to his master had been. Sir Simon had no doubts about Marsh's devotion, and had told Keane so. And Keane had no doubt of it, even now as he stared at the photograph.

Marsh had been devoted to Colonel Paradine.

The question that now arose in Keane's mind was this: had

that devotion of his caused Marsh to become a murderer? Each man kills the thing he loves. Had Marsh, perhaps, killed Colonel Paradine because he loved him? Had Colonel Paradine induced Marsh to do it? And was Marsh's apparent hostility to Mrs. Paradine caused by his determination to protect himself from suspicion? Is so, the man was a scoundrel who was capable of devotion, had the black and the white in him as so many men have.

But the black might prove to be the destruction of Mrs. Paradine.

And then Keane fixed his attention on her photograph and compared the two faces, seeking the secrets of character.

He had seldom been briefed in a case that had given him more cause for thought, which had perplexed him more than this Paradine case, which had even troubled him more. For he was troubled, like a man seeking an outlet from a dark place and not finding it.

This man and this woman—what were they? And why was the man's enmity towards the woman so keen?

The man in the photograph looked eager and determined. Keane sought in the face for cunning.

Long study of human beings, some of them criminal, had led him to seek for character rather in the mouth than in the eyes. Men apparently have more will-power over their eyes than over their mouths. Keane considered the mouth to be the most betraying feature in the face of a man.

The mouth of Marsh was a strong mouth. The lips were closed with a firmness that suggested a will of iron, and they were full lips suggesting sensuality. Sensuality and will Keane found in the curve of those lips, in their pressed firmness, a dominant nature that must surely have known the urge of passion. But—cunning?

He looked at the eyes, then at the cheeks with their prominent bones. The structure of the face was certainly pantherlike. It was a face to attract, perhaps even to startle, women. He saw cruelty of a primitive kind in it, and resolution, but was not sure about cunning. This man looked as if he could strike, but hardly as if he could creep to a crime in stealth, lost among shadows.

Mrs. Paradine's mouth was one of the most delightful features of her face. It was not a Cupid's bow; it was nearly straight, but curved very slightly up at the corners, and suggested to Keane's mind a sort of lazy kindness, careless generosity, indifference to all that was small in life, and acceptance of all that was large and of big value. There was tremendous attraction for men in those lazy lips. A woman with such lips was surely not capable of murder. That was not a criminal face.

And yet, Keane allowed to himself, it was an enigmatic face, a page the writing on which was mainly invisible. There was that strange, not unlovely, even interesting, blankness that made you wonder how much was behind it and of what nature. In the live face the blankness was only to be seen at moments. It was stamped on the photograph.

Hysteria? Keane gazed at the woman.

Fanaticism? He gazed at the man.

While he sat there the conception of a strange defence was forming in his mind. He must talk it thoroughly over with Sir Simon at the earliest opportunity. An afflicted man, longing for death, but unable, from a physical cause, to compass the death he longed for without help. He seeks for assistance from someone who is fanatically devoted to him. He over-persuades. He induces. He causes deep affection to rise to criminal heights. He forces the hand of love to take up the weapon of a murderer. He and his will fade away in death. But the other is left in life to deal with the future as best he can.

What won't a man do to preserve his skin?

It seemed that William Marsh hated Mrs. Paradine.

Keane would deal faithfully with that presumed hatred presently in his cross-examination. He would put Marsh through it! Ah, yes!

A strange thing was this: that Mrs. Paradine had so far nothing but good to say of William Marsh.

The contrast between the man's attitude to the woman and the woman's attitude to the man was extraordinary and very difficult to account for.

Marsh was no doubt of a jealous and possessive disposition. He had wanted to monopolise his Colonel, who had distinguished the whole regiment by his brilliance and valour. Marsh had been very proud of being chosen by the Colonel as his personal servant in private life, and out of that pride, rooted in devotion, had doubtless grown the instinct to monopolise which often causes such devastation in human affairs.

Marsh, in spite of that mouth of his, was, it seemed, no lover and admirer of women.

That could be brought out presently in evidence. Keane was 'on' to that.

Marsh was a celibate, and had been known in the regiment as that rather rare monster, a private soldier who has nothing to do with women; in this being the very opposite of his Colonel, who had been notorious as an eager slayer of women until his affliction overtook him and eventually he married Ingrid Brucke, now Mrs. Paradine. Marsh distrusted women and had often been heard to say so. He thought the whole sex tricky, deceitful and ready to be corrupt if the occasion to be so offered itself. He subscribed to the covering assertion that every woman is at heart a rake. He had 'no use for' women. A rare private indeed, and perpetually chaffed by his comrades for the peculiarity which set him apart from them. Nevertheless, he was respected in the regiment as a very masculine male being who had any amount of courage and would stand no nonsense from anyone.

A peculiar fellow, this William Marsh, a man quite out of the ordinary. Keane must see to it that this latent hatred of woman as a sex was made very clear to the Jury at the trial of Mrs. Paradine. It would account, in some degree, at any rate, for his apparent active dislike of her. In fact, it was a valuable asset to the Defence, for a man who disliked all women, simply because they were women, needed no special reason for disliking the woman who was married to his master and was his own mistress. Special reasons he would no doubt put forth. The Crown would take care of that. But Keane would know how to combat them. His keen mind would grasp all the possibilities. Already, in imagination, he saw William Marsh in the witness-box, he formed in his mind questions that he would put to him in cross-examination.

Looking again at Marsh's photograph, he foresaw the duel that was coming.

And that new theory of Defence which had come into and stuck in his mind?

Keane wondered how Sir Simon would respond to his suggestion of it. There was no quicker brain in London than Sir Simon's, yet such a defence had evidently not occurred to him as possibly effective, or he would, of course, have suggested it long ago. And he had not, although he had been in a difficulty about a defence 'with a stiff, if not cast-iron back to it,' as he had expressed it.

They might be able to prove absence of motive for the murder in Mrs. Paradine's case, or at any rate to suggest it so strongly that a Jury would accept it as a fact that she had no discoverable motive. But that was not enough.

That would be a defence without a spine to it. This new conception of his, Keane felt, would supply a backbone which had hitherto been conspicuously lacking.

But Mrs. Paradine would surely give William Marsh a certificate of character if 'they' allowed her to. They mustn't allow that. But when that word *mustn't* came into his mind, Keane realised something: an enormous quiet obstinacy in the blonde woman from the North.

But surely——

A faint sigh, coming certainly from somewhere in the room, made him start violently. He pushed back his chair, gripped his writing-table, got up, looked all round him.

Someone in the room with him! But he hadn't moved from his chair for the last two hours, and no one had come in. He looked at the door. It was shut. The sigh was not repeated. But he had heard it, expressing life very near to him. There were two tall windows in the room concealed by Nile green curtains, and they were recessed windows. Keane crossed the room quickly and looked into the recesses behind the curtains. No one was there. As he turned from them he saw Sausage, belly close to the carpet, emerging from beneath his writing-table, smiling and stretching, but with a faintly guilty expression in his clear yellow eyes.

"You little devil!" Keane exclaimed. "Why aren't you in your basket?"

Sausage had given a jerk to his nerves that he wouldn't forget in a hurry. He picked the little devil up. Sausage was extraordinarily heavy for his size. He yawned again. He knew that he had done something that wasn't quite the thing, but evidently his deed wasn't going to bear evil fruit for him. Master was merely going to put him where he ought to have been for the last two hours or more, in his basket. There were moments when he couldn't resist his hereditary instinct to creep into dark places, to lie in them deliciously secluded. The furtive instinct of the chase through dense undergrowth coming out in a London house. So he had managed to creep into Master's night-room unobserved and to have a delightful time there close to Master's much appreciated feet. A sigh of satisfaction had brought this surreptitious pleasure to an end. So now inevitably—basket!

Keane returned to his library, but he worked no more that night. He put away his brief and returned the two photographs to his writing-table drawer. But he looked for a long time at the face of Mrs. Paradine before shutting her out of his sight.

She must be made to take a different line about William Marsh. Keane's suspicions about that man were beginning to grow.

X

DURING these days when all London was talking about the Paradine case, Gay and her husband scarcely spoke of it to each other. There was nothing specially strange about their silence on the subject, as they were not given to the intimate discussion of Keane's 'cases.' But both of them felt that their common silence about the Paradine case was not quite as usual, not quite so natural as other common silences which they could remember and which they had never felt uncomfortable in or regretted. There was something definite and intentional about it which made it not quite happy, at times almost painful.

Both of them were aware of this.

Whenever Gay went out in London, into whatever society, people came up to her eagerly asking questions about the great case in which her husband was involved as leading counsel for the defence. Some of them were indiscreet in what they said, though some were fairly tactful. Many women were curious about Mrs. Paradine. What was she like? How was she 'taking' her terrible predicament? What impression had she made upon Sir Malcolm? Did he really expect to 'get her off'?

Though Gay was notably amiable in character she resented these questions, and answered them by saying that she knew no more about Mrs. Paradine than the rest of the public, as Malcolm didn't discuss his cases at home, but kept such discussions for his chambers and the offices of the solicitors who instructed him.

"Ah, you won't tell!" was the usual comment on what was regarded as a transparent evasion. "Sir Malcolm knows how discreet you are, and that's why he feels he can confide in you."

"He never confides in me about his cases," Gay answered one day at a Charity Matinée when this, or a similar, remark was made to her by Mrs. George Blason. "And I don't want him to. A husband's got a perfect right to keep professional secrets from his wife. I should be ashamed of Malcolm if he revealed them to me."

"Secrets!" said Mrs. George, with her smiling impudence, which generally suggested that she was clowning. "But all we want to know is what's the woman really like. She scarcely ever showed in London after her marriage, and none of us has met her. They were nearly always hidden away in Hindley Hall up in Cumberland. There's surely no harm in telling us what sort of woman she is."

"But I don't know," said Gay, almost severely and looking suddenly less ethereal than usual.

"Of course, we've seen the photographs they're selling of her. But in them she is just a beautiful blank, the very best cream laid paper with nothing written on it."

"Well, I haven't even seen her photograph," said Gay. "Goodbye."

"She's very touchy about the Paradine," Mrs. George said to a woman, not an actress but a smart beauty, who was with her selling programmes at exorbitant prices to reluctant stall holders. "I wonder—why."

Her impudent smile had died away and suddenly she looked intense and severely shrewd.

She put a hand on her companion's arm.

"Sally, I shouldn't wonder if there's going to be domestic trouble over the Paradine case."

"Going to be, dear! But it's over. The man's dead!"

"I didn't mean domestic trouble in the *Paradine* household."

When the matinée at which this was said was over, Gay drove to Hyde Park Gardens to have tea with the Flaquers, who were good friends of hers. Lady Flaquer had asked her to look in after the matinée.

Judith Flaquer, though a very different type of woman from Gay, more downright, more satirical, probably less imaginative, was nevertheless a great friend of hers. They had known each other for a long time and appreciated each other's good points. Judith admired Gay's evasive beauty, her delicacy of mind, her curious, very natural charm, and the genuineness of her nature, which was very sincere. Gay, on her side, was attracted by Judith's energetic zest for life, her gaiety, her artistic flair, her Jewish acuteness and the rock-bottom goodness of her heart. For beneath her obvious irony, Judith was very kind. Gay had learnt, too, that Judith could be thoroughly relied upon and never gave away a friend. Usually Gay was a happy being, and she and Judith were at one in an optimistic outlook on life, though, as Judith said, they didn't sit purring like a couple of demure cats and 'numbering their benefits.' But that day, when Gay came into the Flaquers' enormous drawing-room, in which the two grand pianos were scarcely noticed till you came close to them, she was feeling cloudy, and, being very natural and in the house of intimate friends, did not instinctively make an effort to hide it until she saw that as well as Lady Flaquer and Judith there were two strangers in the room. Then, of course, she almost mechanically looked cheerful, but not before the extremely sharp eyes of Judith had wirelessed to her mind the question: 'What's the matter with Gay?'

One of the strangers was a short, very bald man of about forty, neatly but very plainly dressed, with a turn-down white collar beneath which nestled a minute black bow tie, the ends of which were modestly concealed beneath the wings of the collar. From a distance Gay, who could not see far and never used glasses, did not recognise him, but as she drew nearer she realised that though she did not know him she had several times seen him. He was a unique man, a man who stood alone because he was supreme in his own line, an impeccable artist whom no critic, however jaundiced, could ever dare to 'run down,' Señor Bortagas, the famous Argentine 'cellist, in London for a couple of concerts.

The second visitor was also a man and a foreigner. He was a tall, bulky, upstanding Swede with short fair hair growing densely over a powerful head. Lady Flaquer introduced him to Gay as Baron Sedelsward. He was the best living Swedish painter of snow

scenes, and had come over from Stockholm for an exhibition of
his work in a Bond Street Gallery.

Judith's sister, Amy Flaquer, was away paying a country visit.

Lady Flaquer, an animated, rather large woman, with Italian
eyes and a strong foreign accent, though she had lived in London
for nearly thirty years, introduced Sedelsward to Gay, who sat
down next to the Baron, while Judith Flaquer resumed a conversation which she had been having in Spanish with Señor Bortagas.
From time to time, in the midst of it, she sent a rather piercing
glance to her friend, Gay, who was conversing with Lady Flaquer
and the painter.

The painter struck Gay as heavy, but highly intelligent, and
almost naïvely genial and well meaning. Sitting with his big body
leaning forward and his legs wide apart, his large ruddy face
always ready to break into a kindly smile, he talked simply, and
without conceit, led by Lady Flaquer, of the preparations for his
exhibition, and inquired whether Gay would care to honour him
by coming to the private view.

She accepted his offer with pleasure, for his obvious sincerity
and complete lack of pose attracted her. He told them both the
names of some people who were coming and presently added, in
his correct weighty English:

"But I am very sorry that there is one who cannot come, a
half-countrywoman of mine, a very beautiful unfortunate."

"Who's that, Baron?" said Lady Flaquer. "Anyone we know?"

"The lovely Ingrid Paradine who is in great trouble over here."

Judith Flaquer turned her picturesque dark head, birdlike in its
quick motion, towards the speaker, then glanced swiftly at Gay.
Gay's white forehead showed a pucker and her straight eyebrows,
for an instant, were lowered above her hazel eyes.

"You know Mrs. Paradine?" said Lady Flaquer.

"Oh yes! I can remember her when she was in a barber's shop
stirring soap, a slip of a blonde-haired maiden. It was in Copenhagen in winter. I called her the winter maiden. She was as beautiful as frost when the winter sun falls across it. And now! What are
you doing to her here?"

He put the question without any acerbity, mildly, sadly, shaking his head slowly as he spoke.

"She went to America. I did not see her again, but her face

I remember and her long figure, full of grace. Stirring soap she looked like a lady. No; one could not pin her down even to that. Whatever she did was done so simply and naturally that it became a charming thing to do. When one came in to be shaved and saw her there one said: 'It is good, it is delicious to stir the soap.' Such a beautiful neck, she had. That white neck it must not have *it* put round its whiteness.''

He made a horribly expressive gesture with his big, kind-looking hands.

"My husband, and the husband of our friend here," said Lady Flaquer with energy, "will try to prevent that."

And then, rather decisively, she changed the conversation, drawing in Judith and the 'cellist. But presently the Baron, who was evidently a man of memory and one who did not leave a topic he was interested in easily, found a moment to say to Gay:

"But please what has your husband to do with the beautiful unfortunate who once stirred the soap in Copenhagen?"

Gay explained quickly in a low voice. The Baron was evidently surprised and deeply interested.

"He will save her surely," he exclaimed. "I cannot believe that a being so beautiful, so beautiful—like the grace and the beauty of filigree frost in sunlight—can be a criminal. Would your husband come to see my pictures, do you think? I would gladly speak with him."

"He is very fond of art. I will tell him about them."

"I shall have the honour to send him a card with yours."

"Thank you very much."

Gay felt that he wanted to be asked to visit them. But she did not ask him.

When presently he and Señor Bortagas went away Judith Flaquer took Gay to her sitting-room—there were many sitting-rooms in that vast house—to have a *tête-à-tête* talk. Lady Flaquer, late though it was, had someone 'just round the corner in Lancaster Gate' to see before dinner.

"Mamma has too many friends and won't neglect one," Judith said.

"And what about you, Judy?"

"Oh, I simply gobble friendship as a turkey gobbles scraps. But my friends must be somebodies. Mamma is kinder than I am.

She will even go and sit with a bore, if the bore is truly fond of her and wants her."

"Wouldn't you?"

"Not with a real right down regular boring bore I wouldn't."

"But am I a somebody?"

"Of course you are. You could charm a bird from a bough, or a Judge from the bench, wig and all. I can see—let us say—Lord Horfield hopping down drawn by your chirps."

"I should never chirp to Lord Horfield."

"He is an old sinner certainly, but he's very amusing. And he's so thoroughly at home with his own rascality that I have to smile at it. But where's your smile to-day, my own dear Gay? There's a little cloud no bigger than a man's hand about you. And I can see it. But I'm sure it can't presage a great rain like the cloud in Holy Writ. That pucker in the drawing-room at one moment almost became a frown."

Gay hesitated for an instant. But Judy pressed her hand affectionately and she said:

"Mrs. George Blason bothered me at the matinée."

"To buy or sell programmes?"

"No; about Mrs. Paradine."

Judith looked as if she were concealing a sharp expression, burying it abruptly beneath an inquiring, but sympathetic, glance of friendship.

"They are all curious naturally. And you are so near to the throne."

"I may be, but Malcolm keeps me out of his cases."

This time for an instant Judith's face plainly showed a sharp expression.

"But, Gay, do you want to be in them?"

"No. But then how can I tell all these people things? I don't know them. I don't want to know them."

"Other women are more curious than you are, my Gay. We are not so exquisitely detached as you seem to be."

"But your father—does he discuss cases with you all in the family circle?"

"In the *family circle* absolutely never! And we never ask him questions about them."

"I hate asking questions!" Gay exclaimed.

And in her soft voice there was a touch of unwonted violence.

"In etiquette books, framed for the not-knows, this admirable rule is set down: 'Do not ask questions. They may be thought impertinent. Leave people to tell you—if they wish. Only the vulgar probe.'"

"The people I meet evidently don't read etiquette books, Judy. I'm getting very tired of telling everyone that I know nothing about Mrs. Paradine. Give me a cigarette, will you?"

"I thought you never smoked! Is this a long hidden vice suddenly rising to the surface?"

"I've taken to smoking just lately."

"On your next birthday I'll give you a cigarette case. This"— she held out an open ebony box—"is my habitual smoke."

"They're sure to be good, but I'm no judge yet."

Judith held a match for her in a steady small hand.

"Gay, smoking!" she said. "Echo with a cigarette!"

She lit up for herself.

There was something whimsically distressed in her voice and manner.

"Little Gay, generally so unlike other people!"

"But I'm not little!"

"I know. But I like to say 'little Gay.' And if you were six feet tall still I should say it. You know how Italians use diminutives for those they are fond of."

"Dear old Judy!"

"Old as you are little!"

"Yes."

Gay smoked, rather oddly, rather uncomfortably and incompetently, for a moment; then she said:

"I daresay I'm rather a fool to live as I do."

"In what special way do you live, dearest Gay?"

"Incuriously about a lot of things other people are curious about."

"That shows individuality and good sense."

"I'm not sure that it does. One can live only à côté de la vie. And I'm beginning to think that perhaps I do."

"Because——"

"Well, often I don't look at a newspaper for days."

"Think how many lies you are never told!"

"But I may miss many truths."

"You think so—in the newspapers?"

"And perhaps I live half in a dream. And that's very silly. Judy, you perhaps don't realise how many things that almost every woman we meet is interested in, and knows about, I'm ignorant of."

"For instance, precious one?"

"Well—" she seemed to hesitate, then took a decision—"Politics for one thing. I know very little about Politics."

Judith's black eyes, fixed upon her, began to look very penetrating.

"And——?" she said.

"Well—Law, for another."

"Why should you know anything about Law?"

"I'm married to a lawyer."

"That's no reason. Rather the other way. Your husband doesn't want to talk about contracts and torts and cross-examinations and summings up when he leaves the Courts for your drawing-room."

After a pause Judith leaned forward in her chair and uttered: "And——?"

"Topics of the day," said Gay slowly, and looking down. "I don't follow them as I should, as other women do."

"I always think you're wonderfully well up in musical and literary doings, and as for the theatre——"

"No, I meant personalities."

"Personalities?"

"In Society most of the conversation is about people, what they are, and what they do, and how they look, and whether they are what they seem to be or not, and their pasts, and—and half the time I don't know and I don't care. And so I am sure I am thought to be rather a fool."

"Why this sudden sensitiveness and lack of self-confidence in my darling Gay?"

"Well, I'm sure that to-day Mrs. George——"

"Has Mrs. George been hammering you?"

"No. But at the theatre she was talking—of course—" there came a sound of intense irritation into Gay's light voice—"about Mrs. Paradine and I hadn't even seen a photograph of her."

"Ah!"

"And it seems that everyone else has."

"Really?"

"These things make one feel out of it."

"But if you don't care?"

"How d'you mean?"

"If you don't care about all these personalities—why pretend?"

"Sometimes I think I ought to take a little more trouble to know what is going on. *You* read the papers. *You* are up in everything."

"Because I'm simply crammed with curiosity about life. I'm like papa."

"Is he?"

"Of course he is! That's why he revels in his profession. I was meant to be a solicitor, but Providence popped me into the wrong envelope. But you are like Echo and Echo wasn't meant to be a solicitor. You are a charm-bearer. Why be dissatisfied? If you followed all the gossip of the papers, as I do, and rushed to get the photographs of everyone who happened to be in the public eye, as I do——"

"But do you?" Gay interrupted. "I have never seen photographs about your rooms."

"It isn't the fashion to put photographs about. I have dozens in drawers."

"Have you?"

"Yes."

Gay looked as if she were going to say something quickly— and didn't speak. The effect was that of a door handle being turned and the door remaining shut. A moment of silence followed and then Gay got up.

"Must you go already?"

"Yes. It's late. The matinée wasn't over till five."

"You always go too soon, evasive Gay. Shall I fetch up the lift?"

"No, I'll walk down."

As they went down the broad staircase Judith said:

"Don't do things to be like the rest of us, Gay. You are better than most of us. You are a definite individual. Remain one."

"I don't think I'm nearly so definite as you are."

"Can't a whisper be as definite as a shout?"

"Perhaps the modern world we live in is too noisy for a whisper to be heard in it."

"Don't you believe it. A whisper carries. You carry."

"I don't think I do. Oh, there's your father!"

Sir Simon was crossing the hall with his swift alert step. He glanced up and saw them. Judith noticed that he was looking preoccupied. He stopped and waited till they joined him.

"Going, Lady Keane? I wish I had been back sooner. But the Law's a very hard taskmaster sometimes. If you must go I'll let you out."

At that moment a tall footman appeared and went to the hall door.

"Don't come," said Gay. "It's so cold. Good-bye, Judy."

Judith kissed her without a word.

"Good-bye, Sir Simon."

Their eyes met. At that moment each one was conscious that the other was withdrawn in the shell of a persecuting thought.

"Good-bye, my dear. I'm sorry not to have had a word with you. But—" he moved his shoulders and pursed up the lips under his short grey moustache.

Gay crossed the hall and went out.

"What's the matter, Papa?" asked Judith.

"Matter?"

He hesitated for a moment. Then he said:

"Horfield's going to try Mrs. Paradine. And we didn't want Horfield."

He turned away and hastened towards his study.

Judith stood looking after him.

"Clouds to-day!" she thought. "I hope we aren't in for a great rain."

She had a habit of identifying herself with those whom she loved, and she loved both her father and Gay. As she went back to her room she said to herself:

"She wanted to ask me. Why didn't she ask me?"

XI

BARON SEDELSWARD was evidently a remembering man, for on the following morning a messenger boy came to Portland Place with an envelope containing a couple of cards for the private view of his snow scenes, to be held in Bond Street on the following Saturday.

Gay sat down and wrote a polite note of thanks. She felt that she ought to ask him to the house. But she didn't. She would speak to Malcolm about it and hear what he thought. Malcolm was, it seemed, completely wrapped up in his work just now. She didn't suppose that he would go to the View, though he was interested in art and exceedingly fond of seeing paintings. But he was busy, terribly busy. Last night he had seemed to be completely withdrawn in work. Usually when he came home and was with her he threw it off like a load from his shoulders. But last night he had spoken very little, sometimes had not even heard what she said. He had been like a man far away from her at the end of a tunnel, brooding in the dark. And very soon after dinner —they had spent the evening at home—he had gone away to his study.

"I *must* work, dearest," he had said.

"So soon?"

"I'm afraid I really must. I've got such a lot on hand just now. And to-day——"

He had frowned and had not finished the sentence. She wondered what he had been about to say, wondered what had happened of importance to him, and so perhaps to her, that day.

After writing her note to the Swede, Gay collected some patterns which a woman's tailor had sent to her recently and which she wanted to return. It happened that she didn't find an envelope in her sitting-room big enough to contain them and, attended closely by Sausage, she went to her husband's library to look for a long envelope. Going up to his writing-table, she sat down in front of it and pulled out the wide and deep drawer. Keane placed documents of importance in two safes which were in the room and which he always kept locked. In the drawer were envelopes, writing paper and sometimes unanswered letters. But that morning, when Gay opened it, she saw lying on the top of some papers a cabinet photograph turned face downwards. On the back was some writing in Keane's large, very clear, calligraphy. Without meaning to read it, she found she had read it.

'What is behind this shuttered window?'

She hesitated for a moment. Then she searched for a big envelope and found one. She drew it out, shut the drawer, enclosed the patterns she had brought in the envelope and addressed it. Then she got up to leave the room. But when she was near the door she stopped, went back, opened the drawer and turned the photograph over. Beneath it was printed: 'Mrs. Ingrid Paradine.' She took the photograph out. Then she pushed in the drawer and sat down again at the table.

A quarter of an hour later she replaced the photograph face downwards in the drawer, shut the drawer and left the room accompanied by Sausage, who meanwhile had been enjoying a nap behind one of the curtains.

That evening when Keane came back from the Club after his day's work she showed him Baron Sedelsward's card for the Private View.

"I met him at the Flaquers'. He wants you to come if you can," she said.

"Dearest, I've no time for such things," he answered quickly.

"I thought you wouldn't be able to come."

"You go."

"Yes, I think I will. He's a good sort, I'm sure, and you know he's celebrated in Sweden."

"I've heard his name," said Keane, in an uninterested voice.

"As he's been so polite, oughtn't I to ask him to call?"

"Why not? Ask him by all means."

He turned to go out of the room. When he was close to the door, Gay said:

"The Baron used to know Mrs. Paradine."

Keane swung round instantly.

"Know Mrs. Paradine! Where?"

"Long ago, in Copenhagen, where she used to stir soap in a barber's shop. He told me she was like filigree frost in sunshine."

Keane said nothing. He stood for a moment by the door looking at Gay vaguely. Then he opened it and went out.

But the next day, a Friday, he said to her when he came home:

"I find I can manage to go to that Private View after all. I should like to have a look at the Baron's paintings."

XII

ON THAT day, before coming home and before his visit to the Club, Keane had a long colloquy with Sir Simon Flaquer in Bewly Place, whither he drove from Holloway Prison, where he had spent more than an hour with Mrs. Paradine. Since he had first seen her with Sir Simon, he had paid several visits to her alone and had had long talks with her, overheard by no one, though the interviews were watched by a wardress from behind the glass in the door of the room where he saw her. On the day before this last interview he had learnt that the case was to be tried by Lord Horfield.

So—Horfield was to have the last word!

Keane remembered what Gay had said to him about Horfield. He believed it. In spite of often seeming so detached and ethereal, sometimes even so wrapped up in dreams, Gay, he knew, could be observant though she seldom seemed so. She had a sort of apparently haphazard way of stepping right into the truth of things at which he had often wondered, asking himself what led her, by what exactly she was guided aright. She had detected the secret hostility existing between him and Horfield. And now Horfield was going to try the Paradine case.

That was damnable! Damnable Horfield!

A strong word to apply to a distinguished English Judge yet Keane's mind applied it.

It was all very well to glory in British justice. Keane himself had often done that. But even British Judges were men full of faults, pricked by their passions, subject to enmities, to jealousies, to discordances of temperament. They aimed at justice undoubtedly. But is there a man who cannot, in certain moments, be deflected from his aim by dislike, hidden anger, repulsion?

Horfield disliked Keane. They had opposite temperaments, and they both knew it. But there was more in their common dislike than that, Keane believed, at times felt quite certain. Horfield envied him, Keane suspected, had envied him for a long time because of his possession of Gay, because of his luck in having such a delicious creature always with him in his home. Horfield had always openly professed admiration of, and devotion to, Gay. But he had done it in a light, laughing manner, as if it were only a gallant joke, a chivalrous absurdity that of course could not be taken seriously—until just lately.

And again it had been Gay who had caused him to open his eyes. She, who was not given to sharp sayings or to unkind judgments, had said of Horfield that he was a nasty old man. Coming from Gay's lips, that was a very definite condemnation. Keane had seldom heard her say anything so unkind of man or woman before. Horfield must surely have done something to earn that condemnation, but Keane did not know what it was. He could only guess that Horfield had hazarded some remark, or perhaps only some look or gesture, which had enabled Gay to see more deeply than usual into the ugly part of his nature.

That there was an exceedingly ugly part was certain. Many people knew that. For Horfield, though so full of cynical worldly wisdom, had moments of great, even of amazing, carelessness. It seemed as if, now and then, he could not be bothered any longer to play the part of a respectable and dignified servant of the State living up to a high public position, but had to give a fling to his real nature, which was probably compounded of Satyr and Faun. Seldom had Keane come across a man whose brain and whose character seemed to him so disparate. Horfield had the brain certainly of a brilliant Judge, but the character, probably, of a man singularly unfit to sit in judgment on anyone. But in public life by the brain alone a man may rise very high, and even create a sense of awe in his fellow men, if the brain be sufficiently remarkable. For men can be cowed by brain.

Horfield knew that, and he had a great trust in his brain. It had got him out of many difficulties, even out of some dangers.

Perhaps he put too much faith in it.

Horfield to try Mrs. Paradine! Keane felt like one who had received a blow—that he had been expecting. For he had not been buoyed up by any conviction that, in this preparatory stage, things were shaping well for Mrs. Paradine and for him. He went to his interview with her in an unusual state of depression which he did not conceal from her. Perhaps he did not even try to conceal it. There was much of the boy still lingering in Malcolm Keane and some of it he showed that day to Mrs. Paradine. They even talked about Horfield. In Keane's view that was necessary, as Mrs. Paradine was going into the witness-box.

"We know now which of the Judges will try your case, Mrs. Paradine," he said.

"Who is it, please?"

"Lord Horfield."

Mrs. Paradine made no comment, sat still looking at Keane with her beautiful pale eyes.

"You know his name?"

"I have seen it now and then in the papers. But I do not know much about him. What sort of man is he, please?"

Keane hesitated for a moment, perhaps casting about for discretion, but the impulsive part of his nature as usual got the better of him, and he answered:

"He's a humorist and a cynic, a cynic with a lot of bitterness in him, I should think. I don't know whether he has a heart. He's got a first-rate brain. He likes women, especially pretty women."

As he said the last words he looked at her, but he didn't observe any change in her face, any quickening of interest, any sign of awakened coquetry.

"That should be a help to us," he said, as she said nothing. But there was little optimism in his voice. And then he added, yielding to his impulse:

"I would rather have had another Judge for your case."

"Why?"

"There's something in Lord Horfield that I don't trust."

"But he will be there to do justice and you say he has a first-rate brain."

"Oh, his brain's all right."

"Is not that the important thing?"

Keane leaned towards her then, as sometimes in passionate passages of a speech he leaned instinctively towards a Jury, and, putting a finger to his forehead, said:

"I believe I have a pretty good brain, too. But d'you think in a big case, such as yours will be, only brain is needed for the obtaining of justice? There must be heart, too, the key which unlocks the door into humanity. And that's greater, and goes farther, than brain. But Lord Horfield doesn't think so."

Again the pessimistic tone had come into his voice.

"A Judge like Lord Horfield doesn't encourage Counsel to do his best, and I want to do my very best for you. I must do my very best and you must help me. We'll fight Lord Horfield together."

Directly he had said the last words, he realised how extraordinary they must have sounded in her ears. Fighting a Judge! She looked at him and her eyes were examining eyes. The blank look which sometimes made her face strange and unreadable was not in them then. She looked an extremely intelligent woman, fully awakened and on the *qui vive*.

"But how can we fight him?" she said. "Tell me! I do not understand."

Then he plunged into an intimate discussion of Horfield's mentality, as he conceived it to be, and gave her a sort of lesson in the giving of her evidence, having Horfield always in his mind.

Was Mrs. Paradine, he wondered, the type of woman who would have a strong attraction for Horfield? Again he noticed, as so often before, the strange resemblance between her and his wife. Horfield admired Gay very much, too much. Keane hated his admiration for her, because he knew that it was mingled with an ugly and offensive desire. But it didn't fail to occur to the advocate's mind that the faint resemblance between Gay and Mrs. Paradine might be to Mrs. Paradine's advantage when the trial came on. That is, if Horfield's keen eyes detected it.

Even now Keane wasn't sure where exactly it lay. For Gay and Mrs. Paradine were very unlike. Despite the marvellous fairness of Mrs. Paradine, who was much fairer than Gay, and who was slim like a wand, she was much less ethereal than Gay. The painter of Sweden, Baron Sedelsward, had said that as a young girl she had looked like a filigree of frost with the sun shining on it. And it might have been so. Looking at her even now, a woman of well over thirty, one could believe that the comparison, though poetical, had been apt. Nevertheless, Gay, who was not at all like a filigree of frost in sunshine, looked far more delicate, far more frail and evasive than Mrs. Paradine. It was something in expression, in personality, that made that difference between them. Gay had often a far-away look in her eyes which reminded Keane of the sound of an echo, so like, yet so unlike, the human voice which evokes it. Mrs. Paradine's eyes were never quite like that. There was a definiteness of this earth in them; they did not hint at remoteness, did not carry a man into the distances. Gay's expression charmed. It might even be said to purify. Mrs. Paradine's expression charmed, too, but not in the same way.

No, not at all in the same way! Keane had known that for some time. Possibly he had known it ever since he had first seen Mrs. Paradine, with Sir Simon, in the prison reading that book by Schuré. (He had bought that book some time ago.)

But there was a resemblance, surely, in the contours of the two faces, Gay's and Mrs. Paradine's, though Mrs. Paradine's was the larger, and the shapes of the heads, both beautifully formed, were alike; heads that were not foolishly flat behind, and that had brows broad in comparison with the round and small, though not at all weak, chins.

"Why do you look at me in that way?" Mrs. Paradine said, startling Keane, who suddenly realised his carelessness.

Their eyes met then and he was moved to a perhaps greater carelessness.

"I was thinking that you and my wife somehow resemble each other."

"Do we?" she said.

And there seemed to him to be surprise, and something else, in her voice.

"In what way?" she added.

"I don't know exactly. But there is a resemblance, although you are very different from one another. You have something tremendously—" he sought about for the right word—"tremendously definite in you that my wife hasn't got."

"I know. I am coarser in grain than she is."

"I didn't mean that!" he exclaimed, with heat.

"But is not it so? I come from the people. I have been a servant. And I have the servant in me still."

"Why d'you say that?"

"Because it is true," she said, firmly, angrily almost. "I may not look like a servant. I do not believe I do. But I am sure I often feel as a servant feels. Never mind!"

She said it roughly, with a sort of exasperation. He felt passion behind the words. Gay could never speak at all like that. (He had a strange wish just then that she could.)

The wardress was watching them through the glass of the door. What would she think if she could hear as well as see? Keane wished he had the right to order the woman to be off.

He got up abruptly. He wanted to stay, to hear more, to go into this matter and understand it more fully. His mind had suddenly gone to William Marsh, driven perhaps to him by her reiteration of the word 'servant.' He might have to go into this presently, later. But first he must see Sir Simon.

"I don't feel the servant in you," he said, with great gentleness. "I feel only a woman whom I—admire, whom I intend to save."

He bent over the table by which they had been sitting.

"I'll save you!" he exclaimed fiercely. "I'll save you. But you must do as I tell you. Do you hear?"

She nodded, gazing up at him.

"If I can!" she murmured.

In Bewly Place he had a difficult colloquy with Sir Simon, to whom he outlined the defence which his intense consideration of William Marsh had suggested to him. This theory of defence was an entirely new departure and came upon Sir Simon as a shock. Sir Simon's idea had been to dwell upon the absolute lack of any urgent motive for the murder of which Mrs. Paradine was accused. Mrs. Paradine had always shown admiration for, and great devotion to, her husband. Numerous witnesses were at hand who would speak to that. Her behaviour with him had been perfect, and full of the tact that had been perpetually necessary, for Colonel Paradine had, though a hero, been undoubtedly, and for many reasons, a difficult man to deal with. He had been splendid in battle, less splendid in the life of darkness after the battle was over. The Defence of course did not wish to dwell on his faults. But they would be brought out by Counsel for the Crown as possibly having provided the motive that had pushed Mrs. Paradine to the crime of which she was accused. It would be the business of the Defence to make little of them, to water them down as it were. In conversation with Keane Sir Simon had made a great deal of the fact that there was no suggestion of Mrs. Paradine's ever having shown the faintest interest in, not to say fondness for, any man other than her husband since her marriage. There was no damning hint of a lover lurking in the background waiting for her release from bondage to a blind man. She had seemed a wholly devoted wife. A point which Sir Simon had often dwelt upon as telling in favour of the Defence was the fact that Mrs. Paradine had only known Colonel Paradine after he was blinded. It had not been a case of a woman who had loved a man when he was sound sticking to him in physical misfortune. If she had loved him—and it seemed that she had—she had loved him blind and only blind.

Sir Simon wished to present her not as a woman deliberately dedicating herself to self-sacrifice, having a sort of lust for it as many women undoubtedly have, but as an exceptional woman who had fallen in love not merely with a hero but with a hero's blindness. In this prosaic age—and he could be as prosaic as anyone at times—he wished the Defence to strike the romantic note.

"There's any amount of secret romance about," he had said to Keane. "Even in a British Jury. It's our business to tap it. We'll make them think that she loved his blindness, probably would never have fallen in love with him but for it. For—don't you see? —it secluded him, and she's a strongly possessive woman. She wanted someone to herself and she got a hero to herself. Self-sacrifice isn't enough for the defence. We'll go a step further. We'll make self-sacrifice joined up with self-interest, the self-interest which love can breed in a passionate woman. Then where the devil is there any motive for murder?"

"Then who is supposed to have committed the murder?" Keane had put that question.

"Complete darkness, mystery. I've several times got off people accused of murder without ever fixing the crime on anyone else. We can do it in this case, I believe, if we play our cards cleverly. If I could detect anyone else as the criminal of course I should use it for all it was worth. But the flat truth is that I can't."

Now Keane came with his suggestion that possibly William Marsh was the criminal.

"What's put that into your head?" said Sir Simon sharply. "Where do you find a scrap of evidence to back up that theory?"

"One minute, Sir Simon!" said Keane, in his most impressive manner. "What's been troubling me very much ever since I became interested professionally in this case has been the lack of backbone, the lack of spine in the defence we've been contemplating."

"Ah!"

"You've felt it, too, no doubt you must have felt it."

"Well, I should be very glad to get some stiffening into it, even if only some whalebone, if we could do it without casting about wildly, chasing the phantasmal. I like always to feel my feet on solid earth in any case I take up. Of course long ago I considered this William Marsh very carefully. His position in the Paradine household obviously made it possible for him to murder Colonel Paradine if he wished to. I didn't miss that. The veriest booby wouldn't have missed it. But, as I told you, seek as I would, I couldn't find a scrap of cogent evidence against him, while everything I could find told against the notion you're putting forward now, at the eleventh hour, one might almost say, and in the man's favour. His devotion to his master is unquestioned, and—so far as I can see—unquestionable. Nobody connected with the two of them ever doubted it. Even Mrs. Paradine didn't doubt it, and doesn't doubt it now, in spite of Marsh's acute hostility to her. Then where the devil's the stiffening, the spine if you like to call it so, such a theory as yours could put into the case? Has anything made *you* think that Marsh hated his master instead of loved him? Colonel Paradine left him a legacy, it's true, and he may have known, or at any rate guessed, that Paradine would do that. But look at his position while the Colonel was alive! He had absolutely everything he wanted, lived on velvet as regards the creature comforts, and was treated with the greatest possible consideration. There's everything—everything dead against such a theory as you are putting to me. Oh, by the way, you didn't suggest it to Mrs. Paradine to-day, I hope, when you were with her?"

"Of course not. I shouldn't have dreamed of doing that before speaking to you about it."

"My dear fellow, I didn't suppose—you're always delightful to work with. But this damned case is rather upsetting, and as you say the defence does want stiffening. But I really can't see——"

"Has it never occurred to you that this William Marsh is a violently emotional man?"

"That's putting it violently. I believe him to be a man capable of decidedly strong feeling. His devotion to his master showed that."

"And also his apparent hostility to Mrs. Paradine."

"That, too! Yes; Marsh is a man who on occasion feels strongly."

"I believe him to be a fanatic."

Sir Simon was evidently about to say something when Keane stopped him by adding quickly:

"But I want to put another question to you about him."

"Well? Go ahead!"

"Has it ever occurred to you that he may be a man full of cunning?"

"Marsh!"

Sir Simon leaned forward with his expressive and very unEnglish hands folded one over the other.

"I seldom look for the first time upon anyone concerned in a case I have to do with without instinctively seeking for that very quality—cunning. It's elementary with me, I might almost say, the instinct to search for cunning."

"And in Marsh's case?"

"Few people, in my opinion, are not cunning on occasions. Nature, cruel though she is, supplies us with weapons of self-defence. The mind has its claws, the claws of cunning. So I would seldom feel able to rule out absolutely the possibility of a human being's developing cunning in self-defence—pushing out the claws, you know. But I can't say I think William Marsh a typical specimen of a cunning man. I observed him closely in the Magistrate's Court and he gave me an impression of unusual sincerity. The man who's open in his dislikes is very apt to be open in other directions. And in his dislike of our client Marsh seems to be very sincere."

"A very hateful and unnecessary sincerity, if it is so!" exclaimed Keane, with a sudden burst of feeling. "What do you make of that extraordinary scene which occurred in London on the afternoon before Colonel Paradine's death? Doesn't Marsh's presence in the hall at what was evidently a critical moment suggest that he was possibly spying on his master and mistress?"

"It may have been so. On the other hand as a trusted servant he may have had good reasons for being about."

"And Mrs. Paradine's explanation of the cause of the row?"

"What can we do but accept it?"

"Do you believe it?"

"Do you?"

Instead of answering that question Keane said:

"Surely she's been straightforward with us."

"And yet the explanation seems rather thin to me. Such a violent outburst over a mere trifle."

"Bad-tempered men often burst out over trifles."

"That's true. Anyhow we have to accept her explanation. As to Marsh's cunning, isn't it ruled out by the sincerity of his dislike of his mistress so blatantly shown?"

"Mightn't that be an assumption?"

"That is possible, of course. In fact, if there were anything in your theory of Marsh's guilt, dislike and suspicion of Mrs. Paradine would be the obvious line for him to take."

"Exactly! He would be trying to create prejudice against her in the minds of the Jury in order to save his own skin."

"Well," said Sir Simon, with almost pugnacious definiteness, "I may be wrong but I believe Marsh's dislike of our client is honest."

"I don't trust that fellow," said Keane. "I trust neither his appearance nor his manner."

"Mrs. Paradine speaks well of him."

"I know she does—to us. She has had no occasion to speak of him before a Judge and Jury as yet."

After a long pause during which Sir Simon sat very still, apparently in profound thought, he looked up and said:

"What d'you think of Mrs. Paradine's attitude towards Marsh?"

"It's very difficult to comprehend," said Keane, morosely, staring before him.

"There is something between Mrs. Paradine and Marsh that I don't understand at all," said Sir Simon.

"Between them!" said Keane sharply.

"As I said. I have never been able to fathom it. Here we have a woman and a man, mistress formerly and servant. The mistress is accused of murder and is in danger of being hanged."

Keane winced at this and his face reddened all over. He lifted a hand as if in protest. But Sir Simon, without seeming to notice his emotion, continued:

"The servant does not take her part, but on the contrary shows enmity to her and is a hostile witness against her. Nevertheless so far she has stood up for him. She has given him a good character. She has told us that she can only speak well of him. Why is this? What's her incentive? There's something underneath here

that we haven't got at. Now you come to me with this new theory.
If well founded it explains William Marsh's behaviour about Mrs.
Paradine. But it doesn't explain her attitude in regard to him. What
is *she* up to? Can she be simply made up from head to heel of
sheer Christian charity? Another thing! If Marsh were actually
the murderer of Colonel Paradine, wouldn't she be certain to suspect it? In that case wouldn't she have suggested it to us? But she
never has."

"She might not suspect it."

"I don't think you're doing yourself full justice, Keane."

Keane got up abruptly from his seat, put his hands deep in his
pockets and walked towards the window of Sir Simon's sanctum.
As it was winter, and now late in the afternoon, the window was
concealed by curtains and no view was obtainable. Yet Keane went
up to the curtains and stood for a moment facing them. His
powerful shoulders were lifted, almost hunched. His head was
sunk towards his chest. He stayed there for a couple of minutes. Sir
Simon sat looking at him. At last he turned round. There was a
rigid look on his face as if his features had stiffened.

"I'm convinced," he said, speaking slowly, "that Mrs. Paradine
had nothing to do with this murder. When you first briefed me I
confess I had my doubts, and they were very grave. But I have
none now. It isn't so much a question with me of evidence or no
evidence."

"No?" said Sir Simon from the table in a thin voice.

"No!" said Keane, on a deep heavy note. "Circumstances and
psychology may often seem to be in opposition. When they are I'm
inclined to distrust circumstances and trust to my flair—I think I
have one—for getting to the truth of psychology. I've seen a good
deal of Mrs. Paradine now. I've had a number of interviews with
her. I've studied and observed her closely. And I've convinced myself that such a woman as she is couldn't have done what she's
accused of. There is nothing criminal about her! One thing has
specially struck me. I think it was the first thing that made me
think she couldn't be a guilty woman."

"What's that?"

"Her complete lack of fear. She has never said that she was
certain of acquittal, as so many criminals do say. But she has never

shown any fear of condemnation. Even to-day when I told her that Horfield is going to try her case and that I wished we had any other Judge——"

"You told her that?"

"I did. Why not?" said Keane, with a touch of bristling defiance.

"Well, I don't know that it was very wise."

"Oh, I'm frank with her. She can stand it."

"I daresay. Well?"

"Even then when I had given her some of my reasons for wishing it wasn't to be Horfield she never showed the white feather. She seemed to have an almost implicit trust in British justice. I was very much struck by that. It was the attitude of an innocent woman. Mrs. Paradine is innocent. I'm positive of it."

A faint smile stretched Sir Simon's lips. He was thinking of the saying current in legal circles that it was sufficient for Keane to be briefed for the Defence automatically to be convinced that his client was innocent.

Keane didn't miss that slight smile.

"I don't ask you," he continued, almost with menace in his powerful voice, "whether you think Mrs. Paradine innocent or guilty. That doesn't concern me. No man's opinion on the matter concerns me now. *I* am convinced. That's enough for me."

"So it should be! So it should be!" said Sir Simon amiably. "I'm glad to hear it, very glad. It'll put heart, lots of heart, into your defence."

"I'm resolved to get her off, and mark me——" Keane leaned down to Sir Simon and his fine dark eyes blazed——"Mark me, I shall succeed in doing it. Horfield shall not prevent me."

"Horfield's a British Judge!" said Sir Simon, with a sudden rigidity. "We have no right to assume that he would do anything contrary to the strictest, most impartial, justice."

"But you yourself didn't wish him to try this case."

"Because I know he is not sympathetic to you. But I don't doubt his impartiality."

"You know quite well he's a cruel Judge, probably the most cruel Judge who sits on our Bench."

"He is inclined to be harsh in his sentences. I'll allow that. But in this case we know what the sentence, should there be one, must be. For the crime is murder, and this is England, not France where murderers so often go scot free."

"Mrs. Paradine is not a murderess!" exclaimed Keane.

"I was merely alluding to the fact that——"

"I know. But now let us go thoroughly into this line of defence I've suggested."

Keane sat down again by the table, opposite to Sir Simon, who noticed that there were drops of perspiration on his forehead.

"The line I wish to take is this: I wish to suggest that it was William Marsh's fanatical devotion to his master that led him to connive at what was really in essence a suicide."

"A suicide?"

"Paradine's blindness comes in here. He wished to die. He was determined to die, and, being blind, couldn't readily come at the means of compassing his own death."

"A blind man could shoot himself."

"If he could get at a loaded pistol."

"That would be easy enough, one would think, in the home of a man accustomed all his life to the use of firearms."

"Mightn't Mrs. Paradine have guessed his intention and kept them out of his way?"

"Ah! You wish to present her as the would-be saviour of her husband instead of as an innocent, but wholly inactive, member of that tragic household!"

"That may be necessary. If so, I see nothing against it."

"An extra shot in the locker, eh? I don't deny it's an idea! But can you find any evidence of such a desire on his part?"

"I might get some from her."

Sir Simon looked at him hard but said nothing.

"As I told you, I haven't gone into this matter yet with her. I wanted to put it before you first and hear your opinion upon it. It would be an audacious defence."

"Oh, I've no objection to audacity. The point to consider is this —is it watertight? Would it carry conviction? And what would Horfield think of it?"

"That damned Horfield!" Keane muttered.

"Forgive me, Keane," said Sir Simon, more tentatively than usual. "I don't ask out of vulgar curiosity. I'm sure you'll believe that. My reason, I might say, is strictly professional. But is there any serious breach between you and Horfield? He and his wife were dining with you the other night, and it seemed to me that all went quite well."

"An armed neutrality. He doesn't like me. Once or twice I haven't been very tactful with him."

He told Sir Simon about his allusion to the upset judgment on appeal.

"That may have put his back up naturally at the moment. But if there's nothing more serious than that, I hardly think——"

"He's against me, dead against me. I know it."

He stopped, then incautiously added:

"And my wife knows it, too."

"Really!"

"Yes. In fact, it was she who drew my attention to it. She told me Horfield didn't like me. By Jove!"

"What is it?"

"I just remember! She even said one day that she hoped I should never be in a big case before Horfield. And now—that's strange!"

"Did she give any reason for that hope?"

"Yes. She said—well, something about Horfield's being glad to take it out of me if ever he got the chance."

"I can't think——"

"She's always right about things she feels instinctively," Keane interrupted. "I've never known her wrong. She may not be strong in reasoning, but her instinct never betrays her."

"That may be. I delight in your wife. I admire and respect her. But you mustn't get a complex about Horfield. That wouldn't do us any good. And now to return to the matter that puzzles me, and has from the beginning."

"Yes? Well?"

"What is Mrs. Paradine's reason for her attitude in the matter of William Marsh? I shall never be satisfied till I've made up my mind about that. If your theory—I accept it provisionally for the sake of debate—if your theory is correct Marsh's hostility, or assumption of hostility, is fully accounted for: But her apparent goodwill towards him is certainly not explained. Unless—— Aha!"

"What's that?" said Keane sharply.

Sir Simon picked up a lead pencil from a tray on his left hand and tapped the table gently with it.

"Has it occurred to you," he then said, "that if your theory is well founded, Marsh might have been acting in Mrs. Paradine's interests?"

Keane stared across the table.

"Do you mean to imply that if Marsh committed the crime Mrs. Paradine may have prompted him to it?"

"Isn't that possible? Many women have prompted men to the commission of crimes. There's the classic case of Lady Macbeth."

"An invented character!"

"As to that, Shakespeare didn't make his characters do things that are against Nature."

"This seems to me rather fantastic, if you'll forgive me for saying so."

"Or," Sir Simon continued, with a certain quiet obstinacy, "Mrs. Paradine may not have incited Marsh to act, but nevertheless he may have done it in her interest, to save her perhaps from a life of misery with her husband. And she may know that. I'm trying, mind you, to find a cause for her determination to say nothing but good of Marsh. Such a determination might have its cause in fear, or in a genuine, generous impulse of admiration for something big he had done for her."

"She would be an accessory if she knew Marsh had committed the crime for her."

"Better to be an accessory than the murderer."

"I don't believe Mrs. Paradine and Marsh are in collusion. I'll never believe it. Besides, why should a servant risk his freedom, his life, merely to better the situation of his mistress?"

"Even a servant may not be immune to the fascination of beauty and charm in a woman. Ah—and *she* was once a servant herself!"

"What has that to do with it?" said Keane, with sudden violence.

"I have the servant in me still . . . I may not look like a servant . . . but . . . I often feel as a servant feels."

Someone had said that to him. The words went through his mind just then like a trickle of icy water.

"William Marsh is a servant."

Two servants! There might be a natural affinity between them, a natural understanding not to be compassed, perhaps, by anyone who had not been a servant. There is a certain freemasonry of class. Impossible to deny it. Keane was conscious of a sudden ugly thrill of jealousy, fierce and fiery, that went through him like a sharp sword heated in flame.

"Both of these people, this woman and this man, have the servant in them. That might have helped to create a peculiar understanding between them. You see my point?"

Keane shook his head.

"No!" he said, heavily.

Sir Simon did not permit himself to look irritated. He had great self-control, and seldom showed anger or even vexation, though he could be sharp and very definite, even frightening when the occasion seemed to demand it. Now he merely said, in a rather cold voice:

"Just as you like! I should have thought——"

He stopped. Keane had pushed up his lips, which were bunched together. In his large dark eyes there was just then an amazingly unselfconscious look which indicated a mind savagely at work. For a moment he seemed to be completely unaware that he was not alone.

The silence was broken by a clock in the room striking seven.

Keane seemed startled by the thin little chime. He glanced at the clock and got up.

"I must go. It's later than I thought."

Sir Simon got up also.

"We must go into this more fully. There's no time to waste now. To-morrow?"

"Very difficult for me to-morrow."

"What about Sunday?"

"Yes, Sunday. Any time you like—in the afternoon."

"The morning won't do you?"

"No, not the morning."

"Then come to my house in the afternoon. My wife's at home. There'll be people, no doubt. But we can get a couple of hours by ourselves. After four."

"I shall come."

"And bring your wife. My wife and daughter will take care of her, while we thresh this matter out further."

"I'll bring Gay. Good-bye."

As they shook hands, Sir Simon noted that the hand of Keane was hot, like a hand that had just been held close to a fire.

When Keane had gone, Sir Simon said to himself:
"Why wouldn't he see me on Sunday morning?"

He put his papers together, called in one of his clerks, had a
few words with him, got his hat, coat, and gloves, and stepped
out to the lift.

While it was going down he came to a resolve: to talk this case
over with his daughter, Judy.

He had a tremendous opinion of Judy's brain and often wished
that she were with him in the office. His son was no fool, but he
didn't equal Judy in acumen. And Judy never 'talked' when she
realised that talk was inadvisable.

"I'll tap Judy's opinion," he said to himself, as the lift stopped
and Warwick came forward from his beehive chair.

XIII

BARON SEDELSWARD had brought a good many letters of intro-
duction to London, and several influential lovers of Art, including
the Flaquers, had been busy on his behalf. In consequence, his
Private View at the Sampson Galleries drew a record crowd of
the right people. And when Gay and her husband arrived a little
after four o'clock they found some difficulty in pushing their
way in.

Keane seemed irritated in a curiously personal way by the
throng. As they crossed the pavement, and before they had reached
the crowded vestibule, he said:

"What a disgusting squash! Why invite so many people? It will
be impossible to see the pictures properly, and we are supposed to
come for that."

"But do we?" said Gay.

"Some of us do. *I* do, for one," he answered.

Gay lowered her eyelids and her pale face for a moment assumed
its severe expression.

"I know how much you care for good pictures," she said. "Well,
we must do our best."

"If you get the chance, which you probably won't, you might
introduce me to Sedelsward."

"Of course—if I get the chance."

"Oh, somehow you can manage it."

"I'll try. There's Lady Horfield!"

A pair of amazingly high shoulders had come into sight, moving awkwardly towards the first room. A fox fur was throned on them.

"Her shoulders are unmistakable," said Keane. "I wonder if Horfield is here."

"I've never seen him at a Private View."

"And you haven't often seen me, have you?"

"Very seldom. But snow scenes attract you."

The words were spoken gaily, but Keane felt as if there was a sting in them. A sting in words coming from Gay! He was startled and disconcerted. And then immediately it seemed to him that he should have been prepared for it, that a change had just recently been operating in Gay and that he had been subconsciously aware of it. Now that consciousness rose to the surface. He felt stung to a painful alertness.

"I've heard a lot about the beauty of Sedelsward's work," he said, as they edged their way into the first room. "What's he like?"

"He's tall, rosy, heavily built, with kind blue eyes, big hands, tremendously thick and rather coarse light hair."

"I'll look out for him."

"While I look at the pictures," said Gay.

And again Keane was conscious of the sting that can be embedded in apparently gentle words.

"What's the matter with Gay?" went through his mind.

And he felt a sudden very definite creeping of uneasiness. And he thought of a woman, not very far off in body, but thousands of leagues, immeasurable leagues, away in situation, spending her Saturday afternoon in a cell at Holloway. Then his eyes fell on a snow landscape, empty of figures, lit by the dying light of a sun nearly gone over the rim of a Northern horizon, and for a moment he was captured by the beauty and the mystery of that which is inhuman and which is said to belong to humanity. Sweden for the Swedes! But how that snow scene escaped from the power of men, from their puny attempts at proprietorship. And for the moment he was the prey of a simulation of Nature. Only a simulation; but it took him away into a region that was beyond the troubling voices, among which, for the first time, he had to number his wife's.

"Fine!" he muttered. "Fine!"

Moved by an emotion he scarcely understood, he took hold of Gay's arm and gently pressed it.

"I must know the painter of these pictures," he said.

"He's nearly sure to be in the big room."

"If we ever get there. There's another beauty!"

Looking at the marvellous effects of light upon snow, he was led to think again of a Northern woman, and of that painter's comparison of her to a filigree of frost in sunshine, and the cruel tragedy of her situation sent an intimate pain through him. And with this pain there seemed to be mingled a new understanding of all the vast spreading pain of life. And in the midst of that jostling, gossiping crowd he felt horribly emotional. If people knew how emotional he was! If Gay knew! For even she, he believed, did not know. And because of his nature he felt very lonely in the crowd.

"I see him now."

Gay's soft voice, without a sting in it this time, had spoken.

"See whom?" he said, trying hard to come back.

"Baron Sedelsward. He's over there. He's speaking to Lady Horfield."

Instantly Keane was able to concentrate. He gazed—they were now at the entrance of the principal room—and saw Sedelsward, in a frock coat and looking slightly official, his naturally rosy cheeks a little flushed, listening to Lady Horfield who, even more congested than usual, and with unmeaning gesticulations of her small flapping hands, was 'making' the conversation that she thought obligatory. A purple toque was perched on her wig with its rusty muddle of curls. Her cheeks were almost the colour of magenta.

"Shall we go to the rescue?" said Keane. "I think it would be a Christian act. I feel she's in dark chaos."

And without waiting for Gay's assent, he moved resolutely in the direction of the painter. Gay followed him. She was still looking grave, less quietly joyous than usual. She watched her husband's tall figure cleaving a way through the throng, and it seemed to her that it was something mental in him at that moment which obliged people to let them through to the painter.

Sedelsward was delighted to see them. He beamed upon Gay, and when Keane was introduced, grasped his hand with a heavy warmth that was almost clinging.

"I am glad to see you, Sir Keane," he said. "I was anxious to know you. I hope——"

But here Lady Horfield's oddly small hand flapped its way to 'Sir Keane,' and her little restless eyes, feverish and distressed, summoned him to attention. Since the dinner in Portland Place with its strange conversation, their relation to each other had changed. Keane was conscious of that, and so, evidently, was she. He saw the consciousness now in her eyes, furtively rummaging in his for response or evasion. Somehow they two were apart, like two people in an alcove with a curtain drawn over it, in a peculiar intimacy. Since that dinner they meant something to each other that they had not meant before it.

He spoke to Lady Horfield and Gay spoke to her, and then the Flaquers, Lady Flaquer and Judith, came up and there was some general disjointed conversation, in which Sedelsward took, or tried to take, part—for he was constantly being interrupted by guests who claimed his attention—and Keane cursed Private Views in his mind and himself for having been such a fool as to come to this one with a hope that was now, of course, to be frustrated.

"You aren't happy here!" said Judith Flaquer's clear, rather ironical, voice in his ear. "You are too big for this sort of thing. An elephant in a duck pond. And you are hating our quack-quack. Why did you come?"

Suddenly Keane longed to be frank, to liberate his soul in sheer frankness.

"I wanted to get to know Sedelsward," he said. "I had a special reason."

He lowered his voice.

"He used to know Mrs. Paradine when she was a girl in a barber's ship."

Judith's dark Jewish eyes looked interested.

"Mrs. Paradine!" she said. "But she is beginning to overshadow our lives."

"*Our* lives?"

"Well, she comes to *us* through papa, though he doesn't speak of her. And she comes to you through her case. And you, I'm sure, hand her on to Gay."

"No—indeed!" he said, with decision.

"Sure?" Judith said.

"I never mix Gay up in my cases."

"Sure?" she repeated.

And her eyes, he thought, were merciless, compelling him to be truthful with himself.

"It isn't always talking that does it," she went on. "Sometimes, more often probably, it's being. Papa now—but I feel he's going to let out to me. Sometimes he does, you know. I call it treating me like a solicitor. He has his rule—'no family in my business'! But now and then he breaks it with me. And I know he's going to break it over this Paradine case. I feel it coming. The solicitor-link between us! I ought to be in the office."

"I wish you were," said Keane, seized by a sudden wish to consult with this clever, enlightened and clear-brained girl about Mrs. Paradine's prospects and his difficulties in connection with her.

"But perhaps then I should be completely overshadowed too. I begin to see Mrs. Paradine as a cloud lowering over all those who come into contact with her. Even papa isn't immune. What will be the end of it?"

"I don't know. But I must have a talk with the painter."

"You never can here. Ask him to dine with you."

"But then——"

"At your Club—to-night. That's what I should do. We'll ask Gay to dine with us. I will—now."

She turned away from him, but not quickly. No intention seemed to be in her movement. Soon he saw her speaking to Gay, and Lady Flaquer taking part in the conversation. He wished he could hear what they were saying but at this moment Lady Horfield spoke in his ear.

"Horfield is going to try her."

The voice, in the midst of the murmur of voices all round him, sounded strangely cavernous, even sinister.

"Do you hear me? Horfield is going to try her."

"I know."

He looked into her small eyes. They were fixed upon him with a sort of fearful significance. She leaned nearer to him.

"I hate it when he tries a woman for—" she whispered—"murder."

Struggling against the painful and bizarre effect which her extraordinary expression and manner had upon him, Keane said:

"Dear Lady Horfield, you shouldn't have married a Judge."

"He wasn't a Judge then. He was nobody. But"—again her voice sank to a hoarse whisper—"Not to me!"

"You ought to be proud of his great career."

"But I'm afraid"—she made a queer movement with her little right hand as if sawing something—"of—you know—when he has to put on the black cap—for a woman."

Keane, in spite of the crowd pressing round them and the heat engendered by it, felt a coldness spreading all over him.

"Try—do your best—don't let him——"

In desperation Keane, forgetting his manners, turned his back on her. He found himself face to face with Sedelsward. The relief was tremendous. But still Mrs. Paradine was with him. There was no escape from her.

"I wanted to ask you something, Baron. Could you possibly dine with me to-night at my Club, the Cleveland, Pall Mall? It's short notice, but I should be so very glad to have a talk with you. No party. We should be alone."

"Alas, I am not free."

"I'm sorry."

"But—wait! Somehow I will be rude, yes. Somehow I will get free. I so much want to talk to you about one I used to know. What time?"

"Eight o'clock."

"I will come. It must be so. Somehow——" he lifted his large painter's hands—"I will be rude."

A puzzled expression came into his kind blue eyes.

"I must find a way—to be rude."

And then someone spoke to him.

"We've captured Gay for dinner to-night," said Lady Flaquer. "We want her really to know Bortagas, and he's coming. Can you manage without her?"

In her brilliant Italian eyes he read smiling comprehension. He
and she were playing a game.

"Of course. I'll dine at the Club."

"You don't want to know why you are not invited?"

"No."

"Incurious man! We don't happen to want you."

Gay did not play the game. She did not even ask her husband
where he was dining. She seemed oddly subdued as they went home
and said scarcely anything. In the house he told her he was going
to meet the Baron that night, "as you are dining out."

"I know you wanted to meet him," she said.

Then she went upstairs with Sausage.

Keane stood looking after her. In the midst of the crowd at
the Private View he had asked himself the question: 'What's the
matter with Gay?' Now in the quiet and the loneliness of his
home he asked himself that question again and, from somewhere,
there came an answer. But it was an answer that, then, he wouldn't
accept. He repelled it. He tried to put it from him, tried to assert
to himself that it was a lie and that Gay of all people, so well
balanced, so full of trust and of loyalty, couldn't believe such a
thing.

Her rather tall and very slim figure turned the bend of the
stairs with Sausage hurrying behind it. And it seemed to Keane
that that figure, still strangely girlish, looked weary and heavy-
hearted. An impulse came to him to leap up the stairs, to take
Gay in his arms and say to her:

"It isn't true! It isn't true! A thought like that comes to you
from the Devil!"

But almost as it was born in him the impulse died, and instead
he went rather furtively to his library, sat down at his table and
opened its long wide drawer.

Something there he must look at!

XIV

KEANE was at the Cleveland at a quarter to eight. He went at once
to the guests' dining-room and ordered a dinner that ought to be
excellent to be ready in about half an hour. Swedes, he knew, were

fond of good eating and were well taken care of in that respect
in their own country. By his appearance the painter, Keane judged,
was no exception to the general rule. England must not let him
down in one of the most famous of London Clubs. Having arranged
about the dinner he got hold of an evening newspaper and settled
himself in a deep arm-chair to wait for his guest.

He presently heard eight o'clock strike in some distant powerful
clock and, in the intervals of reading his paper, cast an eye
occasionally over the hall on the look out for the painter. But the
minutes slipped on and he did not appear. Keane began to feel
restless. His paper no longer interested him. He remembered that
Sedelsward had been engaged for that evening and began to fear
that, in spite of his expressed determination, he had found himself
at the last moment unable to be rude. Perhaps he was not coming.
But surely, if so, he would have sent word either to Portland Place
or to the Club to say so. The quarter-past eight presently sounded
and still no Sedelsward. He was surely not coming.

Keane was startled by the anger and disappointment that took
possession of him as that conviction came to him. By their violence
they proved to him how anxious he was to have an intimate conversation with the Baron. In the whole of London there was no
man whom he wished to meet so ardently as he wished to meet
Sedelsward. And now he was not coming.

He threw down his newspaper and got up. He felt injured and
bitter against the man who had injured him. Sedelsward ought to
have let him know. Common politeness should have prompted him
to send a message. The hands of a clock on the hall chimney-piece
pointed to twenty minutes past eight. Useless to wait any longer.
Keane walked toward the dining-room. But just as he was going
out of the hall the shrill voice of a child fell on his ears calling:

"Sir Malcolm Keane! Sir Malcolm Keane!"

He swung round. In the distance a rosy page boy was just opening his chubby lips to send out another cry as he walked through
the hall towards the big smoke-room on the ground floor of the
Club. He saw Keane and shut them. Then hastening up he said:

"There's a gentleman for you, sir. Baron Saddlewood."

"I'll come."

Keane strode across the hall eagerly, came up to the Baron with
outstretched hand.

"I'm so glad to see you. I was afraid you hadn't succeeded in being rude!"

The big man looked rueful.

"Oh yes! I have succeeded. But I am very much ashamed. A dinner for me, and I am not there. No."

"Leave your coat and hat here. They'll forgive you. A celebrity is so easily forgiven in London."

"But it was Lady Berrill!"

"Lady Berrill! And she had asked you on the night of your Private View! How characteristic!"

"You know her?"

"Of course! Who doesn't? And what excuse did you make?"

"I said the truth, that I had to dine with you to tell you something about Mrs. Paradine."

They were in the guests' dining-room now and Keane stopped by a table in a corner.

That would be all over London to-morrow. Lady Berrill's probably numerous guests would hear it that very night.

"Will you sit here, Baron?"

"Thank you. Till the last moment I was at the telephone. And now I must lunch with her to-morrow. Am I late?"

"Only a few minutes. Here is what we are going to have. You drink champagne?"

"With greatest pleasure."

Keane ordered a bottle of Pommery. He had become grave, was looking preoccupied. The Baron was evidently a charming and well-meaning fellow, as well as a consummate painter. But was he also a sieve?

"Oh, by the way, you'll have a cocktail?"

"With greatest pleasure."

"What sort? A Martini? Sidecar? Manhattan? Bronx?"

"A Manhattan if I may. It is my favourite."

Keane ordered two Manhattans. The Baron began to beam, and when the Manhattans came sipped his with an air of joyous anticipation.

"I like your London Clubs," he remarked, looking round him at the lofty room with its thick carpet and dark green curtains hanging under the gilded cornices. "This is indeed O.K."

And he applied himself with gusto to the turtle soup which had just been served to them.

"This is better, I most truly believe, than Lady Berrill's. A man's dinner, that is what I like."

Already he grew expansive. There was not a trace of self-consciousness in him, not a trace of the pomposity and conceit which so often detract from the charm of a man celebrated for his talent. Keane felt a strong liking for him. Nevertheless he was doubtful as he had not been doubtful when he arrived at the Club. The explanation at the telephone—the lunch to-morrow with Lady Berrill! It would be necessary, perhaps, to give the Baron a hint. But even a hint might seem to be also a criticism. One thing though that was obvious would surely help matters: the Baron was certainly a transparently sincere man. And it is always possible to make a deal with sincerity.

And so when, in due time, after talk about Sedelsward's pictures and the afternoon's Private View, and the differences between Stockholm and London, they reached what Keane thought of emphatically as the business of the evening and the reason for this dinner, he dared to be very blunt with his guest.

Sedelsward, who was a thoroughly well-bred man, accustomed to the world though preserving happily a *bonhomie* that was almost schoolboyish at times, had probably felt, as Keane had, that it would be indiscreet to rush upon the topic that had drawn him towards the lawyer. At his Private View he had shown, without mentioning it, that he had a special reason for being glad to see Keane, but he did not refer to it during dinner until at last, secretly impatient, Keane brought it up.

"My wife tells me you have met someone in whom at present I'm deeply interested," he said. "Mrs. Paradine."

At once Sedelsward's face changed. Under the influence of good food and excellent wine he had beamed with geniality. Now he looked suddenly grave.

"I wished to speak to you about her," he said, with his heavy, almost chanting intonation, which perpetually recalled to Keane Mrs. Paradine's slightly husky and lighter voice, "but as it would be to you *shop* I waited, fearing to be indiscreet."

He turned, looked about him at the other diners, then said, evidently trying to moderate his voice:

"Yes, in Copenhagen I knew her. She was a girl then in a barber's shop. She stirred soap for the shaving. She was a beauty. Everyone noticed her. I spoke to her many times. She drew me to the place. She was simplicity itself, natural as few girls are. But I think she was clever. Yes, she had clever eyes. The poor dear! What is she like now?"

In a few discreet words Keane told the Baron how Mrs. Paradine appeared to him. He had an attentive listener.

"And she is calm even now?"

"Wonderfully calm. She seems to have no fear at all."

"That is surely the courage of innocence."

"I am positive she is innocent," said Keane, with sudden intensity. "But now, Baron, forgive me for plain speaking. You mentioned Lady Berrill just now. You said you are lunching with her to-morrow. May I ask you not to mention to her one word of this talk of ours about Mrs. Paradine? For what Lady Berrill knows in the morning all London knows in the evening. She is the biggest spreader of news in Britain. And I must not be quoted about Mrs. Paradine."

"I shall say nothing to her or to anyone else," said the Baron, leaning on the words.

"That's a bargain?"

"That is a bargain, yes."

"I venture to say this because I wish very much to ask you a few questions about Mrs. Paradine. Your answers may be valuable to me."

"But I only saw her in the shop when she was a girl."

"But you were in Copenhagen, perhaps, at the time of the scandal with which she was connected? I mean when that young scoundrel got hold of her and there was a raid on the house where she was?"

"I was there and heard about it. It was in the papers, too."

"Good! Now please tell me! Was the impression at that time, the general impression, that the fellow who took her away from the barber's shop seduced her, or that she got away from that house an innocent girl?"

The Baron was silent and shrugged his shoulders.

"You don't know probably?"

"I know what the impression was. I do not know what the fact was."

"And the impression was——?"

Again the Baron shrugged his shoulders.

"The man's character—the character of the house——" he muttered.

"They *prove* nothing!" said Keane, with a sharpness of which he was unaware.

"I am no lawyer," said the Baron. "I am merely the man in the street."

And then there was a moment of silence.

"The man in the street, the juryman!" went through Keane's mind.

Just then he almost hated the Baron. And yet he knew very well that he liked him. And how he would presently hate the jurymen who were to give him, or withhold from him, the verdict he had striven for!

"What people would have to be true is often not true," he said, slowly, trying to govern himself, to speak calmly with a certain detachment. "There is a great deal of the unexpected in life."

"And a great deal of the expected, too," said the Baron.

"Have some more champagne?"

"With greatest pleasure."

Keane filled up the Baron's glass.

"And now may I ask you two or three more questions? You forgive me?"

"I will gladly answer if possible."

"Did you know Mr. Austin Powers, the American diplomat who was so good to Mrs. Paradine in Copenhagen?"

Sedelsward smiled.

"Yes, slightly."

"And Mrs. Powers, his wife?"

"I knew Mrs. Powers a little, too, not much, just a little, as one knows people in Society."

"Can you give me Powers—in a few words—as he struck you?"

"He was a very kind man."

"Ah!"

"He believed people were very good."

"Not all people, surely?"

"Most of us."

And the Baron smiled again.

"He wished to believe it and so he did believe it."

"And Mrs. Powers?"

"She—not."

"She distrusted people? You mean that?"

"Mrs. Powers, I think, was what you call a realist."

"That is?"

"Mrs. Powers probably thought that angels are only to be found in Heaven."

"Did she object to what her husband did about Mrs. Paradine? I mean to his kindness to her, taking her away to America in their service?"

Again the Baron shrugged his big shoulders. It was a movement Keane was beginning to get tired of.

"That means, I suppose——" he broke off, then said: "But as a rule American women have it all their own way. They rule their husbands, don't they?"

"So it is said."

"And didn't Mrs. Powers object in such a way as to cause trouble?"

"I do not know. But I do know that long ago Mrs. Powers divorced her husband."

"That means little in America. What were the exact grounds?"

The Baron smiled once more.

"Excess of philanthropy, perhaps. Something like that."

"I think that, like Mrs. Powers, you are a realist, Baron," said Keane, with a touch of something that was near akin to severity.

"I find this world rather real," said the Baron, finishing his glass. "I like it so—at times. Now for instance! We are too real to live on air, as the angels perhaps do."

Keane put an arm on the table and leaned a little forward.

"Your country produced a great author, Strindberg."

"Ah, he was a genius!"

"You have studied his works?"

"Not all. He wrote a great many. But some."

"I have been reading two or three of them lately. He draws some very strange women."

"Oh, we have his women up in our North!"

"Brainy, hysterical, subtle?"

"We have many like that."

"Calm in appearance, perhaps?"

"And the devil underneath."

"Interesting women, no doubt. But could a man *like* them?"

"That depends."

"On what?"

"On how clever they are. A really clever woman can always make herself liked. Everyone liked poor little Ingrid," he added, in a musing tone.

"What has that to do with it?" exclaimed Keane.

"Well, she was clever. Look! She has become a lady!"

"Clever! Is it clever of a woman to get where Mrs. Paradine is at this moment—in the cell of a prison waiting for judgment? Is that clever?"

"But that may be bad chance."

"You believe in chance, then?"

"Indeed, yes. One man or woman may do a thing twenty times and not be caught; another once and the catch is made. So it is in this life."

Keane's fleeting dislike of the Baron, which seemed like something floating above his liking, returned to him.

"And a man or woman may not do anything at all," he retorted, "and be taken for it."

"That is so. It may perhaps be so with poor little Ingrid," said the Baron sentimentally.

"It is so. I'm sure of that."

"I pray she may be released. You have justice in England. But perhaps she is unlucky. To begin with, she got with that abominable young fellow. Then she was in that bad house."

"But she escaped from it and was taken care of by an excellent man. That was surely luck."

"Yes, true. But her name was in many mouths, and that is not good for a girl at her start."

"But in America she worked hard, evidently, and she supported herself honestly, I mean when she left the Powers."

"She became a Swedish masseuse out there, did she not?" said the Baron.

"Yes."

"Our country is famous for its method of massage," said the Baron in a calm voice. "Was that how she met the Colonel Paradine?"

"It was. She had come over to England."

"He never saw her?"

"Never!"

"Perhaps he *felt* her beauty," said the Baron. "That can be. Beauty is mysterious. Even one who cannot see it may feel it. I believe that if I lost my sight and you took me and put me first before an ugly view, say a coal pit or waste ground covered with thistles and rubbish, and then took me and put me in front of a large view of fine country, and, mind, if there was no smell, no noise, to tell me anything, I should know in a moment when I was before ugliness and when I was before beauty. And *she* is surely beautiful as a woman."

"Yes," said Keane, in a suddenly dry, almost formal voice. "She is. Will you take some old brandy with your coffee? We have some marvellous brandy here."

"With greatest pleasure."

"And then we will go upstairs and I can give you a first-rate cigar."

"Delighted. All good things I like much. I suppose I am a materialist."

Remembering the paintings he had seen in Bond Street, Keane said:

"You have the poet in you, too."

Sedelsward looked very much pleased, and perhaps would have naïvely expressed his pleasure, had not Keane added, rather abruptly:

"You spoke of being able to feel beauty even when unable to see it. Now do tell me, Baron! Imagine, as a blind man, being led in front of two women, let us say of Mrs. Paradine and Lady Horfield."

"Ha!" interjected Sedelsward in his heavy and powerful voice.

"First I—let's have it like that—take you in front of Mrs. Paradine. We stay there for a moment. Then we pass on to Lady Horfield, and we pause in front of her. Do you think you would know which was the beauty and which the one lacking all beauty?"

Keane, who while he was speaking looked at the Baron, saw his eyes closed. They remained shut for a moment. Then he opened them.

"I am not sure," he said.

"Well then——"

"Wait! Let me tell you why."

"Do."

A waiter brought coffee and brandy. When he had poured out the brandy in two big glasses and gone away, Sedelsward said:

"You wonder, do you not?"

"A little."

"It is because though Lady Horfield has such ugliness of body, she has so much of the inner beauty that I might feel it and be deceived."

"Inner beauty! You think so?"

"Oh yes! That is a rare woman."

Keane thought of Gay's comment on Lady Horfield and of his two strange conversations with her. He was deeply interested.

"Why is she rare?" he asked.

He pushed the Baron's glass slightly nearer to him.

"I feel she is capable of greatness. I knew it directly I met her. Ugly—yes! Astonishing—yes! Rococo, if you like—yes! But in Lady Horfield there must be something that sets her apart from ordinary women. And even blind I should feel it, and so perhaps go astray, led by the inner beauty. I cannot tell, but it might be so."

"But has Mrs. Paradine no inner beauty to correspond with her outward loveliness?"

Again Keane's voice for an instant became dry and formal.

"That I cannot say. I only remember that as a girl her body and face were beautiful. Of the rest I knew nothing."

After a slight hesitation, Keane ventured:

"And gained no impression?"

"None that I can remember. This is indeed glorious brandy."

"This man's too sincere!" Keane muttered in his mind.

But they would have half an hour or more upstairs in the smoke-room, and perhaps during that hour he might get a little further on. Now, however, Lady Horfield had got in the way. As they went upstairs, Keane found himself dwelling on her. He was vexed, irritated, as a man may be when he wishes to look at someone and finds an intercepting body in the direct line of his vision.

Lady Horfield barred the way—preposterously. Strangely, absurdly, she was beginning to mean a lot in his life. Her small distressed eyes probed into his. What was she after? Why was she trying to establish an intimacy between them?

But he wouldn't have her getting in his way in the smoke-room. "Take one of these Havanas, Baron. No, not that! One of the big ones."

"With greatest pleasure."

X V

WHILE Sedelsward and Keane were dining together, Sir Simon Flaquer was for once spending a quiet evening at home in the bosom of his extremely united family. No guest was present; a rather rare happening, for the Flaquers had such an enormous acquaintance that all sorts of people were perpetually dropping in to lunch, tea and dinner at their hospitable house. On that Saturday night, however, there was only the family, Papa and Mamma, Amy, Judith, and the son, Alfred, a budding, but not yet actually blossoming, hope in his father's business. Conversation at the dinner table never flagged, for among themselves the Flaquers were as vital, as full of 'go' as when they shone out in Society. They always had heaps to say to one another, and touched the life around them at so many points that they were never gravelled for conversational matter.

"You ought to have been at Sedelsward's View, Papa," said Judith. "And it's a pity you missed it, Amy. He's got immense talent, and though he's of course practically snowbound, it's amazing how much variety he manages to get into his pictures. Almost he might induce me to go North when next I start out on my travels."

Amy Flaquer, who had that day returned from a country visit, said she would certainly see the Baron's pictures on Monday. In manner she was less vital than Judith, and her large, amiable eyes were not black, like her sister's, but a shining brown, like the colour that may sometimes be seen in a Scottish burn when the sun strikes the water.

"What a dear man that is!" said Lady Flaquer, in her soft contralto voice that made some people who loved Italy think with pleasure of the best olive oil. "So enchantingly naïve."

"Naïve and yet knowing," said Judith.

"That's a funny combination, Judy," said Alfred Flaquer, a small swarthy youth, with a sharply curved nose and sparkling eyes. "What d'you say, Papa?"

"It's a combination that's apt to upset calculations," said Sir Simon. "Still, I have met people who managed to be, or to appear to be, both cute and simple. They often need watching."

"Simple and sharp," said Judith. "Keep your weather eye on them!"

"Baron Sedelsward isn't sharp, Judy," said Lady Flaquer. "He's intelligent, of course, but there's no edge to him. He happens to combine great bonhomie with plenty of natural intelligence. I wonder how he and Malcolm Keane will get on together."

"How odd of Gay not to come to-night!" said Amy Flaquer. "When it was all arranged! I wanted to see her."

"She telephoned that when she got home she felt tired out with the View," said Lady Flaquer.

"But Gay's never tired, though she looks so ethereal. Did she mean to come?"

"I'm sure she did," said Judith. "Gay's the most sincere creature I know."

"Then why this abrupt volte-face?" said Amy. "What time did she telephone?"

"Not till half-past eight," said Lady Flaquer.

(The Flaquers dined at a quarter to nine.)

"How late!"

"She had actually dressed to come," said Judith. "She told me so over the telephone. Malcolm had gone to the Club nearly an hour before, thinking she was coming here."

"So he doesn't know she's at home alone?"

"I suppose not."

"It doesn't seem like Gay," said Amy, rather pensively. "I'll go round and see her to-morrow. There's something about her that—— I should hate to find Gay off colour. No ill should ever come near to her."

"She's probably tucked up in bed, with Sausage lying at the

foot in a condition of mild and toy-elephantine enchantment,"
said Judith, who then immediately changed the conversation and
involved her father in a discussion about the financial situation of
the Covent Garden Opera Syndicate, with which he had a close
connection. The combination of art and money was well calculated
to call forth the energetic interest and animation of the whole
Flaquer family, and dinner was over, and they left the dining-
room without any further mention of the Keane household or of
Baron Sedelsward.

Sir Simon sat with his family for a few minutes in the drawing-
room. Then he got up and, giving Judith a quick side glance,
said:

"I've still got some work to look into, so I shall smoke my cigar
over it downstairs."

And he went out of the room walking lightly in his highly
polished shoes.

"A game of billiards, Amy?" said Alfred.

"If you like. What about you, Judy?"

But Judith had picked up a book.

"I'm going to have a few clarifying minutes with my beloved
Christina."

" 'When I am dead, my dearest,' " quoted Lady Flaquer. "Was
there ever a more perfect lyric written? I'll come and score for
you, children."

When Judith was alone, she sat for perhaps five minutes with
the vellum bound book in her lap. Then she got up, and a minute
later had softly opened the door of her father's study.

"Here I am, Papa. What is it?"

She shut the door gently. Her father was sitting a long way
down the big room in a deep arm-chair, with a large, light-
coloured cigar between his lips, his legs crossed, his right cheek
resting in his right hand, his right elbow propped on the arm
of the chair.

"Perhaps you can guess?" he said.

Judith walked down the room. As she came to him she said,
as if tentatively, though her eyes were thoroughly convinced:

"Is it by chance the Paradine case?"

"Oh no, of course not!" said her father. "How could it be?"

"What a pity! I should have loved to discuss it."

"From the solicitor's point of view?"

"And the merely female point of view as well."

She lit a cigarette and sat down near him.

"Well, as it isn't the Paradine case what is it?"

"The Paradine case," said Sir Simon, half humorously and half grimly.

"So you were hard at work on it when I came in?"

"I was, very hard at work."

He lifted his elbow from the arm-chair and folded his delicately made hands one over the other, keeping his big cigar in a corner of his mouth. He was looking straight before him. Judith said nothing, just sat by him smoking her cigarette, which she had fitted into an amber holder. At last Sir Simon lifted a hand to the cigar and out of a cloud of delicate smoke said:

"Judy, strictly between our two selves—as solicitors and father and daughter—for this talk can't be entirely legal and the humanities are likely to intrude—this Paradine case is giving me trouble."

"And giving trouble to others, too," remarked Judith.

"There are—undercurrents."

"Most decidedly there are."

"Which I don't like."

"Nor I."

"You're as sharp as a needle. Where have you got to?"

"To a place in which there isn't as much light as I like to see. Having some oriental blood in me I have a passion for sun. In the Paradine case there's too much obscurity for my taste. Undercurrents, Papa, as you say, and holes, and shadowy places, too. Let's hope that it won't end in deep darkness."

"For Mrs. Paradine?"

"I was thinking of others."

"Ah! And yet you don't know very much, only what's appeared in the papers."

"And my feminine intuition?"

Sir Simon leaned forward.

"Let's be frank, Judy. Otherwise we're wasting our time. What does your intuition lead you to infer?"

"Even to you, Papa, I scarcely like to breathe it."

"My life is spent in listening to the telling of secrets," said Sir Simon, with simplicity.

"Even so, ought I to tell you another's?"

"Another's? Is it Gay's?"

"Perhaps not only Gay's."

"I briefed Keane for the defence of this woman. Judy, I wish I hadn't."

"But you believe in him as a wonder in defence, don't you?"

"Of course I do. But—well, Keane's a difficult fellow to handle, a difficult fellow to work with in certain circumstances. Of course we're the best of friends, as you know, but he's so tremendously emotional. And I feel all the time that I'm working with a crescendo."

"I think so, too."

"And with the prospect of Horfield as Judge! Keane hates Horfield."

"And Lord Horfield doesn't like Sir Malcolm."

"And now Lady Horfield—What on earth was happening between her and Keane the other night at that dinner? They looked like a pair of conspirators."

"She was at it again at Sedelsward's View to-day."

"What can it mean?"

"As to *that* I have no idea. My intuition gives me no help *there*. Others would suppose that she wanted something of Sir Malcolm."

"But what?"

"No idea! A mystery!"

"Has it, can it have, something to do with this case?"

"I don't see how."

"Nor I! And yet I have a suspicion that it has, or—or will have."

He smoked for a moment in silence. Then he said:

"Have you ever thought that Keane may be a changeable man?"

"I have thought the contrary."

"But, for an Englishman, he's a man of violent nature."

"But doesn't he blow off his violence in his profession?"

"No doubt that's a fine outlet. Still—it may not be enough. Sometimes, just lately, when I've been alone with him I've felt

as if I were close to a furnace. The ventilation in the room has
seemed to be altogether insufficient. At our last interview he sprung
a surprise on me."

"Can you tell me what it was?"

"I will. Solicitor to solicitor, of course!"

"Of course!"

"It's a scheme for an audacious defence that's just occurred to
him. Time is running short. Keane's to see me here to-morrow
about it, in the afternoon. He wouldn't come in the morning.
I don't know why. But he was very decided and hasty in refusing
the morning. To-morrow if possible we must come to a definite
decision whether to use this defence or not. I shall have to agree
to it or protest against it. And he's terribly hot on it. I can see
that."

With transparent clearness and in the fewest possible words he
outlined to her the defence that Keane had suggested. She listened
with profound attention sitting almost motionless except for an
occasional slow movement of a hand to her cigarette holder.

"That's the line he wants to take," said Sir Simon, ending his
exposé.

"It's clever, audacious, very audacious."

"The question is could we get a Judge and Jury to believe it?
Horfield and a British Jury? You've never seen this fellow, Marsh.
She sticks up for him."

"But he is against her, isn't he?"

"Apparently dead against her. Yet she won't say a word against
him. Why? That's what bothers me, as I told Keane of course.
Various suggestions spring up in one's mind. One I didn't—"
he paused, seemed to hesitate—"well, the furnace seemed to be in
full blast, the windows were shut, and I thought it wiser not to
mention it at the moment. This fellow Marsh, Judy, is infernally
good-looking in a very peculiar way, a mixture of the animal—
panther—and the Knight-errant. A damned extraordinary blend.
If you can imagine an animal in whose eyes at times there was an
expression of fierce idealism, you have it. Keane thinks he's a
fanatic. That may be. I don't know. Anyhow he's marvellously
handsome. He's a servant. *She* was a servant. It occurred to me
. . . I've nothing to go on . . . that Mrs. Paradine may be in
love with him."

"With the windows shut I understand why you didn't say that to Sir Malcolm."

"Ah?"

The exclamation sounded interrogative but Judith didn't make any reply to it. After waiting, Sir Simon said:

"You're very cautious this evening, Judy."

"Am I?"

"Can't you bring yourself to be perfectly frank with me?"

"Solicitor-frank, or mere woman-frank?"

"Well, we might perhaps begin with the woman."

"Tell me something first then, Papa. What is the real under-reason why you begin to wish you had never put this case into the hands of Sir Malcolm?"

"I think you know it, Judy."

"But can it be possible—after ten years of happiness with Gay, delicious Gay?"

"In man and woman isn't everything possible?"

"But has *she* such immense fascination?"

"For him I'm beginning to be afraid she has."

"Do you feel it?"

"With me it's not so much fascination—no! But she makes me like her."

"Like her?"

"Yes. I don't say she isn't very deep. Sometimes I think she is, sometimes I think that on the contrary she's very straightforward. But however it is there's something about her, apart from her beauty, that gets at you, puts you on her side."

"Then the Jury will feel that?"

"Ah, but there's the Judge, there's Horfield to reckon with."

"Lord Horfield is susceptible where women are concerned."

"Not always. And he's got cruelty in him. He takes likes and dislikes. One never knows."

"He likes Gay."

"You think so?"

"Yes, too much."

"It's odd," said Sir Simon, "but this Mrs. Paradine has, at times, a strange fleeting resemblance to Gay."

Judith's expressive dark face suddenly hardened.

"Really!" she said, and her voice sounded hard.

"Don't bristle. Facts are facts even though friendship is friendship."

"Where does the resemblance lie, Papa?"

"I can't tell. But it's there."

"Has Sir Malcolm—have you ever spoken of it to Sir Malcolm?"

"Never."

"D'you think he has noticed it?"

"I should think so. There's a look—sometimes when Mrs. Paradine glances up suddenly sideways for an instant I feel as if I were sitting with Gay. But she's much less ethereal, much more definite than Gay."

"Believe me, Papa," said Judith with emphasis. "Our ethereal Gay could be very definite if the necessity ever arose."

"Does she—do you think she has the least suspicion that——"

"Oh, Papa!" Judith exclaimed, springing up from her seat and going to stand by the fire. "Hasn't Gay loved Sir Malcolm with all her heart for more than ten years? The least suspicion! Of course she *knows!*"

She turned sharply and tapped her cigarette holder against the carved oak of the high chimney-piece. The stub of her cigarette fell into the grate. For a moment her face was distorted, as if with anger.

"Do you mean that she has actually spoken of it to you?"

"Oh no. But between women, such friends as we are, that isn't necessary. I feel in every fibre that she knows. Gay is terribly unhappy, Papa."

"And it's my doing," said Sir Simon grimly.

"Your doing but not your fault."

"No, of course not."

Sir Simon sat a little lower in his chair. His head seemed to set into his shoulders. He looked suddenly less smart and more Jewish than usual, older and less well preserved. The travail of his mind impressed itself abruptly on the outer man. There was silence in the big room for several minutes. It was broken by the sound of a scratching. Judith was lighting another cigarette. Sir Simon looked up.

"Well, Judy," he said. "We've heard the mere woman speak pretty plainly. Now I want to have a word with the solicitor."

"At your service, Papa!" said Judith, in a suddenly business-like voice.

"How does Keane's theory of defence strike you?"

"First tell me! Do you think Sir Malcolm believes this man Marsh committed the murder?"

"He's absolutely convinced that Mrs. Paradine didn't. And Marsh had every opportunity to do it if he wanted to. He was perpetually about his master, did everything for him."

"And does Sir Malcolm think Marsh is trying to save himself at the expense of Mrs. Paradine?"

"It might be so."

"In that case Marsh is an unmitigated scoundrel, even if his motive for the murder was to help his unhappy master to get out of a life that had become a burden to him."

"Yes, undoubtedly."

"Given that Marsh is this unmitigated scoundrel, wouldn't Mrs. Paradine know it?"

"One would suppose so."

"Or at the very least suspect it?"

"I said as much to Keane."

"And what did he say?"

"He gave a very weak reply. He said that she might not even suspect it."

"I think that's nonsense!" said Judith brusquely.

"As solicitor or as mere woman?"

"As both. What was your comment, Papa?"

"I didn't make one. Keane broke off the conversation at that point. I could see he was very much excited and was trying hard to get thorough control. When he took up the conversation again it was on a rather different plane—something about psychology and circumstances, he arguing that when he'd made up his mind about psychology circumstances could go hang."

"That was the lover, I'm afraid, taking charge of the lawyer," said Judith. "It wouldn't hold water at the Old Bailey."

"Think so?" said her father.

After a pause he added:

"Any other observation to make?"

"You know Mrs. Paradine and you've seen and heard William Marsh at the Police Court, haven't you?"

"Yes."

"D'you think this proposed defence of Sir Malcolm's has really anything in it, or d'you think it's only a despairing effort of his, prompted by his intense desire to find some means of saving Mrs. Paradine from the hangman?"

"I can't rule it out as impossible. If I could of course I should have turned it down on the instant. It's a possibility. Several times in the past Keane has launched some audacious, some startling defence, and pushed it home in the face of every obstacle. He has so many successes behind him that I hesitate to say he is wrong. But why—why—why does our client stick up for William Marsh?"

"If she's in love with him!"

"Mind you, I haven't a scrap of reason for believing she is. It just flashed into my mind that she might be."

"But even so, Papa, would she let his evidence do her harm and still not fight him? Wouldn't her love be turned into hatred by his hostility?"

"Suppose she knew that hostility was merely assumed?"

Judith looked frankly surprised. She half shut her big black eyes and seemed to peer at her father.

"Go on, Papa!" she murmured. "I don't get you yet."

"Suppose these two were in collusion, both aware of the truth of this matter? Suppose they were playing a sort of deceptive game for our benefit?"

"Why should they? Where would be the gain? For whom?"

"Suppose Keane's on the right track so far as this, that Marsh did commit the crime but not for his master's sake?"

"Then why, if he was devoted to his master?"

"Suppose he did it for Mrs. Paradine's sake?"

"Do you mean prompted by her?"

"Or by the sight and understanding of her unhappiness with Paradine?"

"But then why turn against her now?"

"Mightn't he have turned coward when the deed was done? Mightn't his deed have been too much for him? Many men, on impulse, do things that they're not really up to. Such men suffer afterwards from mental and moral collapse. They aren't equal to their own deed. You take me?"

"Yes, of course."

"Marsh may be one of these, and now to keep suspicion away from himself, he shows this hostility to her."

"But then, wouldn't she fight him?"

"Depends on her character. A woman may do anything, or *not* do anything."

"But you say she stands up for him!"

"So far she does, in private, to us."

"So far?"

"Keane seemed to think she might possibly sing another tune presently. On the other side, knowing she was in Marsh's hands, if there's anything in my suggestion, she might be trying to placate him and to get on his soft side."

"You mean that possibly both of them are driven by fear, he of suspicion coming on him, she of his giving the whole thing away if she showed the least sign of hostility to him?"

"It might be so. But I'm in the dark. Of one thing, however, I'm absolutely convinced, and I told Keane so: there is something between Mrs. Paradine and this fellow Marsh, and we haven't yet found out what it is."

"I wish I had a chance to see her."

"I wish it, too. But that's impossible, Judy."

"I believe I could *feel* the truth."

"I doubt it. I've seldom been more puzzled by a case. And now this dreadful complication is introduced into it."

"You mean—Sir Malcolm?"

"Yes. And the further complication of the enmity between him and Horfield."

"Well, but an English Judge, Papa!"

"I know, I know! Still, in practically every relation of life the human undercurrents play their part and have their influence. No man is free, entirely free, of this mysterious influence. Mind you, I don't for a moment doubt that Horfield on the Bench has the clearest intention to be absolutely impartial. Nevertheless, I consider it would be better for us if this case were to be tried by another man. I'll say no more than that. And I wouldn't say as much as that to any living soul but you."

He got up from his chair slowly.

"Well, Keane and I must come to a definite decision to-morrow on exactly the line we're going to take. I wish he could have given me the morning."

"Why couldn't he?"

"He didn't say. Where's your mother?"

"They're all in the billiard-room, I think."

"Let's join them."

He moved towards the door followed by his daughter, but suddenly stopped.

"I know why Keane wouldn't see me to-morrow morning."

"Why, Papa?"

"He wants to have an interview with Mrs. Paradine first. That's it! Why didn't I think of that before? Judy, have you seen any signs of my beginning to go gaga?"

Judith put an arm through his.

"Not yet, Papa."

"I'm not asking my daughter, I'm asking the solicitor."

"Not yet. He'll tell you when he sees any symptoms."

They went out of the room arm-in-arm.

XVI

JUST after twelve o'clock that night, Malcolm Keane put his latch-key into the door of his house. There was a light in the inner hall. He glanced into Gay's favourite sitting-room on the ground floor, but it was, as he had expected, in darkness. Gay, of course, had come home. He went back to the front door, locked and bolted it and put up the chain. Then he went upstairs. When he reached the landing where Sausage slept in his basket he found the little dog's bright yellow eyes fixed upon him, sleepless and apparently furtive.

"Halloh, Sausage!" he murmured, bending down.

But no wag of the tail replied to his greeting.

"What's the matter, Sausage?"

The little dog looked oddly subdued and guilty.

"Aren't you well, eh?"

Keane put out a hand to stroke the brown head. Sausage lowered his head as if expecting a slap. Keane knelt down by the basket and coaxed and caressed the little fellow. Sausage licked his hand, gave a deep sigh and seemed more at ease. But when Keane left him and, going to Gay's bedroom door, tapped and then gently opened it and went in, he found Sausage creeping at his heels.

Gay was in bed with the light on, reading. She looked up.

"Well, Gay, did you have a pleasant evening with the Flaquers?" Keane said, coming up to the bed with Sausage.

"I didn't go."

"Didn't go? Why?"

"I had a headache, neuralgia, I think. It was so airless at the Baron's Private View. Perhaps that was it."

"But now? Have you got it now?"

"Resting has done me good."

"Here's Sausage wanting to speak to you."

"Sausage has been very naughty again," said Gay, but holding out a hand to the dog, who stood up with his large forepaws pressed against the bed.

"What's he done?"

"While I was up here he was evidently left alone in my room downstairs, and he tore two of the sofa cushions and worried them to pieces. Baker told me and I was forced to give Sausage a slapping."

"An access of some old savagery!" said Keane. "Shame on you, Sausage!"

"We'll forgive him now," said Gay. "But I wonder if we shall ever be able to break him entirely of that extraordinary habit? He's good for weeks and then suddenly he goes for a cushion."

"He's unregenerate, I suppose. But so are many who are not dogs."

Gay looked at him but said nothing. He was caressing the dog, who, feeling himself reinstated, began to show symptoms of ecstasy.

"Now, back to your basket, Sausage!"

His tail held on high and his long, elephantine ears flapping joyously, Sausage retired to bed.

When Keane, who had gone with him, came back, Gay had put out the light.

XVII

THAT night Keane slept badly. Although he did no work after coming home, and after the episode with Sausage went immediately to bed, sleep did not come to him. He had the habit of sitting up very late and that no doubt was against sleep, but also his mind was too full for sleep. Gay, Lady Horfield, Sir Simon, Sedelsward, Mrs. Paradine, William Marsh—they were all visitants to him in the darkness, they all had something to tell or something to withhold from him. He was painfully conscious of the mystery connected with each one of them and of his separation from each one of them because of that mystery. He was sad when he thought of Gay. The union between them had been so close and had seemed to have in it some breath from eternity. But now she put out the light to shelter herself from his approach, from further communion with him. And he dared not blame her for that. Her new mental attitude threw a terrible light on the path he was treading. The fact that he could not go to her frankly and ask her why was proof to himself of the change in him, a change he had never conceived of as possible. One does not ask a question when the answer is being shouted by the thing in one that tells. He would never ask Gay why. But could the silence between them endure for ever?

His evening with Sedelsward had added to the acute disquietude already within him. He liked Sedelsward, who was obviously a transparently honest and sincere man. But Sedelsward's knowledge of the world—as the observant imp with the searching, not to be deceived eyes is generally called—had disconcerted him. It was obvious that Sedelsward, in spite of his solicitude for 'poor little Ingrid,' whom he had so much admired in Copenhagen, did not believe in the lily being stainless that grows in the dust. And he had, without intention, caused Keane to feel terrible thrusts of retrospective jealousy. With Sedelsward, he had touted for negatives that had not been given him. The Baron's fundamental honesty of mind had refused what was being surreptitiously asked for. The light he had cast upon the American episode in Mrs. Paradine's life had been particularly abhorrent to Keane, who now continually dwelt upon Powers, the philanthropist, who had rescued Ingrid from damnation. Was it impossible that even philanthropy could exist in an entirely pure state in this world of eternal contradictions?

What had been Powers's real relation with Mrs. Paradine?

And William Marsh?

Sir Simon's assertion that there was something which he couldn't understand between Mrs. Paradine and Marsh stuck in Keane's mind, seemed to create a perpetual ache in his mind like the ache of neuralgia in the body. But he would somehow pierce through to the heart of that mystery. When the morning came he would go to Holloway Prison and drag out the truth of that. He was not an eminent lawyer for nothing. He had capacities that didn't come at the call of the ordinary man. Mrs. Paradine was not dealing with a fool. If Sir Simon was right—and when was he not right about such intricacies of human psychology?—he, Keane, would force Mrs. Paradine to trust him with the truth of that matter.

He could not, he would not, defend her in the dark. She must be made to understand that.

It was two in the morning when Lady Horfield asserted herself in the darkness of Keane's bedroom. He saw her dressed in red, one of the strong colours which she usually wore—as if because they simply couldn't suit her—portentously large, yet with those little flapping hands like fins that seemed to belong to another body than hers. And the little dark eyes in the congested face were piteously expressive of dread and were calling on him for—something. Yes, that was certain. Lady Horfield wanted something from him, some understanding, some help, some sympathy. She was afraid of Horfield. When he came home, after putting on the black cap, she was afraid of him. She had managed to say that, to be definite about that. But there was certainly something else that she wanted to say and had not yet dared to say. And in the darkness Keane stumbled like a searcher trying to find it. But his brain by this time was tired. Emotion seemed to have burnt it out. And at last sleep was coming to him.

But how strange the brain is! Just before falling asleep, he saw something sharply defined against the background of darkness. It was Sausage worrying a big sofa cushion.

And it seemed to have some strange and terrible meaning which he was unable to divine. But while he was staring at the frantic efforts of the dog to dismember the cushion, a shutter was drawn abruptly over everything.

When he woke, it was Sunday morning and nine o'clock, and Sausage was scratching at his door to say good morning.

Sometimes on Sunday mornings when they were in London, Keane took Gay to church, either to St. Paul's Cathedral, to St. Andrew's, Wells Street, or to St. Anne's, Soho. He was fond of first-rate church music and so was Gay, and though not a strongly religious man—for he doubted whether any religion embodied the truth—he often liked a quiet hour in a church, which rested his mind, or to hear a fine sermon, which set it working. No arrangement had been come to between him and Gay about the employment of this Sunday morning, and when he went into her room to greet her she said to him:

"Are you coming to church this morning, Malcolm? I thought of going to St. Anne's."

"I wish I could come too, but I've got to work," he said. "I must go to Holloway Prison and have a very important interview with Mrs. Paradine, a vital interview, in fact."

"Oh!"

"Yes. I'm not satisfied with the defence we've been intending to put up hitherto. It isn't strong enough. I've thought of a way of strengthening it. But I must discuss it with her."

Something had driven him to so much of frankness. Now he looked at Gay and added, more tentatively:

"So—you see!"

Gay only said:

"Will you be home to lunch?"

"Of course I shall."

"If I meet anyone, the Claytons, anyone we know well, shall I ask them to lunch with us?"

"Yes, do. You can count on me to be there. Come, Sausage!"

He went out of the room, followed by the dog.

That day Gay had breakfasted upstairs. Keane—who was un-usually late in leaving his bedroom—went down into the dining-room to an English breakfast which he always enjoyed on a Sunday. The *Observer* lay folded beside his plate. He opened it and, while he ate and drank, tried to interest himself in the news concerning the troubled world, the perpetually troubled world. But he could not be interested. His mind had been taken possession of by the Paradine case. Until that was over and done with he could not free himself to concentrate on political questions, on musical and theatrical doings, on what was happening in Society. It was a fine winter's morning, and presently through the telephone an inquiry came from a man as to whether he was free for a game of golf at Roehampton. He uttered a hasty refusal.

"Sorry! I should love it. But I've got to work on a case."

That case was a devouring monster with a maw. It was eating him up. But, inevitably, it must soon be over and done with. And suddenly he stared into the future, when it would be over and done with, relegated to the annals of the Criminal Law.

What would that future be for him?

And he confronted turn by turn two futures, and both gave him cause for brooding uneasiness. One indeed was definitely terrible; the other held possibilities of good and evil which he scarcely dared to dwell on. He pushed away his plate. Such appetite as he had had was entirely gone. But he poured out another cup of coffee. It was strong. He was very particular about coffee and it was always first-rate in his house. Without adding hot milk, he drank it down and got up from the table.

Sausage, who had been lying under it, now emerged, showing white teeth in a yawn. Keane remembered his vision of the dog and the cushion in the dark. What does night do to the brain? How fierce and almost demented Sausage had looked! And the cushion had been like a living prey being ruthlessly torn to pieces. What of wildness, of savagery, perhaps, lay hidden in that little domesticated dog?

Gay opened the dining-room door. She was wearing a long sable coat that Keane had given her after winning a big case. He remembered her pleasure at the gift, her girlish joy when she put on the coat for the first time. She always called it 'your coat' when speaking of it. He knew that it held a peculiar place in her feminine affection for beautiful wearing apparel.

"I'm just starting," she said.

Keane went to her and put a hand on the fur.

"My coat!" he said.

"Yes."

The softness of the fur woke in him a curious feeling, perhaps partly physical, of softness, gentleness, an emotional desire to be tender. He had given Gay that soft thing, and with so much love. And there was so much softness in her.

"I love the feel of sable," he said.

"So do I."

She stood there quite still as if waiting for something, and under the straight brows her hazel eyes looked wistful and yet, he thought, proud. He longed to be able to take her in his arms and be with her as he had been for ten years, and perhaps he would have taken her in his arms if she hadn't spoken just then. She said:

"Must you absolutely have your interview in Holloway now? Couldn't you have it this afternoon instead and come with me to St. Anne's?"

Then instantly the softness went out of him and he felt rigid with defensiveness. He took his hand from the sable.

"Impossible!" he said quickly. "This afternoon I must have a long talk with Sir Simon. You know we're going to the Flaquers'."

"Yes. Good-bye then."

And she went quickly out of the room. He made a movement to follow her but she turned and said:

"Don't bother to come to the door. Baker is there."

A moment later he heard the front door shut. She had driven away.

"Baker!" he called.

"Yes, Sir Malcolm?"

"Please whistle a taxi!"

"Yes, Sir Malcolm."

In St. Anne's Gay found it very difficult to pray and the beautiful music sung by the choir did not soothe but tormented her. The Rector preached the sermon. His subject was the forgiveness of enemies and the sin of ill wishing. Gay listened intently. He was a good preacher and a man full of worldly wisdom and shrewd common sense, not a saint and an ascetic but a man who could be understood by the ordinary man and woman and who could understand them. As she listened she asked herself if she had ever fallen into the sin he was speaking about. It was, she thought, a particularly ugly and furtive sin. She examined her conscience and could not charge herself with a natural inclination towards ill wishing. But she knew that that very morning a terrible wish had torn its way through her whole being. It was a wish that someone should be condemned, that someone should not live but should die. Yes, she had been capable of having that wish. She was startled by her own possibilities. She felt afraid of herself. When the sermon was over and she knelt down she made an effort to pray. But the effort didn't lead to anything real or fine. She got up from her knees repeating to herself: "I can't help it. I can't help it." London seemed a hideous, dreary town to her as she went out into Soho.

Meanwhile Keane was in Holloway Prison.

While driving there he had made up his mind to be very calm, very lucid, very legal during the coming interview with Mrs. Paradine. He was now well aware of the danger that was threatening him, a danger rooted in his own clamorous nature, and had strongly resolved to control it. He was no longer a young man. He had reached middle age. It was time that his passions were stilled. A boy might run loose. A man in his position, married, known, on the top of a fine career, who had given hostages to fortune, simply must not. His own natural impetuosity made him angry and anxious. His temper was altogether too strong, his capacity for feeling too fierce. But he had a powerful will. Without it he could not have got where he had got. He was a famous lawyer; this was a case. He was being handsomely paid for his services by the Defence. His business was to do the very best he could for his fee. That done the whole matter would be at an end so far as he was concerned. Mrs. Paradine would live or die. In either event she would pass out of his life. For the time his whole brain was at her service. He repeated that to himself as he drove through the Sunday streets.

"Brain—brain—brain! There's nothing else of me concerned in this matter. My brain's got to do its best, its very best. That's all!"

And he remembered Horfield's remarks in the Cleveland Club about emotion being the greatest enemy to a career unless it were held in stern control, and about the inexorable something which must underlie, like a foundation of stone, the building up of a great career. Keane had been inclined to combat Horfield's assertions, moved partly by his secret dislike of the Judge, but there was truth in what he had said.

"Lawyer and client—that's what it's going to be from this time forth! Anything else can go hang!" Keane said to himself. "By Jove, here's the prison!"

As he got out of the cab and went into it he repeated to himself: "Brain—brain. This is work for the brain."

It happened that day that by chance he ran across the Governor of the prison, Colonel Blythe, who happened to be coming out of the great building as he was entering it.

"Halloh, Sir Malcolm!" said the Governor, stopping to shake hands. "You're going to see Mrs. Paradine?"

"Yes. I have an urgent matter to talk over with her, and there isn't too much time, though I doubt if her case will come on at the Old Bailey before the beginning of March."

"No, I suppose not. Well, she gives us no trouble, poor woman. She's got remarkable will power."

"Yes? How d'you deduce that?"

"She seems in such complete command of herself. No tears, no temper, no irritability. A sort of—of deathless calm. The Northern temperament, perhaps. I don't know. I've never had to do with a Scandinavian prisoner before. One can't help liking her—everyone who's had anything to do with her here likes her."

"Why's that?"

The Governor, a small man with a brick-red face and steady grey eyes, looked surprised.

"But don't you?"

"I do," said Keane, throwing a very unemotional sound into his voice.

"Well then—as I say, so we all do who have to do with Mrs. Paradine. I'll just come with you. And then I must be off."

"Oh, don't bother to——"

"No, no! I'll just say good day to her."

When Mrs. Paradine had been brought to them escorted by a wardress, the Governor said:

"Good morning, Mrs. Paradine! Here's a welcome visitor—Sir Malcolm who's working for you!"

Mrs. Paradine smiled at the Governor. She looked at that moment so entirely at her ease that it was difficult to realise that she was a

prisoner facing an accusation of murder. Only the bareness of the
room, the strangeness of such a woman standing with two callers
in such surroundings, suggested that she was not free, was not a
cordial, self-possessed, unselfconscious hostess greeting two welcome visitors. And once again Keane marvelled at his client.

When the Governor had gone—he only stayed for three or four
minutes—Mrs. Paradine sat down on one of the two hard chairs
and said:

"I didn't expect you this morning."

She spoke as usual in the rather husky voice weighing a little
on the words, as Swedes do, and Keane asked himself:

"Why do I like that husky sound? Why do I like these accented
words, this suggestion of almost chanting? Is it beautiful? No.
Surely Gay's clear light voice is more beautiful. But this voice
troubles something right down in my heart."

"I had to come," he said, in his legal voice. "Since I saw you
I've been thinking perpetually about your case, and I've had a
long talk with Sir Simon Flaquer. This afternoon I'm to have
another long talk with him."

"Yes?"

"I'm not satisfied with the defence. It isn't strong enough. It
lacks backbone. You can take this from me. I'm an old hand at
defence and can judge where weakness and strength lie as no
outsider can, as even you couldn't. Unless we can strengthen it
when the trial comes I may find myself in great difficulties. I have
in the past, as you probably know, managed to pull off things by
strong emotional appeals to Juries, by bursts of eloquence, by fierce
determination to get a verdict somehow. But your case comes up
before Lord Horfield and nothing of that kind is likely to have
any weight with him, especially coming from me. With some
Judges it does have a certain influence. I have sometimes seen that
a Judge is against me, and yet been able in my final speech for
the defence to unsettle him sufficiently to snatch a verdict. There
are emotional Judges, and I have more chance with them, being
what I am, than with a Judge like Lord Horfield. Now, Mrs.
Paradine, you must trust me implicitly and——"

"I do!" she said, earnestly, and looking straight into his eyes.
"You do! That's good! That's what I want!"

He had a longing just then to take both her long hands in his and hold them fast as he went on speaking. But there stood the silent figure behind the glass, that cursed wardress who would never leave Mrs. Paradine alone until she was free, or sentenced. And he gripped his left hand with his right and continued:

"You mustn't mind if I'm brutally frank in what I'm going to say to you."

"I shall not mind," she said.

And he noticed that suddenly the strange white blankness came into her face, and over her face, shutting her out from him.

"Why's that?" he thought.

And he was troubled, wondering for a moment whether it might be, though he had never before suspected it, a symptom of fear.

"I have to be utterly frank," he said. "For your sake."

"I wish it," she said.

But still she looked completely blank. And even her voice sounded blank.

"Very well!" he said.

He paused, collecting his thoughts. He had, since his last interview with Sir Simon, made up his mind quite definitely what line he wished, and meant, to take in her defence; it was a line giving scope for his peculiar talents, one which was, as it were, in accord with his temperament. It was audacious; it was startling; it was even sensational. (And Keane knew very well that he was, when fully strung up to concert pitch, a sensational advocate.)

"You know that I believe in your innocence," he began.

"I hope so," she said, in an expressionless voice, which he felt she had deliberately forced to be expressionless.

"But believing and proving are desperately different things. There's a great deal against you, and we must face that. To save you I consider, in fact I'm absolutely convinced, that we must lead the Jury to suppose that the onus of the crime of Colonel Paradine's death lies on a pair of masculine shoulders. We must shift the burden definitely—as definitely that is as we can—from you not on to space, as it were, but on to another. Someone's got to carry it, someone's got to shoulder it. I've been in murder cases in which I've got off the accused and yet left the truth of the crime in the dark. Who the murderer was has never been found out. It was so in the Leith case. It was so in the notorious Ratcliffe case. In both I was successful. In both the perpetrator of the crime has remained unknown. But I can't take a chance this time. Now tell me—and you must be absolutely truthful with me or I shall never be able to save you—haven't you got it in mind all this time who murdered your husband?"

Instead of replying to this question Mrs. Paradine startled Keane by putting one to him.

"Tell me first, please," she said, and the blank sound had gone out of her voice, was replaced by a sound of determination, "whether you are inventing a murderer or whether you believe you have found one?"

"Inventing a murderer!" said Keane. "What do you mean, Mrs. Paradine?"

"What you said just now implied to me that you had been looking about for a weapon in my defence. I want to know whether you have a conviction that you know who the murderer of my husband is, or whether you have been looking about for someone whom the Jury might be made to suppose might be the murderer. There is a difference between the two, is there not, please?"

Keane sat without speaking for a time that seemed to him very long. It was really about three minutes. Mrs. Paradine's question drove him to examine closely into his own brain, and, more, into his own heart. He had to convince himself of something before he answered her. At last he said:

"I believe the murderer of your husband to be his former servant, William Marsh."

While he spoke he looked hard at the woman opposite to him. He was on the watch for some sign of emotion in her, of acceptance, of rejection, of eagerness, perhaps of disgust or anger.

"I knew you were going to say that," she said calmly, and he hadn't detected the least quiver in her face full of Northern beauty.

"How could you know?"

"I think it is fairly obvious that, failing me, William Marsh had greater opportunities than anyone else for destroying my husband. He was perpetually with him in intimacy. When you spoke of 'masculine shoulders' I knew at once whom you meant. But it is no use."

"What d'you mean by no use?" asked Keane, in his defiant

manner, instinctively squaring his broad shoulders, raising his head, and looking aggressive. "Do you suppose that I should ever think of putting forward a defence that was no use?"

"Marsh adored my husband. Everyone who knew them knows it. Witnesses could be called from everywhere to prove it, from the regiment, from the household. Even I could not deny it. And I shall give evidence."

"Ah!" said Keane sharply. "That's just what I have to discuss with you, your giving of evidence."

"We have discussed it," she said, firmly.

"Not with this new line of defence in our minds. Do you know" —he spoke in his most impressive voice—"that, though I shall do all I can for you, I can't save you unless you help me *in the way I want*. You must help in my way. You must not stand out against me obstinately and cling to your own views of how things can be done. I know better than you do what will be needed to save your life. Do you hear me, Mrs. Paradine? To save your life!"

"I am listening."

"I ask—no, I require—you to put yourself in my hands, to believe that I know much better than you can, how you can be saved."

"What can I do but tell the truth?" she asked. "What more do you want of me than that?"

"I want that you shall not do yourself perhaps irreparable harm by bungling the truth."

"I do not think I quite understand."

"Your evidence in this case will be vitally important—you realise that?"

"Yes. I am not a fool, Sir Malcolm."

She did not say it either angrily or with cold brutality. She said it quite simply as one may make an obvious statement of fact, obvious but which nevertheless at the moment necessity seems to call for. In spite of the apparent simplicity, however, he was startled, feeling that he was suddenly confronted by a new facet of her character.

"I realise that very strongly, Mrs. Paradine," he said.

He paused. At that moment he felt hostile to her, as a man can only feel hostile to a woman who has made a very great impression upon him.

"I am no fool either," he then said. "And therefore I like to see exactly where I am going and to walk firmly. We, you and I, can leave the stumbling in the dark to just the fools. Now there is something which I don't understand and which I wish you to clear up for me."

"If I can!" she said.

"I think you surely can if you have the wish and intention to."

"What is it—please?"

"I don't understand—and neither does Sir Simon Flaquer—your attitude to William Marsh and his attitude to you. We can't ask him about it. He isn't our witness and we haven't access to him. But you can surely help us if you choose to. And it is very important indeed that you should. Marsh is, or seems to be, hostile to you. If he persists in his hostility there's no doubt that in the trial he may do you most serious harm. You on the other hand have never had a word to say against Marsh. And you have given me to understand—I don't think I'm wrong in this—that if you should give any evidence at all in reference to Marsh it would be in his favour. Now that won't do. So——"

But here she interrupted him.

"You said 'seems to be,' Sir Malcolm!"

"Eh?"

"Marsh 'seems to be.' What am I to make of that?"

"How can we be sure that what appears to be in his case is? I don't know this man, Marsh. But I have considerable experience in the weighing of human character. Marsh is certainly no ordinary man. I've heard and seen enough of him to know that. He may be deceptive. He may be cunning. He may be wicked. You—tell me what he is!"

"I have known him only as a most faithful devoted servant."

Mrs. Paradine said this with a sort of slow earnestness, pushing out her round white chin a little as she spoke and fixing her long pale eyes on Keane, who, remembering the reiterated assertion of Sir Simon that he was positive there was some secret understanding between Mrs. Paradine and Marsh, felt baffled by this statement and inclined to doubt its sincerity.

"Are you playing with me, Mrs. Paradine?" he said, with impetuous sternness. "Don't make my difficult task harder than it need be. It seems impossible to me that, given Marsh's peculiarly hostile attitude to you, you have only known him as that. Considering what Sir Simon and I know to have happened in that house up in the North facing the Cumberland Fells, the shut-in drama there ending in your husband's death in London, I cannot believe that you *only* knew Marsh in the way you describe. Can't you be frank with me?"

"What is it you want me to tell you?"

"Exactly why, in your belief, Marsh is hostile to you. The *real* reason."

"He has never told it to me. But I think he was always acutely jealous of me."

"Why?"

"Because I married his master. He is a man who does not like women. There are such men and he is one of them. They think that everything evil is housed in women and that men who are linked with women are always the prey of women."

"Is Marsh a fanatical man?" asked Keane, leaning forward.

"Yes, I think he is," said Mrs. Paradine.

"That's my opinion, too," said Keane, and then for a moment he sat quite still, plunged in thought, but always with his eyes on the woman sitting over against him.

Through the glass the patient official watched them, hearing nothing. Keane had forgotten her. He was thinking of Sir Simon's remark to him: 'I don't think you are doing yourself full justice, Keane,' and what had called it forth. Of course he had known at that moment that he had no defence to offer, that he was strategically in a hopeless position. If William Marsh had had anything to do with Colonel Paradine's death she must suspect it, even if she was not certain of it. It was to be noted that she had not taken up his, Keane's, blunt assertion that he believed William Marsh to be the murderer. That omission surely pointed to the fact that she had no wish to enter into a discussion of that matter. But Keane was there in order to enter upon that discussion. And something in Mrs. Paradine's steady simplicity was making him feel tremendously obstinate. While he sat in silence he was considering what course to take, whether to be subtle or brutal, to wind his way into her mind or to attack her with sharp determination demanding the exact truth of her conviction.

"You have given me those two reasons, jealousy and hatred of women, for the attitude of William Marsh, his hostility or apparent hostility to you. Suppose I accept them as sufficient. Then I'm left —Sir Simon and I are left—wondering at your attitude towards Marsh. It would be strange if we weren't, wouldn't it?"

"Would it be wise, in your opinion, if I showed enmity to a man who devoted his life to my husband's service?" she said.

And again Keane was startled and felt that she was showing him a new facet of character.

"Wise!" That word was surely revelatory.

"Is she cleverer, this woman, is she more far-seeing than I am?" he thought.

And his mind bristled and his whole being felt strung to alertness.

"He was very well paid," he said.

"Everyone who has had to do with Marsh has been convinced that he was deeply devoted to my husband."

"And you mean that *that* is the point?" asked Keane.

"There would be plenty of evidence to that," said Mrs. Paradine.

"Still money often leads men, and women too, to profound dissimulation."

She said nothing.

"Doesn't it?" he said.

"I suppose sometimes it does."

"Very often. You have told me that, like me, you think Marsh is fanatical. Do you think he is cunning, too?"

"Why are you trying to make me speak against Marsh, Sir Malcolm?"

"This woman, for all her apparent simplicity, is as acute as the Devil!" thought Keane.

"I'm simply trying to get the exact truth about Marsh from you," he exclaimed. "It's vitally important that I should know it. Is Marsh a cunning fellow in your opinion? Please tell me."

Mrs. Paradine seemed very definitely to hesitate. At last she said:

"Probably most people have some cunning in them."

"Sir Simon over again!" thought Keane.

"And you think he's not without it?"

"Perhaps not—entirely."

"Do you realise that you are gradually beginning to give me

a different view of William Marsh from the view you have hitherto given?" he asked.

"You asked me to be absolutely frank with you. I am trying to be."

Again she spoke so simply that he was almost disarmed. Yet he couldn't forget the new glimpses of character she had, perhaps deliberately—he wasn't sure—given to him that morning. He began to think it was possible that she was really a remarkable specimen of the *Maîtresse femme*. And the thought shot through his mind:

"Possibly that's why I——"

And then it seemed to him that he snapped the thought off short as strong fingers can snap a twig. There are thoughts that frighten a man.

With that new suspicion in his mind Keane resolved to lay some cards on the table.

"The time's arrived," he said, again finding his legal voice, "for me to tell you what I've come to the conclusion is the line we must take if we're to put up a successful defence—on which your life hangs."

Directly he had uttered the last word he realised its hideous significance for her, but he tried not to show that he had realised it, and continued unemotionally:

"I've carefully considered the whole situation, and you must take it from me that this defence is our best chance, and perhaps our only chance."

He then, with his usual lucidity, outlined to her the theory he had put before Sir Simon Flaquer in Bewly Place, that Colonel Paradine, finding his life in blindness utterly intolerable, had wished to end it and, impotent to get at the means owing to his affliction, had opened his heart to his faithful attendant, William Marsh, and had eventually persuaded Marsh to lift the burden from him and enable him to go.

"Elsewhere!" as Keane solemnly expressed it.

Mrs. Paradine, whose face, Keane noted, was again overspread by the blank expression so characteristic of her in certain moments, listened without making a movement, and probably with absorbed attention. It could hardly be otherwise, but that blankness prevented him from knowing. Perhaps it was a symptom of her withdrawal into the very depths of thought. That possibility occurred to him. Sheer mental concentration might be the cause of the banishing from her features of all expression. Anyhow he seemed to feel the intensity of her attention overspreading him as he spoke.

"This line of defence, if successful," he presently said, "while exonerating you would not irretrievably condemn William Marsh. He would be left in the position of a man who had connived at, let us say, had even caused, death, not from a hateful motive but from a motive of almost diseased affection."

"Diseased affection!" she repeated slowly.

And her face looked heavy with pondering for an instant.

"There is evidence that your husband, brave though he was, did not bear his affliction patiently, that he was terribly miserable in it."

"He was."

"And embittered by it."

"Can one, ought one to be surprised at that?"

"Perhaps not! No! I'm not judging him. I'm merely stating a fact that is useful for this defence. He had enormous influence over Marsh."

"Enormous."

"There Marsh's fanaticism comes in. A fanatical man, a man of violent temperament and emotions will commit acts that the average man might shrink from with horror."

"I suppose he might."

Her voice was now as devoid of expression as her face.

"This would be, as I see it, a sort of assisted suicide."

"Ah!"

"I believe it would be possible, given the right sort of evidence" —as Keane said this he looked away from Mrs. Paradine—"to get a Jury to take this view of what happened."

"Ah!" she repeated.

Keane looked at the figure separated from them by glass. What was passing through that figure's mind? Their words did not reach her. But could she be utterly unaffected by the thoughts those words expressed?

As Mrs. Paradine said nothing more Keane at last said:

"You fully understand my meaning?"

"Of course!" she said then. "But where do you expect to get this evidence from, Sir Malcolm? What you call the right sort of evidence?"

"Are you not going into the box?"

They looked at each other in silence. Keane's body was bristling.

"It's my duty to get you off. I intend to get you off," he heard a low voice, his voice, saying, then:

"You are in great danger," the voice added.

"I know," said the other voice in the room. "I know that better than you do."

"In this defence I shall rely greatly on your evidence. Your life may very well depend on the evidence you give and the way in which you give it."

Silence.

"And now," Keane said, forcing a brisk and he hoped ordinary sound into his voice, "I'll tell you what I shall want from you."

XVIII

WHEN Keane left Holloway Prison that day he realised two things: that he had not penetrated to the bottom of the matter of Mrs. Paradine's true relation to William Marsh, and that he had not discovered whether she believed him, or knew him, to have had a hand in the death of her husband.

What would Sir Simon think of that lack of discovery?

Keane didn't exactly look forward to their meeting that afternoon. Still he would have news for Sir Simon. His morning's interview had been anything but unfruitful. Among other things he believed that he had succeeded in shaking Mrs. Paradine out of the curious calmness which had apparently wrapped her till now. He had spoken brutally of the danger in whose shadow she stood. And he thought he had frightened her. If so, if she had been more frightened by him, by what he had said, by his way of saying it, his manner and look when he had said it, than by the actual situation in which she had been placed for so long, he certainly must have obtained power over her. That was something gained. Yes, he had some power over her.

The exultation that conviction brought him gave him the measure of his previous lack of confidence in his influence over her. He had been dogged by the sense of humiliation that sometimes accompanies the dawning of an emotion which a man suspects may turn out to be unconquerable.

In the taxicab he looked at his watch. It was already past one. Lunch was at one. If Gay had invited any guests they would already have begun lunch. They would not have waited for him.

He felt an overwhelming aversion from the thought of being in company, of having to make conversation, to be cheerful, amusing, lively. It was possible that Gay was alone, more likely that she had found someone to join them. Several intimate friends of theirs went regularly to St. Anne's, Soho. She was bound to have met them, to be already seated at lunch with some of them.

Yielding to an irresistible impulse he leaned out of the window and told the chauffeur to go to the Cleveland Club instead of to Portland Place. From there he would telephone to Gay telling her that he had been kept so late that he had thought it best to lunch at the Club instead of butting in on a lunch party that was half over.

He wouldn't telephone immediately; he would wait till towards two o'clock.

It was a few minutes past two when he telephoned. The butler answered, then Gay came to the telephone and told him the Otways were lunching. They had waited for him till a quarter-past one and had then given him up. She had explained where he was.

Keane frowned when he heard her voice saying that.

"Being so late, I thought it best to come to the Club," he said hastily. "So as not to interrupt you in the middle of lunch. Do tell the Otways how sorry I am. I'll be home in time to take you to the Flaquers'."

"Very well," said Gay's voice.

He rang off.

He left the telephone irritated by a guilty feeling. By nature he was frank, outspoken, sometimes brusque and overbearing, but not insincere or a lover of underhand dealings. Gay must be wondering. Or—perhaps she was not wondering?

He was becoming terribly preoccupied with the problem of Gay.

There were very few men in the Club. He avoided those whom he knew, went to the upstairs smoke-room and sat down in an armchair in a corner. He didn't smoke, but sat back and shut his eyes. Something within him felt tired. And he was ill at ease with himself, terribly ill at ease.

The knowledge that this was so made him realise what an exceptionally happy man he had been during the ten years of his union with Gay. He had been so happy that he had not thought much about it, as a man does not think about the process of breathing. It had been perfectly natural to be a happy man living a happy life. Why not? It was the right thing. Men ought to be happy. A man ought to be happy with his wife. Marriage was intended to create and foster happiness. Very often it didn't, but that was because of the crookedness, fickleness or sheer folly of men and women. They wouldn't stick to happiness. They didn't know when they had it. Recklessly they often flung it away.

What was he doing?

The interview he had just had with Mrs. Paradine in Holloway had enlarged his view of her, but it had also unsettled his opinion about her. He had believed her to be simpler than he now felt her to be. He had always realised that she was intelligent and that despite her great naturalness of demeanour there was something important in her, something unusual and strong that set her apart and above the average woman. Her apparent simplicity was not the simplicity of a fool. He had always known that. But now he began to doubt whether the simplicity of her outward manner, of her approach to others, was echoed by any inward simplicity of nature. She was, perhaps, on the contrary, a woman of extraordinary complexity.

He remembered Lord Horfield's remark, after seeing her photograph, that she was perhaps one of those women who have hysteria in them.

Thinking for a moment of hysteria, he tried to imagine Mrs. Paradine completely out of control, to imagine her in a passion, or breaking down under the influence of fear or grief. What would she be like then? She had always hitherto succeeded in dominating herself when with him. Only that day he suspected that he had succeeded in shaking her. Deliberately he had dwelt on the great danger she was in.

But was it possible that she had not realised long ago the extremity of that danger?

Keane had known accused people, some of them guilty people, who till the very last moment had been convinced that they would 'get off.' They were like the many human beings who, seeing people die all around them, cannot feel that the finger of death may at any moment touch them.

But he had shaken Mrs. Paradine that day. She had certainly caught the infection of his anxiety about her fate. And he had meant that she should catch it.

He could not imagine what she would be like in an outburst of fear or grief. He felt certain that she would face her trial with at any rate an admirable appearance of calmness. When he was with her he usually felt that she was calmer than he was. She had said that she trusted him implicitly. But didn't she trust herself more? That white blankness of hers was surely a shield. Perhaps it concealed acute fear, perhaps something quite other than fear. In either case, an extremely sharp intelligence was surely at work behind it.

He had been struck, he had even been startled, by her more than once during their interview. The first time had been when she had asked him whether he was 'inventing' a murderer, and had pointed out to him the implication carried in his remark about shifting the burden. Then a phrase of hers had surprised him— 'but it's no use.' 'No use' to bring Marsh forward as the murderer of Colonel Paradine! The effect of that phrase upon Keane had been strange and almost sinister. That invention no use! And if it were of use—what then? Of course, she might have meant that even if Marsh were the murderer it would be impossible to make anyone believe it. But had she meant that?

Then when she had said: "I am not a fool, Sir Malcolm," and later, when, going back to a phrase of his, after he had got well beyond it, and interrupting him, she had said: "You said 'seems to be,' Sir Malcolm," picking out the vital point in his series of remarks and then adding: "What am I to make of that?" That going back had shown that her mind was keen and alert, that she meant to grasp fully everything that he said to her, that she knew when she did and when she did not understand his drift.

Her remarks about Marsh had interested him, of course, but she had not enlightened him enough. He had felt, when he was speaking of Marsh, that she was giving him the surface of her mind, not the depth of it. And yet she had been frank. She had said that she believed Marsh to be a fanatical man, she had spoken of his dislike and distrust of women. Those were the reasons she had put forward as accounting for Marsh's hostility to her, those and his jealousy. And after Keane's following question about her strange persistence in praising Marsh she had asked that extraordinary question: "Would it be *wise*, in your opinion, if I showed enmity to a man who devoted his life to my husband's service?" The word 'wise' suggested that all her praise of Marsh was perhaps a deliberate assumption of admiration because she believed it to be good policy to praise Marsh.

Thinking over the whole of the conversation in the prison, Keane was fortified in his impression that in dealing with Mrs. Paradine he and Sir Simon were dealing with an infernally clever woman. Being himself clever, he could not avoid that conclusion, though it was far from being sympathetic to him. They had spoken of cunning that day. Was she a definitely cunning woman? If so, had she, who was in such great danger, pondered long over that danger and made up her mind on the best way to meet and fight it?

He began uneasily to wonder whether when with importance and authority, the authority of a famous King's Counsel, he told her that she must put herself entirely in his hands she had not secretly felt that her hands were more able than his!

Nevertheless, he believed that she had made up her mind to give the sort of evidence which he had suggested to her. She had not positively said that she would do it, but she had not said that she would not do it. And—he had been struck by this—she had never interrupted him with any assertion that he was suggesting to her to perjure herself in the witness-box.

Had he been suggesting to her to perjure herself?

He did not know. The defence he wanted to make, he was now determined to make, might be recapitulation of the sheer truth. It was possible.

Yet he knew that when he and she had been talking together he had had the feeling that they were two conspirators. He had had that feeling, but he hadn't cared. He had been carried away by his dramatic impulse and by something else. Possibilities had crowded upon his imagination. He had seen himself in Court conducting that strange defence with enormous mastery, startling the Court, holding the attention of the Jurors and the fascinated crowd, had seen himself as a spellbinder. And he had felt the recklessness of his sensational talent, and the determination to sweep this woman of the North along with him to a victory gained by his brilliance, his daring, his audacity. Never mind whether the defence was well founded or not so that it won through, won the case and saved her from the hangman.

But—there was the Judge, there was Horfield.

.   .   .   .   .   .

Although Keane had told Gay over the telephone that he would go to Portland Place in time to take her to the Flaquers', he did not do it. When he opened his eyes and got up from his chair, he found that it was already four o'clock. He badly needed some air before sitting down to his fateful talk with Sir Simon, and he resolved to walk from Pall Mall across the Park to Hyde Park Gardens, and during the walk to make up his mind exactly how he was going to tackle Sir Simon. And he went a second time to the telephone, and when the butler answered, explained that he would meet Lady Keane at Lady Flaquer's, as he had been kept at the Club and found he must have some air before undertaking more work. He would therefore walk to Hyde Park Gardens across the Park instead of returning home and driving there.

He did not ask to speak to Gay, though the butler said:

"Shall I fetch her ladyship to the telephone, Sir Malcolm?"

At that moment he didn't want to speak to Gay or to hear her voice.

The walk did him good. He went slowly and lingered in the Park, and did not arrive at the Flaquers' house till it was nearly five o'clock. By that time he felt cool, capable, and ready to be convincing. He knew that Sir Simon was a man who could not be played with or fobbed off with displays of emotion and dramatic force. The appeal to reason and intellect would be necessary with him, and it must be a strong one to carry him.

"I must be very careful, too, how I deal with my new conception of her!" Keane thought, as he pushed the bell.

When a servant came he explained that before going up to the drawing-room he wanted to see Sir Simon in private.

"Sir Simon's already waiting for you in his study, Sir Malcolm," said the footman.

"Good!" said Keane, stepping in. "Is my wife here?"

"Yes, Sir Malcolm. Her ladyship is in the drawing-room."

He went in front of Keane across the hall, opened the door of Sir Simon's room and showed Keane in.

"Hulloh, Keane! Aren't you a bit late? I was expecting you sooner," said Sir Simon, getting up quickly from the writing-table at which he was sitting studying a document under a green-shaded lamp. "Your wife's been here for over half an hour. There are several people upstairs."

"Let's forget them. I can think of nothing but this case. I've been spending the morning at Holloway with Mrs. Paradine. That's why I couldn't see you this morning."

"So I supposed," said Sir Simon, dryly. "Come and sit here. Have a cigar."

"I will."

"Your wife tells me you weren't at home for lunch."

"No. I lunched alone at the Club. I wanted to keep my mind free from tittle-tattle."

He clipped the cigar he had taken from a box and added:

"A case such as this completely engrosses my mind. I shan't be free of it till I've got my verdict."

There was a touch of defiance in his voice as he said the last words, and he threw back his head before he bent it to light the cigar at the match Sir Simon held for him.

"I think I've got her to agree to the defence I want to make,' he added, as he sat down.

"Really!" said Sir Simon.

"Yes. And now I want to get you to agree with it, whole-heartedly. For we shall have to go into this with our coats off; stripped to the buff, I might say."

"Ah?" said Sir Simon.

He was not smoking. After offering the cigar box to Keane, he had taken from it a cigar for himself, but after a moment of hesitation had put it back and dropped the box lid. Now he was standing up by the log fire looking down at his varnished boots.

"Yes. If I ever meant to win a fight, I mean to win this one. But it's going to be hard work, and so I told her to-day. I think, in fact, I gave her a jolt."

He said this in a hard, determined voice and without emotion.

"Ah—indeed!" said Sir Simon.

This time, as he spoke, he looked up.

"Yes, I believe so. Perhaps she hadn't fully realised what great danger she stands in."

"Very odd, surely, if she hadn't."

"You must know that many prisoners remain strangely optimistic to the last, and are astounded apparently when they are condemned."

"That does happen undoubtedly. Yes! Tell me"—he gazed into Keane's face which was below him—"Tell me, did you tackle her about her relation to Marsh and his to her?"

Keane's eyes suddenly stared, as a man's eyes sometimes stare when he wishes to lower his gaze but is resolved not to.

"I told her I didn't, we didn't, fully understand her attitude in regard to Marsh."

"Well?"

"She said Marsh was jealous of her because of his devotion to his master, and that he hated and distrusted women."

"And then?"

"Then I spoke of her contrary attitude to him, the reverse of the hostility he showed. In reply to that, she asked me if I thought it would be *wise* of her to show hostility to the man who was known to be entirely devoted to Colonel Paradine."

"Wise? Was that the word she used?"

"It was."

"H'm!"

"Further, she asked me why I was trying to get her to speak against Marsh. Eventually, I got her to acknowledge that she thought Marsh fanatical and that he was not entirely devoid of cunning."

"You got her as far as that?"

"Further even! But it wasn't a very easy job."

"One wonders why still—unless you know."

"Know why she's so reluctant to speak against Marsh?"

"Yes."

"Won't you sit, Flaquer? I think it would help me if you sat down—here."

He pointed to an armchair by his. The movement looked nervous.

"If you'd rather—certainly."

He dropped into the chair with the ease and lightness characteristic of him.

"Is that better?"

"Yes. We're on the level now."

He uttered a faint laugh. And, like the gesture, it suggested a nervous condition.

"I don't know—still," he added, after the laughter. "Unless the explanation is that she has been governed hitherto by that belief in the unwisdom of saying a word against a man who was wrapped up in her husband."

"But then, your defence? What's to become of that?"

"I told her I intended to take the line least inimical to Marsh."

"The line of—didn't we call it 'assisted suicide'?"

"I daresay we did. Anyhow, that's what it comes to, or as near as makes no difference."

"And what impression did you get of her reaction to that?"

"I think it struck her very forcibly. I think it made a very great impression upon her."

"Then it was a new idea to her—eh?"

"Apparently."

"That means then that if your theory of the assisted suicide is well founded she, living in the house at closest possible quarters to those two men, yet had no suspicion of what was happening. Isn't that rather odd? How would that affect the minds of the Jury, to say nothing of the Judge?"

Before Keane could make any reply to this there was a gentle tap on the door. Sir Simon frowned.

"I specially said——" he began.

Another tap.

"Come in!" he called sharply.

The door opened and Judith Flaquer showed herself.

"Terribly sorry, Papa! But Mamma told me I must let you know that Lord and Lady Horfield have just come and are in the drawing-room. Forgive me, Sir Malcolm, if you can!"

She vanished, shutting the door.

"To say nothing of—the Judge!" repeated Sir Simon, with a grim smile at Keane. "I'm afraid, Keane, we really can't leave Horfield to the women. This is most unexpected. I've never known him to honour us on a Sunday before, though his wife sometimes comes. We must finish our talk later. Oh, you can take your cigar upstairs."

But Keane cast it into the flames and got up.

"What can have brought Horfield here just now?"

"Ordinary politeness, I suppose."

"Oh no!" exclaimed Keane. "Oh no!"

"Then—" said Sir Simon, moving towards the door. "What else?"

"Did he know we were to be here, Gay and I?"

"I didn't tell him. Fact is I haven't seen him just lately."

"Damned nuisance his coming!" muttered Keane. "But we must finish our talk to-night. Are you dining out?"

"Yes. With the Satterwaites."

"And we have to go to the Charlestons in Park Place. Could we both get away early, and meet for an hour afterwards?"

"Certainly."

"You come to me—will you?"

"Very well."

"I'll be home without fail by eleven."

"I'll come as soon as I can."

In the big drawing-room upstairs they found a small crowd of people. Gay was there, on a sofa in the farthest part of the room from the door talking to Lord Horfield, whose thin body was seated on a green and gold chair with a round back and a hard cushion covered with striped silk. Baron Sedelsward, in an official-looking frock coat and an all round white collar, was standing near Lady Horfield who was gazing anxiously up at him from a small armchair which was almost swallowed up by her bulky form. Her little hands, in white kid gloves, were making meaningless gestures in front of her ample bosom on which rested a necklace of claret-coloured beads, large and barbaric. Bortagas was there talking to Judith and Amy Flaquer; Mrs. George Blason, with her cloud of black hair done in a new way which made her look Roman, was laughing with Latrobe by a window; and Lady

Flaquer, seated in front of an enormous round tea-table, was surrounded by people, among whom were several young men. Other
people, mostly women, with four or five elderly men, were scattered in groups about the room, which, vast and high, was perfectly
adapted for big receptions. Two tall young footmen in livery
moved to and fro carrying refreshments here and there on silver
trays.

There was somehow a slightly pre-war atmosphere in the
drawing-room. The Flaquers, although anything rather than old
fashioned in their minds, still kept up a certain amount of opulent
state in their way of living; still received on Sundays when they
were in London, still found time for genuine conversation and for
seeing their friends in calm and at leisure, were never to be seen at
Night Clubs and seldom at restaurants. They were enormously
hospitable but always in their own house. About their gatherings
lingered a slight, and agreeable, flavour of the salon. People who
came to them seldom hurried away. They had the pleasant faculty
of retaining those who came to them. A certain young man, who
perhaps posed for being Edwardian, had said of their house that it
was the last oasis left in the vast desert of London.

"One sits under a palm tree there and hears a sound of water
instead of being up to one's neck in sand with a sky of brass
over one's head."

A gay hum of conversation pervaded the room but Keane was
looking grim and even harassed as he entered it followed by Sir
Simon. His eyes crept rapidly and, he felt, furtively, over the
throng as he walked towards Lady Flaquer, seeking out Gay, and
as he reached his hostess he saw her with Lord Horfield. Horfield's
thin flat back was turned to him, but he caught Gay's eyes fixed
upon him and smiled quickly, and perhaps—he wasn't sure—
apologetically. It seemed to him, but he had immediately to look
at Lady Flaquer, that Gay's eyes gave him no greeting, only
regarded him gravely. Her lips were moving. She was speaking to
Horfield.

After talking for a moment with Lady Flaquer and some of
those close to her, Keane was aware of a flickering whiteness not far
off, coming and going like the quiver of light on a wall. He looked
and saw Lady Horfield waving a fin at him. He nodded and smiled.
But the fin went on waving. In its awkward motion there was

something imperative—or begging was it?—he was not sure which. For Lady Horfield was as distracted in her movements as she often was in her conversation. Anyhow she wanted him to come to her. That was obvious. And, half reluctant, half desirous—for there was something about her that both repelled and attracted him since their strange and secret intimacy had abruptly begun—he turned from the tea-table and made his way to her.

After shaking hands with her he gripped Sedelsward's hand and greeted him.

"None the worse for the dinner?"

"No indeed. All the better. Last night, Lady Horfield, Sir Malcolm gave me a dinner fit for a *man*, and I, being I hope a full man—" his cheery yet observant eyes glanced at two or three rather frail looking foreign artists who were not far off—"thoroughly enjoyed it. It is good to eat, drink and smoke what is first rate. I fear that I am earthbound, not fit yet for the Heavenly places."

Then, beaming with geniality, he spoke to an elderly woman near him in order to leave Lady Horfield and Keane free for the conversation that the former was evidently anxious to begin.

"Is it possible—do you think that—I wonder whether——"

She looked quickly round her.

"Can I get you something?"

"No, thank you. I have had tea—at least it was coffee, but still —it is so hot and—" she almost whispered—"noisy here. I was wondering whether——"

"Come with me. I'll find a quieter place for you."

Immediately she heaved herself up, her left shoulder seeming to rise first as if violently leading the rest of her big body.

"Where shall we——"

"The veranda at the back of the house."

"Can we—I don't want to—all these people. I want to talk to you."

As they went she caught sight of Gay and her husband. Lord Horfield was leaning forward and talking with a smile on his long intellectual face, which looked so easily mischievous or cynical as his humour influenced it or his temper impressed it.

"There they are—together!" said Lady Horfield. "They don't see us—they are too—"

She broke off and moved sideways towards the big veranda that ran along the whole end of the drawing-room at the back of the house. But Keane knew that they had been seen by Horfield who, as if prompted by a sixth sense, seemed instinctively to be aware whenever his wife was in awkward movement. Keane had caught a side glance from his sharp grey eyes as Lady Horfield and he passed in the distance.

"Here's a quiet corner!" he said.

"Yes—nobody! People—they like to be where there are others, plenty of others. But that confuses me—then my brain goes like a —that firework—do they call it a Catherine wheel?"

"There is a firework with that name."

"Why?"

"I don't know," said Keane, sitting down beside her. "Does it matter?"

"No, no, it doesn't. You're right. It doesn't."

She laid her little hands in their tight white kid gloves on her two knees. She was looking terribly anxious and distressed, even more so than she usually did.

"Can I trust you?" she said, in a very low voice.

"Yes, of course. What is it? I feel you have something on your mind."

"I have."

"But can I be of any help to you?" he said, wondering immensely why she seemed to have some imperative need of him.

"I don't know."

"Then——"

"But all the same I must speak about it."

"I am ready to hear anything. Do tell me."

"It's a secret—between us."

"Certainly, if you wish it."

"I only tell you because you are in it—in a way. That is—you have something——"

She lifted one hand and flapped it down on one knee.

"I don't like—I hate—Horfield to try murder cases."

"I remember you said to me——"

"Especially when it's a woman," she interrupted. "I don't think any man, or body of men—" she was suddenly becoming lucid, it seemed—"should have the power to sentence a woman to be hanged. It's wicked. It's against nature. It does terrible harm to —I mean such a power is bad for the one who has it. I am not a feminist—is that the right word?"

Keane nodded.

"It is! No! But I feel for women. I feel for them terribly. They hang on to men. Do you realise *how* they hang on? It is like ivy— you know! They say in these days they don't—but it isn't true. They would like to. It is natural to them. And when they laugh at it all and say they don't, that is blague, Sir Malcolm, blague and disappointment, the feeling that there is no man who wants them to cling. But if they have the chance—ah!"

Her red face worked: her small dark eyes almost disappeared in the moving folds of wrinkled flesh. Again she flapped her hands.

"Sometimes in spite of all they must cling. And it is like cling- ing to steel all—all covered with icicles. Women should be for- given a great deal. No man should sentence a woman to hang. Christ would never—— And now again Horfield is to try a woman. I can't bear to think—oh, get her off! Get her off!"

She touched one of his hands, then swiftly withdrew her hand.

"You *must* get her off. If you don't—I can't bear him to come home again and say: 'It's over. She will hang!' It will make me hate him, and there is nothing so awful as to hate the man you love. Love and pity should rule in the world. We all have so much to be pitied for—men, too, though less than women. You too, I'm sure—— Yes, I'm quite sure!"

Her little eyes had suddenly become piercing.

"But perhaps you don't know it—yet. But you will. I feel that. Sometimes I feel things and when I do I am always right. But tell me, and you must say the exact truth! Do you *expect* to get Mrs. Paradine off?"

"Yes!" said Keane, with solemn emphasis.

Her red face looked suddenly less distressed, indeed almost calm. She sighed, opening her little mouth, which accorded with her hands but not with her body or face.

"I ask not for her sake but for *his*," she said, gathering a kind of fierceness again as she spoke.

"His?"

"Horfield's. What do I care for others? And yet I ought—but

—some of us—women—we *can't* get away from the one thing. It's for him. He mustn't have the chance——"

She broke off, staring at Keane with eyes which seemed to demand his complete comprehension.

"What chance?" said Keane.

He was profoundly interested in this conversation which he felt might have great importance for him, though how precisely he wasn't yet certain.

"To *enjoy* doing it! That's so awful for the soul."

Her manner had become almost terrible. Despite the grotesqueness of her appearance there was even something in her that was dominating. Her awkward body towered as usual. But there was something else that towered, something of the inner woman.

"Doing what?" Keane said, ruthlessly, determined if possible to force her into complete confession.

"Cruelty, the chance of indulging in—you know! There's a word for it, but we mustn't use it, mustn't even whisper it."

"Can't you tell me the word?"

"Oh, no! Never! I would never say it—even in my own mind. I hardly dare to—but I want to save him from finding his happiness in such a dreadful—he can't help it. It isn't his fault. It has grown upon him gradually since he became a Judge. With power, you know. These things come with power. When he was young it was different. But even then—don't think I'm speaking against him, but there are times when all one's service should be to truth, and there is something that is greater than any man, even the man one loves. I want—yes, that's it!—to protect him, to keep away—— I can't help being religious—I've tried, because he isn't. He doesn't believe in anything, and I wanted not to be religious so as to be able to agree with him. He laughs at it, you know. He says it's all bunkum to keep the poor quiet. You know—hoping to get something better after death. But—so this time I come to you, because you're defending her. For sometimes I feel that if he comes back after giving the death sentence and begins to tell me and—there are times, aren't there, when it's awful to smile. Some smiles might almost damn a man's soul I think. So—don't give him the chance. Keep it away from him. Get your verdict from the Jury before he sums up and then——"

At this moment, with a light step, Lord Horfield came into the veranda, smiling. With astonishing swiftness Lady Horfield heaved herself up out of her chair.

"Are we going?" she exclaimed, in a muffled voice.

The Judge held out his thin whitish-yellow hand to Keane.

"How are you, Keane?"

Keane, who of course had got up too, was going to make the usual conventional assertion of perfect health but Horfield didn't give him time.

"I think your wife is wondering what has become of you," he said. "She didn't ask me to find you, but she managed, in woman's way, to convey to me without words that my conversation was no longer interesting to her. To get back into her good graces I let in the Swedish Baron who paints snow to our *tête-à-tête*, and undertook this secret mission while she was busy with him. But I'm not in any hurry to go, Sophy, are you? It isn't surely time for evening service yet, is it? Or is it?"

He spoke, as usual, rather slowly, languidly almost, and in a careless lounging sort of tone.

"My wife is one of the few still left—I'm speaking of Protestants —who remains persistent in religious exercises," he added to Keane. "I content myself with Swedish exercises. I attack the soul through the body. She goes the other way about it. One way may be as good as another, for it seems that body and soul are closely linked together. But I prefer my way."

His long grey eyes, slits almost between the puckered eyelids, kept their hints of a smile, but Keane had the impression that something had stirred him to an unusual emotion.

"I like an athlete as my instructor better than a priest. You call your clergy priests, don't you, Sophy? She gets as near as may be to Roman Catholicism, you know, Keane, wets her feet in the Rubicon but doesn't cross it. Ah, Miss Judy, we are being suitable."

"Suitable?" said Judith Flaquer, coming into the veranda, with an inquiring look.

"Yes. As it's the Sabbath we are discussing religion."

"That only breeds quarrels."

Her dark eyes, which often moved rapidly sideways, went from one to the other.

"We are too well bred to quarrel."

"I don't believe it. There are no such monsters as that. The animal that's in us all knows that we can be stripped of our manners whenever he chooses. And religion has always caused the shedding of blood."

"Ah, but that was in the days when people were in earnest about it," said Horfield. "And Sophy is almost the only survivor remaining of them."

Lady Horfield, who had all the air of a guilty woman in tumult, at this direct thrust was driven to speech.

"Oh, you mustn't say that, Horfield. I'm sure that even in these days there are people—I don't mean who shed blood but—that was never right even if—but there are churches in London that still—look at St. Martin's in the Fields!"

"I won't. It may be a fine building, but I would as soon look at Madame Tussaud's or Charing Cross Station."

"What I meant was how it's crowded! But you are only joking. He is joking," she explained to the others. "You mustn't——"

"——take me seriously," Horfield interrupted her. "Laugh, as when I make a pun on the bench."

He looked suddenly hard at Keane, who had the impression that he was about to say something startling, but at that moment Lady Horfield lunged forward, left shoulder leading, and broke up the group. For a moment she looked like something voluminous in flight, driven by a following wind. Then she was brought up short by the crowd that was still in the drawing-room, though people were just beginning to go away.

Keane found himself by Mrs. George Blason.

"One never sees you now, Sir Malcolm. People are saying that the Paradine case has swallowed you up. Is it true?"

She fixed her large eyes upon him with searching intentness.

"If so, do persuade it to expel you again before we've all quite forgotten you. Don't be permanent inside it. Behave like ectoplasm, which comes and goes and is again absorbed, expelled, regurgitated, when least you expect it. D'you know that the celebrated Mrs. Batte, considered by scientific occultists the greatest medium in London, was caught out only last night faking ectoplasm! And what d'you think it was?"

"Tell me!" said Keane, making a fierce effort to be interested.

"A mixture of very porous cheese-cloth and white of egg. And she'd made a small fortune by vomiting it in the darkness the spirits love to people with guinea tickets. I admire her. Her powers, it seems, are physical, not spiritual. Now they say she's going to be had up. Why? Why shouldn't we deceive fools if we can?"

"You don't need to be provided with fools, Mrs. Blason. You can deceive clever men."

"Could you be deceived by a woman, I wonder?"

Her eyes seemed to him to become more penetrating as she said that.

"Of course I could."

"But you've had so much experience with criminal women. Hasn't it made you doubt us all?"

Keane paused for a brief instant before he answered this; then he said:

"Having experience of criminal women such as I have had——"

"And are having!" interrupted Mrs. Blason with smiling swiftness, still keeping her eyes steadily on him with a searching gaze.

Keane stiffened and his dark eyes flashed angrily.

"Are having, Mrs. Blason! I don't think I quite understand."

"Oh, well, I suppose we mustn't prejudge a case that is sub judice."

"What case are you speaking of?"

Mrs. Blason was a hardy creature and boasted that she was afraid of no one. In spite of the warning that blazed from Keane's eyes she pushed her handsome head slightly forward, lifted her white chin, half shut her eyes and murmured in her delicious dark voice:

"The Paradine case, to be sure!"

Keane, without knowing it, clenched his hands, which were hanging at his sides.

"I don't admit for a moment that I am gaining any experience of the criminality of woman by my connection with that case," he said.

"Oh, I'm not afraid of your K.C. eyes, Sir Malcolm! I'm not in the witness-box nor am I in the dock, you know."

"Those who dare to prejudge any case until they know what the full evidence is, sin against Charity in a way I consider unpardonable. We all have need of far more charity than we are ever likely to get. My sympathies are very often much more with the prisoners I have to do with than with the people outside who are tearing their characters to pieces in complete ignorance of the circumstances that brought them to prison."

"You believe in smoke without fire, then?"

"Of course I do! And so does every man who knows much of the world in these sensational days."

"Well, I think, if one looks closely enough, behind every cloud of smoke one will find at least a spark. It may be only one, but it contains the spirit of fire, the fearful vitality of fire."

"You are a cynic, Mrs. Blason."

"And what are you, dear Sir Malcolm? I have made you angry. Forgive me."

"I am not angry. I know your passion for farce. But I can't give myself wholeheartedly to farce when a human life is at stake."

"Lord Horfield!" said Mrs. Blason, seeing the Judge near-by apparently looking for someone.

He came nearer.

"I am having the most terrible dressing-down from Sir Malcolm."

"Why? I expect you deserve it thoroughly. But why?"

"Because I said that when you see a cloud of smoke, if you look closely enough you'll always find at least a spark of fire behind it. What do you say?"

"By a cloud of smoke do you mean a cloud of scandal?" said Lord Horfield. "And by a spark of fire do you mean a spark of truth?"

"Now why pin me down, as if you had your wig on?"

"Does she?" the Judge asked of Keane, who was standing by, looking thunderous, almost menacing.

(Except at times, when he was in Court, he was seldom fully aware how exceptionally expressive his face could be, unless he chose to attend to it, when he was influenced by any strong feeling.)

"I imagine so," said Keane. "But she's merely trying to pull my leg. I'm fully aware of that."

"Indeed, I am deeply in earnest. You do me wrong, Sir Malcolm. But we haven't had your answer, Lord Horfield. And I mean to abide by it, because you're a Judge and must know these things."

"I think," said Lord Horfield, with pellucid, silvery clearness, and opposing a sort of ivory coolness to Keane's ill-concealed irritation, "that there is usually some definite reason for even, I won't say a cloud, but even the faintest wreath of smoke."

"Exactly! the spark!" said Mrs. Blason, acting exaltation.

"In my long career at the Bar and on the Bench, I've come to the conclusion that those who get into difficulties with the police, even if they get safely out of them again, as many do, have almost invariably given some cause for the suspicions they have aroused. Even accused who get off, and rightly get off, are often potential criminals who have hovered on the brink."

"But you go even further than I did," said Mrs. Blason. "You probably think that there's often fire without smoke. Sir Malcolm, you ought to be more angry with Lord Horfield than even with me."

"I'm not angry with anyone. But I prefer not to suspect too easily."

"You forget, Mrs. Blason, that Sir Malcolm shines in defence," said Lord Horfield. "And that what a man shines in is apt to colour his mind."

Keane shrugged his broad shoulders and pressed his lips together.

"A man ought to believe in his job," Horfield added.

"Oh, but you lawyers are actors! We all know that. I never go into a Court of Justice, but I read the accounts of what goes on in them. And really, my intellect often shudders at the melodramatic appeals counsel make to Juries and even—do forgive me —at the so-called humour that drops, like melted margarine, from the bench. Don't tell me that you lawyers are always in earnest. No, you act as we poor mummers do on the stage."

"Mrs. Blason has caught the modern disease of eternal disbelief," said Keane.

"You mustn't expect Sir Malcolm to share your charming cynicism," said Horfield lightly. "He's no doubting Thomas. On the contrary, he believes without seeing any points of nails or having any need of thrusting a hand into a wounded side. He is so identified with his job—and it's a great one!—that the mere act of defence induces belief in him. That's a legend in Chambers."

In spite of himself, Keane reddened and felt the blood rise in his face.

"Yet I've heard it said, Judge, that you think I should make an excellent actor," he said, with difficulty controlling his powerful voice.

"Who told you that?"

"I've heard it."

Lord Horfield looked at him intently.

"I believe you are endowed with the histrionic faculty," he said. "On the other hand, I believe you convince yourself that what you are saying is true when you make a speech for the Defence. That is why you have such a great effect upon Juries. For the moment you believe. Later, it's the business of the Judge to reduce things to their proper proportion. And I think that's why you hate Judges."

"I—hate Judges!" said Keane.

"Don't you?"

It seemed to Keane that something within him made a violent effort to prevent him from committing a great indiscretion, but was overcome by a more powerful factor in his nature.

"Not all Judges!" he said, with biting emphasis. "And now, forgive me, but I really must look for my wife. We're dining out to-night and then I have further work before me. I must have half an hour's rest before dressing. Good-bye, Mrs. Blason. I'm afraid I shall never convert you to a more charitable view of poor human nature. Good-bye, Lord Horfield."

He turned away abruptly, and they watched his tall, upright figure moving towards Lady Flaquer.

"Our friend is in a somewhat emotional state," observed Lord Horfield, musingly. "A pity he works himself up so over his cases. They must take a lot out of him."

"He's not fashioned by the Creator in ice, like you."

"*You* ought to know better than that!" he said, in a low voice, touching her hand.

"There's a certain soufflé which is soft and quite hot outside but when you dig down with your spoon you come upon ice. If one dug down into *you*——"

She didn't finish her sentence but let her gaze sink into his.

"I hope your wife doesn't know what you are," she murmured in an under-voice.

The Judge suddenly lowered his brows.

"Oh, Sophy is not without a modicum of intelligence," he said.

For an instant he looked moody, and Mrs. Blason realised fully his age. Then Judith Flaquer came up to them and he returned at once to the smiling and light self-possession, not free from an occasional tartness, which was his social armour.

Keane found Gay with Bortagas, the 'cellist, and Baron Sedelsward. When she saw him she smiled.

"How d'you do, Malcolm?" she said. "Have you had a pleasant day? I hope so."

She added to the musician:

"Let me introduce my husband to you, Señor Bortagas. He's heard you play and longs to hear you again."

"Yes, indeed!" said Keane, with fervour, as he grasped the musician's broad and plump hand. "Your art has given me some of the best moments of my life."

He stopped, then added, as if the remark were forced out of him:

"Great playing rests me as nothing else does."

He looked at Bortagas's prominent, almost bulging dark eyes. "I wish I were a great player like you instead of a lawyer. Your work takes you into the farthest regions of beauty known to us mortals. Mine takes me into the Law Courts, where there's practically no ventilation even."

He spoke the final words in a half-joking voice, as if suddenly aware that he had, perhaps, been too serious and making an effort to get back to something more appropriate to the moment. But Bortagas moved his round, bald head as if in serious approval.

"You are right, Sir," he said, with a strong foreign accent. "I am—je suis vraiment très fortuné, très heureux d'être musicien. Mais les voyages! Ah, Monsieur, les voyages!"

And he began to speak in bad French with an almost incredible vivacity of his sufferings from sea-sickness when on his great tours.

"Maintenant j'ai essayé les airs. Je monte dans les avions. Je voyage dans le ciel. Mais c'est la même chose, Monsieur, toujours la même chose. Ah, mon bon—" he clapped Keane on the shoulder, then threw up his hands and lifted his eyes to the ceiling—"je vomis quand même!"

With intense earnestness and an utter lack of self-consciousness, he claimed their sympathy and kept them busy listening to a minute account of his physical sufferings upon all the oceans and in all the skies of the world, until the crowd in the drawing-room began rapidly to thin and it became absolutely necessary to call a polite halt. Gay did this with supreme tact inviting Bortagas to call in Portland Place, when she would give him an infallible recipe against sea-sickness.

"If it acts, Madame, I am yours for ever!" cried the 'cellist. "Je suis à vous, âme et coeur!"

And he bade them *au revoir* with the naïve cordiality of an old and valued friend. While Gay was bidding good-bye to the Baron, who had listened in smiling silence to the 'cellist's torrential vivacity, Bortagas added to Keane in English:

"You are right about great music, Monsieur. It takes into the region of gold, where not vice nor virtue is, but purity serene of Eden's Garden before any fig-leaf comes. But Jazz! I spit upon it! So!"

With volcanic energy he clapped his plump hands and made the motion and even the noise of spitting.

"I will come to see you. Je viendrai. The medicine I will drink. Au revoir!"

As Keane was saying good-bye to the Baron he felt a sort of nudge on his left side. It was very slight but there was certainly meaning in it, and he turned sharply and found Lady Horfield beside him.

"Are you going?" she said, in a low but portentous voice.

"Yes. Good-bye."

As he took her little hand he felt that it trembled in his, fluttered almost like a bird whose whole life seems to beat against the hand that holds it, beat in an ecstasy of small terror.

"Good-bye."

She bent her tousled black head towards him.

"Your wife——" she said.

"Yes, what is it? You want to speak——"

"No, no! Not to-day! But—but be careful of her!"

She gazed at him with tragic intensity, then suddenly swerved round and moved away, looking to right and left like one suspecting an ambush.

"How very strange Lady Horfield looks to-day!" said Gay, joining him.

"She always looks strange," he said. "What a great little man that Bortagas is! As naïve as a child, in spite of his genius. How a man like that refreshes one after——"

He broke off.

"After whom?" asked Gay.

"Well," said Keane, with sudden decision, "I was going to say Lord Horfield."

"Lord Horfield! He's been very charming to me to-day," said Gay, with a sort of defensive obstinacy and almost mutinous determination very unusual in her.

"You find Horfield charming?"

"He can be when he chooses."

"I'm glad someone thinks so," said Keane.

As they went down the big staircase he said to himself: "Can Horfield really be a Sadist?"

And a thrill of horror went through him.

XIX

KEANE took his wife away from their dinner with the Charlestons in Park Place early.

"I'm awfully sorry to leave you," he said to his hostess. "But I have to be home before eleven. I have an important interview about a case I'm concerned in."

He had not mentioned to Gay that Sir Simon was coming that night, but in the car going home he told her.

"I promised him I'd be back at eleven," he said. "I hope you don't mind leaving so soon. This case I'm involved in at present doesn't leave me much time for amusement."

"I don't mind," said Gay. "Why should I mind?"

After a moment of silence he added, feeling for her hand:

"All this work keeps me away from you, but you don't feel lonely, do you?"

She made a slight movement. He realised that she wished to avoid his hand without letting him know it.

"Oh no! I'm accustomed to your being busy."

"Presently I shan't have quite so much to do."

When he said 'presently' he was thinking of the time, drawing near, when the Paradine case would be over, when for good or ill it would be but a finished law case in which the decision had been given. It seemed to him then that his hands would be empty, that there would be nothing to fill up his hours. Other cases meant nothing in comparison with this case which was overwhelming his mind. Without it what would he do? He saw before him in the distance of time a procession of empty days.

"But you are always busy," he heard from Gay.

"Not as just now. But you can have no idea how an—a big —how an important case engrosses the mind. One carries it about with one wherever one goes. One can't get rid of it."

As he spoke an emotional desire took hold of him, the desire to be reconciled with Gay. They had never quarrelled, yet in these last days all their former happy ease with each other had disappeared. Without the happening of anything that could be called definite between them the perfect intimacy of ten years had ceased. Only now he realised how perfect it had been, the union which imperceptibly had been attacked and overthrown, union of bodies, minds and hearts, now when he felt continually self-conscious with Gay, doubtful what to say to her, awkward when there was silence between them, acutely separate from her. Like most strongly emotional men he was very sensitive and could not remain unaffected by the emotions of those he was linked with by circumstance. This subtle change in his relation to Gay was beginning to become exceedingly painful to him. He realised that if it continued and increased in definiteness it would make his home life almost insupportable. And it was his fault that it had come about. He knew that. Not for a moment did he blame Gay for the marked change that he had noticed in her manner to him. She was only replying to something in him. Acting on impulse, as he often did in ordinary life, and without weighing up chances, he said:

"Gay!"

"Yes?"

"You aren't getting a little bit jealous of my work, are you?"

It seemed to him that in the travelling car she managed to move a little further away from him. After a moment she said:

"How can you ask me that, Malcolm—after ten years?"

He thought she said the last three words as a child might have said them, a child speaking in the dark encompassed by a vague sense of fear.

"Ten years!" he said. "It's a long time!"

And with the marvellous rapidity of which the mind is capable in critical moments he visualised mentally the ten years of his life with Gay, ten bright shining years that she, he knew, was recalling.

"Long enough for you to know that I have never been jealous of your work. A woman who can be that—jealous of a man's work—has no right to marry a man worth marrying."

"But was I worth marrying?" he said, with a sort of bitterness.

"I thought so," she said, simply.

And her simplicity cut into him like a blade making a wound. There was in Gay something so true, so fundamentally sincere, that she was strangely disarming at moments. There was a nudity in her sincerity that seemed irresistibly to call for a similar nudity from him. He had often felt that. He felt it now.

"Do you think so now?" he asked, treading, in despite of himself, on dangerous ground.

"I don't change my views easily," she answered. "Once I have arrived at a definite opinion about someone it would take a great deal to make me alter it."

There was something at that moment dry, almost academic, in her voice and her choice of words. He realised that she was trying to escape from the personal question, to get on to general ground. Should he let her escape, or should he oblige her to give him a definite reply to his piercing question? He hesitated. If he forced her to reply he believed that she would certainly tell him the exact truth of her mind. Gay was like that, a natural truth teller. He could not conceive of her telling him a deliberate lie. But would it be wise to press just now for the truth? While he was hesitating, divided between a painful curiosity and a feeling that bordered on dread, the car stopped.

"What's the—surely we aren't there!" he said, startled.

"Yes, it's Portland Place! And there's Sir Simon's car waiting."

As the chauffeur opened the car door Keane whispered:

"I'll try not to be very late."

"Oh, you mustn't let anything interfere with your work. It's too important. I'll just say good night to Sir Simon."

She passed quickly into the house.

Sir Simon had just come and was laying down his coat and hat in the hall.

"We're devils, aren't we, your husband and I?" he said, taking Gay's hands. "My wife says she'll sue for divorce and make the Law co-respondent. Can you forgive me for turning up at this hour?"

"I admire hard workers. Will you have anything?"

"No, thank you. I've just dined, and wisely, not too well. My head is as clear as it ever can be. Well, Keane, we must get to it, I don't want to be out too late. Your wife's a forgiving woman."

As he took Gay's hand again in good-bye he couldn't help look-ing keenly at her, and he detected a momentary expression of acute suffering which she tried immediately to cover up with a smile.

"It's this difficult case that bothers us," he said.

"I know; the Paradine case."

"But it will soon be over."

"In March, I suppose?"

"Yes, in March."

"I hope you win it," Gay said, speaking, he thought, as if she forced herself to say it.

Her face became stern as she spoke, as the face of one who is making a fierce physical effort becomes stern.

"May your deliberations be fruitful!"

She turned to her husband who was standing behind her.

"Good night, Malcolm!" she said, in a much lighter tone.

And she turned to leave them. But just as she was at the foot of the staircase the butler came forward with a solemn face.

"I'm sorry to tell you, my lady," he said, "that Sausage has been at it again."

"What! another cushion?"

"Yes, my lady."

"Which one?"

"We missed him this evening, my lady, and made a search. We found him at last in the big drawing-room. The door must have been left open, and there he was lying on the floor, a mass of down, with one of those gold-coloured cushions all torn in pieces beside him."

"Where is he now?"

"In his basket, my lady, looking very ashamed. He daren't come down to you."

"Give me the whip, Baker."

"Yes, my lady."

"Don't think I'm a brute, Sir Simon. I shall only rub his nose in the down and thrash the floor. And I hate doing even that. But this terrible habit of Sausage must be stopped. It's a throwback to his ancestors, I suppose. Dachshunds are really sporting dogs, I believe. But there must be a permanent close time for my cushions."

"The whip, my lady."

"Thank you."

Gay took it and went upstairs.

"She doesn't like doing it," said Sir Simon.

"No. Gay has a tender heart."

"Cherish it," said Sir Simon, then added quickly: "So many women are cruel. We must honour those who are not, eh? Well, now to work. We must forget even the sins of Sausage. Where do we go? Upstairs, I suppose."

"No. I thought we'd have our talk down here."

He opened the door of the room in which he sat so often with Gay.

"We shall be well away—from everyone."

As he spoke he glanced towards the staircase. Sir Simon noticed it and knew he was thinking of his wife. The library, where Keane usually worked, was not far from her bedroom.

"No one will disturb us here. We shall be right away from——"

He stopped short.

"I'm repeating myself. A bad habit."

He shut the door.

"Whisky? Perrier? A cigar?"

"Nothing, thanks. I've been thinking over our talk of this afternoon and one or two points occur to me. But I wish you'd tell me something. What is your real opinion of Mrs. Paradine? Absolute truth if you can give it to me. Is she, or is she not, infernally clever?"

"Infernally!"

"Oh, I stick to the word," said Sir Simon obstinately. "Mind you I confine the adjective to her brain. Cleverness carried be-

yond a certain point has an infernal character, seems to smack
of something caught up out of the beyond where perhaps there is
black magic. Who knows? For what do we know?"

"I see nothing infernal in Mrs. Paradine's intelligence. Why this
question—just now?"

"Our talk this afternoon suggested it to me. One or two things
you reported of your interview with Mrs. Paradine this morning
made me wonder whether she isn't, perhaps, cleverer than you and
I are even running in double harness. And that would mean something."

"Decidedly."

Keane leant forward in his chair, his hands on the arms of it,
in an attitude of waiting.

"Now for them! The first thing that struck me specially was
her remark to you about wisdom. Would it be *wise* of her to show
hostility to the man who was known to be devoted to her husband?"

"Ah!"

"So that struck you specially, too."

"But give me your reason for——"

"It suggested to me that she had perhaps carefully thought out
a scheme of conduct that it would be admirable for her to adopt
if she were accused of her husband's murder, and that part of this
scheme was this attitude of hers about William Marsh. It suggested to me that she wasn't so much looking to us to tell her the
wisest line to take in her defence, but had, perhaps long ago,
made up her mind what line *she* intended to take and was convinced that she had selected the best one. This would mean that
she was ready to back her brain against anyone else's, ours included."

"If it were so wouldn't she by now have told us the line she
intended to take?"

"She might be holding back, humouring us, playing with us
so as not to put us off. She might come out with it later. I've
known women keep things back from their solicitor and counsel
till the very eve of their trial, until the trial itself."

"I'll make a note of that," said Keane, in a colourless voice.
"Well, that's number one. Number two?"

"Her request to know why you are trying to get her to speak

against Marsh showed a wary spirit, exercised in connection with you her defender not her attacker. 'That,' I thought, 'is a woman who's intensely on the alert and probably suspicious of everyone.' Cleverness is far more apt to be alert than dullness. Intense cleverness in anyone usually connotes intense alertness. Don't you think so?"

"I—yes, it usually does."

"Now we come to the great impression you say was made upon her when you outlined to her a defence that might possibly induce the Jury to take the view that the murder of Colonel Paradine was a sort of assisted suicide."

"Did that show infernal cleverness?" asked Keane, with a strong hint of sarcasm.

"Suppose she was acting?"

"Acting!" said Keane sharply. "She was not acting. I feel sure of that. I am positive that the idea that the murder of her husband might have been accomplished at his own request had never occurred to her."

"It seems to me very strange that—but wait a moment! You and I, I believe, have formed very different opinions of Mrs. Paradine. You of course have realised her intelligence, self-control and courage."

"Certainly I have."

"But are you giving her credit for the brain that I'm sure she possesses?"

"I believe so."

"Then if your theory of the murder is correct—" Sir Simon watched Keane narrowly as he said this—"which I'll assume for the moment, could such an intelligent woman, having lived for a long while with these two men, and knowing, mind you, that *she* had nothing to do with her husband's death, have missed entirely the possibility that if Marsh were the murderer he had acted in collusion with Colonel Paradine? Is that likely?"

"They might easily have deceived her. They would naturally take every precaution. Is it likely that Marsh, if he did what I suggest, would be careless in such a matter? You think I do less than justice to Mrs. Paradine's intelligence. But what if you do less than justice to Marsh's?"

"Then Mrs. Paradine had no suspicion? That's your view?"

"I'm positive that she had never thought of what I suggested until the moment when I suggested it."

"And she seemed greatly impressed by it?"

"Immensely! It was evident to me that it fell upon her darkness like a ray of light. I believe that she had really felt till then that it was impossible Marsh could be the murderer, but that she then realised that he might be."

"Your faith in her sincerity is certainly immense," said Sir Simon, but quite without sarcasm.

Keane, who all this time had been leaning forward in his chair holding the arms of it, now got up like a man feeling the imperative need of a change of position. Standing, his hands thrust into the pockets of his trousers, his head raised and with a suddenly pugnacious look on his face, he said:

"Flaquer, let's come quite into the open. I said to you this afternoon in Hyde Park Gardens that we must strip to the buff for this life and death contest. And it's no manner of use, I see now, for you and me to try to work together amid clouds of misunderstanding. I think there's a terrible division of opinion between us in this Paradine case, although we're both for the defence and you briefed me. You've never flatly said so, but I can't help feeling nevertheless that though you are her solicitor, and quite rightly doing everything you can for her, you believe Mrs. Paradine committed this murder. Isn't it so?"

Sir Simon was evidently in no hurry to reply. He was silent for nearly a minute, but he eventually looked up and said:

"I don't feel sure about it but I'm afraid she did."

"And yet you haven't found out her motive!" said Keane, defiantly. "You are ready to believe such a thing without discovering a motive for it. Is that reasonable?"

"If you mean that I haven't discovered a motive of passion, that I can't find a lover, you're right. But there are other motives for murder. A woman's life may be made intolerable to her by the man she lives with though she may not love another man. A woman may make a sacrifice and find it's too great for her. A woman may imagine a man to be entirely different from what he really is and find out she's made a fearful mistake. There are two Colonel Paradines. That's evident. One was a hero. The other was a bully, a tyrant, unfaithful, cruel—not physically, the other way

—with women, heartless and entirely untender, except perhaps in his moments of lust. I know that man through and through. He's typical of many men, the type that's splendid with men and a curse to women. Good heavens, Keane, you know the type! Great masculine virtues, but another side that's indefensible, not to say abominable."

"Given all that—and I give it you freely—why shouldn't she have left him? Why murder a man when you can walk out of his house into freedom?"

"And what about poverty? If Mrs. Paradine is acquitted of this crime, she leaves the Court a rich woman."

An expression of contempt distorted Keane's face for an instant.

"I beg your pardon!" he said.

"Why?"

"I'm aware that I—forgive me! You told me once that you *liked* Mrs. Paradine."

"I do."

"How can you when you think of her as you do, when you are able to attribute to her such an atrociously sordid motive for a horrible crime? Like! Such a word to use in connection with such a woman—if she were such!"

"I'm a man. She's a woman of a natural charm that I can't get away from."

"You might love such a woman. That I could understand."

("Yes—undoubtedly!" thought Sir Simon.)

"But liking's a different matter."

"Love her I couldn't," said Sir Simon, with unusual simplicity. "I'm a family man and I happen to love my wife, and always have since I met her in Venice a good while ago. But there's something about that woman, Mrs. Paradine, which gets you. I don't know that I can define it. There's an ease, an apparent naturalness, straightforwardness, lack of feminine tricks and wiles that— damn it, I do like her! I can't help it. But, as a man who knows the world, and facing facts, I have to realise that in the depths she may be at times a very dangerous woman. I like her but I can't read her. Among all the women I've had to do with outside of, and in, my profession, she's one of the queerest. That blank look of hers—you know it!"

"Yes," said Keane, but reluctantly.

"That hides a lot, Keane. No woman who isn't absolutely wanting in intelligence looks as blank as Mrs. Paradine sometimes looks
without a reason. She puts up the shutters when she doesn't want
people to see what's going on in the room. D'you know what
I wish?"

"What?"

"I wish that my Judy, or your wife, could spend a couple of
days with Mrs. Paradine and give us her impressions afterwards."

"Oh, I don't need to go to women for my impressions of other
women!" exclaimed Keane, with a hint of violence. "Women, the
best of them, are horribly prejudiced when dealing with their own
sex. All this talk of feminism and the solidarity of woman doesn't
alter the basic fact that women are far more cruel to each other
than we men are to other men. By God! I should like to drive the
women out of every Jury that sits to try the case of a woman."

"There will be women on the Jury that tries Mrs. Paradine, and
Horfield will be the Judge."

"I shall save her in spite of them all. I shall save her."

He walked down the room and came back. His head was now
bent and he stared at the carpet.

"I shall save her!" he muttered again.

He stopped in front of Sir Simon.

"You believe in me as a good advocate, don't you?" he said.

"In a certain type of case you're the best advocate I know."

"And this Paradine case belongs to that type, doesn't it?"

"It does."

"Now I want you, Flaquer, to be perfectly frank with me.
Do you, with your vast knowledge of criminal cases at your back,
expect to get Mrs. Paradine off?"

"I think it's just possible. I shouldn't care to say more than
that."

"That being so, don't you think this is a case in which audacity
and ruthless determination are called for? What's the good of
timorous caution in such a case? What's the good of trying to
make bricks without putting in any straw? Ever since you briefed
me and I went to Holloway and met Mrs. Paradine, I've been
living with this case day and night. It's obsessed me. I've never

been able to get away from it. From the first I recognised what a great difficulty the Defence was in owing to the fact that, apart from Mrs. Paradine, there appeared to be no one on whom suspicion could be fastened with any hope of creating a belief in the minds of the Jury that it was well-founded. It seemed to me that the defence was, as it were, struggling in the void. True that Mrs. Paradine's motive for the murder was not particularly strong. That was a point in our favour. If there had been a lover—as there was, for instance, in the Maybrick case—we shouldn't have had a chance. But there was apparently no lover. There's no evidence of a lover, is there?"

He bent forward, gazing into Sir Simon's face with intent eyes. "None that I know of."

"None! None! Very well! A point in our favour—but only negative. Realising how little we had in hand for the defence, I've been searching ever since I came into the case for something that would help us. And naturally my mind's been dwelling on this William Marsh. We've already talked of that. I needn't recapitulate. I saw light at last, as I told you. Owing to circumstances, Marsh's proved devotion to Colonel Paradine and so on, it was obviously very difficult to connect Marsh with the crime in such a way as would carry any weight with a Jury. My theory of a murder suggested, even demanded, by the victim, gets over that. I saw my chance when I thought of it. I saw *her* chance. You must realise the possibilities such a defence contains. Yet I feel you're hanging back. I wouldn't see you this morning because I had to see her first and find out what her reaction would be to it."

"And what was it exactly?" Sir Simon interposed. "You said she was greatly impressed and so forth. But what, in your opinion, was it *exactly*? It's important that I should know."

"Favourable! Favourable!"

"Favourable?"

"In the sense that she didn't turn it down. She saw its possibilities."

"Possibilities! Did she give you the impression that she thought such a murder was a conceivable fact?"

Sir Simon was watching Keane very narrowly at this point in their conversation, and he received a great surprise. For he saw the usually exceptionally expressive face of his companion suddenly become blank, and its strange blankness recalled to him memories of the face of Mrs. Paradine.

"Yes!" said Keane.

And his voice, to Sir Simon, sounded blank.

There was a moment of silence, and it was an awkward silence. Both men felt it to be so. There was a stiffness in it which was painfully apparent to them both. As Sir Simon did not break it, Keane at last shook his broad shoulders—a characteristic habit of his when in Court—and exclaimed:

"My dear Flaquer, I feel your reluctance, I divine your doubts, but I mean to carry you with me. Now look here!"

He sat down again in his chair by Sir Simon and laid a hand on his arm. His manner had completely changed and the blank look had vanished from his face. He looked eager, persuasive, friendly, but there was determination about his lips.

"I know your record. The whole Bar knows your record. You're a man of audacity. You don't boggle at trifles. In your time you've put up extraordinary fights for your clients. If you hadn't, you wouldn't be where you are. We, at the Bar, haven't forgotten the famous Morse libel case and your defence of Sir William Morse in that. We haven't forgotten the great gambling case in which you got off Captain Sachell. Flaquer, you're the most audacious solicitor in London, and everyone knows it. So why should you throw cold water over me when I come to you with a proposition that I confess is a startling one? Has it come to this, that you won't subscribe to a defence unless you're absolutely convinced that you believe in it? Come, come, Flaquer! You and I are old hands in the Law and we know that in these great legal fights lawyers have sometimes to compromise with their consciences. It's a battle of wits. We have to sharpen our weapons to a fine edge. Don't hold back because you're pursued by doubts. Neither of us *knows* who murdered Colonel Paradine. We have to deal with the 'may be.' And I'm convinced that my 'may be' gives us our greatest, perhaps our only chance of winning this case. Say you agree! Leave the thing in my hands. And I swear to you that Mrs. Paradine shall go out of the Old Bailey a free woman."

Sir Simon received this outburst—for it was an outburst—in silence. He sat still in his armchair, his lips pressed together, his thin legs crossed, his fine hands folded one on the other, his eyes steady and, perhaps, hostile in their cold fixed gaze. Keane's allusions to the Morse libel case and the case of Captain Sachell had evidently gone home to him. Keane realised that with a satisfaction that was pitiless. Sir Simon's secret opposition, which of course he was aware of, had roused all Keane's fighting spirit. And moreover, he was in love with his theory for the defence as an actor may be in love with a part.

"Leave it to me and I pledge you my word we shall win," he said, to break the silence.

And, without knowing that he did it, he pressed his muscular fingers hard on Sir Simon's arm. Releasing his arm quickly, Sir Simon said:

"I don't think I lack audacity, but I like to know where I'm going. I wish you'd tell me something, Keane, as frankness"—a slightly embittered smile flickered over his lips—"is the order of the night. You asked me a leading question just now about Mrs. Paradine. Let me ask you one about William Marsh. You want to put up this defence. And I don't say it may not be the best we can find, given the circumstances. But do you believe that Marsh was the murderer of Colonel Paradine?"

"I think it's quite possible," said Keane immediately, like a man in a hurry. "Given the Colonel's acute misery and almost crazy irritation under his affliction, of which there will be ample evidence at the trial, I think it's quite conceivable. And as you talked just now about Mrs. Paradine being queer, let me tell you that Marsh is no ordinary individual either."

"That's true!" said Sir Simon, musingly. "And you actually got her to say she would go against Marsh? Did you—did you frighten her? Did you succeed in doing that?"

"I believe I made her realise thoroughly the very great danger of her situation. And I'm not sure, strange as it seems, that she had fully realised it before. Now she certainly does."

"Be quiet for a moment, please. I must give all my mind to this," said Sir Simon.

"Right! I'll give you as long as you like. Meanwhile, I'll just go upstairs and bid Sausage good night."

"Sausage!" said Sir Simon.

His voice was surprised and he looked at Keane with surprise.

What an odd mind that could switch off from such a topic as had engrossed them to a dog! Long afterwards, when destiny had been accomplished, he remembered that moment of his astonishment, and mentally endowed it with a significance which that night escaped him.

"Yes. He's in disgrace, poor little chap. I must just give him a paw."

And Keane went out of the room.

Left alone, Sir Simon sat in profound thought without moving. Mentally, he was reviewing the entire Paradine case as it had come under the microscope of his penetrating brain. And he was doing something else, too. He was considering the drama that, as it seemed, was connecting itself with that case, a drama arising out of another drama and perhaps containing within it—he did not know —seeds of catastrophe. Although he had such an exceptionally close and intimate knowledge of human nature in its criminal aspects, had been the repository of so many ugly, sometimes hideous, secrets, he had not become a hardened cynic, although he had become an exceedingly sharp and wary man of the world. Like many Jews, he had a sentimental side, though as a rule he carefully concealed it. A devoted family man, his affections were very strong and tenacious, and, because of that, he greatly respected strong affections in others. Unfaithfulness was foreign to his nature, and though he was perpetually dealing with the painful results of unfaithfulness, and acting professionally for wholly unfaithful people, he had never got thoroughly hardened to what he regarded as one of the cardinal defects in human nature. Entirely happy in his own home life, and considering family life, in its better aspects, the foundation stone of human happiness, he respected and delighted in a similar happiness to his own in others. For a long while he had had a great regard for the Keanes, and it was based really on the great regard they had for each other. They were, he thought, unfortunate in having no children to cement their love, but without this cement they were an ideally happy couple. Now the cloud had come and he was responsible for it. This, though he knew himself to be entirely innocent, distressed him. And the fact of the cloud had killed all his former ease in the company of Keane. Sometimes, indeed, he could not help feeling hostile to Keane, for he was a great admirer of Gay and was even devoted to her. And he hated to see even Gay drawn into the meshes of that drag-net, the Paradine case.

And yet—he had confessed it—he liked Mrs. Paradine, and could not see her quite as a *femme fatale*.

Keane's allusions to those two cases, the Morse and the Sachell cases, had touched him shrewdly, and they had been meant to touch him. He had fully realised the pitiless feeling which had prompted Keane to that thrust. A man may know in the secret place where he often abides that certain of his less scrupulous actions have not been missed by his fellow men, but he does not care to be informed of the fact. And Sir Simon, who had not a little professional pride, resented Keane's remark about lawyers sometimes compromising with their consciences. It had seemed to draw him into a connection with Keane that in his present frame of mind, and having Gay in his thoughts, was very unpleasant to him. He understood why Keane had been prompted to this outburst, but he couldn't forgive it nevertheless.

"The Paradine case is becoming the very devil!" he thought. And, a rare thing with him who loved difficult cases, he began to wish he had never undertaken it.

And now this William Marsh business!

He dismissed thoughts of self, thoughts of the ethereal Gay, and concentrated on the case. He had a great belief in Keane's powers as an advocate, but he knew very well that if those powers were to have their fullest scope, Keane must be allowed to take his own way, must even be given every encouragement in taking it. Like all strongly emotional men, Keane had his ups and downs. When he was up he was brilliant. But in moments of depression he seemed almost to wither. Opposition from his opponents in Court often spurred him to his best efforts, but opposition behind the scenes from anyone who was working with him was likely to have the contrary effect. This was a touch and go case. Did Keane see the best way to deal with it? Had he, perhaps, vision? Was his idea for the defence a veritable inspiration? Or was Sir Simon's obstinate reluctance to agree to it founded on an obscure instinct which he ought to trust, although in truth he did not fully understand it? And if he refused to agree to Keane's project—what then?

Sir Simon's stark immobility was broken by a violent movement.

He uncrossed his legs, the upper part of his body shot forward and he gripped the arms of his chair. At the same moment a slight flush tinged his cheeks and his lips parted.

It had occurred to him that if he manifested opposition to the defence Keane was now evidently determined to put up, and stuck to it, Keane might retire from the case.

"Have I found a way out?"

Sir Simon got up. Suddenly he felt restless, unable to be still. A cigar box lay on a table near to him. He went to it, opened it, took out a Havana, clipped it, lit it, and began to smoke. While smoking he moved slowly about the big room, walking softly and lightly.

Two women were in his mind. He visualised them both: Gay with her wistful, yet formerly joyous, charm now tempered to a sadness which she tried to conceal by an abruptness, occasionally by a brusqueness, not natural to her; Mrs. Paradine with her fascinating pallor, her large silver grey eyes and primrose pale hair, her tall very slim figure, long narrow white hands and serious simplicity, or simulation of simplicity. They stood before him as enemies and seemed to say to him:

"For which of us do you stand? On whose side are you? Will you fight for me—or for me?"

Gay against Mrs. Paradine—Mrs. Paradine against Gay! And the test! Sir Simon longed to put Keane to that test. Gay was his friend. He was fond of her. He admired, perhaps even loved, her in an almost fatherly way. But Mrs. Paradine was his client. He had undertaken her cause. She was paying him to fight for her life. He had a tremendous duty towards her.

He had his conversation with his daughter Judith in his mind. Judith and he had gone pretty far with each other. They had dared to go to the brink of a tragedy. But had they, perhaps, exaggerated the trend of events, or even altogether misread it? Possibly they had. A cloud—yes! It had come over a happy landscape. But mightn't it disperse as quickly as it had formed?

Very seldom indeed did Sir Simon fall into that common habit of many men, the habit of trying to trick his own brain. But that night for a moment he did try to trick it. For a moment he tried to believe that Judith and he had made a mistake. Really they had not much to go on, not very much: slight changes of manner;

an appearance of happiness marred; unwonted reserves; an apparently waning intimacy between two people hitherto closely united; a new expression in well-known eyes.

"Are we wrong? Perhaps we are. In that case——"

In that case there was no call to take any special action surely. But the two women remained. And in Sir Simon, despite his sophistries, persisted the desire to put Keane to the test and, perhaps, to strike a blow for Gay at the same time.

If—Keane might retire from the case. He was a man of strong temper. Opposition enforced it. A quarrel between him and Sir Simon, one pitting an obstinate will against the other, might lead to an explosion and Keane's retirement. And then possibly things would come right again between Gay and her husband. For once out of the case Keane would be cut off entirely from Mrs. Paradine. Their connection would automatically come to an end. Sir Simon was minded to strike a blow on behalf of Gay. The temptation was great.

But possibly a woman's life was at stake. And then he saw a woman's happiness, Gay's, set in the balance against a woman's life, Mrs. Paradine's. And he did not know what to do.

The door opened. He turned round.

"Oh, Keane!"

He held up his partially smoked cigar.

"I've stolen one of your Havanas."

"My dear Flaquer!"

"How's Sausage?"

"Very much ashamed of himself, very penitent. But I think I've made things better. I left him composing himself to sleep. His final sigh followed me down the stairs."

Keane took a cigar and poured himself out some more Perrier water.

"Well?" he said. "Have you reached any conclusion?"

He spoke in a calm impersonal voice. His manner, Sir Simon thought, was the manner of a man holding himself well in hand. Whilst out of the room he had perhaps reconsidered and repented of his recent outburst.

"Suppose I can't go with you, Keane? Suppose I can't see my way to work with you on the lines you propose? What then?"

Keane's face changed, set itself in a stern expression.

"Do you mean that you reject my suggestion for the defence?"

"You spoke just now of compromising with conscience. Your implication seemed to be that I should not have much difficulty in doing that."

"My dear Flaquer, I assure you I only meant——"

"One minute, Keane! But supposing that in this Paradine case I didn't see my way to compromise? Supposing that your suggestion for the defence seemed to me immoral?"

"How immoral?" Keane interjected defiantly.

"Wouldn't it be immoral to try to fix the guilt of a crime on a man one believed to be innocent?"

"I don't propose to do that. I suspect William Marsh. I strongly suspect him."

"*You* do! Very well. But suppose that I don't? Can you expect me to stand by and be responsible, with you, for a veiled attack, if it be veiled, on an innocent man? Do you expect me to make such a compromise with my conscience as that? Just now, though, to tell you the truth, you gave me the impression—I may be wrong—that, in putting up this defence you've thought of, you and I would be going hand in hand into—what shall I call it?— into a sort of conspiracy."

"Conspiracy!"

"That seemed to me the suggestion underlying your words. Old hands in the Law—compromising with conscience—not holding back because you're pursued by doubts. Now wait a minute! Let us suppose something."

"Go on!"

"Let us suppose that I agree to this defence, go hand in hand with you. The trial comes on. Your prediction comes true. Mrs. Paradine is exonerated and set free."

"What more can we want than that?" exclaimed Keane with vehemence.

"One moment! Suppose further that owing to your, our efforts, William Marsh is arrested and charged with the murder, is brought to trial, condemned and hanged? And suppose all the time *I* didn't believe him guilty? D'you think I should be able to sleep after such a compromising with my conscience?"

After a pause Keane said:

"I think you're splitting hairs, Sir Simon."

"How so?"

"If such a trial took place it would be a fair trial. Don't you believe in British justice, then—after all you've said to me about it?"

Sir Simon didn't miss this veiled allusion to Horfield, which was really in the nature of a taunt.

"Even British Justice may make a mistake. Now and then, very seldom, I allow, an innocent man is condemned. You haven't forgotten the Beck case, I suppose?"

"Of course not. But aren't you assuming a great deal? Really, Flaquer, I hardly understand your opposition to my suggestion. One would suppose you had some under reason that you haven't disclosed to me."

"A very simple reason would be that I don't believe in the guilt of William Marsh. That would be reason enough."

"Then is that your only reason?"

As Sir Simon didn't answer this question Keane said:

"If it is I think you could leave the matter in my hands. I'm sure you've done as much before in the course of your long and often sensational practice. What we have to do, our job in fact, is to win for our clients. Nothing else really should concern us. I confess that I don't understand your—forgive me—half-heartedness to-night in this matter."

In reply to this thrust Sir Simon merely said, in his calmest manner:

"If I can't agree to go on with this case in the way you are pressing on me, what then, Keane?"

"Is that an ultimatum?" Keane said.

"I want your answer to that."

"Really, Flaquer," said Keane, in the rather overbearing way which had several times put him wrong with the Judges. "If I'm to make a success of a case I must be trusted. I must conduct it in my own way."

"But if I feel I can't stand for this defence?"

"D'you mean that you'd retire, that you'd decline to act any further for Mrs. Paradine?" said Keane, as if startled.

"Certainly not!" said Sir Simon sharply, secretly taken aback by this, probably quite innocent, turning of the tables upon him. "Do you suppose I would prejudice a woman's chance of life by such an action? Why she would be damned before ever the trial began! What could induce you to suppose——"

"Well then what do you mean?"

"Mean? Simply this, if I can't agree to your proposition, if I turn it down so far as I'm concerned, what then?"

Keane looked hard at Sir Simon for perhaps a full minute. Then he said in a hard resonant voice:

"Whatever course you take, Flaquer, I shall not retire from this case. I've put my hand to it. I shall carry it through. And, one way or the other, I shall carry it through to success."

Sir Simon realised that Keane must have divined his half-formed intention, though probably not its reason. Anyhow he now knew that there was nothing he could do to help Gay.

"Give me to-night to sleep on this matter," he said, with unusual brusquerie. "To-morrow I'll give you an answer, as to whether I can fall in with your views or not."

"Certainly. Mind this! I look upon it as our only chance. Think of the woman."

"I am thinking of—the woman," said Sir Simon, frowning. "And now I'll be off."

At the front door he bade Keane good-bye with unusual coldness.

"He's put out because I tackled him fairly and squarely," thought Keane, as he shut the door.

Without being aware of it he opened out his chest and thrust forward his chin.

"By God, I'll carry this through in spite of them all!"

XX

AT TEN o'clock on the following morning a messenger boy knocked on the front door of Malcolm Keane's house and delivered a letter marked *immediate*. No answer was asked for and the boy, after leaving it, walked away whistling.

"A letter for you, Sir Malcolm, by messenger," said Baker, going into Keane's library. "It's urgent, sir."

"Thank you, Baker."

Keane took the letter and recognised Sir Simon's neat and very small handwriting. Directly Baker was out of the room Keane opened the letter.

"Now then for it!" he murmured. "But I don't care what he writes. Whether he agrees or doesn't agree *I* don't retire from this case."

Since the previous night he had had the conviction that Sir Simon had it in mind to get him out of the case, or at any rate had thought of that as a possibility which would not be altogether disastrous. This conviction over which Keane had brooded in the dark hours had roused all his fighting spirit. But it had roused something else, a suspicion which he had honestly striven to drive out of his mind but which nevertheless remained there embedded. It was an ugly suspicion and he knew it for ugly. He felt as if a part of him rejected it and as if another part of him wouldn't, perhaps couldn't, let it go. His suspicion was that perhaps Gay had something to do with Sir Simon's strange wish to oust him from the Paradine case at the eleventh hour. Had they, without his knowledge, spoken together about the case? Or had Gay spoken of it to Judith Flaquer and had Judith Flaquer passed on what she had said to Sir Simon?

Gay and Judith were intimate friends. Judith, Keane knew, was greatly attached to Gay. He was sure that if a difficulty ever arose between himself and Gay Judith would side with Gay. Had those two talked over certain aspects of the Paradine case together? Had Gay, perhaps, hinted, or said, that his concentration upon it was—abnormal? And had Judith gone to her father and told him what Gay had said?

The mind works fast and intensely at night. Suspicions grow in the night and often take on monstrous shapes. Keane actually came to feel in the night that there was, perhaps, a secret conspiracy against him in which Gay, Judith Flaquer and Sir Simon were involved. A sense of guilt in himself produced this suspicion of guilt in others. (For such a conspiracy, in his present state of mind, he counted as guilt.) And under the weight of this suspicion his heart grew hard. It seemed incredible that he should feel hard and hostile towards Gay. Yet it was so.

"These women shall not interfere with me. I'll not have women trying to interfere with me in my profession."

A sensation of being ill-used had encompassed him. With it had come a great sense of loneliness. The responsibility was laid upon him of saving a beautiful woman, still young, from the hangman, and instead of eager help and sympathy from those around him he was met with coldness, with suspicion, even perhaps with direct hostility and the intention to prevent him from making his effort to save a human life. And what had he done to bring about this conspiracy against him? Nothing so far except his duty. He had given himself to the case whole-heartedly. That was all—so far.

Gay, Judith Flaquer, Sir Simon, Lord Horfield, Mrs. George Blason with her laughing malice—they were all against him since he had been briefed for the Paradine case. And now even the man who had briefed him, Sir Simon, wanted to hunt him out of it.

But they had all mistaken their man and he would prove it to them.

His eyes were hard as he opened the letter that would no doubt tell him Sir Simon's decision.

Hyde Park Gardens,
January 3rd, 19——

Dear Keane,

I have spent a good part of the night thinking over our conversations in my house and yours. As you know I take all my cases seriously and am seldom lighthearted about them. You and I follow professions which are terribly responsible and probably few realise how deeply we feel our responsibility. And I don't mind telling you the case you and I are in now has given me as much anxiety as anything I have undertaken in the course of a pretty long career. Nearly all night I have been up pondering over your suggestions of yesterday, trying to look at the case from every angle, and to confront every possible danger that lurks for us in it.

As you certainly noticed yesterday I felt a great reluctance to fall in with your views as to the new line you wish to take. On careful consideration—and trying to be strictly honest with myself—I believe this reluctance had its root in my fear lest any attempt to exonerate Mrs. Paradine at the expense of Wil-

liam Marsh might recoil on the defence, owing to the undoubted
fact of Marsh's great devotion to the dead man which, it seems
to me, given the evidence which we expect, must carry great
weight with a Jury. Had you proposed a direct attack on Marsh
with no extenuating circumstances I should, for the reason I
have given, have felt obliged to oppose it. But the ingenuity of
the suggestion you put forward—I'm alluding of course to the
assisted suicide idea—has given me pause. And something else
has given me pause, too: your great success in the past as counsel
for the defence in many difficult cases. If it were not for *that*
I doubt whether I could agree to risk the defence on which you
are so obstinately set. I see its danger plainly. Long experience
has, I believe, given me the faculty of being able to enter with
a sure step into the collective mind of the average British Jury.
Your defence, if persisted in, will certainly at first rouse hostility in that collective mind. But you have great powers and
may quite possibly overcome this hostility. Your influence over
Juries is of course remarkable.

Having all this in mind I have at last come to the conclusion that perhaps I ought not to oppose you. But I think it
my duty to point out to you that the bottom will surely fall
out of your defence unless Mrs. Paradine gives her evidence in
such a way as to back it up. Can you absolutely rely on this?
If her evidence would not tend to back up your theory then I
am inclined to think we should do better to keep her out of the
box altogether. On the other hand if possible I should of course
wish to put her in the box as her personality might weigh with
the Jury, and I feel sure that whatever evidence she did give
would be well given, and that she would be very difficult to
shake in cross-examination.

Forgive me for saying that I'm still inclined to wonder
whether you have altogether grasped the complexity of our
client. She is, I am certain, no ordinary woman. We had better
see her together as soon as possible, or do you prefer first to see
her alone and make *sure* that she will give the sort of evidence
you will want? When you have thought the matter over let
me know.

Yrs very sincerely,
SIMON FLAQUER.

As Keane folded up this letter, he smiled.

"He's had his try to get me to retire from the case, and I've forced him to give it up."

He had an ugly sensation of triumph.

He answered Sir Simon's letter later that day and wrote that he would see Mrs. Paradine again and make certain that she would not let the Defence down in her evidence. It was, in his view, essential that she should go into the box. He was positive that no one could fight for her better than she could fight for herself. When he had seen her he and Sir Simon could have a quiet interview with her.

In the afternoon he again visited Holloway Prison. He had to prepare Mrs. Paradine for the forthcoming interview when he would visit her in company with Sir Simon.

When he saw her he realised at once that since their last interview he had come to a different feeling towards her. He now looked upon her as an adherent who would, who must, stand steadfastly with him against a combination. In this combination he counted Sir Simon, Judith Flaquer and his wife. Although Sir Simon had given in and would no doubt stick to his promise, Keane was still convinced that Sir Simon had quite seriously thought of trying to force him out of the case. He had no doubt of it at all, and was positive that Judith Flaquer counted for something in that amazing attempt. (Already, he had come to think of what had happened on the previous night as a definite attempt.) Judith Flaquer must have been prompted by Gay, or if not actually prompted, have been acting with Gay in her mind. He felt a *bloc*, three people in it, one of them his wife. And to this *bloc* were opposed two people, himself and Mrs. Paradine. Closely they were drawn together in his mind by this conviction, by this visualisation of two against three. For the first time in his life he saw Gay not as lover, not as wife, but as opponent, as one trying to interfere with his life to its detriment, and to the detriment of another. The subtle division between them had developed into something more definite. Their wills were quite certainly in conflict. As he grasped Mrs. Paradine's hand he had a longing to tell her something of his feeling, to explain to her something of what had occurred. He wanted to say to her:

"You might have lost me as your Defender. How would it have been then?"

He had now the absolute conviction that he was the only man living who could regain her freedom for her. And Sir Simon had been minded to prevent that effort. There could only be one reason for his conduct of the night before, and Keane knew what it was. Gay was the reason. Gay hated his connection with the Paradine case. She had never said so. She had never even hinted at it. But he now felt that he had known she had hated it almost ever since he had accepted his brief from Sir Simon. He remembered the occasion when he had alluded to her resemblance to Mrs. Paradine. Ever since then certainly she had hated it, and possibly before that moment. And Sir Simon somehow, probably through Judith Flaquer who was terribly acute, understanding and observant, had got to know of that hatred, and had acted as he had because of it.

All this was in his mind as he greeted the prisoner.

"What is it?" she said, before he had spoken. "What is the matter?"

"Why should anything be the matter?"

"But it is. I see it in your eyes."

"I've had to put up a fight since I saw you," he answered grimly. "And I've got the best of it. There are people who don't quite understand me yet. But they will. They will."

"Had it something to do with me?" she asked, but not eagerly. Eagerness was, apparently, not natural to her.

"Remotely, I think it had. For the time being, you see, my life is——" he stopped, seeking for a word that would not seem too dangerous—"bound up with yours," he ended, with a sudden feeling of recklessness. "D'you realise that I'm living for you these days, and nights too? Your case is my life."

"But what have they tried to do?" she said, ignoring his emotion and sticking steadily to the point that concerned her with a characteristic obstinacy.

"Suppose——" he hesitated, but something drove him on—"suppose they tried to get me to give up your case?"

For the first time then he saw her startled, perhaps even terrified. She caught hold of his wrist and her fingers felt hard almost as steel.

"You would not do that? You would not abandon me? But I depend entirely on *you*. Sir Simon—he is nothing. He is clever, I know, but—compared with you he is nothing. Oh, I shall not let you give me up. No!"

There was a violent autocratic sound in her voice.

"Who has tried? There must be a woman in that!"

"Why should there be?" he said, startled in his turn.

"No man would do that unless he was pushed by a woman. It is not the men who take away women's chances when they are in trouble, it is always the women. Who is she?"

"Never mind!" he said, feeling that he had gone much too far and determined never to mention Gay's name to her in such a connection. "Why bother about it? If I were going to give up your case I shouldn't be here. But now as you care, more even than I'd supposed, for my help, and believe in it and in me, we can work together as we haven't worked yet. Sir Simon Flaquer, after a lot of hesitation, has fallen in with my view about your defence. He'll see you with me——"

"To-day?"

"No, but almost immediately. I've had a letter from him this morning. He's come round to my point of view. But now tell me——" he stared hard at her with ruthless eyes—"suppose we didn't put you in the box at your trial?"

She stared back at him, and waited.

"Suppose we decided it would be wisest to keep you out of it—what would you say?"

"I should say," she said, in a heavy trailing voice, accenting her words, "that you were mad. That is what I should say."

Menace surely came into her eyes, which defied him.

"Sir Simon was right," he thought. "How much do I really know of her?"

"But you told me just now," he said, sternly, "that you are depending entirely on me. Then that was a lie?"

"Outside of me, I do. That is truth. Yes—outside of me."

"But when we narrow it down to the bare bones, it's yourself you depend on, is it?" he asked, still sternly.

"But does not life drive one to that? What is my chance if I have no faith in myself and only faith in you?"

"All very well!" he said, with an anger which he secretly despised but could not control. "But how can you expect me to do my best for you, to give out all I have of power and ingenuity and—and emotion even, when you trust yourself more than you trust me?"

Just then he had an overpowering desire to master her, to rule her, to force her under the yoke of his will.

"I can never take things from another when myself refuses them," she said simply. "I may wish to, but it is impossible. I cannot."

"You are made of obstinacy!" he exclaimed.

For a moment he was too upset to speak. Seeing it she spoke. She said:

"But why should you and Sir Simon wish to keep me out of the box?"

Back again to the point! How unerringly she clung to what was essential in their conversation, discarding the rest.

"We don't wish to if you will give the evidence we think necessary, if we are sure you will do that and not be shaken in cross-examination. But there must be no contest between us and you. Otherwise, it will be perceived by the Jury, to say nothing of the Judge, and you will be lost. Obstinacy has proved the damnation of many a man and woman. We have to know beforehand what we are to expect from you in the trial."

Suddenly he dropped his angry tone and added, almost pleadingly:

"Surely you can see that?"

"Put me in the box and I can do as much for myself as anyone can do for me."

"Perhaps you'd like to conduct your own case!" he exclaimed.

"No. I know nothing of the Law. What I know something of is not Law."

"What is it then?"

"Human nature."

Exasperation grew in him. He had an increasing urge to dominate her. And she refused to be dominated. And yet only a few minutes before she had gripped his wrist and begged him not to desert her. If he could go back to that moment!

"My knowledge of *that* perhaps equals yours," he said. "And Sir Simon isn't far behind us, I fancy, in that respect. However, if you insist on going your own way—go it! After all, it's you who must take the consequences."

He said the last words with sheer brutality. An imperative need to be cruel rose up in him.

"You're ungrateful!" he added. "You—you hurt me."

It seemed to him that he had never before been so deeply wounded.

"I am sorry," she said. "But I cannot be other than what I am. I know I am too outright. That has always been my fault. At least you know where you are with me."

"I hope so," he muttered, "I hope so."

Ashamed of the violence of his feeling and that she must know of it he made a strong effort to get over it. The effort made his voice hard when he spoke again.

"Now, we'll waste no more time. What Sir Simon and I want to know definitely is whether we can depend on you to give evidence which will help us in the defence I've already told you about. Can you do so? If the evidence you will give is purely negative then——" he threw up his hands—"then we are done. I must have something to work with. I can't bite on air. Now then——" he seemed to sink suddenly into the hard-bitten, self-possessed lawyer, unemotional, lucid and keen—"now then, are you going to back me up in the suggestion that your husband's death may have been caused by William Marsh acting, mind you, at the instance of your husband himself? Sir Simon agrees with me that to go on these lines gives us our best chance to win. It may be——" he looked away from her for an instant—"our only chance. I'm inclined to think it is. Can you give evidence which will help to impress on the minds of the Jury that the deed may have been done in that way? You've had time now to think the whole matter over. What is your answer?"

"This is the evidence I can give," she said. "I do not know whether it is exactly what you want. If not, I cannot change it. It is the truth at any rate of the situation before my husband died. Till you spoke to me of it, I had never thought that Marsh might possibly have helped my husband to his death. But now I realise that it may have been so."

"Who did you think had committed the murder—if murder it was?"

"I did not know," she said, simply.

And the blank look came into her face. Confronted by it, Keane said:

"Please go on. Tell me."

She began to speak in a level voice.

XXI

A FEW days later Keane said to his wife:

"I shall have to be out of London for a few days. I hope you won't mind being left alone. Have someone up to keep you company if you like. But I shall only be away for a very short time."

Gay showed no surprise. She only said:

"Oh, I shall be all right. Is it a new law case?"

"No. I wish to visit Cumberland. It is in connection with Mrs. Paradine's case."

"Oh—yes?"

"She and her husband lived at Hindley Hall, not very far from the sea. The house is to let since his death. The village close by is called Hindley. All the people in it were Colonel Paradine's tenants. I shall not stay in the village but at Sedale on Sands a few miles away. There's a decent hotel there, I understand, and I shall have sea air. I feel I need it. I want a binge up before the hard work the spring will bring me. I haven't been sleeping well lately. But I'm going up North of course on business. I'll try to kill a couple of birds with one stone, get some information I want and a tonic at the same time."

"I see. You'll take Finson?"

"No. I shan't want a valet with me. I want to be alone."

"When do you start, Malcolm?"

"I think I'd better go by the night mail from Euston to-morrow. There's a sleeping car as far as Carnforth. Then one goes on down the coast by Barrow in Furness and Furness Abbey. Sedale on Sands is a few stations before St. Bee's and Whitehaven."

"I hope it will do you good. You are not looking too well."

"Oh, there's nothing the matter with me. I'm only a little bit tired."

He hesitated, then added:

"And one can't avoid all the stupid social engagements up here. All the talk, talk, talk gets on my nerves at times. How they talk! How they talk!"

He made a gesture that, for him, was curiously uncouth.

"But I suppose they can't help it. They've nothing else to do. Though, by the way, one of the worst of them has plenty to do."

"Whom do you mean?"

"Mrs. George Blason. If only—but what's the use of wishing for silence in humanity? They must give tongue—like hounds after a fox. It's more physical with them than anything else. And the soul—left out!"

"Perhaps the change will rest you. But surely it will be very cold on that coast in January."

"I don't mind if it is. Let Nature pitch into me. I can bear that."

Again he made an uncouth gesture. Then he went out of the room.

When she was alone, Gay was in conflict. Keane's unexpected announcement had given her a dramatic opportunity for making absolutely certain of something, certain without peradventure. She had only to make a suggestion and surely knowledge would, must engulf her. Given her husband's mood, given the state of his nerves, she felt certain that he would be incapable of acting to her, would be obliged to show the truth of his heart towards her, if she did what many a woman would surely do placed in her circumstances.

He was harassed, unhappy. He had spoken really like a man persecuted. And she had not given him a word of sympathy, had not shown by a gesture, a touch, even by a look, that she was in sympathy with him, was his companion in the trouble he was struggling with. She had been held in frozen ineptitude. All she had found to say was that she hoped what he was about to do would do him good and that January would surely be a cold month in the North by the sea.

Miserable incompetence! But pride had held her as surely, as irresistibly, as chains riveted in a stone wall could hold the body of her. Till lately she had never suspected what a depth of pride there was in her. There had in her life never before been an urgent occasion for its exercise.

She felt frightened of it, ill at ease with it, yet governed by it. It seemed to be eating into her like a disease. Now she was given a chance of casting it out. An opportunity was offered to her. The conflict she was in was caused by the knowledge of this and the struggle within her for or against the seizing of this opportunity.

Pride told her to let her husband go North alone to wrestle with his demon. He had said that he wanted to be alone. Surely that ought to be enough for her. He had perhaps said it to forestall a possible suggestion from her. Yet she did not quite believe that. Her remark about Finson, the valet, had prompted it. When Malcolm spoke he had probably been thinking of Finson; and perhaps of all the everlasting talkers of London. He had not been thinking of her surely? Surely he wouldn't put her in the mob —even now.

Suppose she cast away her benumbing pride, gave way to her love, the love which now was persecuting her, and begged Malcolm to let her go with him to the North, to be with him for those few days by the sea, to make of them a second honeymoon after that honeymoon of ten years ago. Could she do it? But he was going North because of the Paradine case. Mrs. Paradine and her husband had lived close to that place by the sea. Much of Malcolm's time no doubt would be spent at Hindley. He would not want her there. She would be in his way in Hindley. And perhaps, if she suggested going, he would think she was impelled by curiosity, and was trying to force herself into a confidence he had carefully avoided admitting her into. Her mind recoiled at the thought of that. All her natural sensitiveness was in revolt. And yet something hardy in her persisted, would not in a moment abandon the temptation that was luring her on to an action that would be drastic and certainly must definitely prove to her exactly where she stood with her husband, how near to him or how far away from him. If he accepted her the world would be changed for her. If he refused her quite definitely she would—know.

All that day she revolved the great question of conduct in her mind. She wondered why exactly he felt he must go to Hindley, what exactly he would do when he got there. Perhaps he was only going on strictly legal business. Perhaps he had to see someone who was going to be a witness in the trial at the Old Bailey in March.

But perhaps——

And then her unquiet woman's mind wandered through the gardens surrounding a house in the North, stole through the corridors of that house, looked out of its windows, stayed in its rooms, received impressions from its mystery, heard faint voices echoing between its walls, saw figures moving silently through its shadows, saw actions committed within it.

Malcolm might be going to Hindley on business that was not legal. Perhaps he was going to do something for Mrs. Paradine, something that she had asked him to do; or perhaps he was going for reasons not of Law but of sentiment.

And then her unquiet imagination rose in a tragic flight.

That house, Hindley Hall, had been Mrs. Paradine's home for several years. There are people with strong personalities who impress themselves upon places where they abide, linger on there when they are said to be 'gone.'

Malcolm, she knew, had a lot of what is called 'romance' in him Formerly she had been glad of that, had felt deliciously at home with his romance. But now——

As the day wore on—she spent it alone—a conviction was born in her and persisted. It was this: that her only chance against the overwhelming Paradine case which was swallowing up her happiness was to identify herself with it. Hitherto she had always been deep in her husband's life and isolated from his Law. And she had never wished it otherwise. He had come to her for refreshment. She had represented to him the gracious side of life in contrast to the criminal side of life with which so much of his work was identified. Although now and then, very seldom, he had consulted her about some point in a case that had to do with a woman, she knew that he delighted to keep her at a distance from his work in the Law Courts. That atmosphere was not for his Gay. She did not belong to the tribe of women who, when a *cause célèbre*, another Paradine case, was in progress, tried to fight their way into Court to feed upon horror and garbage, and to revel in the naked exposure of the seamy side of humanity. She was a being apart. And she had loved that. But, as she had said to Judith Flaquer, recently everything was changed, and she had the feeling now of someone living only *à côté de la vie*, and, because of that, being deserted.

Perhaps that was partly her own fault. Perhaps it was time that

she roused herself and came to grips with the life that was stretching out claws to come to grips with her. But could she do it? Was
it possible for her? Dared she do it?

There was only one way, she felt: to bury her pride, let her
love loose from its cage, show Malcolm her heart, and ask him
to take her into the Paradine case, to let her be there with him,
to help him in it, if she could, at any rate to bring all her sympathy
and aid him in bearing the burden of it.

After hours of mental debate and struggle she resolved to make
her great attempt that evening. They were going to spend it at
home and alone, Malcolm's last evening before going up North.
She wouldn't arrange any careful plan in her mind. She would
trust to her heart to do the best she was capable of. She had the
feeling of one about to put her fate to the touch, the feeling that
she was about to make a last throw for happiness, that the result
would mean for her all or nothing.

Yes, it had come to that—in silence. How can such a great
change come about without a word being spoken to help it into
being, without a word being spoken in the effort to delay or
avoid it?

Having come to a decision Gay tried to feel normal and calm.
She went to her bookshelves and took out Ramacharaka's *Yogi
Philosophy and Oriental Occultism*, and tried to bury herself in it.
She read again and again this passage:

> "Learn to look intelligently into the hearts of men . . . by
> knowing men you will be able to help them and will also learn
> many lessons that will aid you in your journey along the path.
> . . . Intelligence is imparted."

She read it, but she reduced the plural to the singular and instead
of men she put the name of a man.

"I must be intelligent," she said to herself. "I have been loving.
I know that. But perhaps I have not been intelligent."

She prayed for intelligence.

Sausage lay at her feet, often resting his tawny chin on her
shoe.

·   ·   ·   ·   ·

Before he left London Keane had resolved to try to meet somebody who had succeeded in troubling his mind greatly during the
last few days, and that morning, just before lunchtime, when he
happened to know that Lord Horfield was entertaining some men
at the Cleveland Club, he went into a public telephone office and
called up a number in Sussex Square. Someone, evidently a servant,
answered and Keane asked if Lady Horfield was at home and
whether he could speak to her. The voice answered that her ladyship was at home and asked for a name.

"Sir Malcolm Keane."

In a moment Keane heard Lady Horfield's uncertain voice bark-
ing uneasily to him.

"Sir Malcolm—what is it?—Has there—has Horfield—is there
anything—please tell me——"

"Nothing wrong, Lady Horfield, nothing at all. But I have to
leave London for a few days to-morrow and I should very much
like to have a little quiet talk with you before I go. Is it possible?"

There was a silence, then:

"But where could we—where could we—I don't—I should like
very much—but——"

"I believe to-morrow is the closing day for Baron Sedelsward's
exhibition. Could you meet me there to-day at four? There'll
probably be very few people. We could have our talk there,
perhaps."

Another silence, then an unexpectedly decisive:

"I shall come."

"Good! Thank you."

He rang off at once lest she might waver.

At five minutes to four he arrived at the Sampson Galleries.

As he had anticipated they were almost empty. There were
two elderly women in one of the rooms; in another there was a
thin, furtive-looking man with his pointed red nose almost glued
to a canvas; in a third room two painted girls were gossiping busily.
The snow scenes gleamed under the cleverly arranged lights.

Sedelsward was not there though Keane knew that he was still
in London. But had he been there Keane would not have minded.
He believed in the Baron's perfect discretion.

Having looked quickly through the galleries Keane returned
to the entrance and waited. Just after four o'clock a taxicab

stopped outside and Lady Horfield, wrapped in a voluminous skunk fur, struggled out of it, paid the chauffeur and lunged secretively across the pavement.

She arrived breathless, but evidently affected rather by her mental than by her physical activity.

"How d'you do, Sir Malcolm? Where shall we go? Is it—are there—where would be the best spot for us?"

"There's practically nobody here. Any room will do."

"Let us—the farthest one—that will be——"

"Certainly. Come with me."

"Yes, yes, of course. I hope there's no one I——"

She was evidently agitated and there was a guilty look in her eyes. Yet he felt that there was decision in her and that, having come, she had made up her mind to 'go through with it.'

In the first room they passed the two elderly women who looked away from the pictures to stare rather blatantly at Lady Horfield.

"Oh, I'm afraid—do you think they—so many people know me by sight because of *him*——?"

"But why shouldn't you be here?"

"But with you so late—it would seem—they might easily think——"

In the next room the painted girls stopped chattering to gaze at them, then as they went by murmured something to each other.

"They know me, Sir Malcolm! I'm certain they know me!"

Keane began to feel irritated.

"Even if they do," he rejoined, "they will never think this is an assignation."

"But it *is*! We arranged to meet here, through the telephone!"

"Yes—but not——" he abandoned the absurd attempt to explain what he meant.

"Here! This will do!"

"But there's that odd-looking man! Who can he be?"

"A pointed-nosed picture maniac. Look, he's going out."

"I wonder why he was here."

"We shall in all probability never know that. Why solitary male human beings haunt London picture galleries is a mystery hidden in the womb of time," he said, for a moment giving free vent to ironical appreciation of her absurdity.

"And this is the woman whom Gay calls a rare creature, and Sedelsward declares to be full of the inner beauty and capable of greatness!" he thought despairingly. "If only I could put a curb in her mind and force her to go steady for five minutes!"

"You are laughing at me!" she said, unexpectedly. "And he often does. Am I so—do you find me——"

"No, no, dear Lady Horfield, I'm not laughing at you. I was only making a stupid joke to hide my deep seriousness. The English fear of—but you know what we are!"

They had sat down on a bench in the middle of the room and he laid a hand on her arm to impress his sincerity upon her. In front of them was a vast canvas showing a slope covered with snow and crowned with a thin procession of birch trees outlined in frost. The sky behind them was tinted with the cold yellow of a Northern twilight. In the foreground were two peasants, men, ploughing their way with bent backs towards home and the repose of evening by the stove.

She seemed somewhat reassured by his explanation, but when he said: "Do take off your fur. You will be much too hot," she exclaimed:

"Oh no! It would look too—I can't stay long. I mustn't—Horfield might—perhaps he won't, I don't know—but I ought to be there."

"Where?"

"At home if he should—what is it?"

"First—do please take off your fur. Then I shan't feel that you are in a violent hurry."

As he spoke he lifted his hands as if to help her with the fur. She hesitated for an instant, then obeyed him awkwardly. Her hands were very small but they fumbled. There was nothing neat about their movements. They looked distracted. But at last the fur was undone and her big body emerged, clad in chocolate-coloured silk. He lifted the coat away and put it beside him over the bench.

"That's better."

"But your overcoat!" she said, as if in rebuke.

He took it off immediately, laid it down, then turned to her.

"To-morrow night I'm going up North for a few days and I felt I must see you before starting."

"Why?"

It seemed to him that she was on the defensive. Her small eyes looked suspicious.

"Don't think I'm an inquisitive man, but you and I are good friends, I think——"

"Yes, yes! Good friends! But——"

"And you have honoured me more than once with your confidence."

"I know. I felt I—but perhaps——"

"One minute! Let me just tell you—quietly. Perhaps I should have said not confidence but half-confidence. Now a half-confidence is sometimes worse than no confidence at all. It may lead to confusion of mind, even to beliefs that are entirely erroneous. Can't you, won't you make yourself clearer to me?"

"But—but—what about?" she faltered.

"I thought you wanted something from me. Surely you did. At Lady Flaquer's the other day——"

"I know, I know! But perhaps I oughtn't—Horfield—he—came you remember, and—and——" She clasped and unclasped her hands. Her hands seemed to be writhing—"He didn't say much, but I think—I'm almost sure he—*suspected*."

Her head, with its chocolate and red toque, drooped forward and sideways portentously.

"Perhaps I oughtn't—perhaps it was wicked of me. But—it's *so* on my mind! I'm *so* miserable about it."

"I thought you wanted me to *do* something. Wasn't it so?"

"If you could! But I don't know—my duty is to him. It isn't his fault—he can't help it. These dreadful things—so often people are full of blame but they don't know. Who wants to be like that?"

"Let me help if I can," he said impressively, but gently, too. "I think it's your duty to make things clear to me. Perhaps I could do something. You spoke—you hinted at Mrs. Paradine."

"Yes. Yes. She's on my mind, terribly on it. I can't sleep for thinking of her and what's—if only he wasn't to try her!"

"But surely——"

She didn't seem to hear him and continued, in a breathless sort of way:

"But they always choose him. If only they knew—but they don't, and he's made his name as a criminal Judge. And he's so fearfully clever. But all the same he should never be given such cases to try. It isn't right. But only *I* know that."

"And I," said Keane firmly. "If I haven't entirely misunderstood your meaning."

She looked frightened, almost cringing. Her big body seemed to shrink.

"Perhaps I oughtn't to have—what did you——"

"I leave it to you," said Keane. "But I think, now things have gone so far between us, it would be best to be frank. Perhaps then I could do something."

"You're defending her—poor woman. That's why I—otherwise, I should never have spoken, never!"

"Lady Horfield—tell me!"

It sounded like a command from one who intended to be obeyed. Her head shook for an instant as if she had the palsy. The red pouches under her eyes worked, and her face was distorted. Keane felt terribly sorry for her, but he meant to be ruthless with her. He wasn't going to let her off.

"Tell me! I'm fighting for the life of this poor woman. If you know anything at all that could affect her fate, it's your sacred duty as a woman to tell it to me."

She bent closer to him and said in a whispering voice:

"Never tell anyone, but—he *wants* to sentence them. If he can't, he's unhappy like—like someone deprived of food, like someone who goes hungry. And—and—he vents it on me. But that's not what I—I'm more afraid of him, much more, when he comes home happy and satisfied because—you know!"

In spite of the grotesqueness of her appearance and manner, or perhaps even partly because of that, Keane felt for an instant bound in sheer horror. He had forgotten where they were. He was no longer conscious of the snow scenes around them. He was in a stark isolation of the mind shared by this hideous knowledge which she had given him. Not for a moment did he doubt the truth of what she had said. Something within him knew it was true. Preposterous though this woman was, he felt that the truth must be in her. She was certainly in her tragic earnestness fantastically sincere.

"Don't condemn him!" she whispered into his silence. "I am so sorry for him, so, so sorry."

Two tears came out of her eyes and trickled over the red patches of skin beneath them.

"He can't help himself. God has made him so. It must be that——— We mustn't———" Her voice died away. "How can we blame———" it came again—"All my religion doesn't—we *are* in his hands. Free will—I don't think———"

Her head trembled.

Keane's eyes were always upon her in a look which had become a fixed stare.

A Sadist Judge! And he was going to plead before that Judge for the life of a woman, for the life of Mrs. Paradine. It was a monstrous situation! A Sadist, who required, in his very flesh, a condemnation, would direct the Jury about the fate of Mrs. Paradine.

"Pity him as I do!"

"No!" said Keane with harsh emphasis. "I'm thinking of the victims. They are those who should be pitied."

A passion of indignation was rising in him urging him to action. He felt a great need for action, but what could he do?

"You began to tell me this at Lady Flaquer's," he said. "It seemed to me that you thought I could do something in connection with—with———" he sought for some expression that wouldn't be too impossible—"with this trouble of your husband's. What did you think I could do?"

"You're a great lawyer. They all say so and I feel it. Get her off. Don't let him have *her* on his soul, too. I can't bear it. There mustn't be another. If there is———" She stretched out her little fin-like hands in a desperate gesture. "Help her to escape him! They tell me there's no one like you for getting them off. That's why I come to you. It's wrong, perhaps. I oughtn't to do it because I'm his wife and I—he's everything to me. But I felt I *must*. He can't help it. It's not his fault. He has been made like that. And———" again she whispered—"it's getting worse. He needs *it* more and more."

Just for a moment, when she said that, Keane felt a flash of uncertainty, and asked himself for the first time whether Lady Horfield was mad. Odd she always was, eccentric in appearance, manner and dress. But he had never had the least suspicion that she had madness in her. Now for a moment he wondered——

and even hoped. Anything would be better than that genuine truth had come out of her. That she had spoken what she believed to be true he was certain. But possibly she had been prompted by a mind that was astray.

"Don't you believe it?" she said fiercely, interrupting his thought.

Keane looked at her steadily, set his mind on Horfield, and sought for the truth of his heart. He had often looked into the eyes of witnesses, seeking to read what was in them, trying to compel them to give him the truth. This time, though he gazed into the little dark eyes of his companion on the bench, he was really seeking not in her but in himself. Remotely, he surely knew already for certain whether under all her eccentricity she was completely sane or whether she was mad. And the answer came out of this remote something in him which was able to know and knew.

"Yes," he said, "I believe it."

He was silent, and then added:

"I'll do all I can, my very best."

"For his sake," she muttered.

"For hers!" he said, perhaps curtly.

She gazed at him so piteously that he was touched and, in spite of his dislike of Lord Horfield, which had now been increased until it amounted to a grim hatred, he said:

"And for his sake, too."

"Thank you," she whispered.

They sat side by side in silence for a moment. Then Lady Horfield made an abrupt, scrambling movement towards her fur coat.

"I ought to go. He may come back and——"

"Let me help you."

He lifted his coat away from hers and picked up the fur.

"You'll never let him suspect——" she said. "You'll be careful not to——"

"Trust me!"

"And one thing—I ought to——"

The deadly serious, portentous expression that he had noticed two or three times before came into her face.

"Be nice to him—when you can."

"Nice?"

"Yes. He doesn't like you."

Keane felt rigid with enmity.

"That makes it worse. He would be glad to—Try to please him."

"But——"

"At the Club, make up to him. Be pleasant. Charm him—if you can."

"I always——"

"No, no! Sometimes you make him angry. I know it. Before the trial comes on make good friends with him. Do it for *her*, or else—he's very sensitive in a way. He always knows when anyone dislikes him and—it isn't as if you were a woman."

A quiver of almost irresistible laughter at this unexpected conclusion went through Keane, but he controlled it.

"When it's a woman then *he* tries to charm—but not with men. Your wife——"

She stopped.

"Yes?" said Keane, the laughter dying out of him instantly. "My wife?"

"With her he would—I mean, he puts forth all——"

At some distance from them, in a farther part of the gallery, a heavy voice with a slightly chanting intonation said:

"I wish you could have seen them by daylight, but I'm glad you found time to come at all."

A clear, silver-tongued voice replied:

"I had quite a panic when I saw in the *Times* that your exhibition closes to-morrow. Is this near Stockholm?"

"Yes. Djursholm in early winter."

"Get me out—Sir Malcolm, get me——"

"Hush! Impossible!"

"But——"

"Come and stand in front of this picture. I've got your coat. Talk about this picture to me."

"But if he——"

"Those are birch trees."

He raised his naturally powerful and resonant voice.

"I know he'll suspect. I'm——"

"Notice the difference between those peasants in the evening light and Millet's peasants in *The Angelus*. The diffusion of light is quite differently treated. You know the work of Israels, the famous Dutch painter? Did you ever chance to see his painting of a dog drawing a cart over a vast plain with night coming on? With him there's his master, a——"

"Keane! How good of you to help Sophy in her efforts to obtain a better understanding of art! I have never dared to put my hand to anything of the kind. D'you find her an apt pupil? How are you getting on, Sophy? Here's the painter himself to add to your knowledge!"

Keane had been held in horrible expectation of Lady Horfield's collapse into a jelly of fear and guilty confusion, but she gave him one more surprise. Swinging her bulky figure round awkwardly, she faced her husband and the Baron with an intrepidity he had not believed her capable of.

"How d'you do, Baron? I had to come once more, and found Sir Malcolm here. He was kindly explaining to me——" She saw her husband's eyes fixed on her between narrowed lids and faltered for a moment.

"Yes?" he said, softly. "Yes, Sophy? We are waiting."

"It wasn't a lesson," said Keane, greeting the two men with a smile. "But I'm afraid I was perhaps being carried towards the ungrateful habit of the pedagogue and was beginning to bore Lady Horfield."

"No, no!" she ejaculated. "It was only that——"

"Let me show you round, may I?" said the polite Baron, who had certainly seen that something was wrong. "I should like you to see a skating scene I've done in the harbour of Stockholm."

He moved away with her, or rather seemed to move her away, leaving Horfield and Keane together.

The Judge's eyes were fixed upon his wife's fur which, with Keane's overcoat, was lying over Keane's arm.

"I'll carry that," he said, stretching out a thin hand.

"Oh no!"

"With your coat, it's too heavy."

"No, really! Your wife was just going to put it on."

"She found it too hot here?"

"Yes."

"She suffers from blood pressure. Perhaps you knew it?"

"No, I didn't."

"That's partly what makes her talk nonsense. Don't bother to be polite; you know, everyone knows, what nonsense she talks. She might have a stroke any day. I have to take great care of her."

Although he spoke in his usually delicately clear, and even beautiful, voice, and his manner was as smooth and absolutely self-possessed as it habitually was, something made Keane know that he was very angry. Perhaps Keane could not have defined what it was. (Afterwards he thought deeply about it and was puzzled.) The way in which Horfield had looked at the fur often recurred to Keane. And there was, despite his apparent calm, an intense under-current of alertness in him. Keane knew Horfield was bristling but could not have said exactly why he knew. Rather feeling than observation informed Keane. There was at that moment an ugly and fierce communication of natures between the two men. An abhorrent intimacy existed between them which was not expressed in words, which was not even expressed in gesture or betraying features. By subterranean channels they mingled and could not separate.

It was one of the most hateful episodes in Keane's life.

He said something hypocritically sympathetic about Horfield's obligation to take care of his ailing wife, and they moved together round the walls, following the painter and Lady Horfield, who had gone into another room. For a moment they spoke of the pictures. Then Horfield said:

"It seems I'm to try the Paradine case."

Immediately Keane remembered Lady Horfield's agitated injunction. But how could he, for any reason, make good friends with this man?

"So I heard," he said.

He waited a moment; then forced himself to add:

"When I told Mrs. Paradine that, she seemed very glad to hear it. She knows the advantage of coming up before a great Judge."

He listened to himself as he spoke, and thought that his voice actually sounded sincere. If so, he had accomplished a miracle of acting.

"I hope you'll be able to win the case," Horfield said. "I know, no one better, how intensely you feel for your clients."

Another miracle of acting?

"By God, we're a loathsome pair!" Keane said to himself at that moment.

They joined Lady Horfield and the painter, and almost directly Keane got away.

As the Judge took the fur from Keane, he said:

"I'm much obliged to you for being so solicitous about my wife, Keane."

Lady Horfield at that moment looked like a frightened bitch who was expecting a beating.

XXII

When Keane got away from the picture gallery and looked forward into the immediate future, he dreaded the evening at home that lay before him. He had reached the condition of acute restlessness in which a man finds it almost impossible to keep quiet, to be calm, reasonable, as usual. Movement and action seemed an imperious necessity to him just then. He did not know how he would be able to spend an evening in his house alone with his wife.

But why spend the evening at home? There was no reason why they should not go out. Lacon and Ollier's was only a few minutes away. Acting on impulse, Keane walked there and bought a couple of stalls for a theatre where only comic plays, usually uproarious farces, were given. Then he called a taxicab and drove home. He wished that he were starting for the North that night, but anyhow, with those tickets he would get through the evening without feeling absolutely desperate. The play was said to be very funny. Perhaps he would be able to laugh at it. As to Gay—well, he must chance her being amused. Just then, without being specially conscious of it, he was furiously selfish and seeking an escape from himself.

Directly he reached his home he went to find Gay. She was in the downstairs sitting-room reading, or seeming to read, the Yogi book. As she looked up, without noticing the curiously intent look in her face, he exclaimed in a hearty voice:

"I say, dear, d'you mind asking them to put forward dinner? As this is my last evening before going North, I thought we'd make it lively, and I've bought two stalls for the Cosmopolitan. I'm told the play there's the funniest thing in London. But we ought to be there by half-past eight. Can we manage it?"

He noticed that she hesitated and looked very grave, perhaps even distressed, but she only said:

"I'll tell Baker. We shan't have much time."

"Let's have a scrambled dinner. I don't mind for once. Let Saunders know that anything will do. I'll just run up to my room. I've got two or three notes I must write."

But when he got to his room he sat down at his writing-table and did nothing.

"Horfield!" he thought. "Horfield! What can I do about Horfield?"

He did not see Gay again before dinner. They met downstairs and went at once to the dining-room.

During the short dinner Keane forced himself to talk and to assume a lively and energetic air which he hoped would cover his intense secret preoccupation. Talking so much himself, making such a strenuous effort, he was not specially struck by Gay's demeanour or by her unusual speechlessness. Consciousness of himself, of what he must do, of what he must endeavour to hide, possessed him. Intent on the impression he was trying to make on her as an actor he failed to be audience to her.

"Time we were off!" he said presently, taking out his watch and silently thanking God that the meal was over.

In a few minutes he would be helped out by the play.

During the drive to the theatre they scarcely spoke to each other. Movement, the noise of the streets, seemed to Keane to protect him. Directly they were in their places the curtain went up.

The play was very funny and was admirably acted, in the right spirit of farce, swiftly, lightly and with lots of ingenious business. Keane was surprised at finding it more efficacious than he had hoped. He could not entirely forget himself in it, but he was able to be amused, and for a couple of hours or more life seemed less tragic to him. Beside him, however, Gay seemed unable to be caught up by the imp of absurdity. She smiled sometimes, she even laughed, but there was something detached and evasive about her attitude. Now and then, when Keane was apparently intent on the stage, she sent him a deeply inquiring look as if all her soul were rapt in contemplation of him. (Men dread such a look from a woman, even from the woman they love.)

Just after eleven o'clock the curtain shut out the stage and immediately Keane was wholly back in the life he had sought an escape from. It seemed to come upon him instantly with the power of a mighty wave inundating him.

During the drive home he forced himself to talk to Gay about the play and the actors. They were both theatre lovers and usually found plenty to discuss after a visit to the play. Many delightful discussions about acting and plays they had had in the past, cosy talks, in which they had agreed or differed, joyously, good tempered and happy in the divine intimacy which allows everything to be said without even a moment's fear of offence or misunderstanding. Now only he spoke and Gay, perhaps, listened. Now and then she murmured something, but it was murmured only with the edges, as it were, of her lips. There seemed to be little that was mental behind that had any relation to it.

Keane felt a great longing, even a great necessity, to be alone. Already he was greedy for his days and nights in the North. He would not be happy in them, but there would be a sort of safety about them, the feeling at any rate of semi-safety that solitude often brings. He lusted for that. And now there would be the night, shut up in his room. There at least he could give himself up to a profound consideration of the near future with which he had to deal.

In the house he was on the verge of bidding a carefully concealed, but in reality eager, good night to Gay when she said, in a very definite voice:

"Malcolm, dear, come into my bedroom, won't you, and let's have a talk. There's something I want to ask you."

As she spoke, to his great surprise, she put out a hand, took his hand and gave it a long soft pressure. For just an instant he was touched, but almost immediately there came a strong reaction.

"She wants something from me!" he thought.

And he was filled with suspicion and a wish to defend himself against her unknown desire.

"You'll come, won't you?" she added.

"Of course. Why not? But you won't keep me long, will you? I still have some things to see to. Winding up one or two matters so that I may be free for the few days during which I shall be away. Go up, dear, I'll follow you."

He released his hand gently and she went up the staircase.

When she had disappeared he went into the dining-room and poured out a stiff brandy and soda. He dreaded the interview that was coming. From Gay's manner, the pressure of her hand, the expression in her eyes, he realised that she was set upon speaking to him of something that was of vital importance to her, and perhaps also to him. He was convinced, too, that she was going to ask something of him. There had been intensity in the voice that had said: "You'll come, won't you?" But there had been obstinacy, too. She meant him to come, was determined that he should come. In his present mood he felt afraid of her. There was so much on his mind. And perhaps she was going to speak about his obsession, the Paradine case. That would be a new departure for Gay. But the emotional and yet obstinate look in her eyes betokened a new departure. She was certainly wrought up to some definite action that meant a great deal to her, that perhaps required from her a very exceptional effort. He felt certain that it would be disagreeable to him.

Perhaps she meant to try to persuade him not to go North.

At this thought he stiffened with rebellion and felt a cruel determination rise up in him against her.

"I'll soon settle that!" he said to himself as he set his foot on the first step of the staircase.

And he went upstairs quickly, longing to get their interview over.

He found Gay in the gown she had worn at the theatre standing before the fire waiting for him.

"Well, dear, what is it?" he asked as he came in, speaking in a brisk, matter of fact voice that was a lie to his mind.

"Won't you shut the door?" she said, gently.

"Oh—did I——"

He turned round. The bedroom door was wide open. He went to it reluctantly and shut it. When he came back she was sitting in a chair by the fire. He went to stand on the hearth.

"Yes?" he said, looking down at her.

Now that the moment had come Gay found it almost impossible to say what she had made up her mind to say. There was something rigid in her husband's figure, something uncompromising in the eyes looking down on her, that defeated her tenderness. The barrier between them had never seemed to her so definite as it did now. She did not feel that they were strangers to each other in this moment but that they were intimate enemies. For even in her love she felt that she was, in a subtle way, his enemy because her desire was surely in such acute opposition to his, was a fighting desire against his. And her realisation of this was so sharp that it paralysed her determination to put their relation to the test she had decided on. She did not know how to say what she had sworn to herself that she would say.

"Yes, dear?" he said. "What is it? You had something to ask me?"

"I'd been thinking about your going away, going up North in winter."

"Ah!"

His voice sounded sharp.

"It seemed to me rather dreary."

"Dreary!" he said, still in the sharp voice. "Why?"

"Well, your going all alone."

"Alone! But there's nothing in that . . ." (He laughed.) "You know I often go away here and there alone for cases. Birmingham, Liverpool, Manchester—where haven't I been? Where don't I go? Work takes me and——"

"I don't want your work to be—to be a separating monster between us."

"My work a monster! What do you mean, dear? Haven't we been married for over ten years and haven't I been at work all the time? All men worth their salt are workers. Would you

have me an idler? Could you stand having a do-nothing husband?"

"No. But couldn't you take me into your work a little more
than you do?"

"But I thought we'd always felt, both of us, that as my profession happens to be one that obliges me to dive deeply into
the seamy side of life, and life's ugly realities, we'd much rather
you were out of it entirely. You were not made for the ugly
realities and I think we both realised it. Why should——"

But she interrupted him.

"How do you know what I was made for, Malcolm?" she said.
"How do I know even? Perhaps I've only been playing at life
up to now. And perhaps you've only been helping me to play.
I know! I know! You've often called me 'evasive Gay,' and it's
all partly my own fault. It must be. What happens to us does
too often come from us. You've thought of me as an echo: but
I don't want to be an echo. I want to be a voice. I want you to
hear me as a voice. Why should I specially live cradled away
from everything that is real? Why should I live only à côté de
la vie? What is the difference between me and other women that
makes people, you and others, think that I must live a sort of
special life away from the centre, away from the core of things?
Even Judy Flaquer——"

"Ah!" exclaimed Keane. "I knew this had something to do
with Judith! I was certain of it. What has she been saying? What's
Judith been putting into your mind to upset you like this?"

"But, Malcolm——"

"Why can't we be let alone? Why must those who claim to be
our friends come butting in and trying to interfere with our
peace and——"

"But she hasn't!"

"Then why mention her?"

"I was only going to say that Judy is like you in calling me
'evasive Gay' and thinking I ought to be kept out of everything
that isn't serene and comfortable and delightful and easy—easy!
Out of the struggle of life! But you can't either of you manage
to keep me out. Everyone has got to be in it. Perhaps I haven't
realised that, but I realise it now thoroughly. And I want you
to know that, Malcolm, and—and to help me."

"How?"

"By taking me into any struggle of yours and letting me be in it with you."

"But I don't understand. What struggle am I in? What's all this about? I'm in the dark—totally. What change do you want me to make in our lives?"

"Suppose you had married Judy——?"

"Oh—God forbid!" Keane exclaimed.

"She mightn't have suited you! Very well. But wouldn't you have consulted her, have asked her counsel when you were in a difficult case?"

"Does a man want to marry a solicitor?" said Keane, forcing a laugh. "Really, Gay, you are going off the line. I'd as soon be married to a solicitor as I would to Judith Flaquer."

"But she might have helped you and I never do. You don't let me. In this house what am I after all? A sort of cherished pet —as Sausage is."

"You and Sausage! What a comparison! Where's your sense of humour to-night? I come to you not to consult you on legal business but to rest from legal business in your sweet company. I come to you to get away from the pain of life, and you want me to carry it with me to you, to infect you with it, to muddy you with it. I shall never do that."

"Are you sure, Malcolm?" she said, gazing up at him with an earnest intensity that troubled his spirit, plunged him deep in uneasiness. "Do you think you possess the power to keep the pain of life away from me—any longer?"

"Why not?" he said, but in an irresolute voice. "Haven't I done my best since we've been married?"

"Ten years of happiness is a long time. Few people probably have so much. I ought to be very thankful for it, and I am. But one can get a habit of happiness. I think I've got that habit. And what one has a habit of one expects to last, perhaps because one feels that one couldn't do without it. And then when any-thing disturbs that expectation one is afraid, terribly afraid."

"What have you to be afraid of?" he said, trying not to speak brusquely and longing to close a conversation which he felt he had lost the mastery of, if indeed he had ever had it.

Gay waited a moment, then her face seemed to harden with resolution, and she said, in a curiously metallic voice:

"The Paradine case."

Although when he had been alone downstairs after Gay had gone up to wait for him Keane had had a momentary suspicion that she was going to speak of the obsessing case which was altering their lives, he was startled now when she spoke of it and he showed that he was startled. He even made an impulsive movement as if he were going to leave the room, but he checked it immediately, faced Gay and said calmly:

"What about that case, the Paradine case as you, as everyone else, calls it? Have you anything against it?"

The question was a strange one but he put it deliberately, challengingly even, remembering his suspicion that Sir Simon's attempt to compel him to throw up the case had been prompted by feminine influence.

"It seems to me," he added, before she could answer, "that there's a great deal of very ugly, and I might say malicious curiosity about that case. I don't for a moment associate you with it, Gay. I know you too well for that. But for others, women, some of whom we know pretty well, I wouldn't answer. I hope you won't let them influence you with their folly and worse. I have reason——" he hesitated, then went on with resolution——"to believe, I might almost say to be certain, that, for God knows what reason, there has been a desire on the part of someone to get me to retire from the case. Any such wish on the part of anyone won't be gratified. I shall go through with this case and I shall win it. I've made up my mind to that and I believe in my own ability to win a verdict for my client. You tell me you're afraid of the case. What do you mean by that? Are you afraid of my losing it and diminishing my reputation thereby? Or has someone, some woman of course—it could only be a woman—been putting some nonsense into your head? I know there's endless tittle-tattle going about London concerning the case. Mrs. George Blason and others have taken good care of that. But it would be difficult for me to believe that you could concern yourself with the pernicious gossip of idle tongues."

"Please don't believe that," Gay said, not without a touch of pride.

"Then what are you afraid of?"

After he had put this leading question there was a silence so long that, to Keane, it became almost unbearable. Yet he could not break it. He had not, he felt, the power to break it. For some reason not known to him this extraordinary silence was necessary to Gay, and he must let her have it. During it she sat quite still looking down, and though his eyes were upon her he believed that she was unconscious of his astonishment and perhaps unconscious of the length of the pause inflicted by her on their conversation. Thought, some internal debate probably, had killed self-consciousness of the common kind in her and also sharp consciousness of him and his waiting. All through the silence he kept the knowledge that her mind was concentrated on his question and that she would answer it when she could. And at last, when the silence was pressing upon him and hurting him, she did answer it with one word.

"Everything," she said, in a low voice and without looking up.

"But—but that's impossible!" he said.

She looked up at him.

"Have you never felt fear that seems to cover everything, to wrap you round, you and your whole life?"

"No," he said.

But as he said it his mind went to Horfield, and he seemed to understand what she meant.

"I envy you," she said.

And again there was a silence. Their conversation seemed breaking into fragments. He felt that their intercourse was becoming unbearable. Either they must talk and keep on talking or he must go. He could not stand there expecting and enduring these silences.

"Well, dear——" he said at last, as she said nothing more, "I think I'd better——"

"Wait a minute, Malcolm!"

She got up swiftly and stood by him on the hearth close to him.

"I haven't said what I wished to say to you."

"No? Well, what is it?"

And again his body felt rigid, prompted by a mind that was ready with a refusal.

"Can't you take me with you to the North to-morrow night?"

He had not expected that. He had thought that perhaps she would try to prevent him from going North but not that she would ask to come with him.

"I won't trouble you. If you have business to do, of course, I'll keep out of it. I'll only be there when—if you want me— ever. Will you take me?"

She said it very simply, without pressure, but the eyes that looked at him were not simple. They were deeply asking eyes.

"We would just be together quietly when you were free."

"But I'm only going for three or four days."

"I know."

"And the hotel—I'm sure it's exceedingly primitive. A North Country inn, in fact. Nothing more than that. And in the winter! No, I couldn't take you, dear. It's all very well for me. On circuit I've stayed in all sorts of places. What do I care? But you! Gay! Oh, no! It wouldn't do at all. I should feel worried the whole time about your having to put up with discomforts. My mind wouldn't be at ease, and I simply must get rid of—of all domestic preoccupations, and give all my thoughts to——"

He had been going to say "to the case," but pulled up, remembering her terribly drastic and personal remark about it a few minutes before.

"I'm going North in connection with work," he said, "and simply and solely for work. I should be no use as a companion, however much I might wish to be. You see how it is?"

"Yes, I see."

"And then it will be awfully cold up in the North on that sea coast."

"Yes, I expect it would be cold."

"And here it's so warm and cosy and even beautiful."

He looked round the luxurious room.

"The right nest for you."

"I'll stay in it," she said.

And he wished her good night.

The lips that he kissed felt to him very strange, dreadfully alive, not like Gay's lips. The touch of them startled him. Never had a kiss seemed so full of meaning to him in the past.

But what did it mean?

He felt full of guilt as he left the room. He felt full of pain. But he felt, too, full of hard determination.

No one, not even Gay, should interfere with his life. His life was his own. No one, not even Gay, must lay hands on it. He visualised mentally those who perhaps would lay hands on it if they could: Sir Simon Flaquer, Judith Flaquer—Gay. And there was one in the background with satirical eyes, smiling and waiting—Lord Horfield.

At that moment how the Advocate hated the Judge.

XXIII

THE express train from Euston to Carnforth roared through the winter night. Keane lay in the bunk in his 'sleeper,' an electric light just behind his pillow, smoking and reading Strindberg's play, *The Father*. It was late when he put it away, crushed out his cigar and drew the metal shutter down extinguishing the reading lamp. Then he lay still in the darkness.

His farewell to Gay had been brief, kind, but quite unemotional. She had come to the front door to see him get into the car. It had been snowing, but the pavement was wet and shining, not white. The snowflakes melted when they touched the ground. As the car moved away down the broad thoroughfare of Portland Place, looking out of the window, Keane had seen Gay's slight but rather tall figure in the lighted oblong of the doorway with Sausage standing beside her. She had not lifted her hand in a gesture of farewell, but had just stood there looking.

How their life together had changed! It was not Gay's fault. Nor did he say to himself that it was his fault. The fault, if any, lay with Fate. They were in the grip of the inevitable. Secretly, Gay might blame him, but—she did not know. There were things no woman could absolutely know about a man, and he was positive that what now dwelt in him not merely could not be known, but could not even be divined.

It had to be his secret, whether he wished that or not. He lay there in the dark with his secret and the train roared steadily Northwards.

And he felt that for a very short time he was in a desolate freedom. He had needed it, but he felt its desolation. To Gay, he had said that he was going North for work. But it was a queer kind of work he was going to. If he tried to explain its nature, who would understand?

He must visit the place where *she* had lived with *him*. And perhaps he would see again the man he was going to attack; covertly, perhaps, but still to attack. That man still lived up North, he understood, in Hindley village.

A gap of time to fill with thought rather than action! A gap of time in which to prepare for the ordeal that wasn't far off! A gap of time in which to meditate upon the sinister reality of Horfield! As if Gay could have any part in his life in the North!

But how pathetic her attempt had been, an attempt to wring the heart. The fact that it had not wrung his heart had shed a new light for Keane on humanity. It seemed incredible that a man so emotional and so loving as he could be, and had been, should be capable of such hardness, should contain such possibilities of cruelty.

"What are we?" he thought drearily. "The best of us?"

And then it seemed to him that the heart could be an executioner. But who can resist its domination?

Gay in the lighted oblong of the doorway, looking out into the night and the falling snow for a last glance at him, the man of refusal! Why didn't she hate him?

A long shriek, accented like the insistence of despair, cut through the night. Keane stopped his ears. It sounded like the shriek of a woman—condemned.

But there are different sorts of condemnation.

He thought he was not going to sleep, but presently he slept.

When he woke, they were not far from Carnforth Junction. Looking out of the window blurred by sleet, he saw vaguely a stone wall, wet grass with here and there patches of snow, another stone wall, a colt galloping away from the train, some hummocky land that suggested to his mind the nearness of the ocean. In the East there was a spear of very pale yellow light, narrow between ragged clouds. Its colour reminded him of the hair of a woman.

At Carnforth he had to leave the train. There were forty minutes to wait, and he went to the refreshment room and ordered
coffee and a roll and two boiled eggs. The morning was brightening
after a night full of snow and rain. He heard the burr of the
Cumbrian speech.

This had been her country after her marriage with Paradine.
It was new to him, although he had often been in Scotland for
the shooting. No doubt, she had many times changed trains at
Carnforth with her blind husband.

He ate his breakfast with appetite and went out into the brisk
morning air with a queer feeling of expectation. A dark red train
was waiting. He got into an empty first-class carriage.

They passed presently Grange over Sands. By this time, a pale
sun showed his face and lit faintly the vast sands and quicksands
which were uncovered by the ebbing tide. Over them multitudes
of sea-birds were wheeling, sending their shrill cries to the wintry
sky. Far off was the tossing foam of the sea. Looking out of the
window, Keane felt very far away from London. How would it
be if he were a man deliberately escaping out of his habitual life,
leaving it behind him for ever, casting it away as an ill-fitting,
outworn garment?

Beginning again! So transitory is everything, so dreadfully subject to change is any man's life. And yet he sits in it with a
ludicrous feeling of being settled, of permanency. So had he, the
man Keane, sat in his life with Gay. And he had had no premonition. When Sir Simon had spoken to him in the Haymarket
Theatre, no secret instinct had told him: "You're on the edge of a
changed life."

He opened a leather case he had laid down on the seat by his
side, took out some documents and began to study them, but
he often glanced out of the window. He saw many stone walls,
many fields of short grass, then billowing sand dunes fringing
the hidden sea, then presently a tidal river and a gullery with
a straggling village at its edge. Soon afterwards the train stopped
at a wayside station and he heard a North Country voice calling
"Ark-ley! Ark-ley!"

He put down the window and thrust his head out. This, he
knew, was her station. Here, coming from London, she had got

out many times to drive to Hindley Hall which lay inland a very few miles away. The sea wind whistled round his head. A blue-eyed porter stared at him.

"Getting oot, sir?" he asked, in a burry voice.

"No, I'm going on to Sedale."

"Next station, sir. This is the station for Hindley."

"The Hall's to let, I believe."

"It is, sir. The poor Colonel's dead. They're having his wife—widow rather—up for murder. I've seen her many a time. She seemed a nice lady, too."

The train moved on. In about ten minutes it slowed up and stopped in Sedale station.

The station was small and neat, and stood close to the sea-beach. Only a narrow path beyond a railing and a short stretch of rough grass divided it from the shingle and a vast expanse of hard yellow sand which stretched away to right and left as far as the eye could penetrate. In the distance a turbulent sea showed line behind line of foam. The station was filled with its voice and with the sound of the wind that beat on that lonely coast. Only Keane got out of the train which, as soon as his luggage was on the platform, moved away with gathering speed on its journey to St. Bee's and Whitehaven. As it disappeared, Keane was confronted by the Sedale Hotel, a white, one-story building with at one end a two-story red stone addition entirely out of harmony with it. In front of it was a strip of grass ending in the station railing. To the right was a sweep of pebbly ground circling round an oval patch of lawn. The station opened on to this and also the front entrance of the hotel. From it a road led out between stone gate-posts to the country beyond.

"Where to, sir?" said a red-faced porter with a very rough skin, to Keane. "The hotel or lodgings?"

"The hotel, please."

"Right, sir."

And the porter proceeded to put Keane's luggage, marked with a large M.K., on a truck and wheeled the truck out to the shingle.

"Not many staying here, are there?" asked Keane, as they walked in the wind to the inn door.

"No one, scarcely, sir. They coom here mostly in soommer," said the man.

Keane hadn't engaged rooms, not thinking it necessary, and also not anxious to push his name on the attention of the people up here. In Hindley, of course, it was possible that he would come across people who had encountered him in the police court at Bow Street. Well and good! But he had no wish that it should be known that he was coming North. And when he asked the middle-aged landlady, a widow dressed in black, with a large white cap on her grey head, for a couple of rooms, he merely gave his name as M. Keane, and wrote in the visitors' book "M. Keane. London."

He was shown to a bedroom upstairs looking out to the station, and to a small sitting-room downstairs at the end of a passage just below it. By this latter there was a door with a loose brass latch which let you out to the strip of grass between the hotel and the station.

"How long will you be staying, sir?" asked the landlady, when Keane had amiably expressed his satisfaction.

She seemed, he thought, rather awed by his appearance, perhaps by his towering height and his large and expressive eyes.

"Three or four days," he said. "I want to have a look at Hindley Hall. I hear it's to let."

"Yes, sir, or sold."

She looked portentously grave, shook her head, and added:

"Ah, it's a bad business to be sure an' all, what with the poor Colonel's death and now his widow had oop in Loondon for murder. I s'pose you've heard of it, sir, cooming from Loondon."

"Yes. I have seen something of it in the papers."

"They do say the Colonel had made a new will just before he died, but it's never been found."

"Really!"

"Oh, but there's a lot of talk going aboot round here, and no woonder when everyone knew them."

"Did you, then?"

"Not to know, sir, but I've seen them. Her especially."

"Yes?"

"Yes, sir. She'd soomtimes coom driving here and get oot and walk oot there all by herself on the sands. Ah, she was a strange lass of a woman, foreign-like, you know. But one'd never have thought as she'd murder the poor man."

"Perhaps she didn't."

"Well, sir, that's to be seen. Dinner's at one, sir, sooper at seven. And I hope you'll be coomfortable."

"Can I have a trap to take me over to Hindley Hall this afternoon?"

"Yes, sir. What time?"

"Well—say three."

"Three it shall be, sir."

And at three a sort of small wagonette drawn by one horse, with a North Country lad perched on a tiny seat that almost rested on the horse's haunches, drew up before the window, and Keane, sitting sideways and swaying uneasily, set off in the wind towards Hindley.

"Drive me to the Hall, please," had been Keane's direction.

"Yes, sir," said the lad, and whistled to his horse.

"Coom oop, then!"

They turned out of the gateway to the right, descended a sandy road, went under a railway arch and passed a line of small lodging houses which faced the green at right angles to the beach. The tide was now coming up, the uncovered sands were diminishing, and the voice of the sea was louder carried over the sands on a strong wind from the West. There she had walked in the days before catastrophe, alone. Keane looked from the swaying carriage. There was no one now on the sands, but he saw some children playing vaguely on the shingle that edged them. He narrowed his eyes, nearly closing the lids. The sands became a blur, the tossing white foam a faint dazzle of white. A lonely figure moved far away in the vision, terribly alone, wishing, perhaps even needing to be alone, meditating, pondering, daring. Intending?

He shook his shoulders. She was innocent. He would prove her innocent. He must, not only for her sake but for his own.

The carriage turned to the left. They mounted a hill, passed more houses with lodgings to let. On the brow of the hill facing the lodging houses stood an old public house: "The Salmon and Otter," of dingy white roughcast. Over the door was the figurehead of some ancient sailing ship, no doubt long since broken up, a woman with blunt features, streaming strands of dark hair, and wild eyes staring out to all the seas of the world. As Keane looked at her he was seized by a tremendous sense of romance, of the romance that life still holds for those who know how to fuel with force, who can still be swayed by the tides of passion. And he felt terribly young, like a fierce boy, in spite of his middle age. The man of the world with his burden of ugly knowledge seemed to drop from him, discarded, and he was loose in that region where anything may happen, where something tremendous surely must happen, something to quicken the beating pulses and send the hot blood surging through the veins.

And they drove into the country, losing sight of the sea but still hearing its voice in the distance booming over the heathery flats and the network of sand dunes, and presently came to Arkley, and left it behind, and penetrated farther inland till the voice of the sea died away and the quiet remoteness of this Northern countryside, curiously alien to the spirit of Keane, with its stone walls, and its grassy banks, and its rugged farmsteads of stone, and its wintry spirit, was about them, and in the distance rose the bleak and tremendous heads of the mountains of Cumberland.

Hindley village was near. Keane looked out eagerly, noting every feature of the landscape with ardent eyes. They came to the brow of a steep hill. The road was flanked by high banks overgrown with brushwood and ferns. There was a curious gloomy red colour in the road, and there was red in the pools of water that showed here and there.

"Hindley village is down in the bottom," said the perched-up driving lad, turning his ginger-coloured head and profusely freckled face to Keane. "Where d'you want to stop over?"

"I should like to go straight to the Hall."

"Aye? Then that's oop the hill t'other side of the village."

"Take me there, please."

"Aye, I'll take you."

The hill was very steep. The horse took it gingerly, his collar shifting loose on his neck towards his head, the shafts thrusting forward on his flanks. Looking down between the banks Keane presently saw smoke rising among leafless trees, then houses appearing in a deep hollow, then the hollow opening out, meadows, a river swollen with winter rains, reddish in colour, swirling in loops and dimpled with sucking eddies, thrusting its winding way seaward almost level with its banks, in the distance another steep hill crowned by woods.

"There's Hindley village and Hindley river," said the driving lad pointing with his whip. "And oop there yonder in those trees is the Hall where the poor Colonel lived. All the village belonged to him, the fishing and all for miles. But he died in Loondon. I've seen him many times walking, all blind as he was, with Will Marsh. He was a great walker, the Colonel was, oop to the last till his illness took him. We'll be passing the Inn in a minute. It's on the left. The Paradine Arms they call it after the family."

Again he pointed with his whip.

"You can glimpse it there! See those chimbleys?"

"Yes."

"That's it then."

"When I've looked at the Hall I'll go there and have a drink and look round the village. And you can rest your horse for a bit."

"Aye. You can get a good soop of beer at the Paradine Arms."

They were now at the entrance to the village and the lad cracked his whip and drove briskly to make a show for the few people about. Several fishermen in raincoats were whipping the swollen river standing in the wet meadows. Mist hung about the trees. There was an intensity of moisture everywhere, a pervasive watery feeling, but the houses were well built of stone and looked cheery and comfortable. Many of them were obviously 'model' dwellings built on a careful plan within the last twenty years or so, and the Inn looked inviting, clean and homely, with its walls of roughcast, its porch decorated with hanging pots full of ferns, its shining windows, and the blue-grey smoke rising from its broad chimneys.

It took them only a few minutes to traverse the village and then another steep hill confronted them.

"Noo it's a climb an' all!" said the lad, who was evidently now feeling thoroughly friendly. "Coom oop with you!" he cried to the horse.

And they began the ascent.

"Is it far to the Hall?" asked Keane.

"Far? Why, we'll be there in ten minutes noo. It's at the top of the rise."

Sitting right round in the tub-like wagonette to face the hill, Keane looked intently at every feature of the landscape. His mind was placing her here, was trying to conceive sharply of her life here with the blind man.

"Who owns the place now?" he asked.

"I couldn't rightly tell you. There's an heir, but he's not coom yet. And not cooming, they do say, as the Hall's oop for letting. You thinking of taking it, sir?"

"Well, I just want to have a look at it."

"Here's the gate in. There's no lodge, but it's a fine big hoose though nothing like Mooncaster."

"Where's that?"

"Mooncaster Castle, what used to be Lord Mooncaster's place above Mooncaster."

"Oh, of course!" said Keane, to diminish the lad's evident astonishment.

The horse was trotting now on a well-kept drive that wound between plantations, in which Keane noted some fine oaks, ash trees and elms, growing in grass that was heavy with moisture.

"Look at the rabbits, sir!" said the driver. "They want keeping down. Will Marsh used to thin them oot proper when the Colonel was alive."

"Who was Marsh?" asked Keane insincerely.

"The Colonel's body servant, sir. Here's the hoose!"

The drive had widened out into a large open space edged by closely cut turf with flower beds, now empty of flowers, rose bushes and some fine flowering shrubs, now of course derelict in this Northern winter. Confronting them was the Hall, a long two-story building of weather-worn brick, mellowed to a harmonious dim colour by time and the play of the elements, with a plain front broken by a large porch with pilasters. The sloping roof showed many chimneys to some of which ivy was clinging. To the right, as you faced the house, was a brick wall at right angles to it with a very wide door set in it. Beyond this wall, at a little distance, was a range of outbuildings, probably, Keane thought, stabling, outhouses, a garage, and perhaps servants' bedrooms. The wall evidently enclosed a big yard. As he got down from the wagonette he noticed that all the windows on this side of the house were shuttered. The garden, though well kept, was deserted at present.

"I suppose there's someone living in the house," he said.

"Likely there'll be soomone," said the lad. "There's a bell to the side."

Keane stepped slowly into the wide porch, which contained two oak benches, one on each side, found an electric bell and pressed it, then waited. As there was a delay, no one coming, he turned round and looked out at the silent domain sheltered from the outside world by its trees. A silence that seemed to him brooding prevailed. What had been her life here with a blind man?

He turned and again pressed the bell, keeping his finger upon it for a longer time than at first.

Then, soon, he heard steps, the rattle of a chain being let down, the grating of a key being turned in a lock. It seemed to be turned twice; then the big door was pulled slowly open and a man in shirt sleeves and with rough, very dark hair stood in the doorway looking out with stern blue eyes.

It was William Marsh.

"Eh, Will Marsh!" called the lad from his perch. "Who'd thought you'd be here an' all? Here's a gentleman from Loondon coom oop with an order to see the Hall!"

Although Keane was tremendously startled by the unexpected sight of the man he had been dwelling on mentally for weeks, and who formed part of the great plan he had developed for the salvation of Mrs. Paradine, he resolved instantly not to show that he recognised Marsh. Why exactly he came to this immediate resolve he didn't know. Perhaps he had an instinct of self-protection. Or perhaps some emanation from the mind of Marsh affected him. Anyhow he did not show even a flicker of surprise to the man facing him but pulled the order he had obtained from the house agents in London out of his coat pocket, offered it to Marsh and said in a businesslike way:

"I want to look over the Hall and the grounds, please. I hear the place is to let."

Marsh who, on his side, had shown no recognition, held out a big muscular hand for the order, glanced at it, gave it back, then said in a deep, resonant voice, full of strength and masculinity:

"You can come in, sir."

Keane stepped into the house and Marsh shut the heavy door. They stood together in semi-darkness that seemed to Keane full of the scent of desertion and emptiness.

"If you'll wait here a minute, sir," said the resonant voice to

Keane, "I'll be opening the shutters. The house is all shut up, and there's none too much light."

And he walked away, a tall shadowy bulk in the dimness, treading firmly with, Keane thought, a sort of military stride.

"The fellow's terrifically male!" Keane said to himself.

Physical, and perhaps mental, power, but certainly physical power manifested itself in the man immediately at a first contact with him. Standing alone in the dark hall, hearing shutters opened in the distance, seeing the wintry afternoon light filtering in to the empty house, Keane was conscious of a curious combination of qualities that was strongly conveyed from Marsh's personality to his own; the combination was of animalism with austerity.

A tremendously animal body surely, this man's, but perhaps held in check, or at any rate fought against, by something acutely austere in the brain and soul.

Would that unusual combination convey temptation to a woman, to a certain kind of woman?

The grinding of heavy shutters being unfastened and pushed back filled the hall; the wintry light grew in it. Marsh's martial striding steps moved on through the empty rooms and presently sounded only faintly in the distance on the parquet flooring.

Keane waited.

Of course he expected Marsh presently to return, but after a long pause which was filled with silence, he heard a different, much lighter step and the rustling of a dress. Then an elderly woman appeared from a corridor. She looked like a respectable caretaker, wore a print gown, had grey hair twisted into a knob behind a round head, and a large, kind and somewhat pathetic face with a pair of faint eyes that looked newly washed in it.

This was not the housekeeper who was going to give evidence at Mrs. Paradine's trial. Evidently things were changed at the Hall though William Marsh still remained there.

"Good afternoon, sir," she said, in a mild voice that smacked rather of the Midlands than of Cumberland. "Marsh says you've an order to view. Please come this way."

"Thank you."

They went together through the rooms on the ground floor, still full of furniture now shrouded in dustsheets, of cabinets void of bibelots, of pictures covered up, of electric lamps dressed in muslin. The carpets and rugs had been stripped from the floors, leaving bare parquet over which their steps tapped with a dry, unimaginative sound.

The caretaker spoke very little at first, but presently, in a big drawing-room, where Keane stood in a bow window absorbed in contemplation of the scene outside, she ventured on:

"It's a fine view, sir, isn't it?"

"Wonderful!" said Keane.

"But makes one sad, sir, don't it?"

"You find it so? Have you been here long?"

"Well, I come from near Birmingham, sir, and only been up here since a few months before the poor Colonel died."

"Were you in his service?"

"I was, sir, but in the dairy. I was in charge there. The poor Colonel he did love my butter. He said no one could make butter like me. What a death for him, sir, wasn't it?"

"Very sad indeed!" Keane agreed in a colourless voice. "And you knew Mrs. Paradine?"

"Her as they're charging with it, yes, sir. I didn't see much of her, but she come in the dairy sometimes. A beautiful lady, sir, but I couldn't make her out."

"No?"

"Perhaps because she was foreign, sir. She was always very nice but—there was something. One couldn't tell, sir. There were times when she'd look quite funny, sir, almost like a sleep-walker as you might say, sir. But she seemed very fond of the Colonel, sir, and he wasn't too easy with her either, poor man."

"What is your name?"

"Emma Prite, sir. My husband's Albert Prite. He belongs here and bakes in the village. That's really how I come to be here. I married him late in life. And now they've asked me to caretake the house till it's let. Mr. Marsh is only here for a day or two helping to keep the place clean. He don't live in the house. He don't sleep here. You wouldn't get him to."

"Why not?"

"He was too fond of the Colonel, sir. He can't bear the house now but will come up when he's needed—by will power, sir."

"Ah! He's got a will then?"

"Oh, sir, tremendous, or he couldn't be here. He hates the house now because the Colonel's gone from it."

"I thought perhaps he'd show me round."

"Well, he might have. But he came to fetch me. 'You go,' he says. 'It's your duty.' I was busy at the time, but he made me come. And I'm sure I'm very pleased to do anything I can. Shall we go upstairs, sir?"

"Yes. I should like to see the bedrooms."

They ascended a broad staircase and Keane went through the rooms above. In one he lingered without knowing why until Mrs. Prite said:

"This was where Mrs. Paradine slept, sir, and next door was her sitting-room."

"Indeed!" Keane said, now knowing why he had lingered. The room was, perhaps, full of her influence. Again he looked out of a window.

The house stood almost on the edge of a steep descent that resembled a cliff. In front of it ran a broad terrace edged with a low stone parapet, on which at intervals stood vases of stone no doubt filled with plants when the house was occupied. Below this terrace, at a considerable depth, ran the river, guarded and decorated by weeping willows whose tresses hung over the water. On the farther side was a great stretch of water meadows, arable land, and gradually rising ground clothed with trees, and, looking far off in the misty landscape, were the screes holding Wastwater and the giants of the Scawfell range beckoning the watcher on to the Lake District, to Derwentwater, Bassenthwaite, Buttermere, Ennerdale, to Skiddaw, Grassmoor, Glaramara.

A marvellous view but, as Mrs. Prite had said, "makes one sad." The beauty of it was wistful and melancholy, and suggested Life closing in on a man not opening out to infinite possibilities, a landscape of almost tearful loveliness touched in its far off with gaunt and stony romance.

To live in this house with a blind man, who was difficult, even bitter and perhaps brutal because of his blindness! William Marsh as an intimate, though a servant, in the household! Marsh with that striking animality linked with austerity. An extraordinary fellow undoubtedly; a silent quarrel surely enclosed in a frame so remarkable that some might think it magnificent, though others might be repelled by it.

And where was he now?

In a very few minutes Keane knew where Marsh was. Leaving Mrs. Prite for a moment in the corridor, with a casual: "I'll just glance into the rooms on the other side. Don't bother to come with me," he went into a room on the left of the porch before which stood the wagonette, gently opened window and shutter, pushed back a leaf of the latter and looked out. William Marsh was just below in conversation with the driver. Keane looked down on the top of his head thickly covered with dark, strongly springing hair, now roughened and in picturesque disorder with the wind blowing through it. And although Marsh was in the middle of apparently earnest talk, and had his back to the house, directly Keane's eyes were on him he twisted his head quickly and gazed up. And as he did so, pushing his head back, he drew his lips back, too, and showed his big white teeth.

And for a moment Keane saw him solely as an animal, a handsome, staring, panther-like animal.

The two men looked into each other's eyes from below and above for an instant. Then Keane called down:

"Would you be good enough to take me round the garden?"

Marsh seemed to hesitate, then said:

"Very well, sir."

"Thanks."

Keane drew in and was about to draw the shutters to and to close the window when the caretaker appeared.

"I'll do it, sir. Let me."

He let her do it, glanced into a couple more rooms, went downstairs with her, gave her a handsome tip and allowed her to open the Hall door for him. The carriage stood there; the lad was on his perch; but he was alone; Marsh was gone.

"Where's Wi—where's the man I spoke to from the window?" asked Keane.

The lad looked down. His freckled face seemed embarrassed.

"He's gone, sir. He was called away."

"But he was to show me the garden."

"He was called away soodden, sir."

Keane stood for a moment. Then he got up into the carriage.

"You can drive me to the Inn," he said.

He forgot to salute the caretaker who was standing in the doorway.

As the carriage disappeared round a curve of the drive between the trees, William Marsh came from the stable yard through a small door let into the big door. The caretaker was still there in the porch.

"The gentleman was expecting you to show him round the garden, Mr. Marsh," she said.

"Let him expect!" said Marsh, in his rough, powerful voice. "I'm not here for that. I'm here to help with the cleaning and beating carpets. And I only do that because I think perhaps *he'd* have wished it."

He strode into the house.

XXIV

AT THE Inn door Keane got down. He told the driver, who still seemed not quite at ease with him, to have some beer if he liked, and to rest the horse, and to be ready to start for Sedale in half an hour. The landlord of the Inn, an enormous man who had in his time been a famous wrestler, came to welcome the new guest and showed Keane into a cosy dining-room.

"You've been 'aving a look at the 'All, 'ave you, sir?" he said. "Ah, that's been a bad business with the poor Colonel! What'll you like, sir?"

"Just a cup of coffee, thanks."

"I'll send the girl, sir."

He lingered, evidently inclined for some talk, but Keane didn't encourage him, and repeating: "Then I'll send the girl, sir," he went heavily away.

In a few minutes the girl brought the coffee, and bread and butter which Keane hadn't asked for. Keane drank, but didn't eat, then lit a pipe and went out to the Inn door. The landlord, who must have heard him, came at once from the bar and joined him. By this time Keane, who had been sunk in thought, felt more disposed for conversation and began to ask some questions about the village and the neighbourhood, but almost immediately he noticed that the landlord's manner towards him had changed.

It was still genial, but the geniality was obviously mingled with a curiosity which the man was quite unable to conceal. Keane caught the fellow watching him with a sharp, almost ferrety interest, which didn't seem to accord with his mighty frame, but rather to belong to a much less bucolic personage. Evidently the increasing of the flesh upon him hadn't stifled his mind. Keane realised that he was with a creature who, though perhaps beery, was very alert. What had caused this sudden and intense curiosity? Keane's young driver was no doubt having his 'soop of beer' in the bar. The landlord had just come from there. William Marsh had been talking to the driver. Keane realised that probably he was known.

"Will you have a glass of beer?" he asked the landlord.

"Thank you, sir," he replied. "I don't mind if I do 'ave a soop. Agnes!" he roared.

The girl who had waited on Keane hurried out.

"Bring me a pint of bitter."

"Yes, sir."

There was a bench in the porch. Keane sat down on it and drew on his pipe.

"Beautiful country round here," he said. "What's it like in summer?"

The landlord broke into eulogy which was heightened when the bitter arrived and had been put to his lips.

"You'll soon have a tenant at the Hall, no doubt," said Keane.

"I'm sure we 'ope so, sir. We all miss the poor Colonel's coostom."

The landlord hesitated for a moment, then ventured:

"D'you think they'll get her off, sir—Mrs. Paradine?"

Even now Keane wasn't absolutely certain that Marsh had said who he was, and he answered casually:

"Difficult to say. What do the people hereabouts think?"

The landlord's enormous face looked cautious.

"Well, sir, they 'ardly know what to think. There's soom for 'er and soom t'other way."

Keane looked steadily at him.

"What is *your* opinion? You're an intelligent man, a man of substance, able to judge as well as anyone in the place. I should say."

Again the landlord hesitated, looking this time more important, more definitely like the man of substance Keane had called him.

"Well, sir," he said at last. "What I *do* say is why should the lady do it? If she weren't 'appy with the poor Colonel, why not leave 'im, though, to be sure, it would seem 'ard to leave a blinded man? But better leave 'im than make away with 'im."

"Surely!"

"And yet, sir, it do seem as soombody must 'ave done it. And, as I've said many a time no further away than the bar there"—he pointed with his left thumb—"if it wasn't Mrs. Paradine, then who *was* it? Seems to me that's where the danger like do lie for 'er, that there's nobody else to pitch upon for it. But there!" (Suddenly he looked very shrewd, even sly.) "P'raps they lawyers'll find soomone. They're rare ones for lookin' aboot."

And he confronted Keane with a gaze of bland innocence which convinced Keane absolutely that William Marsh had told the driver and that the driver had retold the landlord. This sudden innocence was too definite, too pronounced to be natural. Being now convinced, Keane had a natural longing to call the landlord's bluff, and show that he wasn't such a fool as the landlord probably supposed him to be. The very pointed remark about lawyers being rare ones for looking about was indeed such a 'give away' on the landlord's part that it was difficult not to take it up at once. Yet Keane merely murmured a casual agreement.

"That's their business," he observed. "They're paid for it."

"Aye, aye, sir," agreed the landlord. "And paid well they *do* say, though I've never 'ad to do with them. Was you thinking of taking the 'All, sir?"

"Well, I wanted to have a look at it. It's a well-built place, nice grounds, and a fine view. Can I have the bill?"

The landlord looked rather taken aback at this apparently unexpected request, but he drained his glass hastily to the bottom and with an "I'll fetch it, sir," turned to go to the bar.

"And please tell my driver to bring round the trap."

"Aye, aye, sir. I'll tell 'im."

When the man had gone, Keane knocked out his pipe and got up from the bench. He felt for the moment irritated. The landlord at that moment was probably having a good laugh over his own supposed cleverness with the driver, in the bar. And William

Marsh had coolly evaded the interview Keane had tried to arrange with him. What would have happened during that interview, had it taken place, Keane didn't know. Perhaps very little. Marsh's evasion of it possibly indicated that he had been afraid of it. His look up at the window had been definitely hostile. But he was certainly a man with much self-control. He must have been greatly startled when, on opening the door of the Hall, he had been confronted by Keane. But he had not shown it. Their mutual non-recognition had been due apparently to a common impulse. But if they had walked together through the grounds of the Hall, it would have been difficult to sustain their piece of acting. Knowing the swiftness with which suspicion is roused in the breasts of the comparatively uneducated, Keane was not really much surprised at Marsh's conduct, though he was irritated by it, and felt on account of it like a man 'bested' by another. But he was destined to be genuinely surprised later on by conduct of a contrary nature. For a moment, however, as he stood in the porch of the Inn facing the fading afternoon and the swollen river winding its way towards the Hall through the damp meadow-land, he had a very definite sensation of having made a mess of things. And yet he had gained something. He had seen her former home; he had felt her atmosphere; and he had intensified his impression of Marsh.

A difficult fellow to deal with, undoubtedly; a difficult fellow to handle. A man full of obstinacy and perhaps full of cunning. But also, it seemed, full of heart—but not for the many. Perhaps even not for the few. There are strange beings who must concentrate, who cannot share or divide. Marsh might be one of them. He must have loved his Colonel, and perhaps was unable to love anyone else. Had he—could he have—loved him so much that he had sent him out of this world of trouble?

Standing in the porch, Keane wondered about Marsh's religious belief, if he had any.

"The trap's cooming round, sir, and the girl's bringing your bill," said the landlord, returning.

At the same moment the grinding of wheels became audible on the pebbles strewn in front of the Inn, and the wagonette arrived from the stable yard.

"We shall be seeing you again, sir, likely?" said the landlord, with his shrewd look.

"I think not," said Keane, with great definiteness.

"He'll pass that on to Marsh no later than to-day," was in his mind.

"I've seen what I wanted to see," he added, buttoning up his coat to the chin, for the air was growing colder as evening drew on. "And I'm not staying long in the North."

"Sorry, sir."

"I may be off to-morrow."

The girl came with the bill. Keane paid it, tipped her, said good-bye to the landlord, got into the wagonette and was driven away.

The landlord stood looking after him.

"What did 'e coom after?" he said aloud, as he watched the vehicle growing dim down the road among the mists rising from the river.

Although Keane had given that reply to the landlord he had no intention of cutting short his stay at the Sedale Hotel. But he did not wish Marsh to know this. If he did know it, he might possibly get away from Hindley, or if he remained there might be wary and keep in hiding from the lawyer-chap. For he was certainly filled with suspicion. Whether this suspicion was the sign of a guilty conscience, or whether it was merely due to the natural working of a crude and untutored brain inclined to be doubtful of other men's motives, Keane could not tell. He had not been able to make up his mind about William Marsh, and because of this, Marsh held him in bondage.

During the drive back to Sedale, Keane did not exchange a word with the lad on the perch. The ease between them had been destroyed by the revelation that Marsh must have made at the Hall.

When they arrived at the Inn it was growing dark and there was a blustering wind from the sea.

As Keane reached up to give a tip to the driver, the lad said:

"Thank you, sir. Will you be wanting me to take you Hindley way to-morrow?"

"No," said Keane, with the definiteness he had shown to the landlord. "I only wanted to have a look at the Hall."

And he turned away to the Inn door.

In the passage the landlady met him and hoped he had had a pleasant trip.

"And did you see the Hall, sir?"

"Yes, it's a fine place."

"And it is that, sir. But noo it's like to stand empty, they think."

"Who thinks so?"

"The Hindley folk, sir, because of the poor Colonel's murder. But what I say is, he wasn't murdered *there*, so what does it matter? Meaning to anyone taking a fancy to the Hall. I'm sure I hope some rich gentleman will be taking it soon. We all want coostom oop here in these hard times. Can I send you some tea and toast to your room, sir?"

"Yes, please do. Is the fire burning?"

"There's a fine red fire, sir. I've seen to it myself."

The long drive in the cold air had made Keane hungry. He was glad to get into the warmth of his snug, though tasteless, little sitting-room and to sit down in an armchair before the fire, which, as the landlady had affirmed, was a noble and glorious red.

There were two windows to the room, one facing the same way as the front door of the Inn, the other facing the station and the sea. Venetian blinds rattled above them now, for both had been left slightly open at the top, perhaps to let out smoke from the fire before it had settled down into its present steady glow. Outside the room another rattling joined the chorus of the blinds. This was made by the loose brass latch of the door which opened on to the grass between the hotel and the station railings. Keane got up and shut one of the windows and let down both the Venetian blinds. A maid brought in the tea-tray. When she opened the door, Keane heard the shifting latch more distinctly. It sounded like an uneasy and furtive thing. The wind seemed to lay hands on the two windows and shake them mercilessly. But it was cosy indoors. And after tea he smoked by the fire, looking over some papers which he took from his despatch case. Presently, he returned the papers to the case and sank into deep meditation. He had turned out the gas and sat in the firelight. For a long time he sat almost as still as a dead man, but his face had not the calm austere gravity of the dead. There was a tormented expression stamped upon it. And he was tormented.

If only he could know! If he could absolutely know what she was, this woman for whom he was working! And if he could know what Marsh was! Till now he had not thought that his was a wavering mind, had not thought himself an uncertain man.

But since he had been involved in this Paradine case he had been full of uncertainty. He had had his moments of conviction, but they had passed, they had not remained with him.

He was, and he knew it as he sat by the fire, companioned by the wind from the sea, working in the dark. The defence which he had decided to put up for Mrs. Paradine would be a weapon forged in a mind which wasn't sure, wasn't completely convinced, didn't *know*.

He remembered the saying on the cover of Schuré's book, *L'Ame est la clef de l'Univers*. It was probably true. It was, he believed, true. But how was a man to get hold of that key? How was he to come at a knowledge even of his own soul to say nothing of the souls of others, of those around him, of those nearest to him, who meant most to him? A longing that was angry came to him to force Mrs. Paradine to reveal to him, to lay absolutely bare to him, the secret of herself. He could not make up his mind about her. He had begun by doubting her, by thinking she had probably committed the murder she was accused of. Later he had felt positive that she was innocent and had looked upon those who had perhaps doubted her innocence as his enemies. The spell of her personality had worked upon him powerfully from the very beginning of their acquaintance. He remembered his irritation with Sir Simon Flaquer when they had been driving together from Holloway Prison after the first joint interview with Mrs. Paradine. That irritation had been caused by his suspicion of Sir Simon's opinion of her. And the rift between Sir Simon and himself had grown wider with the passing days till that evening when Sir Simon had certainly tried to get him to resign from the case. Keane knew why. Sir Simon suspected the truth. Keane wondered whether others suspected it. Judith Flaquer was terribly sharp and observant, and deeply attached to Gay. She was a danger. Then there was Mrs. George Blason. Suspicion of the truth, or of part of the truth, must have been at the back of her probing feminine mind when she had spoken to him on that Sunday afternoon at the Flaquers'. And as to Gay, he felt sure now that she knew it.

Was he transparent then? Or did the big things in a man insist upon being known just because they were big?

How the windows shook and how that uneasy latch on the outer door rattled!

He must make up his mind, must get his mind clear about the connection between Mrs. Paradine and William Marsh before he went back to London. That was the cause of his mental torment and restlessness, his uncertainty about that. There was, there must be, some secret shared by Mrs. Paradine and Marsh which he had not penetrated.

He got up from his armchair and stood by the fire. He had the feeling, ridiculous enough, that he was trying to force his mind physically to give to him what he wanted, the knowledge that was withheld from him, as a man might try to force a man physically to give him a treasure hidden in the hand. His whole mind was on the strain. He had come up here driven, vaguely on the track, because she had lived here in the North, and Marsh had lived here, and what had happened had been determined by events up here. He had not made any definite plan of what he would do when he arrived in the North. Something would surely happen there to enlighten him. That had been the conviction at the back of his mind when he had determined to get away. And he had it still even though what had happened that afternoon had brought him no tangible result.

"Something must happen here. I must get to know something here. There was a reason for my coming up here. Otherwise I shouldn't have felt compelled to come here."

A tap on the door startled him tremendously. He flung round, faced the door, and instead of calling out "Come in!" called out in the voice of a startled man:

"What is it?"

The door was opened, and a rosy-faced maid showed herself, and announced in a very low and demure voice:

"If you please, sir, I was to say that sooper is ready."

"Oh! Is it seven?"

"Yes, sir."

"I'll come at once."

"Yes, sir."

As he went out he heard the rattle of the latch and saw it shifting against the wood of the door.

There were only three other people at supper, two nondescript elderly ladies, evidently sisters, who spoke to him and, to his surprise, inquired if he wasn't 'from Cockermouth,' and a fat man wearing a gold 'Albert,' who looked as if he were a commercial traveller. Tea had spoilt Keane's appetite and he ate very little and got away from the 'coffee-room,' as the apartment was called, as soon as he could. The landlady met him in the little hall by the bar, when he was about to turn down the passage which led to his sitting-room.

"Good evening, sir. I hope sooper was to your liking?"

Keane made some polite remark. As he did so he noticed a change in the landlady's face. It was wreathed in smiles but the eyes were remarkably intent, almost 'beady' with intentness.

"This is my little room, sir. Won't you step in and see it?"

She pointed to the open door of a room on the right of the front door. Keane saw a bright fire, a large work-basket standing on a round table with a red cloth, some stuffed birds, a horsehair sofa.

"If you would honour me, Sir Malcolm!"

Ah, that was it! The driver had spread the news.

Keane felt obliged to 'step in.' The landlady followed and immediately shut the door.

"I didn't know before, Sir Malcolm, you was the gentleman who was to stand for poor Mrs. Paradine, sir, at the trial in Loondon. We wasn't expecting such an honour, sir. I've read such a lot of you in the papers, sir, and seen your photo, too, but didn't recall it when you asked for the rooms. Oh, sir, *do* you think you can get the poor lady off? I'm sure *I've* nothing against her, nor anyone here, though there's those at Hindley who thinks different I know. But when it coomes to poison, and such a man as the Colonel was, of course there would be those as——"

"I'm sorry I can't discuss the case," Keane interrupted the good woman in his most formidable manner. "It is what's called sub judice. That is, it's a case not yet tried. And as I'm concerned in it I can say nothing about it. Those are very nice birds."

"Yes, sir," faltered the landlady, evidently greatly taken aback. "My poor 'usband collected them."

Though not given to it she dropped an *h* in her confusion.

"And now I must leave you. I'm going to take a stroll on the front before turning in. Please have the fire kept up, and I should like a Scotch whisky—Black and White if you have it—and a bottle of soda-water put in my sitting-room."

"Certainly, Sir Malcolm."

"Thank you. Good night."

"Good night, sir."

Keane got his coat and cap and went out. He felt all on edge. But it was his own fault for having come up to this neighbourhood where everyone of course knew, or had seen, her, where everyone was talking about her and looking forward eagerly to the trial. Curiosity mongers!

"I'm sure *I*'ve nothing against her!"

He was glad when he was out in the wind and the starless night. He passed through the station, crossed the line, and went down to the sands. And he walked on them for a long time.

It was half-past nine when he got back to the Inn and, remembering the landlady, he avoided entering it by the main door and made his way across the grass strip and the pebbly path in front of his sitting-room to the side door with the latch. In the darkness he had not noticed the figure of a man standing on the pebbles under the projecting eaves at the back of the station, close to the gate he had passed through.

As he reached the side door an express train from Whitehaven roared through the station on its way to the South. Keane stood to watch the rear lights of the train disappearing. Then he pressed down the brass handle of the latch, opened the door and went in.

Just after ten the maid came to his sitting-room to inquire if he wanted anything more. The whisky and soda-water were already on the table. He told her he wanted nothing and wished her good night. An instant later he heard her shooting two bolts top and bottom on the outer door. It was evidently bedtime for the personnel of the Inn. But Keane had no intention of following their example. Work had made him a thorough-going night bird. Before midnight he could not sleep. He lit a fresh cigar and sat down at the round table in the middle of the room. It was strewn with documents and writing materials. He took up a pen and began to write on some manuscript paper. The wind was always strong, and though the tide was not high it carried to him the perpetual sound of the sea. The night was alive with voices. Though perpetually conscious of them Keane was able to ignore them and to concentrate because they were not human voices. But though he was sunk deeply in work, preparing always for the coming case at the Old Bailey, presently he lifted his head, looked towards the window that faced the sea, put down his pen, and sat in the attitude of a man listening intently. He heard the windows shaking; he heard the struggling outer door which the violent wind moved in spite of the thrust-in bolts; he heard the rattle of the latch. And then he heard a knock.

He must have heard one before while at work.

He got up at once from the table and stood by it. After a pause the blow was repeated. It was struck on the outer door. He realised that the gas light in his room could be seen outside through the Venetian blind.

He hesitated. Then he went out of his room into the dark passage, stood for a moment considering with a frown on his forehead, then came to a decision, drew back the bolts and unlatched the outer door.

X X V

IT WAS perhaps strange but Keane did not feel surprised when he found William Marsh standing there in the darkness. He must have anticipated this without being fully aware of it. Otherwise he must have been surprised. Marsh was in a navy blue suit without an overcoat in spite of the keen wind. A dark blue handkerchief was knotted round his throat. His head was uncovered. Directly he saw Keane he said in his deep powerful voice:

"Can I speak to you, sir?"

And Keane, as simply, replied:

"Yes. Come in."

He stood back against the passage wall and Marsh, with a stride, was beside him.

"Am I to go in here, sir?"

"Yes. Go in."

Marsh walked into the sitting-room. Keane shut the outer door and followed him and shut the sitting-room door. Then Keane said:

"I don't know why you have come to see me at this time of night but please sit down. How did you know this was my room?"

"I saw the light, sir. I know the Inn well. And there's nobody much staying here but you, nobody as would have a sitting-room anyhow. And I saw you come through the station and go to the door there, coming from the beach."

"You've been here some time then?"

"I walked over from Hindley."

"To see me?"

"Yes. I had a thought to see you."

All this time they were both standing. Now Keane repeated his invitation and sat down himself. Marsh hesitated for a moment, then said: "Thank you, sir," sat down on the opposite side of the round table covered with documents and loosened the handkerchief at his throat. Keane saw his strange eyes, very blue, with their curiously animal look mingled with—or was it rather at moments replaced by—the Knight-errant expression, go to those documents, then glance quickly away while his lips set together in a grim line.

"Can he know?" Keane thought.

It was impossible obviously, yet Keane felt as if, by some occult faculty, Marsh had pierced through into the core of his mind and knew the danger to himself that had been conceived there.

"Why have you come to-night? What d'you want with me?" Keane asked, after a pause during which he looked closely at Marsh as he sometimes looked at a witness he was about to cross-examine.

"Beg pardon, sir, but I thought it was *you* wanted to see *me*, that's why I come over."

Keane felt taken aback. Marsh's manner was respectful but extremely definite. He looked Keane straight in the eyes with an intensely masculine fearlessness that had no touch of impudence and so could not be resented. There was something soldierly in his gaze and something austere. Yet there was that suggestion of the animal carrying with it a strong hint of male sensuality. This was a troubling man, too definite, too complex for comfort, impossible to ignore or escape from in any attempted flight of mental avoidance. He drew you back, pinned you down. While he was there you had to be attentive to him. Besides his powerful physical influence Keane felt he had a psychic influence. Of the latter he was probably unconscious but surely not of the former. He had beauty that might not be to everyone's taste because it was not of any ordinary accepted type, but was peculiar, not bringing you to it consciously, but rather unconsciously holding you off. There was cruelty in it and dominance, and about the lips a touch of contempt that roused a fighting spirit in Keane.

"But the fellow's superbly handsome in his uncommon way!" Keane thought.

"And what caused you to think that?" Keane asked, in a deliberately light tone.

"Well, sir, you came to the Hall."

"I didn't come to the Hall to see you. I didn't know you were there. I came to see the house."

"Yes, sir, I know. But you asked me to show you over the garden."

"That's true. I did. And you, after agreeing to do so, went off on some lying pretext and left me to be put off by the driver."

Although Keane's words were severe his manner and tone were entirely free from anger, or even irritation.

"Does that leave you any excuse for coming here by night, surreptitiously, and disturbing me at such an hour when I'm busy working?"

Again Marsh's blue eyes went to the documents on the table.

"I'm sorry, sir," he said. "But I thought I'd better come."

He looked down. He had laid his large brown hands, not coarse hands but very muscular, with broad palms and nails curving over on the fingers, upon the table. Now he seemed to be looking at them. Keane noticed two depressions on either side of his straight nose by the slightly arched nostrils, a deep line between his thick dark eyebrows, the cheekbones standing out in the crude gas light. There was something very formidable about the man, formidable in his physique and also formidable in the suggestion of character behind it. But Keane said to himself that Marsh did not belong to the criminal type. And there was absolutely nothing mean or shifty in his appearance. Yet he might be cunning in a deep subterranean way. But there would surely be something big, something unusual and personal to him even in his cunning.

"It's for you to tell me why you thought that," said Keane at last, as Marsh said nothing more.

Marsh seemed to be deeply considering something. He looked across the table at Keane and said:

"What for did you open the door when I knocked, sir?"

"I didn't know it was you."

"Well, but a man comes and knocks in the night and you come straight and open!"

"For all I knew it was a visitor at the hotel shut out, who saw the light in my window."

"That's true. It might 'a' been."

He stopped, then said, with almost harsh bluntness:

"But you wanted to have to do with me, sir. It's no manner of use all this because I know it. I felt it at the Hall when you looked down from the window. Your call went right through into my head."

He put up a hand and struck his forehead gently.

"It's in here and I know."

Brought up against this absolute conviction of the man Keane realised acutely how unorthodox, from the lawyer's point of view, was the situation he was in. The advocate for the defence in dark conclave with a hostile witness upon whom he meditated making a deadly attack; deep night around them; wind and the voice of the sea tumultuously addressing them from without; the sleeping Inn about them. And the reason for this? What was it? On his side—what, and what on Marsh's side? What could they say to each other? What could possibly come of this interview? Danger lurked in it. It was dangerous for him to have to do with this man now that the trial was not far off. Dangerous—unless Marsh knew how to keep things secret. It occurred to Keane at this moment for the first time that possibly Marsh had laid a trap for him and that he was falling into it.

"Why didn't you come to the front door of the Inn?" he asked abruptly. "What was your object in coming to the side door?"

"They've all gone to bed, sir. I didn't want to wake the house."

"But you might have come earlier. You said you were at the station when I came from the beach."

"I didn't care to come earlier, sir."

"Why not?"

"I leave that to you, sir," said Marsh, unemotionally and totally without impertinence.

Keane threw a piercing look into his eyes and kept them on Marsh for an instant before he spoke again. Then he said:

"Am I to understand that you don't wish anyone to know of this visit of yours, this interview?"

"I don't see why they should, sir. It's no business of theirs."

"Remember this, Marsh! You forced yourself on me. I didn't seek you."

"But you came to the Hall, sir."

"That had nothing to do with you. I had no idea you were there."

"But you wanted me to go round the grounds with you."

Keane felt an immense power of obstinacy in the fellow. He felt, too, that to some extent Marsh had the power to read his mind.

"You were there. I wanted to see the grounds. I knew nothing about them. Naturally, as there was no gardener about, I asked you to accompany me. Why, by the way"—he put the question sharply—"did you avoid doing so?"

"At the time I didn't feel like it, sir. Afterwards, I thought perhaps I'd made a mistake in not coming."

Keane got up. He went to the fire, made it up, then thrust his hands into his pockets and turned round, remaining on his feet. Marsh didn't move. He sat, Keane felt, doggedly in his place and he kept his eyes on Keane. Probably he knew the impulse which had brought Keane to his feet and was endeavouring to counter it. Keane believed so. That impulse was to tell Marsh to go, to turn him out, politely, of course, to tell him it wasn't fitting that they should talk together in this secret way, that he had nothing to say to Marsh and didn't wish to hear anything Marsh might possibly have to say to him. If Marsh was laying a trap this would be the best way out. Keane knew he ought to do this at once, and he had got up with the brusque intention of doing it. But then he had dealt with the fire. A subterfuge! A means of delay! And even now he stood for a moment in silence, hesitating to act. He told himself that he was a fool in his hesitation. If another man in his position did what he was doing he would criticise and condemn him. But he stood there. He felt as if he couldn't let Marsh go without making an attempt to get at the secret of his relations with Mrs. Paradine. He was burning with a terrible personal curiosity about them. It wasn't at that moment any care for her and her fate that prompted him. It was this abominable personal necessity to know what had been between them, what was between them now. And Marsh sat there as if he meant to stay, as if he too had something he wished to know, or something he wished to tell. And they were both held in a bondage of silence.

"Better get rid of him! I must tell him to go!" Keane said to himself.

And he looked down at Marsh and Marsh looked across the table up at him, and Keane couldn't tell him to go. Not just yet. Not till something more had happened. The wind still beat about the house and the windows shook, and beyond the room door the outer door, now unbolted, struggled like a living thing, and the latch trembled against the wood and uttered its dry, vital sound.

"And this fellow's come all the way from Hindley in this gale and the darkness to see me. Now he must have something he wants to say. But what the devil is it?"

And it struck Keane that perhaps the best way to find out what it was would be to ask Marsh to go. Then, perhaps, he would be forced to come out into the open. On the other hand he might just get up and walk out into the night without a word. He was capable of that, too, this living enigma. Again Keane wondered whether Marsh, after seeing him at Hindley and considering things, had thought of laying a trap for him, and was there for that purpose, or whether, being perhaps highly sensitive, perhaps even psychic, some mysterious sense had warned him that danger lay for him in the brain of Keane, and this danger had lured him out into the night and brought him to Sedale. There are men who shrink from danger and would go anywhere, any distance to avoid it; but there are men whom it draws as a magnet the needle; they must pursue it to confront it. Only in this way can they conquer the obsession it lays upon them.

"What are you here for, Marsh?" he asked, resolving to face things at whatever cost. "It's a long way from Hindley. You walked?"

"Yes, sir."

"Are you staying the night in Sedale?"

"No, sir. I shall be walking back."

"In this blackness and wild weather!"

"Oh, I've done too much soldiering to mind little things like that!" said Marsh, with a touch of masculine contempt. "This is naught to France in the war."

"Still you must have had a strong reason for coming. What was it?"

"Tell me yours for coming up here, sir, all the way from London. And I'll tell you mine for knocking you up to-night. And that'll be a bargain."

Keane felt rather like a witness 'cornered' in cross-examination; yet, strangely perhaps, he did not resent the extraordinary line Marsh was taking. Afterwards he wondered why he had not done so, and found the explanation in the under things which abolish at moments the class differences, and indeed all the surface differences between man and man, and force men, often against their wills, into a brotherhood that seems to be the deliberate work of destiny.

"A bargain!" he said. "Why should I make a bargain with you?"

"That's in your will, sir, to go one way or the other. All I say is 'tell me and I'll tell you.' That seems to me fair enough."

Keane meant at this point in the conversation to bring it to an end, but the fire of curiosity, of that curiosity which is like a deep necessity to know, overcame him again. He felt that he could not separate from this man leaving things as they were. He must go further with him. Yet how could he bring in her name? She was the only reason of his painful interest in Marsh. Marsh must of course know that, and must realise fully that interest by now. If her name were not mentioned, if her case were not touched upon, what was the good of their being together? Of what use was any prolongation of this interview? A longing, that he felt as brutal, even as coarse and primitive, came to Keane to belch out the truth of his soul to this man, to say: "There! that's how it is with me! And now to your part of the bargain. Uncover your nakedness to me."

He caught hold of his chair, held the top bar of it, twisted it round and sat down sideways at the table.

"You see all those!" he said, pointing at the documents on the table. "I was studying the case you're in, the Paradine case. It's getting near now. Before long it will be decided one way or the other. It's giving me a lot of trouble. In London it's difficult for a man like me to get as much quiet for continuous and clear thought as such a case as this requires. I found I could get out of London for three or four days and decided to come up here.

I went to the Hall at Hindley to see if the place would give me any impression that would help me. Perhaps you'll wonder how it could. But I can't explain. I shall go there probably again to-morrow. I shall visit the grounds. I shall absorb some of the atmosphere of the place. And possibly, when you hear me in the Court at the Old Bailey, you'll partially understand my reason in coming here. Your presence at the Hall was quite unexpected by me. But as I found you there I thought I'd make use of you. You thought otherwise and yet you follow me here. Next time I go to the Hall—to-morrow in all probability—I shall not want you to show me round. I shall prefer to be alone. I've got an order to view, which gives me the right to examine the grounds. You can't prevent me. In a day or two I shall have done what I meant to do, have got all I can get to help me up here, and I shall return to London. And you and I shall meet presently at the Old Bailey and have it out there. Yes, we'll have it out there."

Keane said the final words in an almost menacing tone. While he had been speaking it had occurred to him that possibly by show-ing hostility to Marsh, definite hostility, he might provoke him into an outburst which might prove a revelation of character.

"You're apparently going to be a very hostile witness in this case," he added, after a moment of silence, which Marsh did not attempt to interrupt. "You're not one of my witnesses. You're against me. I didn't come up here to try to get at you. I'm not a budding lawyer. I'm an old hand in the Law. And I don't do what's irregular. My reason for coming up here was a perfectly legitimate one. I came on you entirely by chance."

"But you wanted to come on me, sir," said Marsh quietly.

"You choose to say so!" said Keane, with well-assumed careless contempt. "And now perhaps you'll tell me what you've come here for in this surreptitious manner. And if you don't care to do that, then I'll ask you to go—right away."

"What did I come for?" said Marsh, slowly. "What did I come for? Well——" he looked down, seemed to be considering deeply —"I was drove to it. After you went somehow I couldn't rest till I come here. I thought: 'He wants me. Very well, then, he shall have me.' And I started to come."

"Want you? What should I want you for?"

"But you do, sir. Can you say to the contrary?"

And at that moment Keane felt that Mrs. Paradine in him had drawn Marsh there from Hindley in the night. For an instant it was to him as if there were three in the room, Marsh, himself and Mrs. Paradine; the accused woman, her defender, and the man who perhaps was going to witness against her. Had there been a reason for his coming into the North which he had not suspected till now? Had the woman in Holloway Prison pushed him to it? He had not told her he was coming. She didn't know he was here. Yet perhaps she had pushed him to it in ignorance which was nevertheless linked with some desire, some longing, which guided her instinct and had influenced him without his having been aware of it. Perhaps he had had to come because of something in her. Perhaps it was necessary for her salvation.

Moved by this idea, which at that moment took complete possession of him, and governed by a sense of fatalism which made him feel utterly careless of personal consequences, Keane leaned on the table with his shoulders high, his head thrust forward and his gaze gripping Marsh's.

"It's my business, my job, if you like to call it so, to save the life of your former mistress."

"Beg pardon, sir," Marsh interrupted. "I never had a mistress. Colonel Paradine was my master. I was his batman in the army. He was colonel of my regiment. Later I was his personal servant. I should never have served a woman. It isn't in me to do that. Excuse me for interrupting you. But I had to set you right."

"Have it your own way!" exclaimed Keane, trying to conceal his profound irritation at the interruption, and remembering his detection of fanaticism in this man, a fanaticism which now surely confronted him squarely.

"I have to save Mrs. Paradine's life. They've chosen me as the most likely man for that salvation. Do you realise what you are up against?"

"I don't understand you, sir."

"It seems to me that you're inclined to take me rather casually. You receive me at the Hall, where you're evidently engaged still in some capacity. You leave me waiting and send someone else to see me. Meanwhile you go and gossip about me to my driver. Later, I ask you to show me the grounds. You agree to do so, and promptly bolt. To-night, apparently, you think better of it and walk miles in the dark to get at me. You wait till everyone's gone to bed, and then slink round to that side door"—he pointed—"and knock surreptitiously to draw my attention to the fact that you're there. You insist on it that I want you for some purpose. Any interest I have in you is a legal interest. It arises from your connection with an important case which I'm involved in. Of course I'm interested in you for the time. But once this case is settled and done with you'll mean nothing more to me."

"Well," said Marsh doggedly, "say what you like, sir, I believe you come up here for me. Directly I clapped my eyes on you at the Hall door at Hindley I knew it."

When Marsh said that, Keane thought again of Mrs. Paradine's salvation, and again had an obscure and mysterious sensation that in coming up to the North he had been led, had been compelled to do what he had done by some secret power working for an end he had known nothing of and using him as a means to that end. He was not accustomed to any feeling of this kind, being a tremendously definite man, full of self-assurance, and self-reliance, strong in belief in his own powers and putting them forth as a rule with a thoroughly complete knowledge of why he was doing it. No man, probably, had a more natural conviction of free will than he normally had without thinking about it. So now he was troubled and even perplexed, and he looked across the table at Marsh with a sort of cloudy questioning in his eyes. What Power was using him, and for exactly what purpose? What must he do? How was he to avoid a false step? This man opposite to him had perhaps Mrs. Paradine's fate in his grasp. How was that fate to be taken out of his hands? Or, if that couldn't be, how was he to be influenced, or compelled, not to hurt her? With one part of him, Keane knew that he ought not to prolong this interview and indeed, ought never to have allowed it to begin; but, with another part of him, he seemed to know that he must continue it and that it was of immense importance both to him and to the cause he was engaged in.

"You may be right," he said at last. "But I didn't know it. I'll swear I didn't know it. Wait a minute, will you?"

He got up again from his seat and went to stand by the fire. He was trying to extricate himself from the meshes of mystery in which he had the feeling of being entangled. He must come out of them, must be convinced that he, and not some Power, a stranger to him, was dealing with this matter, would bring it presently to a conclusion.

He felt for his pipe, found it on the mantelpiece and began to fill it. All this time he had his back to Marsh, but was feeling him intensely. He struck a match and put it to the tobacco. A little red glow showed in the pipe bowl, increased and diminished. The marvel of fire! The secret power that caused it! He threw the match into the glow that the grate was full of. He turned round to Marsh. He was yielding to the mystery he wished, with one part of his mind, to get rid of or to dominate.

He saw Marsh looking at his pipe.

"You will have a cigarette?" he said.

"No, thank you, sir."

"Don't you smoke?"

"I won't smoke, sir, thank you."

Keane remained standing with his back to the fire.

"If I came up here for you," he said, "I don't know why."

"Didn't she send you, sir?" said Marsh.

The question startled Keane, not only because he wasn't expecting anything so direct from Marsh, but because it marched with his curious suspicion that perhaps Mrs. Paradine had pushed him to do what he had done, to come up into the North. Were he and Marsh then thinking along exactly similar lines?

"Mrs. Paradine didn't even know that I was coming," he said. "She doesn't know that I'm here. She—she had nothing at all to do with my coming."

"Seems I'm wrong then," said Marsh, with an accent of incredulity.

And Keane wondered whether he was wrong.

"Why should she send me?"

"There might be a reason."

"I don't know what it could be."

"Because perhaps you don't know her as I do."

Again that terrible gnawing curiosity took possession of Keane. He knew it now for the curiosity of a lover. No man but one who was a lover could feel it. It was the supreme curiosity that is only connected with love.

"She's my client," he said, with a coldness that he felt to be a lie.

"I know her as lawyer knows client. That's quite enough for me."

"You may not think it," said Marsh, "but you're on the wrong side, sir, and I tell you so."

When he said that a new idea sprang up in Keane's brain. Was Marsh's extraordinary visit to him prompted by fear? Was it conceivable that he had come with the intention of turning him, Keane, against Mrs. Paradine? Keane was known, even to the man in the street, to the class in which Marsh was numbered. He was the most popular advocate of the day in criminal cases. And the man in the street reads criminal cases. Marsh must know of his power, of his supreme ability in defence, of his influence over minds, of his capacity, unrivalled in England, of getting people off who were accused of crimes. Perhaps, then, Marsh was afraid of him and had actually had the fantastic impudence to imagine that he could influence him against his client, could produce in him doubts of her, and could thus steal away from him some of his thunder. It had seemed to Keane not many minutes ago that if anyone knew, or ever came to know, of this interview, he might be suspected of having tried to 'get at' a witness. Was this interview really owing to the fact that this fellow here, Marsh, actually thought that he might 'get at' an advocate?

The whole of Keane hardened at the suspicion. But for that awful curiosity he would, without a moment's delay, have turned Marsh out of the room. Hating himself for saying it, but unable to govern his tongue, and ready to disbelieve whatever Marsh said about Mrs. Paradine, or thinking himself so ready, Keane put the question:

"You said just now that I don't know Mrs. Paradine as you do, and now you say that I'm on the wrong side of this case. What do you mean exactly? Make yourself clear, if you can."

"She's a lady that takes a lot of knowing, and you can't have had the time nor yet the chance to know her. Why, you've seen her only since she's been in prison."

"Of course!"

"What's that then? Do you think a woman in prison, waiting her trial, is like a woman out in life, free to follow her whim? Can she be gay in a cell, or carry on secret doings, or plot and get away with it as she might out in the world with others to take her cue from or give it to? How much, I ask you, sir—" he seemed to put in the 'sir' with a jerk as an afterthought—"can anyone do shut up all alone? It's people make actions. It's people bring thoughts and prompt them. How do we get to know a woman? By seeing her, hearing her, with others out in freedom, carrying on according as she's made. And men too! I've been in the army for years. I lay claim to know a lot about men. But how did I get to know them? By paying them a visit now and again when they were given cells for something they shouldn't have done? Not a bit of it! By seeing them on the spree, and in the trenches, and at drill and on march, and drunk and getting sober after it, and with women and with each other in the dormitories and the canteen, and here and there in the ups and downs of a soldier's life. That's how! To read a book right you have to turn over a hell of a lot of pages. And so it is with people, but specially with a woman. Believe me, sir, you don't begin to know Mrs. Paradine."

Once he had begun to let himself loose and to speak freely Marsh showed a sort of fiery animation that, as Keane said to himself, is often, even usually, the possession of the fanatic. The words rolled out in his big deep voice and hit on Keane's ears with a force that seemed like the force of stones. And of course Keane was obliged to recognise that there was truth in them. But Marsh evidently allowed nothing for intuition, that mysterious faculty which often guides those who have it more surely than observation.

"So you say!" he said, stiffly.

For he was full of rebellion, just because of the truth in Marsh's words. And he was all on edge, too, with the hostile fear which a man feels when he hears criticism of one whom he longs violently to know thoroughly from one who, he suspects, knows her much better than he does.

"But isn't it true, sir?"

"It may be true in a general way."

"I say it's true in all ways, sir, and believe me if ever there was a woman alive who needed knowing it's Mrs. Paradine. Why, she ain't even British."

"What has that to do with it?"

"No man can ever understand a foreigner, what they call an alien, as he can one of his own country. And they Northern women they're the worst ever to get hold of in the way of understanding. And as to her, sir, well if ever there was a woman of Babylon she's one."

Marsh let out the last words with a sudden gust of concentrated hatred that reminded Keane of the blast from a furnace when the furnace door is opened. The heat of it struck on him, startled him, brought him suddenly to a decision that he would stick to in despite of the gnawing curiosity which tormented him. This conversation must stop, this interview come to an end. He ought never to have allowed it. He oughtn't to have admitted Marsh. There was certainly no question of the salvation of Mrs. Paradine here. He realised thoroughly the implacability of this man. It might arise out of a reasonable hatred, or out of craven fear for his own skin, out of the fervour of a soldier's love, or out of some deep-seated cause inexplicable, which perhaps Keane would never be able to penetrate to. Keane was confronted with it and would no doubt be presently confronted with it again in the Criminal Court of the Old Bailey. Then perhaps he might be able to break it down, but not now. Now he had only to get rid of this man.

He waited for a moment striving for complete self-control, for he was violently excited but determined not to let Marsh suspect it. He laid his pipe down on the mantelpiece, listened to the wind, demanded of his nature to keep quiet.

"I can't discuss my client with you," he said at last in an uneven, unemotional tone. "You sought me out to-night. I didn't seek you at Hindley. My coming on you was a chance. Your visit to me here had nothing to do with chance. I can't be sure why you came. But if it was in order to unsettle me in my relation with my client, and turn me against her and so weaken her case before the Court and do her, perhaps, irreparable harm you've failed utterly. I take nothing from you. I judge for myself. And now, please, I must ask you to go."

Marsh got up at once.

"Very well, sir. Good night to you."

He put up his big brown hands to the handkerchief round his big column of a throat and gave it a pull.

"There's a wind to-night and no mistake," he said.

The heat seemed to have gone out of him, but his blue eyes were stern as they looked hard into the eyes of Keane.

"You'll come to know some day I'm right," he said. "And sooner than later."

Then he went out. He shut the room door gently behind him. In an instant Keane heard the click of a latch, a louder roar of the wind, the bang of a door pulled forcibly against resistance, then the heavy crunching of footsteps on the narrow pebble-covered path that edged the green under his window.

Mechanically he picked up his pipe. He waited for a moment, then went to the outer door and shot the bolts top and bottom. The Inn was in darkness, but the maid had left him a candle to light him to bed. He returned to the sitting-room.

What had been Marsh's motive in coming? Had it been fear and the determination to try to strike a blow for himself? He looked a fearless man. There was something at moments high-minded in his appearance, but there was certainly a background of animalism, and at the core of his nature was violence. This Keane knew and the knowledge came to him from his own violence. Like recognises like. In Marsh's hatred of Mrs. Paradine there was something tremendously personal, something terribly intimate, so intimate that Keane did not believe it could be due even to Marsh's belief in her crime, if he were innocent and had such a belief which was still, in Keane's view, completely doubtful. The intimacy of that hatred suggested a deeply personal motive, a motive in which surely the body must be somehow concerned as well as the mind. The complete man must be in it unless——

Could Marsh be a consummate actor playing a part for his own salvation? If there was anything in Keane's theory for the defence surely that must be assumed. And yet Keane could not believe Marsh had been acting that night. And because of that he felt weakened for the battle, as if some of his armour were inadequate and in consequence he was vulnerable.

Now he had seen the Hall, the house where the drama that had preceded the end had been played out. He could visualise it and its setting, that misty landscape, the winding river in the depth beneath the terrace, the willows streaming to the water, the far off mountains lifting their stony crests to the dark sky.

Body and mind in that hatred, unless it were but a simulation of feeling. Body and mind. But what did that imply?

Keane pressed more tobacco into his pipe but did not light it.

He was thinking so deeply that he did not know what he had done, did not realise what he omitted to do.

Marsh had called her "a woman of Babylon." An absurd expression, but it had not sounded absurd on his lips. It was his way of expressing an opinion of a character that apparently now revolted him, his way of expressing a truth loathsome to him. Or it was his way of telling an abominable lie. There came into Keane's mind the words: "Oh daughter of Babylon wasted with misery. . . ."

Then he was back in London sitting with a woman in Holloway Prison.

"Marsh is a liar!"

He muttered the words. Then he bent over the table, swept the documents scattered over it together and thrust them into his despatch case.

"He's a damned liar, but he'll not influence me!"

He lit the candle and turned off the gas. In the dimness the wind seemed louder. He stood with the candle in his hand and stared at the place where Marsh had sat a few minutes before.

Colonel Paradine's servant, and she had once been a servant.

He stared at the empty chair.

Body and mind—two servants. And he had called her a woman of Babylon. A new conception of a possible reason for Marsh's hatred of Mrs. Paradine crept through Keane's mind. It was immense with black possibilities.

He shivered as he stood there, shivered like the windows under the assault of the gale, like the candle flame in the wintry breath from without.

XXVI

KEANE stayed on in Sedale for four days after his interview with William Marsh at the Inn. In spite of what he had said to the driver he engaged the trap again and drove over to Hindley. He left the trap at the Paradine Arms, then walked up the hill to the Hall. He did not ring at the house door, but wandered for a long time about the grounds, visiting the terrace in front of the drawing-room windows, the shrubberies, the flower gardens that stretched to right and left of the long plain house, the woods that surrounded them, descending by a steep winding path to the river bank and among the tressy willows watching the swollen river hurrying seawards between the sodden banks of the meadows.

As he wandered where she must often have wandered, curled up in his mind like a motionless snake went with him the suspicion which had attacked him in the night when Marsh's footsteps had died away on the pebbles of the path beneath the window. He felt that it did not stir, but just remained, like a thing alive but embedded, still, venomous. He seemed to look upon it sometimes from a distance; at other times he was close to it, watching like a man hypnotised. And there it lay like a thing curled up in its home, from which it obscurely knew that nothing could dislodge it. And it was full of deadly poison. He would presently carry it with him to London, carry it into his house, bring it near, bring it close to Mrs. Paradine. Never would he be able to rid himself of it till he knew the exact truth of the connection between Mrs. Paradine and Marsh, and perhaps he would never know that. If his dreadful suspicion were well founded it would account for Marsh's hatred of Mrs. Paradine absolutely, though it would not so absolutely account for her attitude towards him. But she was, Keane believed, far more complex really than Marsh, peculiar and very unusual though he was. Her surface simplicity, which had charmed him at the outset of their acquaintance, he was now convinced was nothing more than a natural manner, perhaps in-born, not a manifestation of her true character and whole men-tality. He was positive that beneath it she was complex, intensely vital, clear-sighted, clever and possibly ingenious. Her unknow-ableness—he coined the word for his use—fascinated him strangely. Until he had met her, loving Gay, he had always felt that his nature responded instinctively towards that which could be com-pletely understood and completely trusted. He had not felt any lure in the unknown, in that which puzzles the heart of man, which disturbs his intellect, and confuses his judgment. Yet now he had been captured by the exact contrary of what he had hither-to delighted in.

He had left London by a night train and by a night train he returned to London, changing into the express for the South at Carnforth. He dined in the train. Opposite to him at his table for two there was a business man from Carlisle, who entered into conversation and presently spoke of the Paradine case. Evidently the whole of Cumberland was full of it. Without expressing any particular interest in it Keane nevertheless encouraged him to talk. He seemed an intelligent, well-balanced man of an ordinary type, not without shrewd common sense, just the type of man who would be useful on a Jury. His 'trouble,' as he phrased it, about the case, and apparently the 'trouble' of most of the North Country men he had talked with on the subject, was that there seemed to be no ascertainable motive for anyone, either Mrs. Paradine or anyone else, to murder 'the Colonel,' as he called Colonel Paradine familiarly.

"Then Mrs. Paradine had no lover apparently?" Keane said, in a tone of casual interrogation.

"Not that anyone heard tell of," said the man. "Of course there are some who say she might have liked the Colonel's man. Marsh I believe his name is. But there doesn't seem to be any proof of it. And from all one hears Marsh isn't a man who would ever look at any woman, much less his master's wife. It's said he's a rare woman hater. Still I suppose any man living might be caught by some woman. A fellow I know who was in the war has seen Marsh, and he tells me Marsh is one of the handsomest chaps he ever clapped eyes on, but fierce-looking and as hard as nails. The case is coming up before old Horfield. And if any Judge can get at the bottom of it, *he* can. They say that for all he's a Judge he's very hot stuff himself. But he has got a brain."

Keane agreed that Lord Horfield, the Judge, had a brain, paid his bill, bade his companion good night and returned to his sleeper.

So in the gossiping mouths of the men of the North Marsh's name had been coupled with Mrs. Paradine's!

Keane undressed and went to bed, but kept the light on. He did not read, however, but lay there and smoked. And the black suspicion lay with him curled up in its home like a sleeping snake. And all the night long enclosed in the roar of the train he brooded over the problem of Horfield and that other problem which tormented him. His short spell of solitude was over. With every moment he was getting nearer to the place that would see the end. It would all be settled soon one way or the other, be taken for ever out of his hands. But meanwhile his whole nature would be tried to the uttermost. He hoped he would prove equal to the strain that

would be put upon him. He had never 'cracked up' yet, but he
had never before had his whole being drawn into a case.

It was snowing when the train came into London. As it began
to slow down and the first chimney pots appeared in the cold light
of the wintry dawn Keane, already up and dressed, watching the
snowflakes dropping on to the mean roofs of the little houses which
bordered the line and melting away into blackness, felt the sudden
thrust of a spear-like thought through his mind.

Suppose Fate, the incalculable thing men called Fate, took a
hand in this game that must be played out for a woman's life?
Suppose Horfield should be removed from the case by some sudden
accident, by illness or death? Men worked blindly in the dark. The
totally unexpected is continually happening. It was odd that up
at Sedale in all his brooding cogitations over Horfield and Horfield's connection with the case Keane had never once thought of
that possibility. Horfield was *there* and would try the case. Starting
from that point of conviction Keane's mind had beaten about
Horfield. What could he do to influence Horfield? What could
be done about Horfield? Was there anything that could be brought
into play by him, Keane, which could lessen, or remove, the danger
existing in Horfield? And never had it occurred to him that it
was possible that Horfield might be prevented by *force majeure*
from trying the case. He did not know why it occurred to him
now, as he looked at the leaden wintry sky, and the snowflakes,
and the mean little houses waking to their mean little lives in the
dawn. But it sent into him a ray of hope, like a very pale sun-
beam struggling out of the dark.

There are surely fighters in life that are not born of women.

"We shall be in now in a couple of minutes, Sir Malcolm," said
the attendant respectfully. "There's a lot of snow this morning."

When Keane arrived in Portland Place he was met by Sausage,
who bustled to the door directly it was opened and welcomed him
with a joyful importance that was almost official.

"Have you been a good boy, Sausage?" he asked, caressing the
little leaping fellow. "No tearing up of cushions, eh? How has he
been, Baker?"

"I'm glad to be able to say Sausage has behaved himself, Sir
Malcolm."

"My wife's sleeping, no doubt. It's so early."

"I don't think her ladyship has rung her bell yet, Sir Malcolm."

"I'll have some tea at once and just run through my letters."

He went softly to his study accompanied by Sausage.

Letters had not been forwarded to the North. Since he had been there no word had reached him from London. He found a big post laid out on his table. While he was drinking his tea and dealing with the post, he heard a faint noise in the house. It was Gay's bell sounding to summon her maid. He listened. The maid would be there in a moment and tell Gay he had arrived. He must go in and report himself.

The snow was still falling heavily. He thought of his interview with Lady Horfield at the exhibition of Sedelsward's pictures. Henceforth, he would always connect her horrible revelation with snow. He took up another letter. The address was in Sir Simon's writing. He tore the envelope. Inside was a short note marked *Private*.

Dear Keane,

When you are back, I shall be glad to see you. Ring me up in Bewly Place. Time's running short now and we've still a good deal to go into. I want to talk to you about the best line to take with Horfield. We must be very careful not to get his back up. I have met him twice within the last three days and thought he seemed in a rather extraordinary mood. I'll explain what I mean when we meet.

Yours very sincerely,
SIMON FLAQUER.

Horfield again! Keane frowned as he memorised the note, then tore it and threw the fragments into the fire.

But there was Destiny, the mysterious Power that interferes. A touch of influenza—something like that—might transform the whole situation.

Gay's maid, Franklin, appeared at the door.

"Good morning, Sir Malcolm."

"Good morning, Franklin."

"Her ladyship's having her tea, sir."

"I'll go in at once."

But he waited for nearly five minutes before leaving his study.

He was beset by an ugly feeling of being transparent after his sleepless night, and the snow affected him, too. He always felt peculiar in snow. It didn't suit him. He wished that the day were flooded with sunshine. Then perhaps——

He set his lips together hard and went out of the room.

As he came into Gay's bedroom the fire there was just beginning to burn up brightly. Beside Gay's bed on a tiny table was a tray with a small silver tea-pot and a cup and saucer on it. Directly he opened the door, Keane smelt tobacco mingled with another quarrelling perfume. Gay, sitting up in bed against heaped pillows, was smoking a cigarette. On a table not far from the fire stood a large china pot filled with growing hyacinths.

"Smoking already, Gay!" he said, surprised.

He came to the bed.

"Don't tell me you slept with those hyacinths in the room!"

"No. Franklin's just brought them in."

He bent down to kiss her forehead.

"I'd no idea you'd become such an early smoker."

"I like a cigarette with my tea. Did you have a good journey?"

"I didn't sleep much."

He sat down, as in duty bound, by the bedside. Gay smoking before breakfast! He had never known her to do that before. In fact, until just lately, she had never smoked, and had told him more than once that she had never had any wish to smoke.

"You look rather tired," she said, in a gentle, expressionless voice. But her eyes were not expressionless.

Gay had large eyes, and though she was short-sighted, except when occasionally she peered, she had not the blind look some short-sighted people have. Her eyes were kind and soft and very intelligent, but occasionally they sent out a long gaze of scrutiny. And when they did that it was as if all her soul were gathered together in deep and earnest inquiry. Keane knew that gaze well and had loved it. There was something childlike and amazingly unselfconscious in it that had often touched him, had made him want to put his arms round Gay and shelter her from all the attacking troubles and misfortunes of life. It was the look that made Judith Flaquer say, 'little Gay.' But now he saw a new expression in Gay's eyes and it was not unselfconscious, not inquiring. There was surely something negative in it, something like an almost furtive refusal. Her eyes seemed to be saying to him: "No, no—don't!"

And they fell before his eyes.

"What has happened to Gay?" he thought.

And he felt convinced that while he had been away in the North, something had occurred which had tarnished her natural frankness, which made her now strangely selfconscious with him, uneasy in his presence, uncomfortable when his eyes were upon her. He could not imagine what it might be, but instinctively he connected it with Mrs. Paradine, and a fierce curiosity bristled in him. While he had been away Gay had done something, or had been involved in something, which was connected with the Paradine case and which must therefore affect him. And she did not want him to know, or to suspect, what it was.

"Have you had tea?" Gay asked.

"Yes, directly I arrived. Sausage met me. Baker says he's been good. No more destruction of cushions."

"No. My punishment has been effective. Sausage remembers."

She took up another cigarette and lighted it at the one she had been smoking.

Chain smoking! Gay!

"What have you been doing while I've been away, dear?" he asked, trying for a casual tone of voice, but keeping his eyes on her, anxious to surprise any fleeting sign of disturbance or confusion.

She told him, mentioning various small circumstances.

"That all?"

"The first night you were away, after the journey night, I dined with the Horfields," she said.

"Really!" he said, surprised. "How was that? A sudden engagement, wasn't it?"

"Yes. Lady Horfield rang me up the morning after you left and said that as she knew I was alone would I dine with them and go to the Adelphi Theatre. They had a box. I accepted, as I had nothing else."

"Was it pleasant?"

"Quite pleasant."

"Somehow, I can't see you perched up in a box by the side of Lady Horfield."

Gay didn't speak for an instant, but then she said, in a curiously inexpressive voice:

"Lady Horfield didn't come to the theatre."

"Not come! But I thought they asked you expressly because they were going."

"So they did. But when dinner was over she felt suddenly unwell. It seems she suffers from blood pressure. And she had to lie down. She lay on a sofa in the drawing-room, and we waited a little, hoping her malaise would pass. She had vertigo. But as she didn't feel better quickly she insisted on our going without her."

"Oh! So you passed the evening alone with Horfield?"

"Yes. He was very entertaining."

"Was he? Well, now I'll be off and have a bath. I have a lot of things to do to-day."

He went out of the room.

His valet was running the bath. After the railway journey he looked forward to it, a hot bath, but not too hot. He would stay in it for ten minutes, losing some of the fatigue of a sleepless night in the train. He undressed and stepped into the water.

His short interview with Gay had left him strangely disturbed. It was not only what she had told him that had disturbed him, but her look and manner when telling it and even before she had told it. Her selfconsciousness was unusual, and he had the definite impression that at first she had meant not to tell him of the evening with the Horfields. He had also the impression that after she had mentioned the dinner she hadn't wished him to know that she had gone to the Adelphi Theatre alone with Horfield; and had only let him know it because he had made the remark about being unable to see her perched up in a box by Lady Horfield's side. She had waited for a moment after that, and during the pause had evidently made up her mind that it would be best to say what had happened. But she had certainly wished to deceive him; she had certainly wished that he should not know it.

He felt very uneasy.

Somehow, Gay's narrative of Lady Horfield's sudden seizure after dinner hadn't convinced him. He wondered whether the seizure had convinced Gay at the time as genuine, and whether for some reason later she had lost faith in it and, so, had conveyed a doubt about it to him. But Lady Horfield, for all her eccentricities, was certainly neither crafty nor insincere. Keane could not imagine her playing a part to Gay of her own will.

But Horfield might have compelled her. There was something slavish about her in connection with Horfield. She seemed to worship him in terror.

What was the matter with Gay?

Keane had always instinctively disliked Horfield, although he had always admired his gifts and his intellect. But since the revelations, fragmentary and yet drastic, of Lady Horfield, he dreaded and loathed him. Gay oughtn't to be with such a man ever. He hated to think of Gay spending a whole evening alone in Horfield's company. And probably Horfield had taken her home after the play; no doubt he had taken her home.

Suddenly the note from Sir Simon which he had just memorised recurred to his memory: "I want to talk to you about the best line to take with Horfield. We must be very careful not to put his back up. I have met him twice within the last three days and thought he seemed in a rather extraordinary mood. I'll explain what I mean when we meet."

Instantly he connected that statement with what Gay had just told him. He must, without fail, see Sir Simon that day.

The best line to take with Horfield! Careful not to get his back up! And he loathed the man, and moreover had one of those naturally expressive faces that are apt to show feeling with too much sincerity. When he was off guard! But Horfield had said he would have made a good actor if he had not become a barrister. Well, he must prove his powers as an actor, and on the very man who had made that statement.

But it would be difficult going. Still, he must try. Lady Horfield, in that last interview among the snow scenes, had begged him to get on the right side of Horfield. For Mrs. Paradine's sake he must make a big effort. There was nothing else to be done. He must beat down all his prejudices, stifle his loathing, play a part, and play it so well that that cruelly sharp intellect would be deceived. But it would be horribly difficult.

And what was the matter with Gay?

He got out of the bath, dressed, shaved and went down to breakfast.

At breakfast, Gay joined him, and they talked uneasily of one thing and another. Incuriously—as it seemed—she asked him a few questions about his time in the North. He described Sedale to her, told her of his walks on the sands, of the wildness of the weather, of the desolation that lay along the seaward edge of the land. Not a word was spoken of Hindley, not a word of William Marsh.

Horfield was not mentioned again.

The snow continued to fall.

Soon after ten Keane went down to his chambers. A little before twelve he telephoned to Bewly Place. The reply came that Sir Simon was at the Law Courts concerned in a case, but was expected to be in Bewly Place for an hour or two after four o'clock. Keane telephoned that he would be there at five.

Just after five he walked into the hall and met Warwick by the beehive chair. He was greeted with respectful cordiality and was taken up at once in the lift to Sir Simon's room.

Alfred Flaquer was with his father going through some documents with him, but got up at once on seeing Keane, and after greeting him went away.

"How's Alfred shaping?" asked Keane, to say something.

"Not badly. I hope some day he'll be able to take my place without wrecking the firm. Sit down, Keane. Smoke if you like."

"No, thanks."

"Had a satisfactory trip?"

"Well, I wanted to—shall I say imbibe? Yes!—imbibe some of the atmosphere of Mrs. Paradine's Northern home, and to study the case under its influence. And I was able to do that."

"Ah!" said Sir Simon.

For a moment he seemed to be waiting, but Keane added nothing. Before coming to Bewly Place he had made up his mind that he was not going to tell Sir Simon that he had met and talked with William Marsh. He felt certain that Sir Simon would entirely disapprove of that interview, and would only be irritated, perhaps even painfully vexed, to hear of it. That secret meeting between the counsel for the defence and the chief witness for the prosecu-

tion was decidedly not in order. And Sir Simon, though often
daring, sometimes even audacious in his conduct of a case, was
nevertheless a stickler for the legal proprieties, and disliked anything that savoured of irregularity. Of course, if the fact of that
interview having taken place should come out at the trial it might
create a serious breach between Sir Simon and Keane, but Keane
did not believe that Marsh would give it away. And if he didn't
it was most unlikely that the prosecution would get wind of it.

"And so you have come back satisfied?" said Sir Simon, after
a pause.

"I'm glad I went. The sea air has done me good. Wild weather
up there, but I wanted it. And now the great ordeal is getting
near. No more holidays till the verdict is given."

He forced himself to speak briskly and confidently.

"And so you wanted to talk to me about Horfield?"

"Yes."

"Anything wrong with him? You wrote of finding him in a
rather extraordinary mood. What does that portend?"

Sir Simon looked down at his large flat writing-table for a moment, then, keeping his eyes fixed on it, said in a low voice:

"You and I both know that Horfield doesn't, though he's a
Judge, lead what is sometimes called a very *straight* life."

"Agreed!" said Keane, wondering.

"I have known him for an immense number of years, and I
know a good deal about him, a good deal more than he has probably any idea that I know. I won't go into that. Every man has a
right to his own life. But so far as any situation, or event, in Horfield's private life is likely to have a repercussion on our case, this
Paradine case, we are, I think, bound to take notice of it."

"Of course!" said Keane, with increasing astonishment. "But
has anything——"

"One minute! Between you and me, Horfield's troubles in life
have almost invariably come about through his secret preoccupation with women. He's a man, as you know, who seems as cold as
ice and whose complete self-possession strikes everyone who comes
in contact with him. One would doubt his having a heart. It is
certain, however, that few men of his age are so governed by the
desires of the flesh. And when he is so governed, and his desire

cannot be fulfilled—that is, if he meets with resistance when he has been captivated, in his ugly way of being captivated—the reaction on his mind, and it almost seems on his whole nature, is extreme. He goes sour, Keane. That's the best expression for it. The whole man goes sour. Something of the kind has happened just lately. And Horfield has gone sour. That's bad for those near him. That's bad, I'm afraid, for *us*. The fact that a Judge is suffering from suppressed gout has made many a sentence far more severe than it need have been. Men and women have served, en masse, years in prison because of such trifling causes. You will say that there is the right of appeal. Granted! But it is sometimes difficult to find a strictly legal reason to upset a sentence even though it seems cruel. Better the sentence should never have been pronounced than that one should have to lodge an appeal against it. You're with me there?"

"Of course."

"Well, now we are up against the fact that Horfield, for some reason that I am positive is connected with a woman, is in this abominable condition, suffering no doubt himself, and so longing to make others suffer."

Keane looked hard at Sir Simon, wondering whether he had the faintest suspicion that Horfield was a Sadist.

"Have you," he said, slowly, "any idea at all as to who the woman is?"

Sir Simon raised his keen eyes from the writing-table.

"I have had no indication from Horfield as to who she is. But it's quite enough for me that there is a woman who is troubling his life just at this, for us, psychological moment. And for this reason—don't think I'm being super-subtle—it is singularly unfortunate that our client is a woman."

"Why so?"

"He is in the sort of condition, I fear, which might lead him to pay one woman out for his—shall we say ill success—with another."

At that moment Keane remembered the curious and subtle resemblance that Mrs. Paradine bore to Gray. And a dark cloud seemed to be forming mysteriously round him. Without making

any comment on this remark of Sir Simon's, just because it had
penetrated so cruelly into his mind, he said:

"I take what you tell me for granted, relying on your long
experience of Horfield. Now I should like to hear your views as to
what you call in your note to me the best line to take with him."

"I'll give them for what they are worth."

Sir Simon continued speaking for about five minutes. Keane
sat listening attentively. He was schooling his face. No changing
vivid expressions flitted across it. On the contrary it looked heavy
and almost glum because of his effort. When Sir Simon stopped
speaking Keane said:

"I see. I grasp fully what you wish, what you advise."

"I'm sure you do. I think it's important for us to avoid, so far,
of course, as we *can*, everything that might tend to ruffle Horfield. No one—" he smiled slightly—"can be more charming, more
winning than you when you wish to be delightful. Horfield is
more susceptible to manner, more sensitive even altogether, I
believe, than he seems to be. And so——" he lifted his hands in
an expressive and very un-English gesture.

"Lady Horfield over again!" thought Keane, remembering her
fantastic injunction to him to charm Horfield.

"I'll do what I can," he said.

They sat for a moment in silence. It seemed that what it was
necessary to say had been said. Yet Keane did not get up to go.
And at last Sir Simon asked:

"Haven't *you* anything to tell *me*?"

At that moment Keane was debating whether he ought to tell
Sir Simon of the black suspicion about Mrs. Paradine and Marsh
which had come to him in the North. Could the telling of it do
any good to the case? His own feeling of course was intensely set
against speaking of it. In fact it would be torture to him to mention it. Nevertheless, if the fact of Sir Simon, with his keen legal
intellect, knowing of it could in any way help the defence Keane
knew that it was his absolute duty to speak. Knowing it Sir Simon
might possibly make some acute suggestion that would help in the
conduct of the defence. But wouldn't it be a deadly sin against
Mrs. Paradine to speak?

"I don't know that I have," he said, slowly, and still quite uncertain whether he would speak or not.

"No?"

"Things float through one's mind of course."

"Yes?"

"It's difficult at times to know which have some importance and which have not."

"One has to sort them out."

"Exactly. No; I don't think I have anything special to say."

He got up, but as if with some hesitation, from his chair and said good-bye.

As he went into Bewly Place he said to himself:

"I can't tell him ever. It's too foul! And besides, I don't believe it. No, I don't believe it!"

XXVII

WAS Gay the woman?

Keane's mind was beset by that question after his conversation with Sir Simon in Bewly Place. And if she was did Sir Simon know or suspect it?

Directly Sir Simon had finished his exposé of Horfield's character and present mood, indeed even while he was speaking, Keane remembered his impression of the morning that something had happened to Gay while he had been in the North, and that she was anxious to conceal what it was from him. Lady Horfield's sudden attack of illness leaving her husband free for an evening alone with Gay! Gay's quite evident intention at first not to tell him that she had dined with the Horfields, followed immediately by another intention, not to tell him that Lady Horfield had not been with them to the Adelphi! Both these departures from Gay's invariable rule of being transparently open and sincere with him about the facts of her daily life had roused in Keane astonishment and suspicion. His visit to Sir Simon made him almost positive that he now understood their reason. Without knowing it Sir Simon had given the whole thing away.

Gay must be the woman whom Sir Simon had not named, but of whom he had spoken.

If this was so, and Keane definitely assumed it as fact, a new and dreadful complication had been introduced into the Paradine case. And it would be a dangerous one for Mrs. Paradine.

That cursed physical resemblance between her and Gay, even that might now do her harm.

For a moment it seemed to Keane as if the stars in their courses were fighting against her and him. A feeling of desperation came over him. It was mingled with a feeling of dreadful curiosity.

He had left Bewly Place on foot. The snow was still falling and there was a fog, though not a dense fog, feeling its way through the town. He walked slowly into Bond Street which was still thronged with traffic and crowded with pedestrians who looked mournful in the obscurity. The sadness of cities seemed to hang in the air, the sadness of human hopes and of human endeavours cherished and pursued in a fever of longing under dark skies. Snow lay here and there rapidly melting. In the lamplight the snowflakes looked like white aliens who, coming here from afar, had missed their way to a purer, more delicate region. Berkeley Square beyond Hay Hill was heaped white with snow.

Keane made his way there, then paused and stood still trying to make up his mind about something; whether to go home or to go to the Club. If he went to the Club it was probable that he would find Horfield there. He was drawn to Horfield by the awful curiosity and hatred which had now taken possession of him, a sort of nightmare sensation which he wanted to fight, as a man wants to fight imminent peril in a nightmare, but which, as in a nightmare, he felt powerless to resist like one bound by an impalpable power. At home there would be Gay.

Berkeley Square was not on his way home. Yet he had come there. It would be easy to get from there to Pall Mall. Across Piccadilly, past the Ritz and the top of Arlington Street, down St. James's Street and he would be there. But was it wise, in his present state of suspense and emotion, after a sleepless night in the train, to try to come in contact with Horfield? He felt it was not wise, but mechanically he walked towards the Berkeley.

He had the sensation of one being pulled by another more powerful than himself. And he gave in; he had to give in and pass through the snow to the lights of Piccadilly. And presently he was standing at the foot of the broad flight of steps that led to the wide portico of the Cleveland Club.

He looked at his watch. It was past six o'clock. Quite possibly even if Horfield had looked in at the Club, as he often did in the late afternoon, he had now left it and gone home to his house in Sussex Square. Better perhaps if he had. And yet that awful curiosity made Keane long to encounter him.

Keane went into the Club. There were men whom he knew in the hall but Horfield was not among them. He left his outdoor things in the cloak-room and mounted the broad staircase to the first floor. Several rooms opened on to the upper hall. Keane looked into the card-room. Horfield sometimes played Bridge. But he wasn't among the Bridge players. Beyond was the Silence Room. A few men were there in armchairs reading or meditating, or perhaps sleeping. Not Horfield!

To the right of this upper hall there was a long room lined with bookshelves but not a silence room. Here members often had tea and sat reading the papers and talking. It was perhaps the most friendly, most cosy room in the Club. There were two big fireplaces, one at each end, several writing-tables, and of course the usual settees, sofas and huge armchairs. Often a cloud of tobacco smoke hung in the air. Behind many of the armchairs there were electric reading lamps with red shades, which members turned on and off at will.

Horfield might be there. It was here that Keane had had tea with him the last time they were alone together at the Club. Keane opened the door and went in.

The long, rather dimly lit chamber was deliciously warm, and at the upper end, near the door, there were several groups of men talking, smoking, having drinks or tea and toast. The big fire blazed. Against the walls some of the reading lamps were turned on and, sunk in armchairs, men were busy with the evening papers. It was a typical picture of Club life in London, friendly, sociable, unpretentious and amazingly comfortable.

Quickly Keane glanced round him. He saw several men whom he knew and nodded to one or two of them, but he did not see Horfield. An elderly waiter, whom he had known for years, approached him softly and murmured:

"Can I get you anything, Sir Malcolm?"

"Yes, Simes, you might bring me some tea and toast. I'll go down to the other end of the room."

From where he stood Keane could see that very few men were there. He felt rather weary after a busy day and the sleepless night in the train. His brain was very much alive but something else in him was weary. If he were not fated to meet Horfield so much the better. In this seductive warmth he would sink down and for an hour give himself up to physical comfort and complete repose. He didn't want to be drawn into talk by any of these men.

He walked down the room, chose an armchair at some distance from the second fire, and sat down, picking up, as he did so, *The Evening Standard*. Opening it, he was about to glance at the leading article when the elderly waiter again approached him and murmured:

"I'm just bringing your tea, Sir Malcolm. Lord Horfield is over there in the corner, sir, if you wanted to see him."

The waiter, a privileged servant, had often seen Keane and the Judge in conversation.

Without raising his eyes from the paper Keane replied:

"Good! I'll go over to him after I've had my tea—here."

"Yes, Sir Malcolm."

The waiter retreated. When he had gone Keane, still holding the paper, looked over it surreptitiously. Where was Horfield? How had he missed Horfield? Had Horfield seen him?

His desire and intention to give himself up luxuriously to complete repose had left him. He looked quickly to right and left, he looked beyond the fire. And then in a far corner at the end of the room, with firelight playing faintly over him, he saw the figure of a man sunk in an armchair, his thin arms spread out on its arms, his long fingers holding its edges, motionless as a corpse, his eyes apparently bent down and gazing at the carpet. It was Horfield, alone, apart, either meditating profoundly or perhaps dozing; certainly, in either case, not observant of his surroundings. Indeed Keane had the impression that he was entirely unconscious of them. His narrow pale face, his long and narrow but intellectual head, showed in the dancing firelight, but the lamp behind him was extinguished. No one was near him. Keane sat quite still looking at him.

In a moment the waiter brought the tea. Keane dealt with it cautiously, trying to make no noise. He was enticed by that motionless figure and wanted to go on observing it.

Now he had made up his mind that Horfield was wide awake, and that his eyes were open but concealed by the drooping lids. He did not know why he was sure of that, but he was sure. There was something definitely sleepless about the still figure. The face looked malicious, Keane thought, profound and malicious. He remembered that phrase of Sir Simon: "Horfield has gone sour." Gone sour because of a woman! And he had a curious and sinister impression. It was this: that the man over there, still in the firelight, was brooding over Gay and meditating harm. And the harm he was meditating might reach out to another woman, might strike Mrs. Paradine. What had happened exactly between Horfield and Gay of course Keane did not know. He could only surmise. But that was not a very difficult process. If Horfield had dared to offend Gay by plainly showing his ugly side to her he could not long have been left in doubt of her feeling for him.

Keane was afraid of her scorn and indignation, afraid of her expression of them to Horfield. While he had been up in the North here in London Gay had perhaps been making a deadly enemy of Horfield. He had come back to London, received from Sir Simon Flaquer, perhaps the shrewdest man in London, the injunction not to get Horfield's back up, had resolved to put forth all his powers of dissimulation and self-control in order to get on the right side of Horfield if possible, and now, while he had been away, unknown to him and to Sir Simon, Gay had probably nullified in advance all his efforts. In his absence Gay had been fighting against him and against Mrs. Paradine. If his supposition were well founded, and he was by now convinced that it was, then his departure from London had been a fatal move. It was as if destiny were fighting against him and had sent him out of London, had deliberately got him out of the way in order that Gay might be enabled to commit the irrevocable action which must inevitably make Horfield definitely his enemy. For Horfield, repulsed by a woman, would certainly stick at nothing to vent his anger upon her, and would not hesitate to strike at her through her husband. And Mrs. Paradine would be involved in the punishment inflicted.

"It seems I'm going to be a curse to the woman I'm trying to save!" he thought desperately. "It would have been better if I'd given in to Flaquer and resigned from the case."

Just for a moment he was weakened and felt in a mood to throw the whole thing up. Gay fighting against him, Gay making the fatal move which might bring to naught all his efforts, all his plans. Why couldn't she have—? But there he pulled up. He was startled, even horrified, at his own furious impulse.

"In God's name what am I coming to?" he thought.

And for a moment he was afraid of himself.

Making by accident a brusque movement he overturned his tea-cup. It rattled against the metal tray it was standing on. Keane picked it up hastily and set it in the saucer. Then he looked across at Horfield in the distance. Horfield was still sitting in the same position, low in his chair, his arms stretched out, his feet crossed one over the other. But he had raised his chin, his eyes were wide open, and he was staring fixedly towards Keane, still with the malicious expression on his pale face. He did not change it as Keane met his gaze, nor did he move. And Keane wondered whether he was recognized, or whether the Judge, immersed in thought, was looking steadfastly at an object, in this case himself, without consciously seeing it.

He poured out another cup of tea and sipped it, not looking at Horfield. When he had finished he again looked towards him. The figure was still in exactly the same position, with the chin raised and the eyes apparently staring straight at him. Was he seen or unseen?

He got up and walked slowly towards the fire.

As he drew near to Horfield he saw that the thin lips were smiling, and before he came up to him, the clear silvery voice said:

"I was wondering whether you were trying to give me the cut direct."

He stretched out a hand. Keane was obliged to clasp it.

"I wasn't certain whether you saw me though you seemed to be looking at me."

"I was looking at you," said Horfield. "Is this too near the fire for you?"

"No."

Keane sat down. Now he must prove whether, as Horfield had said, he had the power to be a good actor. He had now, he felt sure, an additional reason for detesting this man, but he had a tremendous reason for entirely concealing his detestation. And that reason must, for the present, be pre-eminent. Later, perhaps, he could hate in the open. Later, when Fate had cast the dice.

"You're soon back," said Horfield. "Did you have a successful journey?"

He asked the question without curiosity, in the casual way of Society.

"Oh, yes," said Keane, in much the same tone. "By the way, how's your wife? Gay told me she was suddenly taken ill and was obliged to give up the theatre."

"Oh, it was nothing," said Horfield, with a faint smile. "Dear thing! she will eat what she knows won't agree with her: shell fish, peaches, nuts. My wife has few faults, but she's a wee bit greedy. But so are most of us. In her condition she ought to be more strict with herself. However, I was hardly a sufferer, for I had your delightful wife to myself for once. You know my feeling for her. I think her the most charming person in London."

"She told me you were very entertaining," said Keane, with simplicity.

"Entertaining—did she?" said Horfield.

And just for an instant it seemed to Keane that he lost control of his voice. Its smooth and eminently melodious timbre was marred by an edge of sharpness.

"Yes, you always amuse her. And though she's so quiet and often so serious she has a very strong sense of humour—thank goodness."

And then they talked about sense of humour.

"What a conversation!" thought Keane. "Considering what our two minds are really up to!"

And he was amazed at his own facility and at the things he found to say about that very precious sense. And he was disgusted, too.

"A couple of cursed humbugs!"

But the most deep current of surprise in his being was set going by the knowledge that he was able to be as he was with this man, who, he felt sure, had insulted Gay. That was almost incredible, and set a seal on the vast change that had operated in him since he had known Mrs. Paradine. He now knew, as never before, the capacity for change that exists in a human being, for he experienced it in himself. He sat there in the firelight wooing Horfield! And he looked on at himself, listened to himself, almost as a man might look on at, listen to, a monster.

They touched upon humorists of the past. Horfield spoke of Sidney Smith and Theodore Hook. They discussed the respective merits of Whistler, W. S. Gilbert, Oscar Wilde and Brookfield as humorists. They compared different types of humour. Max Beerbohm was mentioned and Herbert Beerbohm Tree. Coming down to the moment they debated about Bernard Shaw in old age, Noel Coward's satirical gaiety, what amused the young ones now who couldn't find a laugh in the whole of Dickens. Mrs. George Blason was spoken of, and the humour of women analysed in its separateness from the humour of men.

And underneath it all ran the deep flowing hatred of Keane and in Horfield—what? Keane could not tell for certain. Horfield was an accomplished man of the world, and very seldom let his mask slip. Only now and then, while they talked, did Keane think he caught a bitter look in Horfield's long narrow eyes, a menacing expression about his thin, very flexible lips. He might have 'gone sour,' but he did not seem very different from the normal Horfield, who was usually satirical and inclined to a biting humour even when nothing had happened to irritate him.

While they talked, it occurred to Keane that there was a way by which he would probably be able to find out definitely whether what he suspected had occurred between Horfield and Gay. And he resolved to take it. For it was vitally important for him to know whether the danger Mrs. Paradine stood in had been increased since he had been out of London, by any conduct of Gay's.

"I should like to make up to Lady Horfield for her disappointment about the theatre the other night," he said, when a pause came in the conversation.

Horfield looked interrogative.

"How?" he asked. "I think my wife's got over it."

"I didn't suppose she was dressed in sack-cloth and sitting in ashes. But why not make up another theatre party? You and your wife come and dine with us in Portland Place and we'll go somewhere. Have you seen Mrs. George Blason in her new play, *The Uttermost Farthing?*"

"No."

"I'll get a box for that then. Which nights are you both free?"

Horfield obviously hesitated. His face did not change. There was no evidence in it of confusion, perplexity or reluctance. But he hesitated and did not reply immediately.

"Perhaps you're very much taken up," suggested Keane.

"No. It would be delightful. Now, let me see!"

He drew out of the inner pocket of his black double-breasted jacket a little book, opened it, and turned the leaves slowly. Keane had the impression that he was giving himself time to decide what he was going to do. His eyes were bent on the book for a moment and his mouth looked grim. But suddenly he began to smile as if something amused him. And he looked up.

"What about Thursday next? We've nothing that night."

He was still smiling, but his eyes looked hard and determined.

"Splendid!" said Keane. "I'll book a box and Gay shall write to your wife."

"But you are sure she and you aren't engaged?"

"I don't think so. Anyhow, I'll make that all right. So please put it down."

Horfield sent a searching glance to Keane, who immediately realised that by his impulsiveness he had roused in the Judge suspicion. He damned himself for his carelessness. He had been driven by his eagerness to know, to make sure whether anything had happened between Horfield and his wife. Horfield of course had not let him know, but when he got home Gay surely would. He was impatient now to get home.

"If we are engaged I'll suggest another night," he said. "I'll telephone this evening. Will you be in?"

"Yes. We have some people to dinner. But telephone all the same. It will only take me away from them for a minute."

"I believe *he's* anxious to know how Gay takes it!" Keane thought.

When he reached Portland Place he found Judith Flaquer in the downstairs sitting-room with Gay. Hitherto he had been fond of Judith, but since his painful conversation with Gay before leaving for the North he had felt differently about her. He still liked her really, for he had every reason to, but he feared her obscurely, and he had the conviction that she had guessed his secret and was ranged on Gay's side against the man who had it. Judith, he knew, was solid with Gay where any question of Gay's happiness and peace was concerned. She was a good friend, one of the best. For that very reason he felt uneasy about her, and wished now that he hadn't found her in the house. As he came in and saw the two women together, he wondered whether Gay ever gave to Judith her full confidence. If she did—but Gay had a curious and charming reticence. He could scarcely believe that, like so many women, she would babble all her secrets even to a friend.

"It's late. I was just going," said Judith, greeting him. "I came with a message from Mamma. She wants you both to dine with us next Thursday. Mrs. George Blason has given us a box for *The Uttermost Farthing*. Will you come? Gay says you have no engagement."

"But we have!" said Keane abruptly, startled, and for the moment captured by an absurd feeling that again Judith Flaquer was trying to put a spoke in the wheel of his life with Gay.

"Really!" said Judith, for once looking taken aback. "I didn't know——"

She glanced towards Gay, who was looking astonished.

"I made one just now."

He turned to Gay. He was vexed at not being able to tell her in private and closely to observe her reaction to his information, but that couldn't be helped now. Circumstance had taken him in the net.

"Yes," he went on. "And—oddly enough, it was to go to that very play, *The Uttermost Farthing*. I've got a box for it for Thursday, and just now at the Club I came across Horfield and asked him and his wife to dine with Gay and me here on Thursday and go with us. And he accepted. I'm so sorry."

"Then we're out of luck," said Judith, looking at Gay.

"I knew nothing about this," Gay said, slowly.

"No, you couldn't," said Keane. "It's just happened unfortunately."

"Couldn't it be changed?" Gay said. "I might telephone."

"To whom?" Keane asked, sharply.

"To the Horfields."

"No, dear, that wouldn't do. I wouldn't on any account put Horfield off now he's accepted. He's an important man and a Judge. I couldn't do that. Remember," he added with an attempt at jocularity, "I must keep in his good books, as I have to plead before him."

"Ah—in the Paradine case!" said Judith.

"Yes. And perhaps in other cases, too. Your father would see at once that I couldn't put the Horfields off after they'd accepted an invitation to my house. It would be—it would be infernally rude. But do explain to your dear mother how sorry I am at this unlucky coincidence. We shall meet at the theatre and then I'll tell her myself."

Before Judith could say anything, Gay said:

"Then Lady Horfield knows about this engagement, Malcolm?"

"She may, she probably does by now. But I arranged it with Horfield at the Club, as I said."

When he had said this, there was a decidedly uncomfortable silence, which was broken by Judith.

"Well, better luck next time!" she said briskly. "Good-bye, dear Gay."

She went to Gay and kissed her gently, then turned to Keane. "Good-bye, Sir Malcolm."

Keane thought her voice, when she spoke to him, was cold.

"You do understand that I couldn't possibly turn the Horfields down?" he said, with pressure.

"I suppose not. No. But Justice!" she fixed her penetrating dark eyes on him. "Can't you trust Lord Horfield to deal out even-handed Justice regardless of likes and dislikes? An English Judge!"

"I'll see you to the hall door. Of course one must. But still, your father would see that a K.C. must treat an eminent Judge with all proper respect, both in and out of Court."

He went out of the room with her.

When he came back, Gay was still there waiting for him.

"I'm sorry about this muddle," he said. "But it couldn't he helped. It's nobody's fault."

"Of course, you couldn't know," Gay said. "There are things one doesn't know."

She said the last words with a strange and profound emphasis, though in a very low voice.

"So many things," she added, like one musing aloud, he thought. She looked at him.

"Wouldn't it be better if it wasn't so? Wouldn't it be much better if we all came out into the open with one another, if we let each other know what we are and how things really are with us?"

"Well, but we do with those who are nearest to us," he said, hastily.

"Oh—no! Even with them we walk in darkness."

"My dear Gay!"

"Yes, Malcolm, we do. And it's our own fault. We *could* be quite different. We *could* be sincere. We have the power, but we don't use it. But I am going to try."

He felt afraid of her at that moment. There was something actually stern in her voice, her look, her whole manner. She was making a great effort. That was obvious to him. He seemed to see her mind straining like a body to lift a burden, with muscles standing out and a skin streaming with perspiration.

"Gay!" he said, longing to stop her.

"Malcolm, I don't want you to receive Lord Horfield into this house. I don't want you ever to have him here again, either next Thursday or at any other time. I have—I have a sufficient reason."

"I know you never cared much about him, but I *must* keep in with him. I simply must. I didn't care to explain before Judith Flaquer just now, but the fact is, Judges are as human as the rest of us. They have their likes and dislikes, they are swayed by feelings and passions like other men. It's quite on the cards that I shall be a Judge some day, but if I am, that won't change my character. You yourself told me once that Horfield didn't like me. That woke me up to a danger."

"What danger?"

"That unless I could get more into his good graces I might do actual harm to any clients whom I was defending before him, that I might actually injure them by my presence instead of being more valuable to them than any other counsel could be. Since then, I've resolved, if possible, to conquer Horfield's dislike of me. And at this critical moment in my career I must avoid giving him the slightest pretext for being antagonistic to me."

He paused, then said with intensity:

"A woman's life may depend on that."

"Is it possible, Malcolm, that you think so badly of Lord Horfield as a Judge?" she said. "But how awful!"

"Gay, I'll tell you the truth. This rests for ever between you and me. I think badly of Horfield as a man and therefore I must think badly of him as a Judge. For whatever people may say man and Judge are one. You can't disentangle the man from the Judge. When this case is over, when Mrs. Paradine's fate is decided one way or the other, then you shall do as you like about Horfield. You can close our door to him if you wish. I won't ask you not to. But till then—till then I beg you not to hinder me but to help me with Horfield. I have my—my duty to my client, that unfortunate woman in Holloway waiting to know her fate. I know you too well to believe you could ever lift a finger to do her harm. Till the case is over—very soon now—you and I must conceal our hatreds. You're the wife of a man who has to battle for a woman's life, and you must help him, you mustn't stand in his way. I know you're too full of mercy to do that. We've both of us got to bear with Horfield for a little while longer."

"A little while. But when this case is decided you'll still be a Counsel and Lord Horfield will still be a Judge."

"Oh, I don't care then! Let the Heavens fall then!" he exclaimed with violence.

And he hurried out of the room.

When he had gone, Gay waited for a moment looking at the door. Then she picked up a book and sat down, very gently and as if carefully, in a chair. She opened the book and put it down open on her knees. But she didn't look at the pages. Presently, she leant forward with her elbows on her knees, in a graceless attitude —Gay, who was always so graceful—put her face against her hands and sobbed. She sobbed and sobbed, and her whole body shook.

"How terrible to hate as I do!" she thought. "I don't want her to live. I don't want her to live!"

XXVIII

THAT evening Keane telephoned to Lord Horfield, who came to the telephone, summoned by his butler.

"It's all right about Thursday. We shall expect you to dinner at seven-fifteen, if that's not too early," Keane said.

The Judge's clear and charming voice replied:

"That is very satisfactory. Sophy is enchanted at the prospect and is already considering what dress to wear. Give my thanks for the invitation and my best regards to your delicious wife."

"I will," said Keane, frowning.

"Good-bye," said the delicate voice.

Keane came away from the telephone hating himself.

Briefly, he told Gay that the Horfields would be there at seven-fifteen on the Thursday. She made no comment on that, and the subject was not mentioned between them again. Since her stern effort at sincerity and plain speaking, which he had so ruthlessly countered, she had withdrawn into herself. In the wintry weather she had become like a frozen woman. It was better so. Anything rather than expressed sincerity! Keane was terribly afraid of sincerity, in his home. But he desired it above all things elsewhere, he was greedy for it, he longed to provoke it.

Dreading the Thursday, knowing that it must be inevitably a date memorably ugly in his life, he resolved to dedicate it wholly to effort, to the full exercise of his will-power in more ways than one, and in the afternoon of that day he drove to Holloway Prison, filled with the determination to be drastically plain-spoken with Mrs. Paradine. He must keep Gay from speaking at all costs, but at all costs he must force Mrs. Paradine to speak. The trial was close at hand now. He could not, feeling as he did, go forward any more in the dark. Since the visit to Hindley and the night scene with Marsh, he was ravaged by the terrible curiosity which was not merely the legitimate curiosity of the lawyer but the necessity to know of the man who had shed the lawyer and stood out as the stark human being.

And always the black suspicion was there, coiled close in his mind, his companion wherever he went.

"She must tell me! I've got to know!"

He arrived at the prison determined to overpower her secrecy. The time was short now. There was no time to lose. He was in the mood to stick at nothing in the effort to achieve his purpose. As he entered the prison he resolved:

"If all else fails I'll terrify her."

There was cruelty in him that day.

When he saw Mrs. Paradine he was struck at once by a physical change in her. She was thinner. Or she appeared to him to be thinner. And this loss of flesh caused her to look, he thought, more ethereal, and in consequence more like Gay. The resemblance between them was accentuated. He noticed that immediately.

As the trial drew near the strain of uncertainty, soon to be converted into certainty, was telling on her, and at last she allowed, had to allow, that to be seen. For the first time since Keane had known her he felt the pathos of her situation tug at his entrails. Hitherto he had been full of pity for her but it had not been the pity that goes deep into a man and actually wrings his heart. Something in her look and demeanour had subtly prevented that. Now that something was removed, at any rate for the moment.

She greeted him with a sort of restrained eagerness, as if she were very eager but did not want to show it too much.

"It seems such a long time!" she said, in her rather husky and trailing voice.

He took her hand, glanced at the female officer who was watching them behind the glass pane, and sat down. If only that woman were away!

"Shall I ever, even for a moment, be able to see her quite alone?" And then he thought of her free, and his heart beat faster.

"I've been out of London," he said.

"Yes?"

"I've been up to Hindley."

Her lips parted but she did not speak. Her pale eyes looked astonished, then intent as if with suspicion.

"I stayed at the Inn at Sedale on Sands and visited Hindley from there."

"Why did you go? What was there to go for?" she asked, leaning, he felt, on the words.

"I was tired. I'd been working very hard, working at night. I wanted some good air, to be alone." He looked hard at her. "You drew me up there."

"I? But I am here."

"Perhaps some of you lingers there. Who knows? Anyhow you sent me up there, or drew me. It doesn't matter which. I visited the Hall. I went into the house, into *your* room where you used to sleep. I walked on the terrace, in the gardens, down by the river. It was in flood. I breathed in the atmosphere of the place that was your home."

He paused. She waited, with her eyes fixed upon him. He saw the blank expression beginning to creep into her face, like something pushed into it from behind.

"Don't!" he said, sharply. "Don't!"

"What do you mean? What am I doing?"

"Doing! You are trying to keep me out, to shut the door against me. The time for that's gone. You've got to let me in—or I shan't be able to save your life."

Her eyes seemed to grow wider.

"You will—you will——?" she said, and waited.

"I shall fail at the trial. Unless I can put my heart into this case I shall lose it. And you keep me in the dark."

"I do not know what you mean," she said, with stolidity.

And in spite of what he had said the blank look overspread her face, exasperating him.

"When I went over to Hindley Hall," he said, leaning towards her and speaking in a low, urgent voice, "I rang at the front door. It was opened by William Marsh."

He saw her heavy white eyelids quiver but the expression of her face did not change.

"He took me into the house but left me there, and a woman, a caretaker, came to show me the rooms. I opened a window in the front of the house, I looked out and saw Marsh below. He was telling my driver who I was. I called down and asked him to show me over the gardens. He called up that he would. But when I went down he was gone."

He stopped speaking. Mrs. Paradine did not say anything. She sat still. Her figure looked rigid.

"I left for Sedale without seeing him again."

He thought that her figure relaxed.

"That night in the Inn I sat up late. I had a sitting-room on the ground floor next to a side door that was opposite to the station railings. Perhaps you know it?"

She did not say anything.

"I was working there. The people of the Inn had locked up and gone to bed. I heard something. I listened. Then I heard a knock on the side door. I went to it, unbolted it, opened it, and found William Marsh there."

He noticed that the blank look seemed to become more marked. A vagueness, almost like that of an idiot, had overspread her face. All intelligent expression was blotted out from it. Even her beautiful eyes were dull as if a glaze had mysteriously covered them.

"He had walked all the way from Hindley to see me."

"Why?" she murmured vaguely.

"I let him in. We were together for a considerable time. We spoke about you."

Her eyelids quivered again.

"He told me that I didn't know what you were. He told me that you were a woman of Babylon. Do you know what is meant by that?"

Not a look, not a gesture, answered him.

"That man hates you most bitterly. I want to know why."

When he said the last words he was aware of a sudden relaxation that seemed to be communicated by Mrs. Paradine's spirit to her body and to run mysteriously all through it.

"As we know that you didn't murder his master, what's the reason?"

"He does not like women."

"What's the good of telling me that? This is a personal hatred fastened on an individual. If Colonel Paradine were still alive it would exist just the same. I'm absolutely certain of that."

"Marsh does not like women."

"Oh, don't talk futilities to me!" Keane exclaimed roughly. "You're dealing with an experienced criminal lawyer not with a schoolboy. For God's sake realise that and don't hand me out banalities. I won't have it!"

He made a violent movement as if to get up, remembered the officer and checked it.

"I am speaking the truth," she said, obstinately. "There will be evidence to that."

"Don't keep on telling me what I know, or—or I shall——"

He stopped short. He was trying hard for self-control. The presence of the officer so near them exasperated his nerves. For a moment he didn't dare to say more. He shut his eyes and de-

liberately relaxed all his muscles. But though his eyes were shut
he seemed to be staring at something coiled up like a motionless
snake, that black suspicion of his. After a moment he opened his
eyes.

"My interview with Marsh," he said, "his attitude, his words,
his whole manner, the look in his eyes while he was speaking to
me, made an impression upon me that I can't shake off. Mrs.
Paradine, we hate, if we hate at all, those most with whom we
have had most to do. We hate, if we hate, in intimacy. We hate
the known not the unknown. You say that Marsh doesn't like
women."

"It is true."

"Others say he's a woman hater."

"Yes. And it is so."

Speaking slowly and heavily Keane said:

"Since I have been with Marsh something seems to say to me"
—he touched his breast—"a man who is a woman hater would
hate most of all the woman who, by her power of seduction, had
compelled him to forgo his hatred of women."

He waited, then added:

"For a time. It might be only for a *night*."

Her tall figure shivered slightly. He noticed that, and a deadly
sensation of nausea came over him. He realised the terrible difference between suspicion and certainty. Leaning on the table by
which he was sitting, leaning heavily, he said:

"Mrs. Paradine, Marsh has belonged to you."

XXIX

WHEN he came home to dress for the dinner at which the Horfields
were to be present Gay was painfully struck by her husband's
appearance. His face, always pale with a clear ivory pallor, had a
curious almost yellow tinge which suggested ill-health; his eyes
looked furtive and feverish; his hands were restless, and his whole
manner was disordered, like that of a man on the verge of a
nervous breakdown. She couldn't help staring at him in amazement, and almost with fear.

"What's the matter?" he said sharply.

"The matter?"

"Yes. Why d'you look at me like that?"

"I was afraid—aren't you feeling well?"

"Perfectly well. Never better. My holiday up in the North did me good. I feel ready for anything."

He snatched at his watch.

"Just time to take a quick bath!" he said. "Quarter past seven for dinner, wasn't it?"

"Yes."

"I can just manage it."

He hurried out of the room.

For the first time in her life Gay felt not only afraid for, but of, her husband.

She went to her bedroom to dress for this detestable dinner with a heavy heart. She felt utterly alone in this house which was her home. She even felt out of place in it, like an unwanted intruder who nevertheless did not know how to get away, or where else to go. The prospect of the dinner and of the long evening at the theatre horrified her.

Since Keane had insisted that the dinner must take place, again and again she had asked herself whether he had understood her reason for wishing him to refuse any pretence of friendship to Lord Horfield. She had not explained it, but he must surely have understood. And yet if he had would he have insisted? Had he fallen so low as that? Or did he really put his duty to his client, regarded simply as client, before everything, even before his duty to his wife? If instead of Mrs. Paradine he had been defending a man would he have acted in the same way, have made to his wife a plea as intense? His almost wild exclamation as he hurried out of the room had given the lie to such a supposition.

"Let the Heavens fall then!"

Mrs. Paradine saved then Gay could treat Lord Horfield as she liked. Malcolm wouldn't care. The verdict given—supreme indifference! But now she must do her part to help towards the consummation he desperately wished for.

"And I don't know whether that woman is guilty or innocent. And I don't believe Malcolm cares. He may have cared once, at the beginning, but does he care now? I don't believe he does. Innocent or guilty she's got to be saved. That's all that matters."

Franklin said presently:

"What dress will you wear to-night, my lady?"

"Anything, Franklin, anything! I don't care! Something black.
Yes, black. Lady Horfield's sure to be in orange colour or scarlet.
I don't want to clash with her."

She hesitated.

"And not one of my best gowns."

The maid looked surprised.

"Something very plain—ordinary. I don't want to dress up to-
night. I don't want to look my best, as if I'd taken trouble. Get
out the dress we care for least."

"Indeed, my lady?"

The maid went doubtfully, looking troubled, into the narrow
room lined with cupboards where Gay's dresses were bestowed. My
lady not wishing to look her best! The dress we care for least!
This mood was beyond Franklin's understanding. However, she
obeyed orders, and brought out a black evening dress which she
had never much cared for, and showed it to Gay with a "Will this
do, my lady?"

"Yes, yes. What's the time?"

"Just on seven, my lady."

"So late?"

For an instant Gay's face was contorted in a grimace which
startled the maid.

"Is her ladyship getting a tic?" she thought, as she got Gay
into the dress that she didn't care for.

"Get me a cigarette will you, Franklin? And then you can leave
me. I want to be quiet and smoke for a few minutes."

"Yes, my lady."

"Thank you. A match! That's it."

When Franklin was close to the door about to go out Gay called
to her:

"You might ask Baker to send me up a cocktail."

"Yes, my lady."

Franklin went out in amazement.

She returned a few minutes later with a cocktail.

"I don't know what they call it, but Baker says it's a good one,
my lady."

"It'll do. It'll do! You can leave me now."

Franklin departed.

Only five minutes more and 'they' would be here. Gay drank the cocktail, set the little glass down and lighted another cigarette.

Had she been right or wrong in giving way about this dinner? At one moment she thought that she was weak and even degraded because of her obedience, at another that she would be doing her duty in receiving the Judge in spite of what had happened. If possibly a woman's life, and especially *that* woman's life, might be placed in jeopardy by her refusal, then surely the sacrifice she was making was praiseworthy. The intimate cruelty of that sacrifice lay in the fact of the hideous desire which she could not get rid of, which was always with her. She was going to fight her own sin, a sin of the mind, or even of the soul. Could such an action be wholly weak, wholly blameworthy?

But it was an ugly business, oh, what an ugly business it was! She felt unclean as she got up to go downstairs, got up to make her début as a hypocrite.

They were not going to use the big drawing-room on the first floor that evening. Immediately after dinner they would have to start for the theatre. Gay found her husband already downstairs standing before the fire in the room where they generally sat. Sausage was beside him. Both of them seemed to be staring into the fire.

"You've been quick, Malcolm!" she said.

Sausage wagged his tail.

"One doesn't want to keep a learned Judge waiting," he said. "We've got to be at our best to-night."

He spoke with a sort of earnest determination.

"Any prejudices we may have we've got to put away. I care for sincerity as you do. But there are times when one must conceal one's hatreds."

"Hatreds!" she said, startled by the sudden violence which he put into the last word.

"Lord and Lady Horfield!" said Baker, opening the door.

And Lady Horfield, for once in black, lunged forward followed by the Judge, who wore the white carnation of a blameless life in his buttonhole and looked, Keane thought, icily smart, icily imperturbable.

The honours for acting in Portland Place that evening, before the professional acting began at the theatre, were carried off, strangely enough, by the two men. Keane was strongly aware of that, and he thought the capacity they showed in deceit marked them out as morally inferior to the two women though it perhaps stamped them as the cleverer sex. He had absolutely made up his mind to be successfully histrionic. Since the interview in Holloway Prison that afternoon he had the feeling of a man whose destiny it was to be tried in the fire. A sense of fatalism had descended upon him such as he had never been conscious of before. Obscurely he knew that he would be made to tread in dark places, that perhaps he must penetrate even to the unholy cavern of the Furies. That was inevitable. There was no possibility of escape from it. All that he could do was to go forward as boldly as possible, calling on all his strength, resolved not to be overpowered by whatever might happen. What had occurred that afternoon seemed to have stung him into a sort of ecstasy of determination. He was as a man on his knees before his own power of will. He had the recklessness that is often the forerunner of despair. But he concealed it behind a charm of manner, a cordiality, a simulation of gaiety and ease which were assumed for the benefit of Horfield. The time was short. He must manage to erase from the Judge's mind his former errors of conduct. He had been a blundering fool with Horfield, he had been much too sincere with him. He must make him forget that, but without going too far the other way. Horfield was clever enough to be made suspicious by gush, though he was probably not insusceptible to delicate flattery, even from a man. Keane remembered what Lady Horfield had blurted out about her husband's awareness of what people felt towards him.

Horfield met him, or seemed to meet him, half-way, frigidly at his ease apparently, dominating in intelligence, resting confidently on his well-tried brain as a good swimmer rests on a wave which he knows will not drown him but bear him to his bourne. He was very talkative, but never hurried in his talk. One of his charms as a conversationalist was that he never seemed to be making an effort, nor to be self-consciously desirous of creating an impression of brilliance. And he was always ready to listen to anything worthy of attention. Even his wife's cluttered incoherences were that evening received by him with a smiling

blandness, such as a kind man reserves for the vagaries of a child.
"She can't help it, poor dear! Let her be!" his manner seemed
to say, and he refrained from his usual faintly malicious comments
on her perpetual self-contradictions.

The fact of his having 'gone sour' he succeeded in concealing
during dinner. Keane, secretly intent and untiringly observant,
could not detect any change in his usual manner to Gay. There
was no trace of selfconsciousness, no hint of suppressed enmity. It
was difficult to believe that this man was laying himself out to be
agreeable to one from whom he had recently had the most drastic
rebuff that a man can receive from a woman. And yet surely that
rebuff must have been administered. For gentle though she was,
Gay could be exceedingly definite. Keane felt sure that she would
have left Horfield in no doubt at all of her feeling towards him.
And the knowledge that Horfield now denied to him he seemed
to be receiving from Gay.

Neither Lady Horfield nor Gay was at ease. Lady Horfield,
it is true, was never at ease when her husband was with her in
company. But that evening in Portland Place was certainly one
of her worst evenings. Keane was positive that always at the back
of her mind was a terrible sense of guilt connected with him. She
had had to make her revelation, but she was ashamed of having
made it, ashamed and yet capable of making it again could it be
unmade. She was torn between a dread of having been treacherous
to her husband and the conviction that her God had desired her
to speak. She stood between the man she loved desperately and
the woman she pitied with all her woman's soul. Keane felt her
as vital tragedy. There was in that clumsy, almost elephantine
body, a power of intense and even beautiful feeling that stretched
arms to him.

That evening at dinner, in spite of her obvious efforts to be
social, sociable and even lively, there was in her demeanour much
that suggested a guilty creature mentally cringing in fear of being
found out. Keane, and certainly Horfield, had frequently seen
people in her condition trembling in the witness-box before and
after cross-examination. They were not always guilty, but nearly
always they were conscious of something they considered it imperative to conceal, and, being sensitive, were cursed by the feeling
of being transparent. All their features seemed to show this, but

especially their eyes, in which the soul was mysteriously visible, stooping and drawing back. Again and again, during dinner, Keane saw the Judge's cold steel-grey eyes, long and narrow and often half shut, fixed on the red face of his wife, while his lips smiled as if his mind were subtly amused. Now and then these eyes were turned on him, and then Keane had the questioning fear of the uneasy witness. "Does he know? Has he found out?" He certainly must know that there was a peculiar and surreptitious intimacy between Keane and his wife, but surely its nature could not be known to him. And yet—Keane was not sure. During a long and brilliantly successful career, Horfield had been trained in all the exercises of penetration. His whole life was a voyage of mental discovery. It was his business to find out what others were trying to hide. Could his own wife's mental processes escape him? That seemed almost impossible. Yet if he knew the reason of her intimacy with Keane, surely he would have done something to punish her for what he would certainly regard as a monstrous betrayal. And evidently he had not punished her. He seemed just as usual with her except that he was slightly more lenient with her than he normally was, and there was nothing in his manner to Keane which was out of the common.

Nor was there anything unusual in his manner to Gay. He was certainly a consummate master of deception. There was even something, Keane thought, almost inhuman in Horfield's capacity for hiding what he considered it absolutely necessary to hide. He was sometimes careless, at moments even reckless, but surely never when he had made up his mind that he wouldn't be.

Like Lady Horfield that evening, Gay failed to hide the disturbance of her mind, but whereas Lady Horfield was unnaturally loquacious and uneasily cheerful, Gay was frozen in a difficult silence which she strove in vain to throw off. Keane knew that she was wishing to play her part, was anxious to be a humbug— Gay!—but the novelty of the task and its difficulty evidently defeated her temperament. She smiled and looked amiable, she even succeeded at moments in forcing a spurious eagerness into her demeanour, but this eagerness died away as abruptly as it came, and by its arrival and passing only drew attention to the abnormal speechlessness and pallor that kept Keane on tenterhooks. He was torn between admiration and anger, admiration of Gay's inability to be successfully insincere and anger with her for not playing up to Lord Horfield as he had begged her to do. So many women whom he knew, whom they both knew, could have done it, done it with ease, even with mischievous pleasure. But Gay—no! It seemed that she couldn't be anything but the true, the eternal Gay. In a way, even now, he was able to love her for that. But he was filled with uneasiness for the result of her incapacity which seemed to rebuke his capacity. For he was, he believed, making a success of hypocrisy, but, if so, his success was cancelled out by Gay's failure. What then, was the good of it all? His object in giving this dinner, this theatre party, would not be attained. Perhaps he was a fool to have insisted upon it.

Luckily, being only four at dinner, the conversation could hardly be other than general, and therefore it was fairly easy to cover up, or at any rate make the best of, Gay's inability to be lively in talk; but with three hatreds gathered together round a table accommodating only four people, to Keane the very air seemed to be vibrating with electricity. Gay, he knew, detested Lord Horfield; Lord Horfield must now be concealing acute enmity to Gay; he himself had a horror of Horfield. On one point he had not been able to satisfy himself. He did not know what was the nature of Lady Horfield's feeling towards Gay. She certainly knew of the ugly attraction Gay had for her husband. Obscurely, in her confused way, she had even warned Keane of it. But she had never let Keane know exactly what she felt about that, and even now he did not know. Aware of Lady Horfield's passionate love for her husband, it would have been natural if he supposed she hated Gay. But he had never had any evidence of that. And he was not even sure that Lady Horfield, with all her secret intensity, had any capacity for hatred. She was, perhaps, only sorry for Gay as she was sorry for Horfield. Having the intuition that is seldom left out of a woman, she probably divined the inherent straightness of Gay. At any rate, she had never shown jealousy of Gay, and she did not show it now.

As they were going to see Mrs. George Blason act, it was natural that they should talk of her, and Lord Horfield made some interesting remarks about the 'evidence,' as he called it, which she supplied of character on the stage, and the evidence she handed out to the world in private life.

"Which is the real Mrs. George?" he said. "When I first saw her on the stage, I thought I was in the presence of an ethereal and intensely sensitive woman, highly imaginative, by temperament inclined to wistful melancholy, even perhaps to tragedy, deeply thoughtful, strongly aspiring. You may say all that belonged to the rôle she was playing. But I saw her in various rôles, and always, however different they were, was conscious of that strange personality behind them, or underlying them. The artiste, too, was always closely linked with nature and truth, and is still, as no doubt we shall find this evening. But when I met Mrs. George in Society I was confronted by an arch humorist, a brilliant buffoon, who turned everything not to tears—as Duse, for instance, did—but to laughter, by a marvellous clown, careless of truth as long as she could get applause for an exhibition of wit, and who would sell the souls of most of us for a bon mot that would go the round of the London dinner tables. Where is the real Mrs. Blason? Are we to look for her in her art, or in her life? What would you do, Lady Keane? How would you set about to look for her?"

"I don't know," Gay said, in a dull voice. "I have never thought about that."

"But," he persisted, with smiling obstinacy, "what are you guided by when you seek for the truth of a person?"

"I should go by actions," said Gay, with apparent reluctance.

"Has it never occurred to you that actions can be performed with intent to deceive?"

"I think deceit is much more often latent in words. It is more easy to say than to do. Anyone can say a kind thing, but to do a kind thing means taking trouble, and the result of it is more definite. An unkind person can say a kind thing quite easily, but couldn't easily do a kind thing."

"You are a terrible realist. Isn't she, Keane?"

"I think she is," said Keane, looking at his wife and looking away.

"Difficult to deceive," added the Judge.

He looked at his wife.

"And what's your opinion, Sophy?"

Lady Horfield started.

"I don't know—I didn't quite catch—I——"

"Are you a realist? What do you judge people by?"

"Oh, I—but I don't think, perhaps—in the Bible it says, 'Judge ..ot that ye be not judged.' "

"A poor look-out for me!" said Horfield, "considering that I do nothing else."

"Oh, but I didn't mean—— You *have* to!—It's your profession."

"I have supposed so."

"But still——" she hesitated, glanced feverishly at Keane, seemed to make a great effort, then added: "But you can be a merciful Judge."

Lord Horfield lifted his left eyebrow.

"Yes?" he said, interrogatively.

"I think that's what the Bible really means."

She seemed to struggle mutely against something then came out with:

"That if we judge others harshly we shall be judged harshly ourselves."

"Indeed? When?"

"At the last!" she said, with intense earnestness.

"And when's that?" he persisted, with a smile.

"Oh, Horfield—you know!"

"My wife believes implicitly in the last day," said Horfield. "Probably she is almost the only woman in London who does. She is highly imaginative. I have often told her," he added, in a more metallic voice, "that a Judge's duty is not to be merciful but to be strictly just."

"But men's views of what is strictly just differ," said Keane.

"True. But a man can only go by his own lights."

"Or his own darknesses!" Keane muttered, before he was aware of it.

Recollecting himself, and angry at his slip, he changed the conversation, and began to speak of the play they were going to see.

"We are sitting close to the front," he said, "the second row of stalls."

"But you said you had a box, Malcolm!" Gay said, surprised.

Keane looked taken aback. Another slip! Was he developing into a careless fool?

"I thought I had," he said hurriedly. "But a mistake had been made. The box had been sold already. So we have to put up with stalls."

He saw Horfield's eyes go from him to Gay. Gay looked down. She knew her husband had just told her a lie. And he had told her and Judith Flaquer another lie when he had said he had a box for *The Uttermost Farthing.*

"Shall we——?" she said to Lady Horfield.

"Yes. I should like——"

She reared herself out of her chair. Keane glanced at his watch. "We've still a few minutes. Horfield, you'd like some port? Then we'll follow you almost directly, Lady Horfield."

When the two women had gone, Keane went to sit by the Judge. There was an instant of silence, then Horfield said mildly: "This is really superlative port. What year is it?"

"Eighteen-seventy."

"Ah! One of the great years. You are lucky to have some of it."

"I've laid down several dozen. Let me send you a few bottles."

"You are too good, but I mustn't rob you of such a precious vintage."

"But remember you promised me some of those marvellous Havanas!" said Keane, in a cordial, half-joking way.

"By Jove! So I did!" said Horfield. "You'll receive them almost immediately. I meant to have sent them for Christmas."

"And you'll receive a few bottles of this," said Keane, touching his glass.

It seemed to him that something, the wine, no doubt, had lured Horfield into an unusually mellow mood. For a moment there had been something actually genial in his voice, even in the glance of his usually satirical eyes. Perhaps somewhere there was a soft spot in this man. Was there not a soft spot in every man if one only knew how to reach it? A sudden impulsive desire came to Keane to conquer Horfield, to take a risk in the attempt to overcome once for all Horfield's undoubted dislike of him, which must have been increased by what had happened with Gay. Keane was known at the Bar for his audacity in big cases. At moments he could be almost reckless. His difficulty was to hold himself in, to proceed always with adequate caution. He had a moment of audacity, of recklessness now. He drew his chair nearer to the Judge, and said:

"It will be a great pleasure to send you the wine, but I hope you will come here sometimes and drink it out of my cellar, as you are doing now, when the great case in which we shall both be concerned so soon is over and done with."

He noticed a fleeting expression of astonishment transform the Judge's pale, narrow face. It should have warned him, perhaps, but it was gone in an instant, and he continued:

"It's the case of my life and I'm glad I shall plead it before you. I believe it's current gossip among my brethren of the Bar that I'm a cantankerous fellow and difficult to deal with when I'm deep in a case, and I've sometimes felt angry with myself at my occasional lack of complete self-control. I daresay, in fact I know, you've noticed it. No one regrets it more than I do, when the heat of the occasion is over and I can look back at things and see them in the cold light of the past. But I simply can't help putting myself in the place of my clients and feeling for them intensely. You know Bunyan's words, so often quoted: 'There but for the grace of God go I'? They're nearly always with me when I'm pleading for a client."

"But they would apply surely rather to one who was guilty than to one who was innocent!" dropped out Horfield, turning his glass round in his long yellow-white fingers and holding it up to the light. " 'But for the grace of God' could scarcely be used in connection with one of the blandly guiltless. Don't you agree?"

"I see your point. But it's so easy to feel completely sinless when one has never been found out. I find it difficult to compass the self-righteous sensation that evidently warms many undetected sinners. And I'm free to confess that even the guilty can sometimes tug at my sympathy."

Keane was secretly searching for the Judge's humanity, but he hadn't found it yet, and he was trying to get *en rapport* with him, desperately trying, putting away resolutely his dislike and dread of him, concentrating on that soft spot which he was now resolved to believe existed in him.

"Life's been so difficult for many of them. So many of them are the victims of life."

"You'll forgive me for thinking, Keane, that to dwell long on that view of the criminal might easily entangle you, or any other man, in a net of sentimentality," said the Judge.

Again he turned his glass slowly round and raised it to the light, watching the ruby glow of the wine with half closed eyes. Then he put it to his lips and sipped.

"Marvellous wine!" he murmured.

And he sipped again. And at that moment, remembering Lady Horfield's scrappy yet terribly definite revelation, Keane saw the red wine as blood and the sipping Judge as the legendary vampire. Yet still he strove, urged on by a passionate determination not to allow the fate of a woman to be determined by any remissness on his part.

"What is sentimentality?" he asked.

"Misplaced sentiment, sentiment directed into a wholly unworthy channel."

"I hope I'm not guilty of that," Keane said, with a touch of hasty warmth. "But I've noticed that those who are naturally devoid of sentiment themselves are apt to call any exhibition of feeling in others sentimentality."

"Just half a glass more, if I may!"

"I beg your pardon! Let me fill it up. Such wine can't hurt you."

"Have we time?"

"Yes, another seven minutes at least. May I put a question to you, a decidedly personal question?"

Keane noticed that Horfield braced up his exceedingly thin figure, as he heard the last three words, and that his lips suddenly tightened over his long yellow teeth.

"Put any question you like, as the candidate at an election has to say to the heckler."

"You were once an advocate and a very brilliant one."

"I was an advocate—certainly."

"Do you find that having become a Judge has altered your outlook on humanity—let us say at odds with the Law?"

Horfield shot a piercingly sharp glance at him.

"Why should it?"

"I can imagine that it might. I've sometimes thought of myself seated on the bench, conceived of the situation, and it has seemed to me that the rather god-like lifting up of the man to the Judge —or superman in Court—might have a very definite effect on his nature. A Judge has such power for good or ill. I could almost feel that such a power might fill me with one of two differing sensations."

"Name them!"

"Either with dread or with adamantine hardness."

"Why the latter?"

"Mightn't the sense of supremacy breed it?"

"Then what about the Jury?"

"But they only serve once in years—as a rule. And the Judge sits on the Bench week in and week out. Do you feel towards the had-ups now as you did when you were an advocate?"

"What I felt as an advocate I have forgotten," said Horfield grimly. "What I feel as a Judge? I feel simply executive. I am there for one purpose only, to get to the bottom of a case, to receive the verdict, and then to pronounce judgment."

"Unless it's a verdict of not guilty!" said Keane swiftly.

"In that case," said Horfield, and a slow difficult smile stretched his lips, "I have the felicity of sending a fellow creature out into what is called freedom."

"And how you hate that!" thought Keane with intense bitterness.

"That is one of the rewards of being a Judge," said Horfield. "And I can assure you, Keane, that it is a very precious one."

"God grant you may be able to do it in the Paradine case!" exclaimed Keane, with a sudden outburst of feeling that astonished himself.

"That case being sub judice I cannot discuss it," said Horfield, and shut his mouth with an audible snap of the teeth. "Ought we to join our ladies?"

Keane sprang to his feet. He felt as if a cataract of ice-cold water had swept over him drowning him out. The snap of Lord Horfield's teeth, as he shut his mouth before opening it to utter formally the final sentence, had sounded in Keane's ears like the sharp dry click of the door of a condemned cell shut on a prisoner. He reddened to his forehead at the memory of his impetuous and unguarded exclamation. The Judge had spoken exactly like a man who felt that another man was trying to 'get at him,' and who saw through the attempt and resented it. Keane stood for an instant quivering as if he had been struck. Then he recovered himself and said, formally like Horfield:

"Yes, I expect we ought."

He took out his watch and glanced at it.

"We've just enough time."

"Good! I shall carry with me to the play the memory of that port."

The Judge had given way again to the guest.

"Damn you and your politeness!" Keane thought, as he opened the door.

They found Lady Horfield and Gay already in their cloaks and ready to go. As they came into the sitting-room Keane met Lady Horfield's eyes. They were fixed upon him with an imploring and questioning look. He knew that they were asking him:

"Have you charmed Horfield?"

Against his will he frowned, he could not help frowning.

"Well, we ought to be off," he said. "We shall just be in time."

Baker was bringing the Judge his heavy fur-lined coat.

As he was getting into it Horfield said:

"We've got the two cars. Shall we divide? Keane, won't you take my wife in your car and allow me to escort Lady Keane in mine?"

Without looking at Gay—he felt that he dared not look at her —Keane answered:

"Certainly! Delighted! We'll meet in the foyer, then. Lady Horfield, shall we lead the way?"

"Oh, if you—shall we—Horfield, do you wish us——"

"Go on, dear! Go on! We'll follow you."

She went sideways along the hall, her long black dress trailing behind her. Keane followed her without a glance at Gay.

XXX

DIRECTLY Keane's motor car moved away from the house in the direction of Regent Street Keane felt Lady Horfield's small fin on his right wrist and heard her voice saying:

"Why did you invite Horfield to-night?"

"Because of what you said to me at the gallery. You told me to be nice to him. I am trying to be."

"But your wife? She—I don't know—did she wish it?"

Keane felt that his body stiffened. She let go of his wrist. He saw her small distracted eyes staring at him in the dimness.

"Could she? If she had—I scarcely think——"

"My wife is always willing to receive our friends in our house. And you kindly invited her while I was away."

"But it wasn't—Horfield *made* me. You mustn't think that I——"

"Dear Lady Horfield, I should never misunderstand you. I know you are straight, sincere, honest as the day. We are both working for Mrs. Paradine. By the way are you better?"

She seemed to shuffle in her seat.

"Please—please!" she almost muttered. "If I seemed—sometimes I *have* to—it isn't that—don't let us——"

"No, no! We'll leave it. I know how things are now."

"No, you don't. Not really! No one does. You must think I'm a horrible old woman to——"

"I don't. I never could think evil of you."

"But you mustn't of *him*. That's what I mean."

She stopped. Keane was silent.

"He is not himself. Horfield's not himself."

"I don't quite understand."

"Something has happened—I can't tell you."

"Don't!" Keane exclaimed forcibly.

"No—of course! But it's upset him terribly. You don't know. He is emotional. People don't think—but I know. If you knew all I think you would be ready——"

She stopped.

"Ready for what?"

"To forgive him."

"Why should I have anything to forgive Lord Horfield?" said Keane grimly.

"But you may. In his present state—oh, why must it all happen now? Tell me—is she terribly afraid?"

"Who?"

"That poor woman? Mrs. Paradine? It is so near now."

"Mrs. Paradine shows the courage of innocence," said Keane, with a sort of fierce protective determination.

"But—she doesn't know!"

"Know what?"

"About—about Horfield. If she did she might—but perhaps with you—I mean to come. I mean to be there."

"At the trial?"

"Yes. I shall hate it. But I shall come. It may—my being there might possibly—I think he knows how I feel."

Seeing his chance Keane said boldly:

"Does he know that you have divined his secret?"

"He has never said so. We've never spoken of it—never. But he is so terribly clever in finding things out. And I—he thinks me a fool and perhaps—I suppose I am. But—" and again her small fin was on his wrist—"but even a fool who—who loves can see into even a clever man. Oh, I understand him! He doesn't know —but I do! I am the only one that—I pity him so because of that. He hurts me, but I forgive it all—because I *know* he can't help it. He hasn't chosen—but it has come to him—gradually. And now he is getting old—and it's too late. Don't let your wife hate him!"

"But dear Lady Horfield——"

"She might. She is so true and faithful—and away from all that. But if she understood him as I do she wouldn't—and he's so miserable! There are so many ways of suffering, but I think his is the worst of all."

"Why?"

"To suffer because—" she seemed to hesitate, then decided to go on, "because one has—has got twisted out of shape, that must be the worst I think."

"But do you think the twisted, as you call it, know that they are out of shape?"

"Some of them do. He does. With a brain like his he *must* know. And I think—perhaps I'm wrong——"

"Yes? What do you think?"

"That more people than one supposes know what they are and wish to be different—quite different. I do for one. And there are many others. 'It is *He* that hath made us and not we ourselves.' Do you know that whenever Horfield—when he gives way to— what I told you, and perhaps I oughtn't, but I *had* to because you are defending that poor woman—whenever he does, and to other things, too, I repeat that text to myself."

"And place the blame on God?" Keane said, moved irresistibly to the saying of it.

"Oh, no! No! Never!" she exclaimed, in a horrified voice. "That would be blasphemy."

"But then——"

"It's a mystery, all a mystery! But we shall know some day. We must just wait with patience. I try to—always."

Keane moved his broad shoulders. Wait—wait—patience! And a world full of tragedy around one. These platitudes of religion exasperated him, and yet something far down in him respected the deep-rooted belief, the deep-rooted trust, that could utter them with conviction, could cling to their meaning, though happiness crumbled and the very sun of life seemed to grow cold. Yet he could not refrain from saying:

"And if there's the danger of perhaps innocent people going to the hangman meanwhile? What then?"

"I am praying—I am praying for her every night! And for Horfield, too."

"I'm afraid that won't do us much good," Keane said bitterly.

He considered for a moment, then, returning to a subject he had already touched upon but had not sufficiently explored, he said:

"You told me just now that your husband 'probably' realises that you are aware of his tendency towards cruelty, of his secret desire to get convictions when he tries cases. Do you think he has the least suspicion that you have said anything about that to me?"

"I ought never to have told you. I ought never to have said anything. I often reproach myself for it, but——"

"Dear Lady Horfield, the thing's done! Regret is useless. And your motive was excellent."

"I thought so at the time. I said to myself——"

"I know that."

"But nevertheless it seems treacherous on my part. But for a fellow creature, a woman too——"

"You did right in telling me. By doing so you spurred me to do my very utmost for my client. Don't reproach yourself. The secret rests between us."

"Yes, yes, I know! I know you're a man of honour and would never——"

"Of course not. But now please tell me! Do you think your husband has any suspicion that you have said anything to me to his detriment? By that I mean simply—about his wish that those prisoners who come up before him should, if possible, be convicted and condemned?"

"I don't know. Sometimes I—but I don't *know!* Oh, I hope he doesn't, for if he does he will hate you."

"That would put the finishing touch to my difficulties with this case!" said Keane, with an outburst of nervous exasperation. He said nothing for a moment, then added, fixing his eyes on her with a brooding, heavy look:

"But there's always the chance——"

"What chance?"

"Of the unexpected happening."

"What do you mean, Sir Malcolm?"

"Force majeure! It crops up when we are least looking for it."

"But what do you mean?"

"Something might even yet occur to prevent your husband from judging this case."

"Do you mean his death?" she exclaimed, with a sudden shrill note in her voice.

"No, no! But a touch of illness, even a slight accident—one never knows what might happen."

"I would rather anything should happen, anything, than that harm should come to Horfield!" she exclaimed, with a vital fierceness that startled him.

"You don't suppose that I wish him harm. I was only——"

"Anything—anything rather than that!" she reiterated, waving her little hands in a distracted gesture. "Time to prepare! He must have that. And I couldn't—I couldn't go on without him."

"But I assure you——"

"I know! I know! But I can't speak of such a thing. And you mustn't! Even naming it seems to be dangerous. And I can't——"

The car stopped before the portico of the Gloucester Theatre.

. . . . . .

In the car travelling behind them Horfield said, in a low voice, as it started:

"I take this unexpected invitation as a pledge from you that my perhaps too hasty conduct the other evening is forgiven."

Gay made a slight movement, pressing a little more into her corner of the motor. But she said nothing.

"It was a charming way you chose of telling me that we are still good friends. Not a spoken or even a written word, but just a permission given to your husband to let me know that all was well."

"I didn't give any permission. I didn't know my husband was going to give the invitation," Gay said, in a very low voice.

"But when he told you, you were willing! It must have been so. Otherwise the dinner couldn't have taken place."

As she said nothing more he added:

"Could it?" in a soft, and almost wheedling tone that made her sensitive flesh creep.

Remembering her scene with her husband about Lord Horfield, his insistence on their keeping on good terms with him till the trial was over, the reason he had given for that insistence, Gay didn't know what line to take. She was in a hideous dilemma. For almost the first time in her life she felt herself withheld from frankness, inhibited from complete sincerity.

"You must have been ready to hold out the olive branch to a too impulsive man, who ought perhaps to repent in dust and ashes. Ought he?"

There was still the wheedling sound in the clear, penetrating voice, a sort of silvery coaxing timbre that made Gay feel very sick.

"Or perhaps you weren't so startled as you seemed? You must have known long ago how things were. Women always know when they have made victims of too sensitive men, men who can't be in contact with beauty and charm without showing what——"

"Please be quiet, Lord Horfield!"

She saw his thin right arm in its loose coat sleeve make a movement towards her and held her right arm high up with her left hand, stretching her left arm. He failed in his ugly effort.

"Don't be silly!" she added, in a totally different voice.

She had suddenly made up her mind, for Malcolm's sake, and perhaps for that woman's sake, to take this disgusting exhibition of

senile lechery—for so she considered it—in a bantering spirit.
After all the drive to the theatre was short, and she was utterly
resolved that once it was over she would never again let the
Judge be alone with her. She saw his thin figure, emaciated but
smart, lean towards her and pressed against the side of the car.

"But how can I help it? Tell me."

It seemed that her change of tone had encouraged him. There
was a note of alertness in his voice.

"And why is it silly to be subject to fascination? A man who
can't be is a dolt. Some people seem to think that because one
happens to possess an intellect, some learning and taste, and a
faculty for disentangling the complications, human and legal,
that come up day by day before a Judge, one has got rid of the
so-called weaknesses that alone make life worth living. But you
know better, Lady Keane, evasive as you are. And you've proved it
by asking me to-night after our absurd little misunderstanding."

"It was not a misunderstanding," said Gay, failing abruptly and
utterly in her gauche attempt at insincerity, and suddenly reverting drastically to her true self. "There was no misunderstanding. I
knew exactly what you meant and I am sure you knew my
meaning equally well. I haven't changed. Please don't think I
have."

"But then what am I to make of this invitation?"

At this moment a block in the traffic obliged Lord Horfield's
chauffeur to pull up close to an 'island' on which shone a lamp.
Light from it came into the motor car and fell upon the Judge's
long narrow face, yellowish white and lined, on his grey eyes looking out between apparently half-closed eyelids, keen and hard
and inquiring, on his faintly smiling lips. A shining silk hat
placed slightly on one side hid his head. There was something horribly buckish in his appearance as he leaned nearer to Gay and
repeated gently:

"What am I to make of it? For if *you* are still angry with me
evidently your husband isn't."

"Oh, why doesn't the chauffeur drive on!" went despairingly
through Gay's mind.

"Or perhaps you haven't told him you are angry with me?"

He watched her delicate small face with piercing eyes. He
waited, but nothing came from her. She was still making an effort

not to break away finally from the rule laid down by her husband
—no revealing of hatreds till a verdict had been given in the
Paradine case. But her power of self-control was wearing very
thin.

"You haven't?"

Gay looked out of the window and saw a dim vision of stopped
traffic, of vague people passing by.

"You have? You have! And he doesn't mind. Well then why
should we mind? Why should we be more Puritanical, less thoroughly modern than he evidently is? He's so busy now, isn't he?
This case I'm going to have the pleasure of trying almost immediately has swallowed him up. He spoke about it to-night after
you and my wife had left the dining-room. I've seldom seen a man
so strung up, so moved. He's heart and soul for his client, the
most passionate Counsel for the Defence I've come across in the
course of a pretty long career. He even so far forgot himself, dear
Lady Keane—" he leaned a little nearer to Gay—"as to express a
fervent hope that I should be able to dismiss this evidently very
remarkable and fascinating Mrs. Paradine into freedom at the end
of her trial. I was obliged to pull him up. The case being still sub
judice, you see! I couldn't discuss it with Counsel for the Defence,
or it might really have seemed as if I were lending myself to a
veiled attempt to get at me. And that wouldn't have done. But
your husband does so identify himself with his clients. That's
notorious. The Bench and Bar both know it. This time though he
seems to be really passing the measure. The whole of what we
choose to call 'London' seems to be talking about it. It's a mystery
how these things get about, but they do. They do! People talk—
women! Mrs. George Blason, whom we are going to see in a
moment, has been saying the most preposterous things. 'One begins
to wonder,' she even said at a Sunday dinner the other night,
'what will happen in a certain household if the dear prisoner gets
off.' God knows what she was driving at! She didn't explain, left
us all guessing."

With a slight jerk the motor car moved on and the Judge's
face went into shadow.

"One doesn't know—one can only—surmise. But it seems
anyhow that there'll be drama presently at the Old Bailey. Drama!
Are you against drama, Lady Keane? Not on the stage; in real

life—as it's called? But aren't you really assisting at a drama in this wintry weather?"

She heard a movement which she didn't see, for she was not looking in his direction, but was staring desperately through the window out into the night. In an instant she found that he was feeling for her hand.

"I forbid you to touch me!" she whispered. "I won't have it!"

"But if he doesn't mind? Why should you and I cut our cloth to the measure of a husband who doesn't mind?"

"I mind! I mind!"

He was silent for a moment and motionless. The car was now in Waterloo Place. They would very soon be at the theatre. Traffic was thinner here than in Regent Street and the car was going much faster.

"Take care!" she then heard Lord Horfield's voice say, softly. "Take care that you don't make your husband hate you."

Gay listened with a terrible intensity.

The voice went on:

"He's a man of vast possibilities in the region of emotion. What are you trying to hang on to? He's escaped from you. He's elsewhere. But he doesn't hate you yet. That might easily come though, considering the condition he's in. Any attempt to hang on, to get in the way—and the lava would flow out of the volcano."

The car turned into Trafalgar Square.

"Why not placate him? Why not take the line of least resistance, do what he wants?"

"I shall do what my nature requires of me," Gay said.

"And what's that?"

Gay clenched her hands under the cloak of fur she was wearing that night. She wanted terribly to make no answer, but something quite irresistible overcame her.

"I shall keep dirty people out of my life," she said.

The car drew up before the theatre.

As it did so Gay heard a voice murmur, with an intensity of acrid exasperation:

"The triumph of Mrs. Paradine!"

Always afterwards, in the following years of her life, when she thought of that evening, remembering the whole of it, Gay lived again in nightmare. The bit of time presented itself to her imaginative memory in the strange trappings of one of those dreams wherein everything is hideously real and yet everything seems slightly distorted. And always the distortion is towards ugliness and horror. She saw the bright theatre with its well-dressed crowd, the Flaquer family looking down from their box upon the party of four in the stalls, Malcolm, Lady Horfield, Lord Horfield, herself—so it came about, herself in isolation—as a place of torment, a place to be endured. Judith nodded to her and smiled, Sir Simon waved a hand, Alfred Flaquer bowed, Lady Flaquer and Amy moved their lips as if in a murmured greeting, and she, looking up, tried to answer. And it was all a ghastly failure, no real friendship in it. For nothing so sweet and sincere as friendship could exist in that nightmare place. And the curtain went up. And another abode of phantoms was revealed, with Mrs. George Blason as supreme mistress of its darkness. It is strange how often what are called the chances of life link themselves, as if of set purpose, with human distresses, press themselves in among the sorrows that people the human heart as if determined to add to the sum of them. So it was that night. The theme of the play 'got' Gay 'on the raw.' It dealt with a husband, a famous doctor, who, for a reason connected with his professional advancement—he was aiming at a Peerage, was determined to be one of those rare birds who are the Lords of medicine—compelled his wife to feign friendship, and to receive in intimacy, a man of influence who had abominably insulted her. The psychological problem of the play was how far a woman of value is justified in denying her own nature for the sake of love, in trampling down the needs of the soul to satisfy the imperious impulses of the heart. The woman Mrs. Blason represented sacrificed everything for the husband and at the end was left without even the consolation of gratitude. As Mrs. Blason said afterwards behind the scenes, where they went to congratulate her on her performance, the lesson of the play was "Don't do it!" Her big eyes, swimming, it seemed, with the malicious humour of a clown of genius, whose absurdities were probably only an embroidery upon stuff that was acutely intellectual, rested on Malcolm Keane and on Gay as she made that pronouncement, and she added: "But what on earth is the good of ever saying 'don't do it' to a woman who loves a man? She's *got* to be a fool. She's *got* to give gold for ashes. She's *got* to create in him the ingratitude that's bred of the arch-folly of self-sacrifice. Live for yourself and men will die for you. But live for them and in the end you'll make your bed like Job—wasn't it?—among the potsherds. Look at what's happened to poor me this very night! It's a fat part, but how I do despise the wretched being I represent. Every Saturday night when I draw my salary I say to myself: 'Another hundred and fifty pounds to you, Iris, for successfully denying before the B.P. the whole range of your intellect.' I loathe the part but I'll make the play run for a year nevertheless. And now you two men have got to do something for me. You've got to get me in to the Paradine case. Can't I somehow sit on the Jury?"

A nightmare conversation had followed in which the Judge and the Advocate, those phantoms of the Law who must play their tragic parts out till destiny was satisfied, had spoken the words set down for them. And a promise had been made by the Judge. And Mrs. Blason had said to the two women standing by: "And where will you two be, my dears? You won't be allowed on the Bench, I'm afraid."

Gay had seen her husband's eyes fix themselves on her with a look that had seemed to be a look of pale nightmare menace, forbidding her to imagine that she could set foot in the Old Bailey during Mrs. Paradine's trial. And she heard herself saying that she never went to the Law Courts and didn't mean to break her rule in the coming trial. And Mrs. Blason, with her dark-coloured liquid voice, had murmured an ironical: "Evasive Gay!" And Lady Horfield had begun to stammer something about Horfield never wishing her to be in Court when he was judging a case—and had lost herself in involved explanations. And then the Flaquer family had appeared and the nightmare talk had gone on. And only the long pressure of Judith Flaquer's hand had seemed, for a moment, to bring Gay out to the edge of the nightmare, to where the sleepless life of human realities began. And then there had been the silent drive home and the scene at the end of it with Malcolm.

Not a tremendous scene at all in spite of the implications underlying it. During the drive to Portland Place Gay had not considered things and made up her mind what she was going to do, though she had known that she was going to do something decisive, something that perhaps, that probably, most of those who knew her would think her incapable of doing. Events had worked together up to human decision, compelling it—the dinner, the drive to the theatre, the theme of the play, Mrs. Blason's characteristic comment upon it. But Gay had actually gone into the house quite ignorant of what was coming, though what did come was entirely owing to her conduct.

"I'm rather thirsty," she said in the hall. "I think I'll drink some lemon and water."

"Do, dear."

Malcolm's voice sounded kind, ingratiating almost.

"He is trying to thank me for to-night," Gay thought, as she walked into the downstairs sitting-room.

And her heart seemed flooded with disgust. To earn kindness from Malcolm in such a way!

In the sitting-room he poured her out some Perrier, and twisted a half-lemon on the glass pyramid, and tipped the juice into the winking bubbles. And his movements were to her as movements in a nightmare. She took the tumbler and drank. And then at once she said:

"Malcolm, you have required of me something that I can't do, though, as you know, I like always when I can to do what you wish, what pleases you, or what you think is necessary to help you in your profession. I am not going to receive Lord Horfield here again. I feel I ought to tell you at once. If he comes here, if you have him here, then I shan't see him."

She saw his face become rigid, but he didn't look at her as he said:

"I only ask you just for a time——"

"No, Malcolm, not for a time. To-night's the finish of my pretence of friendship with Lord Horfield. If I meet him by chance I'll not cut him. I won't deliberately show to other people my feeling about him. But that's all I can do."

"Gay, I beg you——"

"No, Malcolm!"

There was a silence between them. Gay was waiting for something. It didn't come and she said:

"You don't ask me what my reason is."

"Why should I? Reason enough that we neither of us like him, or ever have really liked him. He's not sympathetic to us. I like Horfield no more than you do. So we've no need to go into reasons, explaining what we both understand already. But I ask you again, seriously, for my sake, for the sake of my reputation——"

"What has that got to do with it?"

"Everything, perhaps. A complete break between Horfield and us at this moment would be very detrimental to me as a lawyer. Horfield, I'm pretty sure, is a revengeful man, and he has the power unfortunately to revenge himself on me—oh, subtly, of course, but none the less with thorough-going completeness—if you make him angry. It's only a question of keeping the peace for a very short time longer. In——"

"There's no peace to keep."

She said it deliberately. But even then he asked no questions. She realised that he was determined that she should not explain. If she did explain, frankly, brutally, she would cut the ground from under his feet, and he would be forced, for the sake of his own pride, his own decency—or the appearance of both—to capitulate. Should she save him, or speak? For an instant, a nightmare instant, she couldn't decide.

"Yes, there is! We're still on apparently amicable terms with Horfield, and I told him to-night that I hoped he'd come to us sometimes and——"

"Malcolm, Lord Horfield has tried to make love to me. The illness of Lady Horfield, poor woman, the other night was all a clumsy pretence. She wasn't really ill, but he didn't want her with us at the theatre. He wished to be alone with me."

"Oh, I know he's a fool about——"

"Then you wish me to put up with his disgustingness?"

Keane was silent, and stood looking down at the carpet.

"To-night again, in the car, going to the theatre!"

Still complete silence.

"Tell me, then, Malcolm! You know now how things are."

Still looking down he said, in a dull voice:

"What am I to do? Horfield has power as a Judge. And I have to try to save a woman's life. A few words from him may turn the scale with a Jury. Can't you see——"

Just for a moment Gay felt guilty, with a nightmare guiltiness, distressing in an even unnatural way. For she knew that she had said irreparable words in the motor car going to the theatre. Malcolm was striving to keep something that was already utterly lost because of her. But she didn't tell him that. For in spite of the cruelty in him that seared her, cruelty caused by the woman in prison whom she had never seen, she had pity for him. She must always have pity for him in misery, trouble, in the darkness of the soul's waste places.

"I'll go away!" she said.

Then he looked at her with startled eyes.

"Leave me?"

"I'll go into the country, to the cottage, till the trial is over. Then there will be no chance of my having to show Lord Horfield any more what I feel about him. And if you must have him here you can have him alone."

"Perhaps that will be best," he said slowly, heavily.

He stood for a moment in silence.

"Very well then. Let it be so."

On the following morning Gay went down to their Surrey home. Franklin and Sausage accompanied her. Keane remained alone in Portland Place till the opening day of Mrs. Paradine's trial. It had all been a nightmare through which Gay had been forced to pass, with sleepless eyes and a brain capable of registering impressions, but not of dealing with them in the ordinary way of a brain unclouded by the influences which usually attack it only when some of its power to fight for itself is withdrawn.

She went away without telling Malcolm that, with a sentence, she had lost for him the battle for the indulgence of Mrs. Paradine's Judge.

XXXI

GAY stuck to her intention. She did not move out of Surrey till Mrs. Paradine's trial began. That year March was a bitter month, for the winter lingered and seemed viciously determined not to be chased away by the breath of spring's influence. The March winds were stingingly keen; the earth was frost-bound on many mornings. On some days snow fell towards twilight; the daylight died in a flurry of snow. When the darkness came on Gay sat in the one big room in the cottage by a wood fire, in lamp-light and firelight. Sausage lay with his chin on a foot, serenely contented. And Gay did some embroidery, or turned the pages of a book, or sat and looked at the fire, and something within her, something remote and machine-like, was numbering the minutes till the day of the trial should dawn.

"I shall stay here till the trial is over. And then———"

But there her mind stopped. She could foresee nothing.

If Mrs. Paradine were found guilty and sentenced—what then? And if she were found innocent and set free—what then? Gay could not tell. She remembered Malcolm's face, her fear for, and even on one occasion of, him; she remembered his manner, after his return from the North, the acute nervous exasperation in which he seemed drowned as in an element, and she could not see him released in either event. And she was bound with him.

Two days before the opening of the trial, she was called by Franklin to the telephone in the morning.

"Somebody wants you, my lady."

"It's my husband?"

"No, my lady. It's somebody speaking from Hyde Park Gardens."

"The Flaquers. I'm coming."

She went to the telephone, gave her name, and heard a servant's voice say that Miss Judith Flaquer wished to speak to her. In a moment she heard the eagerly vital voice of Judith asking whether she wasn't coming back to London.

"No, Judy. I'm staying on here."

"All alone?"

"I've got Sausage with me."

"And you don't mean to come up?"

"No. Why? What is there specially to come up for?"

There was a pause. Then Judith said:

"Would you like me to run down? For the day? I'd drive my little Benz. Should I disturb you?"

"No—no! Do come!"

"Very well. I will. Expect me any time. Good . . ."

"Wait, Judy!"

"Yes?"

"Bring something. Stay the night!"

"Shall I?"

"But perhaps you're engaged?"

"Not if you want me."

"Do—do then!"

As Gay went away from the telephone she wondered almost sadly at her own eagerness, at the sudden sensation of physical, as well as of mental, energy that surged through her. It marked the depth of the abyss of loneliness in which she had been sunk.

"No one in the world can have felt more solitary than I have."

Judith arrived in the afternoon, quite alone, bringing a suitcase with her. What Gay had taken to calling the 'twilight snow' was beginning to fall when they met on the cottage doorstep. The 'little Benz' was an open two-seater, and Judith's cheeks were glowing from the keen air as she kissed Gay and, with kind, penetrating eyes, summed her up quickly.

An outdoor servant came into the drive.

"He'll put your car into the garage. Give Franklin your suitcase. How pleased Sausage is!"

"And you—evasive Gay?"

For answer, Gay gave her a hug that seemed scarcely to come from Gay. That hug gave swift Judith the knowledge of what the loneliness had been.

After tea, in spite of the snow, they took a short walk together on the terrace in front of the cottage, and Judith told Gay 'the news.' But she did not mention the coming trial. Nor did Gay. And both the friends, in spite of their careless and animated talk, were conscious of a reserve existing between them, of avoidances which were the enemies of real charming intimacy. This reserve lasted till after dinner, which they ate at a small table in the big room by the fire. But when later they were smoking cigarettes on a sofa, and the table had been taken away and Judith was sipping her coffee, with the hardihood which was characteristic of her, in spite of the delicacies which she knew how to introduce into even the closest friendship, she said:

"Can we—or can't we—be rather frank to-night, Gay? Not too frank! No! Don't be afraid. I think I know where to stop, even with a friend. But, if you'll let me, I should like to say one or two things to-night."

After a moment of hesitation, during which a slight flush came on Gay's cheeks, she answered:

"Yes? What is it, Judy?"

"Ought you to stay here all alone during this trial that's just coming on?"

"Why not?"

"Ought you to leave Sir Malcolm alone in Portland Place? Is it wise?"

"But he'll be in Court all day, and even at night he'll be immersed in the case."

"Somehow, I feel as if you ought to be there."

"But what good could I do?"

"None, perhaps. Yet I'd rather you were there. Just an instinct! And then—*can* you stay here? *Can* you keep away?"

"I—I meant to. I believe I——"

"Ah, you have had a struggle about it! I knew!"

"Judy, I don't want to come up because if I do—if I'm in town——"

"Yes? What is it?"

"You know I've never yet been to a trial, never seen Malcolm in—in action."

"I know."

"He has never seemed to want me to be in Court. And I haven't wanted to go. But, Judy, if I were in London, I should have to go this time. I couldn't keep away. And I know Malcolm would hate me to be there."

After a pause, Judith said:

"Need he know it?"

"But I have never kept anything from Malcolm! I mean, I have never done things on the sly that I didn't wish him to know about."

"No. I'm sure you haven't. Well then, perhaps you had better stay here. But I don't like your being here all alone."

She drank some more coffee.

"I would offer to stay with you, but I am too selfish."

"How—selfish?"

"I am going to this trial. I can't keep away. And Papa seems to want me to be there. It's a rare thing with him to be nervous, but he's all strung up about this case."

"*You* are going!" said Gay, sharply.

For a moment she sat in silence as if considering something

deeply. Judith sat watching her and smoking. Gay looked very sad, even worn with sorrow, less fresh, less youthful than usual. Little hollows were noticeable under her eyes, and the eyes held a look of painful anxiety. There was even something furtive about them. The clear, open gaze of Gay had given place to a nervous, almost feverish expression, that made her resemble many of London's pleasure-hunting women, whereas formerly she had been definitely unlike them, a woman apart, a rather rare woman who was trying for nothing beyond her reach, but was quietly living a life to which she was suited, and in which all her friends wished to keep her.

"Well, if you go——" Gay said at last.

And then again she was silent. Judith realised that she was mentally struggling, and longed to help her, but she didn't know what to do, not being at all sure of the exact nature of the struggle.

"Judy," Gay began again, this time with great decision. "I want terribly to go to the Old Bailey; terribly. I've never wanted anything so much as I want that. But if Malcolm knew I was there, if he saw me, or if he heard I was in Court, I have the feeling that it would upset him dreadfully. I know it would. I think he was very glad when I left London."

"Perhaps he was. Nevertheless, I believe you had better go back to him."

"Stay in Portland Place?"

"Stay in Portland Place."

"Why?"

"I don't feel that Sir Malcolm ought to be left quite alone just now. He's tremendously strung up, tremendously excited. I know that from Papa."

"But what could I do?" Gay asked, and there was a despairing note in her voice.

"Perhaps nothing. Perhaps a great deal. We simply can't tell."

"But if I go, Judy, I can't keep away from the Old Bailey. That would be beyond my power."

Gay got up nervously and went to stand by the fire.

"I couldn't sit at home, so near, and wait, and not know what was going on."

"I can quite understand how you feel."

"And at the same time, I wouldn't for the world do anything that might weaken Malcolm at such a crucial moment. He—there are things—reasons—this isn't an ordinary case."

"It seems rather complex, certainly," said Judith, in a voice that had become colourless.

"It comes to this, Judy. Either I must keep right out of it and stay here till it's over, or I can go up to town. But in that case I can't keep away from the trial. I can't!" (She twisted her hands, clasping one with the other.) "I had made up my mind to stay here alone. And I could have done it. I could have forced myself to do it. And now you have broken in and upset all my resolution. Oh, Judy dear, do forgive me for seeming so ungracious! I was longing for you to come. I'm thankful to have you here. But all the same, you've upset my—my will. That's it! I want to see Mrs. Paradine, Judy! I want to see Mrs. Paradine!"

"I know, dear! I know. Wait a minute! Let me think what's best to be done. I want to get it clear in my mind."

"Yes, yes."

After two or three minutes of silence, Judith said:

"I may be wrong, but I believe you'd better come up to town. I can't bear to leave you alone down here. I can't bear the idea of your remaining here all alone during the trial. That's one 'for.' Another is that, whatever has happened"—she said the last three words with a sort of gentle but significant pressure—"I'm against Sir Malcolm being left alone in the house during the trial in his present state of strong emotional excitement. That is 'for' number two. You two shouldn't be separated just now."

"We are separated, Judy."

"Hush! Don't say that! Don't believe that! I daresay you think you can be no use to him as he is just now. You may be right. You may be wrong. Anyhow—don't give up. To do that would be weak, as I see it. And now for the 'against' your going to the Old Bailey. I think that might be managed without Sir Malcolm finding out. But you must let me take Papa into the secret."

"Oh, but——"

"You must! You know Papa. And Gay, I'll tell you something. I'm sure he understands."

Gay flushed.

"I shall tell Papa and see how it can be managed. Of course, if you go you go with me. We'll stick together. And of course when it's over, you'll tell Sir Malcolm."

"Yes."

"If it's impossible—I mean if Papa thinks it can't be managed without Sir Malcolm finding out—then perhaps you had better stay down here. But I want you to come up. I think that would be the best for both of you. I rather believe in rushing on the spear. You know what I mean, letting the inevitable find you going to confront it. You'd better see Mrs. Paradine and have done with it. Then perhaps you'll feel better—or worse! Anyhow, you'll be out of the fog. To-morrow, early, I'll go up to town. I'll see Papa and talk it over with him. Then I'll run down again."

"What a lot of trouble for you!"

"Don't be absurd, dearest! I've been longing to do something for ages, but you held off."

"I felt I——"

"Of course you did. And now let's drop it. What did you think of Mrs. Blason's acting the other night? Papa thought it marvellous."

That night when they parted at Judith's bedroom door she said, after kissing Gay affectionately:

"What a pity it is that veils are out of fashion, those veils with dense patterns women used to wear in some year when I wasn't prancing to afternoon parties. Mother met Mary Garden once wearing one at a party in New York, and she told me she couldn't detect what she was like, or even whether she was dark or fair."

"Really!" Gay murmured, looking embarrassed.

Judith gripped her hand.

"If you're going to do it, Gay, you must make up your mind to go through with it. No fumbling! No muddling! No non-Conformist conscience! No holding back. And if we have to go into the public gallery among the left-overs, you'll need a pair of opera glasses. You're so sweetly short-sighted."

She spoke briskly, unemotionally.

It seemed to her that Gay checked the inclination to shiver, as she murmured:

"Good night, Judy."

As Gay went to her room with Sausage at her heels, she said out loud, but without knowing that she spoke:

"A pair of opera glasses!"

It was true that she could not see very far. Perhaps from the public gallery of the Old Bailey she would not be able to see clearly the woman in the dock. Not knowing the Central Criminal Court, she didn't know. When she was in her bedroom, she went to a drawer, opened it, and turned over its contents till she came to a tiny case of stamped leather. In it was a minute pair of very strong glasses which she had often used in Covent Garden Opera House. She sat down in a chair and held the glasses to her eyes for a moment.

"But perhaps Sir Simon will advise against it. And then I shan't go."

Judith Flaquer left very early on the following day, promising to be back in the late afternoon.

"I won't telephone. I'll come and tell you what Papa thinks. Expect me any time after five. Don't worry. Go for a good walk with Sausage. Go out on the Common. Get air. Tire your body and give your mind a good rest."

She let in the clutch and the little car slipped out of sight down the drive.

Gay took the advice about going out on the Common. Sausage was enthusiastic. He had a passion for walks that was insatiable, and his ecstasy in starting, expressed in small leaps, eager barks, much running on and running back to make sure that Mistress was doing the right thing, and intense investigation of hedgerows and frosty grass clumps, diverted Gay's mind for a few minutes. But once they were out on the wide stretching Common, under a dark sky like a blanket of steel, a sleety wind about them, no living thing in sight, no suggestion yet of energy in the earth, no promise in the heavens, of coming light on the horizon, she felt out of all communion with the happy little dog, and utterly forgot Judith's advice to let her mind have a good rest. But she did not forget that she was to tire her body, and she walked far and at a good pace, and only drew near home when the light was beginning to fail, and Judith ought, if she kept her promise, to be nearing the cottage.

As she came into the drive, Sausage, his tail lifted high and his large ears flapping, uttered a muffled bark and ran forward, assuming his policeman's demeanour, wary and suspicious and ready to act with firmness if necessary. Gay turned the corner and came in sight of the house. Judith's little Benz was drawn up before the door.

Gay stood still for a moment. A strange feeling of acute nervousness seized her. What message had Judith brought from Sir Simon? Was she to go or not to go to London? At that moment she had a cowardly longing to stay where she was. It was not unlike a child's desire, instantly gratified in the child's case, to hide its head under the bedclothes when it hears an inexplicable noise in the night. But Sausage, after smelling the car, had run into the house. Gay followed him.

She found Judith, who had only just arrived, in the hall, taking off her leather coat. After their greeting, Judith went with Gay into the big room, shut the door, and said at once:

"Papa says it can be managed. Give me some tea, dear, and we'll talk it over. I'm rather cold and a wee bit tired. But it's good to be here by the fire. So you took my advice?"

"About tiring the body—yes."

"But the mind wouldn't be ordered about! I know. I know. It's an obstinate jade and needs more than the whip, the bastinado. And now we shall have to get to business. Ah, here's the tea, thank the beneficent Powers!"

There was a determined brisk and common-sense cheerfulness in her voice. Gay realised that sentiment was not to have any place in their conversation. Judith was taking charge. Well, it was probably much better so.

Franklin had brought in the tea. When she had gone and the door was shut, Judith immediately went on talking in the brisk, cheerful, common-sensible tone.

"There's going to be an enormous crowd at the trial. Everybody wants to get in. All the Mrs. George Blasons of London are clamouring for admissions. At first Papa seemed very doubtful. He realised that if you don't want to run up against people who know you it would be madness for you to be in the well of the Court. The alternative is for you to get into the gallery, which as a rule is the home of the nobodies. But even there on such an occasion there's of course a risk of your being seen by someone who might recognise you. If you are determined to go you must run that risk."

Judith paused, waited. Gay hesitated for a moment. Then she said:

"You still feel I oughtn't to leave Malcolm quite alone during the trial?"

"Emphatically I do. And Papa thinks as I do. He is anxious about your husband."

"Anxious?"

"Yes. I don't want to frighten you, but Sir Malcolm, according to Papa, is in a highly nervous state. You'd better go up."

"Then I will. And I shall take the risk you spoke of."

"Darling, mayn't I have just one cup of tea?"

"Oh, Judy, do forgive me! What a brute I am!"

"Gay—a brute! Thank you. And I'll help myself to all the rest. I'm fiercely hungry. Tell me something. You're short-sighted. We all know that. Have you hidden away anywhere a pair of spectacles?"

"Yes, but I never wear them. Vanity, I'm afraid!"

"Are they large or small?"

"Very large. Hideous things with those horrible horn frames."

"Are they clearers?"

"No. They were specially made for my eyes."

"Then you can see people through them?"

"Oh yes, of course."

"And do they change your appearance at all?"

"Well, they make me look hideous, and as I never wear them I suppose people might find me changed by them."

"Are they here?"

"No, in London."

"We must have them out to-morrow. Could Franklin fetch them and bring them to us?"

"Yes. But where?"

"I can tell her where."

Judith looked at Gay intensely across the tea table. They were sitting opposite to each other.

"Have you ever worn your hair pulled right back from your forehead?" was her next question.

"Never. My forehead's much too high."

"All the better. Give me another cup, please, dear. While you're doing it I'll fetch my little bag, the little idiotic bag that every woman feels she must carry."

"Oh, but——"

"No—but!"

She went with her springy step out of the room, and came back almost immediately with a very chic black and white bag in her hand.

"I've got something here that's terribly unfashionable now, though it, or rather they, used to be the dernier cri when Mamma was in America."

She opened the bag and produced two black veils with elaborate patterns on them, patterns so elaborate that they made the veils look almost like masks.

"These would conceal almost any blushes, however vivid!" she said, handing them to Gay, and taking her second cup of tea.

"But, Judy, indeed I can't let you——"

"Oh yes, you can! You must!"

"But you would have had a seat in——"

"I'm going with you to the back of the gallery. Papa will see to it that we get seats there. The gallery door-keeper is a devoted friend of his and gets a huge turkey from him every Christmas as ever is. He'll do anything for Papa. Whatever happens, however great the crowd is, Papa has promised we shall get in. But only at the back of the gallery. There you'll be more unlikely to be seen by anyone you know. Still, we must take our precautions. I have bought a black hat that will 'go' with drawn-back hair and a high forehead. You'll want to take off your veil in Court, if possible, and so shall I mine. Otherwise, we should be asphyxiated and see very little. Trust it all to me."

"Then we shall go up early to-morrow?"

"Yes. But we shall only go to the Court when the proceedings have started. You mustn't chance being seen by your husband. I've arranged everything with Papa. In the afternoon you'll go back to Portland Place."

"Shall I telegraph to Malcolm?"

"I shouldn't. Let him find you there when he gets back. It will be a pleasant surprise for him."

Judith said all this in a cheerful, indeed almost gay, voice. Gay quite understood why. Judith was 'taking a line' and meant to stick to it, for the sake of her friend. No sentiment, no emotion —at any rate till they were well en route. Then perhaps—but no need to think of that yet. One might almost have supposed, from Judith's voice and manner and bright, sparkling eyes, that they were two women planning a 'lark.' And the life of a woman in peril! Gay thought of that and sickened for a moment. But she understood Judith, and knew that all was done for her. There was drama ahead and they must brace up, she especially, to confront it. And Judith was trying to help her.

Their evening was passed without any letting down. Everything was decided in respect of the morrow.

Franklin, who could be trusted, was to go to Portland Place, with Sausage, after the hour when Keane would have left for the Old Bailey. She would get the spectacles and bring them to the empty service flat of a friend of Judith's, which Judith had access to, after leaving Gay's luggage at the house and telling the servants that their mistress would be at home in the afternoon. She had some errands to do in town for her lady, and would return presently to wait for her. From the flat, which was in Hallam Street, the two friends would drive in a taxi to the Old Bailey. If all went well and Gay met no one who recognised her, she would go each day to the Old Bailey till the trial was finished, leaving Portland Place after Keane had left it, and getting back there before he came home.

Gay hated what she was going to do. At moments she despised herself for her determination to do it. But she had told Judith the truth. If she went up to London, she must go to the Old Bailey. She had not the power of will to keep away from it. For months now her mind had been obsessed by the Paradine case. She could struggle against it no longer.

She, too, must be on the battlefield.

XXXII

"It's all right, Madam. Sir Simon has told me. Wait here a minute, and I'll let you in at the back. There's a couple of places being kept for you, but I have to get out those that's *in* 'em."

So spoke, or rather whispered, the 'Turkey-man,' as Judith called Sir Simon's friend of the Old Bailey, a rosy-faced, broad-shouldered fellow, with determined brown eyes and the general look of a 'chucker out'—which he wasn't.

"The crowd's something awful," he added. "The Counsel for the Prosecution is speaking."

"People in our seats? But will they go?"

The Turkey-man smiled on one side of his large mouth.

"Will they go, Madam! Why"—he bent to her left ear—"they're being paid to keep the seats warm for you and your lady friend."

As he finished speaking, he straightened up and shot a curious glance at the veiled face of Gay, who was standing by Judith.

"You just keep close to me, both of you, and wait where you are when I go in. I'll be back in a mo—in a moment, that is."

"Come on, dear!" Judith whispered to Gay.

Gay followed her and the attendant.

Now that she was on the point of seeing what she had for many weeks ardently longed to see, was on the edge of revelation and greater knowledge, she felt an intense desire to draw back, to get away, get far away, and to stay far away until this trial which had impended, like a great blackness, over her life for a time that seemed very long, drawn out like an infinite chain of days full of suspicion and tragedy, was over. She was filled with a sensation of fear, even of dread, and with a horror of publicity. Imaginatively, she had already put herself in the place of the woman on account of whom all this machinery had been set in motion. Already, she began to realise the immense difference that there is between the reading of a drama of real life and the actual assisting at the playing out of it. And yet, so far, she had seen nothing except a crowd of idlers in the vicinity of the Court, and now people thronging the corridors inside the building and pressing about certain doors in the vain hope of, by some lucky chance, gaining access to some vantage point from which they could obtain a glimpse of the woman of whom all London was talking.

"Stick to me, ladies!" whispered Sir Simon's friend, moving forward till he got to the door. "And now just stand here. I shan't be a minute."

He passed inside.

He was as good as his word. In a very brief time he reappeared, followed by two nondescript though decently dressed men who, Gay thought, as she peered at them through the pattern of her veil, looked startled and sulky. Perhaps they had already got interested in the trial and were cross at being hawked out of it, although they were being paid for giving up their seats.

"Now, ladies!"

A door swung, and immediately Gay was aware of a voice speaking. It was the voice of a man, rather harsh and strong, and it said:

"This was the home to which this blinded man, Colonel Paradine, this man who had fought for England and been awarded the highest decoration it is in the power of His Majesty the King to bestow on a subject, the Victoria Cross, retired, to live out in darkness the remainder of his life, attended by his devoted servant, William Marsh, and by the lady who, after his great affliction had overtaken him, had become his wife, by the woman whom you see before you in the dock, by Mrs. Ingrid Paradine."

"It's Sir Joseph Farrell speaking. He leads for the Crown," Judith murmured in Gay's ear, as they got to their places at the extreme back of the gallery. "We can stand up here if we want to, since there's nobody behind us. But what a squash!"

"Shall you ladies want anything in the lunch interval?"

"No, thanks. We've brought something with us."

The Turkey-man nodded and went out. The rather harsh voice went on speaking.

Almost directly Judith whispered:

"I don't believe there's anyone up here whom we know. I shall take off my veil. You do as you like."

Gay moved her head in reply. The heat in the Court was great, a stifling heat of humanity packed closely in an ill-ventilated, though large, chamber. And the pattern of her veil prevented her from seeing anything with real clearness. After a moment of consideration she decided to trust Judith and put up her hands to her head.

And as the veil dropped into her hands, and her hands went down to her lap, with her short-sighted eyes, now helped by the pair of strong horn-rimmed spectacles which Franklin had brought to her that morning, she saw for the first time a Court of Justice.

She did not know what she had expected it to be like, yet she had the feeling that it was unlike something that she must have conceived in her imagination, that it was less remarkable, less impressive, more ordinary, and yet somehow more horrid. Although she saw that the place was crowded with people—at least all of the Court that she was able to see was crowded—there was, to her, something dull about the general aspect of it, something ordinary, commonplace, unbefitting a Court consecrated to terrible dramas of humanity.

Then for a moment something, she did not know what, but it must be something belonging to herself, seemed to be laughing at her for being the prey of a melodramatic imagination. Terrible dramas of humanity! Carry it a little farther! Terrible melo-dramas, perhaps? This was simply a place for the cold and methodical threshing out of facts. Facts on the threshing floor. A winnowing place. Why should it be dressed up? An absurd ex-pectation on her part.

And yet there were robes in it, faces looking out from beneath wigs, and certainly looking, in consequence, more expressive and remarkable than if the wigs had not been there.

They were in Court Number I of the Central Criminal Court. The wide open Court, Gay saw through her spectacles, was panelled in light oak. The large dock, placed in front of the public gallery, which only held about seventy people although it was crammed, had sides made of plate glass. Directly facing it and the gallery, raised up on a high platform, sat the Judge, Lord Horfield, curi-ously changed by his wig and robes. On either side of him were the seats reserved for the use of the Lord Mayor and Sheriffs. These were unoccupied. Below, sitting in front of a large oak desk, was the Clerk of the Court, and below him, between his desk and the dock, at a large oak table sat the Police Officers in charge of the case, the prosecuting Solicitor and Sir Simon Flaquer, the Solicitor for the Defence. On the right of this table, rising towards the side of the Court, were rows of green leather-covered seats. In the first three rows sat Counsel. The remaining rows, called 'City Lands,' reserved for the use of the Aldermen and Sheriffs of the City of London, were crowded with spectators, some of them women. On the other side of the table was the Jury box, raised to the level of the Judge's platform. In it sat nine men and three women. To the left of it was the witness box, shaped, Gay thought, like a church pulpit, with a large, fan-like screen of oak behind it to improve the acoustics. Behind the Dock, and on each side of it, were oak benches. And these benches were crammed with people, many of them women. Along the front of Counsel's seats, and on the floor of the Judge's platform, and in front of the prisoner in the Dock, were placed heaps of potpourri. And by the side of Lord Horfield lay a nosegay of fresh flowers.

"Flowers!" Gay whispered, with a sort of dull astonishment.

"An old precaution against jail fever, handed down to us," Judith murmured. "The potpourri's a survivor, too, and not a bad one. The atmosphere's pretty foul."

She touched Gay gently.

"There's Papa! And over there's Sir Malcolm!"

Her keen eyes went to the Dock but she said nothing about it or about the woman seated in it between two officers. Gay could find out Mrs. Paradine for herself. Judith knew that any help from her was unnecessary.

She stole presently a side glance at Gay. But Gay was not looking in the direction of the Dock but at the green leather seats on the right of the table at which the Police Officers and solicitors were sitting. Among the occupants of them one man was standing, the man who was speaking, who was telling the story of the case for the prosecution in the rather harsh voice with scarcely any use of gesture, but occasionally turning this way or that with a sweeping movement, now apparently fixing his attention on the Judge, now on the Jury, Sir Joseph Farrell, Counsel for the Crown.

Gay stared at him through her big spectacles. She was wanting to look at someone else, but put off the gratification of her wish, as a weak person sometimes puts off an evil day knowing nevertheless that it must come. He was a short, broad, sturdy-looking middle-aged man, with a rather large fleshy face on which grew two long grey whiskers. The rest of the face was shaved. Above the eyes sprouted two very short, but exceedingly thick, eyebrows, which looked as if they had been brushed out to make them as prominent and pugnacious as possible.

The harsh voice ran on, slowly telling the story of the Paradines. Just at first Gay only heard it in patches. Her eyes and her mind were so busy receiving impressions, registering them, or trying to get rid of them that there were moments when though she knew the voice was travelling on she did not know what it said, heard it only as a blur of sound meaning nothing to her. At other moments, however, the words seemed to sink into her and become embedded in her mind. She did not know why at moments she heard, at moments she did not hear what Counsel for the Crown was saying. Her mind, she supposed afterwards, must have been working in a queer way, letting some things in, keeping other things out, arbitrarily. And she wasn't in control of it, was letting it run loose, give way to vagaries.

Very strange those grey whiskers! Yet they looked legal.

"Now, members of the Jury, I desire to direct your attention to certain peculiarities which, as will presently be given in evidence, were undoubtedly characteristic of Colonel Paradine and which may prove to have an important bearing on the case. His nobilities, of which probably few Englishmen and women are unaware, nobilities which won him the thanks of his Sovereign and the Victoria Cross, and which, tragically enough, brought upon him the darkness in which he ended his days, were mingled with and qualified by faults of temperament and exhibitions of temper which, natural enough, even perhaps forgivable enough, in one who had lost almost all that makes life worth living, made him nevertheless not an easy man to live with. You all know——"

Lord Horfield with a bouquet of flowers! How narrow his pale face looked between the falling lappets of wig which transformed him from a coldly satirical, yet often smiling and ingratiating man of the world, or abominable furtive lover, into an impassive instrument of Justice. To Gay at that moment he gave an impression of calmness, almost of indifference. There was, as she watched him for a moment through her spectacles, something remote and even puppet-like about him perched up there in wig and robes on his high platform, sometimes sitting very still, sometimes bending and writing.

"These exhibitions of temper were no doubt very trying to those about Colonel Paradine, and were calculated to get on the nerves of any sensitive woman, although, considering the circumstances, there was much to excuse them. Colonel Paradine had all his life been an intensely masculine man, a great sportsman, and what is sometimes called a very gallant man with women. Women had played a great part in his life. He had been an ardent admirer of beauty in women. To such a man blindness was a terrible affliction. He could no longer——"

Gay's eyes travelled back from Lord Horfield and his flowers to the green leather benches. Although she had already seen many people in the Court there were two whom she had not seen yet, whom she had managed instinctively to miss seeing, her husband and Mrs. Paradine. (The latter indeed she had seen for an instant as an occupant of the Dock, but not as an individual woman.) Now at last she looked definitely for Malcolm.

She found him sitting beside his Junior, Mr. Arthur Calling, a small, eager-looking man with a red complexion and a sharp little nose that thrust itself forward above a mouth containing prominent teeth. Malcolm Keane in this neighbourhood looked very large. That was what struck Gay at first, large and impressive in his white wig and black robes with the falling white below his collar and the white ruffles—as she thought them—falling over his wrists. He was rather lounging in his seat, with his long legs crossed and his arms folded. As she gazed at him she saw him frown and uncross his legs, then cross them again. He moved his arms, put his hands on his knees, turned and stared at the Jury. Then he looked at the Dock. But Gay did not look at it. She was intent on this large, and now apparently restless, man in the white and the black, to whom she had given so much, so very much, with whom she had been so happy—ten years of happiness!— because of whom she had suffered and was suffering so intimately, this man who had given her such blessed companionship and who now was teaching her the inner meaning of loneliness, this man master of opposites, who had been her lover and closest comrade, who had become now, in some mysterious and unfathomable way, more strange to her than any other man she had known.

"Hindley Hall, where these two people lived, is a somewhat remote place not far from the Coast of Cumberland, and facing the hills of what is called the Lake District. There were neighbours, of course. Colonel Paradine was a well-born man, one of the County people, belonging to a family universally known and respected in the North. On their taking up residence at Hindley everybody called at the Hall as a matter of course, anxious to sympathise with him and to make acquaintance with his foreign wife. The prisoner in the Dock is a Scandinavian, I am instructed, born of a Danish father and a Swedish mother. Her origin was humble. At one time she served in a barber's shop in Copenhagen, and while there was taken notice of by a young man of infamous character——"

Gay began to listen intently. Her mind no longer caught up certain sentences and let other sentences escape from her as water escapes out of a fishing-net. She concentrated automatically. She was listening to a lucid account of the origin and life of the woman who had assumed such a terrible importance in her own life. But while she listened she still looked at her husband, obliged to try to see what effect the narration was having on him. But now a clear silvery voice interrupted the harsh voice that was speaking.

"What was that you said? A house of bad character—was it? I didn't quite catch."

"Yes, my Lord—of bad character."

"By that do you mean a brothel?"

"I am instructed that it was a house frequented by women of a certain class, my Lord."

"A brothel," said the clear, carrying voice of the Judge. And he bent over the desk in front of him and wrote.

Gay saw her husband make an abrupt movement, turning his head towards the Bench. Then he sat back, folded his arms, and remained motionless. Judith Flaquer's eyes went to Gay. But Gay did not return the glance. She was thinking about Lord Horfield. She was convinced that Lord Horfield had only pretended that he hadn't heard what Counsel was saying and that he had made Counsel repeat it in order that it might be at once driven home to the minds of the Jury. The words 'a brothel' still sounded in her ears, and no doubt in the ears of everyone in the Court.

So Mrs. Paradine had come out of a brothel! Something sickened within her. How different was the effect of words spoken before a crowd and the same words read in a newspaper. There was a terrible nudity in words spoken in Court. In the newspapers there were some rags at least of clothing about them.

"I understand why Malcolm never wanted me to enter into this part of his life," Gay thought.

And he had kept her out all these years—for this. So that she might come 'new' to the Paradine case. A smile that was bitterly ironic twisted her lips. 'Evasive Gay' and her sheltered life! The strings that men pull are of thread, the strings 'the gods' pull of steel. For a moment she stared at her own selfishness, at what she thought of now as her almost vicious avoidance of life. She had believed that she had lived for Malcolm, but she had lived for herself, too. Never wishing to harm anyone of what good had she been in the troubled world? She had kept away. But now, like some woman awakened to a flogging, she was dragged forth from her hiding place and the lash descended upon her. And she felt that she deserved it. She had thought to dwell for ever within the glades of the Garden of Eden, and now she was driven out with a flaming sword to have drastic contact with life. She had shrunk from the ugliness and the horror of life with the thought: "They are not for me." And now Destiny took her by the throat and compelled her into the midst of them. She was indeed having a lesson in the Eternal Ironies.

"When seeking to bring home a crime to one suspected of its perpetration the first thing to do, members of the Jury, is to seek for a possible motive for its committal. Crimes indeed have been committed without any ascertainable motive. Murders have been done and the why of them has never been discovered. The heart of the human being is mysterious, and it is sometimes difficult, if not impossible, to trace the cause of a terrible action to its source in the human brain, that source which has received an imperative message from elsewhere. But just consider for a moment the case of the woman in the Dock before you, of Mrs. Paradine. Here you have a woman who, through the kindness of the American I have mentioned, this Mr. Powers, the former diplomat, had been extricated from what is usually called the underworld, taken away from all her former associations, and introduced into a totally different way of life on the other side of the Atlantic. Whatever Mr. Powers' motive in interesting himself in this evidently beautiful and fascinating young girl——"

Gay, who had just turned her eyes at last to the woman in the Dock, and was feeling furtively for her tiny pair of strong glasses, was startled to hear her husband's powerful voice interrupt the speaker. It said:

"My Lord, I must protest against my learned friend's implication. I understand that Mr. Powers is not to be called as a witness in this case. And therefore I submit that it is not in order to attempt to prejudice my client by hinting at anything to her detriment which will remain unsupported by evidence on which I should have the right to cross-examine."

"What implication do you allege on the part of the learned Counsel for the Crown, Sir Malcolm?" asked Lord Horfield in his most gentle voice. "I noticed nothing calculated to prejudice the prisoner."

"My Lord, there was, in my view, a distinct suggestion that Mr. Powers had some other motive than chivalry and Christian charity in rescuing my client from the dark misery into which she had been foully inveigled."

"My Lord," said Sir Joseph Farrell, "I intended no implication. I merely called attention to the fact that it was not possible to know precisely what was the motive which prompted this Mr. Powers to do what he did do, namely to take the prisoner into his service, after rescuing her from the low people with whom she was, and convey her across the seas to America."

"His and his wife's service!" interposed Keane, with cutting emphasis.

"I find nothing to rule out of order so far in the learned Counsel's opening," said Lord Horfield.

"Anyway I will pass away from that," said Sir Joseph Farrell smoothly, having made his point. "As my learned friend objects I will leave it."

And he continued to deal with the past life of Mrs. Paradine while Gay for the moment forgot her opera glasses.

"She eventually became a trained Swedish masseuse," he said presently. "So she called herself, I understand, although her father was a Dane."

"My Lord!" interposed Keane, again on his feet.

"What is it, Sir Malcolm?" asked the Judge, in a soft, penetrating voice.

"May I point out that my client called herself a Swedish masseuse because she had learnt the Swedish method, famous throughout the world, of giving massage, not because she wished to imply that she was wholly and entirely Swedish. She only complied with custom. And I——"

"Do I understand that you intend to put the prisoner in the box?" interrupted Lord Horfield.

"Certainly I do, my Lord."

"Then in your examination in chief you will be able to bring out any points in her favour to which you wish to call attention."

With a thin, uplifted, yellowish-white hand, he signed to Counsel for the Crown to continue.

Again Judith Flaquer stole a glance at Gay. But Gay was not looking towards her. A small red spot showed on each of her cheeks just above the cheekbones, and she seemed to be staring straight before her into space. But she was not staring into space. She was at last looking towards the prisoner in the Dock. Something had kept her from a close examination of the prisoner till now, intense desire to look, mingled with a creeping fear of looking. But not only that too great desire and that fear had held her back. She hated to mingle her terribly personal curiosity with the cruel and vulgar curiosity of the crowd gathered in that Court. So poor and paltry was their reason for staring at the woman in the Dock, so tragic and tremendous hers. But she had to come to it at last. It was impossible to sit there longer, to hear the recital of that woman's past, to hear Malcolm's rebutted interventions on her behalf, and not to look at her. Already, Gay was beginning to think of her as a woman thrown to the wolves. Already, in despite of herself, pity was stirring in Gay's heart. She must see and judge for herself. (For it seemed to her as if with a look, one woman's look at another, she would be able to divine more than all the lawyers could tell her.)

A moment later she knew that in believing this she had made a mistake. At first she looked at the Dock through her spectacles. But suddenly they became blurred, or something, her painful inner excitement, perhaps, made her think they were blurred. And, furtively, she took them off, glanced to right and left, saw that Judith and her own left-hand neighbour, a stout, elderly woman who looked like an excited boarding-house keeper, were listening absorbed to the speech of Counsel for the Crown, and put her opera glasses up to her eyes.

And then for the first time she saw really the woman who

for so long had troubled her life, had tormented her, had taken away her peace of mind, had even taught her naturally gentle spirit the meaning of hatred. The strong glasses drew this woman close to Gay's short-sighted eyes, which fixed themselves on her in a long glance of intense scrutiny.

But this look did not enable Gay to divine more than all the lawyers could tell her about Mrs. Paradine. On the contrary, she was baffled by what she saw: a tall woman with a pale face and almost silver blonde hair, dressed in brown, with her hands, long, slim hands, narrow and very expressive, lying in her lap unclasped, and her eyes apparently fixed on the short, sturdy man with grey whiskers who was bent, it seemed, on her destruction. She sat very still. There was absolutely no symptom of restlessness in her. She did not look concerned, still less terrified, but de-tached, sitting there in a white composure. And immediately Gay felt her as an enigma, was deeply puzzled by her, was conscious of a great inability to understand her.

It is said very often that woman intuitively understands woman. And perhaps Gay had expected to be able to subscribe to that statement when she put the glasses to her eyes. But she knew at once that it was not true of this case. And she remembered the photograph she had examined surreptitiously in Malcolm's work room, and wondered why she had felt so sure of penetrating this woman's mystery at a first glance. For the photograph had held her at bay. (She knew that now.) And now the living woman held her at bay.

True, she did not see her full face, only side face, and when presently she moved her head slightly three-quarters face. But that was enough.

"I can't read her!" she said to herself.

Was she beautiful? Gay believed that she had something of beauty. She was not what English people call 'a beauty.' Still, her appearance was so uncommon, so typically Northern, so impos-sible to ignore—and this quite apart from the horrible publicity of her present situation—that Gay felt there must be beauty in her. But, apart from her attitude in the Dock, which had a curious, natural grace, a sort of slouching grace, she was surely not ex-pressive. She had a shut face; a strange blankness about it; no suggestion of animation, either feverish or self-confident.

"Is she really like me?" Gay thought.

And she couldn't tell. What, indeed, could she tell about this woman?

Yes, there was one thing she could tell: that the prisoner in the Dock was marvellously self-possessed, marvellously self-controlled. Was it possible that she could be so self-possessed and yet guilty?

Her brown dress—Gay could see through the glasses that it was beautifully made though apparently very simple—was cut sufficiently low to expose the whole of her neck. And it was certainly a beautiful neck, snow white, columnar, and long.

As Gay gazed at it a hideous thought struck into her mind.

"In England death is by hanging in cases of murder."

She could not take her eyes from that neck, and a conviction came to her that when Mrs. Paradine put that brown dress on for the trial she, too, had thought of the hangman; and, not only that, but had intended that others, the Judge, perhaps, members of the Jury certainly, should be caused by that beautiful and uncovered neck to think of the hangman, too.

In the choosing of that dress there had been a very definite intention.

And as she knew this, Gay felt as if suddenly she drew nearer to Mrs. Paradine. A link between them was forged in that moment.

"In spite of all he had gone through in the war, in spite of the terrible wound which resulted in his blindness, Colonel Paradine was no invalid. On the contrary—evidence would be called to prove it—he was a man of fine physique and enjoying sound health. There was no reason, so far as the doctors knew, why he should not live into a good old age. But that was not to be. It was fated that the hand of Death should be laid upon him at a comparatively early age. Someone—it is the business of this Court if possible to find out who—had evidently decreed this. The man who, though often in deadly peril, had yet escaped with his life from the war, was destined to be struck down by a mysterious hand when the war was over."

With what a level, though harsh, utterance the voice of the prosecuting Counsel ran on. Gay had put down her opera glasses. She did not put her spectacles on again. She had a wish to return into her natural short-sightedness—to hide for a little while in her lack of vision. She had seen Lord Horfield, she had seen Malcolm and Mrs. Paradine. They were all in her mind, its possession now. And she must listen for a while, only listen. For already, during the short time she had been in Court, she had convinced herself of Lord Horfield's hostility to the Defence. Others might not have realised it. Probably they had not. But she was aware of it. And she felt guilty, attributing it to herself. Her words to the Judge repeated themselves in her mind: "I shall keep dirty people out of my life." He would certainly never forgive them. She would not have minded that if it had not been for the effect which she felt they would have, were already having in this horrible trial. She tried, indeed, to argue with herself, to convince herself that she was morbidly attributing to herself a power which wasn't, couldn't be, hers. But her effort did not succeed.

She knew that she had rendered Malcolm's efforts to get upon really friendly terms with Lord Horfield useless. But she must concentrate on British justice. Lord Horfield was a British Judge with a big public reputation to keep up. Whatever his private feelings were, he surely couldn't afford to give an entirely free rein to them on the Bench. Perhaps she was exaggerating the result of her defiance, her rebuke, inevitable both of them, although they had brought about her creeping feeling of guilt. She mustn't give way to emotional excitement, mustn't get all the values wrong. And she strove to keep cool, to follow the case with the keen detachment which probably Judith Flaquer had fast hold of. She looked down at her knees and listened, saying to herself: "It's nothing to do with me. I'm not in it. All this that I'm hearing about took place before I knew of this woman's existence. Whether she's innocent or guilty, whether they condemn her or set her free, doesn't depend upon me. I'm only here to listen, and to pray that justice may be done"—and then something within her added—was it reluctantly?—"or mercy shown."

She couldn't look at that Dock and wish that the woman sitting so still in it should be condemned to be hanged. That, at least, was utterly impossible to her.

"Impossible, that's impossible!" she said over and over again to herself, while the rather harsh voice of the man with the whiskers ran steadily on. And she began to realise another life utterly different from hers with Malcolm, the life of the woman, who now sat in the Dock, with the man who was blinded in the war.

Counsel was pushing home certain traits of the dead man which must have made life with him exceedingly difficult. He seemed, Gay felt, to be doing this with a certain reluctance, anxious, if possible, to keep a balance between shining virtues—to create sympathy with a hero—and painful disabilities—to establish a probable motive for the crime alleged against the prisoner. He seemed at times to be excusing what he also was condemning. She saw him as a man balanced on a tight-rope, swaying this way and that, yet somehow keeping his feet. And she began to say to herself: "But was there enough motive for such an awful thing as murder committed by that woman?"

The name William Marsh was several times mentioned by Counsel. Gay began to feel a certain interest in this man, who had evidently been an intimate member of the Paradine household, and was destined to play an important part in this case. His virtues were dwelt upon, his soldier-like qualities, his devotion to his master, Colonel Paradine, in and out of the army.

Gay began to receive an impression that this William Marsh was a man of remarkable character, perhaps even of nobility. But he was going to be a witness for the prosecution. Then he was Malcolm's enemy.

Her interest, already painfully vivid, increased when the speaker, always lucid, unemotional and amazingly competent—complete master of his task and material—came to the question of Colonel Paradine's health.

"Hitherto strong, in spite of all he had gone through in the war, it became suddenly affected. At the end of July in the year I have mentioned, he became suddenly unwell. He had severe pain in the head and there was a sensation of numbness. He complained of these and Doctor Worthingly, of Hindley Village, was called in. Doctor Worthingly attributed the symptoms to a severe attack of dyspepsia. Whether rightly or wrongly it will be for you, Members of the Jury, to judge when you have heard the case out. But I shall suggest to you that quite possibly Doctor Worthingly's diagnosis was mistaken, and that this sudden attack of illness was not caused by indigestion but——" the speaker paused for a brief instant, then added: "—was induced by an outside agent. I shall suggest to you that already, in that month of that year, there was a desire in the breast of someone that Colonel Paradine should not enjoy length of days, but that the hand raised to strike for some reason, quite possibly a reason of sudden fear, or even possibly of sudden repentance—*at that time*—was paralysed and so failed to push the blow home."

The speaker stopped for a moment. Gay looked up and saw that he was staring at the Jury. Then he glanced down at some papers that were lying before him, handled them with great deliberation, lifted his hands to his shoulders, pulled at his robe, cleared his throat and added:

"At any rate the dyspepsia, if it was dyspepsia, seemed to die away. The pain in the head ceased. The numbness—a curious symptom, characteristic, by the way, of poisoning with arsenic —disappeared. And Colonel Paradine seemed to be restored to his usual health."

Judith, at this point, looked round and softly whispered to Gay: "He knows all the tricks of the trade."

Gay raised her eyebrows and shook her head. She didn't understand what Judith meant.

"That pause—look—the shoulders—the robe—all calculated."

She leaned forward again in her seat and looked towards the speaker.

"Criminals, Members of the Jury, are not all of a piece. They have their moments of hesitation, they have their doubts, they are even sometimes attacked by the weakness of a latent virtue, which makes them recoil from a crime and leave it in an unfinished state. In the light of what occurred later on, I shall suggest to you that that was what happened on the occasion of this attack which Dr. Worthingly attributed at the time to dyspepsia. Evidence will be called presently which will, unless I am much mistaken, convince you that eventually this unfortunate hero—for with all his undoubted faults of temper and of morality, Colonel Paradine was certainly a British hero—that eventually he died from the administration of antimony taken in the form of tartar emetic, and, as you will learn, he died in London, in a house in Eaton Square which had been rented by him for a couple of months. But the fact that he died from antimony does not preclude the possibility of a former attempt to get rid of him by the administration of a different type of poison."

Another rather long pause. Then Counsel said impressively, but in a lowered voice, which nevertheless travelled through the Court: "Now as to motive!"

He then gave a graphic account of the life at Hindley Hall after the so-called 'recovery' of Colonel Paradine from his attack of dyspepsia—if dyspepsia it was. Gay listened to it with absorbed attention. He drew Colonel Paradine as a man increasingly miserable and embittered in his affliction of blindness, unable, in spite of his former bravery, to resign himself to this terrible blow administered, in Counsel's words, "by the mysterious hand of that unknown power whom we have agreed to name God."

As he continued, indeed, his rhetoric became gradually more and more flatulent, but he was no doubt accommodating himself to what he had come to consider the probable united taste of the Jury, who were obviously not of that distinguished type which has the covering name of 'the intelligentsia.' And he mixed plenty of fact with his embroidery of adjectives.

"There was nothing of the fatalistic resignation of the Oriental in this heroic V.C. He would have been ready, aye content, to die for his country. To live on in darkness without complaint, without bitterness, without kicking furiously against the pricks, was another matter. Members of the Jury, he could not do it. And who was there in that lonely house to bear the brunt of his misery and to listen to the voice of his complaining? Only the woman whom he had married. *She* had to stand it."

He then gave details of angry outbreaks on Colonel Paradine's part, of which his wife had been the victim, all of which, of course, would be spoken to by witnesses. It seemed obvious that as he was unable apparently to bring forward the usual motive for a woman's murder, namely the desire to be free to give herself, without public scandal, to a lover, he was making the most of the matrimonial misery which had prevailed at Hindley Hall. According to him, this misery must have been very great. In describing it, or rather in touching upon it, he did not spare Colonel Paradine. Nor did he attack Mrs. Paradine's conduct as a wife at that time. On the contrary, he laboured to produce the impression that she endured an almost intolerable life with her husband for a long while with apparently exemplary fortitude, ministering to his wants, keeping him company, reading to him, playing the piano to him, and never returning his outbursts of temper with any reply in kind.

"It seems that she bore with him in a remarkable way, both before, *and after,* the attack of illness to which I have drawn your attention. I suggest to you, members of the Jury, that she is a woman of great self-control, not an ordinary woman, but a woman of exceptional will-power, capable of wearing a mask, not merely for an hour, not merely for a day, but, if necessary, for months on end. I suggest to you also that she is a woman of secret violence, who may appear to forgive but who neither forgets nor forgives any wrong that is done to her, or anything that she conceives to be a wrong. And now I must draw your attention to certain money matters which are of considerable importance in this case."

He then informed the Jury that it would be given in evidence that Colonel Paradine's first attack of illness, the so-called dyspepsia, complicated with numbness, from which he suffered, took place ten days after he had made a new will, leaving his wife in the event of his death an annuity of £4,000 a year. This will revoked a former will made immediately after his marriage, in which his wife was only left £2,000 a year. His estate of Hindley Hall was entailed, but he was a comparatively rich man. Had he died before this last will was made, Mrs. Paradine would have been left only half as rich as she was now. Evidence would be produced to show that she was cognisant of the contents of this will. Until this will was signed, Colonel Paradine enjoyed excellent health. He was miserable, he was irritable, he was sometimes little less than brutal in his conduct to his wife, though there is no evidence that he ever offered her physical violence. But he was perfectly well.

Counsel paused dramatically for a moment to let that fact sink into the minds of the Jury. During that moment Gay put on her spectacles and looked again at the green leather benches. She found her husband. He was sitting bolt upright. His lips were pressed together, and within the framework of his wig his face looked hard and stern. The time for him to come into action was not yet. Gay knew that he was chafing at his enforced in-action, was longing to spring up and get to work on the Defence.

But the harsh voice went on inexorably. It drew the attention of the Jury to a second attack of illness which, "upon my present information as I understand it," overtook Colonel Paradine two months after the first attack, and was of a somewhat similar nature, only more severe. Counsel touched upon the symptoms of this second attack, pains in the head, a feeling of numbness, but with the addition this time of sickness and a sensation of sinking.

On this occasion Doctor Worthingly, who was again called to the house, was more troubled by the state in which he found his patient, and questioned him closely about what he had been eating and drinking. He learnt that just before the attack the Colonel had eaten raw oysters of which he was very fond. These had been sent over by a fishmonger at Whitehaven with whom the Paradines were in the habit of dealing, and were not English natives but Portuguese oysters imported into England. Doctor Worthingly apparently thought that some of these oysters, none of which had been eaten by Mrs. Paradine, or the household at Hindley, might have been tainted and in consequence caused the Colonel's illness. But being somewhat puzzled by the violence of the symptoms he desired a second opinion, and a Doctor Culford was sent for from Whitehaven and met Doctor Worthingly in consultation. The result of the consultation was that both doctors found that Colonel Paradine was suffering from acute dyspepsia, but did not succeed in discovering the cause of it, though they thought that it might be due to the oysters which he had eaten, none of which were left for examination.

"This was their conclusion. It may have been right, it may have been wrong. What happened later, however, might seem to many to put a somewhat different complexion upon the matter."

Counsel then told the Jury that Colonel Paradine seemed to recover from this second attack of illness, but he remained in a very miserable, irritable, and depressed frame of mind, and this— "or some other reason"—led Mrs. Paradine to suggest a visit to London by way of a change. Perhaps she was beginning to find the retired life at Hindley with a blind husband intolerable. But she gave out that she wished Colonel Paradine to be livened up, to have some amusement, and she also gave out that she thought he ought to consult a good London doctor about the state of his health. She seemed at this time to be particularly solicitous for his health, and was heard to say on several occasions that she could not understand why he should have been twice seized with illness, and to express an opinion that country doctors were ignorant fools.

Colonel Paradine fell in with her suggestion. A furnished house was taken in Eaton Square. And the Paradines removed from Hindley and came up to London, accompanied by William Marsh and others of their servants. Colonel Paradine never saw Hindley again. He died while in London, after being there for about two months. Soon after arriving in London, he was examined by the celebrated physician, Sir William Ackley, who found nothing serious the matter with him, except extensive nervous depression, and who recommended that he should take Sanatogen, the well known preparation for strengthening the nervous system, and get as much air and exercise as possible.

Counsel then passed on to the last illness and death of Colonel Paradine, telling his Lordship and the Jury how on a certain night during the visit to Eaton Square, "after a particularly bad day of depression, irritability, and even gusts of fury," more than one of the servants, as well as Mrs. Masters, the housekeeper, had overheard sounds as if a violent altercation were taking place in Colonel Paradine's study between him and Mrs. Paradine, with, apparently, attempts at appeasement from the devoted William Marsh, who went to the room. No actual words were heard, but raised voices. And evidence would be called to prove that undoubtedly some angry quarrel or attack was in progress. William Marsh would give his version of what was occurring, and the Jury would be able to judge for themselves of its importance in connection with what happened later. Anyhow, after this scene, Colonel Paradine had refused to dine downstairs with his wife or to have anything more to do with her, and had shut himself up in a small sitting-room on the first floor, next door to his bedroom. Here his dinner had been served to him by Lakin, the butler, who had remained with him to assist him in eating it. William Marsh was not present at this meal, nor, of course, was Mrs. Paradine. Lakin would give evidence that the Colonel, who was evidently in a fiercely nervous condition and labouring apparently under some extraordinary sense of wrong, the nature of which, however, he did not disclose, drank Burgundy at dinner, and when dinner was over directed the butler, Lakin, to put a glass full of Burgundy in his bedroom in a certain place which he indicated, so that he would know exactly where to feel for it. The butler obeyed his master's order, came back to the sitting-room in which Colonel Paradine was sitting alone, and said that he had done so. Colonel Paradine then said that he wanted nothing more, got up and walked into the bedroom, and shut the door behind him; but did not lock it.

There were two doors to this bedroom, one communicating from the Colonel's sitting-room, the other giving on to the main landing. The bedroom occupied by Mrs. Paradine was opposite to the Colonel's bedroom.

The butler, having cleared away the remains of the Colonel's dinner, then went downstairs and found Mrs. Paradine alone in the dining-room finishing a solitary meal which had been served to her by the footman while he, the butler, was busy with the Colonel. When he came into the room she asked him where his master was, had he finished his dinner. The butler replied that he had and had gone to his bedroom, and added that, by the Colonel's order, he had taken a glass full of Burgundy into the bedroom and left it there. Mrs. Paradine then asked whether William Marsh had gone to the Colonel. The butler replied that when he came downstairs the Colonel was certainly alone in the bedroom. He could not of course speak to what had happened since he came downstairs. Mrs. Paradine thanked him, got up from the table and left the dining-room. When she was at the door she turned and said to the butler: "Is he going to bed, do you know?"

The butler replied that he couldn't say, and Mrs. Paradine then left the dining-room and shut the door behind her.

"Where did she go, gentlemen and ladies of the Jury?" continued the inexorable voice, which, Gay thought, grew harsher as the speech for the Prosecution lengthened out. "Evidence will be called to prove that she went first to the drawing-room which—an unusual thing in the average London house—was on the ground floor at the back of the house, remained there for a few minutes, and then was seen going upstairs. In the meanwhile, as you will presently learn, William Marsh, Colonel Paradine's confidential servant, had visited his master's bedroom to inquire whether he could do anything for the Colonel, and had been told to go away and leave him alone. He wanted nothing. The Colonel was then sitting in an armchair at the foot of the bed apparently brooding. He spoke very sharply to William Marsh, contrary to his usual custom. For though often very inconsiderate, even brutal to his wife, he was generally kind to his servant. William Marsh left the room hurt by his master's behaviour. As he did so he saw Mrs. Paradine go into her bedroom, opposite to the Colonel's, and shut the door behind her. Marsh, as he will tell you presently, lingered for a moment on the landing. He was deeply attached to his master and disliked to leave him all alone in such a condition of evident misery, yet he did not know how to approach him again after being ordered away. This disturbance of mind led him to hesitate for a moment wondering what he could do, uncertain in his mind, unhappy at the turn of events. While he thus stood, to his surprise he saw Colonel Paradine's door open and the Colonel come out. Marsh stood where he was and Colonel Paradine, unconscious of his presence, passed by him and went down a short passage. At the end of this passage there was a lavatory. The Colonel entered it—although blind he was clever at finding his way about in places he was familiar with—and shut and bolted the door behind him. Just as he did this Ellen Smith, the head-housemaid, arrived on the landing from the backstairs, and seeing Marsh standing there inquired if she could do anything for the Colonel. Marsh replied: 'No, we'd best leave him alone. He's not himself to-night.' On that Ellen Smith left the landing with Marsh, and they both went downstairs together, leaving Mrs. Paradine in her bedroom and Colonel Paradine locked in the lavatory. Members of the Jury—I am instructed that not one person of that household, except those two persons, was present upon that first landing of the house in Eaton Square during the quarter of an hour which followed. There is no evidence, apart from any the prisoner may presently elect to offer, as to what took place on that first landing during that lapse of time. But evidence will be given that, after the lapse of about a quarter of an hour, servants in the house heard the piano being played in the downstairs drawing-room. Mrs. Paradine was there playing an arrangement of the well-known Viennese Waltz known by the name of 'The Blue Danube.' No one had heard her come downstairs, so no one could say when she came. She may of course have come down sooner or later.

The servants seem to have assumed that she began to play directly she came into the drawing-room. If so she would have been upstairs for about a quarter of an hour. However, I am instructed that there is no evidence as to that. The evidence is that she was upstairs when Colonel Paradine went to the lavatory, and that some quarter of an hour later she was playing on the piano in the drawing-room. She continued playing for a considerable time, perhaps for half an hour or more. Then the sounds ceased."

Counsel then related what happened that night in the Eaton Square house, as he had been instructed. Mrs. Paradine went upstairs to bed at a little after ten o'clock. Her maid, Fanny Greene, was waiting for her and would give evidence that Mrs. Paradine did not go into her husband's bedroom to bid him good night, but went at once to bed. William Marsh, however, in the performance of his duty, did go as usual to the Colonel's room to help him to bed, but found the bedroom door locked. On his tapping, the Colonel called out in a rough manner: "Go away! Leave me alone!" Much troubled, Marsh obeyed, and went downstairs to his room. He slept in the basement. The other servants retired and the peace of night descended upon the house. It was rudely broken, however, just before midnight by Colonel Paradine, who opened his bedroom door and cried out in a loud, half-strangled voice something which woke his wife in the bedroom opposite.

"She has stated that at first she could not imagine what had waked her—she affirms that she was fast asleep—but that, on listening, she heard her husband's voice calling 'Marsh! Marsh! Marsh!' with a rising inflection as if in agony. It is noticeable," Counsel said, leaning towards the Jury box, and slightly lowering his voice, "that, according to the statement of the prisoner, Colonel Paradine did not call for his wife, whom he knew to be sleeping close to him, but for his servant who slept two floors below."

After a pause, to let this sink in, Counsel described the acute illness of Colonel Paradine, the rousing of the household, the sending for doctors—two arrived at the house within an hour—the complete collapse of the unfortunate man who, after being violently sick several times, sank into a condition of unconsciousness, and in spite of the efforts of the doctors, which Counsel described minutely, died soon after seven o'clock on the following morning. From the first the doctors were of the opinion that Colonel Paradine's condition was caused by some irritant poison and a death certificate was refused. There was no question of disease. The symptoms displayed indicated internal ulceration, undoubtedly brought about by an irritant poison. The doctors suspected the presence of arsenic, but eventually, when tests had been made by Professor Blake, to whom certain organs of the dead man and specimens of rejected matter had been submitted, it was discovered that death had undoubtedly been caused by antimony taken in the form of tartar emetic. Nevertheless—at this point in his speech Sir Joseph Farrell spoke very slowly and emphatically, looking steadily at the Jury—traces of arsenic were discovered in the body, and the doctors would give important evidence as to that. With regard to the antimony it was suspected that the poison had been swallowed by Colonel Paradine in the glass of Burgundy which the butler had placed in his bedroom. But in the hurry and agitation caused by his sudden illness that glass—there would be evidence to the fact that the wine had been drunk, for the empty glass had been noticed by more than one witness, standing on the night table by the Colonel's bed—that glass mysteriously disappeared and was never accounted for.

"The assumption is that it was deliberately made away with," said Counsel. "But I am instructed that there is no evidence as to that. The glass simply disappeared from Colonel Paradine's room and has never been found."

Counsel concluded by describing the arrest of Mrs. Paradine on the charge of being the person who administered the antimony to Colonel Paradine and so caused his death, and finished a long and elaborate opening with these words:

"Members of the Jury, I have to submit to you that there is cogent circumstantial evidence that the antimony in the form of tartar emetic, which undoubtedly caused the death of this unfortunate man, must have been introduced into the glass of Burgundy, which stood on his night table, during the short time when he was absent from his bedroom and in the lavatory, into which William Marsh saw him go, and that the only person who could have so introduced it was his wife, Mrs. Paradine, the prisoner in the Dock, she being alone with him at that time on the first floor of the house and within easy reach of his room, empty while he was away in the lavatory. If you come to the conclusion that it was she who administered the antimony, then she is guilty of wilful murder, and it will be your painful duty to say so."

At the conclusion of Counsel's speech the Court adjourned for the lunch interval.

*   *   *   *   *

During the interval for lunch Gay and Judith remained in their places. They had brought sandwiches with them and talked in low voices as they ate them.

"A queer enough opening!" Judith said.

"Is it? Why?"

"Well—how did it strike you? Did it carry much conviction with it?"

"D'you mean of her guilt?"

"Yes. The Crown didn't seem to have discovered a very strong motive for such a crime as they allege. What *I* want to know is— can you guess, Gay?"

Gay thought for a moment, then said, but rather tentatively:

"There are several things that one would like to know more about. But perhaps you mean the cause of the scene—a quarrel, I suppose—that took place on the day of the murder, if it was a murder."

"You've hit it! What was the row about? It was evidently serious. And that servant, Marsh, was in it."

"Yes."

"I shall be glad when that man goes into the box."

She ate another sandwich, not talking while she did so. She seemed to Gay to be thinking hard.

"Seems to me," she said presently, "that there's something in this case that the Crown ought to have discovered and hasn't. I wonder whether Sir Malcolm knows what it is. From the opening we've just heard would you feel inclined to believe her guilty?"

"I don't know. But he died of poison evidently."

"Yes. That's plain enough."

"And only Mrs. Paradine was up there with him."

"After Marsh went."

"Yes."

"And he wasn't let in to the Colonel's room apparently."

"No. So who was there to do it?"

"The butler poured out the wine and carried it up."

"But why should he wish to kill his employer?"

"Oh, I don't accuse the poor man. No doubt he's innocent. Still one must think of everything."

"Could Colonel Paradine possibly have done it himself?"

"That's certain to be considered. But his blindness makes a difficulty there. I wish I were on the Jury."

"Oh, Judy! Why?"

"It would be profoundly interesting to be taking part in such a case as this. Well, now we shall come to the evidence for the prosecution, and when that's all over—in a day or two, I suppose—Sir Malcolm will make his opening speech for the Defence. That suggestion about the arsenic was very sinister. It seems that on two occasions someone started on the road of crime and then, for some reason, stopped. Why? One would like to know. Perhaps fear. Perhaps pity, or even horror, at seeing the beginnings of illness. Perhaps some other reason one can't divine. That statement about the playing of 'The Blue Danube' struck me."

"Yes. It made me think of our dinner and Arthur Lieberstein."

"And of something else. If she—Mrs. Paradine—had introduced antimony into that poor man's Burgundy, and had the nerve to go downstairs and play lighthearted music, difficult too, while she was waiting for him to drink it, the fiend most surely dwelt in her. But women have done such things before now. Human nature is capable of everything. Papa has often said that to me. And he says you can't tell what people are by looking at them, if they're really clever and subtle as criminals so often are. We shall have to get away before the finish of this day's evidence."

"Yes, we must."

"I only hope we don't have to flee while William Marsh is in the box. My instinct tells me that a lot of this case is going to centre round him. Probably they'll open with the servants."

"And as he was one he may go into the box first, I suppose."

"Or last. Will you have another?"

Judith had spoken always in her brisk, rather casual and detached way. Gay knew very well why. She was determined not to embarrass her friend by any thrust of too intimate sympathy, was determined to keep to an assumption that they two were on a level of interest in that Court; Gay not outrunning her for any personal reason. Of course Judy knew, but she was delicate and didn't press forward her knowledge on Gay's shrinking reticence. At moments her manner was almost legal.

She snapped to the lid of her silver sandwich-box. When next she spoke, it was about the people in Court 'down there.'

"I can see Mrs. George Blason."

"Can you?"

"Yes. She's with Arthur Lieberstein."

"Lieberstein? Is he still in London?"

"I didn't know it. But he's here. And Baron Sedelsward is there, too, though not with them. He must have come all the way back from Stockholm for the trial, because he left after his picture show closed."

"I had no—I didn't think that he was in London either."

"He hasn't been near us. Nor has Lieberstein. Probably they've only just arrived. I don't see Lady Horfield."

"Would she be likely to come?"

"Chi lo sa? Perhaps her husband won't have her in Court when he's judging a case. She always does what he means her to do."

"I'm not quite sure of that," Gay ventured.

Judith looked at her sharply.

"Ah! You're thinking of that afternoon at our house! Perhaps even she breaks loose sometimes."

She seemed about to add something and didn't. Gay knew she was thinking of the curious intimacy, surreptitious too, or at any rate meant by Lady Horfield to be surreptitious, between Lady Horfield and Malcolm. Gay didn't understand it and had wondered about it. But there could be nothing surely in any action of Lady Horfield's that need render her uneasy. Gay held to a strange belief in the rareness of Lady Horfield's nature. She *knew* Lady Horfield was fine. The casket was preposterous, baroque and preposterous, but there was a jewel within it. Of that she was positive. It was as if she had seen the shine of the jewel.

Immediately after the interval, when Lord Horfield had taken his seat on the Bench, a procession of servants came to the witness-box. They were the servants forming the Paradine household at

Hindley Hall, and included the housekeeper, the butler, a footman, Mrs. Paradine's maid, two housemaids, two gardeners and a
chauffeur. The evidence of William Marsh, for which Judith
Flaquer was eagerly waiting, was not reached on this first day of
the trial.

The main object of the Crown in calling the servants was to
establish the fact that Colonel and Mrs. Paradine got on very
badly together, were a miserable couple, unsuited to each other,
leading a troubled and at times an almost intolerable life together,
such a life as a sensitive woman might very well wish to have
done with.

The object of the Defence, on the other hand, was to water
such evidence down, to take all the sting out of it, and to leave
the Jury with the impression that though there were at times
unhappy incidents in the life at Hindley, nevertheless, the marriage was not really more disastrous than any average marriage in
which one of the parties suffered from an affliction that was incur-
able and made for depression. The Defence, of course, also aimed
at presenting Mrs. Paradine as a deeply affectionate wife, full of
admiration for her heroic husband, and bearing patiently with his
unfortunate idiosyncrasies, realising that they were caused by the
misery of his blindness. The most important evidence given by the
servants was that connected with the two attacks of illness which
he had while at Hindley, and with the incidents preceding the
attack in Eaton Square which ended with his death. The most
severe cross-examination was directed to the evidence given by
the housekeeper, the butler, and the chauffeur.

Taking the united evidence of the servants on that first day,
and considering it as a whole, the main fact which emerged—
so Judith Flaquer found, and Gay agreed with her—was that
the servants at Hindley were hostile neither to their master nor
their mistress. It was obvious that the war fame of their master
had made them proud of being connected with him, and ready
to bear with his occasional exhibitions of impatience and irritability
to themselves, and to look with a good deal of indulgence on such
outbreaks of temper as they had been witness of vented on his
wife, their mistress. On the other hand, most of them, when cross-
examined, gave a good account of their mistress, who was evidently
kind to them and even sympathetic. (Perhaps partly because,

having once been a servant, she had a kindly feeling of sympathy for the class from which she had risen.) Exceptions to this apparently general goodwill were found in the housekeeper, Mrs. Partridge, and the chauffeur, Sam Trowl. These two evidently cherished some dislike for their former mistress and seemed to have been suspicious of her, though they were unable to give any specific reasons for their rather lukewarm animosity and doubts about her character. They just didn't care for her. She was a foreigner, and not 'up' to the Colonel, in their opinion. He had evidently been their God, she far from being their Goddess.

All the servants gave evidence as to their master's excellent health before his attacks of illness at Hindley. He had apparently completely recovered from the first before the second overtook him. Mrs. Partridge, the housekeeper, had thought these attacks 'very odd,' and had so expressed herself to Trowl, the chauffeur, who was, it seemed, a special favourite of hers. They hadn't seemed to her 'at all like dyspepsia,' and Trowl had agreed with her. Neither of them had believed that the doctors knew what they were about. But Mrs. Paradine had seemed quite satisfied with the doctors' verdict at the time, though certainly she had later suggested a move to London, and when there had persuaded the Colonel to be seen by a celebrated doctor. But both the housekeeper and chauffeur professed to think that the move to London was really organised by Mrs. Paradine because she was tired of Hindley and wished to see some 'life' and have some pleasure. The housekeeper thought that she was 'fair sick' of Hindley and had had more than enough of the Colonel's company. Trowl thought the same.

Keane's cross-examination was directed towards eliciting that their suspicions about Colonel Paradine's illnesses at Hindley were entirely vague, with no facts to back them up, that they had nothing definite to complain about in their mistress's conduct, and that with regard to the move to London when there, Mrs. Paradine had never shown neglect of her husband, or any frivolous turning away from him to a life of pleasure. He was successful in showing the hollowness of their faint dislike of their mistress, which seemed to rest chiefly on the fact that she was 'foreign' and that they didn't care for, or understand, her 'ways.'

The attention and interest in Court became strongly intensified when more evidence was given about the fatal evening and night in London which had preceded Colonel Paradine's death.

It was obvious from the evidence that all the servants in Eaton Square realised that on that evening before dinner something extraordinary had happened, in which Colonel Paradine, his wife and William Marsh were intimately concerned. The butler and the housekeeper had heard the voice of the Colonel raised in apparently fierce denunciation. This when he was alone with his wife. A shouted summons, as well as a violent ringing of the bell, had brought Marsh to the room. He had entered it and shut the door behind him. A considerable time had then passed. The butler and the housekeeper thought at least twenty minutes. They had not, of course, listened at the door. No one had done that. But they and the other servants had been so perturbed at the thought that something unusual was happening in the house that they had congregated on the backstairs, and in the hall just at the top of those stairs, not out of curiosity, not at all, but fearing lest something—they didn't know what—might come about with the Colonel. By the sound of his voice, he had seemed 'quite out of himself.' And the summoning of William Marsh, one of themselves, had given them all the feeling that they ought to be 'within call.' The housekeeper and the butler stated that they had told the other servants to keep away and attend to their own business, but it was obvious that their authority had for once been disregarded. For all the servants gave evidence that there had been a terrible 'row' between the Colonel and his wife. Yet none of them had heard what was said, so that none knew what the row had been about. And when Marsh had finally emerged from the room and had found the butler and the housekeeper at the edge of the hall— the other servants having hastily retreated, evidently having a wholesome fear of Marsh—he had been very angry at finding them there, and had flatly refused to give them any information about what had happened. But both housekeeper and butler described him as looking 'almost beside himself.'

Keane cross-examined the butler closely about the episode of Colonel Paradine's solitary dinner upstairs and the episode of the glass of Burgundy. He dealt especially with the state of the Colonel's mind as it had impressed itself upon the butler. Lakin was a typical servant of his class, conventional, restrained in demeanour, respectable—at any rate in appearance, and quite possibly in character also—and with a certain sense of his own importance as a person who had reached the top of the servants' world. Merely to look at him, still more to hear him give evidence, put an end to any nascent suspicion that he could have had a hand in the destruction of his master. And in cross-examination, Keane did not attempt to create any suspicion about him. What he did do was to try to establish that it was possible that the glass of Burgundy might have been got at by someone other than Mrs. Paradine before Colonel Paradine drank it. Both the doors of the bedroom were unlocked when the wine was placed on the night table. Could Lakin affirm on oath that it was impossible for anyone to have got into the room and introduced poison into the wine before the Colonel retired there? Lakin considered that it was impossible. The Colonel had immediately gone into the room and remained there. Keane then asked whether it was impossible that someone might have been concealed in the room before the wine was placed there. Lakin was obliged to say that such a thing was not impossible. But he had noticed nothing unusual about the room and felt sure it was empty.

Keane questioned him closely about the condition in which the Colonel was during his dinner, at which the butler had helped him, arranging food on his plate, etc., even cutting some of it up. This part of the cross-examination was obviously directed to establish firmly in the minds of the Jury that on the evening preceding his death Colonel Paradine had been in an abnormally excited state, the sort of state in which a man is scarcely responsible for his actions.

"It seems that the Defence is going to be suicide!" Judith whispered to Gay, as Lakin allowed that his master was in a 'terrible state' of excitement while dining.

"Was it Colonel Paradine's habit to drink wine at night, before going to, or after he was in, bed?" Keane asked.

"No, sir."

"So that this ordering of wine to be put in the bedroom was exceptional?"

"Yes, sir."

"Absolutely exceptional?"

"Yes, sir."

"Never done before within your recollection?"

"Not with wine, sir. The Colonel——"

"I am only asking you about wine. Please answer my question."

"No. I never knew the Colonel to have wine in his bedroom till that night."

"Did he usually drink Burgundy?"

"No, sir. Generally claret."

"So the ordering of Burgundy was unusual?"

"Yes, sir. Sometimes——"

"You have answered the question. I am not asking you anything else."

At this point Lord Horfield intervened and said in a bland voice:

"Just one moment, Sir Malcolm." (To the witness.) "By unusual, do you mean the Jury to understand that Colonel Paradine never drank Burgundy?"

"No, my Lord. But he generally preferred claret."

"He generally preferred claret but sometimes drank Burgundy.

"Proceed, Sir Malcolm."

At this point in the evidence, Judith Flaquer, who had glanced at her watch, whispered to Gay:

"I think we ought to get away now. They'll soon adjourn."

"I'm ready."

In a few minutes they were outside the Court in the midst of a throng of gaping curiosity-mongers. Another quarter of an hour and Judith had left Gay to go home from Hallam Street in a taxi, while she went on in another to Hyde Park Gardens. They would meet on the morrow at the flat where Judith had 'arranged' Gay that morning, and where they now said good-bye to each other.

XXXIII

WHEN Keane came home late that evening, Baker met him in the hall to help him off with his overcoat, and told him of the arrival of her ladyship.

"My wife's come up!" said Keane, astonished.

"Yes, Sir Malcolm."

"When did she arrive?"

"Late this afternoon, sir."

"Where is she?"

"Up in her bedroom, I believe, sir."

Keane stood for a moment as if in hesitation and put one hand up to his forehead.

"Can I bring you anything, Sir Malcolm?" asked Baker, sympathetically.

"No thanks. I'll go up. I'll go up."

He went slowly up the stairs, while Baker stood looking after him.

In the housekeeper's room a minute later, Baker remarked to Mrs. Clemm, a stout and smiling woman who took a lot of trouble off the shoulders of Gay, and who was sitting by a nice fire with a drowsy Sausage in her lap:

"Sir Malcolm's just come in, and he does look played up. This case is taking it out of him. When I told him her ladyship was back he looked quite dazed. He's just gone up to her."

Mrs. Clemm switched off her smile with startling abruptness.

"Seems to me, Mr. Baker," she observed, "that Sir Malcolm hasn't been quite himself lately nor her ladyship neither. But you think it *is* the case?"

"It's this Paradine case sure enough. There's something—let's have a look at *The Evening News*."

"Here you are, Mr. Baker. There's columns about it. *I* think she did it."

"Well, even if she did he'll get her off," said Baker, who had a profound belief in his master's defensive powers.

He sat down and buried himself in the paper.

Meanwhile Keane had gone up to his wife's room to welcome her. Yes, he must welcome her but he wished that she had not returned. Her return would force him to make an effort, and he felt that he wanted to relax for a little while, to relax utterly, to play no part, to avoid all intimacy, especially that, to be quite alone, alone with—the case. Now he would have to smile, to seem pleased, natural, would have to talk, would have to hide the tumult within him. Why—why had Gay come up?

He knocked on her door, then opened it. She was there lying on a sofa. He saw at once that she had a tired and furtive look, but she greeted him with a sort of brisk cheerfulness that was unlike her usual manner.

"I *had* to come up. I couldn't leave you alone in the midst of all this."

"All what?" he asked, in a dull voice.

"This great case. How did it go to-day?"

"Oh, it was only the opening. It went all right. One can't tell at such an early stage. You've brought Sausage, of course?"

"Yes. I think he must be downstairs with the servants."

"What was it like in Surrey?"

"Very cold, too wintry. It's better to be in town."

After a little more uneasy conversation Keane got away and went to his bedroom, saying that he would take a bath before dinner. Just as he had begun to undress he heard a faint scratching at his door, opened it and found Sausage outside with a wagging tail eager to greet him. He let the little dog in and locked the door behind him, then, without summoning his valet, went to 'run' the bath. He had taken off the black-braided jacket he had been wearing in Court and thrown it down on the bed. When he came back from the bathroom he found Sausage standing on his hind legs, with his large forepaws on the bed, sniffing, almost greedily, at the jacket.

"Sausage!" he said, sternly. "At it again! That's not even a cushion!"

Sausage took his paws from the coverlet and touched the carpet with his stomach, lowering his head and showing a pair of guilty yellow eyes. Keane looked from him to the jacket. The noise of the running bath-water was in his ears. He stood as if considering something and his round pale forehead was wrinkled in a frown. Sausage lay still, always looking up humbly at his master. Keane began to undress. When he was in his dressing-gown ready for the bath he stood still again, looked at his jacket and at Sausage, pursed up his lips and muttered something under his breath. The little dog beat the floor with his tail and squinted up at the jacket.

What was master up to?

Keane turned away and went into the bathroom. Sausage stayed where he was; but when master presently came back, walking quickly, he rolled over on his back lifting his legs towards the ceiling. Keane bent down and shook him very gently from side to side, let him go, went to a cupboard in the room, took from a hanger in it a jacket similar to the one that lay on the bed, and, bending down, gave it to Sausage to play with. The dog, surprised, at first hardly daring to believe his good fortune, took hold of it tentatively with his teeth, looking sideways at his master.

"Go for it, Sausage!" whispered Keane, and he pulled at the jacket.

Sausage began eagerly to worry it, but not violently. He was still not quite sure of his ground.

Keane directed the dog's attention to the side pockets which were capacious under their flaps. Sausage caught at one with his teeth, holding the jacket with his forepaws, and pulled, making a rent. Then Keane took the jacket away and examined it. Yes, there was a ragged rent in the pocket.

"H'm!"

He stood staring at the rent in the jacket for a couple of minutes, then put the jacket back on its hanger and began to dress for dinner.

With Gay he passed an uneasy evening. Before they sat down to dinner he told her that directly after dinner he would have to leave her, as he must prepare a very stiff cross-examination for the following day. She remembered what Judith had said at the trial and thought of Colonel Paradine's servant. On the morrow William Marsh would surely give evidence. Perhaps Malcolm was thinking of him, was going to prepare for him.

When dinner was over they separated and Keane went to his work room and shut himself in there.

He did not see Gay again that night. It was two in the morning when he went to bed. For hours he had been brooding over the thought of the morrow. In all the cases he had handled he had never before been in such a difficulty as he was in now. Suspecting what he did, knowing it even as a man sometimes knows a thing he could assert but couldn't prove, how was he to deal with William Marsh in cross-examination without putting Mrs. Paradine in imminent danger? Marsh would lie of course. But would he lie well enough to deceive Horfield and the Jury, would he lie well enough to prevent them from suspecting what Keane now believed to be the truth? For if that truth was suspected, still more if it was discovered, what a terribly strong motive for Colonel Paradine's murder would be unveiled. And if Marsh realised—and of course he must—the implication of the defence, might he not be capable of blurting out the fact that he had had relations with his master's wife, with Mrs. Paradine? It would be a damnable thing to say of himself, but if he found himself in danger might he not say it? Mrs. Paradine had flatly denied to Keane that she had ever had anything illicit to do with Marsh. She had gone farther. She had, when Keane had accused her, asserted that Marsh hated her because she had refused his love. But Keane didn't believe her. He wanted to, but his brain refused him utterly the gift of that belief.

"What am I going to do to-morrow?" he said to himself again and again, as he paced up and down in his study. "How am I going to deal with this fellow? How can I deal with him without injuring her?"

For the first time in his career as a barrister he went to bed on the night before a big legal battle completely uncertain of the weapons he was going to use in it. He would have to trust wholly to the inspiration of the moment.

Before he got into bed he took off the hanger in the cupboard the jacket he had given to Sausage to worry and again examined the rent in the pocket. He even sat down by the bed, laid the jacket across his knees, and stared at it for a long time. And there was something terrible in his absorbed gaze at it, something sinister in his tremendous concentration on it.

At last he got up, shook his head, muttered something, and put it away.

Then he threw himself down at his bedside, laid his head in his hands, and remained on his knees like a man praying. Now and then his broad shoulders quivered as if he were stricken with cold. Before getting up from his knees he took one hand away from his face, felt for the switch of the electric lamp by his bed, turned it and put out the light. And he got into bed in the dark.

When he left for the Old Bailey next morning he looked ghastly and perplexed, and Gay's heart was wrung with pity for him. For a moment, forgetting herself entirely, she saw him as a victim, and believed she was able partially to enter into the blackness of his obsession. Not wholly; she couldn't do that. But she seemed to catch a glimpse of the path he was treading, and seemed to divine, rather than see, the abyss at its end. And her sorrow just then was for him rather than for herself. For a moment she achieved an extraordinary selflessness, such as probably a man never achieves.

But when the car drove away with him she was encompassed by fear. What was going to happen to Malcolm?

A few minutes later she said to Mrs. Clemm: "I shan't be in to lunch, Mrs. Clemm," and left the house on foot.

She met Judith Flaquer at the flat in Hallam Street. On the way to the Old Bailey Judith said:

"Did it go all right last evening?"

"If you mean about my being at the trial yesterday—yes. Malcolm doesn't know."

She paused, then added, almost with violence:

"I shall tell him everything directly it's over."

"Yes, yes, of course!" said Judith, touching her hand. "Go through with it now without torturing yourself. What good does that do? When one has deliberately chosen a path one should walk in it boldly."

"I'll try. I'll do my best."

They both noticed that the crowd in Newgate Street and the vicinity was considerably greater than it had been on the previous day. Public interest in the trial of Mrs. Paradine was evidently on the upward grade. They were conscious of crescendo. As Gay saw the crowd, and looked up at the copper-coloured dome above the Criminal Court, crowned by the bronze figure of Justice, and thought of Malcolm's harassed and ash-pale face as she had seen it that wintry morning when he was starting for the day's work, she felt as if all that there was in the world of curiosity, of gaping hope for the downfall of a human creature, was centred about the building in which Malcolm must play such a vitally important part. And was he fit to play it? Would he last? Always she had been accustomed to see him start off for his cases buoyant, even if anxious, full of self-assurance and the determination to win. That morning he had looked like a man rent with doubts, a man on the edge of his nerves, ill in mind if not actually ill in body. And she thought of the woman in the Dock and of Lord Horfield and was afraid. Did the woman know what she knew? And Lord

Horfield—did he know? He could not surely know, but he suspected. His insolent words to her in the motor car going to the theatre were assurance to her of that.

As on the day before they got in at the back of the gallery, conveyed there by Sir Simon's friend, who said:

"They're at it hammer and tongs, ladies. There's been one or two brush-ups between Sir Malcolm Keane and the Judge. But that's an old story at the Bar. Sir Malcolm's always so hot for his clients and small blame to him. And Lord Horfield he's like steel when flint strikes it, as you may say. They've brought in the doctors already."

"But William Marsh!" exclaimed Judith.

"They've not got to him yet. The Prosecution seems to be keeping him back for a bit. There you are!"

The gallery was packed. Gay and Judith squeezed in and sat at the back.

A doctor was giving evidence about arsenic, how long after it had been taken into the system traces of it remained in the organs, etc., etc. He was a thin elderly man with a hatchet face and an authoritative manner. They gathered that his evidence had been interpolated 'by special request,' as he was due to go to Birmingham to give evidence in another case. In spite of his cross-examination the effect of his evidence was to leave the Jury, and no doubt everyone in the Court, convinced that certainly one attempt, and probably two, had been made at Hindley Hall to poison Colonel Paradine by the administration of arsenic, or rather perhaps to begin poisoning him. The intention, it seemed, must have been to start an attempt upon his life which was meant to be cumulative but was interrupted, never carried to its conclusion. The words 'unfinished murder' were heard in the Court. Lord Horfield's comment on them was:

"A contradiction in terms. Murder cannot be unfinished. The proper expression is 'interrupted attempt at murder.' An attempt can be interrupted. A murder cannot."

Cross-examination, which was short, was directed to the point that a man, who was ignorant of the exact effects of arsenic, and who wanted to take his own life, might easily have made a mistake in the amount necessary to cause death, and have been turned from his purpose by the suffering caused to him by a frustrated attempt at suicide. This was of course allowed by the doctor. On this Lord Horfield made the dry comment:

"It is difficult to see how a man who was blind could measure out poison."

"If necessary I will deal with that presently, my lord," said Keane coldly.

"You see the defence is going to be suicide," Judith whispered to Gay.

"But a blind man!" she murmured back.

"Depend upon it they've got something up their sleeves," said Judith, as the doctor quitted the box.

"Shall we have the other doctors now, do you think?" asked Gay, as a subdued rustling sound pervaded the Court.

"The Hindley ones are sure to be called by the Defence," said Judith.

"William Marsh!" called a voice.

Judith leaned forward. Gay took off her veil, which she had worn till that moment, feeling a desire that she could not account for to be hidden, although Judith had whispered to her: "The ground seems clear. No one up here whom we know." She took off her veil and quickly put on her spectacles. Through them she at first looked at the Dock.

The woman was there in the brown dress. And she, too, like Judith, like many others in the crowded Court, was leaning forward. And her long beautiful hands were holding the ledge of the Dock. The attitude showed her to Gay for the first time as a woman expectant, alive in her mind, instead of as a passive, silent, usually motionless figure, inexpressive, detached, around whom, and because of whom, all this machinery of the Law was revolving.

Then Gay looked at the green benches and saw Malcolm, sitting back, his legs crossed, his arms folded, his eyes fixed on something, his lips pursed together, his face haggard in its framework of wig.

A voice, the harsh voice of yesterday, was saying:

"Your name?"

"William Allen Marsh."

"Your age?"

"Thirty-seven."

"Your means of livelihood?"

"I'm living just now on something that was left me, sir, and doing occasional jobs at Hindley Hall."

The other voice, the answering voice, was deep and strong, and gave to Gay immediately the impression of a tremendously masculine personality; something stern and defiant about it.

"You served in the Scots Guards during the late war?"

"Yes, sir."

"You were batman, were you not, to the late Colonel Paradine?"

"Yes, sir."

"And later on his personal servant at Hindley Hall, and elsewhere?"

"Yes, sir."

Question and answer continued, while the crowd in the Court was unusually silent, rapt, evidently, in attention. Always listening, Gay looked at the witness-box through her spectacles. She had immediately the impression of seeing what matched her hearing, a man whose voice belonged intimately to him, expressed truly his personality. Here was a soldierly fellow if ever there was one, a fellow of strong character, of grit, rugged, not easy to deal with perhaps, but a personality.

Gay believed he was very handsome, but his 'looks' were not of the kind that attracted her, although she loved, too much, a big man, a manly man, a man of dominant personality. William Marsh had something overpowering in his appearance from which something within her shrank, half-doubtful, half-afraid. Her delicacies curled up at the thought of a close approach to him. A suggestion of—what was it?—of the jungle clung about him. There was too much of the animal in him for her. And yet he did not look a bad man. It was not a criminal face. At moments it had even nobility. But she could never be at ease with that man. And she thought of him as a servant in a household of hers. Impossible! She could not have borne it.

He gave his evidence well. Nothing shaky or indefinite about him. He stood up to Counsel, to Judge, and Jury, to the packed crowd in the Court. Yet he wasn't defiant. His manner was simple and straightforward. The impression he made was a good one, the impression of a fearless man, not self-conscious, ready to say honestly and openly what he had to say. And his strong voice carried. Every answer was plainly heard by everybody in Court. And he did not, like many witnesses, try to amplify or embroider. Whenever a mere yes or no would do for an answer that was the answer he gave. When more was wanted of him he added the necessary words, but no more. He was listened to with a profound attention which was the greatest compliment the crowd could pay him.

And, so, his story emerged, a story that undoubtedly did him credit, a story of simple bravery and devotion to duty, and, later, of devotion to the Colonel of his regiment, of good conduct in the army and devout attention to duty in private life.

An excellent record.

Three medals were his, the D.C.M., the M.M., and the Mons Star. He stood before the crowd as a brave man, an excellent soldier, a faithful servant wholly devoted to a stricken master.

Counsel for the Crown rapidly 'placed' him. In a very few minutes there must have been few, if any, in Court who were not thinking well of William Marsh.

"They're making the most of him, aren't they?" whispered Judith. "Have you noticed that he has never once looked at *her*?"

"No," whispered Gay.

"Well, he hasn't. Not once!"

Then, as question and answer went on, Mrs. Paradine came into the story. They were out of the army, Marsh and his Colonel. The blind man was married. The life of retirement had begun at Hindley Hall. And with the coming of that life into the trial the interest of the crowd became intensified. The silence in Court was remarkable, only broken by the alternating voices, both strong, but one harsh and the other clear and deep.

Gay and the crowd gathered that Marsh was 'glad' that his master took a wife. He would have someone to look after him, to see to his house, to console him in his affliction, to bear him company. And so Marsh, his servant, was glad. When his master married he, Marsh, was prepared to like Mrs. Paradine and do everything to please her. The Court learnt that he was 'more than willing' to have a lady in the house. But as the examination proceeded it appeared that this rosy state of things did not endure for very long. Mrs. Paradine was 'nice' to Marsh at first, but presently he became aware that he was no favourite of hers. She did not treat him badly. He could not say that she ever treated him what you may call *badly*. (He seemed at this point determined to be fair to the prisoner.) But she was less cordial to him and seemed often to resent his intimacy with the Colonel. She would show it by seeming surprised when, on coming to the Colonel's sitting-room, she found them together. Such remarks as: "Oh, Marsh is with you!" or "I'll come back later when you're alone!" indicated her dislike of witness's presence. Counsel drew from the witness this impression—not that Marsh was jealous of his master's wife, but that she was jealous of him, and handed it on to the Jury. To be sure it seemed to be dragged out of Marsh, but evidently there it was—a woman's jealousy of a trusted servant, who, because of his master's affliction, was forced to be on very special terms with him.

"Precisely," said Counsel. "But did you ever on any occasion give the prisoner cause for jealousy, by interfering between her and her husband, or otherwise presuming on your position of confidence in the household?"

"Never, sir, to my knowledge. I was most anxious to please the lady. But it seemed I couldn't."

"How did she show you that she wasn't pleased with you?" the Judge intercepted at this point.

"By her looks and her ways, my Lord," said the witness. "She would look sour at me when she found me with the Colonel and go from the room."

"Did Colonel Paradine realise that she disliked your being there?"

"Oh, yes, my Lord. He often spoke to me of it."

"Your impression was that Colonel Paradine realised that the prisoner was not favourably disposed to you?" asked the Judge.

"Yes, my Lord."

"Proceed!" said Lord Horfield to Counsel for the Crown.

Counsel now came to the ugly side of Colonel Paradine, shown specially to his wife. It was evident that he wanted evidence from Marsh that would help the Crown to establish motive, but did not want to put witness's 'back up' by drawing too black a picture of his adored master. In a less harsh voice than usual he asked:

"Now tell his Lordship and the Jury, Marsh, was Colonel Paradine at times, and owing no doubt to his affliction, difficult in the house?"

For the first time since he had entered the witness-box Marsh hesitated obviously.

"Difficult—sir?" he said at length.

"Yes. Was he irritable, impatient, what is often called *trying* in his domestic life?"

"I have seen the Colonel put out, sir."

"With whom?"

"With Mrs. Paradine, sir. She seemed to irritate him."

"She seemed to irritate him!" Counsel repeated, looking towards the Jury. "And did he express that irritation?"

"Sometimes, sir."

"In what way?"

Marsh hesitated.

"Just tell his Lordship and the Jury anything that you noticed."

"The Colonel got angry at times, sir. He was an army man, sir."

"We know that. Well?"

"I have heard him swear, sir."

"At whom?"

"At Mrs. Paradine, sir."

Counsel took this up, and eventually elicited from Marsh details of quarrels that had taken place between the husband and wife.

It was during this part of the evidence that Keane, who was of course listening with intensity to every word that was spoken, ready to interrupt if anything was said which had no right to be said, to the detriment of the prisoner, realised that Marsh was carefully concealing the venomous hatred of Mrs. Paradine shown by him in the Inn at Sedale. There he had called her roundly a woman of Babylon. Nothing less than loathing of her had irresistibly burst out of him. And Keane had expected to see a display of that loathing given in Court at the trial. But now he realised that Marsh could be subtle as well as fierce, and had his reason for damping down in public the fire that had blazed up startlingly in private, when they two had been alone together. And he began to wonder whether the witness for the Crown and the prisoner were mutually afraid of each other, being each of them the holder of a damnable secret in which the other was concerned, and to see a possibility of a verdict of not guilty even without some tremendous effort on his part. Certainly Marsh was being unexpectedly mild in his condemnation of the prisoner—if indeed it could be called condemnation. It was obvious that he did not like her, and was trying to give the impression that she had disliked him, but nevertheless he seemed anxious not to go too far, and even to be scrupulously fair in his evidence. A witness for the Crown, yes, but scarcely a really hostile witness.

Sir Joseph Farrell had now come to the attacks of illness which Colonel Paradine had had at Hindley Hall. He examined Marsh closely with regard to them. Had Marsh been satisfied that they were normal attacks such as might have been caused by acute dyspepsia, or had he had any suspicion that they were abnormal, and that the diagnosis of the Cumberland doctors was at fault? Marsh replied that he 'couldn't understand' why his master had these seizures. He had never known him to be subject to indigestion. The numbness felt by the Colonel had specially troubled him. But he had taken the doctors' word for it that the symptoms were such as might have been due to severe dyspepsia, and had never had any suspicion that anyone had had a hand in the Colonel's illnesses.

"And now?" asked Sir Joseph Farrell significantly.

Marsh looked at him, then looked down.

"Now, I couldn't say as to that, sir," he replied, in a low deep voice that had become suddenly dull.

And a heavy expression lowered over his powerful face.

Gay put up her opera glasses for a moment. She looked through them first at Marsh then at the prisoner in the Dock. Mrs. Paradine was leaning forward with her chin in her right hand, the elbow of her right arm being supported on her knee. She was evidently gazing intently at Marsh. Gay got the impression that, at any rate for the moment, she was totally indifferent to all the people around her. And for an instant she saw the man and the woman, Marsh and Mrs. Paradine, as two lonely beings isolated from the world but strangely connected with each other. And she thought:

"What have they had to do with each other?"

And a new burning curiosity invaded her. She felt at that moment as if she were on the edge of some ugly discovery with which those two were connected. She even felt as if she had some inkling of what the discovery might be. And yet—she didn't know. When she asked herself—what, she didn't know. She was in darkness. But these two—there was something between them that, if it were known, would shed light where now there was darkness.

After dealing with the physical symptoms of the two attacks of illness and the impression made upon William Marsh by them, Counsel questioned witness as to the conduct of the prisoner at the times of these illnesses.

"Did Mrs. Paradine seem upset when her husband was ill?" he asked.

"Not specially, sir."

"Tell us exactly what you mean by that."

"Mrs. Paradine was a lady as didn't show much as a rule. She was very shut in," said the witness.

"And by that you mean——?"

"You couldn't tell by looking at her what she was feeling, sir. We all noticed that."

Nearly all the eyes in the Court were turned towards the prisoner, who just then lifted her chin from the palm of her hand and sat back in the Dock.

"But did she, or not, express herself as anxious about her husband's condition?"

"Oh yes, sir. She said the usual things."

"And what were they?"

"That she hoped he'd soon be better, that he must be more careful what he ate—that sort of thing, sir."

"And did she seem troubled?"

"No, sir, not specially. But she did say the country doctors were fools."

A faint sound of laughter went through the Court. Lord Horfield took no notice of it.

"Soon after this did she suggest a change of any kind?"

"Yes, sir. She wanted us to go to London."

"Did that suggestion come from the Colonel or from her?"

"Oh, from Mrs. Paradine, sir. She thought the Colonel had better have a change and see a London doctor."

"Are you sure the suggestion of his seeing a London doctor came from her?"

"Yes, sir. I heard her myself say that in London they could have a real examination, and see if anything was the matter with the Colonel."

"You felt that she was solicitous about her husband's health?"

"Sir?"

"Did she strike you at that time as being very anxious about her husband's condition?"

Marsh was silent for a moment, like a man considering. Then he seemed to take a decision, lifted his chin slightly, and said:

"No, sir."

"Not?"

"No, sir. I thought she was play-acting."

"Why?"

"By her manner, sir. I thought she was pretending to care and didn't."

"You thought her indifferent about the Colonel's health?"

Again Marsh was silent for a moment, staring in front of him. Then he said:

"I didn't think she cared whether he lived or died, sir."

"Then why wish to consult a London doctor?"

"Woman's pretence, sir. That's what I took it for."

"By the time you went up to London with them what, in your view, was the state of things between your master and mistress?"

"Dog and cat, sir, but she hid it."

"And yet you tell us you noticed it?"

"There's things hid that you can *feel* are there, sir."

"You felt it? That's what you mean?"

"Yes, sir."

"Did you ever express this feeling of yours to any of your fellow servants?"

"No, sir. Certainly not."

"To anyone else?"

"No, sir. I'm not one to talk."

The examination was then transferred to the events in London. Marsh described the sort of life led by his master and mistress there, as far as it came under his notice. It was no better, according to him, than it had been in Hindley. The Colonel was very unhappy, more unhappy, it seemed, in London than he had been in the country. Marsh thought that being there brought back to him vividly all that he had lost by losing his sight. In the country he was at least quiet. In London he seemed to realise with much greater bitterness all that he was missing. His nerves, Marsh affirmed, were 'all to pieces.' But his physical health seemed good. There was no reason to anticipate any return of illness. The London doctor consulted had given a good report of him. So things were on the day when a crisis arrived in the lives of these people.

"Tell his Lordship and the Jury what happened on that evening when you were summoned to Colonel Paradine's study, the evening of the night on which he died," said Counsel.

Judith Flaquer's keen eyes at this moment were fixed upon Mrs. Paradine. She had forgotten Gay at her side, she had forgotten for the moment everything except two people, the man in the witness-box and the woman in the Dock.

"Now is the moment for drastic truth or blazing perjury!" she said to herself. "Which are we going to get?"

She noticed that the sort of slouching grace she had observed had gone out of the prisoner's body. That body had surely stiffened. To her it looked rigid, braced up in the Dock. But the face she saw was a blank. She thought of it as a white piece of paper on which nothing was written.

"Where's her mind gone?" she thought.

Then it occurred to her that possibly at that moment Mrs. Paradine was sick with dread. With sickness of the mind, producing the sensation of sickness in the body, sometimes there comes an amazing blankness into the face of woman or man, as if everything of thought and feeling were blotted out by sheer overwhelming sickness, a wave of engulfing sickness. But was this woman overwhelmed at this moment, or was she, full of a queer and vital intention, blotting by an act of the will all writing out of the paper? Judith couldn't determine, though she stared, kept on staring at Mrs. Paradine, not missing, however, a word that Counsel and witness were speaking.

"I heard the Colonel's bell ringing violently and then his voice calling out for me, sir, and I hurried to go to him. I knew there was something up."

"How did you know that?"

"I had heard voices from the room, sir. The Colonel was almost shouting like."

"Did you hear Mrs. Paradine's voice before you went to the room?"

"Yes, sir, but less than his. I heard her just as I was coming to the room."

"Well, you went to the room. And what happened then?"

"The Colonel and the lady were both on their feet. The lady was standing, but the Colonel was going up and down, as was his way, sometimes, knocking here and there against bits of furniture. He was, as you might say, new to the house, sir. It wasn't like it was at Hindley where he knew exactly where everything was."

"Naturally. And your mistress? The prisoner?"

"She just stood where she was, sir."

"What did you do?"

"I shut the door behind me. I didn't want the others to hear. And they might be curious."

"So you shut the door. And then what did you do?"

"Told the Colonel I was there, sir, and asked what he wanted."

"Tell the Jury the gist of what followed."

"Sir?"

"Tell us, as concisely as you can, what followed. Don't try to give the exact words of what was said, but just the general meaning."

Marsh was silent for a moment. He stood with his large, powerful hands clasped one over the other, looking down, and his handsome face looked very stern. Judith, watching him, found herself wondering whether at that moment he was seeking in his memory for exact truth, or was spurring an ingenious mind in the search for the best sort of lies. But she couldn't divine. His face was like a stern mask.

After waiting, in a deadly silence which seemed to wrap the whole Court like a garment, Counsel said: "Well, tell us!" Silence. "Tell us what happened!"

Marsh still remained silent.

"Explain to the Jury, in the shortest way you can, why the

Colonel had sent for you and what happened when you got to the room," said Lord Horfield from the Bench, in a gentle and persuasive voice. "It is essential that we should know."

Marsh looked towards the Judge.

"Yes, my lord."

The Judge's intervention seemed to give the witness heart, for he squared his shoulders, like a soldier on parade, and said:

"When I come into the room and the door was shut, I told the Colonel I was there. He was so excited I didn't know whether he had heard me come in. And not being able to see me, he mightn't know. When I told him he burst out with it."

Again Marsh paused.

"Well?" said Counsel encouragingly. "Tell us."

"He said that the lady——"

"Mrs. Paradine?"

"Yes, sir. That Mrs. Paradine had given me away to him."

Keane made a violent movement, then sat still, leaning forward.

"What do you mean by given you away?"

"He said that she'd told him I meant to leave him, get out of his service and look out for another job."

Keane's attitude changed. His whole body seemed to relax.

"And was that the reason of his anger?"

"Partly, sir."

"Well?"

"His blindness had made the Colonel terrible suspicious. He usen't to be like that when he could see. He wasn't afraid of anything or anybody then. 'I can judge with my eyes!' I've often heard him say that. But losing them seemed to change him entirely. He couldn't seem really to trust anyone thoroughly—but me, as I'd thought up till then."

"One moment! Didn't he trust his wife, the prisoner?"

"I don't think so, sir," said Marsh, in a heavy, rather loud voice, and with a dogged inflection.

At that moment Judith Flaquer had an odd sensation of definiteness. She seemed to see a man burning his boats.

"Did he ever show distrust of her?"

"I don't think he trusted any woman, sir. He thought he knew too much about 'em."

"What was the rest of the reason for his anger, besides his

anger at being told, if he was, that you meant to leave his service?"

"He was very angry at my having said such a thing to the lady behind his back, instead of coming to him with it. That I should go to her. That was what got him."

"But had you gone to the prisoner with any such statement?"

"Of course not, sir. And so I told the Colonel. But he wouldn't believe me."

"You gave the lie to the prisoner?"

"I did, sir. And I'd give it again," said Marsh, in a loud voice.

Judith bent to Gay:

"It's extraordinary! Even now he doesn't look at her," she whispered.

Gay answered nothing. She was absorbed in the case.

"So Colonel Paradine wouldn't believe you?"

"No, sir. He was fair and out of himself. I never see him in such a state before, though I'd often seen him angry. But never with me like that. That I should go back on him, that *did* go home."

As Marsh gave this evidence, it became evident that his hitherto stern self-control was beginning to wear thin. He began to look strongly emotional and clasped and unclasped his big hands several times. He drew down his black eyebrows and raised them and his powerful lower jaw quivered.

"And I'm sure I don't wonder," he added, suddenly lowering his voice almost to a mutter, as if he were saying that to himself, telling it to his own listening mind.

Keane put both his hands up to his shoulders and pulled at his robe roughly, then turned in his seat and sat sideways.

"Didn't you continue to deny it?"

"Of course I did. But he was fair away and nothing would stop him. You might as well have talked to a thunderstorm."

There was a faint laugh from a woman at this. But no one echoed it. Lord Horfield remarked:

"I shall allow no demonstrations of any kind in this Court. Go on, please!" (To the witness.)

"He kept on talking, my Lord, and wouldn't listen to anything I said."

"Did Mrs. Paradine take no part in this scene?" said the Judge.

"Tell us what her attitude was, please," added Counsel.

"The lady just stood there and looked as blank as a sheet of paper," said Marsh, with sudden fierceness.

"He's described her exactly as she is now," Judith whispered to Gay.

"But when you denied it?"

"She didn't back me up, not she! Why should she? She is a woman."

Marsh's hatred of women was now coming out of him like flame out of a fire hitherto nearly black and quiescent.

"Did you ask her to join you in your denial?"

"No, sir. What would have been the good when it was she who'd put the whole thing into the Colonel's head?"

"And the whole brunt fell on you, did it?"

"No, sir. The Colonel was furious with both of us, with me for telling the lady, as he thought, and with her for listening to me behind his back. He put us both down as treacherous to him."

"And so the whole scene that took place was based on his belief that you meant to get out of his service and had told the prisoner so without telling him?"

"That was it, sir."

"And you say there was no truth in this?"

"No truth at all, sir. I would never have left my Colonel."

"Can you give his Lordship and the Jury any reason why the prisoner should have made such an assertion about you when it was entirely untrue?"

Marsh thrust out his square chin defiantly. His evident emotion seemed to Judith to cause his defiance, as if he brought it up as in a battle a commander may bring up reserves at a critical moment to cover a weakening position.

"I think the lady wanted to get me out of my situation," he said.

"Why?"

Keane at this moment stared steadfastly towards the Dock.

"She didn't care for me being so much with the Colonel."

"Do you mean that you think she was jealous of your position of confidence in the household?"

"Yes, sir."

"Anything else?"

"She may have had other reasons," Marsh said, slowly.

"What other reasons do you suggest?"

"Well, sir, I think she wanted me out of the house. Otherwise, why tell such a lie about me?"

"So," said Counsel, looking straight at the Jury box, "the impression you had was that she had her reasons for getting you out of the house and so told the Colonel a lie about you?"

Keane made a sudden movement, half rose to his feet, seemed to think better of something, and sat down again. The Judge looked towards him for a moment, and a very slight smile stretched his thin lips.

"Yes, sir."

"And beyond jealousy of your influence with the Colonel, and his trust and confidence in you, you can suggest no other specific reason for the prisoner's wishing to get you out of Colonel Paradine's household?"

Marsh obviously hesitated. His broad low forehead, bronzed between the thick, dark hair and the thick, dark eyebrows, was furrowed deeply in a frown. The silence in Court was intense, as if the crowd, made one, held its breath. Finally he said, in a low voice:

"It's difficult to know what a woman's reason is, sir. I think I'll leave it there."

Counsel again looked at the Jury.

"Very well. Then we'll pass away from that."

He bent down, fidgeted rather elaborately with some papers in front of him, and whispered a word or two to his Junior, who whispered something back. Then, lifting himself abruptly, he said:

"Did the prisoner take no part whatever in this scene?"

"Oh, yes, sir. After a bit she did all she could to smooth the Colonel down, but it was all no good. We couldn't do anything with him."

"But when you denied the truth of what she had said to her husband?"

"She swore it was true."

"So she gave you the lie?"

"She did, sir."

"And did the Colonel believe her?"

"He went for me, sir, and her too. He was out of himself."

"What d'you mean by that?"

"He seemed almost demented with it. Poor Colonel!"

The way in which Marsh said the last words made a deep impression on the Court. They seemed spoken as if by an irresistible afterthought, and with such sincerity, such complete absence of any intention of making an effect, that almost everyone present was stirred by them. They came in a sort of groan from the man's heart, it seemed.

"That's true enough, if all the rest is lies!" Judith whispered to Gay.

Counsel waited a moment to let the effect of this sink in, and then passed on to what happened during the rest of the fateful evening and night, so far as Marsh had to do with it; to the Colonel's refusal to see Marsh, to let Marsh help him to undress, etc., etc., as it had been related in the opening.

"So finally you gave it up and went downstairs in company with Ellen Smith, the head housemaid?"

"Yes, sir."

"Leaving the prisoner and your master alone on the first floor as far as you knew?"

"Quite alone, sir."

"After a lapse of time, was your attention drawn to anything?"

"Yes, sir."

"What was it?"

"I heard the piano in the drawing-room going."

"About how long was this after you had gone downstairs?"

"I should say about twenty minutes, sir."

"Did you recognise the tune being played?"

"Yes, sir. It was to do with what they call 'The Blue Danube' Waltz, but there was a lot of other things to it."

"Ah! And for how long did this continue?"

"Quite a bit of time, sir."

"Did anything strike you about this music?"

"Yes, sir."

"What was it?"

"I didn't see how Mrs. Paradine could play such music after what had happened."

"What exactly do you mean by that?"

"After the terrible scene with the Colonel, sir."

"You thought that very strange?"

"Yes, sir—that she should have got over it so soon."

A sort of contemptuous bitterness came into his voice as he said that.

Counsel then drew from him his account of what had happened during the rest of the night up to the death of Colonel Paradine.

"At the time," he ended, "what did you think to be the cause of your master's death? Did you think it natural?"

"Oh, no, sir, never! I knew he must have taken something."

"And did you form any opinion as to how he came to take it?"

"I thought that he might have drunk it in his glass of Burgundy."

"Without realising that there was a deadly poison in the wine. Do you mean that?"

"I couldn't think of anything else, sir."

"You knew that a glass full of Burgundy had been put in his bedroom?"

"Yes, sir. Lakin told me. And I saw it when I went to the Colonel's bedroom and he ordered me away."

"Did the Colonel often drink wine in his bedroom?"

"No, sir, not to my knowledge. But that night he was not himself and might have done anything."

"That's hardly what the Crown wanted!" whispered Judith.

"Isn't it?" whispered Gay.

Judith raised her black eyebrows. She began to wonder how much of the drift of the case Gay really understood. It seemed to her that Gay, in her preoccupation with undercurrents, was missing what lay in sight on the surface of the Paradine case. Perhaps Gay was submerged in a kind of dream. Judith wondered. And while she was wondering, the examination of Marsh for the Crown came to an end, and there was an immediate stir through the Court.

"Now for the cross-examination!" said Judith.

But she had forgotten the time. It was close upon one o'clock, and the Court adjourned for luncheon.

During the interval Judith told Gay that she had seen Lady Horfield in Court. She was sitting in the 'City Lands,' with an elderly woman who looked like a lady's maid, and was actually wearing white, 'poor old dear,' and a white toque with a seagull's feather in it. And then Judith started a discussion of the case in a low voice, testing Gay's comprehension of it and giving her views.

"What impression did you get from that man Marsh's evidence?" she asked.

Gay immediately remembered her strange feeling about Marsh and Mrs. Paradine, that there was some mysterious link between them, remembered how for a moment they had seemed to her two solitary figures, isolated from the world in an intimacy which she couldn't understand, couldn't penetrate. But she said nothing of this to Judith.

"What impression!" she said. "Well, I think he's an extraordinary man."

"D'you think he's a liar?"

Gay was startled by this. In a sort of innocent way, though she was no fool, she had been accepting all Marsh's evidence as the truth of what he believed.

"No. Why should I?" she asked.

"Then did you believe all that evidence he gave about the scene between him and the Paradines on the evening of Colonel Paradine's death?"

"Why not? Was there any reason not to?"

"Well," said Judith, always in a low voice, but in her most downright way, "I believe it was a tissue of lies. I believe right through he was carefully concealing what was the real reason of that violent scene."

"But what makes you think so?"

"I feel it. But wait till Sir Malcolm cross-examines the man. Then we shall see. Oh, how I wish I were a lawyer! Not a solicitor, like dear old papa, but a Counsel like Sir Joseph or your husband. What I would give to have the cross-examination of William Marsh! There's something at the roots of this case that hasn't been dug down to yet. I'm profoundly interested. Those two— Mrs. Paradine and Marsh! What a pair! What a contrast! And, believe me, there's iron in both of them. But wait till they're laid on the anvil!"

"How awful to be a witness!"

"That depends on how much you have to conceal."

When the Court resumed it was crowded almost to suffocation.

It had got about that William Marsh was about to be cross-examined and somehow more people had managed to force, or to wheedle, their way in. Although the weather was wintry—for March was a cruel month that year—the heat of humanity made the Court exhaustingly stuffy. Judith and Gay were tightly wedged in between two strangers, both women. Till now Gay had been on the outside of the line of people at the back, but just as the Judge took his seat on the Bench a woman with a pointed nose, a tight little mouth, and determined eyes, had got in somehow and ruthlessly sat down on half of Gay. After a faint struggle Gay had managed to dislodge her, but she now had scarcely enough room to draw breath in. Nevertheless when she saw Malcolm rising to cross-examine the concentration of her mind on the case and him in it made her forget her extreme bodily discomfort.

His first question startled the whole Court.

"William Marsh," he said, in a strong voice, fixing his large dark eyes on the witness. "Is it a fact, notorious in your regiment when you served in the army, that you hate women?"

That Marsh was startled by this opening was obvious to everyone who was looking at him. His tall body jerked exactly as if it had received a blow. Then he recovered himself and stood rigid like a soldier at attention.

"Not at all, sir. I like a nice woman as much as any man," was his answer.

"Is it a fact, notorious in your regiment when you were in barracks in London, and on active service in France, that you had nothing to do with women and often expressed dislike and distrust of them?"

"Not at all, sir."

"You deny it?"

"I do, sir."

"Very well. We will see as to that later."

And Keane bent down for a moment, murmured something to his Junior, and glanced at some papers.

"All calculated!" Judith formed with her lips.

But she did not see into Malcolm Keane's mind at that moment. While every woman in the Court was gazing at William Marsh and wondering whether in truth he was a hater of women, Keane was struggling with the terrible curiosity of a violently jealous man. That scene in Eaton Square between the Paradines and Marsh, that scene so closely followed by the death of Colonel Paradine, what had really been the cause of it? He didn't know. Marsh had given his version. Keane didn't believe it. Mrs. Paradine's version had been given to him. He didn't believe that either. He was haunted by a horrible suspicion of the truth, and knew that, given his powers as a brilliant criminal lawyer, it was quite possible that if he exerted them to the utmost, in the service of his fierce curiosity, he might be able to force the truth out of William Marsh. But mightn't that truth, if it were what he suspected, prove ruinous to the woman in the Dock? Or could he so manipulate it that it might ruin Marsh and not bring her down? It would leave her, perhaps, completely tarnished in reputation. That couldn't be helped. And it was a minor point as things were. But so long as it didn't endanger her life!

He wanted to know. He felt he must know. And here was his opportunity perhaps. But dared he take it? During the instant while, looking down, he was fidgeting with his papers he repeated to himself:

"Dare I? Dare I?"

The pause had become long enough to astonish the crowd and cause an expression of cold surprise and inquiry to dawn on Lord Horfield's long narrow face when Keane pulled himself up.

"Were you once engaged to be married to a girl called Margaret Wells of Southborough, in Kent, near Tunbridge Wells, and did she jilt you on the day fixed for the wedding, Monday, May 6th, 1912, and go off with a man called Richard Truton?" he said, staring hard at the witness with a brutal expression on his face.

A wave of hot blood flooded Marsh's face up to the roots of his hair and a savage expression distorted his appearance so completely that for an instant he was scarcely recognisable. A fury of astonishment at this by him utterly unexpected question had evidently taken possession of him. His blue eyes blazed as he faced Counsel.

"This has naught to do with the case!" he exclaimed, and his deep voice shook with angry emotion.

"Answer the question!"

"I shall not, sir."

"You're here to answer my questions. Did she leave you standing at the church door, on Monday, May 6th, 1912?"

"My Lord!" exclaimed Marsh, throwing out his left hand towards the Judge in a gesture that was almost wild, "I ask you, what has this to do with my poor Colonel's death?"

"I scarcely see the relevance of the question, Sir Malcolm," said Lord Horfield. "What has it to do with this case?"

"My Lord, in my view anything that tends to throw light on the witness's hostile attitude to my client is strictly relevant to this case. My contention is that the witness is a woman hater, and I am seeking to prove it, and to show the reason for it."

"I shall certainly not rule out any question that I consider relevant to this case," said Lord Horfield, in his most silvery tones. "But I hardly see any relevance in going into the witness's private love affairs of nearly twenty years ago. Anything that tends to the elucidation of character is of course a different matter. But how does this reflect upon character? The jilting of a man, if he is jilted, reflects rather upon the character of the woman who does it."

"My Lord, I claim the right to show the reason why this witness is a hater of women."

"But he has already denied that he hates women."

"My contention is that there is no truth in that denial."

"It is impossible to prove a negative, Sir Malcolm."

"My Lord, I must really insist——"

"I do not see the relevance of the question and therefore I must disallow it."

"My Lord, I must really protest. If I am not to be permitted to do my best for my client my handicap in this case is really too great."

"There is no handicap put upon you, Sir Malcolm," said Lord Horfield, his silvery voice changing to a note of sternness. "It is a lack of respect to the Bench to suggest such a thing. I sit here to show strict fairness to everyone. I rule the question irrelevant. Now please proceed!"

There was a moment of painful stillness in Court. Gay felt herself trembling. Judith, who was looking at Marsh, saw perspiration streaming down his face. While she looked he pulled a big handkerchief from his pocket, pressed it against first one cheek and then the other and passed it across his forehead. She couldn't help feeling intensely sorry for him.

"Very well," she heard Keane say in a hoarse voice. "As I am not permitted to show one of the reasons of the witness's hostile attitude towards my client——"

"I must ask Counsel not to question my ruling," Lord Horfield interrupted, with cutting emphasis.

"Very well, my Lord. I will leave it," said Keane, shrugging his shoulders. "I will leave it."

Again there was a pause while the crowd sat breathless. It was obvious to them that Counsel for the Defence was very much disturbed by what had taken place. The witness, too, looked painfully upset and grim with what seemed to be a mingling of shame and indignation. But the prisoner in the Dock had not lost her blank self-possession. There were people in the Court who began to think of her as a human puppet placed there because it was necessary to have a centre for this machinery of the Law, simply because of that. Her stillness, whiteness, and peculiar inexpressiveness seemed to rule out all suggestion of acute feeling.

And yet surely she must be feeling acutely.

Even Lady Horfield, sitting by her very respectable maid, began to wonder about her. Was the almost despairing pity she felt for her being wasted?

What had just happened had stirred up all the hot defiance, and almost reckless determination to put things through in his own way, which in the past had often got Keane into trouble with the Judges, but which had sometimes contributed to his success. It had also increased his natural vitality till he was conscious of a fury of energy. In the morning, when he had left Portland Place, he had looked and felt haggard, nervous, uncertain of himself. That sensation had gone. He was now tremendously alive. Hatred of Marsh ran all through him. And that cursed Horfield held him back. But he had given the witness a terrible jolt. As he looked at Marsh using the big handkerchief he could see that well enough. And he had not done with him yet. In spite of Horfield he had started well. He had got Marsh into a fever of temper and shame. That girl who long ago had left him to stand at the church door! Every woman in the crowd held that vision in her mind and Marsh knew it. So much the better!

And now to get along farther. In spite of the Judge he wasn't going to spare Marsh.

And he proceeded to question Marsh closely about his attitude to Mrs. Paradine and her attitude to him during the first months of the Paradine marriage, seeking to show that she had always been extraordinarily kind to him and thoughtful for his comfort and happiness at the Hall, while he had from the first shown hostility to her and jealousy of her presence. He put to the witness instances of his uncouth behaviour to his mistress, implying that presently the prisoner would speak to them when he put her in the witness-box, but Marsh was obstinately firm in denying that he had ever felt any personal hostility to Mrs. Paradine, though he acknowledged that he had never taken to her.

"And why was that?" Keane asked.

"Because of her foreign ways and because I never thought she cared for the Colonel."

Keane at once took this up and asked Marsh to give instances of Mrs. Paradine's neglect of the Colonel. Did she leave him alone? Was she unthoughtful for his happiness? Did she seek after pleasure? Marsh's replies to these questions were rather vague and gave the impression that he was fencing with Counsel. But he stuck to it that Mrs. Paradine had never really cared for her husband.

"Give his Lordship and the Jury some reason for this conviction of yours," Keane said at length.

The witness was silent.

"You have told us, and others have told us, that Mrs. Paradine was perpetually where the Colonel was, that she looked after his comfort and that she read aloud to him, that she assisted him in the difficulties brought upon him by his blindness. Yet you say she didn't care for him. What is your proof?"

"One can tell such a thing whatever a woman does," said Marsh, doggedly.

"Have you ever," asked Keane, speaking slowly and with emphasis, "had reason to think she cared for any other man?"

"I didn't say that," Marsh answered.

"Do you say it now?" Keane said, leaning slightly forward.

Marsh was silent.

"Answer the question!" said the Judge, intervening.

"I don't say that, my Lord."

Marsh's appearance and his whole manner at this point gave to the Court the impression that he was keeping something back. Keane of course realised this, and he knew he was treading on dangerous ground. Convinced that Marsh had been Mrs. Paradine's lover, but burning with the desire to *know* whether this was so or not—for even now he possessed no proof that he was justified in his conviction—he felt the need of caution, the desperate need of caution. But this was fought against by the reckless feeling that had come to him since his passage of arms with Lord Horfield, and his growing hatred of Marsh. And then the line he had decided to take in his defence not yet disclosed to the Jury! But if he let this urging recklessness take its course that defence would have to be modified, wouldn't it? And he thought of an assisted suicide different in kind from the one he had spoken of with Sir Simon Flaquer, an assisted suicide in which not only the suicide, but the assistant, desired the death which took place, each one for himself, pity, kindness, blotted completely out, Marsh really a would-be murderer, pushing his master to murder himself, asked to do so but eager to help for his own sake.

For a moment he felt as if his brain would burst with all it carried, and he had, as it were, to let himself go to his own voice, yielding himself passively to the words that it chose to say. And he heard it say:

"Very well. We will leave that for the moment."

And the cross-examination went on, question and answer, travelling on, until Hindley Hall was deserted for London, and the Paradine *ménage* was installed in Eaton Square. Keane felt as if he put his questions mechanically. His mind of course must be working behind them, but he seemed unaware of it. There were things to bring out; he brought them out; the growing misery of Colonel Paradine in his blindness, his loss of all enjoyment in life, his perpetual preoccupation with his affliction, his irritability, his fits of overmastering depression, and so on, and so on. Judith Flaquer realised whither he was tending. Probably many others in Court realised it, too. But Keane himself scarcely seemed to realise it—until the journey to London had been undertaken. And then suddenly his brain seemed to clear, his mind to wake up. Now there must be no more vagueness, no more uncertainty. The crisis had come. The battle with Marsh must be definitely joined.

And still that awful personal curiosity, the curiosity of an unsatisfied lover, tore at him, demanding to be satisfied.

"We now come to your master's sojourn in London," said Keane. "To the last days of his life. What, in your opinion, was the state of his health when you arrived in Eaton Square?"

"Good, sir."

"The trouble he had after those two attacks at Hindley Hall seemed to have entirely cleared away?"

"Yes, sir."

"Did you question him about what the London specialist had said of his condition?"

"I didn't question the Colonel, sir. But he told me."

"And what did he tell you?"

"That the doctor said he was all right, but must be careful in his eating after those two attacks he had at Hindley."

"Which you still supposed to be due to dyspepsia?"

"Yes, sir."

"You are quite sure of that?"

"Yes, sir."

"No doubt about that at all?"

"No, sir."

Keane leaned down and turned over some papers. After a moment he said:

"What was the condition of your master's *mind* at this time?"

"As usual, sir."

"And what does as usual mean? Was he—be careful, please, how you answer—was he very unhappy?"

"I couldn't say the Colonel was happy, sir."

"Did he take any real interest in life while in London?"

Marsh hesitated, like one uncertain about where he was being led.

"Please answer!" said Keane sharply. "You must surely know."

"He couldn't seem to enjoy himself much, sir."

"Is it not a fact within your knowledge that your master had entirely lost all interest in life while in London?"

"I should hardly care to say that, sir," said Marsh, with obvious uneasiness, as of one suspecting a trap.

"It isn't a question of what you care to say. It's a question of fact. Is it not a fact that Colonel Paradine had lost entirely all interest in life by the time you got him up to London?"

"I don't know that, sir. I never asked him."

"And though you were perpetually with him you couldn't tell?"

"I couldn't say for certain, sir."

"Remember you are on your oath."

"I know that, sir."

"Very well. Now I ask you—and be very careful with your answer—on your oath whether you did not hear your master say, not once, but again and again while in London, that he wished he was dead?"

"In London, sir?"

"Certainly, in London."

"He used to complain, sir," said Marsh, speaking with hesitation, "about one thing and another. But I never took much notice."

"You mean that he said so often that he was sick of life and wished he was dead that at last you thought nothing of it?"

Sir Joseph Farrell rose in his seat.

"My Lord," he said, turning towards the Judge, "I object. The learned Counsel, instead of letting the witness speak for himself, is deliberately putting words into his mouth."

"My Lord," said Keane hotly, "I was merely asking the witness whether Colonel Paradine had not expressed a sickness of life to him."

"I beg pardon, my Lord. My learned brother told the witness what, in his opinion, the witness meant. I object to the witness being led on in that way."

"I must say," observed Lord Horfield, "that I noticed that the learned Counsel was putting words into the witness's mouth, but I was reluctant to interfere, as I know the learned Counsel very easily resents interruption."

"I beg your Lordship's pardon," said Keane, with heat. "I resent no interruption that is valid, I only object to being interfered with when I am performing my bounden duty to my client within the regulations as to evidence laid down by the Law. If your Lordship thinks I have transgressed, it is for your Lordship to say so."

"My objection stands, my Lord," said Sir Joseph Farrell,

obstinately. "My learned brother was deliberately leading the witness."

"I think," said Lord Horfield suavely, "that it would be desirable—I will not say more—if the learned Counsel for the Defence would let the witness speak entirely for himself, without putting actual words into his mouth."

"I am quite satisfied with that ruling, my Lord," said Sir Joseph Farrell, sitting down with a smile of satisfaction.

Up in the gallery, Judith Flaquer was frowning.

"Oh, why—why—why?" she whispered to herself.

She shot a glance at Gay. There were two red patches on Gay's cheeks. She did not return Judith's glance. She had taken off her gloves and her hands were clasped tightly together.

"My God, that's a dust-up, isn't it?" said the lady with the hard eyes, on her left. "There's no love lost between the Judge and the Counsel, is there? My word!"

"H'sh!" said somebody.

"Silence in Court!" cried a voice.

"William Marsh," said Keane, in a loud, hectoring voice, as if with the deliberate purpose of provoking and angering the witness, "on your oath do you deny having heard Colonel Paradine, while in London, say that he was sick of his life and wished he was dead?"

Sir Joseph Farrell frowned and looked towards the Bench, but Lord Horfield made no sign, only smiled faintly and moved his lips, pressed together, upwards.

"No, sir."

"What d'you mean by 'no sir'?"

"I didn't hear him."

"On your oath, did he not say that before you, in the presence of his friend Colonel Blake of the Grenadier Guards?"

Marsh moved uneasily in the witness-box.

"I can't call it to mind, sir."

"So that if Colonel Blake comes here and swears that it is so, you swear to the contrary?"

After a pause, Marsh said:

"He may have done, sir."

"Done what?"

"The Colonel may have said so."

"I ask you, did he not say so time and again, in your pres-

ence and in the presence of Mrs. Paradine when you were all three
in the room together?"

"I don't rightly call it to mind, sir."

"So that if I put Mrs. Paradine and Colonel Blake in that box
and they both testify on oath to Colonel Paradine's having said
that—that he was sick of life and wished he was dead—and *in
your presence, mind*, your denial still stands?"

"The Colonel said a lot of things when he was angry about his
blindness. I got so accustomed to them that I didn't take much
notice."

"Then you do not deny his saying repeatedly that he was sick
of his life and wished he was dead?"

"I don't seem to remember it, sir, but he might have done."

"And his Lordship and the Jury are to take that as your considered answer?"

"He might have done, sir. That's all I can say."

Keane looked at the Jury-box and raised his shoulders slightly.
He put some further questions to the witness about the life in
the London house, and finally said, in a voice that rang through
the Court:

"We now come to the day before Colonel Paradine's untimely
death."

A long rustle went through the crowd. Marsh braced his tall
body up in the witness-box, and with his right hand gripped his
left hand by the wrist.

"He knows now he's in for it!" Judith murmured to Gay.

And without knowing that she did it she breathed a long
sigh.

"January the sixteenth," said Keane. "Now on that day how
did the Colonel seem?"

"Just as usual, sir."

"Was he cheerful?"

"Not specially, sir."

"*Was he cheerful?*"

"I couldn't exactly say that, sir."

"Was he on the contrary very depressed?"

"I think he was rather down, sir."

"Do please tell us quite frankly *how* he seemed to you that day."

"Rather down, sir."

"What did he do that day as far as you remember? Take us up to the time when you heard loud voices and the summons to you to come to him."

Marsh slowly related how the Colonel's day had passed.

"That will do. Now where were you when you realised that something unusual was taking place in Colonel Paradine's study, the room in Eaton Square that he used as a study?"

"I had been downstairs, sir, in the servants' hall, and had occasion to come up."

"Why did you come up?"

"I can't rightly remember, sir."

"You leave the servants' hall and come upstairs and can't tell the Jury why you did so? Is that your answer?"

"I think it was to see for the post, sir."

"The post?"

"To look in the letter-box."

"Wouldn't that be the duty of the butler or the footman?"

"The Colonel liked me to bring him his letters, sir. I generally collected them and brought them to him."

"And you say that on that occasion you came up to see if there were any letters left in the box?"

"I believe so, sir."

"Now, William Marsh, I ask you this. Was it your habit to be about when your master and mistress were together, in order to try to hear what they were talking about?"

Marsh flushed with anger and thrust his head forward towards Counsel.

"Certainly not, sir. I should be ashamed to spy."

"And yet on that afternoon—or evening—you just happened to be about, and can't quite remember why. Is that it?"

"I came for the post, sir."

"Do you swear you ever went near the letter-box?"

"No, sir."

"What d'you mean by 'no, sir'?"

"I didn't go to the letter-box."

"Came upstairs for the letters and didn't go to the letter-box!" exclaimed Keane, flinging the words scornfully at the Jury box.

"I was stopped by hearing the Colonel calling out for me and hearing the bell going."

"That's your explanation?"

"Yes, sir."

"And what did you do then?"

"I hurried to the study, sir, and went in."

"Very well."

Keane broke off for an instant. He was struggling with himself, with his passionate instinct to go for the truth of that interview of three in Colonel Paradine's study, to go for it, and try to drag it out of Marsh. If he got it, and it were what he suspected it to be, the whole case would at once take a different and sensational turn. An apparently motiveless, or almost motiveless, crime, would be supplied with a backbone of motive terrible in its sufficiency. But could he so manipulate that motive, if he succeeded in extracting it in cross-examination, as to force the Jury's suspicions away from Mrs. Paradine and to concentrate them upon Marsh? That was the question that beleaguered his mind.

For a moment he looked at the Jury and wondered.

And then he looked at Lord Horfield and wondered again.

"Very well," he repeated mechanically, gnawed by a sickening hesitation and simultaneously driven by a curiosity more urgent than any he had known before in the whole course of his life.

"You have told his Lordship and the Jury what was the cause of the scene that ensued when you got into the room. Do you still adhere to what you said?"

"Yes, sir."

"You are aware that there are very severe penalties for perjury?"

"Sir?"

"That perjurers, men false to their oath, have been sent to prison?"

Marsh made no reply.

"I suggest to you," said Keane, speaking slowly, "that you have invented an explanation of what took place in that room."

"No, sir!"

"I suggest to you that what really happened was totally different."

"No, sir!" said Marsh, thrusting forward his head and speaking with fierce emphasis.

"I suggest to you that the whole of your account of what was said by Mrs. Paradine, Colonel Paradine and you was a tissue of lies, designed by you to cover up the truth of what had really happened to cause Colonel Paradine's outburst of anger."

"I deny that, sir."

"Very well. We will see as to that in a moment. Remember that there will be another witness as to what really happened."

Again Keane looked down at his papers before him as if seeking for some suggestion that would set him going again.

"He's looked at her *at last!*" Judith whispered to Gay. "I believe he's afraid of her. I believe Sir Malcolm's put the fear of God into him."

Gay answered nothing. She was gazing at her husband and did not even hear Judith's whisper.

"Do you, William Marsh, expect his Lordship and the Jury to believe that Mrs. Paradine deliberately invented a cock-and-bull story about your intending to leave the Colonel's service, knowing full well that directly the Colonel spoke of it to you, you would deny it?"

"Yes, sir, she did."

"You say that again?"

"Yes, sir."

"You have lived for a considerable time with Mrs. Paradine at close quarters?"

"Yes, sir."

"Do you consider her a fool?"

"Sir?"

"In your estimation is Mrs. Paradine a fool?"

"No, indeed, sir," exclaimed Marsh, with a deep breathing outburst.

"Aha! Now, then! If she be not a fool, why should she invent such a story, not only knowing it was false, but also knowing that directly it was repeated to you by the Colonel, you would give her the lie?"

"I—I couldn't say as to that, sir."

"What object could she have?"

"I couldn't say, sir."

"And how could she possibly expect to attain it in such a manner?"

"The Colonel might believe her, sir."

"Rather than you?"

"Sir?"

"It would be her word against yours, wouldn't it?"

"Yes, sir. And so it was."

"You wish the Jury to believe then that the Colonel, with whom you had been for years and to whom you represent yourself as devoted, after years of experience of you had absolutely no faith in your word?"

"I say the Colonel believed in me, sir!" said Marsh, angrily and with violent emphasis.

"Believed in you and yet thought you a liar?"

"He did not, sir."

"He did not? Then kindly explain to the Jury how he came to believe the lie which you assert Mrs. Paradine told him about you, and refused to believe your denial of that lie."

Marsh was silent. Perspiration was again visible on his cheeks and his forehead.

"You say she told him you had informed her that you were going to leave his service?"

"Yes, sir."

"After being with him for years, and though he depended on you for almost every personal service necessary to a blind man?"

"Yes, sir."

"He calls you in and you deny it?"

"Yes, sir."

"And you say that you don't want to leave him, and never said you did?"

"Yes, sir."

"And on that the Colonel gets into a fury with *you*?"

"Yes, sir."

"You say that? You ask his Lordship and the Jury to believe *that*?"

Silence from the witness.

"And that the Colonel refused to have anything more to do with you, refused to have you in his bedroom to do your usual service to him, refused to let you come near him until he could refuse no longer because he lay there a corpse?"

Silence.

"You say that? You ask the Jury to believe that?"

Silence.

"Answer me! You are here to answer."

"The Colonel was in such a state that he wouldn't listen."

"*If* he was in such a state and what you assert is true, then he thought that his wife was a truth-teller and that you were a liar? Is that what you tell the Jury?"

"No, sir."

"Explain yourself. Colonel Paradine is alone with his wife. She tells him something about you which puts him into a rage. He calls you in to hear your version. You tell him that what has been told to him about you is totally false. And on that he continues to be in such a fury that he won't listen to a word you say, and never has anything more to do with you. And yet you persist in saying that he believed your word, trusted you, and did not think you a liar! Do you say that?"

Marsh was silent. His face now was damp with perspiration, even his big hands were damp.

After waiting for a time that seemed very long Keane said:

"Do you really expect any Jury to believe that?"

"The Colonel wouldn't listen to me, sir," Marsh then said, in a low, dogged voice.

"Then he believed his wife and he didn't believe you?"

"I never said I wanted to leave him, sir."

"And if I put Mrs. Paradine into the box to tell the Jury that she never said you did—what then?"

Marsh half turned his head and looked at the prisoner. People in the Court, including the Judge, noticed that she took no notice of him. For an instant it was as if he were silently putting a question to her to which she returned no answer.

"I can't help what anyone else says!" then muttered Marsh.

"Speak up, please!" said Keane, in a loud voice. "What was that you said?"

"I can't help what others say!" almost shouted Marsh, turning with sudden ferocity on Counsel.

"Please recollect that you are in a Court of Justice!" said Lord Horfield.

"I'm trying, my Lord. But he goads me to it!" exclaimed Marsh. And he lifted a hand which shook.

"I am here to get the truth from you," said Keane, in a ruthless voice. "I suggest to you that all you have told us about that scene between you, the Colonel and Mrs. Paradine is a tissue of lies."

"No!"

"I suggest to you that what really happened was quite different."

Marsh drew his lips away from his big white teeth and closed them again. Keane fumbled with some papers as if searching for something. Marsh stood staring at him, his face twitching. It was obvious to the Jury, and to everyone in Court, that he was waiting in a condition of dread for what was coming. The staring anxiety in his face was ugly, an expression that needed hiding like a naked deformity. The stern boldness had gone out of him. He looked like one expectant of a terrible blow from fate.

"Quite different!" repeated Keane, at length looking up.

"No, sir!"

"We shall see as to that!" said Keane, making use of a formula he had already employed. "Now tell me!" he added, in a more conversational voice, in a voice indeed become suddenly almost bland. "Long before you came up to London, when you were with Colonel and Mrs. Paradine at Hindley Hall, had she not had reason to complain of you?"

"I don't understand, sir."

"Had she not found your manner altogether too familiar?"

"I don't know what you mean, sir."

"Then I will be more explicit. You have told his Lordship and the Jury that you are not a hater of women."

"No, sir."

"You repeat it?"

"I don't hate women, sir, not at all."

"You don't hate women—now! Is that it?"

"I say I don't, sir."

"I accept it from you *now*. But I suggest that, as I shall call witnesses to prove, you did hate women when you were in the regiment, and that you only got over your hatred when you were in service with Colonel and Mrs. Paradine. Was that it?"

"I don't know what you're after, sir."

"Did not Mrs. Paradine on several occasions at Hindley Hall complain to you of your manner to her, of the familiarity of your manner, and did she threaten more than once, if it continued, to complain to the Colonel about it?"

"Never! That's a lie!"

"And did she only forbear from doing so because she knew how completely her husband had come to depend on you, on account of his blindness?"

"It's a lie!"

"And did you nevertheless continue to persecute her with your impertinences, believing that she would never dare to speak to the Colonel?"

"It's a damned lie!"

"Remember where you are, witness!" interposed the Judge sternly. "This is a Court of Justice and I'll allow no bad language here. Answer in a proper manner."

"I beg pardon, my Lord, but when I——"

"You're not in the regiment here. Remember that."

There was a faint noise of half-hysterical laughter from some woman.

"Silence!" said the Judge. "If there is any demonstration I shall have the Court cleared."

There was complete silence.

"Go on!" said the Judge.

"And," said Keane, taking up the thread of his cross-examination, "was that one of the reasons why she wished to remove from Hindley to London, in the hope that there you would not dare to continue your conduct in a city where she could, if necessary, get outside assistance to bring your conduct to a stop, without perhaps troubling the Colonel?"

"Lies!"

"And did she also think, and hope, that the many distractions to be found in London might divert your impertinent attention from her, and tell you so, and try to arrange that you might get out as much as possible?"

"Never! Never!"

"And did she at last, finding all was no use, go to her husband and beg him to dismiss you from his services?"

"Never!"

"And was that in fact the cause, and the only cause, of the

terrible scene which took place between the three of you in Colonel Paradine's study on the evening preceding the night on which he died?"

"I deny it!"

"And did the Colonel tell you to get out of the house and leave his service?"

"Never!"

"And did he then order you from the room?"

"He didn't!"

"And did you, in spite of that, persist in denying the truth of Mrs. Paradine's allegations, and remain in the house, and even, later on, when the Colonel had dined upstairs, go as usual up to his room to assist him in going to bed? And did he then order you away and refuse to have anything to do with you?"

"It wasn't for that."

"He did order you away?"

"I say it wasn't for that."

"Then what was it for?"

"I've said already."

"Do you still persist in that old story?" asked Keane with scathing contempt. "Do you still expect anyone to believe it?"

Marsh did not answer. His face was now streaming with perspiration. He took out his handkerchief again and mopped his face with it.

After waiting and getting no answer, Keane said, in a cold and hard voice:

"Did you become aware while in London that your master had made a will leaving you an annuity of two hundred pounds a year?"

Marsh hesitated.

"Come! Come!" Keane exclaimed impatiently. "That is a simple enough question of fact. Did you, or did you not, know in London that the Colonel had made a new will and left you money in it?"

With obvious hesitation, Marsh answered:

"I thought the Colonel might perhaps leave me a trifle, sir."

"That's not an answer."

"I didn't know for sure, sir."

"So that if I call a witness presently into that box to testify that you *did* know of the contents of that will, as they regarded you, you say that witness is a perjuror?"

"I thought perhaps the Colonel might leave me something, sir."

"Give me a proper answer. Did you or did you not know?"

"Answer the question!" said the Judge.

"I did hear something of it, sir."

"From whom? From the Colonel?"

"No, sir."

"From whom then?"

"From Mrs. Paradine, sir," said Marsh, slowly.

"She told you?"

"She said something of it, sir. But I didn't believe her."

"Oh, you didn't believe her! Why?"

"I thought she might be kidding me, sir."

"Why should she kid you, as you call it?"

"I never knew what she was up to," said Marsh sullenly.

"Anyhow you had been told that the Colonel had made a will leaving you a considerable annuity."

Marsh looked furtively at Counsel for an instant, as if in doubt what to say, and then replied:

"I did hear something of it."

"Then why not say so at once?"

"I have said, sir."

"So you *did* know!"

Silence.

"Now as to what happened later on the evening of the Colonel's death. Where were you while the Colonel was dining?"

"I was in my room."

"Where was it?"

"In the basement, sir. There were two servants' rooms in the basement."

"So you were in the basement?"

"Yes, sir."

"All the time he was dining?"

"I believe so, sir."

"And what were you doing?"

"Doing, sir?"

"Yes—doing, in your room in the basement?"

"Nothing particular, sir."

"You were not packing your things to leave the house?"

"Certainly not, sir."

"You had no thought of going?"

"Certainly not, sir."

"No intention to go?"

"Certainly not, sir."

"Although the Colonel refused to have anything more to do with you you were resolved to stay on?"

"I was certainly staying on, sir."

"You intended to stick it out, did you, in spite of what had happened?"

"The Colonel hadn't given me warning, sir."

"You say you were in your room. Now, on leaving the Colonel and Mrs. Paradine, did you come on your fellow-servants?"

"Yes, sir."

"And did you have any intercourse with them?"

"I told them to go about their business and not to be listening to what didn't concern them."

"Did you give them any indication of what had happened?"

"Certainly not, sir."

"And you went to your room and stayed there?"

"Yes, sir."

"Now, tell me! What was it made you leave your room?"

"Sir?"

"For what reason did you presently leave your room in the basement and go upstairs to the first floor of the house?"

"I thought I would see to the Colonel, sir."

"But the butler was seeing to the Colonel, wasn't he?"

Silence.

"Did you know that the Colonel was dining upstairs and that Mrs. Paradine was dining downstairs?"

"Yes, sir."

"How did you know that?"

"John, the footman, told me."

"Then you knew that Lakin, the butler, was serving the Colonel?"

"Yes, sir."

"Then for what reason did you go upstairs to the first floor?"

"I just thought I would, sir."

"You had no special reason?"

Silence.

"You just wandered up and hung about that first floor without any particular reason, as you hung about the hall when Colonel and Mrs. Paradine were having that scene in the study?"

"My Lord!" said Sir Joseph Farrell, rising to his feet, "I object."

"State your objection, Sir Joseph," said Lord Horfield.

"The learned Counsel has made a statement in detriment of the witness. He has no right to do that in cross-examination. The witness in evidence has stated that when he went into the hall it was to see if there were any letters for the Colonel. The learned Counsel has no right to state that he was hanging about the hall, as if for the purpose of overhearing."

"I did not say that," said Keane.

"The implication was there, my Lord. I strongly object."

"The witness said he thought that possibly he went into the hall to see if there were letters. He did not say that he went there for letters," said Keane. "He did not remember what he went for."

Lord Horfield turned over some memoranda that lay on the desk in front of him.

"I find on referring to my notes that the witness said these words," he said, lifting his head. " 'I came for the post.' "

"That was only when I pressed him as to why he was in the hall, my Lord. Previously to that he had said that he couldn't 'rightly remember' why he was there."

"That is so, Sir Malcolm. But eventually he recollected himself and said that he came for the post."

"A mere afterthought!" exclaimed Keane, with contempt.

"I think therefore that the objection of the learned Counsel for the Crown is valid and must be upheld. The expression 'hanging about' the hall should be withdrawn."

"Oh, I withdraw it!" exclaimed Keane, flinging out his arms. "Let it go! Now then, Marsh!" he added, almost with ferocity, turning upon the witness and stretching out a finger in his direction. "Have the goodness to tell the Jury exactly why you went upstairs to the first floor without being summoned."

"I thought the Colonel might want me."

"Why should he want you when he was dining?"

"He had gone to his bedroom, sir."

"Did you know that when you came up?"

Marsh hesitated.

"What time was it?" said Keane.

"Somewhere about nine o'clock or sooner, sir, I believe."

"Was Colonel Paradine in the habit of going to bed so early?"

"No, sir."

"Had Lakin, the butler, told you your master wanted you?"

"Oh no, sir."

"Anyone told you?"

"No, sir."

"Did you know that the Colonel had gone to his bedroom when you came up?"

"No, sir."

"What, then, was your reason for coming?"

After considerable hesitation, Marsh murmured:

"I thought I should like to make it up with the Colonel."

"What's that? Speak up! The Jury must hear you."

"I thought I'd try to make it up with the Colonel!" cried Marsh, with the violence of a man on the edge of his nerves.

"That was your reason?"

"Yes, sir."

"Your only reason?"

"Yes, sir."

"Very well! And you say you knocked at the Colonel's bedroom door and went in?"

"I did, sir."

"And then what happened, according to you?"

"The Colonel told me to go away, that he didn't want me at present."

"Now, Marsh, did he say 'at present'?"

"He did say he didn't want me, sir."

"On your oath did he say 'at present'? Be careful!"

"He didn't want me just then, sir. That's how I understood it."

"I don't care what you understood. I want to know what the Colonel said to you when you went to his room. What was it?"

"That he didn't want me."

"That was it!" said Keane, looking at the Jury box. "You wanted to be with him and he shouted out to you to go, that he didn't want you. Was that it?"

Marsh looked down and a deep, incoherent mumble came from his half-closed lips.

"And did you go?"

"Sir?"

"When the Colonel called out to you to go, to get away from him——"

"My Lord!" said Sir Joseph Farrell, rising, "I object. The learned Counsel is again putting words into the witness's mouth that he never used. There was no question of the Colonel's having told the witness to *get away*."

"Go—get away! It's all the same!" exclaimed Keane, angrily, even with exasperation.

"I say it is not the same, my Lord."

"Oh, I withdraw! I withdraw!" said Keane, before the Judge could speak. "Now then——"

"One moment!" said Lord Horfield's penetrating voice. "I have asked you, Sir Malcolm, and now I *tell* you, not to put into the mouth of the witness words he has not used."

"Oh, very well, my Lord! Very well!" said Keane.

He swung round to the witness with a white, angry face.

"Now, then, Marsh, tell us! When the Colonel had told you to go away and to leave him in peace did you obey him? Did you go away?"

"I went out of the room, sir."

"Did you leave the landing?"

"Not immediately, sir."

"It's not a question of immediately. I ask you—did you go from the landing?"

"No, sir."

"You did not go. You hung about outside his door, didn't you?" Keane flung the words 'hung about' at Counsel for the Crown.

"I didn't go directly, sir."

"You didn't go! What did you stay for?"

"I—I don't exactly know, sir."

"Come! Come! When a man is ordered by his master to go, and does not go, he must have his reasons. What were yours?"

"I—I didn't seem to like to leave the Colonel in the state he was in."

"Although it was your own conduct that had put him into that state?"

"It was not, sir."

"You still deny it?"

"It wasn't, sir."

"After the terrible scene downstairs, you persist in denying it?"

"I do!" almost shouted Marsh, raising both his arms in an almost frantic gesture.

"So though the Colonel ordered you to go, you disobeyed him? You remained on the landing?"

"I waited for a moment or two, sir."

"When you were coming from the Colonel's room, after he had ordered you out, did you see anyone?"

"Yes, sir."

"Who was it?"

"Mrs. Paradine, sir."

"What did she do?"

"As I was coming out she was going into her bedroom, sir."

"Did you speak to her?"

"No, sir."

"Nor she to you?"

"No, sir."

"Did she see you?"

"I don't think she did, sir."

"How was that?"

"She had her back to me and was going into her bedroom as I came out from the Colonel, sir."

"Did she shut her bedroom door?"

"Yes, sir."

"And you remained on the landing?"

Silence.

"For how long did you remain there?"

"A moment or two, sir."

"Or perhaps more?"

"I didn't reckon it, sir."

"You waited and you don't know for how long?"

"I didn't reckon it."

"And what were you doing while you waited?"

"Nothing particular, sir."

"Now, Marsh, do you tell the Jury that you had not a very special reason for waiting?"

"I wanted to make it up with the Colonel," Marsh muttered, doggedly.

"Through a shut door?" Keane said, contemptuously.

No answer.

"When you were in the Colonel's bedroom had you noticed anything unusual?"

"Sir?"

"Did you notice a glass full of wine standing on his nighttable?".

"Yes, sir, I did see it."

"Very well. And after seeing it, you hung about on the landing?"

"I stayed, sir."

"And what happened then?"

"I saw the Colonel come from his room, sir."

"What did he do?"

"He went down the passage to the lavatory."

"Did he pass by you?"

"Yes, sir."

"Did he know you were there?"

The witness hesitated.

"*Did* he?"

"No, sir, I think not."

"And you didn't try to attract his attention in any way?"

"No, sir."

"Although you say you were waiting there because you didn't like to leave the Colonel?"

No answer.

"He comes out, passes you, and you let him believe you aren't there?"

No answer.

"You tell that to the Jury?"

No answer.

"Did you hear the Colonel bolt the lavatory door?"

"Yes, sir."

"Now, did the Colonel, when he came out of his bedroom, leave the bedroom door open? Or did he shut it?"

Marsh looked at Counsel and hesitated.

"Did he," repeated Keane, in a loud voice, "shut the door, or did he leave it open? Answer me!"

"He left it a bit open, sir."

"Left the bedroom door a bit open and bolted himself into the lavatory?"

"Yes, sir."

"And you were left alone on the landing with the Colonel's bedroom door open?"

Again Marsh seemed to hesitate.

"Answer!" said Keane.

"Yes, sir, I was, but——"

"Answer my question! You were left alone on the landing with the Colonel's bedroom door open, the Colonel bolted in the lavatory, and Mrs. Paradine shut up in her bedroom?"

"Yes," said Marsh, sullenly.

"Now, Marsh, did you go into the Colonel's bedroom?"

"Certainly not, sir."

"You swear it? Remember your oath!"

"I didn't go!"

"What did you do?"

"Stayed where I was."

"Just stood doing nothing?"

"Ellen Smith, the housemaid, came directly and I went away with her."

"How long was it before Ellen Smith came up and found you lingering on the landing?"

"She came directly the Colonel went to the lavatory."

"That was her cue?"

"Sir?"

"Directly the Colonel shuts the lavatory door Ellen Smith appears on the landing?"

"She came then, sir."

"That's what you say?"

"Yes, sir."

"As the Colonel disappeared, Ellen Smith appeared?"

"She happened to come just then, sir."

"And when she joined you, what happened?"

"Seeing me there, she asked if she could do anything for the Colonel. I said no, we'd best leave him to himself."

"And then?"

"I went downstairs with her, sir."

"So that as soon as Ellen Smith came you found you had no further reason for lingering on the landing?"

"I went with her," muttered Marsh.

"Directly someone came you changed your mind about not liking to leave the Colonel?"

Silence.

"And hurried away downstairs?"

"I went with her, sir."

"Leaving the Colonel still bolted in the lavatory?"

"Yes, sir."

"And Mrs. Paradine shut up in her bedroom?"

"Yes, sir, so far as I know."

"What d'you mean by that?"

"I didn't see her come out."

"Were there two doors to her bedroom?"

"No, sir."

"Then what d'you mean by saying 'as far as I know'?"

"I wasn't looking at the door all the time, sir. Part of it I was turned and looking towards the lavatory."

"What is your implication?"

"Sir?"

"Do you wish the Jury to think that while you stood there on the landing close to the Colonel's door, Mrs. Paradine could have left her bedroom and gone into his and you not see her, or hear her?"

"I don't know, sir."

"Is that what you mean to suggest?"

"I only say that as far as I know Mrs. Paradine was in her bedroom when I left the landing. But I wasn't watching."

At this point Keane put in a plan of the landing and handed it to witness.

"Kindly put a cross against the spot where you were standing when the Colonel went to the lavatory."

After considerable hesitation, witness did so. Keane then handed the plan up to the Judge, who examined it carefully. Afterwards it was passed to the Jury and explained to them.

"Now, Marsh," said Counsel, "his Lordship and the Jury have seen the plan and know where the bedrooms were and exactly where you were standing. Do you still suggest that possibly Mrs. Paradine might have crossed from her bedroom to the Colonel's without being seen by you, and *without seeing you?*"

"I don't say she did, sir. I only say I wasn't looking the whole time, so couldn't speak to it."

"Speak to what?"

"To whether she could or couldn't, sir," said Marsh with acute nervous exasperation.

"Very well. I will take that as your answer!" said Keane, looking towards the Jury. "But just tell his Lordship and the Jury what exactly you meant by saying that Mrs. Paradine was in her bedroom so far as you knew? What did you mean by that?"

"Nothing, sir!" said Marsh with violence, again raising his voice.

"You meant nothing?"

"No, sir."

Counsel then questioned the witness about the further events of the night after the death of Colonel Paradine.

"Were you shocked at his death?" he asked presently.

"Indeed I was, sir."

"Surprised by it?"

"I should say so indeed, sir."

"And to what did you attribute it?"

"To his taking something, sir."

"Do you mean to his taking poison?"

"Something bad for him, sir."

"By that, do you mean poison?"

"I couldn't say what it was, sir."

"Did you, or did you not, think it was poison?"

"I thought it might be, sir."

"Now, tell me, Marsh! Had you before that evening heard of tartar emetic?"

Marsh hesitated.

"Answer the question. It's simple enough. Had you heard of it?"

"I might have done, sir."

"*Had* you?"

"I believe I had heard the name, sir."

"And did you know that tartar emetic contains antimony?"

"No, sir."

"And that antimony is a deadly poison?"

"No, sir."

"And that, taken in the form of tartar emetic, it is easily soluble and has very little taste?"

"No, no, no!" exclaimed Marsh, ferociously, and beginning to tremble. "I didn't! I didn't!"

"I must ask the witness to collect himself and to remember where he is," said Lord Horfield, but not severely.

"But, my Lord," exclaimed Marsh, with the manner of a man almost beside himself, "he's trying to accuse me of poisoning the Colonel!"

There was a moment of dead silence in Court. Then Keane said:

"I accuse you of nothing. I am not here to accuse. I am here to defend. I am here to ask you certain questions and to get your answers for the benefit of the Jury. You say you knew of tartar emetic but knew nothing of its poisonous properties. Is that your answer?"

"Yes," muttered Marsh, holding the witness-box with both hands, and still slightly trembling.

"And do you still persist in your version of what took place in the study between Colonel and Mrs. Paradine and yourself? Remember that Mrs. Paradine will presently go into the box and give her version."

Marsh turned at this point and gazed at the prisoner. The whole of him, his expression, his attitude, his thrust-forward head, his lifted and shaking right hand, seemed to be asking some terrible question. With an absolutely blank expression Mrs. Paradine looked away from him. Throughout the whole of his cross-examination she had shown no emotion. She showed none now.

"Answer my question!" said Keane, in a hard, metallic voice. "Do you still persist in your story? Tell the Jury that."

"If she says the contrary——" muttered Marsh.

"What's that?" asked Lord Horfield, putting a thin hand up to his ear and leaning a little forward on the Bench.

"Speak up!" commanded Keane. "What do you say?"

But Marsh said nothing. He was still staring at Mrs. Paradine who took no notice of him.

"Answer the question!" said Lord Horfield, after the pause.

"My Lord—what does he want?"

"He wants to know whether you still adhere to your version of what took place in the study between Colonel and Mrs. Paradine and you on the evening before the Colonel's death?" said the Judge.

"My Lord," said Marsh, in a low, almost broken voice. "I—I stick to it."

His head drooped forward.

"I have no more questions to ask you," said Keane.

Marsh stared at him for a moment with an expression of intense hatred on his face, then stumbled out of the box.

"There goes a perjured man!" Judith whispered to Gay.

XXXIV

"MY GOD, Keane!" exclaimed Sir Simon Flaquer when the Court rose and they were away and Keane was disrobing. "I simply don't know where I am."

He took Keane by the arm. He was obviously in a condition of acute perturbation.

"Where on earth are you heading for, man? You've thrown over the whole of the defence we agreed upon. I gave in to you, and now——" he flung up his hands.

Keane, with a white face, looked down on him.

"Don't you think I shook him? Didn't I give him a grilling? Didn't I nearly break him?"

"But the assisted suicide? What's become of it?"

"There's room for that yet if we need it. No harm in a double line when one's trying to get to land."

"But your whole cross-examination, all the last part at least, pointed straight at murder—by Marsh!"

"And why not?"

"But you never said—we never decided——"

Keane put away his robes. His wig was already gone.

"Flaquer," he said. "It came on me suddenly that, given the evidence so far, it was just as likely that Marsh was the murderer as that—" he pulled himself up, then added—"that anyone else was. He had the opportunity. He may have made use of it."

"But what is your real theory of the scene that took place in the study on the day of the Colonel's death?"

"Marsh was lying."

"Of course! Anyone could see that. Even a Juryman!"

"Come with me, Flaquer!"

He took Sir Simon aside, bent down, and whispered for a few minutes in his ear.

"You really believe that?" said Sir Simon, giving him a piercing glance.

"I'm practically certain."

"But then both of them had any amount of motive!"

Keane said nothing. His eyes shone, as if with fever. He began to look exhausted.

"I'm going to see her now, at once, before she's driven away. And I mean to visit her to-night. Afterwards, however late it is, I'll come round to you. I must consult with you. I'm not at all sure we'd better not scrap all our witnesses."

"What! Scrap our witnesses! Are you mad?"

"Except Mrs. Paradine! If we do I shall have the last word. And if she gives her evidence perfectly, and is cool in her cross-examination, and I have the last word with the Jury, I believe now we can carry it."

"But—Horfield!"

"I'm not at all sure, as things are now, that Horfield can wipe me out with the Jury, if my speech is the last before the summing up. But if Farrell has the last word—I don't know!"

"Scrap all our witnesses!"

"We'll talk it over, when I've seen her."

Sir Simon stared hard at Keane for a moment without speaking. Then he said:

"Of course I realise that with your power of influencing a Jury it would be a simply enormous advantage for you to speak last. But then there's Horfield."

"I fully realise that Horfield will do his damned best to take the wind out of my sails!" said Keane, thinking of a certain conversation he had had with Gay in his home—how long ago! "But if I once get the Jury I may render all his cursed efforts impotent. And after all what are our witnesses? We've collected the best lot we could, witnesses to character, to her devotion to her husband, the two doctors who never suspected arsenic, Colonel Blake, and so on and so on. But there's no absolutely vital witness except her. And——" he raised his voice slightly like an excited man—"I'm for scrapping the lot. But I've got to see her first. You'll see me some time to-night."

And he was gone, leaving Sir Simon more perplexed than he had ever felt before in a big case for which he had briefed an eminent Counsel. What Keane had just whispered in his ear had startled him out of his usual supreme equanimity, which lay concealed behind his obviously keen intelligence and animated observation. For Keane, forsaking suddenly under an uncontrollable impulse all the reserve which had hitherto prevailed between him and Sir Simon with respect to the case, had given away to Sir Simon his secret theory of the relation which had probably existed between Mrs. Paradine and Marsh. One night he had said to himself, after an interview with Sir Simon: "I shall never tell him." And now suddenly he had told him, in the fewest possible words, blatantly.

"My theory," he had whispered, "of the scene between Colonel Paradine, Mrs. Paradine and Marsh on the afternoon before the Colonel's death is simply this. I feel convinced that Mrs. Paradine and Marsh had had illicit relations together at least once if not oftener. And I believe that somehow—how, we shall probably never know—Colonel Paradine found this out, and that it was that discovery which brought about the terrible scene between the three of them. Of course Marsh lied about it, but I'm confident that in my cross-examination I convinced the Jury he was lying. The man's discredited. My aim was to discredit him and I accomplished it. If I know anything of *her* Farrell won't be able to shake her in cross-examination. And the case is down to this now—Mrs. Paradine against Marsh. No one and nothing else *really* counts."

"The Devil's in this case!" Sir Simon said to himself, as Keane's tall figure vanished in the direction of the room where the prisoner had been taken on the conclusion of the sitting.

He had meant of course to see Mrs. Paradine before she was

taken away to Holloway, but now he resolved not to see her. Better leave her to Keane.

He threw up his hands again in an instinctive gesture of abandonment, which said as plainly as a gesture could: "The whole thing's out of my hands!"

Meanwhile Keane had hurried to the chamber where Mrs. Paradine was waiting with the female officers who were responsible for her safe custody. The crowd outside the Court had become enormous, and they were waiting till a satisfactory means had been provided for spiriting the prisoner away as secretly as possible. Keane nodded to the officers, went up to Mrs. Paradine who was standing and said:

"I hope you're not dead tired?"

"No!" she said.

"I came to tell you that I shall be at the prison later. I must have a talk with you."

She looked at him without speaking. The blankness he so much disliked had gone out of her face. He met her eyes and was startled. For a moment it seemed to him that he saw in them a gleam of hatred.

"What's the matter?" he stammered.

Then he thought of the officers, two solid women with calm sensible faces, who were standing by looking as detached as they could.

"Nothing," she said.

"But——" He stopped.

The gleam had faded out, but her face still looked expressive. He felt that within she was on fire with some tremendous emotion.

"This evening I'll come."

"Yes. You said so."

Her manner, her voice, chilled him, embarrassed him. There was something in both which seemed to rebuke him.

"I'll go now," he said.

"Yes."

"But——" he leaned towards her. "It's gone *well* for you to-day. D'you realise that?"

"Has it?"

"Don't you know it?"

She stared at him in silence as if she were closely examining him with hostility. Then she said:

"I am not a lawyer."

"But, good God!" he exclaimed, feeling a wave of fierce anger go through him. "You're a clever woman! Didn't you realise how I shook the man?"

She looked down.

"Did you?" she said, in a suddenly dull voice.

Keane turned to one of the officers. After the effort he had just been making Mrs. Paradine's reception of him had chilled him to the bone.

"Can't you tell her?" he said, fiercely.

"I'm sure, Sir Malcolm," said the officer, in a deep steady voice. "You did wonders for our lady. I never saw a man more knocked about in the witness-box."

"There!" exclaimed Keane.

He met Mrs. Paradine's eyes again, and again seemed to see the gleam of hatred in them.

"You'll—you'll realise later!" he said, almost stammering.

And he went out of the room without another word.

He left the Old Bailey alone, pushing his way through the dense crowds outside, looking at no one, recognised by many. Never before among his fellow beings had he been so unconscious of them. The pressure of his mind just then prohibited the ordinary exercise of his normal physical faculties, dulled his hearing, obscured his vision.

"What's the matter with her?" a voice within him kept on repeating.

Could it have been hatred he had seen in her large pale eyes?

Out of the crowd at last, he hailed a taxi and drove to Portland Place. He let himself in with his key, went at once to his work room and rang the bell. Baker came, accompanied by Sausage.

"Yes, Sir Malcolm?"

"Please bring me some extra strong coffee, Baker. I'll take it black. Enough for two large cups. And please—is her ladyship in?"

"No, Sir Malcolm. Her ladyship was in about an hour ago, but she's gone out again."

"When she comes in please tell her I'm sorry I shan't be in to dinner to-night. I've got a lot to do. I must go to Holloway and—but I'll write a note while you fetch the coffee."

"Yes, Sir Malcolm."

Directly the butler had left the room Keane bent down and stroked Sausage, who then retreated to blackness under Keane's immense writing-table; then he sat down and wrote this note:

My dear Gay,

Forgive me for not dining with you to-night. I'm over-whelmed by this case. Don't bring it up against me. Till it's over I can't be my own man. I must go to Holloway presently, and later must see Flaquer.

Good night,

M.K.

Baker brought the coffee and took away the note. Keane locked the door behind him, lit a cigar, fell into an armchair and reached out for the coffee.

He left the house again later without encountering Gay who, however, had come in, and who heard him in the hall speaking to Baker before going out; walked down Portland Place in the chill March air, took a taxi just beyond the Queen's Hall and drove in the dark to Holloway Prison.

XXXV

WHEN he reached the prison he saw the Governor for a moment, and told him that he wished to have a very important interview with his client in regard to her case and the evidence she would have to give, and had also to speak with her about a drastic change he intended to make, with her consent, in the future conduct of the case.

The Governor was sympathetic. He had already seen a late edition of an evening paper, and read an account of Keane's cross-examination of William Marsh.

"You shook the fellow up badly," he said.

"I meant to," Keane replied grimly.

The Governor touched a bell and directed that Mrs. Paradine

should be taken at once to one of the 'Solicitors' Rooms' as Sir Malcolm Keane was coming to see her. He kept Keane for a few minutes in conversation, but was very careful not to pump him about the case.

"I hope with all my heart you'll get the poor lady off," he said. "I have a regard for her. She's been so marvellously self-controlled all the time she's been here. What's going on in her underneath it all one can't tell of course. But she's really an extraordinary being."

"Yes!" said Keane.

"Don't you think so?" asked the Governor.

And for a moment there was a searchingly sharp look in his bright eyes.

"Perhaps she is. Yes, I believe she is."

"In her apparent calmness."

"I must say that so far she's got along wonderfully," said Keane.

But as he said it he remembered the extraordinary look he had noticed in Mrs. Paradine's eyes when he had been with her that afternoon after the Court had risen. It had been as if a shutter had been silently drawn back enabling him to look into a room he had never had a glimpse of before.

"Let's hope she'll be able to keep it up till the end," he added.

Again the Governor looked at him sharply.

"You think——" he stopped.

"It's a tremendous ordeal for a woman."

"Yes."

"And it's a fairly big ordeal for me."

"It must be. But after to-day, your cross-examination of that fellow, Marsh, it seems to me she's got a great chance."

"I hope so," Keane said, in a deep voice. "I'll do my very best till the end."

When he had gone the Governor sat for a moment at his table plunged in thought.

"What's wrong with Malcolm Keane?" he said to himself.

There had been a sort of fatal melancholy in the tone of Keane's voice, a sort of fatal melancholy in the expression of his eyes. The Governor realised what a terrible responsibility must weigh on the shoulders of a defending Counsel.

"And she's got such an exquisite neck, too!" went through his mind.

He shook his shoulders in an involuntary shudder.

"Glad I'm not in his shoes!"

Keane nodded to the female officer as he passed beyond the half-glass door into the room where Mrs. Paradine was waiting for him.

"Damn her!" he thought viciously. "Why isn't she away?"

Never yet had he seen Mrs. Paradine in real privacy, free from human observation. The officer, he knew, wouldn't be able to hear what was said in the little room with the table and couple of chairs and the wall of glass. But he hated those watching eyes.

The officer shut the door and stayed outside beyond the glass.

"I'll try to forget her!" Keane resolved.

Mrs. Paradine was standing by the table wearing the brown dress she had worn at the trial. Keane went to her and took her hand. It was very hot, dry and hot, and rested in his unresponsively. From it he got an instant impression of excitement.

"You must be terribly tired!" he said, with deep pity.

"No, I am not. What is it?" she asked, in the trailing voice.

"Sit down," he said, anxiously, and looking at her with painfully questioning eyes.

She obeyed. He sat down on the other side of the small table with his back turned to the officer. He was about to speak but she spoke first, immediately, and with an intensity that was new to him in her; something ungovernable in it.

"You have not kept faith with me!" she said. "No! You have not!"

"What d'you mean?" he asked in amazement, immediately connecting the words with the look he had seen in her eyes.

"We talked together. You laid it all out. You persuaded me. I consented. And now you have gone away from it."

She spoke in a very low voice, as if conscious of the officer all the time she was speaking, but in spite of that there was a fierceness in her voice which seemed to him made more intense by the calculated softness of it.

"I did not agree to what you have done to-day."

"But——"

She broke in at once with the authority of one who felt herself to be in the right.

"No! You persuaded me."

"Persuaded you?"

"About Will—Marsh."

The last word was added, as if because of an afterthought. A dreadful chill struck through Keane. Those three words, and her way of saying them, frightened him. He knew immediately that he was on the edge of an abyss. A depth was below him, lost in impenetrable blackness.

"It was to be that my husband killed himself with help, help of a man who cared for him too much to bear his misery, and was persuaded, because my husband was blind, to help him on the way out of life. *That* was what I agreed to after much persuading. And to-day you have gone away from all that and have pointed to him, to Will, as the murderer."

"But——"

"No! And I am to go into the box, perhaps to-morrow, perhaps the day after, and how do I know now what you will ask me? I do not trust you any more as my Counsel. You go right away from your own words, your own promises."

"What do you mean by calling him 'Will'?" said Keane, leaning across the table, all his mind fastened on that one word.

"I call him what I choose. What does it matter?"

There was a cold defiance now in her very low voice.

"I will not forgive you for what you have done to-day," she added.

A flood of anger surged up through Keane. At that moment he had an impulse to strike her. He seemed in need of physical violence. He clenched both his hands on the table and, making a tremendous effort, leaned back and away from her.

"Forgive me! You! When I am exhausting myself——" he thought of Gay and his long happiness of ten years with her— "and destroying myself and my life in an effort to save you!"

His powerful voice failed him, like a thing gone under in a flood of bitterness.

"By God! That's too much!" he said, in a broken whisper.

And though he didn't know it, there were tears in his eyes.

For a moment he was so completely overpowered that it was

only with difficulty that he restrained himself from crying out to her: "I throw up your case! Find someone else to battle for you!" and hurrying out of the room.

"Forgive me! You—forgive me!" he added, still in a whisper. "And—I've been fool enough to love you."

At last it was told. But of course she must have known it a long time ago.

"I'd better throw up the case!" he said, brokenly, as she said nothing. "If you're not satisfied with my way of conducting it."

They looked at each other across the table like two enemies.

"No, we must go on," she said, inflexibly. "We cannot stop now."

She had made no comment on his confession. It was as if she hadn't heard it. Had she heard it?

"Did you hear what I said just now?" he asked her.

"Yes."

"And you say nothing?"

"I say this: If that is true, how could you deceive me as you have done to-day?"

"Look here!" (He leaned forward again, his two fists on the table.) "What's your objection? The case has narrowed itself down to this. One of three things! Either your husband managed somehow, though blind, to poison himself. Or Marsh poisoned him. Or you poisoned him. I shall never get a British Jury to believe he poisoned himself, being blind."

"You said that the defence was to be that he was helped by Will Marsh."

"Don't call him that!"

"What?"

"Don't call him Will Marsh!"

"As you like!" she said, stolidly, as if it didn't matter at all, one way or the other. "Out of pity and the devotion of a faithful servant who could not bear to see him suffering. I gave in to that. You made me."

"Oh no! I couldn't make you do anything!"

"Anyhow, I gave in. And now——"

"All that's no real use. I felt it in Court to-day. Looking at the Judge, the Jury, I felt I had to make a change, shift my ground. I'm an old hand. I know! It lies between Marsh and you."

He stopped, and added:

"One of you killed him. That's certain!"

The words were a violent murmur. All that they said was still said in low voices.

"The evidence shows that it might have been Marsh. There was the possibility. It was my absolute duty as your defender to show that."

He felt that he had made some impression upon her at last.

For she said slowly, and as if reluctantly:

"That may be. But you broke it upon me without warning, without telling me what you were going to do."

"I didn't know *what* I was going to do till I had the man in front of me and began to speak to him."

He stopped, looking hard at her with terrible eyes, then said:

"Do you love William Marsh?"

"Yes," she said at once, without hesitation.

"Now I know why you have attacked me in this terribly cruel way," said Keane.

And something within him muttered: "Now I know! Now I know!"

For now indeed he knew, had a clue to the mystery. The blow had fallen upon him. But he had a strange feeling that long ago he had divined the ugly truth of this matter, but had refused to face it, because of the spell which had been cast upon him. That spell was not lifted now. If it had been he could not have felt so completely desperate under the brutality of the situation in which he was placed. How to go on when the enemy was within the gates? For this woman for whom he was fighting was really his enemy. She had just proved it. Hadn't she? But something, perhaps the thing in a man of intense feeling that must hope in spite of all, drove him to tear out the whole truth from her if he could.

"Marsh lied to-day," he said.

"Of course!"

She said it with a sort of dreadful indifference, as if speaking of an every-day matter that could be of no real consequence, so obvious was it that of course it had to be so.

"I know what the truth was."

"In Court I guessed that you must," she said.

"Your husband had found out about you and Marsh."

"Yes."

"But how did he find out?"

"I told him."

"You! Ah!" he exclaimed but always in a low voice, mindful even in his painful excitement and misery of the nearness of the officer. "Now I understand all Marsh's hatred of you. You caused him to be basely treacherous to his master, and then, in the end, you told of his treachery!"

"It had to be so. Things could not go on as they were. One cannot bear too much."

"Did Marsh deny it?"

"Yes. At least he wanted to, he tried to."

"What d'you mean? Wanted? Tried?"

"Is there not a saying in this country—truth will out?"

"Yes."

"My husband was blind. He could no longer read in a face. But the blind, losing one faculty, sharpen others. That night, my husband heard in a voice what he could not see in a face. He did not believe Will's denial."

"And Marsh knew that?"

"Of course! Now, you must know how mad you were in your cross-examination of Will. You nearly drove him to call out the whole truth. And then you say you are fighting for me."

"It's you who are mad," said Keane, drearily.

Suddenly he felt terribly tired, exhausted. He looked at the mean table on which his arms were leaning, and longed to lay his head down on it, and to sink away into unconsciousness, to give it all up, to have it all removed from him, or to be removed from it.

"Mad to tell me all this and to expect me to go on and fight for you, and save you. What am I to do? I meant—I had made up my mind before I came here to-night to cut out all our witnesses except you, to trust to your own evidence and my final speech to save you."

"Cut out the witnesses!" she said, for the first time showing uneasiness. Not anger—but just that—uneasiness.

"Yes. It's like this in our Courts. If I call witnesses, as well as you, I have to make my speech for you immediately the witnesses for the defence have given their evidence, and Counsel for the Crown addresses the Jury after me. But if I call no witnesses, except the prisoner, I have the right to speak last. That's how it is. It seemed to me that, as things are, and after what has happened to-day, it would be safest to call only you and be the last to address the Jury."

"Yes?"

"I can usually make a tremendous effect on a Jury."

Brave words, but they were spoken without 'go,' without courage.

"Speak last!" she said. "It will be better. Trust me in the box and speak last."

She made a slight movement, after looking at the figure beyond the glass, and her right hand touched one of his hands. When that happened he realised in a flash the immense physical power this woman had over him. He hated it because it made him feel like a slave, but the whole of him without question acknowledged it. She was evidently the woman among women, who, for some mysterious reason entirely unfathomable by him, had the power to hold his flesh in thrall. And that was the secret of the whole of his obsession for her. It was not a question of spirit but of flesh. And he knew why she had overcome William Marsh, turned him to baseness, made him disloyal, horribly treacherous to the man whom he no doubt loved far more than he could ever love her or perhaps any woman. She had the secret, inexplicable gift that here and there a woman possesses, and by its possession makes men do what are called 'mad' things, not to be ever understood, explained, or forgiven by those who are held far off from her.

He left his hand by hers. He could see she was watching the officer, who must certainly at that moment not be looking at them.

"You will save me," she whispered. "I feel it. But I must not be saved at his expense. Do you hear?"

With a slight creeping movement her hand left his. The officer had moved, was again becoming attentive.

"I shall do things in my own way!" said Keane, savagely. "I can't be ordered by those who know nothing. What do *you* know of Law cases, of Judges, of Juries? Absolutely nothing! And you dare to tell *me* what I must do to get you off!"

"I know what must not be," she said, with heavy obstinacy.

"And what's that?"

"You are not to destroy him. If you do, I shall hate you as I have never hated a man."

For a moment Keane sat silent, staring at her. He realised that probably he had come at last on the big thing in this woman, and that it was in truth very big. Multitudes of human beings, he knew, are incapable of greatness even if the moment which demands it ever comes to them. She, perhaps, must be numbered among the exceptions. If it were so it would help him to understand why she had gained such a terrible influence over him, but it would leave him quite hopeless, bathed in the light of a knowledge that would show him his own destruction.

"And suppose it had come to this, that absolutely the only way to save you is to create in the mind of the Jury the belief that Marsh is the murderer?" he said, still staring at her.

"You have tried to do that to-day. Perhaps you have done it."

"Well—then?"

"You know what I feel about that. I have just told you."

"I cannot help facts. The fact is that there was a lapse of time, very short, no doubt, in which it would have been possible for Marsh to go into Colonel Paradine's room and get at his wine. It was the interval between Colonel Paradine's leaving his room for the lavatory and the arrival on the landing of Ellen, the housemaid. No wishes of yours can do away with that fact."

"I know that. I have always known that."

"What do you wish me to do, then? What am I to do? What can I do?"

"I cannot have Will destroyed. That is all."

Keane got up. For the moment he had forgotten the officer. As he got to his feet he remembered her. But it didn't matter. He couldn't stay still.

He moved away two or three steps, came back and stood by the table.

"I can't help it now," he said. "It's too late. I must go on in the way I've begun. I shall not give in to you. Perhaps—if you don't help me—perhaps the Jury may disagree. That's the most we can hope for—perhaps. Anyhow, I shall act according to my own view of what must be done. And you can do what you like. It will be on your own head. I shall scrap all the witnesses. They'd be no real use to us now. I shall put you in the box. Say what you like there. My questions will be mine—your answers yours! Fight me, of course"—he stared hard at her with terribly seeking eyes—"if you're reckless about your own life. I can't prevent you. Barring the Judge, I shall have the last word with the Jury. If you haven't destroyed yourself by the time I come to speak, I'll do my best for you. That's all I can do. You've made things too difficult for me, as impossible, almost, as you can. In all my life, I've never had such a terrible time with a case."

As he said the last words he seemed to see the Paradine case rise up before him like a huge black shape drawing him on into its devouring darkness.

He turned and went out of the room.

"Guilty! Guilty!" he muttered, as he stumbled into the corridor.

XXXVI

FROM the prison Keane drove to Hyde Park Gardens. During the journey through London he did not once look out of the window, but sat either looking down or with his eyes shut. He felt dreadfully tired, as if he had no force to go on, to face all that was coming upon him. Mrs. Paradine's stony indifference to him as a man, shown with such brutality, had overcome his spirit. He realised now that during the whole of their association she had never regarded him as anything but an instrument, as a weapon in the fight for her life, never as a man of any interest to her apart from that. He meant nothing to her except as a lawyer. And he had fallen in love with her, had at moments even believed that if he managed to save her she might show that she cared for him. The recklessness of her brutality that evening had proved to him the terrible force of her concentration on Marsh. In her passion for Marsh she had even forgotten the necessity of 'keeping in' with the man upon whom probably her life depended. She had only remembered that when she had put out her hand and touched his.

He had no more illusions. How could he have any after that interview?

She must still have the wild hope of winning Marsh back if she regained her freedom. It must be so. And that was the secret cause of the attitude which had for so long puzzled Keane and Sir Simon Flaquer. She had been trying to play for safety with Marsh because she loved him.

Keane only stayed for a short time with Sir Simon. Briefly he told him that he had resolved to call no witnesses but Mrs. Paradine and had told her so, that she had raised no objection and that therefore so it would be. Sir Simon was painfully struck by the dull misery shown in Keane's eyes and by the hopelessness of his manner. He spoke indeed with a certain cold decision, like a man who had absolutely made up his mind to a course of action, but there was no glow of life in him. He seemed to have no keen and fighting expectation of success in the course decided upon. Nevertheless he said as he was going:

"We'll get her off."

When Keane had left him Sir Simon sat for a long time sunk in his chair brooding over the interview. It had occurred to him that perhaps Mrs. Paradine had made a confession of guilt to her Counsel and that Keane was keeping it from him.

Presently he called Judith to him and had a long talk with her. They spoke of Gay.

"This horrible case has swallowed up poor little Gay," Judith said, with deeper feeling than she generally showed. "It's a monster with an insatiable maw. But she's sticking it out bravely. Oh, Papa, why will you men throw away substance for shadow?"

"I've never done it, Judy."

"You're a wonderful exception. What wins the average man, and often the man who isn't average, like Sir Malcolm? It isn't charm, or faithfulness, or devotion."

"What is it, Judy?"

"It's iron will-power combined with that mysterious something which ignores the spirit of man, but knows just how to get at his flesh. Oh, it's rather sickening, Papa."

"Life often is rather sickening, Judy, but we've got to face up to it and do our small best to make it less sickening."

He got up from his chair and stretched his arms.

"I shall be more than thankful when this cursed case is over and done with. But now let's go to your mother and get the taste of it out of our mouths for a little while. Thank God for her and the family!"

.   .   .   .

The case for the Crown was concluded on the following day. A night intervened, and when the Court resumed Keane rose to deliver his opening speech for the Defence.

"Members of the Jury," he said. "With my learned friend, Mr. Calling, I share the terrible responsibility of defending against the awful charge of wilful murder the lady who is before you in the Dock, a foreigner, friendless and alone in a country not her own, but a country, thank God, that has always prided itself on its passion for Justice. I had, I tell you frankly, the intention to call before you numerous witnesses on her behalf, witnesses to speak to her character, to her deep affection and devotion to her husband of whose murder she stands accused, to her self-sacrifice in giving up the life of pleasure and cheerfulness and gaiety natural to a beautiful woman, still fascinating and still young, in order to bring the light of her affection into the darkness of a blinded man. But after hearing the case for the Crown I and those who instruct me have changed our minds. We find so little to rebut in the case for the prosecution that we have decided not to call the witnesses who had been attending here in Court ready to go into the witness-box."

At this there was a stir of surprise through the Court and even Lord Horfield allowed an expression of astonishment to appear on his generally impassive face.

"We shall call no witnesses, Members of the Jury, except—the prisoner."

Here Keane paused for a moment. Then he added impressively:

"*She* will go into that box confident in her own innocence. You will hear from her lips her version of what took place before this tragedy. She will gladly and fearlessly submit herself to cross-examination. That has been her wish from the beginning, her decision ever since the dark shadow of this accusation fell across her life. 'Let me go into the box! Put me into the box!' The plea of an innocent woman, of a fearless woman! And when she has been heard I shall leave the decision in your hands, confident, as I have never before been confident in a murder case, that the decision of the Jury before whom I have to plead will be a unanimous 'Not guilty!' and that the prisoner at the bar will be set free to take up again her broken life and remake it, exonerated by you in the sight of all men from the foul charge brought against her."

Although he had had an almost sleepless night and was feeling distracted by the misery which he was obliged to conceal and by the dread of the line Mrs. Paradine might take when she went into the witness-box, Keane, calling on all his power of acting, opened with a tone and manner of supreme self-confidence, which at once impressed the Court. His voice was full and powerful and persuasive, his manner was serene and courageous. There was none of the nervous fierceness and brutality which he had shown during the cross-examination of Marsh. He seemed another man. His face was pale and drawn and there was a noticeable darkness under his eyes, but his bearing and the sound of his voice contradicted this pallor, this darkness, so strongly that the crowd in Court did not notice them. Almost everyone in Court, even including the Barristers, was infected with the feeling: "This man's absolutely sure of getting the prisoner off."

"Sir Malcolm's wonderful!" Judith whispered to Gay. "Simply wonderful!"

Gay slightly moved her head in reply. She was already past speaking. The sight of Malcolm squaring up for the fight made her feel so emotional that she was afraid of herself, of what she might do. Something within her seemed to be melting. And yet she was aware, too, of something hard and resistant. There was a tremendous giving of herself to Malcolm, but there was also a part of her that was braced up to resistance against him. She wanted him terribly to be great in this, for him, great moment. And at the same time, as from a remote watchtower something of her observed him coldly, critically, something not to be deceived, that refused to be carried away by his capacities, that dissected his motives, and with a piercing penetration saw through his subterfuges. With a passionate attention, absorbed in spite of the conflict within her, she listened while always with the same air of self-confidence, and at times almost light and easy assurance, he dealt briefly with the case brought forward against Mrs. Paradine. She followed on his track like a hound on the trail, always at his heels as he went onward, from Mrs. Paradine's beginnings as a lovely girl in Copenhagen, her almost miraculous escape from the underworld, 'untarnished,' as Malcolm affirmed, though having been subjected to the greatest danger that can befall an inexperienced girl on the threshold of life, her life of self-support and honest hard work in America, her return to Europe, with her meeting and eventual marriage to the wounded and blinded man, the war hero whom she was now accused of having basely destroyed after his escape from destruction in battle.

She followed him up into the North to the romantic home facing the Cumberland mountains, where this woman, still young and full of fascination, self-dedicated to what he called 'a beautiful and touching task,' gave herself up to making life possible for the blind man, ministering to him, consoling him with her affection for the tragedy that had come upon him. All this he dealt with rapidly and concisely, giving a high light, a dramatic touch here and there, but wasting no words. All was done swiftly.

"As in no very long time, members of the Jury, I shall have occasion to address you exhaustively on the whole of this case in my closing speech for the defence," he said presently, "I shall not detain you long now, but I will just put before you a few facts which I have in statement before me."

He then proceeded to touch upon the two attacks of illness which Colonel Paradine had had in the North and which the doctors called in diagnosed as caused by severe dyspepsia, and pointed out that it was Mrs. Paradine who after these attacks persuaded her husband to leave Hindley and visit London partly, if not mainly, with the object of his being examined by a London specialist. Was this a probable move on the part of a woman who had already made up her mind to get rid of her husband, and who, according to the suggestion of the Crown—not bolstered up by any evidence whatever—had already probably made two beginnings of attempts on his life, by the administration of arsenic. Arsenic was certainly found in the body of Colonel Paradine after his death. That was undoubted. But there was no evidence as to whether it was administered to him feloniously by someone in the household at Hindley, who either wished to get rid of him for reasons of their own undiscovered, or who, possibly in a passion of pity for the misery of his life in the dark, was ready to help him to do what he was unable to do without help.

At this point there was a movement in Court and subdued murmurs were heard.

"Silence in Court!" cried the usher.

"There must be absolute silence in Court while Counsel is speaking," said Lord Horfield, raising a hand, and fixing his eyes on the crowd. "I shall allow no demonstration."

Continuing now in an easy and conversational voice Keane pointed out that there was no evidence of Mrs. Paradine or anyone else in the Hindley household having made purchases of arsenic. No chemist had been called to prove that. 'The arsenic mystery' in fact remained impenetrable, and Keane would advise the Jury to dismiss it from their minds and to concentrate their attention upon what occurred later in London.

He then touched upon the occurrences later in London which were relevant to the case, allowing that Colonel Paradine's death was undoubtedly caused by poisoning with antimony taken in the form of tartar emetic, and probably, indeed almost certainly, swallowed by him in the Burgundy which, by his order, Lakin the butler had placed on his night table. Colonel Paradine died from absorbing into his system sufficient antimony to bring about the cessation of life. The question for the Jury to decide was who administered that antimony, who placed it within the Colonel's reach. As to that, without accusing anybody, it was obvious that, as well as Mrs. Paradine, two other persons might have tampered with the wine. Lakin, the butler, poured it out and conveyed it to the Colonel's bedroom. His evidence in the matter had been heard and the Jury could form their own opinion on it. There then was William Marsh, Colonel Paradine's body servant. From the evidence it was obvious that for a time, long or short, Marsh was lingering on the first landing of the house, within sight of his master's bedroom, the door of which was open, Mrs. Paradine during that time being shut in her bedroom opposite, and Colonel Paradine locked in the lavatory. In order to bring in a verdict of wilful murder against the prisoner the Jury must be *certain* that she, and she alone, could have committed it. Keane was confident that such certainty, given the evidence for the Crown, was impossible. He passed away from that to the extraordinary scene which had preceded the murder, the scene in Colonel Paradine's study between him, his wife and William Marsh. Marsh's evidence as to what had taken place on that occasion was, he suggested, false from beginning to end. As to that the Jury had had the benefit of hearing and seeing Marsh in the witness-box and could form their own opinion of his character and veracity. In the box Mrs. Paradine would give them her version of what really took place. And they could compare the two versions and decide for themselves which carried conviction, and which was obviously invented.

After briefly describing Colonel Paradine's death and what followed upon it he closed with an unexpected allusion to what he called 'a very peculiar incident,' which had been brought up in the evidence for the Crown, the incident of Mrs. Paradine's playing 'The Blue Danube' between the time when it was alleged that she had introduced poison into her husband's wine, and the moment when it might be supposed that he had probably drunk it. Could the Jury, could anyone in their senses, be brought to believe that a woman waiting in agonising suspense to know whether her attempt to murder her husband was going to be successful or not would pass away the time in playing waltz tunes on the piano?

His fine voice rang with scorn at this point in his speech.

He concluded by an allusion to the strange lack of motive in the case. All that the Crown had been able to do was to scrape up evidence of marital disagreements such as occurred in nine households out of ten. Colonel Paradine was unhappy because of his affliction and sometimes vented his unhappiness on his wife. Was that a reason that would drive a woman to murder?

"This is, in my view, a case in which no body of thinking men and women could possibly convict," he ended, in an almost casual manner. "I will now put the prisoner in the box, absolutely confident that when you have heard her you will, without hesitation, agree with me."

"He seems perfectly certain of an acquittal," Judith whispered to Gay.

"And you? What do you think?" Gay murmured back, keeping her eyes on the Court.

"Wait till we've heard *her* version of the scene before his death, and then I'll tell you," whispered Judith. "In *that* scene I feel sure the motive for the murder came to light. She's rather beautiful."

Mrs. Paradine looked very tall as she walked slowly to the

witness-box with the two female officers. All eyes were of course fixed upon her. The only indication she gave that she was aware of this was by an increase of the detached reserve which she had manifested ever since the beginning of the trial. There was a sort of white sulkiness in her fair northern face as she faced her Counsel. It suggested a desire to repel the gaze of the multitude of eyes fixed upon her. But it did not suggest any fear of them. Her look conveyed rather a silent, but definite, rebuke of bad manners.

"If you wish, you may be seated while giving your evidence," said Lord Horfield, in his clear, carrying voice when the prisoner stood facing him.

"No, thank you, my Lord," said the prisoner.

Every ear in the Court was strained to get the first sounds of her voice. What sort of character did they express, as they carried this woman in sound to everyone there? For the first time Gay felt a sort of physical contact with this woman who had altered her life, this woman who was supposed to have some queer physical resemblance to her. And for a moment, using her imagination violently, she transported herself to the witness-box. She was there facing Malcolm and he was beginning to ask her questions. How tall and how penetrating he looked! But he was there only to draw out from those answering lips words that would serve as an armour of protection. The brutality that had disfigured him while he was battling with William Marsh was gone from him. His manner was manly but very kind. Kind but not soft. Nothing 'honeyed' in it. Gay had the feeling that Malcolm knew he was dealing with a very courageous woman and was treating Mrs. Paradine as one.

Ingrid Paradine! Gay's mind loitered over the name, Ingrid. It suggested to her character completely different from what she believed to be her own, more practical, less evasive and inclined to lose itself in dreams, keener, more dominant.

"It has been suggested that you left your service with Mr. and Mrs. Powers in New York under a cloud. Is there any truth in this?"

What a curious trailing voice it was that answered, with an almost chanting intonation.

"There was no cloud—no. But I left because Mrs. Powers did not like me in the house."

"Goodness! What a truthful woman!" the women in the Court began to think, almost universally.

"Why was that?"

"Her husband, a man of noble character, had befriended me. She seemed to resent that after we got to America. Her character was not noble. She could not understand. So I left."

Many of those in Court had opened their mouths to laugh at the implication. But something in the witness's manner stopped the laugh. There was a sort of stern simplicity in the two concluding statements. The witness was certainly not playing for humour. There was something startling in her simplicity both of manner and of matter, a directness that seemed to be inborn and that was impressive. Many in Court were already comparing her and her demeanour with William Marsh and his. Some looked from her to Marsh who, in a dark navy blue suit, with a narrow black tie and white turned-down collar, was sitting in the witnesses' seat, leaning back with crossed arms, his eyes bent down, his firm under-jaw now and then quivering slightly.

Those two! A strange pair! Interesting people!

And they had both been servants. Of the man one could easily believe that. A soldier servant. But it was very difficult to credit it of the woman in the witness-box. And many women there were in Court who sympathised secretly with that Mrs. Powers who hadn't 'a noble character.' It is sometimes so difficult to be noble when confronted with a woman obviously far more beautiful than oneself. And it was growing on the Court that this woman had beauty. As she answered and answered, always with that great simplicity and directness, the white sulkiness went out of her face, and she began to seem almost eager to help on the trial—as if it were not hers.

"You never saw your husband before he was blind?"

"Never."

"What was your feeling for him?"

"I thought him a great hero and I loved him."

Heavens! What directness and lack of sentimentality, yet how much seemed to be expressed in those simple words!

"You did not dread the idea of spending your life with a blinded man?"

"No. I thought it a great opportunity."

"How so?"

"To serve him as eyes."

When Mrs. Paradine said that, Keane remembered his first interview with her in Holloway Prison and her 'had to be.'

She hadn't forgotten the suggestion that it would be wiser to put that differently when she stood up before a Judge and a Jury. She had a good memory.

All was well so far. But—where were they going?

"It has been suggested that you had reason to be very unhappy with your husband, that he was often very unkind to you. What have you to say as to that?"

"He was sometimes unkind. What man is not?"

At this there was irrepressible but low laughter from the women in Court. A curious expression of faint surprise came into Mrs. Paradine's face. She looked towards the Judge.

"I only mean, my Lord, that it is difficult always to be kind."

"In what way was your husband unkind to you?" said the Judge. "Was he ever physically cruel?"

"Never, my Lord. But being blind made him often desperately miserable and then he would be unkind to me. But I understood and forgave."

Lord Horfield sent her a piercing look and bent slowly over his writing-pad.

Mrs. Paradine was questioned about her husband's unkindness and without hesitation gave details of it. It seemed evident that she had no wish nor intention to water it down, make less of it than was true. Gay, up in the gallery, and probably many others, got the impression that Mrs. Paradine was trying to be absolutely truthful. Now and then she waited before answering a question, and Gay felt that during the pause she was seeking for words that would express with absolute accuracy what was in her mind as the truth. This, of course, when Keane's question demanded more than a mere yes or no.

One reply that for an instant greatly surprised the Court came when Keane was dealing with Colonel Paradine's two attacks of illness at Hindley. He said:

"Were you greatly upset and alarmed by these attacks?"

"No!" came the firm reply.

Lord Horfield lifted his head and gazed at the prisoner.

"You weren't alarmed?" he said, like one thinking the question had been mis-heard.

"No, my Lord."

"Why not?" asked the Judge.

"I had seen a good deal of illness, my Lord, and though I was very sorry my husband was unwell, I didn't believe it was anything serious. May I explain, my Lord?"

"Yes," said the Judge.

"William Marsh, in his evidence, said I did not seem greatly concerned. That was quite true. I thought, as the doctors presently did, that my husband was suffering from acute indigestion that would quickly pass away. And it did."

"Ah!" said the Judge, and he wrote in his notes.

Keane looked at the Jury to see how they took this. Even he, who had so much experience of Mrs. Paradine, was wondering about her. What would happen presently when he came to the scene in London that preceded Colonel Paradine's death?

This was what happened, after much more evidence had been given, some of it concerning William Marsh's attitude to his mistress at Hindley Hall and her relation to him, which she described as cordial, though she confessed that at times she had found Marsh rather 'difficult.'

"But I forgave that because I knew my husband depended upon him for everything that I could not do."

"We now," Keane said, after a rather long pause, during which, holding his robe near the shoulders with both hands, he had stared down at the papers before him, "come to the afternoon preceding your husband's death. I ask you"—(his tone became very grave) —"to weigh your answers very carefully."

William Marsh raised his head and gazed at the prisoner. There was a curious dusky pallor near his eyes. Judith noticed it from the gallery.

During the long pause, Keane had been thinking with agony:

"What am I to do now? What can I do? If I get her to tell the truth, what I am convinced is the truth, will it break her? Or can I so manipulate it in my final speech that it will save her and wreck Marsh? And then Farrell's cross-examination? Will it be deadly? Had I better slide over the whole thing, leave it more or less in the air? But there's Horfield! He'll miss nothing. Up to

now they have the impression that she's as truthful a witness as
ever stepped into the box. If she lies now, that impression will be
disturbed, or perhaps killed outright! God—I must get on with
it!"

And then he lifted his head and looked at Mrs. Paradine. Really,
at that moment mutely he was asking her what he was to do. As he
looked, it seemed to him that her large, pale eyes menaced him. All
their connection flashed upon his brain and heart like something
seen for an instant only in a burst of fierce light, his first sight
of her in the prison, the impression she made upon him, their many
interviews, always watched by the silent figure outside the par-
tition of glass, his growing interest in her, his obsession for her, his
belief in her innocence followed by terrible doubts, his hideous
conviction of the intimacy between her and Marsh, key to the
whole mystery of Colonel Paradine's murder, the revelation of her
love for Marsh, the love of servant for servant—"I have a lot of
the servant in me still!" a horribly truthful statement—his dreadful realisation that he meant nothing to her as a man, though
everything as an instrument.

A flash of fierce light, all this seen in it like one thing, com-
pact, welded together, indivisible.

And she stood there waiting—the woman of Babylon!

"Is anything the matter, Sir Malcolm?"

The voice of Lord Horfield struck through the deadly silence in
Court. Was there a sneer in it?

"No, my Lord."

Suddenly the acute lawyer woke up in the man who, for a
moment, surrounded by an intent crowd, had almost managed to
dream. The voice of the Judge who, he knew, hated him, had recalled him from the inner region where a man is alone with
himself and that which has moulded him.

"On that afternoon you were in the study alone with your
husband, were you not?"

"Yes."

"It has been given in evidence that certain of the household
heard voices raised, as if in violent argument, within the room.
Was there any disagreement at that time between you and your
husband?"

"My husband was angry about something."

"Can you tell the Jury what it was?"

"It had to do with his valet, William Marsh," the witness replied, slowly, and with apparent reluctance.

"Kindly tell the Jury what it was in connection with William Marsh which upset your husband."

"I asked my husband to find another place for William Marsh."

Marsh leaned forward in his seat, staring at the prisoner like a man hypnotised, his two hands gripping his knees.

"Why was that?"

Mrs. Paradine hesitated. Her eyes went for a moment to Marsh and then returned to Keane.

"Answer the question," said the Judge.

"I didn't wish Marsh to stay in the house."

"Why?"

"He was a splendid servant, but I preferred he shouldn't be there."

"But why?"

"I didn't like his manner with me."

Mrs. Paradine's voice had become very low, and the sulky look had returned on her face. Keane kept his eyes fixed upon her. She was now looking straight at him and he felt that her eyes were trying to forbid him to deal further with the matter he had touched on. A violent gust of anger went through him. This sickening love for that fellow sitting there with his hands on his knees, that servant fellow, persisted in, even in such a moment of imminent danger, threatening to wreck the whole case, infuriated him by its fatuity. Some, perhaps, if they knew of it, might find it glorious. He couldn't. His jealousy made him loathe and despise it. He knew that she was still, at this climax, trying to play for safety with her mind on a possible future; herself released, Marsh still to be won back by her determined will pushed by an obstinate passion.

As if it were possible! Madness! Indeed, degraded madness! But he would not be its victim. And for a moment he saw red.

"What was it in Marsh's manner to you that you disliked?" he asked, slightly raising and hardening his voice.

"I thought it was sometimes too familiar and sometimes too rough."

"Had you noticed that for some time?"

"Yes."

"Before going to London?"

"Yes."

"Up at Hindley Hall?"

"Yes."

Looking directly at her, Keane contracted his forehead in a frown. To the woman in the witness-box it looked like a warning signal. A hard line came on her lips.

"You have heard Marsh's version of what happened that day when he entered the room?"

"Yes."

"Now I want yours. What caused Colonel Paradine to shout for Marsh and ring his bell?"

"He was angry at what I had told him."

"About Marsh's manner to you?"

"Yes."

"He believed what you had told him?"

"Yes."

"And he rang for Marsh to have it out with him?"

"Yes."

There was a strange pressure in the way in which Counsel asked these questions. It was noticed by all the lawyers in Court and, of course, by the Judge. Afterwards it was freely said in legal circles that Keane's examination of his own witness had resembled a cross-examination.

"You swear that?"

After a just perceptible pause the witness answered:

"I swear it."

"So that Marsh's version of all that took place is a fabric of lies!"

"My Lord," interposed Sir Joseph Farrell, rising quickly. "I object. My learned brother is once more deliberately leading a witness and putting words into the mouth of a witness. I object most strongly."

"I was merely asking witness a question," said Keane, showing at once a nervous anger.

"My Lord, the learned Counsel put it in the form of a statement—'So that Marsh's version of all that took place is a fabric of lies!' I object! That is a statement by Counsel."

"The form is objectionable," said Lord Horfield. "I must require the learned Counsel to keep to questions."

"I *did* ask a question," said Keane, abruptly.

"I require you to let witness give her answers in her own words, Sir Malcolm!" said Lord Horfield with cutting emphasis. "Not in yours! You understand me, I hope."

"Oh, your Lordship always makes your meaning perfectly clear!" returned Keane sarcastically.

"Then kindly attend to my ruling! And do not let me have cause to repeat it," said Lord Horfield.

"I hope I always attend to the ruling of a learned Judge, however much I may disagree with it!" said Keane.

Gay's pale cheeks were flooded with red.

"Don't bandy words with me, Sir Malcolm, but kindly go on with your examination of witness."

Keane opened his lips as if to hurl some brutal rejoinder at the Judge. With a disorderly gesture Lady Horfield, in the 'City Lands' wrung her little hands which were encased in tight white kid gloves. Perhaps Keane caught sight of the gesture. Anyhow, he shut his lips, waited for a minute, and then resumed with cold self-possession.

"As his Lordship objects to the form of my question—*not* statement—I will change it." (To witness:) "Do you agree with Marsh's account of what took place in the study between your husband, yourself and Marsh?"

"My recollection of it is different," said Mrs. Paradine.

"Totally different?"

"Not the same."

"Tell the Jury, please! Did you, before Marsh, ever say that he had privately told you he intended to leave the Colonel's service?"

"No."

"Or behind his back—did you say that?"

"No."

"Nothing like it?"

"No."

"Now, Mrs. Paradine"—he leaned a little towards her—"did you give any indication to the Colonel as to exactly why you objected to Marsh's behaviour to you?"

"Indication?" said the witness, vaguely, and suddenly looking blank.

"Surely the Colonel asked you whether——"

"My Lord!" said Sir Joseph Farrell, again on his feet. "I object! These are not questions at all. These are deliberate statements and suggestions."

"I have directed you, and I direct you again, Sir Malcolm, to keep strictly to questions!" said Lord Horfield, with an intensity of sharpness that thrilled the Court.

"As your Lordship pleases!" said Keane, with the smiling contempt which a man might indulge in to a silly, complaining child.

"Kindly show proper respect to the Bench!" said the Judge angrily.

"That shall be my endeavour, my Lord, and I hope to attain to it—however late in the day." (To witness:) "Did your husband ask you to define your strong objection to Marsh's behaviour?"

"He asked me why."

"Ah! And what did you answer? Please tell the Jury."

"I said Marsh was too familiar with me."

"In what way too familiar?"

Witness was silent.

"Please explain precisely what you mean by too familiar," said the Judge.

Mrs. Paradine looked at Keane. He frowned again.

"Kindly attend to me, witness!" said the Judge sharply.

"My Lord?"

"Please explain exactly what you mean by too familiar?"

"My Lord, I was once a servant. Marsh knew that. And—so—he—took liberties."

"Had Marsh discovered that you were once a servant?" asked the Judge.

"Yes, my Lord. He knew it."

"And that was why you wished him to leave Colonel Paradine?"

"Yes, my Lord."

"Continue, Sir Malcolm!" said the Judge, after writing down the answers.

"Had you no other reason?" said Keane.

Witness was silent.

"I must ask you this," said Keane, with determination. "Did Marsh on more than one occasion attempt to make love to you?"

There was a visible sensation in Court, especially noticeable among the many women present. As the question reached their ears every woman in Court, except one, made a movement of some kind. The exception was Gay. Something kept her rigid. Her hands gripped each other in her lap. Her eyes were fastened on her husband behind the big spectacles that covered them. At that moment she was physically a prisoner bound, as if with cords, by her mind, incapable of relaxation.

"The motive! We're getting to it at last!" murmured Judith, who had become restless. "But—why?" she added, in a whisper, "I can't understand Sir Malcolm."

Gay heard her but gave no answer, made no comment.

"He spoke to me now and then in a way that I didn't like," said Mrs. Paradine, dragging the words, as if they came from her lips reluctantly.

"Did Marsh try to make love to you?" persisted Keane.

After a long pause Mrs. Paradine answered, with evident reluctance:

"Yes."

"And did you, or did you not, resent that?"

Mrs. Paradine's eyes shot a glance of hatred at her Counsel, but Keane, frowning, stared back at her.

"I—did," came from her.

"What is that?" said the Judge, putting a hand to his ear. "I didn't catch it."

"Please repeat!" said Keane, in a rather loud voice. "Did you resent this?"

"I did," said Mrs. Paradine, in a slightly louder voice.

"You did! And did you complain about it to your husband?"

"I thought I ought."

"And did you?"

"Yes."

"And was that the cause of your husband's outburst of anger on the day before his death?"

"Yes."

"When Marsh came into the study what happened?"

"My husband was very angry."

"Did he give Marsh warning?"

"I didn't hear him do that."

"Was there an argument, a very violent argument?"

"There was an argument."

"What did Marsh do?"

"He defended himself."

"By that do you mean that he denied that he had ever tried to make love to you?"

"Yes."

"He gave you the lie?"

"Yes."

"And I give her the lie now!" suddenly shouted a powerful voice with a fierceness that startled and thrilled the crowd.

Every face was turned towards Marsh, who had sprung to his feet and was gesticulating towards the Bench.

"This is all lies, my Lord! damned lies! She's a——"

"Take him out!" said Lord Horfield, lifting a hand. "This is gross contempt of Court."

"But my Lord," exclaimed Marsh, still in the shouting voice of a man beside himself with passion. "How can I sit still and hear a woman take away my character? I never——"

Two officers of the Court seized him and made as if to drag him out, but he violently shook off their hands.

"I'll go with you," he said. "Leave me alone. I'm coming."

He turned again towards the Bench.

"My Lord," he said to the Judge. "If there's a bit of justice left in England have me back and put me in the box again and give me a chance to answer her."

"Take him out," said the Judge. "And keep him in custody within the precincts of the Court until I direct you otherwise."

Marsh passed out through the crowd amid the murmuring of many voices. As he went he thrust out his powerful head towards Mrs. Paradine and enveloped her in a glance of intense hatred. She did not look at him but stood perfectly still in the witness-box, looking absolutely blank. A buzz of talk rose all over the Court.

"Silence!" said the Judge, making his usually charming voice as hard as steel. "I will have silence. If I hear any more noise in this Court I shall have the Court cleared."

At this threat there was immediately a silence which was only broken by someone in the well of the Court coughing. Lord Horfield looked angrily in the direction of the afflicted person. The cough became more definite, rose to a paroxysm.

"If there is anyone here who is unable to control their symptoms of ill-health I shall have to ask them to leave the Court," said the Judge.

At this the sound of coughing ceased instantly, but just as Counsel was opening his mouth to put another question to the witness it began again violently and in a higher register.

"I order that person who is coughing to leave the Court," said the Judge. "She is creating a disturbance."

At this an elderly well-dressed woman, scarlet with embarrassment and coughing convulsively, got up in the well of the Court and with great difficulty made her way out, always coughing.

Lord Horfield waited impressively till she could not be heard any more and then turned towards Counsel with a slight gesture of his left hand.

"What with your assertion," said Keane, "and Marsh's denial, and your husband's anger, there was what may be called a 'scene' in the study, wasn't there?"

"Yes," said the witness, in a low voice that could scarcely be heard.

"How long did it last?"

"I don't know."

"How did it end?"

"My husband broke away and left the room in a passion."

"And then?"

"What?"

"What happened then?"

"Marsh left too."

"Did your husband leave the room first or did Marsh?"

Mrs. Paradine stood as if considering. She still preserved a sort of façade of almost blank composure, but it was becoming obvious that she had been shaken by the violent scene which had been ended by Marsh's departure. She looked curiously vague and her tall figure stooped a little in the witness-box.

"Give the witness a chair!" ordered the Judge.

A chair was pushed forward.

"You can give your evidence sitting," said the Judge.

"Thank you, my Lord," muttered Mrs. Paradine.

And she sat down with the two 'officers' on either side of her, ready to minister to her in case of need.

"Which of the two left the room first?" asked Keane, deliberately softening his voice.

"I think it was Marsh—— Yes—Marsh."

"What happened then?"

"My husband went upstairs."

"Alone?"

"I believe the butler went to him. I did not. It would have been no use."

"Please tell the Jury this. Had you any reason whatever apart from the reason you have given, for wishing to get Marsh out of the house?"

"No, none."

"He has suggested that you may have had some secret reason for wishing him away. Had you?"

"No."

"You swear that?"

"I swear it."

Keane then put to the witness a few questions as to what she did previous to going to her bedroom, as spoken to by the witness, Marsh, eliciting nothing from her of any particular value for the defence. After dining alone downstairs she had gone to her bedroom on the first floor.

"Why did you go up to your bedroom?" he asked.

"I wanted to arrange my hair and put some eau de Cologne on my forehead," said the witness.

"Did you see anyone as you went to your room?"

"No."

"You went into your room?"

"Yes."

"And shut the door?"

"Yes."

"While in your room did you hear anything?"

"No."

"You did not hear your husband leave his room and go to the lavatory?"

"No."

"Nor any person enter his room?"

"No."

"About how long were you in your bedroom?"

"Not very long. But I didn't time it."

"Now, Mrs. Paradine, please tell the Jury on your oath—did you visit your husband's bedroom while he was in the lavatory?"

"I did not."

"Did you—remembering he could not see—did you go into his room for any purpose when he was there, before you came downstairs to the drawing-room?"

"I did not."

"You are accused of having poisoned him by introducing antimony, in the form of tartar emetic, into something he took that evening or night—perhaps into the glass of Burgundy by his bedside. Did you do this?"

"I swear I did not."

"Did you have anything at all to do with his death?"

"I did not."

"When you finally came downstairs was anyone on the landing?"

"No."

"When you came downstairs what did you do?"

"I was very unhappy at what had taken place. To try to soothe my nerves I went to the piano and played."

"An arrangement of 'The Blue Danube'?"

"Yes."

"You did this to try and quieten your nerves?"

"Yes."

"What caused you to stop playing?"

"I was tired and went up to bed."

"Did you fall asleep?"

"Yes."

"Did anything wake you?"

"Yes."

"What was it?"

"I was wakened by a voice, my husband's, shouting on, or near, the landing."

"Did you hear any words?"

"I heard a cry of 'Marsh! Marsh!' "

"Now, Mrs. Paradine, please tell the Jury exactly what impression this cry made upon you."

"What impression?" said the witness, vaguely.

"Yes. What impression did you get from this cry?"

"That something terrible was the matter, that something had happened."

"Ah? But this cry of 'Marsh!'—did it sound like a cry for aid?" Keane looked at her and frowned as he put this question.

The witness hesitated.

"I—don't know," she said finally.

"Or did it sound like a comment?"

"A comment?" said the witness.

"For instance," said Keane, with almost sinister slowness, "did it sound like a denunciation?"

"My Lord!" said Sir Joseph Farrell, abruptly rising, "I must really protest. The learned Counsel, contrary to your Lordship's ruling, is again trying to induce the witness to say what *he* thinks would be useful to the Defence. He is manifestly leading her."

"I am not!" exclaimed Keane. "I merely ask her——"

"*I* will ask her," the Judge interrupted. (To the witness:) "Your husband's cry of 'Marsh!' What impression did it make upon you?"

"An impression that something dreadful had happened, my Lord."

"Just that?"

"Yes."

"Nothing else?"

"No, my Lord."

"The question is answered, Sir Malcolm. You can pass away from it."

"If I am not to be allowed to question the witness in my own way, my Lord, it is impossible for me——" began Keane wrathfully.

"I have said that I will not permit words to be put into the mouth of the witness by Counsel, and I now repeat it. The question should have been put as I put it."

"I am quite sure your Lordship's methods must always be better than mine. Nevertheless——"

"Kindly cease to argue with me and get on with the case," said Lord Horfield, sternly.

"In all my long experience of the Law——" began Keane passionately.

Then he stopped abruptly, seemed to make a great effort, and in a cold, dry voice asked the witness some more questions, about the arrival of the doctor, her husband's illness and death. He closed his examination in the following way:

"Did you tell William Marsh that in his will your husband had left Marsh money?"

"I believe I did."

"Why was that?"

"I did it to show Marsh that I had no enmity towards him, no wish to do him harm. I thought he would be pleased and that he would do nothing that would displease my husband."

"That was your object in telling him?"

"Yes."

"Did you ever wish any ill to Marsh?"

"Never."

"You only wished to have him away from the house?"

"That was all."

"Because of what you have told the Jury?"

"Oh yes—yes!" the witness exclaimed, as if suddenly driven out of all self-control by sheer nervous exasperation. "*Yes!*"

The last 'yes' was almost a cry. It was followed by dead silence.

"That is all I have to ask you!" said Keane, with cold abruptness.

And he sat down and bent over his papers.

XXXVII

DIRECTLY Keane had sat down Sir Joseph Farrell got up and stood for a moment as if in hesitation. Then, turning to the Judge, he said:

"My Lord, I cannot help thinking that it would be helpful in elucidating the truth of this somewhat complicated case if the man who has just been taken out gave some further explanation to the Jury. I beg your Lordship's pardon for mentioning this."

"My Lord——" began Keane excitedly, on his feet, "I——"

Lord Horfield held up his right hand.

"This matter lies with me and only with me!" he said. "Kindly proceed with your cross-examination, Sir Joseph."

Keane flushed to the temples and sank back on his seat, moving his lips as if muttering something to himself.

Up in the gallery Judith Flaquer turned with irrepressible impatience to Gay.

"Oh, why doesn't he control himself?" she whispered. "What is the good of——"

She stopped. The stricken look on Gay's pale face checked her and just then a bland voice broke the expectant silence in Court. Sir Joseph Farrell was beginning his cross-examination of Mrs. Paradine.

He began by asking her a few searching questions about her early life. The circumstances of her rescue by Mr. Powers, the American, from 'a certain house of evil fame' in Copenhagen, her eventual departure from the Powers' *ménage* in New York, and her subsequent existence in America, and elsewhere, as a masseuse. Mrs. Paradine replied to him with quiet composure. She had herself marvellously well in hand and showed no traces of the acute agitation she must have undergone during the sensational incidents which had recently disturbed and excited the great crowd in Court. It was obvious that she had recovered from what had happened more rapidly and completely than her Counsel, who, as was apparent to everyone, was in an acutely emotional condition. His handsome face was still flushed with angry blood. His dark eyes showed a fierce light as of burning indignation. And his hands were scarcely ever still. He fidgeted with his papers, plucked at his gown, bent down and whispered to his Junior, sat back and set his lips firmly together, opened them as if to interrupt Counsel for the Crown, shut them again, then seemed to bury himself in his papers almost like a man trying to hide from an ordeal which was rapidly wearing him down.

The curious blandness of Sir Joseph Farrell was in strong contrast with Keane's demeanour so full of acute nervous irritation. This rather short, thick-set man of the shaven lips and the whiskers was almost seductive with his dulcet tones, and his gentle gestures, and his softly inquiring voice and, at times, semi-wistful manner.

"I want to know——" he would say, and "Can you tell me——" and "It would help me if you would explain——" and "It would make things easier for the Jury if you could make clear why——"

But Keane knew the danger of the man from old experience, and showed increasing uneasiness, and the cross-examination continued, passing on from Mrs. Paradine's marriage to the blind man—("you married him merely out of love, not at all because he was very rich and had an excellent social position?")—to the life at Hindley Hall with its difficulties, the two attacks of illness, and the subsequent removal to London. During the cross-examination about the life at Hindley, Sir Joseph put a number of questions concerning Mrs. Paradine's relations with William Marsh.

"Marsh has been described as a woman-hater. Did you find him so?"

"I didn't think he cared about women."

"No? But that manner you had to complain of eventually in London? What about that?"

"I attributed that to impertinence."

"Merely to impertinence?"

The witness hesitated.

"Remember your evidence in chief. To what did you attribute this manner of which you had reason to complain?"

In a low and apparently reluctant voice, witness answered:

"I suppose to the fact that Marsh had been foolish enough to take a fancy to me."

"You had reason to believe that the woman-hater had taken a fancy to you? Was that it?"

"I suppose so."

"But was it?"

"Yes."

"Was Marsh, in your view, a most devoted servant?"

"Yes."

"Passionately attached to his master?"

"He certainly seemed so."

"You thought it hypocrisy?"

"I—I do not care to say that."

"You don't care to say that! Here is the body-servant of a blind man, professing devotion to his master and, according to you, secretly trying to make love to his master's wife. Is that not hypocrisy?"

Witness was silent. During her silence she looked towards her Counsel.

"Kindly attend to me!" (The voice was slightly less bland.) "Do you believe that Marsh was, or had been, genuinely devoted to his master?"

"I suppose so—yes."

"And yet you say that he grossly betrayed his master's confidence?"

Silence.

"If that be true, mustn't such a man be an arch-hypocrite?"

"I—I don't know."

"You are doubtful?"

The voice was very soft, yet urgent. The witness made no reply.

"You were fond of your husband?"

"Yes, very fond."

"You loved him?"

"Yes."

"Did you admire him?"

"Yes."

"Respect him?"

"Yes."

"You have given evidence that Marsh was impertinent to you and made love to you, both at Hindley and in London. Did you ever resent it?"

"Yes."

"Did you ever speak to anyone of it?"

"No."

"Why not?"

"I was ashamed."

"Why should *you* be ashamed? Was it *your* fault?"

"Of course not."

"Then why be ashamed?"

No answer.

"Now, Mrs. Paradine—if, as you say, you admired, respected

and loved your husband, why did you allow a valet, your husband's valet, to make love to you and not complain of it to your husband?"

After a pause, witness said:

"I knew it would upset him terribly if I told him."

"You thought it preferable to let it go on, this servant's love-making, and let your husband believe that all was well?"

"My husband depended on Marsh."

"Didn't he depend on you?"

"Yes, of course."

"Do you think that Marsh was more important to him than you, his wife?"

"No, of course not."

"Then why didn't you complain of this alleged gross insult to you?"

"I hoped to stop it without upsetting my husband."

"What did you do to stop it?"

"I spoke to Marsh."

"Did your speaking have any effect?"

"I hoped it would."

"But did it?"

"I still had reason to complain from time to time."

"And yet kept silence? Didn't seek assistance from anyone?"

"I hated to speak of such a thing."

"You mean that modesty held you back?" suggested Counsel, with the suspicion of a sneer. "Remembering your past, you say that?"

Keane sprang to his feet.

"My Lord, I protest! There has been nothing in the evidence that reflects on the witness's past. I protest against that insinuation."

"My Lord," said Sir Joseph calmly. "There was no insinuation. I merely intended to convey that a lady of mature years, who had been a professional masseuse, and formerly a maid-servant, and before that had had the misfortune to fall into the hands of members of the underworld in Denmark, need hardly have been held back because of maiden modesty from appealing to her own husband against the advances of his valet."

"I did not find anything objectionable in the learned Counsel's remark," said the Judge, looking straight at Keane. "I took it in the sense he intended."

"It was a gross insinuation against the blameless past of the witness," said Keane, angrily.

"I do not think so, Sir Malcolm," said Lord Horfield, in an almost purring voice. (To Counsel for the Crown:) "Proceed!"

Keane threw himself down in his seat, this time pale with anger.

"I will leave that," said Sir Joseph softly, and looking at Keane, who stared indignantly at him.

The next question startled the Court.

"Do you think William Marsh very good-looking?" asked Counsel.

Keane again sprang to his feet.

"My Lord, I object. What can such a question have to do with this case?"

"My Lord, if I am allowed to proceed without these continual interruptions from my learned brother, it will be apparent that the question is cogent," said Sir Joseph, but totally without heat.

"I allow the question," said Lord Horfield. "I must ask you, Sir Malcolm, not to interfere with Counsel. I will interfere if I see reason."

"But, my Lord——"

"Kindly leave it to me."

"My Lord, it is my duty to protect my client and I intend to do so at all risks."

"Sit down, Sir Malcolm!" said the Judge sternly. "I have already said that I allow the question."

For a moment Keane kept on his feet with a defiant look on his face. Then his Junior gently pulled at his robe and whispered something to him, and he yielded and sat heavily down. "Now, please go on!" said the Judge to Counsel for the Crown.

"Do you think William Marsh a very good-looking man?" said Counsel to the witness.

Mrs. Paradine lifted her chin with a jerk.

"No, not at all!" she said, in a hard, sharp voice.

"Ah?" said Counsel. "You have considered that question?"

"You asked me."

"But had you considered that question already? At Hindley?"

"No, never. Marsh was a servant. I couldn't consider him in that way."

"But had not you also been a servant?"

"Long ago."

"Is it so odd for a former servant to think about the looks of another servant?"

"I was the mistress of the house in which Marsh was a servant."

"We know that. But did you not, in fact, think Marsh wonderfully good-looking?"

"I never thought about such a thing."

"Not even when he, as you allege, made love to you?"

"My Lord!" cried Keane, on his feet. "I claim the protection of the Bench for the prisoner!"

"Sit down, Sir Malcolm!" said the Judge. "These questions are quite in order."

"But I say it is disgraceful that——"

"Enough of this! You allow yourself to be carried away by your zeal for your client. I now direct you to resume your seat and to let Counsel proceed."

"But, my Lord——"

"Silence! I am arbiter here. Sit down!"

The Judge made a sign to Counsel for the Crown.

Keane remained standing for a moment. Then with a furious gesture he stooped as if to gather up his papers and leave the Court. He even took some papers into his hands. But then he turned his head and looked at Mrs. Paradine, who was looking fixedly at him. The papers dropped from his hands and he sat down, throwing up his hands as if in protest. A long murmur went through the Court.

"Even when Marsh made love to you, as you say, you never thought about whether he was a very good-looking man, or not?" asked Counsel.

"I have told you," said the witness, with a sort of sulky emphasis.

"Very well!"

Counsel glanced towards the three women in the Jury box.

"Although Marsh lived for months with you in your house, and, according to your statement, made love to you, yet you never noticed his looks? Is that what you tell the Jury?"

"I couldn't think of my husband's servant in such a way."

"He meant nothing to you?"

"Not in that way."

"In what way did he mean anything to you?"

"I valued him as a servant to whom my husband was greatly attached and who had always seemed greatly attached to him."

"You valued him for his attachment to your husband, whom, according to you, he was trying to wrong in the most grievous way possible? Is that what you tell the Jury?"

Witness was silent.

"Please answer."

"My husband was accustomed to Marsh, and as he was blind, I didn't like to upset him."

"For that reason *only* you endured what you allege to have been Marsh's disgusting attentions?"

"I tried to do the best for my husband."

"No *personal* reason?"

"I don't know what you mean."

"I will try to make myself clear."

Sir Joseph leaned forward, and suddenly dropping his bland voice and gentle manner, thundered out:

"I ask you, on your oath, did you not refrain from complaining about Marsh because you were madly in love with him?"

Mrs. Paradine moved sharply back in her chair as if she had been struck, then got up from it and stood facing Counsel. Then, in a heavy, smothered voice, and reddening from her forehead down to her uncovered throat, she said violently:

"A lie! A lie!"

"Were you not in love with Marsh all the time you lived in the house with him at Hindley?"

"That is a lie!"

"Were you not madly in love with him in London?"

Mrs. Paradine leaned forward in her turn, and a smile that suggested an intense bitterness of satire transformed her face; then, with a triumphant gesture, she exclaimed in a loud voice:

"Madly in love with Marsh, and go to my husband and ask him to send Marsh away! Is that what you think? Then you know nothing of women!"

And she began to laugh while the crowd watched her, breathless. Her low laughter was heard through the whole Court. Meanwhile, Sir Joseph Farrell waited, holding his robes and with the expression of a man who still had many shots in his locker. At last the low laugh died away, and the witness said, before Counsel could speak:

"Your own witness has given you the lie—Marsh himself."

"Kindly cease to make statements and attend to me. You are here to answer my questions. Is it not the fact that soon after you married Colonel Paradine, and discovered that Marsh took no interest in women, you resolved to overcome that indifference?"

"It is a lie."

"And set yourself to entice and attract him?"

"It is a lie."

"Had you not great opportunities for being with Marsh?"

"I saw him sometimes."

"Was he not almost always in attendance on your husband?"

"Sometimes he was."

"Was he not continually about Colonel Paradine in intimacy?"

"He often was."

"Did you not pursue him with your attentions?"

"It is a lie."

"Were you not absolutely set on overcoming his indifference to women?"

"No."

"And—" Counsel lowered his voice suddenly and spoke almost in a whisper—"Did you not finally succeed in doing so?"

All the colour had now died out of the prisoner's face, but her long neck was still mottled with red. Instead of answering the question, to the amazement of the Court she turned away from Sir Joseph Farrell and, with an expression of menace on her face, gazed at her own Counsel. And as she did this the crowd saw Keane's eyes look away from her. His head drooped slightly. His powerful shoulders were hunched. He stared down at the floor. His whole attitude suggested guilt as hers suggested a silent and terrible accusation.

"Answer me!" said Sir Joseph. "Did you not finally succeed in your object, and induce this unfortunate man, who, as witness after witness has testified, almost worshipped his master, to be false to his trust, false to himself, and to betray that master?"

"I deny that," witness said, in a smothered voice.

She sat down suddenly in the chair from which she had risen and for a moment looked as if she were going to faint, for her head drooped towards her left shoulder and her body seemed out of control.

One of the female officers touched her and whispered to her. She shook her head, put up a hand to her cheek and pulled herself up.

"Are you feeling ill?" Lord Horfield asked. "Do you wish anything? Shall we interrupt the cross-examination to allow you to recover yourself?"

"No, my Lord. I am—perfectly well. But—these horrid—lies——" her voice died away.

After a moment's pause, while the Court was wrapped in a breathless stillness, Lord Horfield signed to Sir Joseph to continue. During this moment Keane had sat motionless, his tall figure drawn up rigidly, his hands locked tightly together, his eyes fixed on Mrs. Paradine. From the moment of Sir Joseph's saying: "Answer me"—he had abandoned his curiously guilty attitude, the almost crouching posture which he had assumed, and had evidently made a great effort to appear at his ease. But the result of this was not happy. To many in the Court he suggested a man who, rent by a distracted consciousness of shortcoming, was trying to face up brazenly to a situation which he had inadvertently brought about and of which he had lost the control. It was by now obvious to every practised barrister in Court that Counsel for the Crown was cleverly grounding his cross-examination upon the previous examination by Counsel for the Defence. He was drawing a bow at a venture. This cross-examination was surely a suddenly conceived improvisation, suggested entirely to Sir Joseph Farrell by Keane. Lawyers often talked of it afterwards as one of the most unexpected departures in a sensational trial.

"But what the Hell's going to happen to his own witness?" whispered a young eager barrister to an older man sitting beside him. "He's out to prove him a perjuror—nothing less."

"There are perjurors and perjurors, my boy!" whispered back the other. "Just wait till you hear his closing speech; there is such a thing as a chivalrous liar. Doesn't the Divorce Court know it?"

The younger barrister's eyes showed an inward look for a moment. Then he moved his head and muttered to himself:

"I believe I get it!"

"You deny what I have suggested?" persisted Counsel, taking up the thread of his cross-examination.

"You have your own witness's evidence against it," said Mrs. Paradine.

"We will see as to that—presently."

Mrs. Paradine's large eyes widened for a moment and her lips parted. The remark had sounded like a threat, and for the first time acute fear seemed written on her face.

"But at any rate you deny it?" added Counsel.

"It is a lie," said the witness, spacing out the words, and putting a heavy accent on each of them.

Counsel for the Crown looked at the Jury, setting his shaven lips tightly together.

"Now as to the visit to London," he resumed. "You suggested it?"

"Yes."

"What was the *real reason* of this suggestion on your part?"

"I have said—I wanted my husband to see a good doctor."

"Anxiety for his health prompted you, although you thought him quite well?"

"I was not exactly anxious, but I thought he should see a first rate doctor."

"Ah! Any other reason?"

"That was my chief reason."

"Ah! Any other reason?"

"I thought in London I should see less of Marsh."

"You thought that in London you would see less of Marsh. You seriously tell the Jury that that was one of your reasons for wanting to go up to London?"

"Yes."

"Very well."

Counsel then asked a number of questions about the life in Eaton Square, with the obvious intention of inducing the witness to acknowledge that her husband's condition of misery and irritability became much worse after he left the retirement of Hindley Hall for London. On her side, in her answers, she did everything she could to attenuate this alleged condition, which had been spoken to by witnesses.

"I was not unhappy with my husband," she asserted, with emphasis. "I understood why he was sometimes miserable and I sympathised with him. I never hated him for his occasional impatience. I only pitied him."

Presently Counsel said:

"Kindly tell us whether you still assert that Marsh's attentions to you were persisted in while you were living in London?"

A fierce look changed Mrs. Paradine's face and was immediately blotted out, as if her will sprang to the rescue of her momentary inadvertence.

"There was no change," she said, in a colourless voice, that was in direct contradiction with the expression which had just disappeared.

"So that one of your reasons for coming to London had not turned out quite as you had hoped?" asked Counsel, slightly turning towards the Jury.

"No."

"On the other hand there was, according to the London doctor—" Counsel gave his name—"nothing the matter with your husband's health?"

"No, except nervous depression."

"For which Sanatogen was prescribed?"

"Yes."

"Now, on the morning of the day on which he died, was your husband in perfect health, so far as you know?"

"He seemed much as usual."

"In excellent health?"

"He didn't seem ill."

"But somewhat depressed in spirits?"

"Yes."

"Now, Mrs. Paradine, on that fateful day, did you come to a resolution?"

An utterly blank expression came into the witness's face.

"I do not know what you mean," she said, stolidly.

"No? Remembering what happened later you say that?"

"I do not understand."

"Have you ever heard of the expression 'burning one's boats'?"

"I think I have," witness said, vaguely.

"Do you know what that means?"

Witness shook her head.

"I will tell you. It means risking all and coming out with the truth, however horrible and detrimental that truth may be. Now on the day of your husband's death, when you were shut up in the study alone with him, did you not decide to do this?"

"I do not know what you mean."

"I mean—did you not decide that you could not stand your situation in that house in Eaton Square any longer? And did you not blurt out the truth of the whole matter to your husband?"

The witness made no reply for an instant. Then, still looking quite blank, she said:

"I have said that I told my husband about Marsh."

"Now, on your oath, did you not tell your husband that you loved Marsh and had belonged to Marsh?"

"That is a great lie," said the witness, but in a feeble voice that seemed to contradict the words spoken.

"And," persisted Counsel, "was not that the cause of your husband's fury, of his summons to Marsh, of the whole scene which followed, of your husband's leaving the study and shutting himself up in the sitting-room next to his bedroom, of his solitary dinner, of his refusal to allow Marsh to help him to bed, of his ordering Marsh away, of everything that happened, up till the time of his illness and death?"

Witness shook her head.

"Kindly answer so that the Jury can hear you."

Mrs. Paradine, like one making a supreme effort, turned towards the Jury and whispered:

"No."

"But the man's trying to convict his own witness of perjury!" whispered the young barrister to his older companion.

"Because he knows now that Marsh means to come out with the truth if he gets the chance," whispered the other. "Sh!"

"You deny what I have suggested?"

The witness nodded.

"You still assert that what happened was that you told your husband Marsh had pestered you with his attentions and that you wanted him to be dismissed from his situation on that account?"

The witness was motionless and did not answer.

"Do you still assert that?"

Witness nodded.

"Tell the Jury!"

"Yes," the witness murmured, not looking towards the Jury box.

"Very well!" said Sir Joseph, looking straight at the Jury.

He then asked the witness some questions about her employment of her time until, after her solitary dinner downstairs, she went to her bedroom to "arrange your hair and put some eau de Cologne on your forehead."

"Were you in a very agitated condition?" he asked.

"I was upset."

"You realised by that time that you had made an enemy of Marsh?"

After a pause the witness said:

"I did not think about that."

"You had a more important matter to think about?"

"I do not remember what I thought of."

"Do you swear that when you passed to your room you did not see Marsh coming out of your husband's room?"

"I did not."

"You did not know that Marsh was upstairs on the landing, that when he left your husband's room he remained there for a short time?"

"I did not."

"Was your bedroom door completely shut?"

"Yes."

"You swear that?"

"Yes."

"It has been given in evidence that your husband presently left his room and went down a passage to the lavatory. Now, did you hear him go?"

"I did not."

"It has been given in evidence that shortly after, almost immediately, Ellen Smith, your head housemaid, came up to the landing. Did you hear her come?"

"No."

"She talked to William Marsh outside your bedroom door. Did you hear the voices?"

"No."

"She and Marsh went away. Did you hear them go?"

"I did not."

"Later your husband must have come back to his room from the lavatory, feeling his way. Did you not hear him?"

"I did not."

"Do you swear that during the time which elapsed between the departure of Ellen Smith and Marsh and the return of your husband from the lavatory you did not visit his room?"

"I did not."

"And tamper with the glass of Burgundy which stood upon the night table beside his bed?"

"I did not."

"So that you heard absolutely nothing of what took place on the landing, Marsh's coming there from your husband's room, your husband's going and coming, Ellen Smith's arrival, her talk with Marsh outside your door, their departure together, your husband's return to his room? Of all this you heard and knew nothing?"

"Nothing."

"How long did you remain in your bedroom?"

"I don't know."

"What were you doing there?"

"Arranging my hair and getting eau de Cologne."

"You had a lady's maid, Fanny Greene?"

"Yes."

"You did not summon her to help you?"

"No, I had no need of her."

"You preferred to be quite alone?"

"Yes, I was tired."

"After the scene downstairs in the study?"

"Yes."

"When your husband returned to his room did you visit him?"

"No."

"Did you make no effort to see him?"

"No."

"You swear that?"

"Yes."

"You say you were tired?"

"Yes."

"But you did not retire to bed?"

"No; it was too early."

"You went to the drawing-room?"

"Yes."

"And played for perhaps half an hour upon the piano?"

"Yes."

"In spite of this terrible scene which had tired you so much you were able to play difficult waltz music, light music, upon the piano for perhaps half an hour?"

"Music soothes me."

"You needed to be soothed—just then?"

The witness moved her head slowly.

"Were you waiting—for something?"

"What?" said the witness. Then she hurriedly added: "No."

"When you stopped playing you went upstairs to bed?"

"Yes."

"Your maid helped you to bed?"

"Yes."

"Did you sleep?"

"Yes."

"You swear that?"

"Yes."'

"So that after this terrible scene with Marsh and your husband you were able first to play brilliantly upon the piano, and then to go to bed and immediately fall asleep?"

"I slept—after a time."

"We have learned what you say woke you. You heard your husband's voice crying out, 'Marsh! Marsh!'"

"Yes."

"Now did that sound like a call for help?"

The witness hesitated. She was obviously much shaken by the cross-examination and the scene which had preceded it. Her answers now were given in a low voice. Her tall body looked tired. Her pale eyes were usually cast down. Her white face had a dull and weary expression.

"Please answer!"

"Yes," she said, then immediately correcting herself she added: "No, I do not think it did."

"You have given two contradictory answers. Which do you adhere to?"

"It was just a call."

"For help? Why does a man who is ill, in pain, call out a name? Would it not be a call for help?"

"Perhaps it was."

"Now your husband knew you slept opposite to him?"

"Yes."

"But when he found himself in agony, in spite of what had happened in the study that evening, he called not for you but for Marsh. Did not that strike you as strange?"

"I suppose—it was," said the witness, in an almost toneless voice.

"Did not that make a painful impression upon you?"

"I do not think so."

"You were not surprised that your husband did not call for you, his wife, who, he knew, was close to him, but for his servant who was downstairs?"

"I forget."

"Did not that suggest to you that even in his agony he wished to have nothing more to do with you?"

"I do not know. I forget."

There was a fading sound in the voice.

Counsel asked a few more questions about the illness and death of Colonel Paradine. Then said:

"You heard my request to his Lordship to recall William Marsh for re-examination as to the scene in the study which preceded your husband's death?"

"Yes."

"Having that request in your mind do you still swear that your account of that scene is true?"

"Yes," almost whispered the witness.

"That is all I have to ask you," said Counsel.

The witness stood for a moment as if uncertain what to do. Then one of the officers touched her arm. She started violently. The officer whispered something to her. She turned and made her way out of the witness-box and back to the Dock.

Immediately afterwards Sir Joseph renewed his application that

William Marsh might be purged of his contempt of Court and recalled for further examination.

"I take note of your application and will give my decision as to that after the luncheon interval," Lord Horfield replied, looking towards Keane as he spoke.

The Court then adjourned for lunch.

XXXVIII

SIR SIMON FLAQUER caught Keane as the latter was hurrying out of the Court and took him by the arm.

"What's that?" Keane exclaimed sharply, looking round. "Oh, it's you, Flaquer, is it? What d'you want? I'm in a hurry!"

"Then I won't keep you," returned Sir Simon, with unusual grimness. "I only wanted to say—" he lowered his voice to an almost inaudible whisper—"that if Horfield decides to put Marsh in the box again in my opinion it's all up with us."

"I've done what I could!" said Keane, with a frantic gesture. "I'll fight to the last. No man can do more."

"It's just possible of course that Horfield may decide not to."

Keane bent down to him savagely.

"Horfield decide *not* to! Good God, man! Can't you see that Horfield's got the chance he's been waiting for? D'you think he'll let it slip? Not he! Not he!"

He broke away and hurried off. All that he had said had been spoken in a voice so low that no one but Sir Simon could have heard him. Yet the intensity in his voice had been terrific. Sir Simon felt as if an iron door had been suddenly flung open and had let out a red-hot blast from a furnace.

"I wonder where the Devil he's going!" he thought. "To see *her?*"

But when, later, he himself visited Mrs. Paradine Keane was not there. He was alone, walking the London streets, trying to get himself in hand.

When the interval for lunch was over and the Court reassembled he was in his place. He had eaten nothing but he had drunk a stiff brandy and soda just before he came into Court.

As soon as Lord Horfield had taken his seat on the Bench he said, with a glance through half-closed eyes in the direction of Keane:

"Let the witness, William Marsh, who is in custody be brought up before me."

There was a stir through the Court. During the pause which followed it Keane sat looking at Lord Horfield with hatred in his eyes.

The dense crowd waited in silence for the reappearance of Marsh, a silence that seemed massed together, heavy like a mighty weight that bore down all human opposition to its power. It was not as if they were silent, those ranges of human beings, but as if silence lay upon them holding them down. Mrs. Paradine sat perfectly still in the Dock. She, like Lord Horfield, was gazing at Keane, whose eyes were always on the Judge. During the interval she seemed to have aged. Many of those in Court noticed that. Her curious beauty was surely withering in the sight of all men. But she showed no active emotion.

"I can see her now as an old woman!" Judith Flaquer whispered to Gay. "It's awful."

Gay gave no sign that she heard.

There was again a stir in Court. Heads were turned. The tall soldierly figure of Marsh appeared walking stiffly in custody. Mrs. Paradine's pale eyes were directed towards him, but she did not move her body. Marsh did not look at her. His eyes were for the Judge.

"Release him!" said Lord Horfield.

He then addressed Marsh in a stern voice, rebuking him for his contempt, and pointing out to him the grossness of his conduct, "unparalleled in my experience of the procedure of these Courts." Whilst he was speaking Marsh stood rigid like a soldier on parade. Not once did his eyes move from the face of the Judge. Having finished his admonition Lord Horfield added that despite Marsh's grave offence his desire to return to the witness-box would be acceded to. He concluded his remarks by adjuring Marsh to remember the sanctity of a witness's oath, "taken on the Holy Book," and to unburden his soul of the truth in order that "this terrible conflict" might be resolved in the sacred interest of justice.

"Now go into the box!" he said.

"We shall get the truth now—at last!" whispered Judith.

"You asked to be re-heard," said Lord Horfield to the witness. "Do you wish to correct any of the evidence you have given in this Court?"

"Yes, my Lord," said Marsh, resolutely. "I do."

"You know of the penalties for perjury, confessed or unconfessed?"

"Yes, my Lord."

"Very well. What part of your evidence do you wish to correct?"

"About what happened in the study on the day before my master died, sir—my Lord, I mean," said Marsh.

"Was what you testified to about that untrue then?"

"It wasn't true, my Lord."

Without making any comment upon this the Judge continued:

"When Colonel Paradine summoned you to his study on the afternoon before his death what did he give you as his reason for doing so?"

"He said that my—that Mrs. Paradine had been saying something to him about me, my Lord—about me and her," said Marsh, gripping one big hand with the other, looking straight before him, and speaking in a voice that sounded unnaturally loud.

"You told the Jury in your former evidence that what she told her husband was that you meant to leave his service. Was that true or untrue?"

"Untrue, my Lord."

"You told the Court a lie?"

"I did, my Lord."

"Why did you do that?"

"Because I was ashamed of the truth, my Lord, and——" Marsh broke off.

"Yes? And what other reason had you?"

"I didn't care to tell against a woman," said Marsh, in a lower voice, and with less resolution.

"What is the truth? Tell it to the Jury in your own words."

Keane shut his eyes and folded his arms. At that moment he heard again the sounds of the wind and the roar of the sea outside the rattling windows of the Inn at Sedale; he saw Marsh sitting opposite to him in the night. A voice in his ears said: "She's a woman of Babylon—some day you'll know it." That same voice was speaking now. He heard it say:

"When I came into the study my Colonel was in a terrible state. As soon as he knew I was there he turned on me and told me that his wife—Mrs. Paradine there—had made what he called a confession to him."

The voice stopped.

"What was this confession? Tell the Jury," said the Judge.

"The Colonel said she'd told him that—that I'd been with her up at Hindley."

"What do you mean exactly by that?"

There was a long pause. Then Keane heard Marsh say:

"As a man is with a woman he's fond of—that way."

"You mean that you had had guilty intercourse with his wife?"

"Yes, my Lord."

"He told you that?"

"Yes, my Lord."

"And what did you do?"

"Tried to give her the lie."

"What do you mean by—tried?"

"At first I swore it wasn't true."

"And then?"

"In the end I couldn't keep to it, my Lord. I—I—I'd never been given to telling lies to my Colonel, and I couldn't keep it up. He wore me down and at last I told him."

"What did you tell him?"

"Told him it *was* true, my Lord, and that I'd been with her— once."

"Where was that?"

"Up at Hindley."

"Was it before, or after, the two attacks of illness your master had?"

"After them, my Lord, not long before we came to London."

"The prisoner has said that while in service with Colonel Paradine you pestered her with your attentions. Is that true?"

"No, my Lord," said Marsh.

His voice sank to a deep murmur as he added:

"It was the other way about."

"Explain yourself."

"That's clear enough, my Lord, ain't it?"

"No. You must tell the Jury exactly what you mean."

Marsh looked down.

"She came after me and gave me no peace till I—I didn't want to do the dirty on my Colonel. I would have gone through fire for him—and had. But she couldn't see it that way; she said he was blind and would never know. I was all against women. That's quite true, my Lord. But a man's only a man after all, and she knew how to get over me. It was only once but that was enough. He went to his death and I was never able to put it right. I don't say I wasn't in the wrong of it. I was, God knows. But I wasn't as bad as my master thought. Dead that very night! And the last words I heard him say to me was—'Get out of my sight!' And he blind as he was!"

During this speech Marsh's voice sank lower and lower. The last words came from him in a sort of pitiful groan.

"I have only one more question to ask you," said the Judge, after a pause. "Had you any hand in your master's death?"

"My Lord!" cried Marsh. "*I* lift my hand against my Colonel!"

The exclamation following immediately on the dolorous murmur startled the Court by the nakedness of its sincerity.

"That is all I have to ask you," said the Judge.

But Marsh remained standing in the box till his arm was touched by an attendant of the Court. Then he stepped heavily from the box. He stood for a moment looking dazed. Finally he lifted his eyes to the Judge.

"Am I—am I at liberty to go, my Lord?" he asked.

"Yes," said Lord Horfield. "You have purged your contempt."

Marsh turned and made his way out of the Court, looking neither to right nor left. As he went by some stared at him, but many lowered their eyes. There was that in his face which forbade them to look at him.

XXXIX

THAT strange and, as it seemed, ill-assorted couple, Lord and Lady Horfield, dined alone together that night in their big house in

Sussex Square. Lady Horfield had again been in Court, and had returned home with her mind in a condition of violent excitement and upheaval after the sensational events of the day. Lord Horfield had been to the Club for a while as his custom was, and had arrived in Sussex Square about an hour before dinner. They dined when at home always at half-past eight.

The Judge was fond of ceremony in his house and did not even disdain a certain amount of state. He and his wife were always waited upon at dinner by a butler and two footmen. The cook was a Cordon bleu. Everything was excellently done. There were menus, flowers, old silver, beautiful glass—the Judge was a connoisseur of glass—the wines matched the perfection of the dishes. A big wood fire burned on the hearth. Some fine pictures of the English School, two Constables, a Morland, a Gainsborough, an unusually good Copley Fielding, hung on the walls. The wintry weather of an unusually cold March was blotted out by shutters and by curtains of golden brown silk.

And the Judge was evidently in a happy mood.

Whatever effect the events of the day had had upon Lady Horfield, William Marsh, the prisoner, Malcolm Keane, Gay and others, they had produced no fatigue, no depression, no painful agitation, in the Judge. After his repose and cigar at the Club he had come home in excellent spirits, had taken a warm bath, got into evening dress, sipped a cocktail with a touch of old brandy in it, and was now sampling his dinner with the critical appreciation of an accomplished gourmet.

His wife, on the other hand (in bright green), seemed to have very little appetite. She accepted each course as it was offered to her and ate a morsel or two, peeping furtively as she did so at her husband, to see if he was satisfied with her pretence. Then she pushed about the food with her fork, to be doing something, and presently it was carried away by the butler or one of the footmen.

There was not much conversation, but evidently the Judge was not troubled by the occasional, rather prolonged silences. He was enjoying his food, his wine, the warm cosy atmosphere of the spacious, well-furnished room after the somewhat fetid atmosphere of the Court. And apparently his mind was a pleasant companion. For as he ate and drank there was a serene look on his

long narrow face, and now and then he showed his long yellow
teeth in a smile that seemed caused by some agreeable procession
of thoughts taking place unseen, unheard, in the mystery of the
inner man.

At length dessert was put on the table and the men-servants
went out of the room.

"Shall I stay with you, Horfield?" asked Lady Horfield, in an
uncertain voice, glancing at her husband and looking away. "Or
would you rather drink your wine alone?"

"You can stay, my dear, you can stay."

Lady Horfield, who had made an awkward movement as if to
get up, checked it and flumped on her chair:

"Did you enjoy yourself to-day?" continued her husband, in
his agreeable voice. "It was quite entertaining, wasn't it? A good
deal of drama, too."

"I thought—it seemed to me—but of course it isn't often that
I have anything to do with—oh, Horfield, it was terrible."

"He's never sent me that port!" the Judge murmured, lifting
his glass. "And never will now, if I know anything of men."

"What port?" exclaimed his wife, fluttering her little hands.
"Whose port?"

"Keane has some wonderful 1874 port. I praised it the other
night when we dined with him, and he promised to send me some
bottles."

"Then of course he will."

"I don't think so. But we shall see. Perhaps you can remind him
when you meet him again—in a picture gallery."

"Oh, but I shan't ever—of course not! It was only by—I mean
that Sir Malcolm won't want——"

"I don't mind, my love. I like you to have a cavalier. Considering your age—we're neither of us quite in our first bloom—I think
you've achieved a triumph with Keane. And Lady Keane takes it
with admirable sang froid. By the way, did you notice something
to-day in Court?"

"Yes. No—I'm not sure. What?"

"That at times there's an odd flash of likeness to Lady Keane
in Mrs. Paradine?"

"Oh—surely——"

"Yes. It's something about the mouth and at the corners of the eyes. The shape of the head, too. There's a likeness."

His voice for a moment held a sound of warm satisfaction.

"But Lady Keane is *so* different—such a—there's something in her character——"

"I'm talking not of character but of physique!" said Lord Horfield, with a sudden tone of asperity.

"Oh, well—if you mean—but I didn't see it."

"But what do you see, my dear? Now, take William Marsh. When he was cross-examined, did you see that he was lying?"

"I wasn't sure—I couldn't quite——"

"No, I don't suppose you could. And when Mrs. Paradine gave her evidence, did you realise that it was false?"

"But could they both be false? It seems hardly likely——"

"You'd scarcely do on a Jury."

"Oh, I wouldn't be on a Jury for anything. I could never bring myself—the poor creatures who are given into the hands of sinners like themselves. Women too! I hated to see those three women in the Jury box. But perhaps they'll be more inclined for mercy than the men."

"Don't you believe it, my dear. Quite the contrary. Women are merciless to their sex."

He sipped his port.

"There'll be less mercy, as you call it, now that women sit than before, when Juries were exclusively composed of men. How did the last evidence which William Marsh gave, when I had him back, strike you?"

He half-closed his eyes, lay back in his chair, one hand on the stem of his glass, and let his close observation play over her congested features.

"It was awful. It seemed impossible that—and yet there was something——"

"Yes? Go on!"

"One could not think he was lying then."

"Ah! So even *you*——"

He took his thin, yellowish-white fingers away from his glass and sat forward.

"Give me your impression, your **exact** impression!" he said, in a thin, sharp voice.

"Oh, Horfield, I felt then that he *had* to speak the truth, that it was forced out of him in spite of himself. Could a man say such a thing of himself if it wasn't true?"

"That man couldn't—and didn't. We shan't see him in Court again. He's gone, like the scapegoat, into the wilderness. Those last words of his Colonel will ring in his ears till the end of his time on earth, if I know anything of human character."

His face hardened into grimness and he looked suddenly very old.

"She knew to-day that she had lost him for ever, whatever the result—to-morrow," he muttered.

"What—I didn't hear! What did you say? Something about to-morrow?"

"To-morrow I sit till I get a verdict, however late that may be."

"How I shall pray to-night that it may be not guilty!" Lady Horfield exclaimed, distractedly.

Her face was working now and her little hands moved incessantly.

"Pray—pray as much as you like!" said her husband. "Your prayers won't turn Justice aside from her course. Farrell's closing speech for the Crown was a masterly effort."

"I thought it abominably cruel!" exclaimed Lady Horfield. "He *asked* that the poor wretched woman should be hanged. He *wanted* her to be hanged. Don't ask me ever to have Sir Joseph here again, for I really——"

"What folly's this?" said the Judge, showing sudden irritation. "Farrell was for the *Crown*. Didn't you realise that?"

"I don't care what he was for. His speech was the most terrible thing I ever heard. I don't defend treachery—if she *was*. But when a woman's the prey of love for a man—but no man, I'm sure, knows, or ever can know, what that is, for no man can ever—and she had been a servant and taken out of her sphere, and then, perhaps, went back to it in her heart. And there *is* something in that poor wretched man, Marsh, which might——"

"Are you defending adultery?" the Judge asked, in his purring voice. "And treachery to a blind man, whom he pretended to care for?"

"Not pretending! Horfield, that poor fellow loved his master. He was broken to pieces by that, when he said those last words and went out. It made me——" her voice broke; she stopped, recovered herself and said, with awe: "It made me think of Judas. *He* went away—and hanged himself."

"And that fellow probably went to the nearest public house and drank himself silly," said the Judge.

But, as he said it, he looked at his wife with a sort of musing wonder that was not wholly divorced from admiration.

"It seems to me that you pity every scoundrel who cumbers the earth," he added.

"I do! I do pity them!" she said, with the strange, sudden fierceness that revealed now and then the fire burning somewhere far away in the grotesque bulk that misrepresented her to the sons and daughters of men. "Does anyone need pity more than the man—or woman, too, of course—who has sinned?"

"Punishment is part of the scheme," said her husband. "And an extremely necessary part of it."

"But doesn't life punish us enough, doesn't it, Horfield? Why should we hurt each other? We have no right to be cruel. If I am certain of anything, I am certain of that."

Suddenly, with an awkward, even startling movement, she stretched forward over the dining-table, knocking over a glass as she did so.

"Horfield, my dear—don't be cruel any more!" she said, in a trembling voice. "Give it up! You may think it makes you happy, but you're wrong. It doesn't! It can't! It's—it's an illusion!"

Her own sudden lucidity seemed to startle her, for a look of amazement made her face grotesque; she lifted her eyebrows towards the fringe of rusty curls that came down low on her deeply wrinkled forehead, and for an instant her little eyes stared like the eyes of one conscious of wonder, but with an inward expression which suggested that the wonder was caused by herself.

"Yes, yes, yes!" she added, with an indrawn breath. "I can see —I have seen—for a long time."

"You have thrown over a glass!" said her husband, in a voice of steel.

A little red had suddenly appeared in his face, which was mottled here and there in patches.

"Oh—have I—where?"

"There!" he said, pointing.

"So I—how stupid of me! But I am always so clumsy," she said, snatching up the glass and setting it down so violently on the table that the jar broke the stem.

"Oh—give it to me!" the Judge exclaimed, with an outburst of nervous exasperation.

He got up, bent his excessively thin body over the table, gathered up the fragments—the goblet of the glass was unbroken—and went with them to the sideboard, where he stood for a moment with his back to the room, staring at his wife in the mirror let in to the cedarwood panelling.

She had dared—after all these years! He stared like one examining a stranger.

Lady Horfield began to get up.

"Horfield, forgive me! I am obliged—I feel I must———"

"Sit down, Sophy!" he said, turning sharply round.

She sank upon her seat looking desperately up at him.

The Judge came back to the dinner-table and pressed a foot on a place close to his chair. Then he sat down and waited. The door was opened almost directly and the butler appeared followed by a footman carrying coffee on a silver tray. The butler held a smaller tray on which were a box of Havanas and a cigar cutter and lighter.

In silence the coffee was served. Lady Horfield's cup and saucer rattled as she took them with both her little hands.

"Brandy, my Lord?" asked the butler.

"Yes," said the Judge.

Brandy was brought to him.

The butler was about to put the decanter back on the sideboard, when Lady Horfield exclaimed:

"I'll take some, too."

"Oh, I beg your ladyship's pardon!"

"Of course, I never—but I will to-night."

"Yes, my lady."

"That's enough, please."

The butler and the footman went out. Then the Judge said, with his usual slightly sub-acid graciousness:

"You have been talking even greater nonsense than usual to-night, Sophy. I told you not to come to this trial. You are much too excitable and devoid of reasoning power to be able to comprehend the processes of Justice. To-morrow you had better stay at home."

"I will—I will, if only you'll promise me not to give way to——"

"Be quiet, Sophy! How dare you speak like that to one of His Majesty's Judges!"

"Don't sum up against that poor woman. I don't know what she's done—how can we be certain? No one saw her put—— There's no absolute proof. Perhaps she did, but—oh, Horfield, don't have another poor woman's death on your conscience! You think I don't see. You think me a fool. I know that. But for a long time I *have* seen it growing in you, always growing—the need to—how can you *wish* to give a woman to the hangman? No man has the right—you know what I feel for you, Horfield. Don't think I am criticising you. You are so much more than I am. I could never dare. But for once listen to me and resist that awful——"

"Drink your brandy, if you're going to, and then you can leave me alone. You're the victim of a crazy imagination. Because, on account of my profession, I am at times forced to pronounce sentences upon evil-doers, you imagine that I like doing it."

"You do! You do! Oh, Horfield, it's your pleasure. It's becoming your chief pleasure in life to——"

The Judge suddenly leaned forward over the table, stretched out his right hand and seized one of his wife's wrists with his long, bony fingers.

"Have you ever said anything of this to Malcolm Keane?" he said, sternly.

Lady Horfield's congested face lost some of its extravagant colour. It did not become pale, but it seemed suddenly to fade. Her cheeks looked flatter. Her little mouth opened, but no words came from it. One of her fin-like hands beat on the tablecloth. The other trembled in the grasp of her husband.

"Do you hear me?" he asked.

"Yes."

"Have you spoken? In the picture gallery—were you two talking of that?"

"Horfield, I was desperate. Sir Malcolm was defending her. I thought I ought—I thought perhaps if I—he could do more to

help her. It was only that. I felt as if it was my duty—it seemed
to me that perhaps God had laid upon me—as I was your wife—
the duty to try to——"

"You mad woman!" he said. "You old mad woman!"

He let go of her wrist and violently thrust her hand away from
him.

"That's the way a woman loves!" he exclaimed, with a sneering
bitterness. "I suspected this, of course. Your manner with Keane!
And his blundering attempts to get round me! Stroking the dome
of St. Paul's to propitiate the Dean! So you two actually supposed
you could play about with me? What exquisite absurdity! I'm glad
really I've lived to enjoy it. Well, my dear, to-morrow evening
you, and he, too, will know the inner meaning of the title of one
of Balzac's best books. Ever heard of it? *Les Illusions Perdues?* Let
him try to spell-bind the Jury! Let him do his damned best!"

He got up and went slowly over to the wood fire, cigar in hand,
his head a little bent. When he got there he turned round, stood
with his back to it and straightened himself.

"To-morrow, no doubt, when the Court reassembles, we shall
have one of the most florid specimens of burning rhetoric, and
what the Americans picturesquely call 'sob stuff' that has ever been
heard at the Old Bailey. The great actor at the top of his form.
And yet I don't know. He's not far from the end of his tether.
He's on the verge of a breakdown."

He stopped speaking, put his cigar to his lips, drew on it and
let out a cloud of perfumed smoke, following its upward movement with suddenly smiling eyes.

"You and Malcolm Keane have become so intimate this winter
that perhaps he's told you his secret. Has he?"

Lady Horfield who, turned sideways in her chair, was gazing
at her husband with her head drooping forward, stammered:

"Secret? I don't know—we haven't ever——"

"Then I'll tell it to you. Keane is madly in love with Mrs.
Paradine. And to-day in Court, when I recalled Marsh and
had him put back in the box, Keane got his death blow."

"Oh—Horfield!"

The Judge looked at her and smiled.

"You silly old woman!" he resumed. "You muddle along and
don't know where you're going, or what are the true aims of

those you come in contact with. You're just one of the innumerable blunderers who clutter up the world. And you actually thought you could play out a hand of trumps against me without making a mistake. An extra ace up your sleeve and God Almighty put it there!"

With sudden brutality he added:

"Go to bed! I've had enough of you and your folly!"

Lady Horfield heaved herself up, and stood for an instant towering, with one hand pressed palm downwards on the dining-room table.

"I *had* to do it, Horfield! I couldn't do otherwise. I didn't know that he—Sir Malcolm—what you've told me. I never suspected—but that doesn't matter. Horfield, you know I've never thought of any man but you, and I can't bear that you should——"

"Go to bed!"

She went awkwardly towards the door. Her big body was shaking.

"I am a fool, I know, and a muddler. But I can see something. Oh, Horfield, you *can't* find happiness, real happiness in the misery and despair of others. No one can. Try—do try—the other way before it's too late!"

"Go to bed!"

She opened the door and got out of the room somehow.

The Judge threw his cigar into the burning logs, put his thin arms on the high mantelpiece and leaned his head on them.

"Women! The way they talk!" he muttered.

He stayed thus with his face hidden for two or three minutes. Then he lifted his head from his arms, turned from the fire and, walking slowly like an invalid, went back to the dinner-table. The brandy Lady Horfield had asked for was by her dessert-plate untouched. The Judge looked at it, took it up and drank it.

"Her brandy!" he muttered.

He sat down at the table and reached out for his own.

"The verdict—to-morrow!" he whispered to himself, as he lifted the glass.

X L

ON THE following morning, which was bitterly cold and wintry, with a drifting of sleet in the early hours, Gay had a struggle with herself. She had arranged with Judith Flaquer to 'stick it out,' and to be present in Court on the last day of the trial. (Judith was sure that the case would finish that day.) But when the morning dawned, and her maid came in to bring her tea and to light her fire, she was seized by a panic of nervous depression and a longing to go away, right away, to get out of London, to go down and bury herself once more in the Surrey cottage. There, unobserved, not forced to act, she could face the result of this hideous trial in solitude. If she had a sort of breakdown—and she felt on the edge of one—there would only be a couple of servants to conceal it from. Or if she couldn't quite conceal it they would probably not understand either its extent or its cause. Whereas here, in London, there must be observation and talk. Already she had a feeling that Mrs. Clemm and Baker were wondering about her, and discussing her daily unaccountable absences from home, her going away mysteriously on foot, missing lunch and returning in the late afternoon. Malcolm, she believed, hadn't noticed anything. But he was in no condition to be observant. He was wrapped up in his own desperation, and if he thought about her at all thought of her as someone from whom, if possible, he must hide the passions which rent him. At dinner on the previous evening he had made no allusion to the events of the day. He had said very little, had scarcely eaten anything, and immediately after dinner had abruptly bidden her good night and gone away to his library. There he had shut himself up, and she had neither seen him nor heard his step again that night. He had looked very worn and ill, and there had been an expression in his eyes now and then which had frightened her. It was a terribly inward look, like that of a man utterly detached from his immediate surroundings, withdrawn in the vast distance of a mind committed to some desperate enterprise of thought which no one must share. It made her realise with painful intensity the utter solitude of the human spirit in moments of crisis. One flesh? Yes; that might perhaps be called possible. The prayer book asserted it, and human beings accepted the assertion. But one spirit? No! Never!

"Malcolm and I have never been one," Gay said to herself. "And we never can be one."

And yet she loved him, and, strangely, never more than now. She had loved him in the past, admiring him, rejoicing in his confident powers, his success in the usage of them, his masculine strength of body and intellect, his pride in her and their common life. Now she loved him with a passion of pity, with tears of the heart for him and for herself. His suffering seemed to wind itself round her like a shirt of Nessus. She was compressed in his silent despair.

She had promised to meet Judith at the flat in Hallam Street, and she walked there at the appointed time, shivering under her furs in the fierce March wind, clouded in an atmosphere of nightmare. But even when she reached the house and was mounting the stairs to the second floor, where the flat of Judith's friend was, she hadn't decided that she would go to the Old Bailey.

"Probably I won't!" she thought. "And then I'll leave a note for Malcolm and go down to Surrey."

Judith opened the door to her. She, too, was wrapped in furs. "Up to time!" she said, as she kissed Gay. "We must be off at once. Your husband will begin his speech directly the Court sits. Papa is sure the verdict will be given some time to-day. Unless of course the Jury should disagree."

She made as if to come out of the flat at once but Gay stopped her.

"Let me come in for one minute, Judy."

"Of course! But what is it?"

Judith drew back. Gay walked in and shut the door, and at once said:

"I don't know whether I'll come, Judy."

"Oh—you must!"

"I thought—I had some idea of going back to Surrey to-day —instead."

Judith put her hands on Gay's shoulders and looked into her eyes.

"Don't go! I understand. I'm sure I understand. But be brave and stay. I believe it is best."

"But, Judy, will she be condemned?"

"I don't know."

"What does your father think?"

"He thinks the Jury may possibly disagree."

"And if they don't?"

Judith hesitated.

"If they don't disagree he thinks she will be condemned?"

"Papa doesn't know. No one can know."

"Does your father think she is guilty?"

"I'm afraid he does," Judith said.

She moved her shoulders.

"After yesterday! That man's confession!"

"But is it proved?"

"Circumstantial evidence! Still there's a chance for her, what people call a sporting chance. Your husband has worked miracles on Juries before now."

"But it seemed to me—I had the impression——" she stopped.

"Yes? What is it?"

"Oh, Judy, didn't Malcolm do great harm in his examination of her? I don't understand these things. I've never been in Court before. But I couldn't help thinking that Sir Joseph Farrell read something that was in Malcolm's mind, and acted on it, and that——"

She stopped again. Judith said nothing. For once she seemed almost painfully embarrassed.

"If it is so, and if she is condemned—perhaps in consequence of that—what will Malcolm do?" Gay said.

Judith didn't answer that question. Instead she said with deep seriousness:

"You mustn't run away. Don't you see that? But after what you've just said you must see it. I think to do that would be almost like cowardice."

Gay flushed and looked down.

"Don't you agree with me?" Judith asked, gently.

They stood in silence for a moment. Then Gay said:

"I will come. But if she is condemned?"

"And if she is set free?"

Judith simply couldn't help saying it, but directly she had said it she bitterly regretted her words. Her brain had taken charge at that moment and had betrayed her heart. That was how she felt it.

"Let's go!" she exclaimed, cursing that rapier-like brain which she couldn't always control, fundamentally kind though she was. "We must see it through. There are things in life one *must* see through. And this is one of them."

Without speaking Gay turned and walked out of the flat.

Down below they picked up a cab and Judith told the chauffeur to drive to the Old Bailey.

"Going to the trial, lady?" said the man.

Judith nodded.

"I'd give a good deal myself to hear the end of it," he said. "I think she done it. But perhaps Sir Malcolm Keane'll get her off."

"The man in the street has a tremendous belief in Sir Malcolm's powers," said Judith, as the cab drove on. "Perhaps he'll justify them once more to-day. But there's Lord Horfield to reckon with."

"Judy," Gay said, in a faltering voice. "I shouldn't be surprised if Malcolm broke down in Court."

"Oh—no!"

"He looked horribly ill at dinner last night."

"And this morning?"

"I haven't seen him. He didn't come to my room. He always comes, but this morning he didn't."

"Sir Malcolm won't break down. Once he gets on his feet all his powers will come to him. I know these practised lawyers. They are like big actors who may arrive at the theatre feeling at death's door, but directly they walk on the stage and *smell* the audience—a nasty expression that but current behind the scenes—are masters of the job they were made for. You'll see I'm right."

"I hope so," said Gay, faintly.

She thought of the silence and the emptiness of the commons round their cottage in Surrey. And this day was only beginning.

The crowd was dense in front of the Old Bailey. The sensational occurrence of the last few days, spread abroad through the newspapers, had roused the attention of the mob. A fever of curiosity to know the result of the trial had taken possession of the town. In the Clubs men, and quite decent men, were betting on Mrs. Paradine's chances. Mrs. Blason had turned down her thumbs, but many others were not so certain. A member of the Government, notorious for his love of a wager, had offered a hundred to one that the Jury would disagree.

With their faces veiled Gay and Judith got out of the cab and managed with great difficulty, helped by a gigantic policeman, to get into the building which to-day at that moment seemed the centre of a horrible world.

"It's the last day of it, ladies!" said their friend, the attendant, cheerily, as he convoyed them to the gallery entrance. "We shall get the verdict some time to-day. As long as I've been here I've never seen such a crowd. One moment!"

As Gay squeezed into the packed gallery an instant later she heard a familiar voice speaking with the clearness and ease of a practised orator. It was Malcolm's; and it gave her the impression of a man completely self-possessed, determined and lucid. She glanced at Judith who whispered:

"What did I tell you? The big actor who smells his audience!"

She did not know how long her husband had been speaking, but he was now dealing with Sir Joseph Farrell's speech for the Crown delivered on the previous day, and was evidently dealing with it viciously. There was concentrated contempt in his voice as he said:

"Gentlemen and ladies of the Jury, in all my long and varied experience at the Bar I have never listened to such a biased and cruel attack on a prisoner, a *woman* prisoned mind you, delivered with such venom, and supported by so little evidence, as the speech we were obliged to listen to in this Court yesterday."

He continued in this strain for some time, dealing with the opening of Sir Joseph's speech, with his 'brutal sneers' at the prisoner's early association with the noble-minded and chivalrous American who, from purely altruistic motives, had saved a young girl from a life that was worse than death, and 'grotesque endeavour' even to make capital against the prisoner out of the fact that, having studied the Swedish method of massage, 'famous throughout the world,' she had called herself, for the purposes of her profession, a qualified 'Swedish masseuse.'

"Nothing," he said, "has been too trivial, nothing too harmless, to escape the learned Counsel's envenomed attention. The fact of the matter is, as I hope presently to convince you, that it has fallen to his lot to endeavour to make bricks without having any straw in his possession. He has had to try to build up an indictment of this unfortunate lady without having anything really tangible to go upon. He has been hard put to it, and there were moments in his discourse when I was really disposed to pity him. But—" here he stopped for an instant, looked hard at the Jury box, then added—"my inclination towards pity was soon transformed into a righteous indignation at the really outrageous handling of my client by the learned Counsel, who seemed entirely to overlook the fact that in our English Courts what we require in order to convict the accused person is not insinuation, however crafty, not implication, however sinister, but proof. Proof!" He repeated the word, raising his powerful voice till it rang through the crowded Court. "The learned Counsel for the Crown has been sent here to supply proof that my client is a cold-blooded, determined murderess. Let us see if he has supplied it. Nothing else will do. Suggestion is of no use, suspicion of no avail, possibilities, even probabilities, are ruled out. In England, members of the Jury, to bring a human creature full of life, of powers, of yearnings, of that love for the glory of existence which we all alike share, to the scaffold, you must deliver proof that he or she is guilty of taking deliberately the life of another. Now let us see whether the learned Counsel for the Crown has delivered any proof, or shadow of proof, that my client is so guilty. Let us put passion and prepossession aside, and coldly examine into what he has thought fit to offer you for the conviction of my client, and the sending of her, still young, still full of life and great possibilities, into the eternal silence from which there is no return."

Gay was amazed at the energy and force of his voice and manner. Was it possible that this was the weary and desperate-looking man, with the furtive eyes and embarrassed manner, with whom she had dined on the previous evening, the man who, when dinner was over, had slunk away to shut himself up and be

alone till the morning? She had come into the Court drowned
in nervous depression, fearful of what might happen, not merely
to Mrs. Paradine in the Dock but also to her husband in the
place set aside for Counsel. But evidently her fears had been
groundless. It was obvious that Malcolm was in full possession
of all his faculties, full of fight, full of confidence in the result
of his efforts.

But how he hated Sir Joseph Farrell! Or was this merely an
exhibition of feigned indignation for the benefit of the Jury?
Gay wasn't sure, and she glanced at Judith, who was looking
at her.

"Is it genuine, Judy?" she whispered.

"What?"

"Malcolm's anger with Sir Joseph?"

"Horribly genuine!" returned Judith under her breath. "He
knows that Sir Joseph's cue came from *him*. That's why he hates
him."

With a rush Gay's nervous terror returned upon her. She
felt an actual sickness of fear.

But Malcolm was, again coldly, examining the case for the
Crown.

During this section of his elaborate speech for the Defence
he dropped all the arts of rhetoric, withdrew all passion and
wrath from his manner, and made his appeal to the brains, rather
than to the hearts of the Jury.

He dealt with what he called 'the fatuous groping about of
the Crown to discover an adequate motive for the murder which
it was sought to fasten upon the prisoner.' One might really
suppose, he said, that the Crown had not troubled to get up a
genuine case against the prisoner at all. Where was the motive
for such a murder as the prisoner was accused of? The Crown
could only put forward, in the opening of the trial, a tissue
of absurdities about the supposed unhappiness of the prisoner
in her married life. He dealt separately with the evidence of
the various witnesses, servants and others, who had been called
to speak to Colonel Paradine's fits of temper, and so forth, which
had recoiled upon his wife. 'Family jars!' he called them.
"Domestic quarrels and differences such as occur in nine out of
ten ménages. Do people," he inquired, "who are not completely

mad, and so not responsible for their actions, commit cold-blooded murders because of storms in tea-cups, passing tiffs about the trifles which crop up here and there in all lives, and on which opinions may differ? If it were so, what wife, what husband, would be safe?" He put it to the Jury, men and women of experience in the traffic of daily life, whether such a murder as was alleged against the prisoner could have taken place with such a motive as the Crown had absurdly brought forward at the beginning of their case.

All this was lightly and confidently dealt with. But Keane's manner completely changed to deep gravity when presently he said:

"The other, purely impromptu motive, with which Counsel for the Crown later made such melodramatic play in his closing speech—what I may call the William Marsh motive—I will deal with later. That is a very different thing. I will now content myself, and relieve you, members of the Jury, of boredom and weariness, by brushing aside as utterly unworthy of serious consideration the domestic unhappiness motive which Counsel, misreading, as I think, your united intelligence, thought fit to endeavour to interest you in—till he got hold of what he obviously thought something better. Enough of that!"

He made a movement with his right hand, as if brushing something away.

Then, changing his manner, he drew a picture of the prisoner's 'life of devotion in that house in the North, alone with her blinded hero,' representing her as passionately attached to her husband and full of a romantic desire to solace his darkness and bring him the happiness that only a woman's love and tenderness could create for a man who had suffered and must suffer to the end of his days. At this point in his speech he used with great effect the personal knowledge of Hindley which he had gathered when up in the North. With the skill of an accomplished novelist, he created for the Jury a life in which Mrs. Paradine was the heroine, Colonel Paradine the suffering hero. He did not fail to draw the Jury's attention to the fact that no witness had been called to prove that Mrs. Paradine had been a neglectful or indifferent wife. Even those of the servants who were 'vaguely hostile to her' had not dared to perjure themselves by representing her as callous, as a seeker after pleasure. She never absented herself from her husband. Always she was to be found with, or near, him. She bore with his occasional outbursts of temper and moods of despair with devoted resignation and charity.

Mrs. Paradine gradually emerged in his speech as a woman of exceptionally fine character who had dedicated her life to a man whom she loved.

Through all this section of his speech, Keane left William Marsh aside, only just mentioning him as one of the household in attendance upon Colonel Paradine. He concentrated on Mrs. Paradine and her husband, throwing the high light on them, presenting them in a sort of romantic isolation, linked by a deep affection though shadowed by the sorrow inevitably caused by the Colonel's affliction. And so skilful was his handling of the life up at Hindley that he held the crowd in the Court enthralled by it, and sent a shock that was unmistakable from one end of the Court to the other when, suddenly pulling up, after a brief silence, he said in a low but penetrating voice:

"But this close intimacy which I have ventured to describe to you, ladies and gentlemen, was unfortunately not an intimacy confined to two persons who loved each other. There was a third person included in it, a man of unusual character whom you have seen and heard in this Court, the soldier servant of Colonel Paradine, the perjured witness, William Marsh, who has blatantly asserted before you his own crime of perjury, and who, I venture to say, perjured himself again when he did so."

And he went on to deal scathingly with Marsh's character, calling him again and again 'that perjured man,' the 'self-confessed liar, whom you have seen and heard in the box.' He drew Marsh as a dangerous man of intense and furious passions, who, having been turned to hatred of women by a disappointment in love when he was young, had for years lived the life of a soured ascetic, 'bottling up the violent physical desires which ravaged him, and which, having no natural outlet, increased within him like water rising behind a dam, until finally they took complete possession of him and drove him to the persecution of Mrs. Paradine which she has reluctantly—*very* reluctantly—testified to in that box.'

He alluded to the fact, 'so frankly acknowledged by the prisoner,' that she had been born in humble circumstances and had once been a servant, and suggested that Marsh, having come to know of this, had been misled into thinking that he, with his certainly remarkable appearance and impudent self-assurance, would have the less difficulty in gaining his end with his master's wife, more especially as that master was blind and therefore prohibited by his affliction from observing what went on around him.

He dealt at some length with this, by him assumed, 'persecution' of Mrs. Paradine by Marsh, evidently with the intention of hypnotising the Jury into the absolute conviction that Mrs. Paradine's testimony as to that matter was true, and explained her reluctance to speak of it to her husband by the fact that for years Colonel Paradine, deceived as to Marsh's true character, had relied upon him and trusted him absolutely, and must certainly be made most unhappy by such a revelation of his treachery and baseness.

"But at last it *had* to come out," he finally said. "This unfortunate lady could no longer endure this continual and loathsome persecution of a frustrated libertine, and she went to her husband and told him the whole truth."

Leaving aside William Marsh and his baseness for a moment, he then dealt carefully with Colonel Paradine's two illnesses at Hindley, the evidence of the doctors and the removal of the family to London 'at the suggestion of my client.' He did not attempt to minimise the fact of arsenic having been found in Colonel Paradine's body, but contented himself with observing that it seemed very strange that if it was Mrs. Paradine who had administered the arsenic, as to which there was no evidence, and not someone else of the household, or even the Colonel himself, *she* should have been the one to suggest a removal to London in order that a first-rate specialist should overhaul her husband thoroughly to see if there was anything serious the matter with him.

"Does a would-be poisoner do this?" he inquired of the Jury. "Does such an action commend itself to your intelligence as reasonable and likely on the part of a potential murderess?"

Counsel for the Crown had actually had the assurance to suggest that the prisoner had urged the removal to London, and the calling in of expert advice, simply in order to lull all suspicion to rest when she had actually achieved her object and done away with her husband. In doing that, he had surely underrated the intelligence of the Jury. Even a collection of schoolboys would be unable to swallow that, much less twelve grown-up people of mature age and vast and varied experience of life. A woman, fully seized with the resolve to do away with her husband, would scarcely be such a fool as immediately beforehand to get a famous doctor to give him a clean bill of health. Really, the Counsel for the Crown might have tried to find a better explanation of what happened than that. But the fact of the matter was that the learned Counsel was intent upon getting the Jury to believe, willy-nilly, that the prisoner was an amazingly crafty and daringly audacious fiend of a woman, subtle in plotting, ingenious in the inventions of *coups,* far-seeing in the execution of her horrible plans.

"The London doctor—merely called in to throw suspicion later on off the scent!"

And yet this self-same woman later on is presented to the Jury as going to her husband and actually blurting out to him the whole story of a debased intrigue with his valet which he had never suspected, and which, being blind, he never would have suspected.

"A sly, crafty, far-seeing, far-planning fiend, and at the same time a woman so preposterously passionate and impetuous that she rushes to the husband she has deceived, and gives herself and her infamy away to him, without reason—for there is no evidence that Colonel Paradine had ever suspected that anything objectionable, to use no stronger word, was taking place in his household! Is such a woman conceivably possible, or is she merely the distorted invention of a learned Counsel at his wit's end to put a plausible case before a Jury he is afraid of?"

Soon after this contemptuous question, which Keane delivered with jeering bitterness, turning as he did so markedly towards the place where Sir Joseph Farrell was sitting motionless with an impassive countenance and an air of supreme detachment, he came to grips with what he called 'the core of this extraordinary story of human disaster.'

Two attempts at poisoning with arsenic, and no evidence at all to connect the prisoner with the purchase of arsenic or with the possession of arsenic. A successful attempt at destroying life with antimony, in the form of tartar emetic, and no evidence of any kind to connect the prisoner with such antimony! A strange mystery indeed—a strange lack of evidence! No proof at all! Nothing but suggestions, implications, innuendoes! And the whole tottering evidence based upon—what? The frantic assertions of a self-confessed perjuror!

What was it, he asked, that really took place in the house in Eaton Square on the day before Colonel Paradine's death? Three versions had been placed before the Jury, two by the witness, William Marsh, one, and only one, by the prisoner. William Marsh, in his first version, had sworn that the violent scene in the study had been caused by Mrs. Paradine's having gone to her husband and falsely asserted that he, William Marsh, intended to leave the Colonel's service, and had come to her and had confided his intention to her. Later the prisoner had been put in the box and had given her version, that she had been at last driven by Marsh's conduct to tell her husband about it and to ask him to dismiss Marsh from his service. Marsh, evidently roused to fury by this exposure of his perfidy to his master, had got up in Court and given her the lie, committing thereby the grossest contempt of Court that he, Counsel, had ever assisted at. Then a most grossly irregular thing had occurred——

Here the Judge sternly interrupted Counsel and called him to order. There had been no gross irregularity. It was within the competence of the Judge to recall any witness to clear up any point that had been left in doubt, the only purpose of a trial being to elicit the whole truth of the matter tried so that justice might be done.

"I call upon the learned Counsel to withdraw those words," he said.

Keane stood for a moment in silence, facing the Judge with an angry look on his face. Then he said, in a contemptuous voice:

"Oh, very well, my Lord! As you order me, I withdraw!"

He then immediately turned to the Jury and continued his speech.

Then a most unusual thing had occurred. William Marsh had been recalled, although after his cross-examination the learned Counsel for the Crown had not bothered to re-examine him, and had been permitted to make a sort of confession to the Jury, a thing unprecedented in his, Counsel's, experience. And what a confession it had been! An unmanly, repulsive attempt to counter the prisoner's reluctant avowal—how reluctant everyone in that Court must have noticed!—reluctant avowal of Marsh's pursuit of her by the foul, trumped-up assertion that *she* had pestered *him*, with her attentions. Stung by the prisoner's admission of the ugly truth, Marsh had thought to defend himself and ruin her by piling perjury on perjury, throwing the surely natural chivalry due from man to woman to the winds, and showing himself in his true colours, a coarse, brutal liar, a coward and one treacherous to his trust.

Keane then dealt with all that followed after the conclusion of the scene in the study, dwelling specially on Marsh's extraordinary audacity in trying, after what had occurred, to force himself upon the unfortunate Colonel, 'who only wanted never to be with him again.' Even Marsh himself, though a brazen liar, had been forced to acknowledge that his master's last words to him were 'Get out of my sight!' Did not these words point to the truth of the prisoner's account of what happened? Were they not a convincing proof that her version was the true one?

He then examined minutely the incidents already revealed to the Jury, and the conduct, spoken to, of the protagonists in 'this extraordinary drama.' And here he sprung a sensational surprise upon the Jury and all those in Court.

"When I first took up this case," he said, "more than one theory presented itself to my mind. One was this: that the death of Colonel Paradine was an assisted suicide, not an actual murder, not a murder, that is, in the ordinary sense of that word."

He then outlined his reasons for thinking that that might have been possible, considering the Colonel's misery caused by his blindness and consequent growing indifference to life. Without mentioning Marsh by name he suggested that a suicide, in the circumstances, would probably have been very difficult, if not impossible, without the help of someone, and that it had come into his mind that the Colonel might have prevailed upon one deeply devoted to him, *not necessarily a woman*, to help him to get out of life.

"The course events have taken, however," he continued, "have convinced me that that was not what occurred. In my view this is undoubtedly a case of deliberate murder. But I contend that there is absolutely no proof that it was committed by the prisoner.

I do not accuse, directly, anyone else of it, but let us see, examining
the facts without passion, whether anyone, besides the prisoner,
could have obtained access to the Burgundy in which it is as certain as anything can be that the poison which killed Colonel Paradine was placed. Three persons, besides the prisoner, could have had
access to that wine. One was the butler who poured it out and
placed the glass on the Colonel's night-table, another was the
Colonel himself, a third was the prisoner, and a fourth was——"
he paused, then added, "the perjured witness, William Marsh."

He then dismissed the butler from his purview, observing that
he could have had absolutely no motive in committing the crime.
He dismissed Colonel Paradine, who might have had a motive in
taking his own life, but who could hardly have managed to poison
the wine without some assistance from outside.

"Two persons remain, the prisoner and William Marsh."

"At *last* it's narrowed down to that!" whispered Judith to Gay.

"Yes!" Gay breathed, without looking at her friend.

Keane then dealt with the incidents sworn to, showing that
Marsh, 'for some inexplicable reason,' hung about on the landing
outside the Colonel's door after he had been ordered to go away.
The Colonel had left his room and gone to the lavatory. For a short
time his bedroom was left empty, the glass of Burgundy presumably in it. During part of that time William Marsh was up there
on the first floor and Mrs. Paradine was shut up in her bedroom;
during part of it Mrs. Paradine was there alone, except for the
Colonel's presence locked up in the lavatory. There was no evidence as to how long the Colonel remained in the lavatory. Who
entered the Colonel's bedroom during that short space of time and
introduced the poison that undoubtedly killed him into the wine?

"Nobody knows!" said Keane, slowly and impressively. "Or
ever will know for certain. For there is no proof whatever of anyone having entered that room. The fact is that there were two
persons who could have entered it—had they so desired. One is the
prisoner, the other is William Marsh. Which of these two persons
had the most cogent motive for committing the crime?

"You, ladies and gentlemen of the Jury, have heard the evidence,
and have seen, and therefore are able to judge of the characters
of the witnesses. It is for you to decide that according to your consciences. You have had before you the prisoner, whose evidence

was not upset in cross-examination, and William Marsh, who al-most ardently gave testimony that he was a liar and therefore unworthy of trust. And now I have nearly done, but there are just one or two points I should like to deal with if you will bear with me for a few minutes more."

He then came to the curious circumstance of Mrs. Paradine's playing upon the drawing-room piano, between her visit to her bedroom for the purpose of arranging her hair and her retirement for the night.

"The learned Counsel for the Crown," he said, "always venom-ously intent on presenting my client to you as a monster of perfidious audacity, has dwelt upon that piano playing as an in-fernally clever and cold-blooded ruse to make it impossible for anyone to believe that the prisoner is guilty. According to him, this is what the prisoner did. As soon as she had seen Marsh leave the landing with Ellen Smith, through the crack in the partially opened door of her bedroom—no evidence that the door wasn't fast shut, but never mind! . . . such trifles don't trouble my learned brother!—as soon as she had seen that, she stole into her husband's bedroom, poisoned his wine with antimony, and then stole back to her room. The Colonel returned from the lavatory. Then Mrs. Paradine calmly went downstairs, and for half an hour or so played brilliant waltz music on the piano—this while wait-ing for the poison to be swallowed and to begin its deadly work. She then went up to bed, in presumably a happy mood, and retired to rest. She has given evidence that she fell asleep. If she did—according to the learned Counsel—that is only one more proof of her monstrous self-possession and cold-blooded indifference. A monster! He presents you with a monster!

"The prisoner, on the other hand, says that she never visited her husband's room or was aware that anyone else visited it. How easily, were she a crafty liar, might not she have said that she saw Marsh on the first landing, as he saw her, thus seeking, perhaps, to divert suspicion from herself to another. But no, she says that she did not see Marsh. She does not try to suggest that anyone, not herself, might have done the awful deed. She tells the simple truth, even when a lie might perhaps serve her purpose of proving her innocence better. She did not see Marsh and she says so. Hav-ing arranged her hair, and put some eau de Cologne on her forehead, it being too early to go to bed—what does she do? Does what any innocent woman might do, goes to her drawing-room and, to soothe her nerves after the tragedy in the study, plays on the piano for half an hour or so. Then to bed—and to sleep! That is *her* version, I venture to say the version of a perfectly innocent woman.

"Now, one other point!

"The prisoner, according to her evidence, was waked up by her husband's voice. And when wide awake she heard him shouting, 'Marsh! Marsh! Marsh!' "

Keane gave the word out with a harsh denunciatory vehemence which startled and thrilled the Court.

"Now the learned Counsel for the Crown has tried to persuade you that the Colonel in his agony was calling for his faithful and well loved servant to help him, and was deliberately avoiding calling to his wife, who he knew to be sleeping next door—even in his last agony differentiating between a woman he had done with and a man he still clung to. I suggest something very different. I suggest that the dying man—" he stopped, as if scarcely daring to continue—then said: "I will put it in this way. I suggest that the cry was not a cry for help, but a shout of despairing denunciation. I will leave it there, ladies and gentlemen of the Jury. I will say no more than that."

After saying this Keane made a very long pause. Then, speaking more slowly and with less intensity, he dealt with all that had happened immediately before and after the death of the Colonel, and with the eventual arrest of Mrs. Paradine accused of the murder of her husband. He closed a very long and closely reasoned speech, broken here and there by passages of vehement and fiery rhetoric, in an almost strangely earnest and simple way. He said:

"I will not attempt to keep from you the fact that this case has caused me many troubled days and sleepless nights, severe toil of brain and great anguish of mind. I have certainly never had a case given to me that has engaged my sympathy so closely and at the same time caused me such acute and wearing anxiety lest I should be found wanting in the conduct of it. Very early in my acquaintance with the prisoner I came to the conclusion that she was undoubtedly innocent of the crime of which she was accused. On examining into the case, as my duty was, I could find no proof at all that she committed the crime. No poison, either arsenic or antimony, was traced to her possession, and I could discover no cogent motive which could have driven her to so awful a crime as murder. I came to this Court, therefore, on the first day of the trial with almost the certainty of easily obtaining her acquittal. But I cannot but realise now that an element has been introduced into this case which has been a complete surprise to me who never anticipated it. The fate of the prisoner, against whom I contend that no direct proof at all of a criminal intention has been adduced, still less of a criminal action, may, I realise, hang, rightly or wrongly, upon what you, the Jury, believe—whether you believe the evidence of my client or whether you believe the evidence, the, as I consider, irregularly introduced evidence, of William Marsh. That he lied persistently in his answers to my cross-examination of him was of course obvious to me, and to every person in this Court. When he left the box we all knew that we had been listening to the assertion of one who was false to his oath, deliberately and of set purpose false. I contend, with the great Schopenhauer, that a man who shows the cloven hoof once is certain to show it again, that a man who, after swearing on the Bible to tell the truth, lies, will do the same thing again, that such a man's word can never be trusted, that any evidence he may give subsequently is worth no more than dust upon the wind. I hope and believe that you will agree with me. If you trust William Marsh's word, if you rely upon him, in my view you run a terrible risk of causing an awful miscarriage of justice. I feel it my solemn duty to warn you of that. Marsh obviously perjured himself in cross-examination. Then followed the examination, and the most extraordinary cross-examination of my client. Counsel for the Crown sprang upon us the astounding suggestion, obviously an improvisation of the last moment and never contemplated till then by the prosecution, that the prisoner had cherished a guilty passion for Marsh and had even succeeded in bending Marsh to her foul purpose. And Marsh, recalled, swore that this was the case. If you, ladies and gentlemen of the Jury, can bring yourselves to believe such a monstrous proposition, backed up only by the testimony of a perjuror, a proposition formulated at the very last moment when the Crown must have realised that there was practically no case to go to the

Jury, then you may believe that the prisoner had some motive for getting rid of her husband. But just think what it implies! It implies that the prisoner actually went to her blind husband and told him, for no earthly reason, what he would never have found out for himself, the story of her sin. Who but a mad woman would do such a thing? Counsel for the Crown suggested that the prisoner did it in an outburst of frantic rebellion against the life she was leading, that she did it thinking that then she could get away from her husband and that Marsh would be driven out with her, that she did it in an access of passion which made her completely reckless of consequences. Can you believe this? I have had considerable knowledge of life and of human nature and I simply cannot. On one side stands Mrs. Paradine, on the other William Marsh. Take your choice between them, which is the truth teller, which is worthy of your belief, and may God guide you to choose aright."

In delivering this last passage of his long speech Keane, although he dropped all the arts of an accomplished spellbinder which he had previously employed, often with great effect, and spoke with a sort of bare sincerity and with great simplicity of manner, seemed deeply moved, and in speaking the closing sentences his voice was clouded with emotion, and twice he paused as if unable to control it and fearing to break down. Those who, knowing him well as an advocate, were expecting from him a thrilling peroration, were surprised at the almost fading quietude of his conclusion. And yet it moved them greatly. This was not the tremendous appeal of an accomplished orator but the plea of a man who was certainly terribly moved by some emotion which he was with difficulty controlling. His voice shook and almost died away when, after putting the question "Can you believe this?" he added, "I have had considerable knowledge of life and of human nature and I simply cannot." The final words he seemed to utter to himself, to the deeply brooding mind of him.

"I cannot—I cannot!" Did they not go echoing down into him? Judith Flaquer, listening to them, added mentally to them the additional words:

"I will not!"

"Poor Sir Malcolm!" she thought.

And at that moment her heart, which had not bled for the woman in the Dock, bled for him.

The Court had sat unusually late to allow Keane to finish his speech. It now rose for the luncheon interval.

When that was over the Judge would begin his summing up.

It had got about that whatever happened, however long the Jury might spend in debate, unless they were hopelessly divided, and could not see any hope of reaching an agreement, the Judge would remain in the building till a verdict was given.

XLI

LORD HORFIELD began his summing up by saying to the Jury that the case they had to try had been marked by certain features which were, to say the least, unusual and put it out of the category of most murder cases. One of these features was the sudden and unexpected decision of those responsible for the Defence to call no witnesses, with the one exception of the prisoner in the Dock. That seemed to be an afterthought, arrived at seemingly after the case had proceeded some way. And it appeared to indicate that the Defence considered the case against the prisoner to be of comparatively little account. It would be for the Jury to decide whether they fell in with this view. Another unusual feature was the utter failure of the Crown to trace the possession of the two poisons which were undoubtedly employed against the dead man, Colonel Paradine, to anyone in his household. There was no evidence at all that anyone in the Hindley Hall household ever purchased arsenic. Nor was there any evidence that anyone in the Eaton Square household purchased antimony in the form of tartar emetic. Yet it was as certain as could be that Colonel Paradine was twice made ill by arsenic, and was eventually killed by the administration of antimony. A third unusual feature was the fact of the witness, William Marsh, after the extraordinary incident of which the Jury had cognisance, retracting the evidence which he had given, and on returning to the witness-box confessing that in his evidence in chief he had committed perjury. There

were also one or two other features in the case which had struck
him, but which he would leave aside for the moment, and would
probably touch upon, as not unimportant, at a later period in his
summing up.

The Judge then, in an always clear and charming voice and
with transparent lucidity, traced the history of Mrs. Paradine, so
far as it had been made known, from her difficult beginning in
Copenhagen to her marriage with Colonel Paradine. Apropos of
the latter he remarked that such a marriage might have been
prompted only by love and admiration and pity. On the other
hand the Jury would remember that Colonel Paradine's social
position was excellent and that he was a rich man. Ambition
might possibly, therefore, have had something to do with so uneven a marriage, the prisoner having been at one time a domestic
servant and subsequently a masseuse.

Coming to the married life at Hindley Hall the Judge dealt
with it minutely, examining the evidence of all the witnesses,
servants and visitors to the house, a considerable body of evidence
from which emerged one quite definite fact, namely that the
married life of those two curiously mated people, of different
classes and different nationalities, was by no means untroubled.
Colonel Paradine was certainly a man who was 'ill to live with.'
Many instances of this fact had been given in evidence. The Judge
recapitulated them. It would be for the Jury to decide how such
conduct would be likely to affect a young woman like the prisoner, secluded from the world in this somewhat remote place,
buried in the country, and surrounded by strangers, her only
companion a blind man whose mind was painfully affected by his
affliction. Apparently at that time the prisoner, Mrs. Paradine,
had shown a great deal of patience and resignation with her lot.
There was no evidence that she had displayed any weariness of
this curiously uneventful life. On the contrary she had appeared
thoroughly satisfied with it. It would be for the Jury to decide in
their minds whether there was any extraneous reason for this
contentment, or seeming contentment, of a beautiful and still
young woman with such an existence.

In this passage of his speech the Judge's voice took on a faintly
sinister tone and he glanced for a moment at the Jury with an
almost inquiring look on his long pale face.

This existence, monotonous in essence though frequently complicated by the disagreeable ebullitions of the blind man's ill-humour and depression, was presently broken by the two sudden attacks of illness which had been described by witnesses.

The Judge went thoroughly into the evidence connected with these attacks, drawing special attention to Mrs. Paradine's behaviour during and after them.

"She appeared to take them rather lightly, if the evidence is to be believed, but she has explained that by saying that she agreed with the doctors summoned that her husband was merely suffering from dyspepsia. You will note nevertheless that she expressed the opinion—if the evidence is to be believed—that country doctors were fools, and afterwards persuaded her husband to make a journey to London in order, so she said, that he might be examined by a specialist. Whether there is any contradiction here I must leave for your consideration. An additional reason for her desire to get away from Hindley is that connected with Colonel Paradine's body-servant, the witness, William Marsh—if you accept her evidence as true. It is somewhat difficult to understand why a removal to London should have benefited her in this connection, but I will go into that presently. At all events the removal to London took place, a house in Eaton Square having been rented for some months."

The Judge then came rapidly to what he called 'the strange tragedy towards which these three lives had, perhaps for long, been tending,' not omitting, however to touch upon everything in any way pertinent to the case: the visit to the London specialist, his report upon Colonel Paradine's health, and the contradiction between the Colonel's apparent good condition of body and unhappy state of mind which had been brought out in the evidence. Hitherto the Judge had, as some thought strangely, avoided connecting William Marsh closely with Colonel and Mrs. Paradine. But now, with a slight change of voice which immediately deepened the already strained curiosity of all those in Court, he said:

"It is necessary now to draw your close attention to the psychological problem which makes this case so peculiar, and in some ways so unprecedented. In a great many cases of murder, perhaps in most cases, the motive is either mercenary or passionate; that is to say that murder is most often committed either *for* money, or for some reason connected with love, such as jealousy. At the beginning of this case you probably noticed that there seemed no special motive for the murder of Colonel Paradine, if he was murdered. The learned Counsel for the Crown dwelt upon the Colonel's ill-temper and depression, the dullness and loneliness of the life at Hindley Hall, and so forth. But it probably occurred to you, as it did to me, that few murders have been committed because a husband was irritable, and because life with him was somewhat dull and lacking in variety. It needs more than that to drive a human being to commit murder. But of course, remember, it is for the prosecution to prove their case. Then the witness, William Marsh, was brought forward by the Crown, and at once a psychological factor of importance was introduced into this case."

The Judge proceeded to deal minutely with Marsh's evidence in chief and with his character, as it had come before the Jury up to that point in the trial, carefully giving him full credit for all the good qualities placed to his account by the various witnesses who had preceded him. Counsel for the Crown, he observed, went, like Agag, somewhat delicately in the examination of Marsh, and Marsh seemed also to thread his way delicately through his replies. An apparent inclination to caution had seemed noticeable on both sides, and the Jury had probably been struck by it as he had been. But as the examination proceeded a crescendo of feeling was obvious in the witness, which reached a culminating point when Counsel asked him questions about the scene in the study in Eaton Square which preceded the Colonel's death, and which, it might be —the Jury would consider and decide as to that—it might be had led to that death. Here the witness had shown marked personal hostility towards the prisoner and had given his reasons for that hostility. He had sworn that the prisoner had told lies to his Colonel about him, her purpose being to get him dismissed from his employment. The reason for that purpose and desire, according to him, was that she was jealous of him because of the confidence his Colonel showed in him. Other reasons were vaguely hinted at but not expressly defined. The Judge re-read Marsh's evidence about this scene and then added: "At a later period of this trial, when I recalled him, the witness took back all he had said, and swore that, in saving it, he had perjured himself. This being so, it may be desirable that you should treat his first evidence about the scene in the study as unworthy of your consideration. Dismiss it or not from your minds, but take account of it in so far as it tends, in your opinion, to the elucidation of the psychology of the witness. You will, perhaps, agree with me that William Marsh is no ordinary man, but is a man of violent feeling and perhaps of violent passions. Counsel for the Defence sought to show that he is, or was, a hater of women, and cross-questioned him to that effect. The Defence had in reserve apparently witnesses ready to speak to that. But as these witnesses were never called it is for you to consider whether the cross-examination of the Defence established that proposition. Marsh denied it. It is for you to decide whether you believe this denial."

The Judge then went into the question, 'the very important question,' as he called it, of the relations existing between Mrs. Paradine and Marsh, so far as it had been possible to gather them from the evidence adduced.

"It is as well to remember in regard to this," he said, "that the prisoner at one time belonged to the domestic servant class, and that Marsh became aware of this—how, we have not been told. It is for you to consider whether the prisoner is likely to have informed him of the fact, for some purpose of her own, but there is no evidence of that."

At this point in the summing-up Keane showed great uneasiness and half-rose in his seat as if to make some protest. The Judge, however, continued rather rapidly and Keane sank back without speaking, with a tormented expression on his face.

"Here you have a former servant risen to the position of the mistress of a wealthy household, this household containing a man of evidently strong character and violent feelings, formerly batman to the master of the house, completely trusted by him, having served in his regiment through the Great War, and who has known his master for longer than the lady who became his master's wife. Owing to the blindness of Colonel Paradine, Marsh was to him almost more than a servant, a sort of companion and help in every way, perpetually about him at all times. A very special relationship which should be borne in mind in connection with this very difficult case. It has been sought to establish that Marsh, to some extent a woman-hater, disliked the prisoner, that he was jealous of her in connection with his master and that she was jealous of him. There is a conflict of evidence on this point. But there is, of course, a direct conflict of evidence throughout as to the relations between William Marsh and the prisoner. The prisoner has said, apparently with great reluctance which you have perhaps taken note of, that Marsh, although said to be a woman-hater, pursued her with his unwelcome and resented attentions both at Hindley Hall and, later, in London. She says she bore this persecution in silence for a long time, for many months, never saying a word about it to anybody, and that eventually she spoke of it to her husband, thereby provoking the terrible scene on the afternoon preceding the Colonel's sudden death. A strange thing is this, that nobody in the Hindley Hall household, so far as we know, ever noticed anything unusual in Marsh's behaviour to his mistress. Servants, we know, are acute observers, to say no more, of what goes on in any household to which they are attached. Very little escapes their attention. Is it not strange that if Marsh pursued his mistress for months with attentions which she resented, not one person in the house should ever have suspected it? On the other hand Marsh, when recalled and examined by me, swore that the prisoner, having apparently fallen in love with him, pursued him with her attentions and eventually, overcoming his resistance, caused him on one occasion only to have guilty relations with her, thus being false to his blind master, to whom he professed himself entirely devoted. And, again, no one in the household, if this be true, apparently ever noticed this pursuit by the prisoner of one of their fellow servants. In regard to this, I should like to suggest to you a question which your experience of life will perhaps enable you to answer. Which is most likely—that a man such as Marsh, pursuing his mistress with his attentions, should be crafty enough so to manage it that he entirely failed to arouse the suspicions of his fellow servants; or that a woman, such as the prisoner, pursuing Marsh in a somewhat similar manner, should be subtle and clever enough to avoid all suspicion? You know men. You know women. You have seen and heard both Marsh and the prisoner. I leave it for you to decide."

The Judge made a long pause at this point in his summing-up, as if he were considering what to say next. He leaned over his notes and seemed to be reading something. The crowd sat in silence. Most of the Jury were gazing at the prisoner, who remained quite still, looking down. At length, raising his head, the Judge took up again the thread of his discourse.

He drew attention to the fact that ten days before Colonel Paradine's first attack of illness, he had made a new will, leaving his wife £4,000 a year and Marsh an annuity of £200.

"Both these persons, therefore, stood to benefit monetarily by the death of the Colonel. But both were able to lead an exceedingly comfortable and, materially speaking, pleasant life so long as he lived—*unless anything should occur which might cause him to have a change of heart towards them.*"

Again the Judge paused and glanced over his notes.

"Calculated!" whispered Judith Flaquer in the gallery. "He wants that to sink in."

"If, however," the Judge said, speaking slowly, "such an incident did occur, causing such a change of heart as I have suggested, it is obvious that it would be in the interest of both these persons that the Colonel's death should occur before he had time to alter his will. We have it in evidence that a terrible scene took place in the Eaton Square study a few hours before Colonel Paradine's death by poison, and that he was undoubtedly in a fury, and that he left the study and went upstairs and refused to dine with his wife, and dined alone, and, later, refused to permit William Marsh to stay in his room and help him to bed, and that, so far as we can ascertain, he never held any intercourse with either of these two persons again. It seems therefore that he died cherishing intense anger against both these persons. Both of them, therefore, might well consider that they were, materially speaking, in grave danger. Should the Colonel alter his will, both might be left penniless. Whether this fact constitutes a motive for murder I leave to your consideration."

The Judge then described the scene in the study, contrasting the prisoner's version of what had occurred with William Marsh's second version, given after his recall and in examination by the Judge himself; Marsh's first version being ruled out as a tissue of lies on Marsh's own confession.

"Here we have a direct conflict of evidence," he said. "One witness giving the lie to the other. The prisoner's version is that she complained to her husband of Marsh's pursuit of her and asked for his dismissal. Marsh's version is that when he came into the room the Colonel told him that the prisoner had made a confession of guilty intercourse with him, Marsh, and that eventually, in spite of his attempts at evasion of the truth, he was forced to acknowledge that the prisoner's confession was true. The prisoner flatly denies that she ever made such a confession or ever had guilty intercourse with Marsh. Now"—here the Judge spoke very impressively, dwelling on his words—"it is your duty to judge between these two persons, and the verdict you will give must, I venture to say, depend greatly on your judgment of them. You now *know* that Marsh is capable of perjury. He has confessed it. Whether the prisoner is so capable I leave to your decision. You saw and heard her under cross-examination by Counsel for the Crown. Are you satisfied that she was speaking the truth? If not, and if you believe that Marsh, when examined by me, was telling the truth at last, it will be for you to decide whether that truth provided the prisoner with an adequate motive for murder. It has been said that nobody but a mad woman would have blurted out such a confession, as Marsh alleges the prisoner made, to a blind husband who could not see what was taking place around him, and so had no means of finding out the truth for himself. Against that we have the impulsiveness that is often characteristic of passionate women driven beyond the verge of caution by the wild desires of love. It may be—I do not say that it was—that is for you to say—it may be that the prisoner had arrived at a point when she could not stand the life she was leading any longer and was carried away by a determination to end it—to burn her boats, in the well-known phrase. That impulse may have led to confession, and the confession once made—to a further course of action. You are the judges of that. I think it right to remind you at this point that Marsh, when I asked him if the alleged guilty intercourse between him and the prisoner took place before, or after, Colonel Paradine's two illnesses at Hindley, replied 'after.' If these two illnesses were indeed caused by someone who wished for the Colonel's death, that is perhaps significant. The suggestion is that someone had a strong reason for getting rid of the Colonel at that time. Might it have been to leave the road clear to—shall I say a greater probability of happiness? Anyhow, that possibility should perhaps be taken into account by you. I will not say more than that. Why these apparent attempts on the Colonel were not persisted in at that time, we have no means of knowing, so I will not trouble you with that. The removal to London seems to have brought matters to a crisis, and the eventual end, as you know, was swift and brutal, and followed almost immediately upon that terrible scene in the study."

The Judge then went through all the rest of the evidence as to what happened before and after Colonel Paradine's death, pointing out that unless he, though blind, somehow succeeded in committing suicide, his death must have been brought about by one of those who had the possibility of access to the Burgundy which was placed on his night-table. That the poison was introduced into that was made practically certain by the fact that the glass which had contained it mysteriously disappeared. The murderer must have made away with it to prevent the dregs of the wine from being examined. That glass had never been found. One point he made was this. Alluding to Colonel Paradine's cry of 'Marsh! Marsh! Marsh!' he asked the Jury whether they thought it likely that a man in mortal agony would cry out in denunciation of someone, or whether it was not far more probable that he would cry out for assistance? If the latter, then it seemed that Colonel Paradine's mind, in the supreme moment, had turned to Marsh and had turned away from his wife. That, he thought, was a point worthy of the very careful consideration of the Jury, as it would indicate whether the Colonel believed that Marsh, in what had happened—if Marsh's final evidence was worthy of credence— between him and Mrs. Paradine, was the most guilty party, or Mrs. Paradine. If he were instinctively summoning Marsh in his agony, then the presumption was that he trusted his servant, even then, more than he trusted the prisoner.

"Weigh that carefully," the Judge added. "It is a point not unimportant. It is evident that Marsh was most anxious to conceal what had happened—if it did happen—between the prisoner and himself. It was this, one must suppose, which caused him to perjure himself in his first evidence. Had it not been for the prisoner's going into the box, and giving the evidence she did"—he looked towards Keane—"when under examination by Counsel for the Defence, and later in cross-examination, it seems to me as certain as anything can be that we should never have heard anything

of this intrigue—assuming that there was one—with the prisoner.
It was the prisoner's assertions which provoked his denials, and
eventually accounted for the final evidence which he gave when
I recalled and examined him.

"At the beginning of my charge to you, I said that there were
one or two features in this case which had struck me, but which
I would leave aside for the moment and perhaps touch upon
later. It was evident in the mind of the Defence that it might
possibly be effective to bring before the Jury a very extraordinary
suggestion, namely that of an assisted suicide. For this purpose,
one must presume, very much was made of Colonel Paradine's
misery, weariness of life and desire to get out of life. The learned
Counsel for the Defence pressed the witness, Marsh, as to this,
and I had expected, probably you had also, that a strong suggestion would be made in his final speech that there was at any rate
a possibility that Colonel Paradine was assisted to take his own
life by someone whose devotion to him drove pity to the extreme
of committing a crime—for an assisted suicide would have been a
crime. But nothing came of this. The Defence seems to have been
in two minds and finally to have utterly abandoned a theory which
certainly must have been held until very late in the day. I direct
you that there is no evidence whatever which might lead you to
suppose that Colonel Paradine took his own life, either without,
or with, assistance. This is undoubtedly a case of murder and must
be considered only as such. What you have to decide is who had
the opportunity to commit it, and who had the strongest motive
for committing it.

"A somewhat curious point which has come up more than once
in the course of this trial, is the fact that, after the terrible scene
in the study and presumably, indeed almost certainly, after the
deadly dose of poison must have been introduced into the glass
of Burgundy upon Colonel Paradine's night-table, the prisoner
played for half an hour, or more, upon the drawing-room piano.
Counsel for the Defense suggested that if the prisoner had placed
the poison in her husband's wine she could not subsequently have
been in a condition that would have allowed her to play difficult
waltz music upon the piano. He implied that a guilty woman could
not have done this, though a monster might have done it. Counsel
for the Crown, on the other hand, suggested that a criminal of

strong purpose, wary, cautious, determined and of iron nerve, might have done it on purpose, so that later the fact that she had done it might cause all men to think, '*she* cannot have poisoned her husband.' I must leave it to you to decide between these two propositions, merely suggesting to you that in the long history of crime there are innumerable instances of criminals doing the most daring, and one would suppose nerve-racking, things to throw possible suspicion off the scent. Those who are capable of crime are often capable of amazing deeds which they believe will prevent them from being unmasked as criminals. I will say no more as to this piano-playing incident.

"You have in mind the final evidence of William Marsh. Do you believe what he said then, or do you believe the prisoner's account of what happened, namely, that she was pursued by Marsh with pestilent attentions, and at last was driven to appeal to her husband? You have had these two people before you. To which of them do you give credence? The Defence has made no effort to prove that Colonel Paradine died a natural death. Undoubtedly he died of poison—antimony. Could it have been self-administered? If not, by whom was it administered? If you have any doubt on that point, you will bring in a verdict of not guilty. But if, having heard and seen the prisoner and Marsh, having noted their demeanour in the witness-box, and formed an opinion of their respective characters, you come to the conclusion that the prisoner, when Marsh had left the landing outside his master's door, and while her husband was still in the lavatory, stole into his bedroom and placed the poison of which he certainly died in his wine, you will bring in a verdict of guilty. Act without prejudice in accordance with the dictates of your conscience, each one of you. Now go and consider your verdict."

XLII

LORD HORFIELD finished his summing-up of the case at a quarter to five o'clock. The Jury retired to consider their verdict. The Judge left the Bench. The prisoner was conducted below to await the Jury's decision. The dense crowd in the Court broke into a

fidgety movement, into half-whispered or audible talk. Judith, in
the gallery, after a glance at Gay's face, sat in silence. Below
them, visible to Judith, and to Gay if she had put on her spectacles
and troubled to look, Lady Horfield sat mute beside her elderly
maid, Mrs. Pratt. Her face was scarlet and there were beads of
perspiration on her forehead just under the dark curls of her wig.
Her toque was a little on one side. Mrs. George Blason, looking
unusually subdued, was talking to Arthur Lieberstein, but only
in a murmur. She had not missed a word of the trial. Now she
was saying to the pianist:

"I wonder if they'll be out long. Whatever happens, I *must* go
at half-past six. But how I shall act to-night after all this, I don't
know. Acting—after such a reality as this! It seems grotesque."

"The human passions are the stuff on which great acting is
embroidered," said Lieberstein.

"Do you believe Marsh's last evidence was true?"

"Yes. And so will the Jury."

"But then will they condemn her?"

Lieberstein moved his broad Jewish shoulders.

"Unless they think there wasn't enough definite evidence."

"Poor woman! I want to see the end. But I don't—don't want
to see her sentenced—if she is. Do you know what is the strangest
thing of all in this strange story?"

"You mean her telling her husband?"

"Yes. And yet I can understand it. She must have come to the
end of her tether, and her true, wild, violent nature broke loose
suddenly and rushed out like a demon. She had a heart storm. Oh,
I can understand that! Throwing up everything, money, reputation, everything! 'Only let me get out and be myself, my naked,
savage self!' She's a wild thing, that pale, blonde woman, and she
loved her servant lover, and she thought he'd be thrown out with
her, and that then she'd take him and keep him, in spite of his
resistance, his anger, in spite of all."

"But then why kill her husband?"

"She never meant to, but something in Marsh's behaviour in the
crisis decided her to. She must have realised that as long as 'his
Colonel' was alive she'd never get him for good."

"But she'd tried already—one supposes!"

"Because of Marsh, too. But that was before she had conquered him."

"And lost him."

"Poor wretched woman! She's seen his innermost hatred now. It's blasted her. And that's her true sentence. If she's condemned I think it will break Malcolm Keane."

"Why should it?"

Mrs. Blason turned her large eyes, now tragic, upon him.

"Because—" she hesitated, then said in a very low murmur, "Malcolm Keane has put too much into this Paradine case."

Mrs. Blason was unable to stay for the verdict. At half-past six the Jury were still out, and she had to struggle away and get to the theatre.

Soon after she had gone there was a movement in the Court, and a rumour ran through the crowd that the Jury had sent a message to the Judge, asking for his assistance. It seemed that they were in some dilemma and wished to put it before him. After a short pause the Jury were seen filing into their box. Then the prisoner was brought in again. It was noticed that she walked steadily and needed no assistance. It was noticed also that she had withered as a flower from which water has been withheld withers. Always white, her marvellous fairness had degenerated into a ghastly sort of ash colour. Her eyes seemed to have sunk into her head, her face to have wasted till it suggested the face of one worn with fasting or illness. Her lips looked like the lips of an old woman from whose soul the last illusions had fallen away for ever.

"God in Heaven!" muttered Baron Sedelsward as he gazed at her. "Poor little Ingrid!"

He heard a woman, a stranger, next to him whisper:

"How awful! She's all cheekbones!"

Lady Horfield stared at her, clenching those tiny hands. She had taken off her white gloves, tearing one of them as she did so. She was praying—praying. It seemed to her that her fast-beating heart had grown, expanded, until it filled all the bulk of her big, awkward body.

She saw her husband return to the Bench. He looked perfectly calm, self-possessed, very much as he did at a dinner party. Only his wig and red robe altered him, giving him an official appearance. Addressing the Foreman of the Jury, a tall, elderly man, with a refined, intellectual face which now looked strongly emotional, the Judge said:

"Have you agreed upon your verdict?"

"No, my Lord," said the Foreman, in a husky voice.

"Can I help you in any way?"

The Foreman cleared his throat, making a frantic sound.

"We wish—there are some—We think it might be helpful, my Lord, if you would direct us about the witness, William Marsh."

"Yes? Are you in any difficulty about him?"

"The question that troubles one of—some of us—is this, my Lord. Seeing that—" he cleared his throat again frantically—"that Marsh has acknowledged himself to be an oath breaker, a man who deliberately perjured himself, can we—have we the right to accept any of his evidence as the truth?"

The faintest hint of a smile dawned and faded on the Judge's thin lips.

"In my charge to you," he said, speaking slowly and with great clearness, "I suggested that it might be desirable that you should treat the evidence which the witness, William Marsh, subsequently retracted when recalled and examined by me as not worthy of your consideration. I did not suggest that you should treat Marsh's subsequent evidence, the evidence which he himself asked urgently to be permitted to give and which I decided to allow, in the same light. It is your duty to consider and weigh carefully that evidence. The fact that a man tells a lie, or series of lies, once, does not mean that he will never, under any circumstances, unburden his soul of the truth. It is for you, who have heard and seen Marsh, to decide in your minds whether, when I examined him, he was telling the truth—or not. You have no right to assume that *that* evidence *must* be false because he acknowledged that the previous evidence he gave was false. He may have made amends. It is for you to decide whether you think he did."

"Yes, my Lord," said the Foreman, glancing at one of the women in the Jury, a thin, sensitive-looking creature of about forty, with an obstinate mouth.

"Have you any other difficulty?" asked the Judge.

"No, I think not, my Lord. But there were—there was——"

"That will do!" said the Judge, interrupting him. "Now go back and try to arrive at a verdict. I am willing to stay here till midnight if necessary, in order to finish this case."

The Jury then retired and the Judge once more left the Bench.

More than two hours went by, two hours that seemed to those waiting in the Court interminable, leaden-footed, unbearable hours that yet must be endured. Gay sat very still beside Judith. Once Judith bent to her and whispered:

"You wish to stay? If you'd rather not I'll go with you."

Gay's lips formed the words:

"I must stay."

She couldn't go now. She must see it out. But she was so frightfully nervous that she felt like one in the grip of an illness, torn by a dominating disease. In those hours she was in the prisoner's room with Mrs. Paradine, and she was with Malcolm, wherever he was. He had gone out when the Judge went away for the second time and had not returned. But just before nine o'clock sounded from the church clocks of London she saw his tall figure coming in. With head bent down he went to the Counsels' seat and sank down on it. There was a stir in Court. The Jury were coming back. The prisoner was again brought in and took her place in the Dock.

Lady Horfield put both her little bare hands to her face and held her red cheeks. Still holding them she saw her husband come slowly in and take his place once more upon the Bench.

When he had done so the Clerk of Arraigns called the list of the Jury. As soon as he had finished he asked:

"Members of the Jury, have you agreed upon your verdict?"

The Foreman cleared his throat twice convulsively before he spoke. Then he said:

"We have."

"And do you find the prisoner guilty of the murder of Desmond James Paradine or not guilty?"

After a horrible pause the Foreman said:

"Guilty."

The Clerk of Arraigns, on this, was about to address the prisoner when there was a commotion in Court. The figure of a bulky woman towered up in the 'City Lands,' and, lurching forward, tried to make her way out, stumbling and pushing against people like one out of control, or unable to see her way. She was closely

followed by an elderly female companion, who seemed to be trying to assist her.

"Silence!" called an attendant. "Silence in Court!"

But the big woman stumbled on.

The Judge was about to speak and command silence when he
saw that the moving figure was his wife. He shut his lips and sat
perfectly still looking down till the commotion ceased. Then the
dry voice of the Clerk of Arraigns was heard saying:

"Ingrid Paradine, you have been found guilty of wilful murder;
have you anything to say why the Court should not pronounce
sentence upon you?"

Mrs. Paradine, leaning against the Dock, with her withered face
turned in the direction of Counsels' seat, said in a harsh voice
that sounded to many in the Court like the voice of a man:

"It is his fault!"

Then there was silence. The Judge waited; everyone waited.

But as the prisoner did not speak again, only stood like a tall,
withered puppet leaning against the Dock, the Judge assumed the
black cap, and, after saying in his silvery voice that he agreed
with the verdict of the Jury, passed sentence of death.

XLIII

OWING to the density of the crowd outside the Old Bailey Gay
and Judith Flaquer had great difficulty in getting away. The
night was very dark, rainy and starless, and it seemed to Gay as
if all London were waiting in the neighbourhood of the Criminal
Court to hear the result of the trial. She was exhausted when at
last they were free of the jostling mob, and Judith hailed a taxicab and helped her into it.

"To-night I'll drive you straight home," Judith said.

"Yes—do."

Judith gave the chauffeur the address.

"Would you like me to come in with you, Gay, and stay a little
while? Shall I stay till Sir Malcolm comes back?"

"No, no—please! He mustn't find anyone. He'll—I don't think

I'll see him to-night. No. It will be better not. Poor Malcolm! No, I won't see him. He won't want to see anyone. After all he's tried to do—*this!*"

"There may be an appeal."

"Oh!" Gay exclaimed. "I hope there will be. Perhaps then——" She broke off.

"No," she said. "I feel this is final. I know she will die."

"But how can——"

"Judy, I know! When I looked at her just at the end I knew life was over for her, utterly over. I believe she is guilty. Yes, she is guilty. But, Judy, I am certain she had an over-mastering love for that man, Marsh. And it wrecked her. I shall never forget her face when he gave his last evidence. To be hated like that by someone you love, and must go on loving! Poor woman! No, Judy, she won't appeal. She knows there is nothing left for her in life."

"But we all cling to life, Gay."

"Not she—now. I am positive, Judy."

"What did she mean by those few words at the end, just before she was sentenced?" Judith asked, after a rather long silence. "Was she thinking of William Marsh?"

But Gay gave no answer to that question, and Judith did not press her. The strange silence, perhaps, was sufficient answer.

"Gay knows that she meant Sir Malcolm!" she thought, drearily. "But the Court will suppose it was William Marsh."

When the cab stopped in Portland Place Gay pulled down the veil with the pattern, squeezed Judith's hand, and got out.

"Don't wait!" she whispered.

Judith obeyed. She leaned out into the night to the chauffeur and in a moment was driven away.

Gay hadn't got her key. She had to ring; and Baker answered the door.

"Yes, Madam?" he said, on seeing her.

The interrogative tone of his voice made Gay at once realise that with her veil down she wasn't recognised.

"It's all right, Baker!" she managed to say, and she stepped into the hall.

"Oh, my lady, I beg pardon!" the butler exclaimed. "I didn't for the moment——"

"I know."

She spoke through the veil. Baker mustn't see her face just then. "I went to the Court."

"Did you, my lady?" said the butler, evidently astonished. "Is it finished?"

"Yes."

"I hope, my lady——" The butler paused.

"She's condemned to death," Gay said.

And she went away and upstairs.

In her bedroom she took off her veil, hat and fur, and bathed her face again and again in cold water.

A clock on the mantelpiece chimed ten o'clock. A knock on the door announced her maid, who came in accompanied by Sausage.

"Haven't you dined, my lady?"

"No."

The maid's eyes went to the veil which was lying on a chair and examined it with obvious surprise and curiosity.

"Please put it away."

"Yes, my lady."

"And bring me some tea and some toast, nothing else. I won't dine."

"Yes, my lady."

"That poor woman has been condemned to death. And I was there."

"Mr. Baker's just told me, my lady. How awful! What a way poor Sir Malcolm will be in after all he's done."

"Just the tea—and then I'll go to bed. I'm tired."

"You won't take a bath, my lady?"

"No."

She bent down to touch Sausage's narrow head. Her maid went out of the room.

As soon as the tea was brought she bade the maid good night.

"I shall want nothing more. Take Sausage with you. Perhaps—when Sir Malcolm comes home he may like——"

Her voice died away.

"Yes, my lady. Good night, my lady. Come, Sausage! Master!"

Sausage uttered a muffled bark and hurried out of the room.

At midnight Gay lay in bed, wide awake. She had left her door unlocked. One light was on by her bedhead, but she wasn't reading.

Two sentences kept repeating themselves in her mind. One was:
"*L'Ame est la clef de l'univers.*"

The other: "It is his fault."

Had Malcolm understood that accusation? With what a terrible voice the words had been spoken—like a man's voice, harsh and broken, or like a boy's voice breaking when the threshold of manhood is reached. Malcolm must have understood. Where was he? Had he come home? She had heard nothing.

A tap came on her door. She trembled. So he had returned and wanted to see her. She hadn't expected that, though she had left her door unlocked and the light on and was listening.

How would they meet?

"Come in!" she called.

"It's I, my lady! Could I come in for a moment?"

Baker's voice! She sat up in bed.

"Yes, come in!" she called sharply.

The butler showed himself. He had a newspaper in his hand.

"I'm sorry to disturb you, my lady, but I felt I really ought to let you know——"

"What is it? Where's Sir Malcolm?"

"He's in the sitting-room downstairs, my lady. Sausage is with him. He's been home about half an hour."

"But then what is it?" she asked, in a different voice.

"Oh, my lady, someone's tried to murder the Judge!"

"Lord Horfield?"

"Yes, my lady, his lordship!"

"Give me the paper, please! Where?"

"It's the last edition, my lady. I heard a boy——"

"Where? Where? Where?"

He showed her. It was only a short paragraph, in special type.

"Lord Horfield, who judged the Paradine Case just decided, was leaving the Old Bailey on foot-tonight, and was in the midst of the dense crowd gathered to hear the result and, if possible, to see the prisoner's departure, when he was shot by some person unknown. The bullet lodged in his lordship's chest. He fell to the ground, but did not lose consciousness. There was a panic in the crowd, but eventually his lordship was carried to a cab. He insisted on being taken to his house in Sussex Square. Although suffering great pain, he remained in full command of his faculties. He stated that he had not the slightest idea who had shot him. It was dark and the crowd was dense. There is absolutely no clue to the person who made the dastardly attempt, which, it is thought, may have been carried out by means of a revolver fired through a pocket."

Still holding the paper, Gay said to the butler:

"Does Sir Malcolm know of this?"

"Yes, my lady, I told him."

"But didn't he know it when he came home?"

"Oh, no, my lady, I'm sure not. He seemed horrified when I told him."

"Thank you, Baker. You can take it."

She gave him back the paper.

"Shall I tell Sir Malcolm, my lady, that you are——"

"No, no—it's very late."

"Yes, to be sure, my lady. Then——"

"Stop a minute!"

"My lady?"

"Is—does Sir Malcolm look very tired?"

"Oh, my lady, yes—something terrible. He wouldn't eat, but I've opened him a bottle of champagne. I only hope he hasn't taken cold."

"Cold? Why should he?"

"He came home walking, my lady, and without even his overcoat."

"Without—why?"

"He said he forgot it, my lady, when leaving the Old Bailey."

"D'you mean without either hat or coat?"

"Oh, no, my lady. Only the coat. He forgot it in the hurry and excitement, so he said."

"Ah!"

After a pause, as Gay said nothing more, the butler said:

"Then good night, my lady."

"Good night."

The man went out of the room.

Directly he had gone, Gay got out of bed. She caught up something—she didn't know what—wrapped it about her, thrust her feet into slippers and went to the door. But she didn't open it, only stood by it for a moment. Then she came away and went to the hearth, on which smouldered the golden remains of a fire dying out in a smother of wood ash.

She waited there for some time, always listening for some sound from outside. But she heard nothing.

The gold on the hearth gradually faded away. A clock in the room chimed one o'clock. Just after that Gay made a movement as if to hurry to the bed. She had heard a faint sound, like a door shutting. Malcolm must at last have gone to his bedroom. She checked her instinctive movement and sat down on the sofa near the hearth, and again waited.

"What am I waiting for?"

She asked herself that and found no reply. But she felt that she must be up, that late though it was, something more must happen that night in which she must be concerned. Perhaps Malcolm even now would come. But he did not come. And at last, feeling driven to action, though not knowing at all what she was in the end going to do, she softly opened a door which led into a small lobby, beyond which and another shut door lay her husband's dressing-room. In the lobby she listened attentively and almost immediately heard a curious sound. It suggested to her the noise of an animal scrambling about. There was a strong suggestion of violence in it. It did not die away but continued. Sausage must be in there. But what was he doing? Something impelled her gently, very gently, to open the door. The dressing-room was unlit, but from her husband's bedroom beyond some light shone in through the partially opened door, and she was able to see the dark shape of Sausage furiously worrying something on the carpet, dragging it to and fro, then holding it with his forepaws, and tearing at it with his teeth, shaking his narrow head frantically from side to side. She looked, stared, bending forward. It was not a cushion he had got but a braided jacket of Malcolm's. Not a sound came from the lighted bedroom. The dog was so intent upon what he was doing that he did not see her, and after a long moment of rapt contemplation she drew away, closed the door of the dressing-room softly, traversed the lobby and went back to her room. When she was there, she locked the door behind her. Then she went to the door which gave on to the landing and locked that, too.

As she crossed the floor of her bedroom, she was shivering.

She got into bed—but she kept the light on till morning. She was afraid, if she put it out, that she would see in the blackness the frantic shape of a dog worrying something on the carpet, something that belonged to Malcolm, something that he had worn that day at the trial.

XLIV

THE only woman—or man for that matter—of whom Sir Simon Flaquer sometimes made a confidante in professional matters was his daughter, Judith, and it was not often that he opened out without any reserve even to her. But on the evening of the day when Mrs. Paradine's execution had taken place in Holloway Prison, after dinner at home in the family, he asked her to come with him to his library and to sit with him while he smoked a cigar. During dinner he had scarcely spoken a word, and the family had respected his silence. They knew that this had been a black day for him. He was sensitive about the great 'cases' he handled, and the loss of one—a rather unusual happening, for he was famous as a winner—always affected his spirits. As his children were wont to say:

"Papa searches his brain and his conscience with a toothcomb to find out where, just where, he went wrong."

They were sure that at dinner he had been mentally going through the Paradine case with his tooth-comb, and trying to make up his mind how far he was to blame for the tragic result of it.

When the library door was shut Sir Simon said at once:

"This is a terrible day for me, Judy."

"I know it, Papa. Let me get you the cigar box."

"Do. And I suppose a much worse day for that poor devil, Keane."

Judith was looking for the cigar box with her back turned to him, and said nothing for a moment. Having found it, she came towards him.

"Here they are!"

There was another minute of silence while Sir Simon was light-ing up; then she said:

"Is it really true that Sir Malcolm is going to give up the Bar?"

"He has given it up. He's returned all his briefs and is going abroad."

"I knew about his going abroad. Gay told me that, of course, and that she was going with him. But she didn't say that he was giving up work for good."

"He is."

Judith sat down close to her father, and leaned forward with a penetrating look in her eyes.

"Had Gay anything to do with that, Papa?"

"I shouldn't wonder. It's strange enough, all things considered, but I believe she still has great influence over him."

"Can it be the influence that comes from a great forgiveness?"

There was something so peculiar in his daughter's tone when she said that, that Sir Simon examined her for an instant with an almost fierce attention.

"You mean her forgiveness of his—shall we say concentration on that poor Ingrid Paradine who paid for her sin to-day?"

"That, too, perhaps."

"Judy, we must be careful. Remember, we know nothing."

"Nor ever shall know, thank God. It's strange, isn't it, that this Paradine case has driven the man who defended it from the Bar, and the Judge who tried it from the Bench?"

Sir Simon leaned back in his chair and blew out a cloud of smoke.

"Yes, Horfield's a loss—in a way," he said. "One of the acutest legal brains of our day, undoubtedly. But I'm not sorry he's decided to retire. He's a merciless Judge, and he's had a long run."

"Lady Horfield will be glad."

"You think so?"

"Papa!"

"You mean that she'll have him more to herself now that he's bound to be a delicate man."

"Partly that."

"I believe he'll hang on for years now that they've got the bullet out of him. He's tough, both mentally and physically. That fellow—or the woman, for it may have been a woman—who fired that bullet was clever, very clever. Darkness and a dense crowd in a condition of wild excitement! What an opportunity for vengeance. Men are still wondering at the Clubs which of Horfield's victims did it. One of his harsh sentences come home to roost, as it were. That's what everyone thinks."

"Ah!" said Judith, lighting a cigarette.

"For prisoners come out of prison. Judges shouldn't forget that."

"No clue at all?"

"Nor ever will be. Probably the revolver was stolen by some rough in the mob, who saw his chance and took it when it had been dropped and he trod on it. That's my theory, anyhow."

"And probably the right one."

"Plenty of ruffians ready to take such a risk as that."

"Risks!" said Judith, taking up the word. "There's generally something big in those who are ready to take them, isn't there? And perhaps that accounts for the lurking sympathy some of us have for those who we know, or suspect, are criminals. You had it, hadn't you, Papa, for Mrs. Paradine?"

"Yes, Judy. I told you long ago, and told Keane, too, that I had conceived a liking for her. She was fascinating, but it wasn't merely that. There was something almost homely about her apparent naturalness, lack of all pose, which drew you to her. And yet she was certainly very deep. I'm pretty sure that she was one of the fiercest women, secretly, that I've ever had to do with. Her passion for that man, Marsh, proved it. I'm positive that right up to the end of the trial—his final evidence—she believed that if she was acquitted she'd get him and keep him. That was always at the back of her mind and guided her actions. The fact that *once* she had made him false to his Colonel, the great devotion of his life, gave her unlimited confidence in her power over Marsh. It was that which led her to take the terrific risk she took on the day of the murder, when she told the sheer truth to her husband. A burning of all her boats with a vengeance! She played out all her cards on that day, like a true fatalist. Her passion for Marsh was a grande passion, if ever there was one."

"Poor Sir Malcolm!" breathed Judith.

"Ah! To be regarded as a weapon instead of as a man!"

"And to fail even as a weapon! What he must have gone through to-day!"

"I'm glad I didn't have to see him. The last interview he ever had with her was when he went to the prison to try to persuade her to consent to an appeal. She let loose at him before the officers who were with her in the condemned cell, accused him of having ruined her by the line he took for the defence."

After a pause, Sir Simon added grimly:

"I come in there! I gave Keane his head. I was weak with him."

"Why wouldn't she appeal?"

"Judy, there was nothing for her in life, and she knew it. Marsh had shown her the depth of his hatred. That was her sentence, not Horfield's. She met her death with complete indifference. At the last moment the despair of the soul absolutely dominated the natural shrinking of the body."

"That shows which is the greatest. Gay has often quoted to me a French saying."

"Yes?"

"L'Ame est la clef de l'univers."

Sir Simon sat very still for a moment, looking straight before him. Then he said, in an unusually emotional voice:

"Let's hope that hers will be able, even after all this, to unlock the door to *his* soul again some day."

"Her universe still, you think?"

"Isn't it possible?"

"I believe it is. Yes, it is. Poor, great little Gay!"

THE END